THE SILVER DARLINGS

THE SILVER DARLINGS

Neil M. Gunn

faber and faber

First published in 1941
by Faber and Faber Limited
Bloomsbury House, 74–77 Great Russell Street
London WC1B 3DA
First published in this edition 1969
Reprinted in 1975, 1978, 1984, 1986 and 1989

Printed and bound by CPI Group (UK) Ltd, Croydon, CRO 4YY

ISBN 978-0-571-09041-9

FSC
www.fsc.org
MIX
Paper from
responsible sources
FSC® C013604

TO
THE MEMORY OF
MY FATHER

CONTENTS

CONTENTS

CHAPTER I

THE DERELICT BOAT

❦

As Tormad tried to flick a limpet out of the boiling pot, he burnt his fingers, upset the pot, and spilt the whole contents over the fire, so that there was a sudden hissing with a cloud of ashes and steam. Fortunately the fire was outside, round the back of the cottage, where Catrine boiled clothes on her washing day.

"Did you ever see the beat of that?" he asked, hissing through his teeth and flailing his hand in the air.

It was so like him, and she so loved him, that she turned away.

He kicked the smouldering peats apart and began retrieving the limpets, which, being hot, stung him frequently. Holding one in the corner of his jacket, he gouged out its flesh easily with his thumb-nail. Whole and clean it came, and he cried: "They're ready!" delighted after all with his judgement. "I'll put the fire on for you," he said, "in a whip," as he scraped limpets and yellow ash together into a small rush basket.

"I don't need it," she answered. "Never mind. And what's the good of blowing the ashes off that, you great fool?"

"Because I always like," said Tormad, "to leave things neat and tidy."

As he had probably never left anything neat and tidy in his life, Catrine turned from him towards the house. His lids lowered and his eyes glimmered in a dark humour, as following, he looked at her back and the carry of her fair head. She was very light on the foot always, and could break into a run as quickly as she could laugh. When laughter beset her it doubled her up, but if anyone tried to catch her in the helpless middle of it, she would arch her waist and whirl off with a little abrupt yelp. He knew by the way she walked with her head up exactly how she was feeling. She did not want to break down, to discourage him, but the tears would beat her if they got half a chance. By keeping very busy and leaving the house at once, he would not give them the chance. In his twenty-four years he felt full of a great competence. Catrine was only nineteen.

"Yonder's Ronnie," he said, pausing for a moment at the door. "They'll be waiting for me. Let me see, now. You have the scone and the drop of milk. There's the net. And here's the limpets." He stood looking around their simple living-room, with its fire in the middle of the floor, and added, "Yes, that's everything. I'll be going."

"All right, then," she said calmly, standing quite straight, her shoulder to him.

He looked at her side face, his eyes going black. If a fly touched his sympathy, he might half-kill a man to save it. "Very well," he said, "that's fine." He slung the net on to his left shoulder and balanced it, then lifted the limpets and the food. "You needn't come down," he said. "Don't you come. There's no need. Everything's fine."

"All right," she answered.

He should have gone then, but the sympathy in him was his greatest weakness. He stood looking at her.

"Why don't you go?" she asked sharply, without turning her head.

"Catrine," he said gently, "why won't you give me your blessing?"

"Why don't you go?" she cried.

"Catrine——"

"Go!" she screamed. "Go!"

He took the step between them. "Catrine——"

"Oh, why don't you go?" He felt her teeth biting at his

10

chest and her fingers digging into his back like little iron claws. The net fell from him and the small rush basket and the pocket of food. Her tears had won against her and were making her savage. Her sobs were tearing gulps.

He soothed her as best he could, and the Gaelic tongue helped him for it is full of the tenderest endearments. "You see," he whispered in her hair, "it's all for you—and himself. There's nothing here, Catrine; nothing in this barren strip of land for us. And the men who are going to the sea are making money. Could I do less than them, when I have the strength in me not to see them in my way? Be reasonable now, Catrine, love of my heart, my little one, my wild pigeon. Listen now. It's your help I need. . . ."

Under his talk she was quietening—indeed his words had brought a soft emotion into his own throat—and he thought they had never come so near to a grown-up understanding of life together, when suddenly, her fingers gripping his flesh, she threw her head back and looked right into his eyes. "I'll never let you go," she said. "I've got you. I'll never let you go." He knew her wayward moods. But this was something far beyond. It was hard and challenging, without any warmth. Her eyes were suddenly those of an enemy, deliberately calculating, cold as greed.

He looked away, not wanting to believe it, and said, "Don't be foolish, Catrine." Her fingers were hurting him. "Come, now, I'll have to go." He tried gently to free himself from her grasp; but she held on the more firmly. Her strength was astonishing. He made to take a step away. She twisted her legs round his legs, so that he staggered and they nearly fell. He appealed to her again, but she only increased her fighting hold, her teeth deep in his clothes. The strangling pressure on his neck was irking him. Impatience beset him. This was too much. He finally set his strength against her and tore her arms from his neck. "Why are you behaving like this?" he cried, crossing her writhing arms against her body. But she struggled like one possessed, in a wild fury, and he was panting when finally

11

he disentangled himself and left her on the clay floor choking with sobs, her face hidden.

Easing his neck, he looked about him and then down at the gathered heap she made. The anger in his mind was baffled and weary. After all he had done; selling his second beast to help buy the old boat and net; tearing the rocks out of the barren land; striving—striving . . . it was hard on a fellow. He bent down and heaved the net to his shoulder; lifted the limpets; stood for a moment looking at her; then, without a word, turned and walked out.

The ground sloped down to a narrow flatness before it tumbled over a steep face of earth and broken rock to the sea-beach. All that primeval hill-side of heath and whin and moss was slowly being broken-in to thin strips of cultivated land by those who lived in the little cabins of stone and turf dotted here and there with rounded backs like earth-mounds. They had come from beyond the mountain which rose up behind them, from inland valleys and swelling pastures, where they and their people before them had lived from time immemorial. The landlord had driven them from these valleys and pastures, and burned their houses, and set them here against the sea-shore to live if they could and, if not, to die.

The first year had been the worst. Many had died. Many had been carried away in empty lime ships. A great number had perished on the sea. But a greater number, it was believed, were alive in Nova Scotia and elsewhere in Canada and other lands, though fighting against dreadful tribulations and adversities. It had been a bitter and terrible time. Some said it had been brought upon them for their sins, and some said it had been a visitation of the Lord upon the world because of the wicked doings of the anti-Christ, Napoleon. But with Napoleon at last in St. Helena, the burnings and evictions went on; and as for their sins, to many of them, if not to all, it seemed that their lives had been pleasant and inoffensive in their loved inland valleys; and even in an odd year, when harvests had been bad and

12

cattle lean, even now the memory of it seemed lapped around with an increased kindliness of one to another.

Tormad's heels sank into the earth. He was a heavy broad fellow, a little above the average in height, with black hair that sometimes glistened. His eyes were a very dark blue and had an expression in them exasperated and sad. He knew why his wife hated the sea, but she needn't have gone to such lengths to show it. That first winter had been a terror. For one long spell, they had had little or nothing to live on but shell-fish and seaweed. Often they ate the wrong thing and colic and dysentery were everywhere. Old men, trying to live on nothing to give the young the better chance, had become unbelievably gaunt, so that children would sometimes run from them, frightened. What had preyed on Catrine's mind more than anything was the death of her uncle. He had been one of the most heartening men in their little colony—for there were many such colonies along that wild coast—with the gaiety in him that was natural to Catrine herself. He had got nimble at hunting the waves and was daring anyhow. They had cleaned the shore to the lowest edge of the ebb, and one day, following the suction of the receding wave, he slipped, and, before he could get up, the next wave had him and sucked him over a shallow ledge. His arms lathered the water for a moment while horrified eyes watched. Then he sank and did not come up.

Yet it was out of that very sea that hope was now coming to them. The landlord who had burned them out in order to have a suitable desolation for sheep, had set about making a harbour at the mouth of the river, the same river that, with its tributaries, had threaded their inland valleys. Money had been advanced by him (at $6\frac{1}{2}$ per cent. interest) to erect buildings for dealing with fish. All along these coasts—the coasts of the Moray Firth—there was a new stirring of sea life. The people would yet live, the people themselves, for no landlord owned the sea, and what the people caught there would be their own—or very nearly (for landlords over a long period continued to levy tribute on the fish landed). It was the end of the Napoleonic era. For the Moray Firth it was the beginning of the herring fisheries, of a busy, fabulous time among the common people of that weathered northern land.

A foretaste of the adventurous happy years to come was upon Tormad. Round the corner, at the mouth of the river, Helmsdale was getting under way. It was near the end of July and the height of the herring season. Yesterday a boat from the south side of the Firth had had a shot of herring that must have brought in nearly sixteen pounds. Sixteen golden sovereigns for one night's work. It was a terrible amount of money. Four in the crew made it four pounds a man. Four pounds for one night—out of nothing! It so stirred the imaginations of the people that it seemed to them uncanny; seemed to them at times hardly right, as if some evil chance must be lurking somewhere, ready to pounce.

Old men and women from the gable-ends of their wretched cabins saw Tormad going by with the net on his shoulder. They stood still, silent, but others not so old began to come from their little holdings, and already a group of boys were trotting behind Tormad. His young brother, Norman, who was fifteen, strode by his side with pride. He had secretly made up his mind that next year he was going to sea himself.

When he came to the crest, Tormad saw the three members of his crew round the bow of the boat, keeping her stern in the water. They were learning! Others were on the beach, waiting. He went down the short steep slanting path, and out over the stones to the boat, into which he let the net fall with a thud. "I see you have the two lines," he said, and laid the basket of bait beside them. "I think that's everything. Are you ready?"

"Yes," said Ronnie, a quiet lean fellow, with a sallow face, two years older than Tormad. Ian was a year younger

than Tormad; but Torquil was only eighteen, and though
he had been able to contribute nothing to the purchase of
the boat and gear, he was going with them because they
couldn't keep him back. Tormad was full of business. Bending down he took one or two steps forward to see that no
boulder might damage the planking as they pushed off. A
small wave splashed over his feet and he pulled them out
smartly as if he had been stung, just saving himself from
falling on his face by gripping the gunnel. The boys laughed,
for this had often happened to themselves and they liked
Tormad. His eyes brightened in his flushed face. "That's
the baptism," he cried back to them comically. They were
delighted, and came and put their hands on the boat, touching it as if it were a strange horse. Norman gripped it
firmly. Looking up, Tormad saw the people in a line along
the edge of the crest. The whole colony was seeing them
off. He felt the pressure of eyes and decided it was high
time they were away. But suddenly voices cried from the
crest. All on the shore looked up, and presently Tormad
saw Catrine coming over the crest and down the steep
path. His whole face went dark and congested as he moved
up the stones to meet her.

"You forgot your food," she cried, holding the satchel
in front of her and stepping lightly on her toes.

"Did I?" He smiled. He did not know what more to say
so he pulled open the satchel's mouth and gazed into it.
"That's fine," he said, glancing up at her. For one moment
her brown eyes—they were her loveliest feature—looked
at him, and then they looked away, wild and shy. Altogether she was like something that might fly away, her
large mouth smiling and blood-red. There was at times a
gay lightness about her, like blown leaves. They could not
say anything, because of the eyes around them. And the
lids of Catrine's own eyes were fired a little with the recent
weeping. "Well, so long," he said, with a laugh, raising a
hand in homely salute and farewell. As he came back to the
boat, the small stones roared from his heels. "Out with her,

boys!" As the three clambered aboard, Tormad gave the final push and landed neatly in the bows.

"Hold your oar in, Ian," he whispered and began to pull with all his strength. They had had some practice with the oars, bringing the boat up from Golspie, and Tormad soon had the bow swinging round to sea. But he kept pulling so strongly that, before Ian could get a proper start, the bow was almost in-shore again. Tormad now held water, exasperated that they were not making a good start before the people. When the bow went seaward, he dug in fiercely. "Keep her like that!" he cried, giving way with all his force.

On the pull of the oar, Ian's slim body was levered off the seat and writhed like an eel. He had not Tormad's bull-shoulders, but he had all Tormad's pride and would sooner that his sinews cracked than that his tongue should cry halt. But the boat was now gathering way, and Ronnie at the tiller began to feel the kick of Tormad's oar, the excitement in him making his face sallower than usual. His eyes gleamed with the knowledge that he was guiding Tormad's wild strength and sending the boat straight on her course. "You're doing fine," he said quietly. The two oars described a high half-circle, hit the water, and dug in. "Boys, we're making a good show."

The exultance in Ronnie's voice was a great encouragement. Not that Tormad needed any spur, for he could see Catrine standing on the beach where he had left her. His love for her came over him in half-blinding spasms. He could have cracked the oar and the boat and the world. Indeed, if the oar broke in his hands it would be with relief. His mind was mazed with exultation and sorrow, but singing underneath was the song of what he would yet do for her, and knew he would do for her, if God spared him.

That wildness in the house—it was her own wildness, her own mad wildness, to protect him and herself and him to come. He could see her still standing all alone.

Extraordinary how out of a man's greatest strength could mount a softness near to tears.

"Careful, Tormad, or you'll burst your thole pin," said Ronnie. "Careful, boy."

"Not yet," said Tormad. "Keep her going, Ian."

"I'll keep her going till I burst," said Ian.

The shore receded from them, and soon the folk were moving up the beach, and Tormad lost sight of Catrine. The folk were like small animals, like little dark calves. After a while, Ronnie called a halt. "It's our turn now."

They changed places in the boat so warily that she scarcely rocked. Tormad wiped the sweat from his eyes and Ian leaned forward, drawing his shoulders from his sticky vest. Not until that moment did they fully realize that they were by themselves, cut off, on the breast of the ocean.

They had never before been so far from land, and the slow movement of the sea became a living motion under them. It brimmed up against the boat and choked its own mouth, then moved away; and came again and moved away, without end, slow, heedless, and terrible, its power restrained, like the power in some great invisible bull. Fear, feather light, kept them wary, like the expectancy of a blow in a dark place.

"There's no hurry, boys," said Tormad quietly. "I'll be keeping my eyes open now for the signs."

The old Golspie man, who had been white-fishing half a century before herring-fishing started at Helmsdale, had given Tormad certain land-marks by which he might direct himself to the best grounds. Tormad had tried to memorize these marks as well as he could, but, inclined to be over-sanguine and the whole business of buying the boat exciting him, he had not grasped fully the need for the double bearing to give him his angle. Not that he showed any indecision now. "There's Brora yonder," he said. "And that point away far off is Tarbat Ness. Now on this side—will you look?—that's Berriedale Head. You wouldn't think it's six miles off! We have to go three miles out and I

17

shouldn't think we're far off that now. Pull away gently for a little yet, boys, and then we'll try it." No-one spoke, and after they had pulled out, for what seemed a long time, over a sea that must be getting deeper and deeper, Tormad stopped them. "We'll try her at that," he said. Then he gazed around him with what was meant to be a seaman's eye.

They all gazed around, but what they saw was the land, and with a little cry of surprise Torquil pointed to the ridge of a hill going far inland, over the valley of Kildonan. They knew it like the back of a hand, and their minds filled with pictures, with memories of boyhood and familiar scenes This was the time of year when they would be away from home at the summer shielings with the cattle, the happiest time in all the year, living in turf bothies, with the young girls there and many of the old. "Hand me up that line, Ian," said Tormad, who had the limpets at his feet.

From the basket he took four limpets and gouged out their flesh with his thumb. The tackle consisted of a short cross-spar of slim hazel with the line tied to the middle of it and a hook on a short horse-hair snood dangling from each end. To the end of the line, which hung a foot or more below the middle of the spar, was tied a heavy sinker. Upon each hook Tormad fixed two limpets, the hard, leathery surfaces to the inside. "That's the way it's done," he explained, and dropped hooks and sinker overboard. They had half a dozen herring with them which might have been better bait, but the Golspie man had been used to mussels and limpets, and Tormad had taken a fancy to the limpets.

As yard after yard of line was unwound from the fork-shaped hazel stick, they had a new way of realizing the sea's depth. "It's got no bottom to it, I do believe," said Tormad humorously. Still the line went out; and out. "It's not feeling so heavy, I think," said Tormad, as if listening through his fingers. Clearly he was in doubt. He looked at the amount still wound on the stick, and let out more, and

18

then more. Down went the line, coil after coil, and they were beginning to believe that maybe the sea had, in fact, no bottom, when suddenly the pull ceased and the line went slack. "I've got it!" cried Tormad, heaving a breath. They were all relieved, and Tormad went on cheerfully to demonstrate how one must lift the sinker a yard or more off the bottom and then work the line up and down, waiting all the time for the feel of the bite.

They watched him until his mouth fell open. "I think I've got something." He gulped, then pulled—but the line refused to come. It came a little way and then pulled back. "It feels like a whale," he said, his eyes round, his head cocked. "O God, it's something heavy indeed!" Excitement got hold of them all strongly. What if it *was* a whale?

The forked stick was very nearly jerked out of Tormad's hands. He had to let out more line quickly. Then a little more. Leviathan was moving away from under them!

Their hearts went across them. The boat rose on the heave of the sea. Now that they were clear of the land, a gentle wind darkened the surface of the waters. A small ripple suddenly slapped the clinched planking like a hand slapping a face. The sound startled them. Ronnie looked at the sea. "We're drifting," he said. "The oars, boys—quick!" cried Tormad. "Quick, or all the line will be out!" Ronnie and Ian each shoved an oar out, and Ronnie pulled the bow round so smartly towards the wind that Tormad, on his feet, lurched and fell sideways, clutching at the line, which all at once went slack in his hands. On his knees he began hauling in rapidly. The line came to a clean end. Sinker and hooks and cross-spar were gone.

Tormad stared at the frayed end against his palm. No one spoke. Tormad stared at the sea. It came under the boat in a slow heave and passed on.

"When one place is no good, you try another," he said quietly. "Let us go farther out."

Ian and Ronnie swung the oars. Torquil was looking a

bit grey. He had been underfed for a long time, but the blue of his eyes held an intolerant green.

"I wonder were you stuck in the bottom?" Ronnie asked.

"Himself knows," said Tormad.

When they stopped, they did not know quite what to do, for they were frightened now to use the second line. There was no sign of gulls about to signify herring. Nothing but this heaving immensity, treacherous and deep as death. That time he had fallen, Tormad remembered the joke against him in Helmsdale: "Between her two skins of tar, she's rotten." The old Golspie man was supposed to have fooled them—to his humorous credit, because a boat is there to be examined before it is bought. But Tormad had been shy of asking a Helmsdale man to go with him, not merely because of the long distance in the short busy season but also because he could hardly appear as a real fisherman with only the one old net. So the idea he had put about was that they were going to try for white-fish with the hand-line —to begin with, anyway. Accordingly and naturally they had come to sea before the other boats, which would not put out from the harbour for two or three hours yet, as nets were never shot until the evening. There was also the instinctive desire to keep to themselves until they knew enough not to be laughed at, for the folk from the glens were sensitive and had their own hidden pride.

And now the first hand-line was gone.

"We're drifting," said Tormad, who had been staring at the land. Then he noticed Torquil on his knees in the bow, his back to them, his head down.

"What's wrong with you, Torquil?"

"Nothing!" snapped Torquil.

Ronnie looked over his shoulder. "Feeling sick?" he asked gently.

Torquil's body gave a convulsive spasm. He retched, but there was nothing in his stomach. "What's this?" asked Ian, who was next to him, putting his hand on his shoulder.

"Shut up!" said Torquil. He had tied a single hook to

the end of the broken line, and a foot or so above the hook had knotted the line about one of the slim stones that were to be used for sinking the net. "Give me the bait!"

His fingers shook as he handled the hook, and the smell and look of the pulpy yellow bait made him retch again. But he baited the hook as Tormad had done and dropped it over the side.

They watched him, fascinated, until Ronnie noticed the increasing slant on the line and put out his oar. Already experience was teaching them that they must "hold up" a boat against the wind-drift. Ian and Ronnie pulled gently as if to make no noise, for they now had a premonition that something strange was going to happen.

As Torquil worked the line up and down they waited. It was the odd thing always that did happen! Then Torquil's grey face quickened and his eyes flashed. Swiftly he began hauling in the line. In his haste, his hands and arms got meshed in the coils. The rowers forgot their oars. Tormad's lips came apart.

When Torquil stopped hauling, as if something had hit him, they craned over the edge of the boat and saw a great grey back that frightened them. "Stand away!" screamed Torquil, and catching the line low down he heaved. The hook and line parted company as a huge cod fell thrashing on the bottom boards. Tormad lunged at it as if it were a dangerous beast and tried to throttle it. Finally, he lifted it in his arms and bashed its head against the edge of Ronnie's seat. From the stretched-out, dead, but still quivering fish, they lifted their eyes and looked at one another.

"Torquil, my hero," said Tormad softly. He began laughing huskily. They all began to laugh. They swayed and hit one another great friendly thumps.

"We'll do it yet, boys!" said Ronnie.

They would do it. They would do it, by the sign beneath them. The great slippery belly of the sign made them rock with laughter.

But Torquil had now discovered his hook was gone.

When they found it inside the cod's mouth they could hardly retrieve it for the weakness that mirth had put in their fingers.

But now Tormad was busy with the second line. When, after a shout and much fierce hauling, he produced a single little whiting, he could do no more than nod at the dangling fish with helpless good humour.

They got going in earnest. Whether they caught anything in the net or not, here was enough success already to justify a first venture. And presently when a good-sized haddock appeared, and shortly after that a flat fish with beautiful red spots, and then—of all things—a crab, the excitement in that fourteen-foot boat rose very high. But Ronnie failed to land the crab. Just as he was swinging it into the boat, it let go its hold of the bait, fell on the flat of its back on the narrow gunnel, balanced for an instant and tumbled back into the sea. Tormad dived to the shoulder after it, badly rocking the boat, but fortunately for him did no more than touch one of the great claws as it sank beyond reach. Then he caught his oar just as it was slipping from between the pins. What next? They were all laughing and Torquil's sickness seemed completely cured. Their eyes were bright and very quick. They cautioned one another not to take liberties with the boat, but whenever two hands began hauling rapidly, four heads tried to see what was coming up. Each passed a line on after a short spell of fishing. Tormad had a dramatic moment when he struck what he felt was a heavy fish. He swore by Donan's Seat that it was a monster, the biggest yet. His hooks came up as they had gone down, the baits whole. "I don't care what you say," declared Tormad, "that fish was three bushels if he was an ounce." "Do you think perhaps it may have been the bottom?" asked Ian. "No, nor your own bottom," said Tormad shortly. "Bottom indeed! Didn't I feel the jag-jag of his mouth to each side? Man, do you think I don't know the difference between the bottom and a fish's mouth?" "No, it's not the bottom," said

Ronnie. "How do you know?" asked Ian. "Because," said Ronnie, "the bottom here is hard and clean. I let my sinker lie for a little while on it. That's how I got the crab. Pull just a little more strongly—just a very little. We don't want to drift off this spot."

By the time they saw the boats coming out from the harbour mouth they didn't mind who would inspect their catch. It was a fine evening, with the wind, from the land, inclined to fall. They watched the small fleet with an increase of excitement and a certain self-consciousness, expecting them to pass close by and in a friendly way call a few sarcastic greetings. "We'll just answer, off-hand, 'Oh, about a cran or two.' Like that," said Tormad. "Leave it to me."

But the herring boats did not come near them. They watched the oars rising and falling like the legs of great beetles as the small fleet headed south. They were all open boats, one or two of the largest some twenty feet in length. The use of sail on this northern coast was as yet little understood and on this fair evening not one was to be seen.

Tormad began wondering if he had come to the wrong place. They discussed this. "We're doing fine here," said Ronnie. "And it's as well we should have the first night by ourselves." They all agreed with this in their hearts, but Tormad said he wasn't so sure. He didn't see why they shouldn't go where anyone else went. Success had given a fillip to his adventurous mood. Tormad could be put up or down, and when he was up he could be very high. But in the end he smiled. "Ach well, it's fine here, boys, by ourselves and we're doing grand." Often enough the herring boats caught little or nothing. Perhaps they themselves in this spot might be lucky. It would be a joke if theirs would be the only boat to go into Helmsdale with herring in the morning! They laughed. They had made up their minds to distribute all the white fish they caught among their own folk as a first offering to good luck, and now Ian began to mimic old Morag's astonishment when he went up and presented her with the cod. He did it very well, hanging to high-pitched vowels and flapping his hands. Life was good, too!

"They're shooting their nets now," said Tormad. Some two miles to the south the boats were scattered over the sea. Blue shadows came down the hills. Tormad blew up his big buoy until his eyes disappeared. He had got it from the man in Golspie, and though its skin crackled with age it seemed tight enough. He could hardly blow up the second one for laughing, because it was the bag of an old set of pipes to which they had danced many a time as boys. It had a legendary history, for the old piper, its owner, had been a wild enough lad in his day. When he was driven from his home, he cursed the landlord-woman (who had inherited all that land), her sassenach husband, her factors, in tongues of fire. Then he had broken his pipes, tearing them apart. It had been an impressive, a terrifying scene, and shortly after it he had died.

Well, here was the bag, and perhaps it marked not an end but a beginning! They had had a little superstitious fear about using it. But they couldn't afford to buy another buoy, and, anyway, they argued, if it brought them luck it would be a revenge over the powers that be. The dead piper wouldn't be disappointed at that!

The net was made of hemp and, being old, was coarse and stiff, but quite strong. The large buoy, tied to the outer end by a fathom of rope, was first slung overboard; then as Ronnie and Torquil let out the net, with its back-rope and corks, Tormad slipped a flat stone into each noose as it came along on the foot-rope, Ian meantime keeping the boat going ahead for the wind had all but dropped. It took them a long time, for Tormad would insist on hauling at the part of the net already in the sea to make sure that it was going down as straight as a fence. He got wet from hand to neck doing this, without being aware of it. At last he dropped the piper's bag upon the sea with his blessing, adding, "Now play you the tune of your life, my hero, and

24

let himself smile on us from the green glens of Paradise."
Ian rowed away the three fathoms of rope—all they had—
by which they would swing to the net as to an anchor.
Tormad made fast. The oars were shipped. And now it was
food.

Everything was going better than they had expected.
They could easily make hand-line tackle—so long as they
had the line. They talked away, full of hope, as they
munched their dark-brown bere scones and drank their
milk. When they had finished eating, they started at the
lines again, and there was a short spell in the half-light
when they caught large-sized haddock as quickly as they
could haul them in. Then everything went very quiet and
the darkness came down—or as much darkness as they
would have on that northern summer night. They were
tired now, for they hadn't had much sleep the last two
nights, what with going to Golspie and bringing the boat
back along the shore and the excitement of the whole
strange venture. They would stretch themselves out between the timbers as best they could. This they did, and
above them they saw the stars, and under them they felt
the sea rise and fall.

"Does it never go quiet at all?" asked Ian.

"Never," said Tormad.

"A strange thing, that," said Ronnie. "Never."

Their voices grew quiet and full of wonder and a warm
friendliness. They told one another all the queer things
they ever heard about the sea. After a time Ronnie murmured, "I think Torquil has fallen asleep." Torquil muttered vaguely. They all closed their eyes. It seemed to
them that they never really fell asleep, though their
thoughts were like dreams going their own way. Every
now and again one of them stirred; but for long spells they
breathed heavily. The stars were gone, when Ronnie
opened his eyes wide, looked about him and sat up. It was
chilly and the surface of the water dark in an air of wind,
but to the north-east, beyond the distant rim of the sea,

THE DERELICT BOAT

was the white light of morning. And then, out from Berriedale Head, he saw a ship with a light, like a small star,
over her. The star disappeared as he gazed. He wakened
Tormad with his hand.

They all sat up, with little shudders of cold, and looked
at the ship. Canvas was now breaking out both behind and
in front of her high mast. "She'll be a merchant ship," said
Tormad, and turned to see what the herring boats were
doing. He was surprised to find that already they were
beginning to leave the ground. They couldn't have much
herring, surely. Then his face opened in dismay. "The
piper's bag is gone!" he cried. There was no sign of the
corks. He stumbled aft and caught the swing-rope. They
leaned over the sides. As Tormad hauled strongly, the
piper's bag appeared, bobbing and breaking the surface.
And then their eyes widened and their breath stopped.
Tormad began appealing softly to the God of their fathers.
Then his voice cleared and rose. "It's herring, boys! Herring! Herring!" The net was so full of herring that it had
pulled the floats under the surface, all except the end buoy,
which was half submerged.

They forgot all about the ship; they forgot everything,
except the herrings, the lithe silver fish, the swift flashing
ones, hundreds and thousands of them, the silver darlings.
No moment like this had ever come to them in their lives.
They were drunk with the excitement and staggered freely
about the boat. Tormad took to shouting orders. The wind
had changed and, growing steady, was throwing them a
little on the net. "Keep her off," shouted Tormad. "Take
the oars, Ian. The foot-rope, Ronnie." Tormad was now
pulling on the back-rope with all his strength, but could
only lift the net inch by inch. But already herring were
tumbling into the boat, for Torquil was nimble and Ronnie
persuasive. "Take it easy," said Ronnie, seeing the con-
gestion in Tormad's neck. "Take it easy, or the whole net
may tear away. We've plenty of time, boys." "Don't be
losing them," grunted Tormad, his heel against the stern

26

post. "Take them all. Alie the piper is watching us." They laughed at that. The piper had done his part, full to overflowing. It was always the way he had done things whatever. No half-measures with Alie.

"The ship is coming this way," said Ian.

"Let her come," said Tormad, not even turning his head.

But Ronnie looked over his shoulder. His face brightened. "She'll be a big schooner come to take the barrels of herring away maybe."

"Of course," said Tormad. "What else would she be?" And the vague fear that had touched them at first sight of the ship almost vanished.

"Perhaps she'll offer to buy our herrings," suggested Torquil.

"She might easily do that," Tormad grunted out, the sweat now running. "But if she does—she'll pay—the full price."

More than half the net was in and Torquil glittered with scales in the rising sun, when Ian said, "She's coming very close."

She crossed their bow at a cable length, and then, slowly running up into the wind until her great sails shook, she came to a standstill so close that they could see the men moving about her decks.

Fear touched them once more, because they had learned that everything that spoke of power and wealth had to be feared.

"Pay no attention," muttered Tormad. "The sea at least is free."

A voice as loud as a horn called to them, but they were not sure of the words, for what English they had was strange to them even in their own mouths. So they doggedly hauled away at the net.

"There's a boat coming," said Ian.

"Let it come," said Tormad, giving it a quick glance.

Four oars rose and fell smartly and the ship's boat drew abreast. Two men sat in the stern, with long-nosed pistols.

27

One man, standing, asked them in a loud voice if they heard the ship's hail.

"Careful, Torquil," said Tormad softly. "Don't lose the darlings."

Then the man with the loud voice expressed his anger in a terse oath which the four lads didn't understand, though they gathered its intent. But they did not look at the man; they looked at the net whose back-rope Tormad contrived to haul steadily.

Whereupon in the King's name the man commanded them to drop the net and come alongside His Majesty's ship of war and present themselves to the commander, and if they didn't do this quietly and at once, things would happen to them of a bloody and astonishing nature.

"There's three crans in this net," said Tormad to Ronnie, "if there's a herring."

An order was whipped out. Smartly the visiting boat closed on Tormad's bow and in no time a stout rope was passed through the ring-bolt in the stem. "Give way!" The four oars dug in, rose and dug in. . . . But Tormad, on the back-rope, held both boats stationary. "Let go there!" shouted the voice in stentorian wrath.

Tormad, his face swelling with blood and anger, looked over his shoulder. "Let go yourself!" he cried in his best English.

"Ease away!" As they stood down on the fishing-boat, the two near oars were smartly shipped and direct contact was made by Tormad's feet. The man who was giving orders held a cutlass. He raised it above his head with intent to sever the back-rope of the net. Tormad dropped the rope and in a twinkling whipped his right fist to the jaw with such force that the man overbalanced against his own gunnel and went head first into the sea. With the lunge of the blow, Tormad's boat had gone from under his feet and he, too, would have pitched into the sea if he had not grasped the gunnel of the other boat. In this straddled, helpless position, a pistol-stock hit him on the head with

28

so solid a crack that the sound of it touched Torquil's stomach.

Tormad was pulled into the ship's boat like a sack. From the sea they hauled a gasping, hawking, purple-faced man who doubled over his own knees in a writhing effort at vomit. In his surprise he had taken the water down both channels. Presently he lifted his head and glared with mouth askew and made the men jump with an ordering sweep of his fist.

But Torquil now had hold of the back-rope.

There was to be no more nonsense, however. When the pistol-point had no power over Torquil, a swipe from it numbed his arms so that he could not even hit the man who, grabbing him by the neck, thrust him against both gunnels, which were grappled.

Ronnie and Ian immediately tried to haul him away, and there was a scuffle in which both of them were belaboured and finally forced back. Threatened by pistol and steel, they were ordered to throw their net overboard; but the voice of authority behind croaked, "Heave the bloody thing over yourselves!"

Two men remained guard over Ronnie and Ian as their boat was taken in tow.

Alongside the sloop, a rope was passed under Tormad's arms and he was hauled upward, hands dangling, head lolling, with dark blood running down past one ear and under the chin. Torquil was made to climb the rope-ladder, then Ronnie, then Ian.

The commander of the sloop looked over the rail. "Take all the fish and cast her off."

The little incident had provided an amusing diversion for the ship's company. Tormad's senseless body was regarded here and there with a wink and a smile of private satisfaction. He hadn't done badly, he hadn't. The leader of the press-gang was not a favourite.

Men jumped to their stations. The bows fell off. The great area of canvas above a fixed bowsprit stayed to the masthead, took the light morning breeze. The boom of the mainsail clacked over. The square topsail was set, and the royal sloop, white ensign over her stern, set a southerly course.

The long suave lines of the hills by Kildonan caught a mist of rose as the sun came up. The little cabins were still as sleep in the chill of the silver morning. The sea glittered from Berridale Head to Loth, vacant in all that space save for one small derelict boat.

CHAPTER II

HOW THE NEWS AFFECTED CATRINE

❧

There was great excitement in Helmsdale that day. Most of the small fishing fleet beached on the coast south of the harbour as far as Portgower, their crews taking at once to the hills. The three boats from the south side of the Firth that made the harbour, even though each possessed a "permant" (a costly certificate exempting them from the attentions of the press-gang), tied up in haste, their crews leaping ashore, waking folk up and spreading the news. It was better to be sure than sorry in a matter of this kind. Hurry and scurry, with men of all ages, from boys to grey-beards, taking to the glen and the hills, and women running back and fore like a disturbed beehive. They knew what the press-gang could do. Three years ago, in broad daylight, a party had landed, armed to the teeth, and had impressed several men before the simple folk of the hamlet were aware of what was really happening.

They were not so innocent now. And though those in the settlement of Dale had heard the story, the picture left in their minds was that of armed men, marching on land; men raiding the home and taking whom they wanted. It had not occurred to fellows like Tormad and Ronnie that they might be impressed at sea.

The press-gang was, of course, a legal institution, and throughout past centuries had often been the chief instrument of recruitment for the Navy. A fisherman who had not bought himself out—a privilege allowed only in latter years—could be taken by force without redress, and often that force had been exercised with guile and brutality. In the nature of things, it could hardly be a gentle business.

From the hill-tops men watched the royal cruiser for nearly five hours, until her sails sank below the land behind Tarbat Ness, and then some boys volunteered to keep watch until the darkening. Men returned to their homes, and a crew put off to pick up Tormad's boat.

Evidence of the struggle in the boat was clear in the remains of herring trodden to pulp. One man pointed to bloodstains on the gunnel. The four faces grew hard, and eyes, casting about the sea, saw the buoy. The net told its story very clearly, for part of it, in a lump, held dead herring, but the end near the big buoy came up with some living fish.

Few words were spoken as if the men were assisting at a funeral, but one black-bearded man, his eyes on Tormad's boat as she followed dumbly on the tow-rope, said with searing pity, "It's a pure sin."

The bringing in of the boat made a deep impression on those gathered at the harbour. By an odd chance, Tormad had struck the herring shoal, and this luck gave to their old tarred craft, with its profusion of scales and solitary net, an air inexpressibly empty and tragic. The absence of the living bodies could be felt, as if their dark shadows still haunted the boat.

What fun and happy sarcasm there would have been had they come in in the ordinary course, with a curer solemnly offering to engage them, complete with net! But now the three curers were grim as the rest. They had no right, one of them said, to take all the men. They should have left at least one man to navigate the vessel to port. It had been high-handed action and against the law in that respect at least, and he would see about it. He would write the Navy Board. He would write to Dunrobin Castle. But old Murray, the best of the fishermen, shook his head. He had belief neither in the Castle nor the Navy Board, and his experience in such matters was longer and more eventful than that of any other of the group at the corner of the store, for he came of a Kildonan family, though he lived now, with many of his compatriots, in Macduff. "I know Tormad," he said. "If he hit one of the press-gang he hit him hard. It won't be easy for these lads for many a day. You can't attack authority in this life and get off with it. It's sometimes difficult enough to live itself and get off with it."

Then the Dale men came over. Tormad's father went to Murray and asked him about the meaning of what had happened in a quiet voice. No anger, no bluster; a nod now and then, and the eyes staring away through grey screens. What he wanted to know was how long they would keep him. "It's difficult to say," Murray answered. "But it'll be a year or two anyway, I'm feared—unless he might not suit." Murray did not know what to say. "Will it be five years, do you think? I have heard that." "It might. A lot depends." "What is the longest time you have known of anyone?" "Oh, I have known men nearly twenty years in it, but they came out at the end well and strong and with a pension. Some men like it. It agrees with them. It has got that side to it. There's no need to worry in that way. Many men on the south side have joined the Navy of their own free will. . . ." "Twenty years," repeated Tormad's father, looking beyond his own death. "Ah, well," he added quietly, "I'll be getting back. It's hard on them at home. He has a young wife." Then he thanked Murray and departed.

Some of the women-folk appeared at a friend's house. No-one could speak of anything else. All over the coast the news was known long before the day ended. No boats went to sea, less for fear of a return visit from the warship than in communal acknowledgement of the dread visitation.

But the following evening all the boats went to sea and were fairly well fished. Coopers, gutters, and packers were busy as they liked to be, and life went on in this new exciting game of catching prosperity as it swam past.

HOW THE NEWS AFFECTED CATRINE

In Dale, however, the gloom did not lift. It settled deep. There was to be no end, it seemed, to destruction and loss. For some inscrutable reason the affairs of this world were so arranged that there could be no relief now for the old, perhaps no relief for all of them, except in death. Whatever was pursuing them, it was after them with bare teeth. Death would be a sleep and a forgetting, and beyond it, in God's providence, there might be a happy quiet, a pleasant peace. Peace and quiet, and the mind relieved of what gnawed at it.

There was an old way of life behind them that had produced in the centuries proverbial sayings and rhythms of poetry and music. But this did not help many of them now—for when despair found its ultimate rhythm, the eyes in, clined to stare and the hands to fall.

Catrine had not gone to bed until midnight. Her action over this time was strangely without any reason. It began with a dream she had three nights before. This dream had nothing to do with the sea, though it had to do with water. The scene of the dream was by the banks of a burn that ran into the Helmsdale River, not far from the Church of Kildonan. She had passed the ancient cross cut on the rock and the wood that in her own tongue was known as "The Wood of the Cell of Mary", and then she had come on Tormad standing between two birch trees above where the burn falls over a rock into the haunted pool. This was not her own home area so that each little place with its name and legend produced a vivid pause in the imagination. The pool was said to be haunted by the spirit of a young woman who had been deserted by her lover and had died of a broken heart. At certain times—under the waning moon, for example—her voice could be heard moaning or rising out of the harsh throat of the pool in curses upon her faithless lover. In parts here the banks are high, with broken rocks and overhanging rowan trees, and altogether the scene on an early September day of bright sunlight was wild and beautiful. In her dream she saw Tormad's face as she had seen it that first time, but with so much deeper a penetration that she was aware, as she walked along laughing and excited, neither looking at the other, of every movement, shy or exaggerated, of his body as the clearest expression of the disturbance in his mind. Again her two girl companions must have been with her, for she was conscious of their presence, though actually she did not see them in her dream. Suddenly, then, Tormad and herself were above the haunted pool, and now they were alone, with the pool below them no longer a boiling pot but a calm sheet of water like a loch, a loch that somehow in a moment stretched away from their feet. This was all perfectly natural, as if they knew the place well. But while they stood there, the emotion that held her mind in exquisite expectancy was touched by a thrill of fear and she looked over her right shoulder at a wood a little way off. In this wood, the tallest trees were rowans, heavy with clustered berries of a menacing blood-red, the clusters leaning slightly towards them, as watching faces might lean. As she looked, out of the wood came a black horse, and at once fear got such a hold of her that she gave a sharp cry and clutched Tormad's arm.

When Tormad saw the horse, he smiled. "That's my horse," he said. He was amused at her fear and a little proud of his horse, for it was a finer beast than anyone could hope to see in the valley of Kildonan, with a gloss on its skin and a powerful arch to its neck. As the horse approached, sinking its head and lifting it in a strong graceful way, her fear increased to terror. Tormad soothed her a little but not very much, because he was still amused. "You must have a ride on my horse," he said. At that her terror got such a hold on her that she gripped Tormad with both hands and buried her face against him in a frenzy. He loosened her hands and looked at her in a strange smiling way as if his mind were now remote from her a little and critical. This look, though in no way unfriendly, left her stricken, unable to move a muscle. Then Tormad turned to the horse, caressed its shoulder lightly with his open hand, and, in a mutual understanding where Catrine was an intruder, leapt lightly on to its back. As the horse pranced and curvetted some yards towards the wood, Tormad looked down on her with the same smile. Then he turned his head away, and at that moment, as though checked by an invisible rein, the horse reared up, swung round, and, forelegs coming down in a thud, galloped straight into the loch. At first the water was lashed to froth, but quickly they were in deep water, where the horse sank out of sight, taking Tormad with it. Tormad slid beneath the surface, leaning back without making any movement, and in an instant the loch was smooth.

She so clutched the Tormad who was sleeping by her side that he muttered, "What's the matter?" She began to tell him her dream in a terrible urgency. He made one or two vague hushing sounds and patted her. "Yes, yes, go to sleep." And then again, with protest, "Go to sleep now," his breath thick. Between each sound he made he fell asleep, and in the morning remembered nothing about it.

And in the morning she did not care to tell him. For though, in her dream, her experience had had a reality vivid beyond anything she had ever known, in the daylight it was, after all, no more than a dream—with all the blessed relief there was in that. Usually any dream she might have vanished shortly after waking, but this one remained complete in every detail. She could even remember—though without being able quite to re-experience it—the vivid compelling quality it had had, the quality of being absolute and inexorable. She wanted to tell Tormad the whole dream in detail, but found she could not. The same reluctance kept her from even mentioning it to anyone else. And she tried to make herself believe that this reluctance sprang from the superstitious folly of the dream itself. For the black horse was no other than, of course, the water kelpie of legend, the supernatural water-horse that lured unsus-

pecting humans on to its back in order to rush with them
to its lair at the bottom of the loch. Only a few old women
still believed the water kelpie existed, and even they were
mysterious about it rather than frank, though the old
stories repeated round the peat fire at night could make
the hair rise on a young head.

All the same, this dream remained with her, and probably
it was the strongest element behind her fierce irrational
clinging to him before he had left their home to go to sea
in his black boat. All that evening she had kept going out
and in, looking at the boat which was little more than a
black speck on the sea, until at last she lost it in the gathering dark. She did not go to bed until midnight, sitting in
the lonely house by herself, for she would have no-one to
stay with her. When the silence got too oppressive, she
put her head round the partition and spoke to the cow, a
friendly old beast that mooed back at her.

This was the first night she had ever been alone in a
house, and she became so sensitive to its silence that she
heard far-away sounds. Then she took herself in hand and
said that this was nonsense, that she was no longer a girl
but a grown woman with a child to be born in the new year.
She had thought of leaving the fire burning, but now she
smoored it as usual, covering the red embers with grey ash so
that they would be alive in the morning. She was suddenly
very tired, as if some great virtue had been drained out of
her, and when she got to bed she fell into a profound sleep.

She awoke with a start, with the awful fear that she was
late for—she did not know what. The morning light came
in through the tiny window on the edge of the thatch and
down through the smoke-hole in the thatched roof. She
dressed quickly, combing back her hair with her fingers as
she went out at the door. At once her eyes picked up the
little black speck, though it had moved some way from
where it had been last night. The humped cottages of Dale
were all asleep. Everywhere were quietness and peace on a
lovely summer morning. But the other boats—where were

the other boats? She could not find them. Away, far, far off, she could see a slim thing, straight as a finger, stuck on the sea, but could not recognize it as a full-sailed vessel. If the other boats had come home, why hadn't Tormad? What was he staying out there for so long? Had he not got fish and did he not like to come home?

She went back into the house, drew the red-embered peats from the ash and, nestling them together, red edges down, blew them into a little flame. Then she leaned back on her knees, lifted her eyes to the small window, and for a long moment, her lips parted, remained still. In the faint gloom of the soundless cottage her face, hearkening for the message of her spirit that had gone beyond her, caught the nameless quality beyond beauty.

Hurrying from herself, she made the bed, tidied the room, put new peats to dry around the fire, then lifting two wooden buckets, set out for the well. It was on the way to the well that she saw the heads and bodies of men moving on the top of the mountain above her. She stared at them with wide-open frightened eyes, slowly turned and looked around her. Over the brow of the ground below and to the right she saw a man coming. He went to the house of Tormad's father and disappeared inside. She forgot the well and began walking slowly back to her own home, her eyes never leaving the house where the man had entered. She set the buckets down quietly and stood at the door. Her ears caught a woman's smothered cry, the sharp keening cry, and such a weakness went over her body that she felt her knees give way.

So it had come.

Her breathing grew rapid and a buzzing went into her head. She started to run. Tormad's mother caught her white face in the doorway and cried. "They've taken him! They've taken our Tormad!" They were all in the room and the Helmsdale man said once more, "It's the press-gang. They took the four lads this morning at sea."

Catrine could not understand, and stared at the Helmsdale

man and then at the others. "Of course, they'll be all right,"
said the Helmsdale man gloomily. "They'll be quite well."

"They're gone! We'll never hear of them!" Tormad's
mother was stout and kind-hearted and warmly emotional.
In her grief she was crying out. Her husband was hitching
up his trousers. The two girls, in age between Norman and
Tormad, stood weeping. Norman's lips were quivering,
but there was anger in his brows against the way his
mother was carrying on.

Catrine turned back to her own cottage without saying a
word. Her brain had grasped at last what had happened. Of
all the many fears she had had, the press-gang had not
been one. Men had said that the end of Napoleon was the
end of the press-gang.

Something had happened which she had never expected;
and what might have happened—Tormad's death—had not
happened. Tormad was taken from her; but he was alive.
She sat on the small stool staring into the fire. Then she
got up, and looked around, and listened. She did not know
what to do. There was nothing to do for anyone. She made
to go to the door, but turned back. She walked round the
room, stopped and touched things blindly. She kept going.
She began to move quickly. She had better go and tell her
mother. But she wanted no-one, no-one except Tormad.
Dry convulsive sobs caught her breath. She got to the floor
and buried her face and bit her wrist. She did not know
where she was or what had happened to her, for her mind
was not her own. Grief would not properly come. She felt
dry and hot as in a fever.

This dry, barren state of the spirit remained with her. If
she made weeping, whimpering sounds, they were on the
surface. She could not stay long with anyone, and soon folk
saw that she was avoiding them. In the evening her mother
came to her house, sat down, asked about the cow, and
talked quietly of small things—until Catrine saw that she
intended to stay the night, to sleep with her in Tormad's
place. At that a feeling of horror went over her in a deadly

hush. Out of this hush came fear and cunning. She waited, until at last her mother said it was time they went to bed. "You needn't stay with me," said Catrine quietly; "I'm all right." "No, I'll stay," answered her mother. "You should have someone with you." "I'll manage fine," said Catrine. "I would rather be alone." "That's not natural," answered her mother. "It wouldn't be right." "I don't want anyone," said Catrine. "Either I'll stay with you here", answered her mother, "or you'll come over and stay in your own home." "This is my home," said Catrine. The quiet fatal fight between the two women went on until the mother saw she could not break down her daughter's spirit, and at that point Catrine said, "I would be all right if I had Isebeal with me." "Very well," answered her mother. "So long as you have someone."

Catrine went home with her mother and brought Isebeal back. Isebeal was twelve and came quietly, feeling grown up, though frightened, too. But when Catrine took her hand and pressed it as they walked hurriedly, something of relief and conspiracy came to her from her elder sister and brightened her. Once inside, Catrine shut the door and said in a friendly voice, "Now we're fine!" She put the peats closer together and made the flames dance up. Then she skimmed a basin of milk and put the cream in two bowls. Over the cream she sprinkled a little dry oatmeal and, sitting by the fire, they supped their bowls.

"Good?" asked Catrine.

"Yes," answered Isebeal, shyly.

"Will you like staying here with me? I didn't want mother to stay or anyone big and grown-up. Big people are very sad sometimes."

"Yes."

"There's black marks all round your eyes. You've been weeping, too. Are you tired?"

"No," said Isebeal. Her lips began to tremble. Her eyes grew bright.

Catrine looked away. A few small sobs started. Catrine

laid down her bowl. "I shouldn't have said that. Never mind, Isebeal." She put her arm round her.

"I don't—want—to cry," sobbed Isebeal.

"I know. I know," said Catrine, taking the bowl from her thin shaking hands. "It comes over you. You can't help it. Isebeal, my dear, my own little sister, my little darling sister." Her arms round the trembling body, her chin touching the top of a head as fair as her own, Catrine made soothing sounds, as she stared into the fire.

When Isebeal was quiet, Catrine, still holding her in her arms, said confidingly, "Now I'm going to make a little bed all for yourself on the floor. Won't that be fine? I would have taken you into my bed, but we might then both be restless, and that would be bad for us, because if a girl doesn't get sleep she pines away. This will be a little game all to ourselves, you in your bed and me in mine, and we'll never tell a soul. Will we?"

"No," said Isebeal. She smiled happily when she was bedded down. In a little while the clicking of Catrine's needles sent her into a deep sleep.

On the following day, Catrine met Norman, Tormad's brother, at the well. Norman was embarrassed because he was fond of Catrine and did not know what to say.

"Is your mother feeling better?"

"Yes," replied Norman.

"There's no more word of anything?"

"No."

"What are the men saying in Helmsdale?"

"They're saying that they put up a good fight anyway," said Norman, with awkward pride.

"Did they?"

Norman was gratified by the catch in her voice, but did not look at her.

"Yes. Tormad wouldn't be the one to give in easily, they're saying."

"How—do they know?"

"Because of the signs in the boat. The herring were

41

smashed to porridge. You can see the red marks on the gunnel."

"Red marks?"

Norman nodded. "The press-gang didn't get it all their own way."

"Blood?"

Norman looked at her. She was white as a sheet, her eyes staring at him.

"It was just a fight," he muttered awkwardly.

She kept staring, and then began to sway.

"What's wrong? Catrine!"

Her lips drew back from her clenched teeth, and he saw the shudder go over her body as she sucked in her breath. Against the weight of his arm, she sat down. After a few seconds, she pointed to the buckets. He began to fill them. When they were full, he looked around. No one had seen them. Her left hand was pressing into her breast.

"Is there anything the matter?" He spoke in a low, frightened voice.

"No, Norman. Just give me a minute."

He waited, and then carried her pails home. She thanked him at the door, giving him a strange drawn smile. "Don't tell anyone. It was only a stitch."

"Are you feeling better now?"

"Yes."

When she had left him he turned and walked away, tears in his eyes and gnashing his teeth, because of the great fool he was.

That night Isebeal, asleep in her shake-down, was a help to her, for as the dawn came in she was caught by a clear, disembodied feeling, which was rather a lack of any feeling at all. It was like death, with a dull urge in it to get up and go away. Just to get up and go away, away beyond life altogether and never come back. She felt herself walking away, light and cool, over the ground and over precipices.

She got up and began to dress, slowly, like one asleep. Isebeal gave a small whimper, like a puppy in a dream.

42

HOW THE NEWS AFFECTED CATRINE

Catrine looked down at her little sister's face. In the half-light, it had all the tender purity, the unearthly frailty, of a young angel's face. Catrine got down on her knees and stared at it until she no longer saw it. Her head drooped; her eyes closed; and for a little while she half slept. But when she got back into bed she was as wide awake as ever.

She hadn't slept a wink last night. Two or three times she had heard Tormad's footsteps coming to the door. And more than once his body had formed in the dim room. But to-night he did not come. To-night nothing could come to her because her spirit was dry and arid. Heart and feeling were gone out of her body. She simulated her friendliness to Isebeal. She wanted to be left alone. Her body itself felt like a shell, a husk in its grave-clothes.

This pallor of living began somewhere at the back of her mind to be bloodstained in the next two days. It was as though in dream, in another life, she heard the words: *Blood: rowan-red.* The words were soundless, a haunted rhythm, but their colour was bright as rowan berries or arterial blood.

She returned now and then to the ordinariness of life with a clutch of fear, followed instantly by the cunning which helped her back to the detached state of being fey. She did her work, attended to the cow, and spoke to people normally, though with reserve.

It was the fifth night after his capture that she saw Tormad again. She lay between sleep and waking, in the bodiless clarity beyond fever, when, without any warning, any dream-scene, he appeared before her. He stood up-right, but with his head slightly lowered, looking at her. His features were not clear as in daylight, but shadowed as in sorrow. He did not speak, he could not speak, but stood there mute, asking her forgiveness. And she knew why he asked her forgiveness: not for anything that had happened between them, not for anything in the past, but because he was dead. The power of the emotion in him, its desire to help her without being able to help, its essence of the inmost man, the soft generous man she knew so well, its appeal to her, with the glimmer in the eyes searching for her understanding, so wrought upon her that her own love mounted through her in a warm flood and she cried to him in a broken cry, and awoke fully, and in the wakened moment saw him fade backward into the far wall.

Going about the crofts after that night, Catrine was grave and calm, though sometimes she would smile to Isebeal and talk to a neighbour sensibly and even lightly. But in bed now she would often weep to herself. One night her weeping wakened Isebeal, who started up in fear, crying out aloud. Catrine caught her, took her into bed beside her and put her arms round her, hushing her in a broken voice. "I am just missing Tormad," she explained, and little Isebeal clung to her in understanding and they wept together. From that night Isebeal slept beside her in Tormad's place and Catrine never woke her again.

Just as the detached fey feeling had grown into the fatal urge to go away over horizons and precipices, so now this saner mood worked upon her to leave Dale and go away to live in a new place. She began to hate this place into which they had been driven; felt its dumb misery everywhere; but especially she feared and hated the sea. When the sunny weather broke into wet cold days, and the sea grew leaden and angry, the misery crawled along her bones in a way which sometimes, when she was sitting beside the fire, produced involuntary shudders that more than once startled Isebeal.

Then one day, quite suddenly, she decided definitely that she would go, and the following evening she spoke of what was in her mind to her mother, the two of them being alone. Before her marriage, she would often order her mother about with a cheerful affection, and there was indeed between them a strong bond of sympathy. At first her mother was startled, but Catrine had always been a good worker, with clever hands and sound sense behind her high spirits. "I feel I must go away for a time, anyway, and I was thinking I would go to Dunster and stay with Kirsty Mackay. Many a time she asked me. I would like to go."

"And what will happen to the croft?"

"I thought of giving it over to Angus." Angus was her elder brother. "He is wanting a place of his own, as you know, because he would like to get married. What else is there for him, with the others growing up? Otherwise you will lose him. Besides, I am hardly fit to break in the ground. Then about Tormad's share in the boat—nothing is being said about that just now, but it will have to be settled. I would like to give it to Norman, his brother. I can see they would like to get another crew going. You will never stop them, because they must get money and there's money in it. I have been turning it all over in my mind."

Her mother was appalled, yet began quietly enough, "But what about yourself and Tormad? It may be some years before he will come back, but, who knows? he may come back soon, any time. And where would you be then? Besides, you could hardly ask Angus to come in here and him perhaps to get married and then one day ask him to go. I know how you feel, and you could go away on a short visit well enough, but you must be sensible. No, no. Even yourself—in the condition you are in—no, no, you must keep your home, for it's your man's home, and hold it for him you must. You cannot give away his croft and his boat like that. That's the one thing a woman can never do on her man—give away what he owns in this world. . . ."

When she had finished, Catrine sat silent. Her mother, whose brown hair was greying and whose features were regular, looked at her sideways with the concentrated assessing look one woman can give another.

"I was thinking," said Catrine, "if it was a fine day I would go the day after to-morrow."

"You couldn't walk it alone, for it's a long, long way, and the coach is dear."

"Oh, I would walk it easily enough. I'll have a talk with Angus to-morrow. The cow is giving a good drop of milk and that would be something for you."

"And when would you come back?"

"I could see. There would be no special hurry, if it was convenient to Kirsty."

"Well, we'll see. But you won't say any of the foolishness to Angus or to Norman that you said to me. How you could have had it even in your mind to give away your husband's croft and boat and them so bitterly come by! It vexes me that you could have thought of it. But I know—I know. It's been hard on you. Very hard. And maybe the little change will do you good. Things can be very bitter, my dear, and I can see how you have suffered. But—you must keep your heart up. More than ever now, and you as you are. One day Tormad will come back——"

"He will never come back," said Catrine quietly.

"Catrine!" cried her mother sharply. "What words are these?"

Catrine said nothing, looking into the fire.

"Catrine, what do you mean? Aren't you afraid of a judgement? Take back these words. Take them back!"

"He will never come back to me in this world," said Catrine, her features calm and pale.

Her mother's voice broke into a cry of fear, of dread, for her daughter's words were a temptation, a mortal sin.

"Don't weaken me, Mother."

"My white one, you are overwrought, you don't know what you're saying."

"He came to me," said Catrine, "when he died."

There was a stark moment, and her mother's whisper. Catrine turned to her, drawing a loud breath through her nostrils, and buried her face between her mother's breasts.

Her mother held her wildly sobbing body, rocking her gently, crooning, "Catrine, my little daughter, my own love, hush, my darling . . .", the tears running slowly down her face.

CHAPTER III

CATRINE GOES INTO A STRANGE COUNTRY

T he morning was fair and the sky clearing into wide blue fields, when Catrine turned her back on her home.

"Come on," said Angus, for the members of the family were still smiling and he was afraid they would break down and make a scene. Faces were watching them all over the place. "Where are you going?" he asked Isebeal with a frown. Isebeal paused, looking at him from under her brows as if she would cry any moment. Then she backed in behind Catrine and grabbed her skirt. "Go away home this minute," said Angus to her angrily, and walked on.

Catrine turned and smiled to Isebeal. "You'd better go," she whispered. But Isebeal merely held hard, trying her best to keep back her sobs.

"Go home, will you!" said Angus in a low furious voice.

"Never mind her," said Catrine. "She'll just come a little way."

It was not the time for argument, and Angus stalked along and up the brae, carrying Catrine's small bundle.

When they got to the new road, Catrine turned and looked back. The family were waving to her from their home. She saw her mother's still figure. From every home folk were waving to her, from every little house, except one. The narrow strips of ground were green with grain and with potatoes, and at the top of these strips, where they were trying to tear new soil from the heather and boulders, men rested on their picks and spades, and here and there an arm went up in greeting and farewell. Above them, on the mountain-side, the children who were herding the cattle looked down on the scene.

"Come on," said Angus and moved off.

Catrine's eyes went back to the deserted cottage and out to sea. She stood very still for a time, and then for a little while longer, though her sight was blurred, until she had conquered her emotion. Isebeal saw the white teeth bite on the trembling lip as the head turned away, and she followed her sister quietly as her shadow. As if he knew what was happening, Angus never looked back but kept straight on though at a slackened pace.

Nor did he glance at Catrine when he allowed them to overtake him.

"It's going to be a fine day," said Catrine in a clear, light voice.

The tone heartened him and he said it had every appearance of being a fine day, "We can go back home now!" and he glanced sharply at Isebeal.

"Ach, never mind her," said Catrine. "She can come a little way and then you can both go back."

"There was no need for her to come," he remarked. "She won't be able to walk it."

"Don't be foolish, Angus. There's no need for either of you to come far with me."

"And what would mother say when I went back?"

"How far are you coming?" she asked.

"Most of the way," he answered.

She stopped. "You'll do no such thing," she said firmly. "You'll come one mile, and then you'll both go back."

This was more like the Catrine who had ordered him about many a time. "We'll see," he said, but in an easier tone.

He left the road, taking the short cut that went down into a wide gully. Catrine smiled to Isebeal, took her hand, and followed him.

It was steep going up the opposite slopes and more than

48

once Catrine had to stop for a minute to ease the hammering of her heart. She felt weak and a little light-headed, with a small trembling in her flesh at the unaccustomed exercise; but her heart felt lighter than it had done for many a day, as if the sun were brighter here and the air cooler and more friendly. Sometimes Angus was well ahead of them.

When they were going down into the great ravine Catrine asked Angus if they hadn't come far enough.

"I'm going to see you over the Ord at the very least," he said, and went plunging down. The Ord had a reputation as a place for robbers in the old days.

They all rested by the little burn at the foot of the ravine, and Angus, with a vague smile, asked them how they were getting on. "Fine. Aren't we, Isebeal?" "Yes," answered Isebeal, glancing at her brother.

"You're a little monkey," he said.

At that she smiled shyly to Catrine. Angus got down and took a long drink out of the burn. His hair was much darker than the girls', and his eyes, in marked contrast to Catrine's brown ones, were a greeny blue with a sharp light in them under strong but finely-cut eyebrows. "When you're ready we'll go," he said.

After a long climb they came out on top of that world of ravines near the edge of a high precipice. The sea was below them, its great floor rising slowly. Far as the eye could stretch northward the coast line was a wall of rock, ending hazily in a remote headland.

"This is the Ord of Caithness," said Angus, "and that's the Caithness coast."

A coast of precipices and wings and perilous depths. A coast of hard rock and sea. She turned her head to the heather moors that rose slowly inland, with the mountains behind. The mountains and the moors and the warm sun on them, brown and soft and playful. She kept towards the inside of the road, the cliffs and the sea like down-rushing dizzying wings in her breast.

When the road had left the cliffs and was wandering inland a little, she stopped. "Now you have come far enough," she said. "I'll manage fine."

Angus began to protest, but she paid no attention to him and, taking Isebeal in her arms, kissed her. Isebeal did not cling to her, for she knew the moment had come, and so kept her face as stiff as she could.

"Good-bye, Angus."

"This is nonsense," he said in an impatient voice.

But she took the bundle from him, though he was not for giving it up, and shook his dead hand. This seemed to annoy him still more, and saying he would see her as far as Langwell, anyway, he strode on. She caught him at once and held him. For all her strong effort at restraint, Isebeal began to cry. "You'll go back now," said Catrine firmly. "I will not," replied Angus, looking past her, his brows drawn. "Don't be foolish, Angus," said Catrine sensibly. "Good-bye. Good-bye, Isebeal. Good-bye." And Catrine, holding the cloth bundle by its knot, backed from them a yard or two and then turned and walked away At a little distance she swung half round, and waved to them cheerfully. Angus was still standing and looked as if he might come striding after her, so she hurried on.

When she looked back again, they had turned and were going homeward. A little time afterwards, when she looked back, she saw them against the sky, and though they were now much smaller in size, she could see that Angus had Isabeal by the hand. She remained quite still, staring at the two clear-cut figures. As if her thought had overtaken them, they stopped. She felt Angus's keen hill eyes searching for her. She could not wave or make any sign. His arm went up and then little Isebeal's. She answered and turned away and went stumbling on stupidly, her sight dimmed.

All her body felt stupid, and her mind, and the only feeling she had was a dumb bitterness.

In the course of time, wearied, she came to a well near the roadside. In these great primeval moors, there was no human habitation, and as she stood for a moment looking around, the desolation touched her with a strange feeling that was not quite fear, as if the brown were the brown of some fox-beast that would not harm her but still was invisibly there. Yet, like the fox, she was a little hidden away herself from all she had been before, and in this lonely weariness she lay down in the heather. From being wide awake she passed in a moment into a sound sleep.

The sky was now a milky blue and the sun warm. The tiny buds on the heather were pink-tipped. The water trickled from the well through a tongue of green grass, and a wild flower here and there drooped suddenly under the weight of a noisy bumble-bee excited by the honey scent that was already stealing over the heath. As she slept, her lips came slightly apart, showing the tips of her teeth. Though her mouth lost its shape a little, it remained generous, the lips rich, delicate and blood-suffused. Near her ear, the skin was pale and fragile as from a long illness, but even here sleep brought a breath-soft warmth. Her hair was fair, of that even fairness that would not draw a second glance. Her nose was not cut finely like her mother's, neither were her eyebrows, yet now in rest they smoothed down the family chiselling to a simple mould, and in the clearness of her brow was a quality like light. As she slept, her features, fine in the bone, recalled an innocence and smallness of early girlhood.

Her sleep was troubled by a dream in which hundreds of horses' hooves came thundering down upon her, wild black horses of the Apocalypse, and, opening suddenly, her eyes blazed and the innocence was consumed.

When she saw the stage-coach come rolling down the slight incline, with its four horses crunching the gravel under their galloping hooves, she flattened again like a wild thing, fearful of being seen, and only when it was well past did she lift her head and gaze after it until it disappeared. The carriage road and the stage-coach, newly introduced to these northern wilds, signified to such as Catrine the traffic and pomp of the great world, its ruthless power and speed, its cities and its wealth.

As she sat up and gazed around, the desolate moor came about her in a friendly way. She looked at her right foot and picked a piece of heather from between two toes. Then lifting her bundle, she continued on her way, keeping to the grassy verge of the road that was soft to her feet. Her jacket and skirt were a homespun tweed, crotal-brown in colour, and the cloth she put round her head was green, but now she carried this cloth on top of her brown bundle, for she liked her hair to be free under the sun.

In time she came to a small burn, and feeling somewhat weak from hunger and the exhaustion of many days, she sat down and from her bundle drew out two round bere bannocks stuck solidly together with butter. As she ate, a lightness of happiness blew in upon her mind. Living in Dale had become like a nightmare. And here, at least, was a sunny new world in which she was free, in which she was alone, in which she was glad to be alone—until the thought of her solitude actually touched her. Then, for a little time, she wept freely, even turning over into the heather and gripping it.

But the tears were doing her good, and deep in her mind she knew it, for they were a weakness she would have to get over, but meantime they were an indulgence—and—anyway, life had been hard to her.

Self-pity, however, had not got very far when she felt that the world outside had grown ominously still. Slowly she lifted her head and saw the legs of a man standing beside her. Without raising her eyes farther, her heart in her mouth, she reached for her bundle and, knotting its corners, got up.

As she did so a pleasant voice asked her if there was anything wrong. He was a lusty shepherd of over thirty, with a weathered face, blue eyes, dark brown hair, a crook in his hand and two dogs at his heel.

She did not understand his English, for he spoke in a

southern dialect, but she could see that his intention was to be companionable.

A paralysing shyness came over her. After a first glance she looked away and, saying the only words of English she could remember, "No, thank you," moved on.

He walked by her side, offering to carry her bundle, his voice laughing and adventurous. But when he put a hand on her bundle, she started away and, as he followed, swung round and faced him.

"Ye needna be feared o' me," he suggested, with searching merry eyes, inviting eyes.

"Leave me alone," she said precisely and walked on again.

He laughed, not at all deterred. "Ah, come on," he said, "be friendly. Ye're a lang way frae nowhere an' I'll see ye there." He talked on in a wheedling chuckling voice, close by her side. She paid no attention to him. He asked her where she was going, where she had come from, and other questions, but she did not reply. "Ye're a dour ane," he said, "and ye sae bonnie. I'm no' gaen to eat ye."

She stopped again and faced him. Her quickened expression and blazing eyes made her very attractive. Behind his laughing face she saw excitement concentrate in a green glint, a seeking light. He swallowed and chuckled.

Her terror heightened her angry expression. "Please to leave me," she said sharply.

"Please to leave me!" His mimicry was meant to compliment her, teasingly. "Now, be sensible——"

"Leave me!" The words were a scream and a lash, and they steadied him. She would fight madly.

"Wha's touchin' ye?" His smile grew sardonic. "I was only offering to help."

She turned abruptly and walked on, head up. He followed, and for a moment she felt blind physical forces balancing behind her. Then he stopped, cried some words she did not understand, and gave vent to his laughter. Something wet touched her bare calf and she leapt, squawking with such terror that the sniffing collie sprang back.

The shepherd whistled his dog and gave her a wave and a last laugh.

She strode on, forcing her knees to their work, trying not to be sick.

There was a long slow slope she had to climb before she could get out of his sight, and she called to her spirit. Half-turning her head at a little distance she saw him out of the corner of her eye coming slowly on. Her fear and horror of him increased. Her breath went in and out in short panting gasps. If she had had the energy she would have lost her head and broken into a wild run; but now it was as much as she could do to keep going, and once or twice as in nightmare she felt her body falling down and screaming like a trapped hare. There was a piercing whistle, and a wild "No! no!" answered in her mind. Into view on her left shot one of the collies and a long way out began rounding up some sheep. He was still coming. Her breath now was sobbing, but her brows were still strong and her eyes had a trace of the intolerance that so often characterized Angus's. By this last remnant of primeval anger her legs were kept going, and when at last she mounted the low crest and saw on the slopes, rising to the horizon beyond a deep glen, the outlines of cottages, she was so heartened that, out of sight of the shepherd now, she broke into a run. Almost at once she pitched by the shoulder, but she was soon up again, walking and running, caring no more what wild sobbing noises she made.

She was a long way on before she saw the shepherd on the crest behind, against the sky. At once, she walked with decorum. Like an ominous watchman, he remained there darkly on the crest, so that she hardly saw the deep-wooded valley below her.

But when it was clear to her that he was not pursuing her any more, and a dip in the ground hid him finally from her sight, she paused and, her weakness drowning her in a warm flush, fell backward against the heather. Her eyes closed and she breathed open-mouthed, as in a stertorous sleep.

It was a lovely deep glen, with two valleys, each containing its river, coming to a point far below her at a short distance from the sea. The other river was hidden by high rising ground, broad-browed, that lay between the valleys, but this one wound its way by cultivated fields and green pastures up into the hills. When, haunted still by the fear of the man behind her, she sat up and her eyes rested on a large house it suddenly came to her that this must be Langwell.

How often she had heard of it, how often Kirsty Mackay had told her the history of each member of that family from which Mr. Sage, the grand old minister of Kildonan, had taken his second wife. This, then, was the house. If she would go there, mentioning Kildonan and Kirsty's name, she would surely be welcomed by someone. And how avid Kirsty herself would be for news! She should go, she told herself. But somehow she could not go. She felt shy; and then—they would ask all about her, and . . . The afternoon was wearing on and she had a long way to go yet.

So she passed Langwell House, crossed both rivers, and climbed the steep mile-long hill with a slow weary mind. But when she came to the cottages of the folk, each on its little croft, and a man or woman by the road called a greeting, she grew heartened, and presently asked an elderly woman if it was far to Dunster.

"It's far enough and you walking," answered the woman, looking at her shrewdly. "But the road will take you there. Have you come far?"

"I have come from Helmsdale," answered Catrine.

"Have you indeed?" said the woman, with proper astonishment. So she took Catrine into her cottage and made her sit by the fire, though it was a warm day, and gave her a bowl of milk and a scone thick with butter and new cream cheese. Then she proceeded to question her politely but firmly.

Catrine gave her parents' names, the part of Kildonan they had been cleared out of, the number of her brothers and sisters, the size of their new home in Dale, and other and more particular information, and received in return as much as she gave, complete with commentary and judgement and an eye to see that the guest was eating properly. But Catrine did not tell her of Tormad and what had happened to him. "I am on a visit," she said, "to a friend of my mother who lives in Dunster, and it's time I was on my way." "A friend of your mother? Well, now! And she's living in Dunster? How many have come from the terrible evictions in the glens of Sutherland to this coast and it bare enough. Let me see now: she'll be Widow Sutherland likely?" "No," said Catrine, "she's Kirsty Mackay and she's a far-out relation of her who was housekeeper to Mr. Sage in the manse of Kildonan before he married again." "Kirsty Mackay, you're telling me? Kirsty Mackay?" and raising her eyes to a corner of the ceiling she drummed her knee as if it were her memory. A few more questions left her still baffled, however, muttering, "Kirsty Mackay? Kirsty Mackay?—no, it beats me. But," and she brought her eyes down, "if you step up with me the length of my good-sister's, she'll know surely, for her man, who is my own brother, is at the sea and is in Dunster often enough." Catrine politely declined this invitation on the plea that she was late as it was and would no doubt readily find out where Kirsty lived when she reached Dunster itself. The woman at last told her how she would know Dunster, and blessed her, and hoped she would find her friends in good health when she arrived.

As Catrine walked away, a smile came into her eyes, for the inquisitive elderly woman is always a source of amusement to the young. This intimate knowledge warmed her pleasantly and she now felt in better heart than at any time during that day.

From the road the ground sloped gently down to the top of the cliff wall, and as she wandered on past the cottages, each of them standing back a little from the road, she wondered if they had always been here and decided that very likely they had not, for folk of her kindred liked living in sheltered glens, on inland slopes, not on the windy tops of cliffs. Probably more than one of them had come from her own country, for it was years now since the first clearance.

Thus occupied with odd thoughts, and accepting and giving occasional greeting, she came in time to the brow of a broad valley, with a river running through it and little birch woods on the slopes of grassy braes. It was a gentler valley than any she knew in her own country and everywhere she looked it seemed a different shade of green. Nowhere did the slopes tower into mountains, and only when she turned her face inland did she see the familiar eternal dark brown of the moors heaving to long smooth lines against a remote sky. There were croft houses behind her and on the wide slopes beyond the valley that rose so slowly to a distant horizon, but her eye followed the river, whose course was a mass of boulders, for the stream was small, until it ran into the sea where the cliffs had vanished, leaving a stony beach curving round a fairly wide bay. But on each side of that bay the cliffs started again, though she could only see the cliff to her left hand, and it had the abrupt shape of a headland with feet always in deep water.

The shoulder of a green brae shut out the greater part of the foreshore in front of the curving beach, but Catrine saw boats in the river mouth, the coming and going of men, dark patches of nets spread to dry, a great pile of light-coloured barrels and, in a quickening of fear, she began to wonder where Kirsty stayed, hoping with a sudden passionate hope that it was not near that busy cold-green drowning sea.

There was a long house over to her right, and as she went towards it a young man and a grey-haired woman came out. They stopped at sight of her and waited. Catrine addressed her inquiry to the woman.

"Kirsty Mackay? yes, surely," answered the woman with a pleasant smile. "She lives away up there, towards the moor, though you can't see her house from here. Are you going there?"

"Yes," replied Catrine, gladdened that Kirsty's house was inland.

"By your tongue I can tell you have come from Sutherland. Am I right?"

"Yes. I walked over from Helmsdale to-day."

"You what?"

But Catrine refused the command to accept hospitality, saying she had been entertained so recently that she could not eat again.

Catrine liked this old woman, who was so gracious in manner that she did not press her invitation. "Well, you tell Kirsty from me that if you refused to cross my doorstep it was not for want of the asking." Catrine smiled and promised to do so.

"But how can you tell her if you don't know my name?" asked the old lady as Catrine turned away.

"That will be easy," replied Catrine, a faint colour coming to her cheeks and a glance of compliment to her eyes.

"Well now, indeed," remarked the old lady, whose smile brightened her face with intelligence and humour as she turned to the young man beside her, "and sometimes we have criticized the Cattach!" (meaning, the native of Sutherland).

The man gave a small easy laugh. He was twenty-five, fair, with blue eyes and tiny reddish freckles on the backs of his hands and here and there on his face. His expression was pleasant, slightly aloof perhaps and critical, but friendly. He did not speak.

"Wait!" called the old lady. "How do you expect to get there until we tell you the way?"

When Catrine saw that an answer was awaited, she replied simply, "You said that she lives towards the moor in a house that can't be seen. I'll ask when I get there."

The old woman nodded, satisfied. "I doubt," she said, "if I am conferring any favour on you by telling Skipper Roddie Sinclair here that, as he is going your way, he may go so far in your company as to point you the very house. And though you needn't be afraid of him, still a pleasant-looking girl might always be advised not to let any man readily inside her reach."

"No, no," said Catrine too quickly. "I'll manage fine. Thank you very much." She obviously did not wish company.

The old lady laughed and turned back into the house.

"That's Granny Gordon," said Roddie, with complete ease. "She is clever and likes playing with words. I'm going your way, and when we get up the glen a bit I'll show you your house." He looked at her bundle and, with a word, took it from her. "You must be pretty tired as it is," he explained, "after coming all that way."

"I did feel it once or twice, but I rested, and it's been a lovely day. You needn't trouble, please——"

"It's no trouble. I'm going home in any case. You have never been here before?"

"No."

"Are they doing well at the fishing in Helmsdale?"

"Yes, I think so," she said.

But when he began to ask her how many boats were fishing, what was the biggest individual shot, the number of boats from the south side, and similar questions, she was a little sorry to confess that she could not answer him with more precision, because his voice had the simple earnestness it would have talking to a man. Within a minute she was at ease in his company and explained the situation in Dale.

He nodded. "The folk in Dale don't go to sea, then?"

"Not yet," she answered.

"They will," he said simply. "We have made a begin-

59

ning here. It's the coming thing. By the way, wasn't it from Dale that the lads were press-ganged?"

She did not reply and he turned his head frankly and glanced down at her, for he was six feet in height. She was looking in front, a quickening in her face. At once he decided that perhaps some of her own relations had been lifted, and asked lightly, as if he had seen nothing, "But perhaps you don't care for the sea?"

"Not much," she murmured.

To ease the moment, he began pointing out where, on the slopes beyond the river, the stage-coach changed horses and indicating other local points of interest, such as the inn, the market hill, a shop, the small thatched cottage that was a school. When they had crossed the bridge they turned sharp left and began following the bank of the river inland.

She liked the scene now very much, with its flat, well-cultivated fields standing back from the stream towards green braes and, on their right hand, a long ridge of grey rock, with low birch woods growing down over its brow. If not so wild and romantic as places she knew in Kildonan strath, still it had a beauty of its own, a quietness and ease like this man's manners.

"You have good ground here," she said.

"Yes, this is old fertile ground, but higher up, where you are going, it's not so good. Did you have to dig it out of the moor at Dale?"

"Yes. They are still digging it out, and sometimes there are boulders as big as rocks. The whin roots themselves can often be tough enough."

"They can indeed," he agreed, and went on to tell her of local difficulties encountered in clearing the soil, all in a friendly, informative way. Presently they came to a high stone wall, very thick at the base, and running back from the river to a large knoll on their right. There were other evidences of similar walls about this knoll, as though in times long past it had been a fortress or strongly protected place of some kind now fallen upon ruin. The tumbled

stones were a grey-blue softened with lichen. She asked
him what it was.

"The old folk call it Chapelhill," he answered. "It seems
there was a church here at one time, though I have heard it
said that long, long ago it was a monastery and the name it
had was the House of Peace."

"The House of Peace," she murmured in a tone of soft
wonder.

He gave her a side glance and smiled. "You like that name?"

"Yes," she answered, confused slightly, for the name
had been like a benediction sounded softly in her mind.
All in the moment her eyes had brightened and a quickening come to her skin as if the far, soundless echo of peace
had entranced her. They were both aware of what had happened, and if it made Catrine slightly self-conscious, it
otherwise did no harm; for Roddie pointed to a round
tower, still of some height though in ruins, too, on a tongue
of ground that rose between the main stream and its principal tributary which had their confluence in a pool on their
left hand. "That's an old fort, or dun," he said, "though
the professor—that's the name we give the schoolmaster—
calls it a broch. Anyway, it's so old that no-one knows much
about it, for he says it goes back to long before the coming
of the Vikings. It has two little rooms, round rooms, built
into the wall inside. They could build in any case; I'll say
that." Then he did a little thing that she was ever after to
remember. For a short distance the path was built up with
great boulders to protect it from the river floods. "That
fellow," he said, "has been slipping for some time, and if
he's not stopped now he may go." Thereupon, straddling
his legs, he stooped and, getting his hands under the edges
of a great thick flagstone, slowly heaved it back into position. She saw his neck and upper arms swell and his face
redden in the sustained effort. Then he stood up lightly and
dusted his hands, not as any ordinary person might, carelessly palm to palm, but with quick explosive flicks of
finger-tips against finger-tips from the distance of an inch

or so; and in the couple of steps it took him to regain his balance properly he seemed to walk on the outer edges of his feet, jauntily. "This path is useful," he explained, "for bringing things up from the shore. Here, when we break in ground, we like to manure it well with seaweed and fish guts. No manure like it for giving ground heart. You wouldn't do that away up in the strath of Kildonan?"

"No," she answered, still conscious of his explosive strength, for he was not heavily built.

They crossed the tributary by stepping-stones and proceeded up its right bank through a wide display of wild roses, from snow-white to deep crimson. She exclaimed at the unexpectedness of the pretty sight. There were two long pools beyond, and then the land narrowed upon the small stream in an intimate way that touched her fancy. The banks rose steeply, with faces of rock, grey salleys, small vivid green birches, the drooping fronds of large ferns, foxgloves and other wild flowers, all in a tangle, while the water dropped from little pool to little pool or slid in cool glissades down sloping rocks, slippery with clean green summer slime.

"That's your place now," he said, coming to a stop and pointing to a long low house, thatched with rushes, its head much higher than its tail as it lay into the slope of the ground. "And if I'm not mistaken," he added, "that's Kirsty herself wondering who in all the world I have with me now."

His quiet assessing humour brought from Catrine a quick glance and smile. She thanked him and took her bundle. "I go this way," he said, "and I have to hurry, as I'm late for the sea. Good-bye." Giving her an easy, friendly smile, he turned and crossed the burn, having asked in all their talk neither her name nor her business. This complete and natural lack of interest in her affairs was so refreshing an experience that she went up the slope towards Kirsty with a deepening smile of expectancy and the stranger's turmoil in her breast.

And then Kirsty saw her, and exclaimed, and shook her by the hand, and said that she couldn't believe her eyes. They were grey, keen, and searching, for Kirsty was a practical woman, given indeed at times to a precision of manner that many thought hard and unsympathetic. Catrine felt the penetration and knew Kirsty was wondering what trouble had brought a young wife, barely four months married, on so long a journey from her husband, and was suddenly disconcerted and touched with dismay. But she smiled and said simply, "I had a longing to come and see you."

"Indeed, and why wouldn't you? Come you away in now. And did you walk all the way?"

"Yes."

Kirsty exclaimed again, and looked more shrewdly than ever at Catrine's face, then paused near the door to say "There's the old man himself taking the peats home."

Catrine saw Kirsty's father, walking beside a small horse that was dragging a sledge of peats from the moor.

"He's failing on me," said Kirsty. "But that's the way of things. He's never got used to this place. Sometimes I tell him I think he's going dottled. Come in. It's tired you must be. Sit there. And how did you fall in with Roddie Sinclair?"

Catrine explained, and conveyed at the same time Granny Gordon's greetings.

"You're making friends early. And there's nothing wrong with that young man until he takes drink. Well! well! so here you are. And how's Tormad himself?"

Catrine did not answer.

Kirsty came to a standstill.

"He's been taken from me," said Catrine, not looking up.

"From you? Do you mean he's dead?"

"He was out fishing in a boat and a ship of war caught them and took them away."

"A ship of war?"

"The press-gang."

"The press-gang!" Kirsty sat down abruptly. She stared at Catrine piercingly. Then she said with great force, "The dirty brutes, the coarse, dirty brutes. How long ago?"

Catrine told her. There was something tonic in Kirsty's wrath. "The place was getting the better of me, so I remembered how you'd asked me to come, and so I thought I'd come for a change."

"You were right, and I'm glad to see you. We may not have much here, but you're welcome to what there is. My poor girl, you have had a hard time." She got up. "It's terrible news indeed. I wondered when I saw you coming what it was. I thought maybe it was no more than some small trouble that we could put right. You would think poor folk hadn't enough misery and worry already. If only we could have the law on them! Wait now, till I bring you a little of this night's milking," and she left the kitchen.

Catrine got up and looked out of the small window. Dismay came back and quietened her to the stillness of the evening outside. Had she made a mistake in coming, been wrong in thinking there was anywhere in the world she could go or anyone in whom she could find solace? Kirsty seemed harder than she had been, was not so tidy in her person, and somehow there was a faint gloom or misery of poor living in the air.

As she looked out the small window, she had a quite vivid memory of herself as a little girl, being taken by her mother to call on Kirsty or of Kirsty's coming to their home, and of the invariable question, "Now, are you wondering what it is I have got for you?" Kirsty always had something for her, some little present or maybe just a round hard white sweet from her hidden hoard. But the memory of it was bright and young.

Suddenly Catrine knew that an end had come to the vision of her running childhood that she now saw in her mind as if it were far outside.

Was this the vision she had been hunting, without knowing it, when she had left Dale? The question hardly formed, for the vision passed like a glimmer of light and, turning, she looked about the kitchen with cold, alien eyes. Age touched her features with a drawn fear and, in the gloom of the interior, her pale face seemed straining upward for flight. Her eardrums became intensely acute and all in a moment she had a wild terror of hearing Kirsty's footsteps return. Then she heard them coming; footsteps, blind footsteps. Her heart stopped and she all but cried aloud.

She was sitting on a three-legged stool as Kirsty came in. The porridge-pot was bubbling over the fire, suspended from the roof-tree by a heather rope coated round with soot to the thickness of a man's wrist, and here and there glistening like ebony. The fire stood in the middle of the floor, hedged about with flat stone. The chimney was a hole in the roof, square-boxed with wood. But in the dim light, with the yellow tongues of flame idly flapping over the black peat, the fine display of blue-patterned plates and dishes on Kirsty's large dresser glimmered cosily enough. Kirsty had many and special household gods, for her father had had a comfortable holding in Sutherland, which he had rented, not like the numerous cottars from year to year, but on lease. When the lease had fallen in, the landlord had refused to renew it. And that was the beginning of the evictions.

The news of what had happened to Catrine had now had time to take complete possession of Kirsty's mind and gave her an added energy. She spoke continuously, as she moved about getting the simple supper ready, and the drive of her voice and her questions brought Catrine to herself.

Presently Kirsty's father came in. He was a tall man of seventy with a slight stoop and grey steady eyes. "Look whom I've here for you!" called Kirsty. He paused and looked for some time, and then in a voice quietened by surprise, said, "Is it yourself, Catrine?"

"Yes," she answered, smiling and shaking hands.

He kept looking at her in wonder as if she were herself

and something more. "You have grown a big girl," he said and becoming fully conscious of her hand, gave it a firm shake.

Catrine felt embarrassed and a small lump rose into her throat as she kept glancing from side to side, smiling.

"And have you come on a visit to see us?" he asked.

"Yes."

"Very good, very good. And how is your father and mother and all of you?"

"They're all fine, thank you."

"They're not all fine," said Kirsty, putting swirls of air through the peat smoke. "A terrible thing has happened to her. They have taken her man." Her voice rose, as if her father were dull of hearing. "Tormad, her man. You'll have forgotten she was married. The press-gang came and took him away. She has no man now. They have taken him away, the coarse, dirty brutes." She laid a horn spoon on the small deal table with a bang that rattled the four knives in its little drawer. She went on talking while her father regarded Catrine.

"I forgot for the moment you were married," he said. "Forgive me; you look so young. I'm sorry to hear this."

"Sit in," interrupted Kirsty, "and take your porridge. Folk have to eat though the heavens fall. Sit in, I say. This is your place, Catrine. And this table, drat it, if you move it off the one spot you'll never get it steady." The floor was of clay and Kirsty had upset the under-pinning of the table's unsteady leg. But she soon had it fixed firmly again.

"When did this happen?" he asked.

"Be saying the grace," interrupted Kirsty. "There's plenty of time for talk. The child is starving."

He raised his hand to his forehead and reverently repeated the "Grace before Meat" that is to be found in the Shorter Catechism.

When they had eaten and he had got all the news, he fell into an abstraction by the fire. Kirsty gave a sideways, knowing nod to Catrine. "He's getting like that," she said, in a private voice with a nonchalant humour. "Never mind him. You must be feeling tired, and it's your bed you need. We'll get him to take the Books, and then we'll pack him off to his own bed. He sleeps next door. The bed here is big enough for both of us and it's cosy—if you don't mind sleeping with me, eh?"

"No," said Catrine.

"You *are* tired, lassie," said Kirsty with one of her shrewd looks.

"Yes," said Catrine, turning away, a strangling in her throat. She did her utmost to fight it down, afraid the terror of the bed would overcome her. She knew that she was unreasonable, that this was her inevitable destiny. She fought hard. "I am—this is—foolish——" The sob came.

"My poor bairn," said Kirsty, patting her firmly on the back. "There now—don't give in. You must get used to it."

From his abstraction, Kirsty's father roused himself and looked at Catrine.

"We'll be taking the Books at once," said Kirsty before he could speak. "The bairn is tired after the long journey." The peats that stood on edge she shoved closer together, and at once bright flames sprang up, lighting the dying day in the kitchen. The old man took the Gaelic bible and, stooping a little towards the fire said, "We will read in the twenty-third chapter of the Book of Psalms." He knew it by heart.

At once Catrine lowered her head and in her lap her small hands clenched.

The Lord is my shepherd, I shall not want. He maketh me to lie down in green pastures: he leadeth me beside the still waters. He restoreth my soul: he leadeth me in the paths of righteousness for his name's sake. Yea, though I walk through the valley of the shadow of death, I will fear no evil. . . .

Catrine could listen no more. It was a cruel irony that had made the old man choose this chapter to read, for it was the last that Tormad and herself had read together, the night before he had gone to sea.

There had been something very intimate in this reading of a chapter of the Bible after they had got married. They had been shy about it at first, smiling like embarrassed children who were playing at the game of being responsible and grown-up, Tormad clearing his throat and being solemn, while she sat upright and still, like the mother of a family of sons. Tormad hadn't read very loud, as if folk outside might hear, yet had kept his voice steady and had even raised it a bit towards the end. What a lovely experience it had been, warm with the very breath of their love, bringing them together in the ways and traditions of their folk, shyly establishing them in manhood and womanhood, encircling them about with strength and assurance. They thought of the words he read with a certain wonder, as belonging to remote places and remote times, and they hardly dared think of God at all, putting between them and Him the dark veil, with a little fear, a natural humility, thus reserving for themselves the brightness of their human lives, its moments of love and mirth and rapture, this side the veil.

But there was one chapter that all the children knew, and, in its metrical form, a verse or two of it were often recited by them as their private prayer before jumping into bed; for it was familiar in its cadence and full of pleasantness. A curious thing about it, too, was that the words were always drowned in memory except those picturing the green pastures and the still waters. But they remained, shining and green-cool, like a memory of a summer day, spent perhaps up the glen, where no houses are, at a distance from home.

And on that last night, with the childhood cadence in his voice, Tormad had read of the green pastures and the still waters.

Old David and Kirsty got to their knees, and Catrine, following them, buried her face in her palms. She did not hear one word of his prayer, her mind and body blinded, and when they were shuffling to their feet, she had to keep to her knees. They looked at her and turned away, saying no word, and in a few seconds she got up.

At once Kirsty spoke loudly to her father. "Now you'll away to bed. It's late it is."

"Very good," he said mildly, and turned to Catrine. There was that steady look for a moment, his eyes clear open and yet faintly veiled, almost as if he were looking at her from a distance with the unearthly calm and consideration there might be in the eyes of God.

"Good night, Catrine," he said. "I hope you will sleep well."

"Good night," she answered him.

"Good night, my poor girl." His voice, gentle and full of profound pity, went with him as he walked away.

In a little while they had done all they had to do before preparing for bed. Kirsty lifted the big peats off the fire and smothered their burning edges in the ash-hole beneath.

Deep gloom invaded the room with the smooring of the fire, and in its partial covering Catrine sat very still.

"Aren't you getting ready?" Kirsty asked.

"Yes," Catrine answered, and with slow movements of her limbs, as if her clothes were very heavy, she began to undress.

CHAPTER IV

THE FIRST HUNT FOR THE SILVER
DARLINGS

❦

S ome two years before the seizure by the press-gang,
while Tormad, like many other young men along
these northern coasts, was scheming to get a boat
of his own, for he was strongly in love with Catrine and
wanted to marry her, Roddie Sinclair had become the
youngest skipper in Dunster. It was the year that marked
the true beginning of the herring industry, a memorable
year in the history of that land and of its sea fisheries. To
Roddie, his elevation came unexpectedly enough one blus-
tery April forenoon as he called at the inn with a string of
white fish for sale.

The inn-keeper, emerging from the bar door, all but
ran into him. He was a short man with a burly body and
sharp dark-blue eyes that looked small in his fat face. At
any time his manner was energetic and business-like;
now, as he gazed at Roddie, his eyes seemed to grow even
smaller.

"Come in," he said abruptly, ignoring Roddie's reference to the string of fish, and, turning on his heel, led the
way into the empty bar. Roddie followed, his wonder
growing as Mr. Hendry lifted the flap at one end of the
rough deal counter. Roddie now hesitated, but Hendry
jerked his head sideways and onward, "Come on," lowered
the flap as Roddie passed and, going through a door into a
narrow darkened passage, shouted, "Johan!" His wife, a
tall buxom woman, appeared, and before she could greet

Roddie, Mr. Hendry swept the fish to the kitchen with a jerk of his head. "I want to speak to you," he said to Roddie, and ushered him into his small private room.

Roddie had never had such honour paid to him before, and would politely have forborne looking about the small dim chamber with its little cobwebbed window, had not the inn-keeper turned his back upon him in order to take from a recess in the wall a bottle with a dark label bearing in large white scrpt the word "Special". Roddie knew now that the news or business was of some importance, for Hendry acted thus only on very particular occasions, and was, in consequence, referred to among the folk themselves as Special.

"Sit down," he said impatiently but not inhospitably, as he poured some of the liquor into a coarse tumbler. "You had a dirty morning."

Roddie sat down on a narrow form against the inner wall, accepted the glass with a word of thanks, adding, "It was dirty enough."

"Any of the other boats out?"

"No," said Roddie. "It didn't look very good, but I thought it would take off."

"And it took off?"

"A bit. Once we got beyond the shore swell it wasn't so bad."

Mr. Hendry nodded emphatically. "I was in Wick yesterday. I have good news for you."

"Have they got hold of him?"

"Who?"

"Bonaparte," said Roddie, for Special's suppressed excitement seemed to imply little less. But Waterloo was still some weeks ahead and Hendry gave a laugh. "They'll get him, too," he said. "But I have got more important news. By God, and it is! Do you know what the Parliament is going to do? It's going to raise the bounty to four shillings a barrel!" He almost shouted the words.

"Four shillings," repeated Roddie in a small voice.

THE FIRST HUNT FOR THE SILVER DARLINGS

"Yes, four shillings. It's not law yet. But it will be—and in time for the coming season."

"That should help things on," said Roddie.

"Help things on!" Hendry gave his abrupt impatient laugh. "By God, boy, don't you see what's going to happen? Don't you see that the sea in front of our doors is going to be a gold-mine? That we are now at the beginning of what will mean fortunes for those who know how to take advantage of it? The news is running along the coasts like wild-fire. The Wick curers can hardly contain themselves. They're going to dump salt here, in Lybster, in Helmsdale —ay, and in Whaligoe and Sarclet and every little creek that can beach a boat. And the same on the south side, from Fraserburgh to Cromarty."

"There will be a lot of boats at it in that case," said Roddie with his diffident smile.

Hendry looked at him. Then he sat down. "Listen to me," he said. "In the past, the sea has meant little or nothing to us here. A few small boats at the white-fishing, a few cod and ling split and dried. Plenty of cold, dangerous work and damn little for it beyond a mouthful of food. Then came the Fishery Officer and a bounty of two shillings for every barrel of herring cured on shore. You know what followed on that?"

Roddie nodded.

"Fellows with little knowledge of curing and less knowledge of markets thought they could come in and make money quick, sure of the two shillings. Many of the fishermen did not get enough to pay for the two or three nets they bought. It hardly touched us here at all. But, by God, my boy, it's going to touch us now."

Roddie did not speak. He was subdued by Special's enthusiasm and this man-to-man talk in the inner sanctum.

Mr Hendry leaned heavily on the little table in front of him and drummed it with the fingers of his right hand. "And if it's going to touch us," he said, craning towards

Roddie, "why in the name of Providence shouldn't men like you and myself benefit, the men of the place?"

"I hope we will, Mr. Hendry."

"Hope is no use, my boy. Not hope or faith, but works. Works, my boy, as Sandy Ware would say. What's the damned use of your little boats with two or three nets—even for those of you who can buy them? You don't want to make a pound or two—you want to make a hundred pounds!"

Roddie looked at his glass with a slightly embarrassed expression.

Then the inn-keeper, in a strong but quietened voice, broke the silence dramatically. "I have made up my mind to set up this year myself as a curer in Dunster."

Roddie looked at him. Hendry held his eyes. "I may not offer so much a cran as some curers who may come from Wick or elsewhere, but what I offer I'll pay. Will you fish for me?"

"Yes," said Roddie.

Hendry nodded twice. "I have been watching you," he said. "You are a real seaman and the best of the young men. I want eight of the best local boats to fish for me. I am prepared to pay seven shillings and sixpence a cran for every cran landed at my station—whether I myself sell the herring or not. What do you think of that?"

"It's a big offer," said Roddie with a restless movement. He was beginning to feel excited.

"However, that's not what I specially wanted you here for. What's the size of your boat?"

"Thirteen feet keel, but she's not all mine."

Mr. Hendry did not take his eyes off Roddie. "Have you any money?"

"Well," said Roddie, looking away, "it's maybe not very much."

Hendry nodded, appearing to appreciate this reticence. "How would you like," he asked, "to skipper a boat of twenty-feet keel?"

Through the silence Roddie brought his eyes to the inn-keeper's face. The faint diffident smile remained, but the eyes themselves narrowed like a cat's, with a penetrating greeny-blue glint in them. Then they looked away. "You're making fun of me now," he said pleasantly, but with a slight gulp.

"Yesterday I bought the boat—and the nets—and the gear," said Hendry. "She is lying in Wick, all ready to be taken up."

"Is she?" remarked Roddie smoothly.

"She is. She's not new, but I had her gone over by a friend who's a boat-builder. He said she rings like a bell."

"She should be sound in that case," observed Roddie.

"She has a mast and sail."

Roddie remained silent, not looking at Special.

"She is yours to skipper. Yours. You can choose your own crew and go and fetch her. Are you prepared to do that?" asked Hendry, who had not removed his eyes from Roddie's face.

Roddie looked out of the small window for a moment, and then said, "I am."

Hendry nodded. "That's the sort of answer I like. No shilly-shally and waste of time. Now for terms. There are two ways of making our bargain, and the first is this: I'll hold the ownership of boat and gear and take half your earnings; the other half you'll divide between the crew and yourself, keeping, of course, a bigger share for yourself, because you'll not only be skipper but responsible to me for the boat. How does that strike you?"

"That's very generous," said Roddie. There was silence for a moment. "If I lost her," he added, "you would have to give me a few years to pay—that's the only thing."

"If you lost her," said Mr. Hendry, "you would not have to pay anything. I'm the owner."

Roddie's mouth closed and the spittle slid down his throat. His fingers began turning the glass round and round. "That would be too much." His face was warm.

"The second course is this," said Mr. Hendry. "I'll make over the boat to you now at exactly the same price as I paid for her. You'll be her sole owner and you'll owe me the money. That money will be the first charge on the boat and will have to be paid before you or your crew draw anything. When it's paid, the boat is yours—and you'll owe me no more."

Mr. Hendry saw a momentary quiver in Roddie's throat. He turned away and, taking a glass from the cupboard poured himself a small dram.

"Well?"

"I don't know," murmured Roddie.

"Say what's in your mind, man."

"I would like to own her," said Roddie in a small voice.

"I thought you would. That's the spirit. Watch your dram."

Roddie had forgotten the glass, which was tilting perilously at his knee. He lifted it and flushed, turned it slowly round, then raising his head, said simply, "I have seven pounds of my own. I'll take them down and give them to you to-night."

Mr. Hendry looked at him. "Very well," he said, "if you want to. But I won't take the seven: I'll take six."

For an hour thereafter Mr. Hendry eased himself of his bottled-up enthusiasm for the rising wealth of the herring fishings. He wanted to see the place going ahead, he said. He wanted to see life and money about, money pouring into the place like a river. "We're behindhand, man. We're dead. You're the coming generation. I've been watching you. It's for you to lead. I'm giving you the chance. I can do no more."

"I'll do my best," murmured Roddie, his eyes glittering.

He walked up the riverside in a half-dream. So overcome was he that he went into the privacy of a birch wood and sat down. His clothes were wet and the day cold, but the shiver in his flesh felt warm. The dram of whisky had gone a little to his head, for his stomach had long been empty.

75

In the core of his excitement was a remorseless strength, and it now consciously took the form of an intense loyalty to Special. Folk said that Special was a hard business-man, with only one craving in mind and body—for money. Yet he had offered the boat to Roddie on the most generous terms, taking every risk. If he had hung on to the ownership and the half share, he might in the end make far more money than he had paid for the boat and still have her. Now he had handed her over, and if things went wrong might never get his money back—and in any case, would get no more. Lord, it was fine of him! The skipper-owner of by far the biggest boat in Dunster—at twenty-three!

Roddie could not move out of the wood until he had got some of his habitual calm back. Never in his life had he been so stirred. Fantasies of great shots of herring, that would not merely pay for boat and gear but, above everything, that would justify Special's trust in him, took the place of thought. And in the utmost fantasy there was a characteristic underlying force, a fighting grimness, a narrowing of the eyes.

In his inner room, Mr. Hendry continued with his own thoughts. He was satisfied with the way the interview had turned out. For he had not merely been taking a chance with Roddie. His was the long view, covering not only the workings of one boat, but seasons of fishing fleets far into the future. You have to have a bait or net before you can catch anything! Hendry was in his early forties, when worldly ambition is strong.

He could not figure with pencil and paper; indeed as far as writing was concerned all he had laboriously learned was to sign his own name after a fashion; but his head seemed all the clearer for that. A cran of herring was slightly more than a barrel. When he had got his four shillings bounty for the barrel, the cran would cost him actually about three shillings, or, say, four shillings, after gutting and packing. To that he added the cost of salt and barrels, including coopers' wages, commission to the foreign merchant, the cost of a young reliable clerk. The foreman and clerk he wanted were both in Wick and he knew he could get them. The foreman was at present a journeyman cooper, named George Bremner, who would jump at the chance of a foreman's job. George was as keen on coopering as Roddie was on fishing. Mr. Hendry had gone over and over every working and financial detail with his first cousin, who had recently set up as a curer in Wick, including the notice that had to be given to the Fishery Officer covering the few thousand bushels of salt to be stored at Dunster for the coming season.

But though Mr. Hendry might thus appear by nature to incline towards speculation, actually there was nothing he feared more than a blind risk. Accordingly, he had concentrated particularly on the selling side of the business, and here he had got in touch with a commission merchant for the Baltic. There were two ways one could sell abroad: either through a commission merchant at an agreed price or by direct shipment at a price that on a flooded market might be less but on a scarce market might be very much more. There had never been any doubt or hesitation in the inn-keeper: it was the commission merchant for him every time! The profit might be limited—so long as it was certain. His mind being thus clear, he had been early on the scene, and had accepted a price up to eight hundred barrels, which was a large smack's cargo.

Now with the four-shilling bounty and the price per cran to which Roddie had agreed, he could not for the life of him see a smaller profit than ten shillings a barrel, and it might well be a shilling or two more. But even at ten shillings on 800 barrels his profit would be £400.

All that remained to be done was to fill the 800 barrels.

He knew the effect that his treatment of Roddie would have on Dunster and he was prepared to provide certain boats with nets at a figure profitable to himself. He would make them scrape together whatever money they had to pay part of these nets at once. Boat crews would go shares in this debt. They would be dependent on him. He would treat them reasonably. They would be his men, and if incoming curers offered better money, he would tell his men to hang on to the end of the season and trust him. This was only a beginning. They would want bigger boats, money advanced. . . .

But supposing the boats caught nothing, not even one barrel? Then there would be no money due to the fishermen, none to the gutting crews, the salt would keep. . . . He worked out his dead loss and knew he could stand it easily. He would always work out a dead loss, before starting up, say, in Helmsdale, in Lybster, in Wick itself. . . .

His mind could not dream. It got congested with excitement. And, by God, with a roaring fishing here he might make enough profit in drink to cover all his working expenses this year! . . .

As he emerged from his private room he met his wife who asked him, "Did you remember to pay Roddie his threepence for the fish?"

"What fish?" asked her husband. Then, remembering, he snorted with sarcasm and entered the bar as if he had been treated to a peculiar kind of joke.

On a Saturday night, about a fortnight later, Roddie and the three members of his crew entered the bar. It was crowded, for already the inn-keeper was finding business brisk. Now he at once and abruptly hailed Roddie. The flap was lifted. "This way, men." Down the passage he roared, "Johan!" His wife appeared and took command of the bar.

The men in the bar looked at one another, but did not say much. Their eyes were bright. The new boat had made a tremendous impression. Roddie and three of a crew had sailed her into the bay. No man grudged Roddie his high distinction, because he was not only a daring and persevering seaman but also had the quiet independent mind that would curry favour with no one. There were those who said he did not know his own strength, and in his twenty-first year, at the November market, with three glasses of whisky inside him, he had thrashed three men and might have killed one of them had he not been powerfully restrained. But normally he was mild-mannered and pleasant and very obliging.

It was the first time the three members of his crew had ever been in the inner room and they sat on the form to Roddie's right, like scholars in a row. Next to the door was Red Daun, a rounded stocky figure, with close-cropped red hair, small eyes, and great strength for a slow heave. He was three years older than Roddie. His palms occasionally took the weight of his body and moved it from hip to hip.

Don Sutherland was six feet two inches, dark, good-natured, slow-mannered, and about Roddie's own age. He sat quietly, prepared to listen. The youngest of the crew was Rob Maclean. He was only nineteen, but had a habitual solemn expression beyond his years. When he was six, grown folk would ask him questions in order to hear his "old-fashioned" replies. He was very dark, of middle size, with rather small features, and listened with an occasional crinkling of the eyelids. He could tell a legendary story as if it had all happened to himself.

From the recess in the wall the inn-keeper took down his bottle of "special".

"Now you've brought her home, we'll wet her!" he said heartily, and poured out five drinks. "Well, boys, here's good luck to you! I know you'll do your best and not let me down."

Roddie politely stood up and the others followed him. "Here's good health to you, Mr. Hendry. We can do no more than our best, but we'll do that. We would like to thank you very much. Good health!"

"Good health!" echoed the three.

Then they politely sat down.

"Have you agreed on everything among yourselves?"

"Yes," answered Roddie.

"Fine. It's not for me to interfere in your business, but

79

you know how, if I can help you, I will. And if things don't turn out as well as we have every reason to expect, there will always be another season for you to pay off your debt."

"Thank you," said Roddie. "What we have agreed is that when you are paid back, we'll share expenses and what we'll make among us equally."

"That seems simple enough," said Mr. Hendry. "But what about your own personal position as skipper? I mean, someone must have the final say in things."

"That's true," answered Roddie simply. "I'll have always the final say. But the money due to you must come out of the boat's earnings. All of us, therefore, must have a share in the boat equal to that amount."

"Very good. But what if anyone wants to leave—or has to leave—the boat?" asked Mr. Hendry, looking closely at Roddie.

"In that case," said Roddie, "I'll pay him out his share, and that's the end of it."

Hendry nodded slowly. "You have a clear head, Roddie —and a generous one. You might have kept an extra share for yourself. I hope"—and he looked at the three others— "that you appreciate this."

"We do that," said Rob. "But it's the way he would have it himself." His solemnity sounded comical, and they all smiled.

"Well, Roddie, as I say, it seems clear and generous."

"You were more than generous to me."

Mr. Hendry closed his mouth, then nodded once or twice. "All right," he said. But the quiet way in which Roddie led his men brought enthusiasm upon him, and in a moment the latest news of the rise of the fisheries was flowing in a torrent. "The Moray Firth is burning, from Fraserburgh, along the whole south coast, Macduff, Banff, Buckie, Lossiemouth, Brochead and a score of villages besides. We've got to go ahead. No half measures now. The money will be flowing like the river. As one man said in Wick: the creels of silver herring will turn into creels of silver crowns. And by God, boys, Dunster has to go into the lead. You'll have to fish up. Boats from the south side will be here. You'll have to beat them; you'll have to show the Wickers and Buckers a thing or two. You're the leaders now and I'm relying on you."

"We'll do our best," said Roddie.

"I know," answered Hendry, but as if that weren't the point, as if the affair were bigger than the mere doing of one's best. They felt this undertow of excitement, this bigness, this portentous looming of tremendous things.

Mr. Hendry let them out by the back door of the inn, for in their present mood they wanted to be by themselves to go over again and again every aspect of their position. Although they took a dram now and then they were not used to more than the customary small glass, and Hendry's generous portion had gone a little to their heads.

They withdrew into the shadow of a wood. Rob broke the silence by remarking in his dry, solemn way, "He seems anxious for us to do well." In their excitement they began to laugh softly.

Meantime, Mr. Hendry had returned to the bar. He stood still and cast his eyes over the silent, watching faces. "You, James, and you, Alastair, and you, William—will you come in?" He lifted the flap and the three skippers filed through without a word.

Never had Dunster known such talk, such expectation, such secret groupings and meetings. Where husbands or sons were shy or backward their womenfolk encouraged them. Women who knew how to spin hemp taught others. In the meeting- or ceilidh-houses at night nothing was talked about but the coming fishing. "Creels of silver herring will turn into creels of silver crowns" became the joke that never lost its gleam. There were two creelmakers in Dunster, and they worked all day and far into the night.

Yet this busy expectation was quite consumed in the

81

fires of excitement that spread throughout Dunster when unknown curers, and boats, and fishermen, with Scots tongues that few could understand, turned the foreshore into Babel in the first week of July.

Along the cliff-heads, from every cottage door within sight, eyes watched the fleet of boats as in the late afternoon they put out to sea. Hope and rivalry ran high.

But the first few days were almost blank, such herring as were caught being small or in poor condition. In the early morning the crews of women and girls gathered for the gutting, waited until the boats came in, and slowly drifted home. Despondency touched the quickened spirit of Dunster. Hendry could not sit still. The fishing would last only about seven weeks, and already one week was almost gone. From Scrabster round to Wick there had been good shots caught and landed. Then word came that the herring were off Clyth. On the Friday afternoon, Roddie's boat, the *Morning Star*, was the first to put to sea. He had decided to go and meet the herring. Up went his brown sail in a pleasant wind off the land. South-side boats were soon after him, and tailing far behind came the small local craft on their oars.

"That's Roddie leading the way," said young lads from the cliff-tops. The bellying sail sent a thrill through them. The sail was the thing! Watching it, fascinated, they felt charged with adventure and great deeds.

But in the morning it seemed that luck had still avoided Dunster. Small boats drew up on the edge of the tide and fishermen carried their empty nets behind the gutting stations to spread them on the green. Then a boat arrived with three crans of full herring, another with two, another with five. Voices began to rise. The creels poured their silver treasure into the gutting boxes.

But George Bremner stood idly beside Mr. Hendry. An hour later the total catch of nine boats out of their fleet of ten was four crans. The tenth boat, the *Morning Star*, had yet to come.

THE FIRST HUNT FOR THE SILVER DARLINGS

It was a small fishing, voices cried, but it was a beginning! A few of the larger boats were still to come, however. One arrived with seven crans, a second with only a creel, but the *Thistle* of Buckie put in with the top shot of the day, eleven crans.

Mr. Hendry could not contain himself, and above the hubbub shouted in English to the skipper:

" Any sign of the *Morning Star*?"

" Ay, he's comin'."

" Has he any herring?"

"Judging by the maas aboot him, I'd say he hes; but he wis well to the east'ard of us."

The Officer of the Board of Fisheries, who now arrived on the scene, had a look at the herring.

"They'll take the 'Crown Full' brand, Officer?" said the curer concerned.

The Officer nodded. "Yes, I'll give you the 'Full' brand for them all right," he answered with a smile. .

The branding of the Crown with a hot iron on the barrel of cured herring indicated the quality and assured the payment of the four-shilling bounty. Herring of the best quality, herring that were not spent, had the word "Full" branded below the Crown. The foreign merchant accepted these brands, and bought and sold on them, in a faith that was never let down.

The curer to whom the *Thistle* was engaged began poking sly fun at Mr. Hendry, who grew more restless with his voice tending to rise into a shout. He was defiant, because inwardly he was fearful and cast down. If only the *Morning Star* would arrive with, say, twelve or thirteen crans, by God, that would show them! He stumped away to keep his anxiety within bounds. If, on the other hand, Roddie arrived with no more than a creel or two. . . . Feeling his hopes crashing in upon him, Mr. Hendry was unable to pursue the thought further.

But when, at long last, the *Morning Star* was seen coming round the Head, low to the sea, as if nearly sunk, Mr.

Hendry stood dead still. A voice cried, "By the Lord, he's in them to the gunnels!"

Women excitedly crowded to the crest of the beach, shoving their way among the men and boys. The *Morning Star* approached slowly under four oars, followed by a whirling cloud of maas (gulls). The early breath of sea wind had taken off and the water swung and glittered under a bright sky. The two after oars were shipped and Roddie, at the tiller, guided the forefoot of his boat gently on to the sloping shingle.

"She has thirty crans," cried George Bremner, "if she has a herring!"

But Hendry could not answer him. He could not speak. Indeed the boat wavered before him and he impatiently swept the back of a hand across his eyes. Then he roared at Roddie, "Well done!" and waved his fist.

Roddie smiled.

That Saturday evening, the inn was besieged by a vast crowd, more varied and strange-tongued than in all its history, and it had a clan battle of sorts to its credit or discredit.

A few grey-beards from outlying crofts wandered down to warm themselves at the fires of life that had come to Dunster. Had they accepted all the hospitality offered them by open-handed seamen they would never have managed home on their own feet. As it was, two of them experienced slight, but not unpleasant, difficulty in following the uneven paths.

"We are living in strange times," said Donald.

"Strange times, indeed. What with Boney off to St. Helena besides," replied Lachie.

"The world is growing young."

"And we are growing old, sorrow take it."

"When I looked on that young fellow and thought to myself that in one night he had made more money than we will make off a croft in a twelve-month—it was hard to believe. There must be a terrible lot of money in all the world."

"Think of Wick and Fraserburgh and Helmsdale and all the other places on the Moray Firth—it beats me where the money can come from."

"It's enough almost to frighten a man. Do you think it can last?"

"I have a misgiving myself. It seems hardly right."

"Even my feet are astonished," said Donald.

"Let us take it easy," said Lachie, whose own feet were a trifle wayward.

The two old men sat down and looked back towards the inn and caught a distant glimpse of the high sea. They spoke of the harshness of landlords and of the ills that had befallen their folk. They recalled pleasant days of their distant youth. Perhaps happiness would come to the folk again and more money than ever they had known. For the sea was free to all. They looked upon it, bright still in the darkling night.

"Do you know, man, Lachie, when I saw that lad Roddie, tall and fair, with his blue eyes and his quiet ways, I had the sort of feeling that he had come himself up out of the sea like—like one sent to deliver us."

"Had you now?" asked Lachie, with a glance at Donald.

"I just saw him like that."

"Who knows? Perhaps you're right. It felt to me myself like the beginning of strange and wonderful things. But maybe we'd better be going, or they will be saying stranger things to us when we get home."

Donald's blue eyes glimmered like a boy's as he stared away at the sea. Then his grey beard doubled on his chest as he got carefully to his feet.

CHAPTER V

FINN AND THE BUTTERFLY

Τhe first day he had seen the two white butterflies flitting about the cabbages, little Finn had stared with great astonishment, but after a time had summoned courage to approach them, whereupon they had risen high over his head and got tossed away on the air like flakes of snow. This had excited him keenly, and when he asked his mother in the evening, as she tucked him into bed, what they were, she said they were called "grey fools".

"But they're not grey, Mama."

"What colour, then?"

"White."

"That's right. You're Mama's clever boy, aren't you? And when you grow up to be a big man . . ."

But he was not interested in her words and words tonight. "Where do they come from, Mama?"

"Oh, well, you see, they come from—from many places."

"Do they? What places?"

"Many and many a place."

"Do they come from Helmsdale?"

"Yes."

"And do they come from Canada?"

"Well, I don't know if they come from Canada. They would have to cross the sea."

"What's the sea, Mama? Is it a big, big place full of water?"

"Yes."

"How big is it?"

"It's very, very big. It's bigger than all the moor at the back, away, away to Morven, and farther than that."

"Is it? It must be awful big."

"Yes. Now, come, say your prayer and go to sleep, for if little boys don't sleep they won't grow into big men, and what——"

"Mama? Couldn't the grey fools cross above the sea in the air?"

"They might. But it would be such a long, long way that they would grow tired and then what would happen to them?"

"What?"

"What do you think?"

"Would they fall into the sea and be drowned?"

"Yes. Just as little boys will be drowned if they fall into the river. And that's why I have told you never to——"

"Did you ever know anyone who was drowned, Mama? Did you, Mama?"

"Yes."

"Who?"

"Now go to your sleep. I can't stay here with you all night. Come. *To-night as I lie down*——"

"Mama, tell me, where do the grey fools go when they fly away from the garden?"

But altogether his mother had been very unsatisfactory, and her final admission that it was God who made grey fools was nothing new, for God made everything. You can always tell when an old person is going to say it is God.

But the butterflies excited him in a way nothing had ever excited him before. They appeared suddenly out of no-where, like magic, and were white, white. They would wait on a cabbage leaf until you almost had them and then —they were off, not like a bird, but drifting up and down in the strangest way.

Until one day he so nearly caught one that he leapt after it in the air and fell. This time the butterfly merely flitted to another young cabbage, and being angry against it for making him fall, he stalked it with a stone in his hand.

But once again the butterfly eluded him, and he threw the stone at it. The butterfly drifted over the low wall, and he ran after it and saw it meet another butterfly. Together they danced in the air, until one slanted away and alighted on a green leaf. Finn was so eager now that, once over the wall, he rushed up to the butterfly as if he might be swift enough to stamp on it with his foot.

The butterfly arose and, drifting on in its careless, aggravating way, drew Finn after it. When it had passed from view over a bank, he ran his hardest to surprise it on the other side.

And he so very nearly did that both his excitement and his anger increased.

It was at that moment that death entered into his heart. He would kill the butterfly.

His hair was dark and his eyes brown—if not so brown as his mother's, and on his child's skin—he was four and a half years of age—there was a faint flush of blood and guilt. So he had to keep going after the butterfly and away from home.

He went on and on, round little bushes and under big boulders, and sometimes the grassy bank was so steep that he slid on his bottom and then his kilt came away up and he was all bare from the waist down. His kilt was crotal-brown for his mother had made it out of her old skirt, and his jersey, which Granny Kirsty had knitted, was brown, too. His feet and his legs were a delicate tan, and his head was bare. He had lost the butterfly altogether and here he was at the stream clawing his thigh where a flat prickly plant had stung him. He would have waited to attack the plant for stinging him if it hadn't been for the butterfly and the guilt in his mind. He looked back up the slope to make sure that his mother wasn't after him. She would be very angry. She said last time that she wouldn't spank him that time, but that she would next time. This was next time.

FINN AND THE BUTTERFLY

The butterfly wouldn't wait when he cried "Wait" to it, and then it had made him fall, though he had meant no harm to it, and then it had run away. His expression became all the more sober for a queer self-conscious smile in it, and, standing still, picking at a bush, he looked up the brae again. When the wordless inner argument was concluded, he felt anger against his mother as well as against the butterfly. Whereupon he moved along the bank looking, with moody right, into the little pools.

He saw a brown trout. He saw two, he saw three, and as he couldn't count beyond three the next number he saw was eighteen. One big fellow went under a flat stone quite close to the edge on the other side, and where he went in the water was dirtied with brown stuff that rose up in a tiny cloud, so that you knew exactly where he was.

It was a difficult business, crossing the burn, because of the jumps between the boulders, but by wading through the stream where it ran out of the pool, and hanging on to a boulder at the same time, he needn't jump at all and the only real difficulty was keeping his feet on the slimy stones, they were so slippery. The water didn't come right up his legs and he could lift his kilt with one hand. In the middle, however, when he let go the boulder behind him, he found he could neither go forward nor back, and stood swaying and slightly stooped. The small round stones under his feet wanted to slip away. If he moved, he would fall. The only thing left in the world to do was to cry for his mother, to cry loud, loud. But even while he was beginning to cry he took the step forward. The water came to his knees, he let go his kilt, and with a mighty effort lunged for the next boulder a whole foot away. His courage was rewarded and, hardly having cried to his mother at all, he drew himself out of that desperate spot, with its treacherous footing, and very soon was wading across the last shallow, with such carefree ease that he slipped and fell as neat as a penny on his bottom.

At this, having run the gamut of the emotions in so short

a time, he had full right to weep bitterly and angrily, but the flop had been so sudden and complete that its astonishment also made him want to laugh, and by the time he climbed on to the bank and found that no irreparable damage had been done, the uncertain sounds faded out altogether and he glanced around not displeased to find that his misadventure had passed unobserved.

Now for that trout!

He discovered, however, when he carefully surveyed the position, several natural obstacles of considerable, if not unsurmountable, difficulty. From the other side, the water above the stone had looked little more than up to the ankle, whereas now it was up to the knee. The ground sloped down into the centre of the pool, and though it was a little pool, it was deep as a bowl. Accordingly, if he slipped, he would surely be drowned. So he proceeded into the water with the utmost care, leaning sideways towards the bank as he tested each foothold. His kilt, which was sopping wet, became a great embarrassment, because he wanted to keep it from getting wet again. Holding the front part of it high up, he lowered himself slowly into a sitting-down posture. He began to wobble, and thus compelled to let the front of his kilt join the rest of it in the water, he was at once denied all further view of the stone.

On the bank he stood squeezing the water from his kilt but looking at the stone. To tell the truth, he was also just a little afraid of the trout, for it was a monster of four inches and darted with a yellow gleam like lightning. Roddie had told him that a trout did not bite anything except worms, but that an eel would bite your finger as fast as look at you. Besides, to get his hand right down to the stone, he would wet all his jersey, and it was perhaps a little wet as it was.

He would like to do something to that trout for wetting all his kilt on him. He would like to hit it a good hard wallop whatever. Casting around him (with a first glance in the direction of home), he saw a bunch of hazel trees growing nearby, with the young shoots, twice as long as himself, coming straight up out of the ground. If he got a stick and gave it one sharp prog under the stone! What a fright the trout would get, and maybe it would kill him! And then he would catch the trout and take it home and his mother . . . He glanced up, not too sure that his mother would forgive him even then, though he was taking food to the house.

As he rounded the hazel trees a butterfly rose from his feet. He knew at once it was the same butterfly, by the way it flew, side to side and up and down, laughing at him. It was like a fool, the way it went. It settled; and slowly, without looking at it (except out of the very corner of his eye), he moved towards it, but not directly. He got within a few feet, but then could not restrain himself from rushing. The butterfly rose and danced on through the air, down the burnside.

He followed it at once, without thought, because he had had by the pool for a moment a queer dread that his mother's head and shoulders would rise large and menacing over the edge of the brae. If he went farther on then he would be hidden from that near horizon.

The burn wound its way down between the steep braes, and sometimes he had to climb and sometimes to slide, but soon he came to a part he had never seen before, and then he knew he was safe from his mother's eye.

The uneasy, half-smiling expression on his face, he stopped to pick a grass and to chew it, looking cautiously around him at the same time. He had lost the butterfly and was not thinking about it. He was thinking of his mother and what she might do to him. She had no right to do that to him. She had not.

He began to go on, away from home, away, away from that place where his mother was, in a strange mood that was near to tears and yet far from them.

But the world itself was strange, too. There were grey rocks and great, green ferns, and in time he came to another

little burn, and these two joined into one. He crossed it at
a very shallow place because beyond it was the biggest
wood he had ever seen, on a steep hillside, and no one
would ever find him in that wood, though he himself could
lie and watch and see who was coming. Perhaps his mother
would come and she would be crying and crying, thinking
he was drowned.

The thought of her crying made him feel sorry for her, but
it also did him a lot of good. He would be greatly missed.

At that moment his eye landed on a tiny blue object
poised on a primrose leaf. He was bending down to touch
it when it took to the air. It was a small blue butterfly, the
bonniest thing he had ever seen, and his eyes grew round
in brightness and wonder. He ran after it in a rapture, but
when he got up from his second fall it had vanished. Where
did you go? Where? Where? He followed into the wood.

Though the trees and bushes were not high, still they
seemed high to him, and being in full foliage, he found that
they shut out a view of the ground down by the stream. It
was a bit frightening in the wood, too, because the trees
were still and had queer twisted shapes often. When he
listened and tried to see past the trees, he could hear little
birds singing, and once a rabbit gave him a fright.

He could hardly have climbed up through the wood were
it not for a narrow, slanting path used by sheep and cattle.
This invited him on, and every step he took made it more
difficult for him to go back; and though the going on terrified him under his heart, yet it also gave him the feeling of
one fated to go away. Not that he was going away, away,
yet, but—but near it; so near it that anyone else would
think he was.

Every few yards he stopped and nibbled and gazed about
him, and occasionally his expression grew so self-conscious
that someone might have been watching him; and once his
face for a moment grew shyly merry in the most engaging
way. Then he came back to thought of the blue butterfly,
and craned round trunks, and stared at unusual shapes for a

long time. Sometimes when he stared like that his round, shining-clear eyes would lift to a disturbed leaf without movement of his head, and when he went on a few paces he would slowly turn his head and look back as if he weren't looking at the thing he had been staring at.

There was something in this wood a little bit like what there was in the butterfly, only it was very much stronger than he was, just as he was stronger than the butterfly. Now and then the wood was like a thing whose heart had stopped, watching.

This faint panic might in an instant turn to wild fear; but the instant never came, not quite. And the chequered sunlight was everywhere, full of an aromatic warmth, through which the notes of the little birds fell unafraid.

All the same, when at last he saw he was getting near the top, he went on without stopping once, and would have been very tired had he not emerged and gazed down and around upon the whole world.

He saw more houses than ever he had seen before, and one house—one house—seemed familiar and yet strangely small, and he could never have been certain it was his own home if he hadn't seen black Jean and red Bel, the two milch cows, tethered beyond the house in the rough grass towards the burn. They were small also. Like a discoverer, he was proud and excited, and then had a great longing for the home he could see.

But no one was about the house, neither his mother nor Granny Kirsty, and it looked indeed a dead and deserted house. It terrified him the way it lay. His breast became a conflict of many emotions.

But whatever it was deep down that had possession of him now, he turned and walked away. And he went a little blindly, in great sadness, in pity for himself, and with a terrible longing for his mother that yet had in it something alien and withdrawn.

At that moment he saw the white butterfly, the lovely thing that had lured him from his home.

FINN AND THE BUTTERFLY

Like the gay fool it was, it flitted and poised, with the airiest inconsequence, until it settled on a green leaf and flattened its wings. When little Finn sat down, the up-curled edge of the leaf hid the butterfly from his view. On hands and knees he went slowly towards the leaf through the coarse old grass. He did not raise his head or rush the last yard. He had had his lesson more than once. From the grass he slowly lifted his right hand to the near edge of the leaf and then pounced, bringing the leaf and himself head-long into the grass, but with a wild fluttering under his palm, a mad flickering and tickling. He did not let go. He crushed, he crushed, and felt the butterfly break. Instantly he drew back his hand. His palm was covered with silvery dust. On the broken leaf the butterfly lay dead.

He wiped his palm against his breast and looked around. Guilt was glittering in his eyes and congested in his face. He got up and went away, slowly at first, but then with steps that broke into a run. When he fell he gave a squawk, got up at once, and with a backward glance ran on. When he was out of sight of the spot he stopped. He had killed the butterfly. A smile struggled to come into his face; his eyes kept glancing brilliantly. He performed small acts of bravado, stamping down a bracken, kicking the grass. His mind was in a mounting tumult. He trod on his familiar prickly leaf and the tumult broke. Curled up in the grass, he wept and sobbed wildly, drenchingly, until he was com-pletely exhausted.

No-one came to him. He was all alone in the world. As he went slowly on, he saw a house up the slope to his left. He bore away, and when the collie dog barked from the gable-end he crouched under an overhanging bank peering round now and then at the dog. A woman came out and asked the collie what it was barking at, as if she were expecting someone. "You old fool," she said to the collie, and went away. The dog sniffed the corner of the low wall in front of the house, scraped the ground, and growled; then turned after the woman.

Some time after that he found himself on a small green field, with a hill in front and immense ruined walls running down from it. For the first time his loneliness came upon him in a great fear. He was so little that he could not run away and stood exposed in the centre of all the light in the world. As he tried to walk out of that field he felt great weights on his knees, but he got out of it, away from the walls, and round the corner of the hill. Here were high rocks with massive boulders at their feet shutting off the upland on his left hand. In front, a rolling field was cultivated. He thought first of going down one of the rigs, but he held to the base of the hill on his right, for there were no walls on this side, until he saw the river. His tiredness was now so heavy upon him that he began to whimper at sight of the river and could not go any farther. The whimpering filled all his mind so that he had not to think any more of what was going to happen to him. He lay down on his right side, pulled his knees up, and hid his face with his arms and hands, whimpering as into his mother's bosom in the moment before sleep overtakes. The earth's bosom was warm with the sun and soon little Finn was sound asleep.

The sun woke him in its own time, and after a first bodily stirring his eyes opened and he remained dead still. Then his eyes roamed in slow wonder, widened with fear. For one terrible moment he was lost in the abyss of Nowhere, in a nightmare of sunlight and strange appearances. Vividly intense, it yet passed in an instant, and the world of memory stood in its place.

He got to his feet and saw a man down by the river. For several seconds he could not move because he knew it was Roddie, and Roddie had stopped.

Finn turned to go back along the base of the hill. Roddie called, "Is that you, Finn?"

Finn did not answer, but kept on steadily. "Here, Finn!" Finn did not turn round, and when he knew that Roddie was coming after him he began to run.

Roddie very soon overtook him, but whenever he caught

him Finn began to struggle violently, saying, "Let me go! Let me go!"

"But Finn, Finn, my little hero, where is it you're going?"

"Let me be!" and he twisted so fiercely that Roddie had to let him down lest he rupture himself.

Crouched at Roddie's feet, face to the grass, he refused to answer any questions.

"Well, I don't think that's a nice way to treat a fellow," said Roddie, sitting down beside him. "Anyway, aren't you coming back home?"

"No."

"Oh," said Roddie, "I didn't know you were going away. But you haven't got anything with you. You can't go away without taking your packet of bread and milk. A man must do that or he can't go at all. I'm going off to Helmsdale to-morrow morning and I'm going home now for my packet of bread and milk. You wouldn't like to go to Helmsdale, would you? That's a long way off, if you like; over the sea, beyond the mountains, across the Ord. I have been getting my boat ready. You can see the spots of tar on my hands, if you look. Look!"

Finn turned his face just far enough to see the splotches of tar on Roddie's fingers and palms.

Shortly after that Finn was walking with his hand in Roddie's. Roddie had promised to take him in his boat, saying Finn would be a great help to him, especially if he was a little older.

But when they came to the place where the two burns met and Finn realized he was drawing near home, he hung back upon Roddie's hand. Roddie talked persuasively, but Finn tugged strongly.

"Look!" said Roddie. "Look! there's 'God's fool' watching you."

Finn saw the butterfly and stared. His body went all stiff.

"Did you never see one before?" asked Roddie. "There's

often one or two of them about here. If you come with
me——"

"No!" screamed Finn. "No!"

Roddie, squatting, put his hands round him, but Finn,
losing his head in his violence, beat Roddie in the face,
screaming wildly.

"Tut, tut, tut," said Roddie, throwing back his face,
"what a fighter you are! Surely you are not frightened of a
little thing like God's fool. God's fool would never hurt
anyone."

"No," screamed Finn, "not God's fool, it's—it's grey
fool." And he stamped the ground and again blindly attacked Roddie.

Roddie wondered for a moment, for though the real
name of the butterfly was God's fool (*amadan-De*), and
though it was also called grey fool (*amadan-leith*), still the
distinction should merely have interested little Finn, and
certainly not have produced this frenzy. Then his eyes were
arrested, and he said to Finn, "Hsh, here's someone coming."

But the thought of anyone's coming only made Finn
worse, and he screamed louder than ever, refusing even to
look, for an intimacy in the hush of Roddie's voice communicated the awful fear that the person coming was his
mother.

Catrine stopped, her hand to her heart in the characteristic gesture, then she came running. She never looked at
Roddie, her deep-brown eyes round and wild, her face pale,
as if she had been a long time with ghosts. She snatched up
little Finn, one arm under his damp kilt and one round his
shoulders, pressing him against her breast. He struggled,
but his struggles had no meaning, no outlet. "My darling,
my own one," she murmured passionately, and put about
him in no time such a smothering atmosphere of love and
endearment, that his struggles grew tired, and even his
weeping fell away into snorts and hiccoughs. But he could
hardly afford to give up this tremulous weeping even if he

had been able (which indeed he wasn't), because all else was lost to him except the knowledge that his mother should have been angry and spanked him, and instead here she was loving him. But at any moment she might remember and change. To be spanked before Roddie was now a terror beyond all others. Thus his position was very complicated and pitiful, and its sad desperation broke in his throat.

Roddie looked on with his detached smile, thoughtfully, until Catrine suddenly faced him and asked, "Where did you find him?"

"Oh, we were just down the road a bit," he said, nodding backwards with his head. "Can't Finn and I have a walk together if we like?"

But she was far beyond humour. "Surely," she gasped, "you hadn't him at the shore?"

"Not quite, perhaps. But, you see, Finn and I have arranged to sail together, so, you see——" He stopped, before her expression of horror and fear.

"You wouldn't dare!" she gulped, her breathing beginning to come rapidly again.

"Well, all right. I sort of promised, because—well, never mind." He smoothed a splotch of dry tar with the ball of a thumb, regarding it with his head slightly tilted.

"Where was he?"

He met her eyes. "As a matter of fact, I found him taking a rest in the House of Peace."

She stared at him until she saw that what he said was true. Then a swift change came over her face, softening it in a wild glancing way, and immediately she turned and walked hurriedly off, though even in that moment he had seen the glisten of reaction.

Yet Catrine did not break down, did not even weep, though the tears ran down her face, and wen she got into a hidden nook she wiped her eyes with the back of her hand before sitting and taking Finn on her lap. Her shoulder shook two moss-yellow bees out of a purple foxglove, but she hardly heard them. She gave Finn a little secret hug against her breast, and then, lowering her head, said softly, "Tell Mama where you went?"

He would not answer, but buried his face where it had been a moment before. However, in a short time she got him to mutter: "I was chasing God's fool."

"What's that? Who said God's fool?"

"Roddie. It's not God's fool, is it? It's grey fool? Isn't it, Mama?" His voice broke, threatening hysteric sobs again.

"Yes, yes. It's grey fool. Roddie had no right to say God's fool. That's an old name—and it's a sin to use God's name. It's grey fool, as Mama told you."

Feeling comforted, he said, "I saw a little one, a little blue one. It was—it was—lovely. Did—did you ever see a blue one?"

"Yes."

"Where?"

"In the strath of Kildonan."

"Was that when you were a little girl?"

"Yes."

"Long ago?"

"Long, long ago."

His eyes opened thoughtfully, in silence.

"Did you chase the butterfly?" she asked.

He moved with confusion and muttered, "Yes."

"Was it chasing the butterfly that took you away from home?"

He picked at the bodice of her dress. "Yes."

"Tell Mama," she whispered.

He tried to raise his eyes but failed. Then he said, "I killed the butterfly," and smothered his sobbing mouth against her.

Though Catrine might have killed many butterflies to save him a scratch, she found herself without words. She caressed his back, and stared over his head at the intermingling of terrors and meanings in life, hidden, but there.

Her lips trembled. The meanings had started to take her son away from her. Already the terrible knowledge of good and evil was in him. He had killed the butterfly.

Coming up in the late evening of the same day from the sea, Roddie decided to call on Catrine. He would hardly have called at such an hour had he not taken some drink.

But the crew had visited the inn for final instructions and farewell, and Mr. Hendry, in his enthusiasm over opening a station in Helmsdale, had taken the inevitable bottle of "special" from its recess.

It was, in truth, a memorable occasion for Dunster because now for the first time a local boat was leaving its shores to fish from a distant port.

These last few years the prosperity of Dunster had greatly increased. There was hardly a household that did not directly or indirectly make a few pounds out of the summer fishing; and these few pounds, in a simple economy, put the household beyond fear of want. There was an enlivening increase in activity and warmth and life. Out of assurance and hope the natural gaiety and passions of the folk expanded.

Roddie had done particularly well—though, for that matter, no better than the three members of his crew. The debt on the boat had been paid off and, if he liked, he could at any moment now buy out the other three shares. Not that he ever thought of doing such a thing. But he saw that the boat was kept ship-shape and in first-class trim and that each member of the crew was responsible for his own nets. Already he was dreaming of a larger boat, for there were three now in Dunster as big as his own.

He had not been anxious to go to Helmsdale, for he knew the home grounds well, and knew in particular when it was no longer possible to make the river-mouth in a heavy sea. The season before last, five boats had been smashed and many nets lost in a sudden storm, and when all hope for the *Morning Star* had gone news came that Roddie had

sailed her into Cromarty in the wake of a Buckie boat, with
every net intact.

Hendry's reliance on him to lead his new Helmsdale venture to success had touched his spirit and perhaps his pride.
He had consented at once and, with reasonable weather,
they were to set off to-morrow morning.

In the deep twilight of the summer night Catrine's home
looked quiet and still; indeed everything looked quiet and
still, the grey stones and the bushes, the rising ground, the
slow lines of the horizon against the remote clear sky. As
Roddie involuntarily stood, he heard the sound of the running burn, not consciously but as the sound of waters at a
great distance, for his eyes were held by the cottage.

The land, the quiet land, which for ever endures,
threaded by women and children, in the bright patterns of
their lives. Remote from the sea, from the turbulence of
oncoming waves, from the quick movement, the excitement, from the mind of a man like Special, with his flow of
silver herring that changed into a flow of silver crowns.
There's money in it, men, money, money.

Money. The power, the wizardry of it, set a man walking on his own feet. But Roddie was careful at the same
time to keep low down towards the burn, because there
would be little sense in letting a belated neighbour see him
going towards Catrine's at such an hour. Irked at having to
do this, when at last he climbed the slope and went towards
the cottage, he walked lightly, strung up against any sound
even in himself. At the low end of the house, he paused till
his breathing moderated, then went past the byre door to
the kitchen window on noiseless feet, careful not to disturb
the collie.

Slowly he brought his head past the side of the window.
Catrine was sitting beyond the fire, one hand, with elbow
resting on knee, stretched towards the peat, arrested by
thought or reverie in the very act of smothering the live
embers. He saw her features against the red glow, warm
and soft, not only with her own beauty, but with all

women's beauty. It was a picture a man might glimpse once in a lifetime, and have a vision of women afterwards in his mind that time or chance, good or evil, would never change. Like the still landscape that had troubled him a moment, when he first looked up at the cottage.

A profound sorrow moved in him and a desire to lift her lightly in his arms and gently.

This emotion must have touched her for she suddenly raised her eyes. He saw her hand grip her chest, heard the strangled intake of breath, and he moved his open hand back and fore quickly to quieten her. She could not know him; he had to tell who he was; something of fear and horror touched him. "Catrine, it's me, Roddie. Roddie."

The collie growled and barked.

Her chest began to heave from the deep breaths that went in through her quivering mouth. She got to her feet and came slowly to the window, her fallen hand quietening the dog. The fire now behind her, she was more pale than a ghost against the dim night-light. She withdrew from his words, and in a second or two they faced each other across the threshold.

"I'm sorry I'm so late," he said. "We're off in the morning, and I was wondering if I could take any messages for you to your people."

"You gave me a fright," she answered. "Won't you come in?"

"It's very late."

"Who's there?" called Kirsty, from the middle room.

"It's Roddie Sinclair," Catrine answered. "He's off to Helmsdale in the morning and he's wondering if we have any messages."

"What hour is this to come round?" demanded Kirsty, "and decent folk in their beds."

"We've been working late, getting the boat ready," called Roddie, the relief of humour in his voice. "But if that's all you have to say to me, I'll be going."

"Ah, you, Roddie! But when you go to Helmsdale you'll

come amongst decent people, and if anyone asks for me, you'll remember me to them."

"I will that," cried Roddie. "And I'll tell them you wouldn't go back to the Cattach country though you were paid for it."

"You rascal," she said. "It's the good stick you need. And don't keep that bairn out of her bed."

"Won't you wish me luck?"

"No."

"Why that?"

"Because it's not lucky," declared Kirsty. "Don't forget to say your prayers, and may Himself look after you."

"Thank you," responded Roddie.

"Will you come in?" Catrine asked, smiling now.

"It's late," he said. "I shouldn't have come at all, only I didn't——"

"Come in for a minute. I was just thinking of bed."

Roddie followed her. "No, no, don't touch the fire. I'm going."

She pressed the peats together and they broke into a bright flame.

"So there he is, quiet enough now." Roddie looked at Finn's sleeping face over which the shadows flickered. "He had a day and a half."

"Yes," she murmured. Their eyes rested for a little on the child. "It was kind of you to come."

As his head turned round she smelt the whisky in his breath. He smiled now in his detached pleasant way. "I would have asked you earlier but you were in such a hurry to be off with him to-day that you hardly saw me."

"That worried me, too. I should have thanked you, but I was all upset. I was sure he was drowned. I was sick with fear. I cannot tell you the awful—awful experience it was. I must have seemed demented." Her hands and arms started writhing a little as she smiled. Otherwise the horrible memory had left a quietness in her manner.

"Was he away long?"

"Hours and hours. We searched everywhere, the hill, the burn, crying on him. . . . What was he doing when you found him?"

"He had been asleep."

Silence fell between them.

"You'll remember me to those at home if you see any of them. Tell them we're very well."

"I'll make a point of seeing them. Surely. If there's anything I could do, you know I'd do it."

"I know."

Silence came about them again.

"Won't you sit down?" she asked.

"No. I'll be going." He stood quite still. "Well, I'll be going."

"Thank you for coming."

He turned his head and looked into her face. Her smile was open and friendly and her dark eyes glimmered with light. He removed his eyes as if he were doing it thoughtfully. The characteristic smile came to his face, tilting one corner of his mouth a trifle in a light humour. "So long," he said pleasantly.

She followed him to the door.

"Good-bye," she said, not offering her hand. "Take care of the sea."

"The sea!" She saw his face in profile steady against the night. Then he turned upon her a long searching look, drawing something out of her. But before she could feel the discomfort of this he nodded "Good-bye" and walked off.

CHAPTER VI

THE LAND AND THE SEA

W ith an expert jab of the elbow, Williamson released the brake and the four horses thundered
across the bridge, the stage coach swaying as it
swung round on the right-hand turn and took the incline on
the east side of the river. Some three hundred yards and he
drew them to a standstill at the change-house of Tighdubh,
on the left of the road. While the strappers got busy,
Williamson sat like an emperor looking down over two
naturally terraced fields at the sweep of the bay between its
cliffs. There was the usual small crowd to watch the great
event of the day, and when a respectful interval had super-
vened an elderly voice asked if there was any news of the
fishing in Helmsdale.

"Good fishing to-day," said Williamson to the bay.

"Any word of Roddie Sinclair?"

"Dunster boat had twenty-one crans." Without looking
at anyone, Williamson climbed stiffly down in the great
coat that he wore winter and summer, with the difference
that in winter the lapels framed his ruddy face with its
clipped, pointed, ginger beard and in summer lay flat. He
moved up to the stables to comfort himself, while the
horses were being changed.

Kirsty, who had been paying one or two visits—she
dearly loved a talk with Granny Gordon about families in
the fine old days before the clearances—came home in the
first of the evening and told Catrine the news.

"I'm so glad," said Catrine, standing still and looking
away. She saw Dale and Helmsdale, the boats on the sea.

Suddenly she ran after Finn, crying, "Where are you going?" He sped on, shouting with laughter and, looking back over his shoulder, stumbled and fell. But he did not cry as she gathered him up. She spoke rapidly to him, laughing and leaning back, and then ran away from his pursuit right round the house. When she felt quite herself again, she came back to find Kirsty already out of her visiting blacks.

"You're coddling that boy too much," said Kirsty, who felt thát Catrine should not have run off at such a moment but should have hung about her welcoming her back, and asking for all the news she was bursting to tell. Finn gazed at the drawn visage of Granny, with its straight furrows going down under the chin in a way that made you feel she was going to bark the next word at you—which she sometimes did—and hesitated. Often when she looked harshest she was near to the point of yielding something. Now her right hand went into a deep pocket in her skirt and there was a rustling of paper. "You're wondering, aren't you?" she said to Finn, making a face at him. He was not intimidated. On the contrary, his eyes gleamed. And presently the hand emerged with a round hard white sweet which Finn accepted in concentrated silence. "Where's your manners?" "Thank you," murmured Finn. "See you don't choke on it," added Kirsty. Still without removing the paper-bag from her pocket, she handed one to Catrine.

Catrine asked for Mrs. Gordon. "She's very well," replied Kirsty. Catrine asked one question after another, until, mollified, Kirsty at last got down to her news.

Kirsty dealt in facts about living or dead people, and though Catrine might not have known them, still they came out of the background she knew and gave it a movement of colour and life like the lines in a tartan. It was an extraordinary background, too, even tumultuous at times in its far-flung riot of adventurous living. Kirsty's father had been a leaseholder or tacksman, not on a very large scale, it is true, but yet in the material realm on a more secure and affluent basis than was the ordinary clansman or cottar who had made up the bulk of the population. Often these tacksmen traced kinship to a ruling chief or landlord through a mathematical system of cousinhood, linking up younger sons and daughters in an intricate yet clearly defined pattern. Because of the restricted economic outlet, however (for an acre of land is constant), the large families of these tacksmen had themselves to become cottars or crofters and in this way over untold centuries a feeling of blood-relationship had come to pervade a group or clan, and not only to one another but to the heads or rulers of the clan themselves. For the most part this relationship was so tenuous as to be completely indefinite, and in practical living was forgotten, yet it lived on in the blood, and if, say, a man's name was Mackay, he instinctively felt, to the point of fighting for it, that he held the honour of all the Mackays in his keeping.

In the bloody aftermath to the Jacobite Rising of 1745 the clan system was smashed; and what was left of it was swept away by the chiefs themselves in the notorious treachery and brutality of the clearances that began at the end of that same century and continued sporadically for two generations. Yet, though political and economic revolution might come overnight, the pulse of the blood does not change so readily nor the secret paths in tradition's hinterland get blotted out at a stroke, not generally, anyway.

Again, however, because of the restricted economic outlet, all the members of the tacksmen's families could not find reasonable holdings amongst the crofters, even if they had wanted to, which they didn't—so long as any more alluring outlet presented itself. Soldiers of fortune they became rather than traders, and their names, thinly disguised, linger over northern Europe and, at odd times, still come into prominence. As with the tacksmen's families, so with the crofters'; and in that outer world, where merit and courage had the staying power, many an odd twist was given to fortune's wheel.

107

With the clearances came enforced mass emigration, and in Catrine's short lifetime, boatloads of her own desperate people had been shipped to Canada, where, working through terrors and distress and death, they were building up new generations in a new land. They were emigrating, too, to Australia. Men she could all but remember had fought and been killed in South Africa, and men she could remember had been slaughtered in the terrible battle before New Orleans. Colonizers, explorers, fighters, traders, from Hudson to India, from the plain of Waterloo to the Blue Mountains of the Cape. Such geographic names were familiar on Kirsty's lips, not in any vague way but connected with someone she knew or knew about.

It was her mention of Langwell that first arrested Catrine's attention; and for a little while thereafter she hardly heard what Kirsty was saying. She could see Langwell House on the other side of the deep-wooded glen, but what she felt was the dark sensation of the shepherd over the ridge behind. For in recent months this shepherd had visited her more than once in her dreams. The memory of each of these dreams or nightmares was a horror. He came at her slowly, with his full intention hot and blood-dark in his face. She retreated backward until her legs could no longer move and her throat drew so taut that it cramped and would let no sound pass. Only when she felt his hot breath on her face and the grip of his hands about her was she released to a struggle that, however, could not push off his overpowering, smothering weight, and only when she felt herself growing weak did the last remnant of her strength in a desperate thrust succeed in awakening her. She was naturally afraid lest her very fear of having this dream would only help its recurrence and, growing accustomed to it, she might lose the strength to fight successfully. Deeper than that, too, was the awful suggestion she had got of the body's possible treachery and, far below that, of the horrible dark ultimate compliance of a mind that was hardly hers.

THE LAND AND THE SEA

"The Langwell connection was through the father, Major George Sutherland, who was the second son of the then Laird of Langwell. The Sutherlands of Langwell were an important family with a pedigree going far back into the ancient line itself. As well as Berriedale, they also had Swiney, down Latheron way, and again from a second son you get the Sutherlands of Swiney. However, this Major George Sutherland had been in the army, and when he retired on half-pay he leased the farm of Midgarty, in Loth, from the Countess, or I suppose I should say from the Earl of Sutherland, for though it was her land, he was her husband, if there's not much else to say about him. Well, this Major George was twice married. To the first wife he had eight daughters and two sons, and to the second a son and a daughter. The second wife, whose maiden name was Robinson, had an unfortunate end, poor woman. She had fallen sick and the doctor recommended medicine for her— a dose of Epsom salts, in truth, it was. But by a terrible mistake, for people were not much used to Epsom salts, and that for the good enough reason that they did not need them, was she not given a dose of saltpetre instead. Saltpetre is the stuff they made their gunpowder out of. So she died. Ay, it was a terrible tragedy. All the daughters married, except one who died young, and good matches they made. Janet was the oldest and she was married on one of the Grays of Skibo, who was a West India planter. He had a great fortune, but seemingly they were not happy together—many a dreadful story there is about him—so they separated, but without taking a divorce. I'll tell you what happened to her again. Next came Esther. This, too, was a hard case, because didn't she make a secret match of it with a son of Sheriff Sutherland of Shibercross. Her husband, who was a lieutenant, died the year after they were secretly married and then to get her widow's pension she had to produce her marriage-lines. There was great talk about it at the time. But perhaps I told you her story before?"

"Yes," said Catrine.

"Now it was the third daughter, Jean, that Mr. Sage, the beloved minister of Kildonan, married as his second wife, and so we get the Kildonan connection, through Midgarty, to the Sutherlands of Langwell. Well do I remember the day Jean was brought to Kildonan manse. It was coming on for the middle of December in the year 1794. . . ."

"Were all the daughters of Major Sutherland of Midgarty equally unfortunate?" asked Catrine presently when she got a chance.

"I was coming to that," said Kirsty, "because it's through Kildonan again that we link up with Tarboll, where Robert's bastard son, also a Robert, was brought up, about whom I heard news to-day from Mrs. Gordon. Not that the other daughters come into it, though when you come to think of it, it was a strange enough family, for all that did happen, to happen to them. But it's only like what happened to many and many. Take my own family. Where are they but scattered to the four winds. Two brothers in the Americas, one in Australia, one dead through howking the stones out of this ground we live on, a sister in London whose husband is half the time sailing the seas, and the youngest, Ruth, married to that runaway shepherd in the Borders, God help her, poor lassie, for of us all, she was my favourite."

"But she loved him?"

"Faugh! Him! What she saw in him beat me, as I told her many a time. But she made her bed and she'll lie on it, lumps and all. My father died the winter you came, howking out the same old stones. And I am all that's left, like the kail runt. However, I'm going through my story, and I've no patience for anyone who does that. Where was I? Yes. Well, as I say, Mr. Sage was married on Jean, the third daughter. The next was Williamina, and she became wife to Robert Baigrie, a retired captain of a merchantman in the West India trade. . . ."

Catrine's attention began to wander back into the old

days at Kildonan, and though she heard Kirsty's voice and
half-followed the intricate genealogical patterns it wove,
more and more the bright days of her girlhood ran in her
mind, and presently the voice fell away into the distant
monotony of water plunging into a pool . . . the haunted
pool . . . Tormad and herself . . . the red berries of the
dream. . . . She drew back and listened to the voice.

". . . It was a strange wild story and difficult to follow
all the ins and outs of it. But back to the West Indies
Robert went. That was in the year 1810—the year after
my father was told there would be no renewal of his lease.
Well, he became the chief counsellor to the king of an
island there—Haiti, it was called. The king's name was
Christoph, or Christopher, after Christopher Columbus, it
was said. However that may be, poor Robert died shortly
afterwards. And it was his bastard son who was brought up
at Torboll. So now we come——"

"Mama! Bel's in the corn!"

At once the two women arose and went rushing out,
followed by Roy, already barking and in such intemperate
haste that he took the two feet clean from Kirsty on the
threshold and left her sitting and looking after him in helpless, if not silent, wrath. On he sped, followed by Catrine
and Finn, the hens that had been gathering with an idea of
going to roost flying out of the way in the noisiest excitement, and even the old rooster kok-koking and running
with less than his usual dignity. The two calves had heels
and tails in the air; the five tethered ewes bleated warn-
ingly to the five lambs that broke off a headlong race to
suck with the fiercest proddings, while the stirk and the
heifer in the little dry-stone enclosure, between an impulse
to dance and the curiosity to watch, succeeded in making
abrupt movements and choked sounds. Alone amid them
all black Jean regarded the scene with quiet irony and,
perhaps, more than a little satisfaction, as it had not been
too pleasant contemplating Bel devouring the good corn
Corn, full grown but still green, has a soft, mashy, memor-

able taste in the hour of cud-chewing, but it does no beast any good to remember the wild, tickling thrust that debauches the palate at the first mouthful.

Like the arrow sped Roy, with Catrine on the wind behind. Bel made a valiant endeavour to get her tongue round as much of the cornfield as it could encompass even with Roy leaping at her throat. Roots and all came tearing out, drenching Roy with the good earth as she swung her head to give him a toss. Whereupon, angered, he nipped her flank; and at that down went her head and up went her heels, and with the great mouthful swinging from her jaws she, too, began to run, kicking and dancing, like a two-year-old in spring, with her full and aged udder walloping from side to side and spilling its treasure on the air.

"Come in, ye fool!" roared Kirsty at the dog. She was now on the trot, with a stick in her hand.

"Roy!" yelled Catrine. Finn followed his mother with a bliss that was near to terror. Down went the stick across the slap in the stone enclosure and out came the stirk and heifer to join the two calves in the chase after Bel. In his stall, the garron whinnied, while, evening though it was, the old cock crew and clearly felt the better for it, if a little self-conscious.

Breathless, Catrine at last managed to grab the tether and hang on while Bel pulled and Roy yapped. "Roy!" she called in desperation, for Bel swept her careering along. "Roy!" croaked Kirsty. "Roy!" yelled Finn. And Roy, feeling the consensus of opinion against him, drew off. Kirsty addressed him with the lather on her lips and then added, "Come here!" He came near enough to tempt his mistress to hit him a blow, but permitted the earth to take the actual impact and Kirsty's arm the jarring discord. With a harsh imprecation (which was the only thing Finn properly heard), she hurled the stick at the brute. But long experience had taught Roy that anything thrown by a woman would hit him only if he tried to dodge it. So he created a diversion by rounding up the stirk and heifer in expert fashion, while Catrine hammered home the stake of Bel's tether.

"Ye old fool, you!" said Kirsty, approaching Bel with the stick behind her back, while Jean, a few yards off, looked on with profound impassivity. "Take that!" she cried. "And that! And that!" Bel took them, sinking her quarters to the impact and glancing round with the white of a guilty eye. "And that—ye ill-faured wicked old bitch! At your time of life you ought to have more sense."

It had been a very exciting ten minutes, enjoyed by all, and not least by Bel, who swung her barrel-shaped belly, as she licked a haunch, with some of the abandon more natural, perhaps, to youth. But she had grace still and her heart was young. To Jean she directed her hind quarters and when that canny beast could no longer restrain a muffled deep-throated "Hoo!" Bel responded in a natural way with nonchalance.

Meantime, Kirsty was inspecting the damage done, her whole body glowing with righteous wrath. Cultivation of the soil in all these parts was in long narrow strips or lazy beds, with hollows or rigs between. Three women cutting with the small hand-hook could take the broadest strip before them and leave nothing standing. The men came in behind to gather and bind and stook. Though, for that matter, folk worked according to the labour available, and to a great degree communally or by mutual assistance.

Bel had cropped the ears from about a couple of square yards. "You couldn't have driven that stake in hard enough," Kirsty accused Catrine, who now had a wooden bucket in one hand and the smallest three-legged stool in the other.

"It was yourself who did it," said Catrine. "You shifted her just before you went out."

"Did I? In that case, she's been up to her tricks again," and she nodded grimly. "We'll put her to the market, that's what we'll do with her." Nodding even more grimly, she entered the house.

THE LAND AND THE SEA

"How does Bel pull the stake out, Mama?"

"We don't know. But perhaps she pulls first from one side and then from the other and in that way loosens it."

"Perhaps she kicks it with her foot, the way Granny does with her heel when the stone is over at Jean?"

"I shouldn't wonder."

"If I lay in wait for a long, long time watching, and Bel couldn't see me, then I might find out. Mightn't I, Mama?"

"You might, indeed."

"Yes, and I'll see, and then I'll tell you, and then everyone will know. I'll get up early in the morning and watch and watch . . ."

Catrine starting humming her milking song, and black Jean stood quietly. With the pitcher half full, they went towards Bel.

"Why don't you take the cows in at night, Mama?"

"Because it's healthy for them to be outside when the weather is good."

"And the byre doesn't need cleaning then?"

"That's so. And they start eating in the early morning."

"Yes. And they'll have more milk. Tell me, Mama . . ."

Bel acknowledged their arrival with a sulky "Moo".

"What way was that to carry on?" Catrine demanded, clapping her flank gently.

Bel knew all about such blandishments and was not disposed to give in easily. When Catrine had to move her stool after the restless beast, Finn said in a commanding tone, "Stand still, you wicked old bitch."

Catrine's face opened. In a hushed voice she asked, "What words are these?"

After a glance at her wide eyes, Finn turned away, pivoting on one heel, growing ever more embarrassed and beginning to laugh.

"Finn, come here."

His laughter gurgled out of him in the merriest way, his face flushed. He was very embarrassed, and when she called

114

him again, he hopped away one step, two, and then ran, his laughter strung behind him in bubbles.

Catrine was very shocked, and pressed her forehead against the cow's side. She tried to hum, but a wild inward mirth surged up. She closed her eyes and softly shook.

For what she had really heard was the sound of his laughter, that infectious gurgling sound, so innocent, so natural, gone all self-conscious and merry and entrancing.

There were passages of communion between them when she felt the very texture and essence of this little boy, who was her son, in moments of indescribable ecstasy. Sometimes, of course, he was wicked and bad-tempered, and more than once had so far forgotten himself as to assault Granny. But to anyone who really understood him (felt Catrine) that was—that was . . . After all, he was only four and a half and you couldn't expect him to be a little saint, even if you wanted him to be. And those times when he wept, feeling he had been unjustly wronged, and his eyes . . . that brightness in his eyes, and the poor little fellow crying as if his heart would break. Yet if you sympathized with him then, he would hit you a wallop and get angrier than ever. But when he was really good, gold wasn't in it. Though, for the most part, he was just happy and companionable and full of endless questions. . . . The running of his living body ran through her blood, and she got up and patted Bel with a gentle hand, murmuring, "Poor old lass!" with bright gleams of suppressed humour. "Did you get your whackings?" she asked. "Was it sore then?" "Moo," said Bel, who knew all about these soft tactics, yet swinging her head in a half-mollified way. Jean tore up a mouthful of grass and looked across at this touching scene with no more than an exaggerated out-thrust of neck.

Then Catrine smoothed her features to an innocent solemnity and returned to the house.

It was longer than the average croft house, with two doors. Through the bottom door one entered to the animals' stalls; through the top door to the kitchen. Above the

115

kitchen were two rooms; the first, little more than a closet, was where Kirsty now slept, and the second or farthest-up room was the guest chamber, where Kirsty had all her special furniture and ornaments.

From the surplus of summer milk were made the butter and cheese, of which they sold or traded some, retaining enough to last them through most of the dry period before calving-time. While the various evening duties were being performed, Catrine ignored Finn or regarded him with a cool, remote look. On his part, Finn ignored her, being busy about invisible affairs of his own, though pausing occasionally to look round his shoulder with a solemn but knowing countenance. His worst moment was when sleep overcame him and he was put to bed while Kirsty, in the calm that had come upon the house with the summer twilight, took up the thread of her story. He was defeated the moment she began, because he knew her voice would go on and on for ever, and so he hated her and grew petulant and, finally, to the shattering of his dignity (not to mention the hope of re-establishing relations with his mother), he had to be forcibly undressed. But he held out against saying his prayer, and Catrine had to threaten him with God's displeasure.

"You're running on a thrashing, my young man," declared Kirsty. "No, I'm not!" he shouted, weeping. "You'd better give him one or two, Catrine," said Kirsty. "No! no!" he screamed. "Now, Finn," said Catrine quietly but raising her eyebrows in conspiracy, and soundlessly forming "hush!" on her lips. For an instant he looked into her great brown eyes with their solemn appeal, then waggled his head in rebellion. But, in the end, he stuttered the words after her, and sleep did not take long to defeat him. Catrine had known quite well what he had passionately wished. He had wished Kirsty to go away to her bed so that he could say his prayer to Catrine alone. Not that he always wanted to do this: but he wanted to do it then to save his dignity.

And perhaps, for less obvious reasons, too, because one

116

night, a week later, with Kirsty gone earlier than usual to her bed—it had been a heavy, sultry day—he said to his mother, with the firelight still playing on the walls as he lay on his back in the hushed hour, the queer hour of stories and strange things:

"Mama?"

"Well? . . . What is it?"

"Why is a word bad?"

To save her face she did not look at him, but regarded the problem thoughtfully, and out of her wisdom answered, "Just because it's a bad word."

Though he recognized the logic of this as irrefutable, yet he was not quite satisfied.

"But what makes it bad?"

"What," responded Catrine, "makes you bad sometimes?"

The question was personal and hardly fair, but he strove to be objective and simply asked, "What?"

What, indeed?

"I don't know," said Catrine. "All I know is that we mustn't be bad and that we mustn't use bad words."

"Who made them bad?"

"The Bad Man," answered Catrine.

His eyes opened. "Mama," he whispered, "where does the Bad Man live?"

"You know where he lives."

"In the Bad Place?"

"Yes."

At that moment something fell outside with a clatter and the door shook. Little Finn cried in fear to his mother.

"It's only the wind getting up," said Catrine.

The gust caught the house and shook it with a snarl. A small eddy ran along the floor and met another one over the fire in a spiral of smoke and ash. Then the gust passed away to the moor in a high-pitched whine. As they listened, another one came. Catrine went to the door and swung the wooden bar into its slot and this stopped the door from rattling. Very rarely was a door barred at night, for only a suspicious or frightened nature would shut out anyone who had need to call.

Finn had his own little bed, but she decided to take him in beside her until he went to sleep. This she did, holding him in her arms and murmuring to him, until he fell off. The wind had now a continuous rise and fall in its whine. Sometimes it was sustained for long seconds at its highest pitch. She thought of the little ricks of bog hay that Kirsty and herself had cut and left down on the flat ground. They would be tossed away, though the low birch bushes would catch great wisps. The wind came from the sea. . . .

She thought of all the local boats at sea, and was touched by fear. She had seen the fury of a winter storm in Dale, had seen it smash and send its spume hundreds of feet high over the cliff walls. She thought of Roddie and his crew. She liked Roddie very much, but now the horror of what might happen to them all was more than the thought of any individual or of herself. Her hatred of the sea had gone deep as an instinct.

In the grey hours of that morning all Dunster came awake, and men and women buttoned and wrapped themselves firmly and made for the cliffs. The gale was blowing fair in on the beach, the very worst airt for boats any distance along the coast. But by great good luck the herring signs had been off the bay, and the boats had been shot a mile or so out, between the Head and the cliffs to the west. The real danger now lay not in the force of the wind but in the seas the wind would whip up and smash on the beach before they could reach it.

The smaller boats hauled their few nets as swiftly as they could and were soon on their sweeps, coming with the wind at a great pace. The seas were rising rapidly, having the whole weight of an ocean, east by north, behind them. The tide was half in and the worst of the boulders covered. As a boat grounded, the crew leapt into the surf and heaved.

Soon there were sufficient men on shore to give new-comers immediate help. The beach in that morning gloom became a scene of extraordinary activity, with dark bodies rushing and voices crying above the seething waters and the high whining of the gale.

From the cliff-tops the women of the crofts could see the boats coming, and struggled down to the beach, and watched their menfolk advancing and retreating, grasping and hauling, on the edge of the mounting surf as in a wild, infernal dance.

The larger boats, with drifts of twenty nets, lay on a back-rope and found it a dead weight, hard and unyielding under the great pressure of the storm. Many cut clear; others that hung on too long in a desperate effort to save all they could, had to face a beach where high waves were curling over, smashing, and sucking down the shingle in a white roar.

But all boats made the beach, and the bulk of them were hauled clear without any damage done. Indeed, beyond the starting of a few planks and the abandonment of some nets, the Dunster fleet was intact and its fishermen, apart from a minor bruise here and there, unharmed.

As the crowd drifted away from the shore the feeling of delivery was upon them, gratefully in the high-pitched voices of the women, but with the pleasant quiet that follows fighting exultation in the hearts of the men. When a small boy appeared, his father took him by the hand.

Realizing what might have happened had the boats been shot a few miles along the cliffs to the west, many said that Dunster had been fortunate and that news of another kind might well reach them from other fishing stations before the day was done.

The first of that news came with the stage-coach. Mr. Hendry was inmost of the group that gathered round, when Williamson drew his horses to a standstill.

"I made a special point," answered Williamson, "of asking in Helmsdale when I came through. All the boats were accounted for except two—the *Esperance* from the south side and the *Morning Star* from Dunster."

Through the silence Williamson climbed down stiffly.

"No word at all?" demanded the inn-keeper in a sudden loud voice.

"No," said Williamson, pausing to look at the bay where the great combers were smashing on the beach in intermittent booming and a continuous roar. He seemed extraordinarily detached, untouched, like fate.

Mr. Hendry swung abruptly round and went stumping back to his inn at a rapid pace. There he yoked pony to gig, and to a group at the corner shouted, "I'm for Helmsdale." Whipping up the pony, he was off; nor did he stop when man or woman cried to him, but yelled in abrupt response, "I'll be back!"

Mr. Hendry's wealth had been mounting these last years. Helmsdale, his first out-thrust into the greater world, had already assured him of a profit that in the few remaining weeks should handsomely increase. Roddie had become more than a fisherman to Hendry; he had almost become a talisman. Next year, Lybster. The year after, Wick. And then . . . . Not so much money, money, money now in the glitter of silver crowns, as that vast ultimate thing called a fortune. His banker at Wick received him in his parlour.

Now if Roddie and his crew were lost, Mr. Hendry had the superstitious feeling that it would take the heart out of Dunster and in some malign way smash up his designs.

"Hup!" and he used the whip on the sweating horse. Anything to get away from the desperate knowledge, plain to landsman or publican, that no boat could have headed into that sea, that no boat had any place to run for but the harbour or the rocks. Unless, of course, it had beached somewhere along the sandy southward shore or perhaps even have made Portgower—a mocking hope, for in either case word would have been in Helmsdale long before the stage-coach.

Far below him the cliffs of the Ord boomed and he
thought he felt the gig take the shudder from the earth.
The distant strand, southward to Brora, was a broad belt of
white. Any boat attempting that beach would have been
tumbled over and over like a wooden bucket. He cast his
glance over his left shoulder and far as eye could travel was
a waste of white-capped seas. "Hup! hup!" cried Mr.
Hendry peremptorily, taking, at the same time, a firm hold
on the reins, for he did not want the brute to come down.
As he was rounding the last of the long serpentine curves,
Dale below him and Helmsdale still hidden, his ever-lifting
eye thought it saw something like a boat on the waters
going into Helmsdale. He lost it at once and kept staring
and nearly had a nasty accident, for, given her head at the
wrong time, the poor brute, with the weight of the gig
behind her on the fairly steep decline, had broken into a
mad, hopeless gallop, and he had to exercise all his skill
and strength on pulling her out of it. It was touch and go
until the decline eased and he drew her to a standstill. She
was quivering all over, with restless head and terrified
eyes. Torn between the desire to curse her and to soothe
her, he succeeded only in yelling futile questions. But his
wrath he communicated, and she began backing senselessly.
At once he realized this as preliminary to a mad bolt. He
had over-driven her and now her nerves were quivering
like her flesh. And she had not to back far to send the whole
outfit headlong down the slope towards the rocks. Immediately he left his seat to get at her head she would bolt.
A wheel jarred against a providential boulder on the road-
edge and threw the gig forward upon her. He caught her
strongly on the rebound, and then in a firm, commanding
voice, crying, "Steady, there! Steady! Steady!" eased her
forward. She danced but he held her, and at length in a
lather of foam brought her to the Helmsdale stables. But,
shout as he would, no one answered. This maddened him,
and he leapt from the gig. "This is the way the Cattach
does business," he explained to the trembling beast. Not a

121

soul outside either! What a place! Man, woman, nor child! He quickened his short steps to a waddling run and came on the whole population lining the harbour wall. As he pushed his way through, one or two men exclaimed angrily at him, for two lads on the edge of the wall had nearly been shoved over. They might have been flies for all he cared. He got to the edge and looked down. There was the *Morning Star*, with the crew shaking their nets, and Roddie, standing aft, with uplifted face, talking quietly to seamen above him.

He did not hear a word Roddie was saying, heard nothing but a buzzing of blood in his ears, while he gaped on the quiet picture of boat and men as if it had been conjured out of another world.

"That you, Roddie?" he shouted at last in so loud a voice that every face turned to him.

Roddie saw him, smiled, and nodded in a friendly way. Mr. Hendry elbowed a passage along the wall until he was right over the boat.

"We all thought you were lost!"

"Not quite," said Roddie, while his boat rose and fell under him and pulled on her mooring-ropes.

But Mr. Hendry was staring at the silver fish. "Herring!"

"Just two or three crans," answered Roddie. "We lost s even nets."

But the inn-keeper, staring at the fish, did not seem to understand. At length he exploded, "By God!" and with a wave of a fist that hit a man in the ear cried, "Come on up and have something!"

"Whenever we redd the nets," replied Roddie in the same quiet voice, "and get the herring out."

"Great way on you to-day, Hendry," said Simpson, a Wick curer.

"Hullo! Hullo!" cried Hendry. "Is Dunster showing you how to do it?"

"Well, they did bravely, with the help of God."

THE LAND AND THE SEA

"It's the help a few of you could be doing with about here."

There was chaff and sarcasm while the creels of herring were brought ashore to the gutting station.

Mr. Hendry found a delightful air of brightness and relief about the little fishing port, and admired, as always, the solid stone buildings, as good as anything in the biggest ports. Nothing like them in Dunster. The many boats tied together or beached in the river mouth; the safety of both the missing crews—the *Esperance* had made a forced landing in a creek down the coast; the movement of strange young men and women full of life, of grey-bearded bodachs and tight-shawled cailliachs, of boys and girls playing and quarrelling and shouting in any case; the whole stir of busy money-making appealed to Hendry strongly. "Leave the nets and come with me," he cried impatiently to Roddie. "Dammit, you've got the whole night to spread them. Come on!"

A dram all round and the best meal the inn could provide. The crew did not appear tired so much as very quiet. They smiled in a silent, dazed way.

Only on the road to Dunster did Roddie explain what had happened. For the rest of the crew agreed that Roddie should take a chance of going home that night. To-morrow was Saturday, when no boats went to sea, and so, after a good sleep, the rest of the crew might then walk home and all could return together on Monday morning.

"We had intended walking home most week-ends," Roddie explained as they set out, "but between Monday and Saturday you don't get much sleep. We've got a good shake-down, comfortable enough; and it's cheerful when things are going well."

"Man, I'm fair delighted. Hup! She nearly killed me this morning. We'll have to get down and walk. It's too steep for her." He was still clearly excited. Roddie staggered a little and got a supporting hand on the gig. "Just the road heaving a bit," he explained.

"Get on board," ordered Hendry. "Meg'll pull you all right."

Roddie shook his head. "It's no bad thing to have the earth under your feet." Still that quiet dreamy manner. It worked like a ferment on Mr. Hendry.

Roddie, behind the wheel, let the gig pull him in long strides. Now and then he regarded the solid purposeful body in front with a vague smile, which he sometimes turned on the sea, and sometimes on the heather rising back to the mountains. It was nó bad thing to have brought your crew and yourself back alive. Anything else hardly mattered a great deal.

But it was everything else that mattered to the inn-keeper. He was fully holding his own with the best of the other curers, and in some strange way felt responsible for Roddie's seamanship. In his elation, he was jealous of the fine stores and curing yards in Helmsdale. "You wait!" he shouted above the crunch of the wheels. "You are training skippers. You'll train more. The time is at hand!"

"The skipper of the *Esperance* was telling me you can't get boats for love or money. It's all building, building, he said," remarked Roddie with an effort.

The inn-keeper laughed. As if he didn't know all about that! "What would you expect? And building means money? Of course! Very well. Every man who has a stirk to sell has a stirk to sell. Every wife who has two pounds in the shottle of her kist to bury herself or her man, has two pounds. There's such a thing in Wick as a bank. There's what is called security. There's . . ."

Roddie listened. On each of the first three days of the week they had averaged barely three hours' sleep. All through last night and this morning they had fought the sea to the last of their strength. What had haunted him in the dreadful hours was not drowning but the bitterness of having made an error in judgement. His brain was so exhausted by the tearing roar of that sea that it now appre-hended Special's words remotely but with the clarity of something told in a dream. The lack of outward excitement, the glimmer of the eye staring into this incredible future conjured up before it, had a stimulating effect on the inn-keeper.

"O Lord, I'm thirsty," said Roddie, as they got into the gig.

Mr. Hendry foraged under the seat and from the folds of a hemp sack produced a black bottle. "Have a pull at that. It's special."

Roddie shook his head. "I'm so dry, I want to drink a whole burn, you'll excuse me."

"Wait," called Mr. Hendry, "wait till we get to the Grey Hen's well. Hup, there!" On they rattled and bumped. "So you don't think I'll get the factor to build stores and salt-cellars and packing-sheds?" cried Hendry.

"Knowing the Laird, do you think it's likely?"

Small eyes twinkled upon Roddie in sarcastic humour.

"You haven't much faith in lairds and their factors?"

"We haven't much cause, perhaps," remarked Roddie.

"No, by God," said Hendry. But he could not help a short laugh, the point he had to make was so good. For his own pleasure he therefore had to come at it cunningly. "Why," he asked, "were the crofters burned out of their houses, swept from the glens?"

"We know why," muttered Roddie.

"They were evicted, because the lairds would make *more money* out of sheep. You know that, as you say, but have you learned the lesson of it? Money, man; money. Why does the laird have a fish factor taking his share of the cod and haddock the small boats bring in to our river mouth? Why does he have a ground officer going over the crofts and houses? To ask after your health, is it? What happened to you the year before last, when your father and yourself and the rest of you had taken in from the rank moor that extra bit of a field on the top side? I forget how many years you were at it, but I don't forget this—that your rent was put up ten shillings."

"I know that," said Roddie. His mouth was ashen dry.

"But you're wondering what that's got to do with building curing-yards? You have a lot to learn, my lad, in the ways of the world. You can take it from me that I wouldn't bother myself asking the factor to claw his head unless he'd get more than lice out of it. No. And apart from what he'll make out of the buildings and curing-stations and boats' dues, it would pay him, man, out of the increase in rents alone. Think of what ten shillings added to each croft rent would mean, in total, from Dunster itself. Think of the new families, the new houses springing up. It's as certain as we're driving this road, that soon my rent will be doubled. Ay, or trebled. And if I was to complain, he would say, 'Go!' He can say that whether you complain or not. Did you complain when the ten shillings were put on to you? Not you. You knew better. And when you're a successful skipper, making a wad of notes, would you take the road out of Dunster rather than pay, say, two pounds more rent? Would you?"

"I mightn't mind then."

"Exactly. And he knows it. The old laird at Buckie, years and years ago, used to buy the boats himself, and make the fishermen go to sea. And if the weather looked a bit rough and they didn't feel like it, he would be down on the beach, driving them to sea with a big stick. And that's gospel truth. Ask any of your skipper friends from the south side. And he got more money out of them than ever he advanced on the boat! A heap more, Roddie, my man. And there was no golden herring season in those days. All line fishing. And that reminds me, by God!" He became excited again. "With the bigger type of boat we'll be able to tackle the great-line fishing in the early part of the year. Cod and ling, boy. Cod from the Skaet Hole. I'll be able to arrange—whoa!" he yelled, pulling Meg on her haunches. "The Grey Hen's well."

Roddie had heard of this well, and somehow had expected something more striking than a mossy water-hole in an expanse of bare moor. But, oh, the water was spring-cold and crystal-pure and pressed against the dry heat in his mouth, chilling it, chilling it. . . .

"Stop," cried Mr. Hendry, "or you'll get a knot in your gut."

Roddie lifted his face and stared at the well before making the effort of heaving himself round and, sitting, slowly wiping his nose and mouth. "That was good," he said. "Good." The water trickled from the well through a tongue of green grass, and here and there a wild flower drooped under the weight of a bee, though Roddie was not so observant as Catrine had been at this spot five years before. The scent of the moor, the faint honey scent, took his nostrils in a memory too old for him to do more than acknowledge it with his slow smile.

"Come!" said Hendry. "They'll be waiting for us."

Roddie looked about him. He must remember this well. Lord, but he would like to throw himself down and sleep. Sleep through the bees and the heather, with the wind soft and the sunlight yellow and old. "Ay, I suppose so," he said, and they got back into the trap. The road sloped gently downward now for a long way.

"You're sleepy—what?"

"Oh, a bit," admitted Roddie.

"You had a bad night?"

"It was a case of hanging on. I'm vexed over the loss of the nets, but they were solid with dead herring. We took a turn on the back-rope. As her stern rose the net tore away. We cut away then."

"Never mind about the nets. I'll provide you with new ones, and they won't cost you much more than they cost me! This very gig will take them back with you on Monday morning."

Roddie was grateful. "We could sail up for them."

"Keep your sailing for the herring! Why didn't you make for shore, like the other boats, when you saw it coming?"

This had been Roddie's torture question in the long hours. "For that matter," he replied quietly, "it came on us very quickly, and if I had been with the bulk of the boats, I might have followed them. The usual fishing bank is out to about three miles and runs between the Ord and Loth Bay. I'm friendly with the skipper of the *Esperance*. He knows the coast to Peterhead like the back of his hand and has had many a shot on the Guilliam off Cromarty. Well, anyway, he believed the shoals were working south, and I followed him, some miles to the south'ard of the last boat of the fleet, and would have followed him farther, but we came on good signs, as I thought, and we shot. The wind struck us like the side of a house. We hung on for a bit. I didn't like it. 'We'll haul and run, boys,' I said. But we found herring in the nets. We strove away. Soon it was nothing but white drift and hauling on the back-rope was like hauling on iron. We could make no more of it. We'd give the squall a chance to take off, if squall it was, and lie to the nets. The sea began to rise. We had either to cut and run now or hang on and chance it. The loss of the nets would wipe out the season. I put it to the lads. We decided to hang on."

"By God, that was a decision to take!"

"One thing helped us or we would certainly have been swamped. The nets, of course, acted as a solid anchor; but the boat was well found in rope, and we swung to the nets on a long cable, which gave as the sea took us, and then slacked off for the next one. It made riding easier, if you understand me."

"Yes, yes. I'm glad she was well found. Hup! I said I would have no old rotten gear; nothing but the best. I saw to that."

Roddie smiled. "We rigged up the sail to throw off the lighter seas, but in one gust it blew over on us with a slap that knocked Daun senseless. He was bailing at the time. We thought he was dead. Some time in the morning there was a terrific lump. I thought we were away with it. But,

O Lord," murmured Roddie fondly, "she rose to the seas, she took them like a bird."

"A fine boat, what! Hup, there! Gee up! And it was like that all through the night? When did you haul?"

"We started well before midday. The wind had taken off a little, but it was slow, tough work. The near nets were lightly fished, but the outer nets were solid. Herring—they have a queer effect upon you."

"Have they now? What!"

"But in these last nets the herring were drowned and heavy as lead."

"Cheer up! A good shot will buy more nets. So then you made for home?"

"Ay, with a peak of the sail, while the lads lay dead among the herring. But I got them up before we crossed the bar. They have their pride."

"I should say they have! Here, man, take a swig of this."

"I think I will. Your health!"

"And health to yourself," responded Hendry. "Now, now then, dammit, here, curl up."

"I believe I will," said Roddie, letting himself fall sideways. For the last few minutes he had been growing light-headed. Within the restricted floor space his knees drew up to his chin in the slow motion of one dealt a deadly blow, and his head slumped. Open-mouthed, his breath came from him in noisy gusts.

Nor did Hendry attempt to waken him until some miles from Dunster he saw two lads coming on the road—scouts from the headquarters of suspense. "Roddie!" he cried, shaking the sleeper's shoulder, but without receiving even a grunt. Then he caught the reins firmly. "You'll do your best, Meg," he said, and he took the whip in his right hand.

The lads drew to the roadside. One was Duncan, Roddie's younger brother, and the other David, brother to Don Sutherland. "Any word?" they shouted at the inn-keeper's menacing figure.

"They're all right," bellowed Hendry, galloping past. At once the lads broke into a sprint in order to get a supporting hand on the body-work of the gig which hid Roddie from view. But Hendry swung round, lifting his whip. "Leave go there!" he yelled so fiercely that the lads stopped as if they had been hit.

There were men and women and children along the road now at short intervals. "They're all right! All safe!" bellowed Hendry. When folk got the news their eyes brightened, they smiled, and then, in their delight, they laughed to one another, crying, "Old Special's as full as a fiddler!" The wild flourish of his whip made them rock with mirth. But the bumping of the iron-shod wheels under springs stiff as boards shook Roddie's teeth and bones, and a final thump on the ear opened his eyes. He slowly pulled himself up and when the young sprinters behind saw his head appear, they missed a step and a breath.

Two stops, and on each occasion a mother with her hands on Roddie's arm and tears in her eyes and a ring of neighbours.

For rumour had it that the boat was lost with all hands. It was the solitary and for ever enigmatic passenger on the stage-coach who had said it to someone never identified. And by way of confirmation Williamson himself "had all but said it" to one of the strappers in the stable. "You could see it on him," was the strapper's sad comment.

Roddie was not embarrassed by the press of folk or by the silence that hung on his few words of description, for he was part of the warmth of kinship, the natural love of life, that moved them all. His father was there, a tall viking of a man, with a sandy beard, and Roddie moved over to them, for they had looked on. "You've got back, Roddie," said the old man with Roddie's own quiet smile. "Yes," said Roddie with a nod. Then Shiela, who was twenty and vivid, came against her brother, caught his wrist in both hands and murmured, "Oh, Roddie!" His young brother, Duncan, moved away, but the old man called to him.

Duncan pretended not to hear and, sliding out of the company, began to trot up the river-side until, out of sight, he broke for home like a hare. His mother was waiting, all alone.

Roddie refused Hendry's invitation to the inn, but thanked him for what he had done.

When at last they had crossed the burn above the Steep Wood and were, as a family, heading for home, Roddie, turning casually round, saw Catrine, who had been coming at a little distance behind them. "Oh, I clean forgot," he said, "to speak to Catrine McHamish. I have a message from her mother for her." He turned on his heel. "I won't be a minute." After going a little distance he hailed Catrine. She looked over her shoulder and went down towards the burn to meet him. The father thought it was a natural and kindly thing for his son to do, and kept on his way, followed by his silent, quick-glancing daughters.

"Hullo, Catrine," said Roddie. "I couldn't get a word with you in that crowd."

She smiled. "We were all glad to see you."

Her eyes were so bright, with such a warmth in her face, that his tiredness went over him in a soft wave.

"I may look in to-morrow night and give you the news. Your mother and all the rest are fine, and everyone in Dale asking for you."

"Were they?"

"Yes. And tell Kirsty that I have some special messages for her."

"Won't she be delighted!"

"Tell her they are from an old admirer of hers. Tell her that's what I said—no more."

Catrine laughed, and behind the red of her generous mouth her teeth were milk-white. So deep-red and soft were her lips sometimes that it was as if she blushed there.

"And now I'm off," said Roddie, and he turned and left her.

131

CHAPTER VII

FINN BLOWS HIS TRUMPET

There were no fewer than five marriages that
autumn. Indeed the autumns now were becoming
the merry and marrying time of the year, for
young men with money in their pockets from the fishing
could approach young women with a few pounds of their
own from the gutting and contemplate setting up house
even if not backed by much land. The year before, Daun
had at last got married to a girl who had found difficulty in
making up her mind about him, he had wanted her so much
and she was so sure of him. Don was two years married
and had two of a family. Amongst the men of his age
Roddie alone seemed unaffected.

That autumn he gave a curious reply to one who probed
him on this. The reply was freely quoted and hung in the
minds of men and women with a strange wild sanction. It
was the evening of the eventful settling-up day, when
curers paid fishermen, and fishermen paid everyone, from
shopkeeper to creel-maker. It was the evening of the flowing of money—and of talk rising through liquid refreshment into song. Even geography was enlarged. Names
that had never been heard before took on a rich significance.
The Helmsdale-Dunster catch was already becoming
known as a Baltic cure. Soon high-canvassed schooners
would come, ship the barrels, and sail out into seas where
for days on end no land would be seen. The Baltic. In itself,
what a roaring, staggering barrel of a name!

After the settling-up, Hendry stood rounds on the house
straight from the bottle's gushing neck. Special! "Give us

a toast, Roddie." And Roddie, amused, his six feet of sure manhood balancing lightly, looked around. What could he toast? He could toast the inn-keeper. He could toast the hope of seeing curing yards in Dunster that would rival those in Helmsdale. And something like this was in his mind as he raised his glass. There was a pause, a complete silence. He looked at his glass. His smile deepened. "Boys," he said softly, fondly: "To the silver darlings!"

There was a roar of acceptance. Above the hubbub a droll voice cried, "And here's a darling to yourself!"

They all turned on Roddie, eyes gleaming. "High time, Roddie; high time, boy!"

They hushed as they saw he was going to speak. Simply he said, "I have married the sea." His smile was detached and friendly and mocking. And the sea roared up in them.

One of the marriages lasted five days. In truth, there were such dancings and goings-on that the catechist and evangelical preacher, Sandy Ware, stirred up the embers of hell and damnation and carried them around with him. Not that he blamed the folk so much, for folk were simple and sinful everywhere. They were due to be damned: it was his duty to tell them that, and he believed in doing his duty, and did it. But the real fault lay, the source and fountain-head of the fault, with the Established Church of Scotland, that in its Laodicean moderation, consequent upon its en-slavement to temporal power and privilege, was selling God's kingdom for the comforts of a manse.

But the folk, in the flush of joyful living and the assur-ance that money brings, did not listen to him as earnestly as they might have listened.

The hill market in November was the biggest in living memory. Crofters were thrawn to a degree rare in the experience of the dealers and haggled uncompromisingly through a dozen advances and retreats to the splitting of a final sixpence. Money! They wanted the last farthing they could get.

Even in folk who could have no possible connection with the sea, the bargaining spirit was unusually strong. Some of the more cunning dealers intercepted crofters before they reached the Market Hill, in the hope of spotting good beasts and tempting their owners with a direct cash offer.

"Well, Mistress, and what's this you have?"

"It's a cow," said Kirsty.

"So it is," agreed the dealer. "At least," he corrected himself, "she was in her day. Where are you going with her?"

"I'm taking her to the market," said Kirsty, "and if you have no more to say you'll oblige me by getting out of my way."

"To the market? Bless me, woman, do you expect to sell her?"

"I do."

"Do you now? And what do you expect to get for her?"

"Five pounds."

"Five pounds, did you say?" He went up to Bel and, pulling down her lip, had a look at her teeth. Bel threw her head away, her soft eyes glancing with fear. The dealer laughed, not unpleasantly, for he was a big, bushy man. "What do you feed her on?" he asked. "Saps?"

"Come," said Kirsty, with a jerk of her head to Catrine. "I thought this fellow was a dealer."

The man chuckled. "So this is your stirk, too?" he said, giving Catrine at the same time a humoured glance, and dropping his eyes for a moment to the dark, round-eyed slim little boy at her side. "I suppose you'll be wanting five pounds for this, too?"

"Seven," said Kirsty.

"Well, I'll offer you four; and to save it from dying on your hands I'll give you two for the old rickle of bones. How's that?"

"It's wasting time," said Kirsty. "Come!" And she began hauling on Bel.

Further interchanges proved equally fruitless, and in a

few hundred yards the great concourse on the Market Hill came full upon Finn's distended gaze.

He forgot his mother; his hazel switch trailed by his side. His mind could not take in the scene, for the upward slope, far as the eye could see, was a mass of human beings. Bellowing cattle, bleating sheep, barking dogs, a continuous uproar of voices; and the whole hillside moving. It was incredible and terrifying. A young horse curveted and whinnied at his back, a dog brushed past him, a man yelled in an angry voice. The horse came dancing round. "Finn!" screamed Catrine. He dashed for her. She caught his hand and shook his arm angrily, telling him he was not to wander but to stay by her. He looked back at the horse. A small boy was blowing a trumpet with lines of the most beautiful colour upon it. "Stop that, curse you!" yelled the man with the horse at the boy. The boy ran away a little distance and blew harder than ever. There were many boys dashing about with complete fearlessness. One or two of them, seeing Finn's solemn face, paused to laugh. They knew at a glance that he came from the hills, was outlandish, ignorant of the ways of the civilized world, Mama's pet and soft, all dressed up in a little stiff doublet and round bonnet with a feather in its side.

Kirsty took up her stance by the side of a dry-stone dyke. "We'll stay here," she said. She had not been put out in the least by the dealer. On the contrary, the encounter had braced her into a confident commanding mood. For her mind was quite clear. Four pounds ten for the stirk and three for Bel. If she couldn't get that she would just take them home again. The offer of two pounds had been hopeful. It might even be wise to part with Bel at two pounds fifteen. With that reservation she was now ready. "Well, young man, and what do you think of the market?" she asked Finn, her eyes twinkling through her solemn countenance.

Finn was unable to think. His wits had run away. He pulled restlessly at his mother's hand. "I told you you shouldn't have come," said Catrine.

"Nonsense!" said Kirsty. "What are you frightened of?"

To Catrine's great astonishment Kirsty had taken Finn's side against her. Finn had learned all about the market, for he was now nearly five years of age and nimble and tireless on his feet. But Catrine had been very positive against his going. She was sending him over to Widow Grant's for the day. Finn had stormed and wept. And then Kirsty had appeared with a hazel switch. "The beasts get frightened," she said. "And it's no easy work hauling them on the rope. But if you have a clever young man with a stick behind, it's easy as blowing your nose. Will you come with your Granny, Finn?"

And it was Kirsty now who gave him heart from the masterful confidence in her eye. The trouble lay in getting used to all this tremendous hubbub. He had been afraid of the silent wood when the butterfly had led him on the strange road that goes to the back of the world. But the wood had remained still. This dark forest heaved and rolled with a tumultuous life, with straining ropes, the harsh voices of strange men, the peering faces of mocking boys. He had to be so quick inside himself lest a thing sprang on him that he wanted to cry, to cry to his mother to take him home, back to the quiet of the house, the braes and the burn, where he was safe. But, standing close by his mother, he did not cry.

Time wore on. He got more used to the rough men who, paying no attention to Kirsty or his mother, handled Bel and the stirk as though they owned them. Bel never failed to make them grin, and then they would accost Kirsty with a sarcastic sally. Finn hated them and was very sorry for Bel. Usually, Kirsty gave as good as she got. "She's only rising fifteen," said a stout wit with ponderous gravity. "What do you feed her on?"

"Ginger-bread," promptly replied Kirsty.

There was a loud laugh all round and the dealer so enjoyed her sally that he offered two pounds ten and, against her four ten, raised his figure to two fifteen.

"I cannot throw her away," said Kirsty. "Too much good meat has gone into her."

"Ginger-bread!" cried the dealer, and laughed mightily as if the joke were his own. "I'll leave the offer with you for a while, Mistress."

Catrine bent down to catch Finn's murmur: "Mama, what's ginger-bread?"

"Do you see the brown cake that boy's eating? That's ginger-bread."

"Is it good?"

She pressed him to her side and smiled. "Wait you."

Ever more folk were appearing, out for the day's fun, groups of young men and women, all dressed in their best, full of mirth and anticipation and a readiness to laugh at little or nothing. Finn saw Roddie coming with three or four other men; saw his eyes brighten, his hand wave. "Hullo!" he cried as they all came up. Out of the banter, Roddie squatted down and spoke to Finn specially. Pride and incoherence so choked Finn's utterance that he could neither say yes nor no to Roddie's offer to take him round the market.

When Roddie straightened up, Rob was talking to Catrine in a quiet, earnest way. "I met your sister Isebeal," he said, "in Helmsdale. It was her first season at the gutting." Catrine was deeply interested, her face smiling and slightly flushed. "I spent a Saturday night over at your place," Rob went on. "I got on very well with your mother."

Don laughed. "Come away up with me and get your fairing," he said forcefully.

"Thank you," said Catrine, "but I can't leave just now."

"Rob will stand by," said Don. "He never was a hand for the girls any more than Roddie here!" His large body was full of pleasantness and good nature. He was out for the day.

"Off you go!" said Kirsty to Catrine peremptorily. "I have a few things to ask this young man."

Finn soon realized that hitherto he had stood on the out-

skirts of the market. He was now in a tremendous press of
people and to save him from getting crushed Roddie hoisted
him on to his shoulder. At once he beheld the long line of
stalls going away up the slope, each laden with things he
had never seen before in his life. Fat women behind the
stalls were shouting their wares, and now and then shouting to one another or to men digging more things out of
boxes behind. There were great piles of ginger-bread and
glittering ornaments of silver and gold in every size and
shape; red gooseberries and green gooseberries and nuts
in little hills; oranges and apples; sweets and toffees of
every colour and description. Near by, a man standing on
a box was shouting at the top of his voice. He had come
specially to present to the people the greatest bargains the
world had ever seen. Into a beautiful case, satin-lined, containing three knives and three forks made of solid silver
and ivory, he, before their living eyes, with thumb and
finger, placed a golden sovereign; then he snapped the case
shut and offered the lot for fifteen shillings—a fraction of
the cost of the cutlery alone. Would no one make him an
offer? Even ten shillings? . . . "Ladies and gentlemen, I
have been offered five shillings! Five shillings! ! Is it for
the empty case alone, sir? What's that? . . . I gather, ladies
and gentlemen, that this gentleman, who is contemplating
the blessed state of matrimony . . ." There was a roar of
laughter at this lucky shot.

Everyone was smiling or laughing. Don held up to Finn
a flat cake of ginger-bread. "Now," asked his mother,
"what do you say for that?" "Thank you," said Finn. He
did not like to eat it at once, but when they weren't looking
he tried a mouthful. It was soft and melted into a clammy
mess that was unbelievably good. Don gave Catrine a
bag of sweets. Then Roddie asked her what she would
have. All the young men seemed to be buying fairings for
the young women. One girl had a bag like a pillow-slip.
They all had bags, except Catrine. The girls laughed a
tremendous amount, and the young men made jokes and

138

took jokes against themselves with good nature and swaggering gestures. Finn saw a mound of trumpets, each striped in blue and red, exactly like the one the boy had blown at the horse. He could not take his eyes off them. There were many other kinds of toys, too, but they were nothing to the trumpets. Roddie lowered him to the ground, the better to get at his reserve money, and so Finn got a closer view of the trumpets. The woman behind the stall seemed to know that he would like a trumpet, though he had never told her. He got very embarrassed. "Here you are," she cried, "and good luck with it, my little gentleman!" She held one out to him. He backed away, against Roddie's legs. Roddie took the trumpet from the woman and handed it to Finn. Finn stared at the trumpet and slowly put out his hand. "Oh, my word!" exclaimed his mother. "What have you to say to Roddie for that?" But Finn had nothing to say. He remained dumb. "Leave him alone," said Roddie. Catrine looked at Finn and on the point of pressing him to remember his manners, remained silent. Finn changed the ginger-bread from his right to his left hand and the trumpet from left to right. He could hold things better with his right hand. But he had not the courage to raise the trumpet to his mouth.

Presently, however, when he saw the others had forgotten him, he put the trumpet to his lips and said, "Zoo!" But it did not sound as it had done with the boy. More firmly he called "Zooo!" into it. Still it remained dead. There was something wrong with his trumpet! It was broken! It would not sound! His distress became acute. Roddie was kneeling beside him. "Blow into it, like this—phooo! . . . No, no, don't make a sound, just blow." Finn blew, and the trumpet sounded loud and high, clearing a path for itself over the world.

There were two more incidents of that day that were to remain in his memory. One stall consisted of an inclined table on which were spaced out attractive articles of every kind. Each article was surrounded by a circular wall with a hole an inch wide at the top. After paying a penny, you were permitted to pull back a handle at the low right-hand corner and let it go with a bang, whereupon a marble shot up to the top of the table, and returned, bouncing from one enclosure to another. If you were very lucky, the marble entered one of the little holes or gates, and then you were presented with what was inside the enclosure. Roddie insisted on Finn's having a shot. "Pull it back yet—back yet—now!" Finn let go. Off on its wild career went the marble. Then down—down—it was going in!—no—down —down . . . nothing. In these few seconds Finn lived such a long time, that the marble fell back into the bottom of an exhausted world. "Have another shot," said Roddie. Finn felt all weak with the terrible excitement, and if he got nothing again he would hardly be able to bear it. His face deeply flushed, his eyes glittering, he let go the knob. But he had not pulled so hard this time and the marble barely reached the top. He could have cried to have the shot over again, but the marble, describing a gentle curve, hit against the edge of a little gate at its first contact, knocked against the other edge, wobbled, and fell in. "Hurrah!" cheered Roddie. And Finn was handed a lovely brooch, with a large glittering gem in the middle of it.

Roddie and Finn came to a tall mast surrounded by a crowd of men. Roddie heaved Finn on to his shoulder. "For strong men only! Ring the bell and get your money back!" shouted a crow of a man with a club foot and wisps of lank hair; whereupon he caught up a great hammer, its wooden head bound with iron, and, swinging it full circle, hit a knob which sent an iron pointer travelling hurriedly up the mast to tinkle a bell at the top. Strong men, who could have broken the showman on a knee, tried to ring that bell and failed. Twice Don got it a couple of inches from the top. "Very hard luck, sir! Very hard cheese indeed!" cried the sympathetic showman. Whenever he said "hard cheese" the crowd laughed. "Break the mast, Don," cried Roddie. Don, who had already been in Mr. Hendry's refreshment booth, looked around until he found Roddie's head. He smiled. "Come on, Roddie, and ring this dam' thing, or I'll never get home." "No, no!" said Roddie, laughing. But the crowd now had caught sight of him. "Come on, skipper!" They would not leave him alone. They made way for him. "Don't let the crew down!" cried a greybeard. Roddie lowered Finn to the ground and left him on the inside of the ring. As he lifted the hammer, he said humorously, "It's all in the turn of the wrist!" Finn felt his heart swelling in a terrible anxiety. Roddie looked up the whole length of the mast. "She'd carry a good sail, boys!" Before anyone could laugh, the hammer had swung round in a flash; the pointer shot up with invisible speed to a ring and clatter at the top as if the bell had burst. In the momentary silence of the crowd, Finn's body quivered. "Come on, Don," said Roddie, with quiet but commanding humour. Don obeyed. Roddie whispered something in his ear. Down came the hammer swiftly; up shot the pointer and the bell just tinkled.

Don was delighted and insisted on hauling Roddie round to Hendry's booth. "Wait till I put Finn back to his mother." "Is this the little Cattach?" asked Don with a friendly smile to Finn. He put his hand in his pocket and offered him three pennies, but Finn was too shy to take them. "And he's got a little pocket in his doublet, too!" Don put the pennies in the pocket. "Now," he said, "you'll come and drink a glass of ginger-ale." "But we can't take him into the booth," Roddie objected. "Let the boy be," said Don. "His country was kind to us." Without more ado, he led the way.

Roddie smiled. After a dram, Don's good nature got very persistent. There was no sign of Catrine anyway, and there would be no drunkenness in the booth yet, though some of the dogs outside were beginning to snarl, and when the dogs fought, their owners, if they had a drop too much, fought also.

The jostling, swaying crowd inside the canvassed enclosure, open to the sky, frightened little Finn, and Don lifted him on his right arm. This was the one real day in the year (though there was also a spring market) when quiet, law-abiding men of the countryside permitted themselves some licence. Bargains were struck, palms spat upon, hands shaken, and final agreement sealed over a dram of "special". With good money in the pocket and the heart open, a friend was a friend, and if he hadn't been seen since the last market, there was a lot to be said. There were many friends. The world was full of friends. "Hullo, is that you, Robert, my hero? God bless me and how's your old father? . . ." Finn was deafened with the voices. He had never seen men like this, easy and confidential, swaying to one another, here with solemn confidential faces nodding sadly over a tale of family grief, there with shoulder-slapping mirth. Mr. Hendry's voice barked out its commands. Dave shouted to a servitor, but failed to attract the overwhelmed lad's attention. "Blow a blast on your trumpet, Finn," urged Don. Finn did not like to blow, but at last he let off a splendid blast. Everyone looked at them. "A ginger-ale and two specials!" shouted Don. Mr. Hendry recognized them. "Ha, you!" he cried. And then a man, who knew Finn, saw him. "Is that my little Finn I see?" He was a brown-bearded, broad-shouldered man, with a face happier than any boy's. He waved to Finn with an exaggerated prim womanish gesture that made heavy men lean back. "Peep-bo!" he cried. At last they had to stop him, and a voice yelled, "Wull, you're drunk!"

Wull was up near the serving counter and he looked down the booth upon figures standing and figures sitting on the long wooden trestles, swaying lightly, his eyes lost in a benign, silent mirth.

"Boys," he said to them softly, in so confidential a tone that everyone listened, "boys—I'm full as the Baltic." As a noted smuggler, Wull was enjoying the perverse happiness of drinking whisky that had paid duty.

.   .   .   .   .

Catrine was waiting for them when they came out. Her smile was a little awkward as she tried to dissemble her concern. "I was frightened you had got lost," she said, looking reproachfully at Finn.

"Why would he get lost?" asked Don. "Surely the poor fellow can have a drink with the rest. Eh, Finn? Are you going home with your mother or are you sticking by Roddie and me?"

"Come, Finn," said Catrine.

Finn hesitated. Roddie and Don laughed. "That's the boy!" said Don. "Away home, woman of the house, and leave the young man to enjoy himself. The fun hasn't started yet."

"Come, Finn," said Catrine firmly. She took his hand.

"Finn, Finn, my boy," said Don, shaking his head, "that's what they do to you."

"Have you sold?" asked Roddie.

"Yes, I'm glad to say," replied Catrine. "And at a good price."

"Kirsty will be pleased!"

"Yes." Catrine nodded. She was somehow a little constrained now and looked extremely attractive. Her eyes in the sun were not dark, they were nut-brown, a fathomless brown, shot through with light. Her mouth made any other woman's prim and pale. "Thank you very much," she said, flushing a trifle as she felt the men's eyes, "and particularly for looking after Finn."

"Really going?" asked Roddie.

"Yes, oh yes. I must."

"My young man—and where have you been? Drinking, I hear?" It was Kirsty, her face portentously solemn. Finn backed away. Don picked him up. "What have you to say for yourself?" she demanded, and poked him in the stomach.

Now Finn's stomach, what with ginger-bread, gooseberries, toffee, and a large bottle of very fizzy ginger-ale, was tight as a drum, and when Kirsty poked it there came through his mouth a prolonged, an incredible eructation. Even Kirsty laughed, nodding her head like a witch.

That night Finn had a thousand things to tell and more questions to ask about the strange world he had seen, once his mother and himself were alone and Kirsty in bed. In minute detail he described how Roddie had rung the bell.

"He must be awfully strong, Mama?"

"Yes."

"Do you think he's the strongest man in the world?"

"I couldn't say. Perhaps he is. Do you like Roddie?"

"Yes," said Finn. "And when I'm big I'll go to sea, too, and be a skipper."

"Mama does not want you to go to sea. You must never go to sea. Do you hear? Never."

"Why?" He was astonished at her vehemence.

"Because I don't want you to. Because people who go to sea get drowned. The sea is an angry cruel place. You must promise me never to go to sea."

"Will Roddie get drowned?"

"I hope not. Will you promise never to go to sea?"

"Can't I sail the little boat Don gave me?"

"We'll see. But not yet."

"I want to sail the little boat," said Finn moodily.

"Haven't you your trumpet? Isn't that enough for you?"

"I want also," said Finn, "to sail the little boat."

"We won't talk any more about it just now. Go to sleep." Catrine left him.

Finn knew the pool in the burn on which he was going to sail his little boat. The boat was painted red and had a mast with a piece of cotton tacked on to it. The boat was longer than his foot. Don told him how to put it in a pool and push it off. Then the wind would come and hit the sail and the boat would go away, away, sailing to the other side. He could take his trumpet down with him, and when he pushed the boat off he could blow on his trumpet and cry, "There she goes! Look out, everyone!" Then he would

144

cross the river and meet her when she arrived. It was such a long time to the morning. If Mama would not give him the boat it would be awful. If he promised to be very, very good she might give it to him. He had given her the brooch. He had said, "Mama, you'll have a fairing from me", just as the men said it to the women at the market. He had felt a little shy about it, so had done it as casually as possible. His mother had looked at him, as if she could not believe her eyes. "Oh, Finn," she had said. "Oh, Finn, how lovely!" And then she had snatched him up and smothered her face against him. Her face got all flushed and her eyes glistened. Anyone would think he had given her his trumpet. The trumpet had a little handle, by which you could lift it smartly to your mouth and drop it down again. Once or twice he thought his mother was going to lift him and kiss him at the market and before Roddie. He would have been desperately ashamed. But she hadn't done it. He had kept the brooch until they were on the way home. He must watch that she never got the chance to do it before boys and men like Roddie. Roddie was the greatest man in the world. If he said he would be very, very good perhaps she would let him sail the boat in the morning. She was sitting so very quiet before the fire with her back to him. She would be thinking of the market, too, of all the strange and wonderful and lovely things in the world. What a great and happy place the world was! But you had to be big and grown-up before you could do just what you liked.

"Mama?"

His mother did not answer. She was crouched over the fire, her shoulders drawn down.

"Mama?"

But she did not turn round; she did not speak. He sat up and stared at her. The world rocked in anguish. "Mama!" he cried. "Why are you weeping?"

CHAPTER VIII

THE SPIRIT AND THE FLESH

"How can we trace the way of the spirit, how can we tell in what manner it was united with this clod of earth? No man can trace and no man can tell. It is enough that He who formed it did also unite or marry it to the body. For nothing is more clear than that the body which is carnal could not of itself create the spirit which is of God. What an astonishing mystery it is thus to see heaven and earth married together in the one person, to see such a noble and divine guest take up its habitation within the mean walls of flesh and blood. But as the mean walls of flesh and blood shall in corruption return to the earth, so shall the divine spirit, which was created a rational spirit, conscious of good and evil, so shall it appear before the Creator of the spirits of all flesh, before the dread Arbiter and final judge. Woe unto each one of us on that day. Woe unto you in whom the spirit all the days of your lives has been polluted by the raging flesh. . . ."

Mildly in this fashion did the catechist, Sandy Ware, pause to expound his reading in Genesis (Chapter ii, verse 7), before proceeding in more direct terms to indict the carnal self-seeking of the day. Little Finn, standing by his mother's knee, kept his round, dark eyes on the mouth which opened and shut between the hair of the upper lip and the thick, square-cut forest on the chin.

In wide, Highland parishes, it was not easy for the minister of the parish church—the only church—to keep in close contact with the individuals of his flock, and so a god-

THE SPIRIT AND THE FLESH

fearing man, of some scriptural accomplishment, was appointed here and there to instruct the people in doctrinal truth as it is expounded and made finally clear in the one hundred and seven Questions and Answers agreed upon by the Assembly of Divines at Westminster and called the Shorter Cathechism.

Normally the catechist went from house to house, but sometimes many were gathered together in one house for the convenience of the catechist, particularly if he were as well known as Sandy Ware and his services demanded in places far from his own district. For Sandy was not only a catechist, not only an expounder of doctrinal subtleties, but also, on occasion, a preacher of fluency and force. Roddie, who was now sitting with elbows on knees and the flat of his hands supporting his cheeks, had heard him in Helmsdale preaching to the fishermen. He had also been to Wick, pulling the drunken brands from the burning. Sandy and men like him had for some time been raising their voices against the constitution and spiritual inadequacy and backsliding of the Established Church itself, calling for its disestablishment, its dissociation from the worldly forces that govern it, calling for its reform and the uprising of the pure evangelical spirit.

Nearly thirty persons were gathered in Widow Grant's house. It sometimes astonished Finn that though Widow Grant was very holy, she could yet speak to him in an ordinary voice, and sometimes even smile. She now sat with lowered head staring at the winking peat. All those present were slightly tense or excited, because they wondered how they would come out of the ordeal of "the Questions". And it was a relief when at last Sandy had cleared the ground for the main engagement and, casting his eyes around, let them rest on Finn, the youngest.

"I wonder," he said, "if this young man could tell me: WHAT IS THE CHIEF END OF MAN?"

Finn replied: "*Man's chief end is to glorify God and to enjoy him for ever.*"

147

"Very good," said Mr. Ware, his whiskers breaking against his chest as he nodded. Then he looked thoughtfully at Finn for a moment, for he remembered how as a little boy he himself had repeated for years the two words *chief end* as one meaningless word. "Now could you tell me the meaning of the words *chief end*?"

"It means," said Finn, "the chief thing that man has got to do."

"A little Daniel!" declared Mr. Ware.

Kirsty raised her chin a couple of inches and her closed lips moved out and in, combatively and with satisfaction.

"WHAT RULE HATH GOD GIVEN TO DIRECT US HOW WE MAY GLORIFY AND ENJOY HIM?" Mr. Ware asked her.

"*The word of God, which is contained in the Scriptures of the Old and New Testaments, is the only rule to direct us how we may glorify and enjoy him,*" replied Kirsty, evenly.

"WHAT DO THE SCRIPTURES PRINCIPALLY TEACH?" asked the catechist, going round with the sun.

"*The Scriptures principally teach what man is to believe concerning God, and what duty God requires of man,*" replied Shiela, Roddie's sister.

"WHAT IS GOD?"

"*God,*" answered Roddie, "*is a Spirit, infinite, eternal, and unchangeable, in his being, wisdom, power, holiness, justice, goodness, and truth.*"

Through the number of persons in the Godhead, the decrees of God, his work of creation and his creation of man, his providence, up to sin, its definition, and man's fall, all was plain sailing. The first stumbling occurred with Robert Duncan, who was thirteen years old and one of a family of ten. "WHEREIN," asked Mr. Ware, "CONSISTS THE SINFULNESS OF THAT ESTATE WHEREINTO MAN FELL?"

"*All mankind by their fall——*"

"No, no," interrupted Mr. Ware, "that describes the misery of the estate whereinto man fell. First we must have a definition of *the sinfulness* of the estate itself.

"Oh, yes," said Robert, so quickly that a faint smile

148

THE SPIRIT AND THE FLESH

showed here and there. "*The sinfulness of that estate where-into man fell, consists in the guilt of Adam's first sin, the want of original righteousness, and the corruption of his whole nature, which is commonly called Original Sin: together with all actual transgressions which proceed from it.*"

"That's better," said Mr. Ware, "but perhaps you will learn to repeat it a little more slowly, so that we may all have time to apprehend the meaning of the words." He stroked his beard. "Now . . ."

As he went deeper into the mysteries there were momentary hesitations here and there, but the first real break came with Simple Sanny, who was in his thirties, with a brown hairy face and small acute eyes.

"WHAT IS ADOPTION?" Mr. Ware asked him.

Sanny opened his mouth thoughtfully and scratched his chin. "I know the *justification* one better," he said.

"We have just had WHAT IS JUSTIFICATION?" remarked the catechist.

"Oh ay," said Sanny, "so we had." His quick eye turned upon a faint noise suspiciously like young laughter at Mr. Ware's back. Encouraged by this, Sanny said, "I'll give you the first commandment instead—if that will suit you."

"We are some way from the commandments yet," replied the catechist, with some severity, "and we do not bargain in these matters as we do over a stirk at a drunken market. A very drunken market, from what I have heard."

Sanny glanced up out of the corner of his eye. Was the catechist getting at him? For Sanny's simplicity and malice were an irresistible attraction to merry-making boys and men; and, in truth, at the fair he had been so well treated that he had slept the night in a ditch near the Market Hill.

"Ay, it was all that, from what I have heard myself," he now replied with an air of simple and sad innocence.

Some clearing of male throats and a choked nasal sound from a boy did not ease Mr. Ware's severity. But it encouraged Sanny still more. "Ay," he said, shaking his head and sucking in his breath, "ay, there was one man there

149

and he told me what adoption was, and it's his words that will not go out of my head, but I know fine they are not the right words. He could not mislead me there," said Sanny. "No fear."

"Silence!" cried Mr. Ware.

"He didn't use bad words, if that's what you mean," muttered Sanny, hurt now. "He only said: 'Adoption is jail without the option'!"

"Silence, you blasphemer!"

Sanny had gone too far and knew it. Everyone knew it. Mr. Ware's eyes were sunken a little in his head and they now glowed. He stood like a prophet who might well call down doom upon them, the everlasting wrath. Before his denunciations, Sanny curled in upon himself like a whipped collie. But Mr. Ware could, on a breath, almost find excuse for him, for this poor, witless man who to gratify the hunger of a cunning vanity would try for a blasphemous jest in God's temple itself, because of the ever-growing carnality and sin of those amongst whom he moved, those who should show him a far other example. The more wrought upon Mr. Ware became the richer and more powerful grew his language, lifting him at last to the cry: "Asses' heads or doves' dung was not Israel's meat when the lepers were sounding the trumpet. Lord, hasten the day of sounding the trumpet with the lepers, of battering Jericho's towering walls with Joshua's rams' horns. When will the worm Jacob thresh the mountains? When will the anointed stripling David come from the wilderness to the slaughter of the Philistine that is Israel's terrification? When will Moses come down from the Mount and see how our Aarons have made the people naked? Lord, hasten the day when our idolizing mirth will be turned to a repenting grief."

Little Finn gazed on the figure of Sandy Ware with awe. The uplifted head with the out-thrust beard, the hands raised a little like tentative supplicating wings, the deep, rolling fluency of the voice, the up-curling eddies of blue smoke, the gloom of the rafters, the watching faces, the bowed heads, and passing in the midst the ritual, awful figures of Joshua and Moses and David, with the walls of Jericho tumbling down at the sounding horn on the plains of Israel.

A quietness came on the company and Mr. Ware resumed his catechizing, drawing forth the benefits which in this life do flow from justification, adoption, and sanctification, from belief in Christ and the resurrection, working on through obedience and the moral law to the meaning of the commandments, and so to a recital of the ten commandments themselves, together with amplifying statements of what is required in each and forbidden, so that their meaning be completely apprehended. To Wull fell the answer: *The third commandment is, Thou shalt not take the name of the Lord thy God in vain; for the Lord will not hold him guiltless that taketh his name in vain;* and to Catrine: *The seventh commandment is, Thou shalt not commit adultery.* But it was when the commandments were left behind, onward in that rarer air of *repentance unto life* and sacrament as an *effectual means of salvation,* that the young and many of the old stumbled. Even Roddie got lost among the six petitions, for here there was no word in the Question to suggest the beginning of the Answer. Catrine hesitated once, but quickly picked herself up. Kirsty never hesitated. In the same even, indifferent voice, she repeated the conjoint wisdom of the Westminster divines as something she had long been familiar with, and did not require anyone in particular to challenge her on the matter now.

When Mr. Ware had addressed them on the state of their knowledge and had exhorted them to be ever more diligent in cultivating the one and only way of salvation, he got to his knees. They all followed him. Finn got down, too, though his mother paid no attention to him. Mr. Ware prayed in a deepened, humbled voice, with every now and then a husky rising urgency as he wrestled in travail with the Holy Spirit. The fervency of supplication became a rich

151

tapestry of text and biblical figure and Eastern scene, with Christ amid the money-changers in the temple, walking by the golden grain in challenge to the orthodox, lifted on high at Calvary, Christ the Redeemer. "O Lord, lead us not unto temptation but deliver us from evil; take us, we beseech Thee, in Thy gracious hand and lead us by the green pastures and by the quiet waters that flow from Thy holy spirit."

When they were on their feet, Sandy Ware was quiet and smiling and shook hands with each one. Then the folk scattered to their homes in little groups. Roddie took Finn's hand as he walked with two men behind Kirsty and Catrine and Shiela. At the door of Kirsty's house they all paused. Kirsty invited them in, but Roddie's father, who was a good-living man, said it was time they were home.

"I hope," remarked Kirsty to Roddie, as they were moving off, "that you feel a better man now?"

"Well, I know it could not have made you better anyway," replied Roddie.

"Hmff!" snorted Kirsty, giving him a sharp, humoured look.

Roddie laughed, saluted Finn, and said, "Good-bye, Catrine."

"Good-bye," said Catrine.

"Hmff!" repeated Kirsty as the three came inside; "Sandy setting up to be a preacher! Him criticizing his betters! Sandy Ware, who learned the A B C in his father's byre, talking about *heavenly* wisdom being more than *college* learning. It would be far better for him if he helped his poor wife and daughter to work their big croft than stravaiging about the country, all dressed up, teaching those, who know better, how to behave themselves."

Finn gazed at her, his mouth fallen open.

And when Catrine had put him to bed (he went without a murmur) he lay gazing up at the rounded soot-blackened ceiling but pursuing images of his own, wondering what a leper was and what sort of trumpet he had and what the horn looked like that tumbled the walls of Jericho. For Finn knew a little about trumpets, and it was news to him that they could knock down walls. But whenever he wanted to ask his Mama a question, there was Kirsty's endless voice: ". . . And that was Donald Sage, the greatest Christian minister and man that ever spoke with college learning from any pulpit. She was a strange woman, his second wife. I was there when he brought her home to the manse at Kildonan. And what a home coming it was! He came himself riding on a grey horse, and she beside him sitting sideways on a garron. Eppy Mackay, the housekeeper, went forward to meet them, bowing at every third step. Oh, Eppy knew her manners! We could do with more of her manners here, and less of this evangelical style, with its plaguing the Lord, who knows too much about us already for our comfort. And there waiting were Mr. Sage's four children. The two lassies were in tartan gowns, their hair nicely braided on the forehead and smoothed with pomatum. But Eppy had kept her skill for the two boys. With ordinary white flour, she had powdered and combed their heads. There were brogues on their feet and white worsted stockings on their legs, tied below the knee with red garters. The kilt and jacket—it was all the same tartan— were seamed together into the one piece and opened down the front with yellow buttons. . . . And the dance afterwards when Eppy put the flour on the elder's bald head . . ."

Finn fell asleep.

As Catrine sat alone by the fire, in a habit that had grown upon her at this hour, she heard her son dreaming.

She began to dream herself.

Running in and out her mind was a little girl in the strath of Kildonan, all bright and full of life and sometimes of half-dreaming reveries that went along the slow ridges of the hills against the sky. But the mind shut itself in a quick snap against anything so slow that it grew frightening, and the body ran off in a shout, an ecstasy of life, with hardly even a look behind. Tormad in the woods. Tormad—with mind and body thrilled to an unbearable stillness, until she felt she would dissolve, fly into bits, unless . . . ah, the crush of his arms, crushing all the bits back into shape, and the relief of it, the unutterable, divine relief, and the sudden exquisite lack of care, of caring no more, of letting go. . . . Tormad—and the red berries. . . . Blood-red magic.

The letter had been written by a man for Ronnie in the West Indies last year. Ronnie had been ill but was getting better. The letter also said that Ian and Torquil, when last seen, were well. There had been no mention of Tormad. It almost seemed as if a previous letter never received had been written wherein some final word may have been said about Tormad. Either that or Tormad had been separated from them in the beginning. . . . Tormad, standing before her, in sorrow, as if blaming himself for leaving her . . . and fading away into the wall. . . .

Little Finn breathed quickly in his dream.

The birth of Finn in the awful quiet of the gloaming, among the straw in the byre. She had gone in to see Kirsty's father, who was now committed to his bed and who, they both knew, was dying. Perhaps it was because she had known him in this final stage of his life that she had grown to love the old man, he was so gentle, with that strange, far-away look that pulled the strings of the heart. Gaunt his face had grown, too, and his patience was beyond belief, beyond what was natural in human being, and now and then expressed itself in gentleness, in a faint smile of regret at having to trouble anyone. He was like a man out of whom long ago the heart had been taken but who now had received back the essence of the lost heart's kindness.

"I want to speak to you, Catrine," he said, and at that, as at an irrevocable summons, her own heart stood still. "Are you happy here?"

"Oh yes," she answered.

"It may be difficult for you at times." His voice was weak and he paused, as if unaware of the passage of time. "I have been talking to Kirsty. This will be a home for you as long as you like, and should it so happen in the order of things that Kirsty will be taken before you, and you will still have no home of your own, then it is my wish that you would have this home, for yourself and the child."

Catrine shut her teeth hard against her uprising emotion. Never had she shown any complaint to this man, never anything but what little brightness was in her.

"My family are gone from me—all except Kirsty, but she has been a good daughter to me and will honour my wish."

Her head drooped. She could not speak.

"At first I thought that a new young life like yours would have tired me. But you brought lightness with you, and kind, willing hands. You have been a great help to us, and somehow you have brought peace to my last days. I want to thank you, Catrine; for my time has come upon me."

The tears were now streaming down her face and her body was trembling.

"You have had a hard life for one so young," said the voice, quiet now as if disembodied. "But His ways are inscrutable. I had hoped to live long enough to see your child born, and so have made it easier for you, but it is not to be."

Catrine lost control of herself, and fell on her knees by the bedside, and buried her face, crying, "No! No!"

His long, worn hand came gently upon her head. "May God bless you, my child, now and through all your days."

Her face was such a mess of emotion and blinding tears that she could not look at him, but got up and hurriedly left the room, without thanking him or saying one word.

By the door she brushed past Kirsty, who merely remarked in a matter-of-fact voice, "Have a look at Bel. I hear her mooing."

Blindly she went into the byre. Bel threw her head round, showing the whites beyond her great liquid eyes. Her calving time was upon her.

Catrine stared at her and suddenly felt sick. Her knees weakened, sweat broke out on her brow, and she staggered towards the new straw, got to her knees and rolled over. With the pains came terror, but she bit the scream into her lips.

All the flesh of her body gathered itself together, terrified but fighting-wild, gathered and strained, blood running from her lip, her hands knotted in the straw.

Outside, Kirsty's voice called, "Catrine! Catrine!" It was the high death-cry, and in the midst of her own torment, Catrine knew it, and it did not weaken her but on the contrary increased her fighting urgency.

To the byre door came Kirsty, still crying "Catrine!"— and saw Catrine in the straw and little Finn being born.

That matter-of-fact astringency in Kirsty, which she had instinctively turned to from the emotional dissolution of Dale, as a dog will turn in its sickness to green grass, had been all firm hands and confidence, death put aside in the urgent needs of life. "You're all right, my lassie. Bel herself couldn't do it better." And the firm hands worked deftly.

Finn gave a little whimper in his sleep.

Catrine got up and soothed the dream from him, then returned to the fire, and began lifting the peats back and smooring those with red embers in the ash-pit.

What lovely days, too, she had had in her life! How lovely life could be, how bright and beautiful! And, in a way, loveliest of all had been these last few years with Finn.

Down on the braes below the house, with the small birch bushes, the grey boulders with cool ferns in the shadows, primroses and violets, smooth bare-cropped green hillocks, the sunlight on narrow alleyways winding and hidden amid the golden gorse, daisies and buttercups and dandelions, the burn singing its low, unending song from the throats of the little shining pools, and Finn's restless body and Finn's voice. The herding days of summer. For beasts could not always be on tether, and whenever possible Catrine had to herd them, so that they could visit all the rich pockets of grass on the steep, broken ground, and yet, in their freedom, not be allowed either to stray from their own ground or on to the cultivated land.

What happy hours, what moments of delight—sheer delight that sometimes frightened her and brought a momentary shadow across the sun; from the feel of Finn's body, the sound of his merry laugh. There was that moment in the hiding game when, half-terrified at last lest she had disappeared altogether from the world, he would suddenly come on her behind a bush—followed by the swift meeting, her arms round him, her face burrowing with bubbling sounds into his breast, and laughter shaking from him like notes from a tumbled music-box.

The tired hour when she took him on her lap and sang the old lullaby, so old that it must have made itself out of the heart of a mother in the beginning of time, and so new that it was Catrine's own heart in its deepest fondness—carrying them both away, together, close together, until she had to stop singing and bring them to a warm huddle in the lap of the living moment.

Occasionally she would look around, near and far, to make sure that sensible folk were not watching. For often she felt as young as Finn himself and would suddenly clap her hand over her mouth to smother the yelp of laughter. If she possessed nothing in the world but Finn, she had enough, enough, for ah! Finn was her own, her very own.

And all that lovely time was ending. For next summer Finn would be old enough to do the herding himself, old enough to have his own ploys, to sail little boats and logs, to dam tiny shallows and guddle yellow trout, too old for a daisy-chain, too restless and grown-up for her lap. But—she would understand. With the point of the poker she slowly drew the ashes over the small, scattered embers that glowed like red jewels. She would try——

Finn screamed. She dropped the poker and dashed to

157

him. He kept on screaming as he clung to her wildly. "My legs!" She bared his legs, soothing him: "My little calf! My sweetheart! It's only a dream." He muttered something about a wall; but already the dream had gone, and gulping and half-sobbing, he was sinking down into sleep. In a minute he was quiet again.

On what dangerous journey had he been all alone? She stood still in the darkness for a moment, but the night was more silent than her wondering mind.

In the morning, however, Finn suddenly remembered his dream. It was the first dream he ever had remembered and its clearness so astonished him that he looked around to make sure he could escape unseen. This was fairly easy if one moved away, bit by bit, interested in this or that, as if one weren't going anywhere. Once round the corner of the house, he ran. Down where the burns joined, there was a drystone dyke taller than himself. He had climbed it once, but the stones on the top were shaky and he had got a fright. If one of the stones fell on you it would kill you! Well, he had seen this wall in his dream, but it was a much bigger wall, though it was the same wall, too. Now there was something about this wall that had always seemed to threaten him, to dare him and yet to threaten him, with a queer sort of expression on its face formed by the curious shapes of the holes between the stones. The wall had to be tumbled down for it was a bad wall. "Go forward and sound the trumpet!" cried a great man behind him, who was Moses, though he looked like Sandy Ware. There were many people behind, as Finn went forward. The trumpet hung from the branch of a tree, as Finn had sometimes hung his own trumpet, but this was a much bigger trumpet than Finn's, and not straight but curved like one of the great horns on a Highland cow. Both the wall and the trumpet grew bigger as he drew near. But he took the mouthpiece in his lips and blew all the breath that was in him. The trumpet roared like a bull, and at that one or two

158

of the stones on top started to shake; then the wall began to sway; he turned and ran as the wall fell, but the stones came after him, leaping over the grass, and he stumbled, and the stones leaped on to his legs. . . .

When he reached the drystone dyke, he was not altogether surprised to find it still standing. It was standing there exactly as it had always done, the same grey stones with the holes between.

He gazed round about him as at nothing in particular. He looked up at the sky, but without lifting his head much. He tried to whistle carelessly. Suddenly he ran off home.

CHAPTER IX

THE SEASHORE

❧

"I can feel him," said Finn, "I can just touch him," his mouth open and his face flushed. He withdrew his arm from the hole in the cairn and quickly removed a few more surface stones. Oscar, the young collie, whimpered, but Donnie told him to shut up. In went Finn's arm again. Donnie watched Finn's eye and so knew what was happening. There was a scrabbling sound as Finn pulled out the rabbit by the hind legs. "Get down!" roared Donnie to Oscar, kicking him off with his knee. The rabbit squealed as Finn held him up and hit him smartly behind the ears with the edge of his open hand. He hit him several times, and then once or twice more to make sure. It was a young but full-grown rabbit. "Boy, he's fat! Feel that," said Finn. Donnie felt the broad back and nodded. They were connoisseurs of trout and salmon and game, not merely because their spoils were few and therefore precious, but also because they had to hunt with extreme wariness, lest gamekeeper or ground officer or other minion of the laird come upon them. For the smallest offence against the rights of "the estate", a whole family might summarily be evicted from their croft and the holding be let at an increased rent to one of the many applicants for land and a home in these growing days.

Finn was thirteen and Donnie one year older. Donnie had called on his friend Finn to try to inveigle him to go to the shore. It was a fine, sunny morning in early August, and the boats would be coming in. Finn had said that of

course he couldn't go because he was herding and there was
no-one at home but his Granny. So he had driven the beasts
down the brae to the lowest part of the holding—a place
they liked because the grass was green and succulent. Finn
did not let them go there normally: he kept it in reserve for
those special occasions when he wanted to absent himself
for an hour or so. He then had accompanied Donnie as far
as the House of Peace and was standing talking to him,
heavy with disappointment at not being able to go to the
shore, when Oscar had suddenly started a rabbit. The rabbit had come straight for them, as its burrow was in the
brae at their backs, had seen them and doubled—and finally
slipped into this occasional refuge of the cairn.

Finn's blood was now up. "I'll tell you what," he said.
"I'll go to Granny and tell her you and me are going after
rabbits at your place and I'll be sure to bring one home."

They discussed this at some length, and Donnie was left
to secrete the rabbit in the hole from which it had been
drawn and to block up the hole with stones, while Finn ran
swiftly back with Oscar at his heels. He drove the cattle up
the brae and behind the house.

He was never sure of Kirsty. She could be extremely
strict and harsh, and yet might suddenly agree on something you thought utterly hopeless and even wrong.

She was washing potatoes by stirring them with a stick
in the big iron pot as he went in. She looked up at him with
her shrewd eyes and witch-like face and barked: "Well,
what is it?"

"I was wondering," he said, mildly, "if I could get off
for an hour or so. Donnie is wanting me up at his place."

"Oh, indeed! And what is Donnie wanting you for?"

"There are one or two rabbits," he said, "eating the
corn on them, and Donnie says he knows how he would get
them if I went with him at once."

"And why at once?"

"Because the dog bolted a rabbit into a cairn, and the
two of us working on a cairn could pull rabbits out."

"And what about me and all the work to do myself while you're off pulling other people's rabbits out?"

"I'm sure of getting one rabbit home with me. That's certain." Finn spoke in a moody embarrassed voice, not looking at his Granny.

"And what if anyone sees you?"

"No-one will see me," said Finn.

"It would be just as well," said his Granny. She stirred the potatoes. "They're eating the corn, are they?"

"Yes."

"No rabbits should be allowed to eat corn," said Kirsty. "You can go—but don't be long."

"All right," replied Finn. "The cattle are behind the house." He strolled slowly out, but when he got to the lower gable-end, he took to his heels—and immediately pulled up to drive Oscar home. Oscar's tail disappeared, while his eyes in their desperate pleading all but wept. Finn was merciless, growling and hissing.

Donnie saw him coming, and fell in. They threw snatches of merry talk as they ran. "It was the rabbit eating your corn did it," cried Finn.

"Well, that was no lie," cried Donnie.

"No, but it was lucky!" cried Finn.

They both stopped to have the laugh out, then ran on again.

The sea! the sea! the boats coming in!

The lightness and brightness of the sea, and boats, and fishing, and fun!

But when they came in sight of the stir on the long flat green before the beach, Finn pulled up. Pointing to the shelter of the river-bank, he said, "I'll go round this way. You have a look to see where my mother is working and come and tell me on the edge of the sea."

"Right you are," said Donnie, and off he set. The boats had been in some time, for curers liked to have their herring in salt at the earliest possible moment after being caught, and Mr. Hendry was full of more than the usual

business ardour in this and other respects. The animation
of the scene excited Donnie. Fishermen were already
spreading their nets on the outskirts of the gutting stations,
one net overlapping another, so that each drift was a long,
rectangular darkness upon the green grass of river flat or
sloping brae. He watched the barefooted men walking
smartly in a line, for he knew who they were or where they
came from. "Was there a good fishing to-day?" he asked
one man, coming up with a net on his shoulders. "Only
fair," said the man. But there seemed to be an enormous
number of herring in the wooden gutting boxes, which
were bigger than the floor of a room, with sloping sides
that the women could bend over. And there they were,
bending over all sides, rows of women, their heads bobbing
up and down as they stooped, caught a herring, gutted it,
and flung it into a basket, bobbed again, gutted, and flung,
their hands working so quickly that you couldn't see
exactly what the blade of the knife did. The old women
worked like lightning, but the young women were glad to
straighten their backs when a basket was full, and were on
the look-out for a joke at any time. And here was George,
the foreman, of important and sometimes stentorian voice,
whisking salt from his scoop with expert gesture. Donnie
backed away and went along the stations, looking for
Finn's mother. It was difficult to know the women with
their wrapped heads and odd garments unless you could see
the individual features.

"Hullo, Donnie! Does your mother know you're
out?"

"Yes," said Donnie, and then blushed at having been
caught so easily. There was a laugh and he backed away
again. Then he saw Shiela; and, in another moment,
Catrine, dumping her shallow, empty basket on the herring. A big enough pile there to keep her going for some
time, he decided. Shiela saw him and waved a bandaged,
bloody hand gaily, but before Catrine could spot him he
went away hurriedly.

"He seemed to be looking for someone," said Shiela to Catrine.

"Did he?"

"When he saw you he ran."

"No?" She paused, then had to look at the gutted herring in her hand to see whether it was full or spent.

But by this time Donnie was on the beach where all the boats were drawn nose up. And he had a great bit of luck, for as he passed the *Morning Star*, that had come in late, he paused to watch big Maria taking a creel of herring along the gang-plank. It very rarely happened, but still there was always the chance of a slip. And slip Maria did, clean as a whistle. The creel, keeping to the gangway, came hard against the side of the boat and so most of its contents were saved, but Maria hadn't time to lift her skirts, though she lifted them as she waded out, exposing a breadth of flank that she thought men might be better employed than laugh at.

Donnie was bursting with delight and listened to all the sallies with attentive ear.

This slight misadventure ran along the boats and up over the beach to the gutting stations like a warm wind, and when Maria appeared with her creel, which had been filled up, George looked her over with his quick professional eye. "What have you been doing to yourself, Maria? You're very wet."

"I didn't do it to myself," said Maria.

Some of the women had to stop gutting because their hands grew feckless in laughter.

Maria was a large, straight-backed, heavy woman of a slow tread. She was used to the creel, like all the women of the crofts, and bore it on her back with the same ease, whether loaded with manure, peats, fish, or any other material. Croft and sea were still so allied—and would be for many years—that the older women brought the customs of the land to the boat, and on occasion even carried their men on their backs, wading through the water to the

164

gunnel to save them from getting wet before they adventured on the cold sea. Not that there were very many women of Maria's heroic proportions in Dunster, and for the most part the men—especially the younger crews—did their own carrying, but still the fishing was based on the household, and where the men were there the womenfolk were gathered, giving life its extra warmth and excitement. Whether paid in fish or pennies, Maria reckoned she did as well as any of the gutters.

Donnie found Finn talking to Roddie. "Only three crans," Roddie was saying, the folded net balanced lightly on his shoulder. "Does your mother know you're here?"

"No," said Finn. "Mind, don't tell her."

"All right." Roddie smiled to this fast-growing lad who, though slim, had little awkwardness in his movements. "You'll find the handline in the stern of the boat."

Though the sterns of the boats were in the water, for the tide was flowing, the slight wash of the sea on the beach made it a poor place for fishing except for those useless finger-length fish they called "sellags". Finn knew a much better place, where the water was deep beyond a sloping skerry, with a capital sandy bottom for flukes. With the handline and two herring, picked from among the ballast stones, Finn and Donnie slipped away to the skerry.

They had a moment of terrible excitement when, squatting on the rock, they saw a dark-mottled flat fish about a foot long approach one of the two baits. "Don't move," whispered Finn intensely, for it was Donnie's "chance" of the line. The water was of a perfect transparency. The flat fish came right up to the white bait, put its nose to it, and the bait disappeared. At once Donnie jerked and pulled and had him. He hauled rapidly and was on the point of heaving the fish out of the water when the second hook caught in a cleft of the rock.

"Watch, or you'll break the line!" cried Finn.

"I'll lose him!" cried Donnie.

"Let him go!" yelled Finn. "Let him go!"

THE SEASHORE

But Donnie couldn't bring himself to let the fish go.
Finn snatched the line from his hands and slackened it. At
once the flounder went nose down to the bottom, naturally
drawing the hook from the crevice as it did so. "Now,"
said Finn, handing the line back, "haul away—but canny!"

Donnie hauled, and up the sloping, barnacled rock came
the flapping flounder. This was the real fish of the deep sea,
such as the winter small boats caught far off the land.
Thrilled with wonder and excitement, they touched the
skin with their finger-tips.

"It's your chance," said Donnie, in no way hurt because
Finn had snatched the line from him.

"You see," explained Finn, "Roddie gave the line to
me, and it would be an awful thing if we broke it."

"Yes, but I wouldn't have broken it. I thought it might
just come out of the crack itself."

"I know," said Finn, nodding generously. He took a
piece of flesh from the herring's back, trimmed it with his
nails, and neatly hid the hook in it; then, getting to his
feet, he stepped warily down to the edge of the water
where it lapped on the rock and threw both baits as far out
as he could.

"That was a good throw," said Donnie.

"It'll do," said Finn.

They squatted and waited, seeing all sorts of interesting
things, from tiny crabs to little reddish fish that they
assured each other were the young of the cod; coming out
of and going into the narrow forests of coloured seaweed
that grew around the foot of the rocks. Tall fronds of the
tangle, leaves of dulse, bushes of long, swaying streamers
that moved in the pulse of the sea like eels.

"Isn't it fine here?" said Finn.

"It's great," said Donnie.

"And the other boys are fishing off the boats," said
Finn.

"For sellags!" said Donnie.

The sarcasm was rich and throaty. A reddish rock cod

over a foot long came sailing round the corner of a submerged ledge. Their breathing stopped. He sailed over
their baits, straight to the ledge they sat on, nosed the
weed, passed still farther in, then turned and began to go
out. But as he now approached the baits, well above them,
obviously not seeing them, Finn gave a gentle pull, so that
the baits not only moved but even rose an inch or so. This
movement was observed by the wanderer and he went
down to investigate. He kept his nose quite a time in front
of one bait as if he were sniffing it delicately. He opened
his mouth and the bait shot in. Finn tugged—and successfully landed this new variety of prize.

They forgot about time, crofts, cows, and humanity.

The climax came when it was Finn's chance. As the baits
lay on the sandy bottom, there emerged from the outer
forest an eel of such length that fear struck them straight
to the heart. It was longer than themselves and its sinuous
progress was terrifying to behold. It moved like the father
of all serpents. They had involuntarily exclaimed on in-
drawn breaths, and now Donnie said, "Don't!" He meant:
Don't let him take the bait. And Finn knew he shouldn't.
Yet he could not draw the line away, held at once by a fearful curiosity and an instinctive need to pit his courage
against the desperate moment. The eel saw the bait, un-
dulated down to it and promptly sucked it in. Finn pulled
—and the eel, writhing into a knot, held. Finn pulled till
the line bit into his hand, but could not raise the whirling
eel. "Watch he doesn't pull you in!" shouted Donnie. And
in truth Finn had all he could do to hold against the eel.
Indeed the eel snatched some line from him. "He's going
to break the line!" he cried.

At that moment there was a tremendous shout from the
shore.

"Your mother and Roddie!" exclaimed Donnie.

In the flush of embarrassed weakness that went over
Finn, the eel gained more line.

Roddie was shouting at them through cupped hands.

Then Donnie understood and yelled, "Finn, we're surrounded by the sea!"

The eel had gained the forest of seaweed.

"Come on!" screamed Donnie.

Panic was in Finn, too, but there was also the pull on the line, pulling at his hunting instinct, his courage He suddenly lost all fear of the eel and tugged angrily, madly, with all his might. The snood broke at the eel's teeth and Finn landed on his back. As he got up he glanced sideways and saw his mother stumbling down towards Roddie, who was on the tide's edge. Then he turned his back on them and rolled in the line.

Donnie was already splashing his way, the water to his waist. Finn deliberately lifted the four principal items of the catch by sticking a finger under the cheek of each and slowly climbed off the skerry and deliberately selected his spot. Donnie had struck in too quickly and was nearly off his feet. It was shallower, taking it at a slant. With the seawater over his hips, he felt for each foothold carefully, casting his eye around at the same time. Roddie had waded in to steady Donnie and haul him out. When Finn saw Roddie coming towards him, he shouted, "I'm all right," in a gruff voice. Roddie stopped, and Finn, still holding to his line and fish, waded out.

His mother's face was very pale. She was also so angry that for a moment she could not speak. Then her voice issued thick and thin at the same time, asking him what he meant by coming here when she had told him never to come. What did he mean? And her voice cracked. It was an ugly voice. The way she was behaving shamed him. His face grew darkly flushed. He did not look at her. And all in Roddie's hearing.

Roddie had politely turned away and was now talking to Donnie as they went back towards the curing stations Donnie was telling him about the great eel.

His mother suddenly stopped and turned her back. Finn glanced round and saw her shoulders heaving, though she kept quite straight, with her head up. The folk who had been coming, attracted by the shouting, now paused and, after exchanging a word and a laugh with Roddie, went drifting back.

Finn went on, hoping Roddie would not look back; but after a minute he did and Finn saw, by the way his eyes steadied a moment and narrowed, that his mother must still be standing with her back to them. Finn looked on the ground and slowed up, a dark smile twisting his face in moody embarrassment. He stooped to squeeze the water from his clothes, then followed Roddie as he moved on again. Half-turning his head, he saw his mother coming. He sloped away from the path to the beach. His mother called him, but he paid no attention, and went along until he came to Roddie's boat. There he tightly wound the end of the line on to the forked stick and left it in the stern where he had found it. A bitter impulse came on him to throw the four fish into the sea, but he resisted it. Some men who were looking after the boats called to him cheerfully about his good fishing, but he hadn't much to say. They knew what had happened, for half the world must have heard the shouting, and he avoided the humour in their faces. Going off along the beach by himself, he presently turned up the bank of the river, leaving Donnie waiting for him over at the curing stations. He did not want Donnie or anyone else. He had not liked that concentrated look in Roddie's face, a look of silent condemnation, condemnation of a situation for which he, Finn, was to blame.

He walked without hurrying his steps, for his mind was dark and angry and he was not running away from anything. When at last he came to the cairn by the House of Peace, he drew the stones away, pulled out the rabbit, and pushed it up under his jersey. Then he threaded the four fish on a hazel stick, crossed the burn, and went up by the big pools towards his home.

He heard Kirsty's voice yelling at the cattle before he

saw her. His eyes narrowed and his mouth gave a small twist. This was the next of it!

"My lad! where have you been all the day?"

Then she saw the fish and looked piercingly at him. "To the shore!" she said in almost a small voice.

"Donnie had to go a message and I went with him."

"So! You told your Grannie a lie?"

"I have the rabbit here," he replied, giving the bulge in his jersey a thrust. Without looking at her, he walked slowly on.

"Did your mother see you?"

"She did."

As she accompanied him, Kirsty's head kept nodding as if it were on a swivel and couldn't stop, the lips tight. "And what did she say to you?"

Finn did not answer, and they entered the house, where he laid down his varied catch.

Kirsty looked at the rabbit, the flounder (of which she was very fond), the rock cod and the two lythe, and nodded once or twice grimly. "Where did you get the fish?"

"At the shore," replied Finn, turning to walk out.

"Come here!" she called peremptorily. "Do you think you can live without food?"

"I don't want anything." And he went out, ignoring her further summons.

So! thought Kirsty, it was like that! It would be! She put a small pan of milk on the fire. For a quick dish when he was hungry, Finn liked nothing better than milk brose. When the milk was boiling, she poured it over a fistful of raw oatmeal in a wooden bowl, stirred, went hurriedly out, and sent Finn in. She looked after him with an expression in which there was a glimmer of amusement. The man was stirring!

After eating, Finn drove the cattle towards the edge of the moor, then sat down by a clump of gorse, and presently saw Roddie and Donnie appear in the distance. They stopped and looked in his direction, but Finn remained hidden and so they crossed the burn and went towards their homes. Roddie would now try for a couple of hours' sleep, before going back to lift the nest and put to sea again. Some time afterwards, Shiela and Catrine appeared. They stood talking for a long time together before they parted. Shiela was married and had two of a family. Her husband had been on one of the first boats to come in and was already asleep. His mother lived with them and looked after the croft and young children when they were both away. Through the bush, Finn saw Catrine go up towards the house. He did not deliberately hide. In fact, he got to his feet before she could have reached the house and idly strolled down the brae.

No-one came near him until, a long time afterwards, Kirsty's voice shouted him to supper. Slowly he drove the young beasts into the enclosure and tethered the two milch cows. He knew he must go in, but he put off as much time as possible, so that he might eat alone.

Kirsty came and called again. Then he went in. He did not look at his mother. The skeleton of the flounder, clean as a new comb, lay on Kirsty's plate. She put a lump of butter on his rock cod and remarked abruptly, "Say your grace." He lifted his hand to his forehead and muttered into its palm. She closed her lips, denying herself. When he had finished eating, she rose and went out. Between his mother and himself no word had passed.

But he could see that between Kirsty and his mother there had been quite a few words, and he had the odd feeling that Kirsty had stuck up for him.

He did not return to the house until it was time for bed. Catrine had to be up and off very early in the morning. His mother and himself still slept in the kitchen and he now strongly wished it were otherwise. As she sat before the fire, her back to him, he said his simple prayer silently, stripped to his shirt, and slipped in between the blankets. Then she smoored the fire, as she always did before undressing, kneeled, and got into her own bed.

In the darkness, the awful burden of their silence was easier for Finn to bear. He was glad that was over! One would think his mother was stricken dumb the way she went about! He had got through it much better than he had expected—because he had got through it intact. He was whole, and if his mind was dark it had a queer smile in it, bitter a little, but still his own. He got this feel of himself, knit together, in the round, under the blankets, his own body curling up, his very own. It was fine!

Only he didn't feel in the least sleepy. He was as wide awake as anything. And—he had won his way. He had gone to the shore; he had come back; and here he was. Roddie might look like yon—but what did he care? The monstrous eel came out of the forest of seaweed. The clear water, with the faint green that seemed to make it clearer; the slow-waving weed; the sea. He had held on! He hadn't let go. . . . The sea: what a size of a place it was! And soon the schooners would be coming to take the barrels away to foreign places, the large ships with the tall masts and the great sails. He had seen one last year from the cliff-heads, though no-one knew that but Donnie. Their own boats took out the barrels of herring and loaded them on to the schooner. Sometimes they needed an extra man on the schooner and he was called a sailor. Sailors sailed the seven seas, sailed all over the globe that "the professor" had in the schoolroom. If anyone tried to keep you back, to keep you shut into a croft—you could go away and sail over the seven seas to strange lands, and so be free in yourself to wave your arms to distant things, to shout, and to go with other men on adventures. . . .

His mother moved restlessly in her bed, and at once his mind gave a whirl like a caught eel. He knew perfectly well she was wide awake and wanting to say things. He felt the dark dumb burden that was pressing down on her and decided to go to sleep at once. So cunningly he slowed up his breathing and let it come regularly and more and more audibly.

" Are you sleeping ?"

It was a deep, sad whisper. He did not answer.

"Finn."

The way she called his name, softly, drawn out a little, like a far-away forlorn bird's cry, touched the quick of his heart. Swift responses came pressing up inside him, but he breathed steadily.

Then he heard her turn away, and the world rolled over. Her soft shuddering sigh sank into the dark places where all is formless and incomplete.

This incompleteness could not be borne. The responses got past his throat to press against his eyeballs. It was difficult to keep breathing regularly. It was too much. Having to swallow the tears in his throat broke his effort, and a choked sound got out before he could bite on it.

She heard. She sat up. She was coming. Oh, he knew it! She shouldn't come now! He hated her coming to find him broken.

She knelt beside his low bed and put an arm out over him. He turned away angrily, pulling the clothes about his shoulders.

"I'm sorry, Finn," she said. "Won't you speak to me?"

"Go away." The tears were getting completely the better of him now. He bit the bolster.

"Listen, Finn. You mustn't be angry with me. The sea has not been kind to me. And then—we have been living here, though it is not our croft, our home. I cannot do a man's work, taking in new land. You and me—we are wanderers, who found a home. The only way we can pay back is if you——" She stopped, for though she knew what she was going to say was true enough—how she herself was making a little at the gutting for the use of the house, the need for working the croft properly and breaking in land lest the ground officer get at them, for Finn to concentrate on the home and grow up into a man to take the burden from Granny (there was no extra man here as on other crofts)—all were not so much reasons, however true, as excuses for covering over the ultimate truth, which was simply her fear of what the sea might do to Finn; and because she knew this, and was honest in her ultimate self, she stopped talking; her hand fell limp and her head drooped. There was no way of making the boy understand. No way. She saw it was inevitable and natural. This was the beginning of the new loneliness.

But her stillness was invaded by the movement of Finn's body. She heard him gathering his resources, choking back his sobs, and then, as if he understood in his own way all that troubled her, he got out: "I'm sorry."

"Oh, Finn," she said swiftly and stretched both arms over the clothes, buried her face, and sobbed.

"Don't cry, Mama!" he said, his own tears gushing again. "Don't cry." His groping hands got caught in her hair.

She did not lift her face until she had control of herself. His hands on her head, fumbling to comfort her, had a deep effect upon her, and she had all she could do to keep herself from kissing his fingers wildly.

"Now go to your bed, Mama; you'll get cold."

"All right," said Catrine, as if accepting his wise advice; "I'll go. Good night, Finn." Her voice was happy. She offered him no endearment.

"Good night," he answered.

Life was light again as thistledown. His mother had obeyed him as if he were a man. He loved her. He would fight for her. He would fight ten thousand. . . .

And though they both felt wide awake as sunlight, yet in a very short time they were in a deep sleep.

In the year, there were many particular seasons: the long festival of the New Year, when folk visited one another's houses, the men with a snatch of song in their mouths as they advanced with their bottles and offered the strong product of the barley, which was tasted after a little speech of good wishes for health and happiness; the preparing of the land for the spring sowing; the cutting of the peats in May; this new and overpowering excitement of the herring fishing in July and August; and, lastly, the harvesting of the crops, followed by the November market and the long winter nights of inside work, when women carded and spun and knitted, and men and boys sat round the fire discussing the world and telling stories.

Of these, harvest-time was still in some profound sense the most significant. When the last sheaf had been cut and stooked—or carried in as a trophy—a man's eyes going over his land were satisfied. Whatever befell now, there would be meal in the girnel and straw for the beasts. It cleansed the mind, satisfied manhood, and released care. The rest was in the hands of God.

Then a man might look at a woman in the gloaming, in the dim light of a barn, under the great harvest moon, and see her hair like the ripened corn or dark as sleep.

The harvesting that followed Finn's struggle with the eel and the quarrel with his mother, brought with it an incident that worked deeply in Finn's mind. It was the custom for friendly neighbours to assist one another, and when the grain had been stooked at Roddie's home, Roddie and Shiela and Duncan had come down to Kirsty's. They were a happy party and the work had gone ahead in great style. Kirsty had appeared with bread and cheese, whisky and barley-water, to celebrate the beginning, and the proper words had been spoken and the right blessings invoked, for Kirsty knew how a thing should be done decently. Sandy Ware might talk of pagan practices: that did not worry Kirsty. The last sheaf was cut on the edge of the dark, and though there were folk who feared Kirsty's tongue and thought she was hard, yet a few dropped in in the passing, for it does the heart good to see a harvest gathered anywhere at any time. Moreover, if Kirsty offered a dram, one could rely on its being "special"! So faces were smiling in the kitchen and every taste of the liquor was a speech.

Finn, who was always conscious of Roddie's presence

anywhere, suddenly missed him and went out. The moon was rising and the new stooks were casting shadows. It was so lovely a night that it made him feel restless. The day's labour lay warm and sluggish in his blood. Manhood was troubling his body with its premonitions of things to come, and the stooks were Kirsty's, but they were also partly his, in the way that stooks were a man's product, as articles made of wool were a woman's. Roddie had said, "You have a good harvest here, Finn." And he had looked it over and answered, "Not so bad." The quiet, moonlit land and the peaked stooks like little folks' houses: he gazed at them a moment as at something intimate and strange in his own mind, and wondered where Roddie had gone. Probably into the byre, where a man naturally goes now and then to be out of sight of womenkind. He went quickly, from the generous impulse the night put in his breast, and came on them just inside the byre door, Catrine with her face white and scared and Roddie, a yard from her, silent. They looked at him but did not speak, and in that queer, still moment Finn's breast seemed to crush together and fall down inside him. A great awkwardness held his body so that he could not move.

Roddie greeted him, but there was no warmth in his voice; it was quiet and cool; not angry or annoyed, but quiet and distant, like something smooth and fatal.

Finn felt his body twisting. He wanted with all his heart to take it away, but it would not come. "Some more folk in," his mouth muttered.

"In that case, I'm off," Roddie said.

"You'd better come in and say good night to Kirsty," Catrine suggested in a curious withdrawn voice.

Finn got out of the door, but before he had managed a couple of clear steps Roddie called, "Good night." Finn felt his mother coming behind him, but did not turn round, nor did he go into the house, passing the door as if he had something to see to.

But he walked without seeing the ground he trod on,

though his feet took him down into the hidden alleyways among the gorse bushes. He stood and gazed over the burn, silver-bright under the moon, but could not gaze long, so restless he felt, with a flutter in his mind, like the flutter of a tumbled bird.

Roddie and his mother.

He had never dreamt of anything between them. He knew all about flesh relations. He could not think, and chewed stalks of grass, and did not know what to do. A tremulous feeling began to beat up in his chest and made him feel sick.

Roddie was thirty-eight and Catrine thirty-three. In Finn's thought they were fixed in their courses like the sun and the moon. They were old people.

His mother's face had been white and scared and somehow extraordinarily pitiful.

Suddenly he hated what he had seen, hated it in dumb, frightened anger, hated its bodily crush, its tragic pallor, and moved swiftly on to the moor, as if the ghost of his father had come up behind him.

After that night Finn cunningly hid things inside himself, yet at the same time found a greater release in life. Not only did the croft work occupy his mind in a more manlike way, but he also looked for companionship outside the home. Increasingly his evenings were spent in other houses with lads of his own age and older, gay evenings, with songs and story-telling, and, above all, with talk of the sea. The great rendezvous for sea-talk was the kitchen of Meg, the net-maker. And one Monday evening Finn scored a triumph there—and took into himself a new and haunting disquiet.

It was a memorable Monday from the first entrance of "the professor" into the long, low thatched building that was his school. Education was a voluntary affair, but respect for learning was deep in the minds of the folk, because it came out of a very ancient tradition, the tradition of the bards with their classic poetry, in epic and in song, and their extensive knowledge of history, particularly the real and legendary history of their own race. While each scholar took a peat with him every morning, on Monday he also took a penny.

The long plank seats were crowded with boys and men, smooth-faced and heavily bearded, when "the professor" strode in and, whisking off his bonnet, dumped it upon a wooden peg, completely unaware that he had also removed his wig. Eyes gleamed and young bodies squirmed to repress their mirth at sight of the wigless head. But prayer first. Then a chapter of the Bible. Mr. Gordon went for his hat to collect the pennies and discovered his wig. "Ha," he said, "ha, now I understand! Hm!" He put on his wig and with his hat held out in front of him moved along the back seat collecting his pennies. While he turned to the next seat, two boys slipped from the off end of it into the back seat. The bulk of the school saw the manœuvre and waited. Along came Mr. Gordon and saw nothing. The two young rascals had saved their pennies. Beards shook at them, but the eyes above were merry. For the professor had obviously got some sort of bee in his wig this morning.

The reading was perfunctory; the writing, as always, strictly supervised, but no more; so it must be the arithmetic. It was.

"Most of you here are interested in the industry that is concerned with catching white herrings. Very well. Instead of directing our attention to the consideration of number in an abstract way, I propose to-day to apply it to this particular industry. As a people you may be in danger, as you have been in the past, of being taken advantage of by governing forces superior in possessions, in craft, and in knowledge—particularly in knowledge of arithmetic. I should not like it to rest at my door that, in this matter of preparing you to judge your own respective positions, I had failed in so elementary a duty as providing you with the necessary knowledge."

178

They liked this sort of talk for its difficult words and the fine rhythm of the sentences rather than for its meaning. Moreover, Mr. Gordon was inclined to be a rebel against "authority", as his ambition to enter the ministry had been balked several years before by "governing forces".

He was a tall, lean, drooping man, with a manner often absent-minded but occasionally extremely pointed and alive. Obviously he had been thinking over the questions which he now proceeded to put to them:

"How many women are there in a gutting crew, and what do they do?"

"Three. Two gutters and one packer."

"What do they jointly earn for gutting and packing one barrel of herring? You!"

"Fourpence," said the fisherman.

"How many herring are there in a barrel?"

All were very interested now, and as the number varied according to the size and quality of the herring, Mr. Gordon agreed: "There can be 800. So let us call it 800. Now what I want you to tell me is: What does a woman get for gutting 100 herrings?"

He turned away to give them time. "Well? You, Donald."

But they were troubled.

"Take it home with you and bring me the answer tomorrow," said Mr. Gordon, before they had proper time to work it out. "Now," he continued briskly, "we have in our midst a lady who is a distinguished craftswoman in net-making. I assume you know to whom I refer?"

"Meg," said one of the boys who had saved his penny, and the school laughed.

"How much is paid to this lady for the making of a net?"

"One pound."

"What is the length of a net? You."

"Twenty-five fathom," answered a skipper.

When Mr. Gordon had this translated into fifty yards
and had discovered that the depth of the net was fourteen
yards and that the mesh from knot to knot must be one
inch, he asked for the number of meshes in the net, and in
due course was given the correct answer.

"Now," said Mr. Gordon, "each mesh is contained by
—how many knots?"

"Four."

"Four. Agreed. Well now, how many knots are there
in the net?" He dusted the chalk from his palms and was
turning away when he said, "What! Already?"

The answer given was four times the number of meshes.

"You all appear to be agreed?" And then it was that
Finn made the impatient movement with his hand. "Some-
one seems to be troubled," remarked Mr. Gordon, giving
Finn time.

He walked up and down the floor, with a dry smile.

They all got troubled. They began to make dots on their
slates and saw at once that four times the number of meshes
was absurd.

"Well?"

Finn raised his head. "The number of knots along the
top is 1,801. The number down from that 504. So there
are 505 lines of 1,801 in each. The total"—he paused to
add on his slate—"is 909,505 knots."

"Very good, indeed. I compliment you. Excellent." He
was so delighted that he drew a small net on the blackboard
and illustrated the problem at length.

"Finally," said Mr. Gordon, "how many knots does
Meg—I mean the lady who makes the net—how many
knots has she to tie to earn one penny, ignoring fractions?"

This time there was no catch. Meg had to tie 3,789 knots
for one penny.

The number was so large that it made them twinkle with
mirth. She fairly earned her penny!

At home that evening Finn got up to go out.

"Where are you off to now?" asked Kirsty.

"Over to Meg's."

"It's no business of mine," said Kirsty, pressing spiritedly on the treadle of her spinning-wheel.

Catrine looked up at him from her carding-combs and smiled. "Don't be late."

He walked out without answering. The dumb mood was on him as he entered at Meg's door, and he was taken aback when greeted with, "Here comes the professor!" There was laughter. "Tell Meg about her knots!" cried Wull. Then Finn understood and flushed.

George, the foreman, paused in his measurement of the meshes with a yard stick. Meg, seated at her new net, turned her head and welcomed Finn: "Come away, *laddie*." She spoke the word in English. She often used an English word, and her voice had the south-side accent, for her mother had come from Macduff. Sometimes when they were in a good mood they would mimic her accent and English words. She was a little woman, tidy as a provident hen, her head sleek with dark hair that showed no grey though she was over sixty. Her house was astonishingly clean, with plates and bowls gleaming from high dresser shelves in the light that leapt and winked from the fire and burned more steadily from the cruisie-lamp near her shoulder. This lamp was no more than an iron saucer, filled with clear fish oil, from which a wick burned. The wick was the white pith of a bulrush looped where it lay in the oil, the lighted end leaning against a shallow spout in the rim of the saucer. This was the common lamp, but folk did not use it unless at labour, because oil was dear. Meg made her own oil, keeping all the livers she could get from the fishermen in a little barrel. In the last few years since cured herring had become plentiful, Meg had found it much easier to get white-fish livers.

There were nearly a score of persons in the room, and often it was packed to the door. Bearded young fishermen, a few of the older men like Wull, lads crushed together, and two or three married women and unmarried girls, apparently anxious to study Meg's art, but otherwise intent on keeping the fun going.

Finn's entrance created a great hubbub, and while he was having his leg pulled, George resumed his measurement and counting. Then he clapped Meg on the shoulder. "Very good," he said, quietly for him.

But Wull was watching. "Big enough to let whales through, George?" he called.

"They are right," said George, "according to law."

There was laughter at that, for sometimes, behind his back, George was called "According-to-law". Wull's eyes twinkled, for he liked to be the author of merriment. "They may be right according to law, but are they right according to the herring?" he asked.

This droll question did not allay the mirth for it was deeper than it seemed, but a young woman falling backward among the boys set up a noisy tumult.

It was at this moment, as he turned his head away, smiling, from the scrabble on the floor, that Finn encountered Una's face, the dark eyes full upon him. She was twelve years old.

There had been one memorable morning in Finn's young life when, cautiously approaching a grey boulder in the burn, hoping to see a yellow trout, he beheld the long straight back of a sea-trout. The excitement had been so intense that it quivered with something like fear.

Once—and only once—he had seen a squirrel in the Steep Wood. He had been sitting quietly and, hearing a strange sound, had turned his head. From a fork in a tree, the unknown, beautiful wild thing had looked down at him.

Una was not unknown to Finn, but she lived a considerable distance from his home, on the other side of the river. Never before, however, had her eyes thus rested upon him.

In the bewildering stress of the moment, he turned upon unoffending Donnie and cried, "Watch who you're shoving!" and dug him in the ribs with his elbow.

"You should take some lessons in arithmetic from Finn," George was answering Wull. "Or the professor. They seem to know a lot about nets!"

"What's wrong with arithmetic? Isn't it according to law, too?"

"Pach!" snorted George. "If Meg there makes thirty-six meshes to the yard, how many will there be after the hemp has been in the bark and the sea once or twice? Ask the professor that."

"That's true enough," said Daun. "They shrink a good lot."

"Of course they shrink," said George. "And according to law a mesh must not be less than one inch from knot to knot at any time. It's herrings the net is for, not sellags."

George was pleased with the laughter, for actually the mesh was on the big side, measuring a bare thirty to the yard. But here he was not merely keeping on the right side of the law, he was also following out Mr. Hendry's private policy, for in the matter of price, big herring were better than small herring. The agents for the foreign market wanted them big. True, the large mesh might not catch so many herring, and if that was against the fishermen's interests now, still, in the long run, it might not be. Who could say?

For what was deemed a terrible calamity had befallen the herring industry: the Government had stopped payment of the bounty.

Finn had listened to endless arguments over the last two or three years. Mr. Hendry at first had said that they might as well haul their boats and close down. From four shillings on the barrel the bounty had gone down to three shillings, to two shillings, to one shilling, to nothing.

There had been meetings in Mr. Hendry's little room, meetings on the shore, meetings everywhere.

But if the price per cran had been reduced, the fishing had not stopped. On the contrary, all over the coasts, it had

gone ahead in a striking manner; and it looked now as if it
might even still increase. So that the tension of concern
was lessening, and Wull could say to George:

"You and your bounty! Why should the Government
pay the curer the bounty? It's the fisherman who should
have got it anyway. Didn't he catch the herrings?"

"And who paid the fisherman?" asked George.

"The curer," said Wull. They all laughed, Wull with
them.

"Would Meg be making this net? Would the thousands
of pounds that came into Dunster these last years have
come in, if it wasn't for the curer? Would——"

"Would you be here yourself?" interrupted Wull.

"No," began George.

"Ah, that would have been the greatest loss of all," said
Wull, wagging his head sadly.

They shook with the mirth they loved.

Una did not laugh; her eyes lighted up and glanced.

They were wide-spaced, and in the dim light looked
black. To Finn, her clear face seemed so vivid, so unusual,
that he wondered how others did not want to stare at her.
He was inclined to be boisterous. Meg removed the small
S-shaped piece of stiff wire; hitched the net forward, and
fixed the wire again. The part of the net she was working
on was attached to the wall and reached her in a downward
slant. The flat bone needle, with its body of twine and
pointed end, slid in and out with remarkable speed. A
couple of hitches—over, under—in movements quicker than
the eye could follow, and she was on to the next knot. The
rasp of the needle could be heard quite distinctly, and sometimes she smoothed it with a touch of coarse fat. She spoke
little when the men were talking, but sometimes she told
very interesting stories of life around Banff and Macduff
when she was a young girl.

"How could it pay the Government to pay the money
out?" asked Wull.

"It paid them all right," said George.

"If you think it will pay you to give me four shillings—put them there," said Wull, holding out his hand.

"That's all you know," George snorted. "You can't see farther than your nose."

"Put them there—and watch if I can't see farther than my nose."

"If I put four shillings there with this hand and received back five shillings from you with my other hand, I would be better off, wouldn't I?"

"You would be a living marvel," said Wull.

Una glanced up at her sister Mary, who was nineteen, and full of frolic; then Finn saw Una looking at him, though he wasn't looking anywhere near her.

"What's wrong with you," said George, "is that you know about as much of the world and its commerce as Meg's needle there. Here we are sending our barrels of herring——"

"And well-coopered barrels, I admit that," said Wull with an innocence.

"All over the world," cried George, who was getting angry. "Ireland, the West Indies, the Baltic——"

"You send the fulls to the Baltic." Wull nodded with understanding.

"And—and what does that mean?"

Wull's mouth opened respectfully.

"It means," cried George, "that we are exporting all that. Money, export trade, sea-carrying trade, possessions abroad—and what does all that do, but increase the wealth of our country? And if the wealth of our country is increased, then the revenue is increased. And it's out of that revenue that we got our four shillings. They gave us four shillings and got five back. But there are some who would need a few more brains to see that."

It was a point! For a moment their little world opened out into the great world. They glimpsed regions far beyond the waters of their creek.

Una's eyes looked from one face to another while she sat

quietly by her sister. Clearly this was the great world for her, with the surge and clash of personalities like the roar of the sea What was said did not matter except as it moved and swayed bodies and brought living words from their mouths and the warmth of fun.

But George was getting heated, and Wull, who could not let a personal thrust pass, was sarcastically hitting back. Other voices were taking points up. "George is right," said Daun. "There's something in it," said Hamish Sinclair, scratching his ginger beard. "If the Government gets more money——" "But if the money——" "It doesn't matter about that. It's purely a question of the money——"

Discussing money gave a man a feeling of importance. Some of the girls got talking together, because the "points" about money, over which the men could become so heated, grew very dry after a time. Occasionally a girl would say to her brother, "Ach, be quiet!"

For the unity of the gathering was getting broken up. In twos and threes men argued under the louder noise of George's main argument. The young lads listened. The girls got talking about their gutting experiences and more personal matters.

Meg's needle went on, over—under, weaving the net that would catch the bigger herring for the bigger price, the white bone glistening in arabesques of movement.

When George felt he had sufficiently dominated the scene, he took his departure, carrying his measuring stick with him. But even the few things that were said behind his back created argument. A pest on their arguments! Men were like that!

They began to go home. Mary cried merrily to Meg, "We'll be back to see you with the new moon."

Outside, the old moon had just risen. It was a clear night. Dark bodies parted, sometimes calling back from a little distance with a girl's laugh, then disappeared their various ways. Una looked small as she walked beside Mary.

Finn went home the top road with Donnie—the shortest
way from Meg's to Donnie's house. Thus they did not
require to come near the river and the ruins of the House of
Peace. Finn now knew about the ruins' being haunted and
how grown men, with the exception of Roddie, would not
pass them alone at night.

They talked away about the fishing and George and
Wull and argued some of the points over again. For one
day each of them would be the skipper of a boat. They
would sail the sea and catch so many herrings that it would
not matter whether there was a bounty or not. They began
to tell each other how a skipper knew when there was
herring about. Gulls and porpoises and whales. They
talked in the friendliest, confidential tones as the whale
grew in size before the inward eye, grew until each jaw
was bigger than the floor of a room, as big as a field—it
might easily be as big as a field, mightn't it?—a great
monster of a whale?—and then when the jaws closed . . .

"What would you do if he came up beside your boat?"
Finn asked.

"I would spit in his eye," said Donnie, "and that would
blind him."

They laughed, feeling they could master the whale all
right.

"What would you do?" asked Donnie.

"I'd shove the oar down his throat," said Finn.

Something scurried from their feet and they leapt. It
could only have been a rabbit. But Donnie, to cover the
scare they got, said it might have been a hare. A rabbit
would have more sense than come near them! Their hearts
were beating from the silly fright. But it was not so silly—
if it was a hare.

"You heard about Dave?" Donnie asked.

"What?" asked Finn.

"He was going to sea—when he saw Margad on the path
in front of him. He turned back home and said he wasn't
feeling very well. The boat went to sea without him."

"I heard that," said Finn.

Everyone knew that Margad was a witch. And everyone knew that a witch could turn herself into a hare. They glanced around and thought they might as well have a look at what was going on in old Lachlan's house, which they could now see.

Lachlan's house was a famous gathering-place—the real ceilidh-house—before Finn was born. Lachlan himself was nearly eighty now and his memory as good as ever, though the old fiddle-bow had grown husky, and indeed was used very rarely and only when a drop of whisky inspired him to forget the fulminations of such as Sandy Ware, who denounced the violin as the devil's instrument. Above all, Lachlan was the great story-teller. You could listen to him for hours, and listen to him again the next night. He had a niece, Anna, living with him. She was a quick-witted, pleasant woman of thirty, and the girls called to see her and the young men called to see Lachlan.

As they approached the house, they heard singing. Involuntarily, Finn paused, and the rhythm went all through the night, over the land, and quivered in his heart.

"Come on!" cried Donnie, quickening his steps.

Finn followed. But when they were come by the house and Anna's clear voice rose alone in the next verse, Finn paused.

"Come on," said Donnie.

"No, I think I'll go home," said Finn. "It's getting late."

"Come on in, man."

"No. You go. They're all alone at home. Good night." He turned away.

Donnie looked after him, but he knew Finn's domestic difficulties.

When he got round the house Finn paused again to listen. The rhythm of the song was more intimate to him than his own face. With lips apart, he held his breath.

When all the voices surged together, rising, his body quivered as if sluiced in chill water.

Anna's voice had made him think of his own mother.

Life in the dim night, under the stars, over the land, the old, old land, the curved thatch, the still birch trees, the surge of the singing, rising as smoke rises from a fire, spreading out over the immemorial land, under the dying moon.

He walked away.

By the time he came to the top of the wood, the cool quiver of the song had passed from his cheeks, and the dark things of the night were about him again. Not that he was exactly frightened of a hare or of any dark thing, but it was as well to be wary, so that the heart wouldn't jump too quickly into the mouth. Down along the top of the wood was the place where he had killed God's fool. Beyond, he caught a moonlit glimmer of the pool that lay to the west of the House of Peace. They said it was a monk, with a cloak and cowl, who haunted the ruins. There was a story which told that long, long ago a man with the second sight saw the monk in broad daylight standing in front of a little round house, like a large bee-skep, and saw going towards him a Viking with a battle-axe. The monk stood quietly and the Viking swung the battle-axe and split his head.

Finn was not frightened of the House of Peace in the daylight. To tell the truth, he rather liked being there then, though the stillness of the lichened stones would sometimes make one wonder. But the darkness was a different matter. What was hidden in the dark was the marrow that was hidden in the bone.

Other boys were more frightened than he was Donnie would not go down past this wood in the dark though you paid him. Many men, too—like Daun—were frightened of the dark. He had not heard all the stories that they had heard, because he had had to stay at home, stories about a ball of fire hurtling over the ruined broch; of music coming through Knocshee, the fairy hill; of the headless horseman . . . he had just heard bits from Donnie. Kirsty told only true things about folk she knew when she was young in Kildonan. His mother. . . . There was the glitter of the burn below him. It was his own burn, and the sight of it quickened his heart. He heard its voice—but it had more than one voice now, quiet-speaking voices, low down in the dark hollow. He had to cut through the voices, right through them, and then he was up the slopes—not running (never run)—and into the house. A long story told by his mother about an underground passage, a passage that went right under the Helmsdale river, flashed through his mind, not in thought nor in memory, but in sheer vision. The place was called "The Maidens' Field", and the subterranean passage could be seen to this day—a mile or so below Suisgill. It was called "The Maidens' Field" because of the two girls who followed the two calves, when, playing and skipping, they suddenly ran into the passage. The girls followed, and followed, in the dark, until one of them and both the calves disappeared, leaving the other girl all alone. She groped along in mortal terror, until she could get no farther. She now stood in a low chamber—and overhead heard voices. She pressed wildly against a flat stone in the roof, screaming for help, and the stone moved. This stone was the hearthstone of a house in Learabail, and when it moved under them the family ran out yelling with terror, for they thought it was the Devil himself coming up. But when they plucked up courage to come back, and found the girl, then they knew what had happened. For the mother of the girl who was lost was a witch who had pledged her daughter to the Devil, and the calves . . .

Down through the dimness beyond the burn Finn saw a tall, dark figure come silently. His flesh ran together and his knees trembled. A curlew's cry pierced the air, and fell away forlornly towards the House of Peace. Finn's skin went cold as rime. The figure came to the edge of the burn, crossed it, disappeared, and through æons of time Finn waited—until it reappeared, first the dark head against the

bright water, then the dark body, coming towards him. He
sank down through his knees. The figure came on, and just
before the great cry of terror got past his throat, he saw it
was Roddie. And suddenly he could not speak, could not
move, and when Roddie had passed, he lay for a little in the
trance of his own horror.

Crossing the stepping-stones, he slipped and the shock
of the cold water helped to steady his trembling muscles.
When he got to the low end of the house, he leaned against
the wall until he began to shiver from genuine coldness.
He knew Kirsty would be in bed, because she had had a
fevered chill a month or so ago and had never quite thrown
off its effects.

Catrine looked up at him as he entered, the firelight on
her face. Her look steadied; her eyes widened. She got up.
"What's wrong, Finn?"

"Nothing."

"You're white as a sheet."

"Nothing," he said with a touch of impatience. Why did
she *have* to notice anything? He did not want to feel angry
with her.

And now she was silent! "I slipped," he explained
casually, without looking at her, "crossing the burn, and
wet my feet."

"Sit here." She went and put some milk in a pan and
began to warm it, and handed him a towel so that he could
rub his legs.

"Were you over at Meg's?" she asked in a conversa-
tional voice.

"Yes," he answered, rubbing his feet and his toes slowly
with concentration.

"Were there many there?"

"A good few."

She poured him a bowl of milk, then sat down and went
on with her knitting. He drank it slowly, to fill in the long,
silent minutes. There was a vague heavy mood upon
him that he could not break. More and more this sort of

191

mood seemed to be deepening between his mother and himself.

He would have liked to ask if there had been anybody in, but he could not. His mother seemed calm and a little sad, as if nobody had been near her.

He had thought Roddie would have been at Meg's.

It would be more comfortable in bed. "I think I'll go to bed," he said in an easy voice. At once she stirred, as if she might break in on him because his voice had been natural, but he gave her his shoulder as he went across to his bed.

Once in between the blankets, he turned his face to the wall. He did not want to see her sit by the fire or smoor the peats.

When the room was in darkness and his mother in bed, he felt more at ease. To-morrow he would spend all day at the flail in the barn, threshing oats. It was heavy work. He liked winnowing in a fine wind.

He would not quite let the question as to where Roddie had been touch his mind.

The last vision he had was of Una's eyes. Eyebrows and eyes and face formed in the dark, out of the dark.

Strange the difference between Meg's house with George's "Money, money", and old Lachlan's house with the singing voices. . . .

His mother did not sound restless. He fell asleep.

CHAPTER X

THE COMING OF THE PLAGUE

❦

Before Finn was two years older he was at sea. It came about in a tragic manner, for his land was visited by what people called the plague, but which was, in reality, a form of cholera. Never had such a disease been amongst them before, and when the first rumours of it reached Dunster folk spoke of it in low voices. Their dread of it went beyond reason. They apprehended it in the imagination, and feared the evil of it more than they feared death, as though its uncleanness, its taint, its corruption, would not only destroy and rot the body but pursue the living quick beyond the grave itself. Their instinct of recoil was an instinct of pure horror.

Sandy Ware said it was God's judgement upon them for their sins, for the carnal pleasure that turned its worldly face from the Almighty to make merry with Mammon. "When the silver herring were swimming into your nets God was forgotten. With money in your hands, you danced. The great ships came and took your barrels away. Away to the ends of the earth. The ends of the earth are very far away. But all ends are under God's hand. The ships came back. The ships brought more money for merrymaking. Yes! But what have the ships brought now? The flapping of the wings of the black bird of corruption and death! I cry unto you to repent while yet there is time. . . ."

But a fisherman who had been visiting his wife's relations in the country near Wick came home and, three days after, fell sick and started retching. When his bowels ran

193

nothing but a watery fluid like whey, the folk knew the plague had come to Dunster.

Finn had been friendly with this young seaman, for his older brother, Don, had until last year been one of Roddie's crew. In fact, this seaman was the David who, with Duncan, had sprinted behind Mr. Hendry's gig when it had brought Roddie home from the storm he had survived off Helmsdale.

He was now a man of twenty-four, six months married, and his young wife, hearing that her mother was ill and touched a little by homesickness, had prepared to make the journey on foot, for it was the beginning of the herring season. But as her husband judged she was not in a fit condition to do so, he had gone himself.

When he walked into the house and found the mother alone, in bed, her face incredibly emaciated and her sunken eyes half-closed, he was struck dumb. The atmosphere was sour and bitter and got him in the throat. He had called a greeting on entering, and now he saw the eyes slowly focusing upon him. He went to the bedside and asked, "What's wrong?" There was a movement of the hands, repelling him, shoving him away. Her voice was low, a whispered hoarseness he could not understand. Then, after a gasping sob, she lay exhausted. He listened for someone in the house. There was no sound. Into the appalled emptiness of his mind, a high-pitched voice cried his name from outside.

He went out and there was Nan, his wife's elder sister, wringing her hands, her face pale as chalk, some twenty yards from him up the slight slope. Beyond, were one or two others he knew. He walked towards her. She backed away, crying, "David, go home! Go home at once!"

He realized now that he had been in the presence of a woman dying of the plague. He stood quite still, but perhaps because he had already been in the presence, there moved in his mind a deep revulsion against thus leaving a helpless woman to die alone.

"Is no one looking after her?" he shouted.

"We can do no more. She drove us out." Nan wrung her apron. She was in terrible distress. "I am frightened for the bairns." She had three young children, the youngest not yet weaned.

"But someone must look after her."

"No more can be done." Her voice rose to a scream. Her body writhed in a demented way.

"It's all right," said David, nodding and half-turning his back. She ran away, crying loudly and pitifully, as if she could not bear to stand still any longer.

David was in a desperate position. He could not just walk home straight away, arriving in the dark early hours with this dreadful news, all the more dreadful because indecisive. He would just have to tramp back here again for the final news.

The sour, diarrhœtic smell was still in his throat. He took out his snuff-box and dosed himself so heavily that, seasoned as he was, he sneezed. He rasped and spat. Those behind heard him.

He was fond of his wife's mother. She had always had such good sense, and been so cheerful, and helped him when he was tongue-tied. Her husband had died when the third child had been born, and she had kept everything going herself. All three were married, and now she would die alone—to save them. That was the kind she was, by God, thought David. He wished Rob, her son, were here. Nan had always been of the teasing kind, and often enough had angered him.

Suddenly, not wanting anyone to come and speak to him again, he walked down into the byre. The cattle were gone. They, too, had been removed! He felt the loneliness as he had felt it in the house, seeping about himself and the dying woman, cutting them off. A dumb anger began to smoulder in him. He knew that eyes were watching the house, wary, frightened eyes, inimical to him, herding him in with the dying woman in the doomed house.

He went out and saw a boy of about fourteen standing at a little distance with a pitcher and something wrapped in a white cloth. The boy laid the pitcher and the white cloth on the ground, and cried, "This is food for you." Then he turned and ran up the slope towards the house to which Nan had retreated.

David walked slowly to the food, and when he came to it a great rage seized him and he had all he could do to stop his right foot from kicking pitcher and parcel over the green. He saw the furtive heads without looking at them. When the blood-flush had passed from his eyes, he stooped, lifted the pitcher of milk with one hand and the oaten bannocks that slithered inside the cloth with the other, and strode down to the cottage. He would make food for his mother-in-law.

As he entered at the door, the smell got him again. She was lying on her back perfectly still, her face livid, her half-closed eyes showing only the whites. The words died in his throat. Without knowing quite what he was doing he laid pitcher and bread on the table by the head of the bed and took a step towards her. "Mrs. Keith," he said. She did not move. "Mrs. Keith!"

He had never seen a dead person with open eyes. He wanted to touch her brow to see if she was cold, but could not. His eyes glanced about for something with which to poke the body. There was the long black tongs. God, he did not know what to do. "Mrs. Keith!" Then in an instant, his vision heightened by his tense emotion, he saw the body stiff as dark clay, with no breath, no last vestige of movement, left in it. Before him lay the stillness of death.

From big, gulping breaths his mouth stuck in a dry slime that had the taste of the evil smell in the house. His hand shook as he lifted the pitcher from the table, and from his lips the milk dribbled on to his breast. As he placed the pitcher back on the table he saw there were two pitchers. The other was the one he had brought in. He wiped the milk from his breast. He was trembling all over.

THE COMING OF THE PLAGUE

At the door he pulled himself up, and breathed the sweet air that was blowing upon it, for he had already noticed that folk were keeping to windward. He went out and walked deliberately towards the house where Nan was. Twenty yards from it he paused and shouted loudly, "She's dead!" Then he turned on his heel and headed for home.

A lot of his anger and rage had been put into that last shout, and the thought of this was some satisfaction to him for quite a long way. In the gloaming he came to a pool in a little stream on a lonely part of the moor, and swiftly threw off all his clothes, scattering them around him on the heather. The water had an icy chill and he turned over and twisted in it, twice keeping his head under for as long as he could. From the bottom, he clawed fistfuls of sand and fine gravel and rubbed chest and arms and head, liking it the better the more it hurt. Naked, he jumped about on the moor until in a wild moment his feet fell into the steps of the Highland fling and he gave a throaty roaring laugh of challenge. His clothes he shook and flailed against the heather, like a madman knocking dust out of them. Dressed and shivering, he set off at a rapid pace, often running long stretches at a time.

Just after midnight, he came down on his own home in the heavy dark. The window was up on the edge of the thatch, above his head, for the house was an old one with extremely thick walls. Because of the shaft of light, he knew Ina was not in bed. All was silence. There was no one in but herself. He cleared his throat and passed on to the door, which he pushed open, at the same time crying her name. "Ina. Come here."

He saw her changing face, as she stood motionless. Her closed hands came up against her cheeks.

"Don't get excited," he said. "Take it calmly."

"David!" She stumbled a step or two towards him.

"I can't come in just now. I have something to do——"

"David! Is mother——"

There was a long moment. "Yes," he said simply. He

seemed to see her face, though the light was now behind her. Then she staggered away and flopped down on the floor.

He entered a step and stood watching her. He knew she had not fainted completely because there was a slight squirming motion in her body. Then, however, she lay quite still, her face to the clay. He sent his mind to help her so strongly that his own body went death cold.

Presently she stirred, whimpering; then all at once sat up and stared at him with a wild open face. She had brown sand-coloured hair with pleasant features and blue eyes that now glittered darkly.

"I can't come in, Ina. For God's sake try and take this calmly. Think of the child in you."

She waited.

"Your mother died when I was there. I was in time." He took a deep breath. He looked away. "There's nothing wrong with me, Ina. Absolutely nothing. I'm all right my-self, but—but they told me not to go near anyone for a day. It's nothing. It's just to make sure. I happened to go near a—a sick house."

Her voice came small and hoarse: "She died of the plague?"

"Yes. Listen to me, Ina——"

She did not listen. Her face went blank. "Mother," said her mouth in an appalled whisper.

He turned away and stood with his back to the outside wall by the door. When he heard her crying on her mother he became restless and irritated. She should think of herself, and as his irritation increased the tears came streaming down his face. She should think of the child anyway. What was the sense in weeping and carrying on like that? He grew angry, because her desperate, heart-broken voice brought the tears streaming down upon him readily. He felt the push of her empty fists on the floor, the burden of her awful grief, and turned away down to the corner of the little barn.

The truth was he no longer cared about the death of the mother. All interest in her had passed from him. He could only think of the taint. And he felt he had defeated it, expelled it from the outside of his body. If only—if only he had left that second accursed pitcher alone. Perhaps her mouth had been to the very spot where his own lips? . . . Yet it had been pretty full. There was every chance he was all right because the all-important thing he had not done— he had not touched the body.

After a time Ina grew sensible, and became extraordinarily calm as she realized the nature of the danger he was in. Not that he told her all he had been through. "Nan sent me home at once," he said. "It's just having been near the wind of the trouble. So I thought, for one night, I might curl up in the barn. You can always cry to me if you want me." Her mother had been properly attended, doctor and all, right to the end. Nan had kept away because of the children. He spoke on, giving her time, though he was not a talkative man.

That night he slept heavily. On the second day he was back in the house as usual. On the third, he went down to the inn and bought a bottle of "special". Two men were ordering a drink and called for an extra one for him. They were talking about the fishing and he was glad of their company. He left, carrying the bottle with him. The alcohol was going to his head, and this annoyed him, for though he drank very little, still a small whisky should hardly trouble his feet as it was doing. In times of illness, folk were always anxious to have a drop of whisky in the house as a restorative medicine. Suddenly he felt the liquor in a swirl in his stomach, and before he had gone three paces up it came. At a little distance a woman, bringing water from a well, saw him and stopped. He was bitterly ashamed for though men might take an extra drop at special gatherings, such as markets and rent-day, it was a deep disgrace to be seen the worse of drink in the broad light of a working day. However, he felt much better now and said nothing about the incident to his wife when he got home.

Against inclination, he took some supper, but shortly after they retired to bed he had to get up. His wife had been in a silent, miserable condition all day because she felt this was the day on which her mother was being buried and neither of them was there. David had offered to go, but an inscrutable fatal mood held them in its grip as in a circle which they could not step out of. "I'll go if you like," David had said.

She wondered what was keeping him outside. She grew alarmed. The minutes drew themselves out to a tension so fine that she heard the dark whisper of voices being borne on the wind to the sea. Such a mortal heaviness came on her body that she could hardly drag it to the door. "David!" she called. And when there was no answer, his name came the next time from her mouth in a scream.

She heard him coming, saw the deeper darkness of his body draw near and pause. "Ina," he said quietly, "don't be frightened. You must help me. There's only the two of us. For God's sake don't break down, or we're lost."

The low, clear appeal in his voice helped her, drawing resources of strength about the dissolving turmoil in her breast.

"Are you ill?" she asked.

"Yes," he answered. "I think I've got a touch of it."

The plague!

In that silence, wherein they could not see each other's face, their love passed between them in a red glisten of anguish. Out of this love came release and action.

"If you put out a blanket I'll make a bed for myself in the barn and sweat it into the straw. You'll find I'll be better in the morning."

She bustled now, taking the warm blankets from their bed.

"No, not gruel," he answered her. "Fill a big bowl with hot milk and grind a little of yon black nut into it."

THE COMING OF THE PLAGUE

They became eager allies, conspiring in the dark against death.

Twice during the night she stole down to the barn. The second time there were no sounds of sickness, and she scarcely breathed his name. He must be sleeping. She got back to the house in a little run and fell to her knees by her bed and prayed to God. "Save David. Save him, save him, O God." When her emotion rose with her cry and whelmed her mind, her mouth still cried, "Save him! Save him!"

And when she had made her prayer she buried her face and cried through her sobs, "O my darling! My darling!"

In the afternoon of the fourth day David died, his strong body emaciated, his face bony and gaunt.

The carpenter, a small man, very skilful with his hands, and often of a broad humour, made a coffin so dovetailed and tight that he swore no breath of foul air could ever come out from it. One or two men, lounging in his shop, smiled uneasily. The carpenter's eyes twinkled. "If it's fated, it's fated. But I'm giving fate little chance. You needn't be frightened to carry David in this box. May he have his share of Paradise. He was a decent lad."

The uneasy problem of who was to keep watch over the dead, and coffin the dead, was answered by Ina herself. Her husband's folk and her own, she warned off, speaking to them at a little distance from below the wind.

On the seventh day after the funeral Ina died. The coffin was ready, and David's father entered the house and put her into it, and they buried her beside her husband on the following day, watch having been kept near the house, with singing and praying, all night.

When the burial was over, David's father, who now kept by himself, approached the dry thatch of the infected house with a flaming torch and set it on fire, and did the same to the barn, removing from either place none of the belongings of the dead.

Far and near, folk saw, or climbed to see, the burning house, and as the red flames rose above the dark smoke young women wept openly with a queer personal anguish, and old women cried sad, broken words of sorrow, and men stared at the red flames, the cleansing flames, as at some dread rite to the old dark gods.

In that way the plague came to Dunster. The two men whom David had drunk with in the inn were shunned. The inn itself was avoided.

One day Catrine said to Finn, "I would like you to go to Dale to see how all are at home. I was dreaming about them last night. Would you care to go?"

"Yes," he said. "I don't mind."

Kirsty was inclined to be a little short in the temper and irritable, because through the broken winter she had never quite picked up her strength. There had been no long spell of hard frost to clean trouble away. Even the little snow that had fallen turned overnight into slush and mud. Sleet on a dark spring wind, and cold searching through every cranny in the walls and joint in the bones.

Catrine was diplomatic in her approach, but Kirsty was forthright. "Yes, anywhere out of this cold hole. And if he never came back, it might do him no harm."

When Catrine was alone with Finn she said, "I can't quite make her out, but I think she means you to go."

"Well, when are you going?" Kirsty asked him the following day.

"I'll go any time, Granny," Finn answered simply.

"The sooner the better," said Kirsty.

Finn looked after her, feeling she was blaming him for the thought of going, accusing him (and therefore, in some measure, his mother) of desertion. But Catrine, divining his thought, shook her head behind Kirsty's back, and when Kirsty had gone outside and left them, she said, "She wants you to go."

"I don't know," Finn muttered, looking out the window.

"It's her humour to make us feel like that. But you'll have to go now. She'll see to that."

Finn understood this, and all at once wanted to be away, to be gone from this place, anywhere. He was conscious of having toiled hard at the spring work and the peats.

"You'll take a change of shirt and stockings with you," said Kirsty that night. "We'll see what the weather is like in the morning."

The morning was overcast but dry. At parting, Kirsty gave him a wintry smile. He hardly looked at his mother, though he had been conscious of her about him, making him eat a good breakfast of porridge and milk and two eggs and packing something for his hunger on the journey. It was the first time he had ever been away from home and he felt excited. "Stay a week, anyway," his mother had said. "And if Granny asks you, stay longer. The change will do you good."

As he topped the hill beyond Langwell, and faced the empty stretches of moor towards the Ord, his spirit mounted with the tall wide day and a rare happiness came in about him. He liked being on the road, moving in freedom to a new place, and his home seemed little, and far away, and shut in. All Dunster, indeed, seemed dark, lying under the shadow of the plague, held by it, clamped down.

Soon he began watching for the Grey Hen's Well, and when at last he came to it, he smiled eagerly and drank. Then he unrolled his little bundle and brought out his food. His mother's invisible hands were all round it, and without distinctly thinking about her, he yet felt comforted. He had a little snuff hidden away in a twist of paper, and taking it out he snuffed openly and sneezed. But nobody saw him sneeze. It was a grand day now and all the better for the lack of sun because it made walking easier. He stretched himself out in the heather, where his mother had lain a few months before he was born, and looked up at the sky. What a tall great world it was for adventuring into and doing active things! A rush of the width and happiness of that summer world came down the wind from the clean,

strong mountains, and unable to lie any longer he got up
and went on.

As he descended the slope into Dale he met a man and
asked him which was his Granny's house. The man looked
steadily at him. "Where have you come from?" "Dunster." "That's the house," said the man, pointing; and at
once walked away.

At the door he was met by a grey-haired woman whose
dark-brown eyes looked for a long moment at him and then
glimmered. "You're Finn," she said, and this surprised
him only a little. "Yes," he answered, feeling shy, for it
seemed to him that her face, with its finely-cut nose and
eyebrows, was distinguished. Then her eyes searched for
his mind. "Are you all well?"

"Yes, thank you. My mother wanted me to come and
see how you were keeping."

She let out a deep breath and took him in, full now of
questions and hospitality, treating him like a high and
welcome guest, and seating him in a chair before the fire.

But he had seen the searching look and knew now why
the man had walked away.

During the next two days he saw that folk were avoiding
him, though Angus was kind and took him into Helmsdale
to visit Isebeal, who was married there. Isebeal was so
overcome with joy that she shed a tear or two while laughing and welcoming him. He admired the tall buildings and
yards and the harbour wall that banked the river. The fishing had started, and the whole place was busy, but no-one
went near the upper part of the village. The plague had just
come to Helmsdale.

One of a group of men at the end of a store called to
Angus. They were disputing about a Reform Bill, which,
according to one fluent speaker, would yet give the people
power to curb the high-handedness of the great lairds.
Angus agreed with the man, adding that the only thing
wrong with it was that it did not go far enough. Finn liked
Angus because he was quiet and strong. And he liked also

the flavour of the talk because it was defiant. One of the men asked who Finn was and Angus replied that he was his nephew, but did not say he came from Dunster.

By this time Finn knew that he was disappointed in his visit, and though his cousins and other children now began to accept his company more freely, they would ask him questions about the plague, and what it was like to look at, when they got him alone. Thus he gathered that the folk in and around Helmsdale believed the plague was so virulent in Dunster that houses were being burned every day. He stayed a night with Isebeal, and she asked him so many questions about his mother and what was happening on the croft—she had been there more than once—that he grew homesick.

On the Monday morning he said to his Granny, "I think I'll go home to-day."

She begged him to stay, for from his answers to her simple questions she had seen that his mother had sent him to be out of harm's way. But Finn replied politely, "I must go, because they're needing me on the croft." In the end he agreed to stay until next day, and that evening everyone was very pleasant to him, as though they would make up for any disappointment he had experienced, for it was extraordinary how they all knew one another's feelings without speaking about them. In the morning his Granny said tentatively, "I think, Finn, your mother would like you to stay longer."

Finn now knew quite well what she meant, but replied as if he didn't, "I must go. There's a lot to do."

She saw he understood, and her eyes filled with a gentle light. "Very well, Finn; you know best."

"I'll tell mother how you asked me to stay," he remarked, not looking at her.

She laid her hand on his shoulder. "I know you'll always be kind to your mother."

He was glad to be on the road again. He hated that quick uprise of emotion that nearly brought tears to the eyes. It could be very awkward. One little cousin with black hair, named Barbara, kept waving to him, but he only waved twice back to her.

And then at last the precipices, the Ord, the great sea-wall of rock all the way to remote Clyth Head, the moors, the mountains, and the freedom of going back home!

It was blowing fairly hard and the great shore of sand stretching mile upon mile from Loth to Brora and beyond, with the waves curling slow and white, was a startling and memorable thing to see; but, ah! the rocks, the precipices, they were his own, and he remembered the day he had climbed down for the gulls' eggs with Donnie on top screaming to him to come back. And when he had climbed back, using only one hand (for the other held ten eggs in his round bonnet), he found Donnie shivering and white and so angry that he wanted to fight. Donnie had said that the deep water, swirling against the rocks far below, had cried to him to throw himself over. Finn now smiled, remembering.

There was a wise humour in the smile, that moved his sensitive mouth and crept up around brown eyes which, unlike his mother's, had one or two pin-point grey flecks in them. He was tall for his fourteen years, going lightly on his feet, his face up. The face had the same kind of distinction that he himself had found in his Granny's, but the clean-cut regularity of bone was less noticeable, more smoothed over. When his eyebrows gathered in swift concentration all his features came vividly and arrestingly alive. His hair was dark-brown rather than black, though to a first glance it looked dark enough.

Down into the deep Langwell glen and up the other side, and here were coast-line and sea again, and far in the distance the outline of the land of home. It was difficult to keep the smile away from the mouth sometimes, though now he was near houses and greeted an occasional fisherman or scholar he knew. Then, less than a mile before he came to Dunster itself, he saw a girl coming along the road all

alone, and if there had been any side-path or other means
of escape, he would have taken it in the shock of the
moment. His feet he could manage, though they seemed to
hit the road an instant too soon or too late, but the idiotic
way his face wanted to crease up was almost beyond him.
At ten yards the difficulty of straightforward advance was
an elaborate form of torture. Just as he was passing he
threw her a glance, and in a tone positively hearty, said,
"Hullo!" She answered, "Hullo", but quietly, out of a
dark, entrancing smile.

Undeviating, chin up, and eyes above the horizon, he
held a steady course.

He was in Dunster before he realized it, because it had
taken quite a little time to tell himself the sort of fool he
was. He had spoken to a girl three miles back, and even
inquired after her father, quite at his ease. He knew Una's
mother as well as her father, and could have made a joke,
asking: "Has she started on a net yet?" He could have
made a score of jokes. If only (he thought) she were coming
towards me now, how differently I would behave! Just to
test himself, he might take a walk out this way of an evening, as if he were going somewhere. Then she would see
that he was neither up nor down!

After that Dunster struck him as being a delightful
place, everywhere full of things he knew, of houses and
fields and small woods, of slopes and hollows and the river
going down to the sea. He paused on the edge of the brae
and saw a man coming up the shore road and knew at once
it was Roddie. They would meet at the bridge. A laugh of
pleasure surged inside him. It was good to be home!

"Ha!" cried Roddie, smiling. "The wanderer has returned!" Roddie shook hands with him. "And how are the
Cattachs?"

Finn felt grown-up and so free from awkwardness that
when Roddie told him of two more cases of the plague he
felt grave and responsible.

At the House of Peace, Roddie paused. "I don't want to

alarm you," he said, "but I'm just wondering if you should go home. The truth is your Granny is not very well." He spoke on quietly, in a reflective manner. "You know how that chill sat on her? Well, two or three days ago, she thought she would pay a visit to one or two of her old friends. It was a nice day and she probably overtaxed herself, but she hasn't been too fit since. I wonder if we——? I don't think your mother was expecting you back so soon." Roddie's brows gathered. "Do you think you should go home or come up with me first—till we see?"

"I—I think I would like to go home," said Finn.

"I know." Roddie nodded. "All the same, in these times we have to go a bit canny and think of others. The only point is that your Granny called innocently enough at Seumas Maclean's, and she's not the one to run away at a sneeze. The thing comes on a healthy person so quickly, that you never know . . . In fact, it was only after she left that Seumas Maclean properly went down. He's being buried to-morrow."

Finn did not speak. Roddie glanced at him.

"There's just the one thing," said Roddie, "and it's simple enough. If your Granny doesn't show any sign by the end of the next two days she's all right. But we cannot be quite certain until then. I am sure your mother would not like you to go home for the next two days. You can understand that?"

"Yes," said Finn.

"Anyway, there's no hurry on you. Come up with me and we can talk it over. There's a nasty swell and we're not going to sea to-night. So we've been barking the nets."

As they went up by the edge of the wood Finn looked back across the burn and over the slope to his home. There was no-one about the house. The beasts were on tether. A curious desolation in the scene caught at his heart, followed by a swift stab of physical pain at the realization that, if his mother took it, he would never see her again. The ground wavered before his eyes and he had to lift exhausted legs against the brae. An overpowering desire to go home to his mother came upon him. He had to stop. He couldn't go on.

Roddie glanced back at the quivering pale face, then glanced away.

"Come up and have something to eat; we'll get in touch with your mother in the evening. That's arranged."

Roddie went on slowly and did not once turn round again. Finn had his eyes clear and his face composed by the time they came to Roddie's door.

"My mother fell and hurt her leg yesterday, so she's keeping to her bed," Roddie said in his casual voice. "Come in."

As Finn entered, he saw Roddie's father sitting by the fire. The face turned to him and, with the native welcoming instinct, the old man got up and stretched out his hand. "Well, Finn, you have got back from your travels?" He was taller than his son Roddie, with a fresh complexion and a beard that still had a shade of brown in its silky grey. His manner of natural hospitality, slow in movement, but expressive in the eyes, gave him an air of dignity that now attracted and warmed Finn, gathering his elements into that need for social behaviour which in itself is a pleasant form of courage. Finn answered the old man's questions about Dale and Helmsdale, not in an awkward word or two, but with a care for language and, where necessary, even at some length, and always with the polite *you* in place of the colloquial *thou*.

In the midst of the conversation, Shiela blew in with a swirl of air, crying his name in welcome. "I saw you coming," she said. "And how are you and how are they all in Dale?" She bustled about. "Cut up the fish, Roddie. Haven't I to look after two households now?"

Finn said he was sorry to hear of the accident.

"Ach, it's nothing. She'll be on her feet in a day or two." Shiela was full of life. Finn heard her voice talking to her mother in the next room, for manifestly the old lady had elected to leave the kitchen bed meantime. Soon the two pots were on, one with potatoes in their skins and the other with salt cod.

"Two such handless men in a house I never knew," declared Shiela, as she now settled down to get Finn's news.

"And what's the talk in Helmsdale?"

"They were talking about the Reform Bill," answered Finn.

"Were they?" cried Shiela, and she roared with laughter. She was very fond of laughing. "Haven't I heard them at it? We'll soon have the burns running with milk and honey." She looked at him almost gravely behind her dancing eyes as if she were thinking two sets of thoughts at once. "Wouldn't that be fine, Finn? Eh? Your Granny is not very well, but she'll soon be all right, my hero." She put her hand on his knee, for she was kneeling by the fire coaxing the peat. "The Reform Bill!" She laughed again. "When you grow up to be a man, Finn—and you're almost that already—I hope you'll have more sense than men often have."

"And what were they saying about the Reform Bill?" asked her father.

Shiela at once became silent, deference and laughter in her eyes as she looked into the fire.

"Uncle Angus was saying that he didn't think it went far enough," replied Finn.

Shiela squeezed his knee, delighted with him.

The old man nodded. "And was that the general opinion?"

"I think it was," Finn answered.

When the old man had said the Grace Before Meat, Shiela put a lump of butter on Finn's large piece of cod and told him to eat, whatever else he did. Finn now found himself very hungry. Roddie seemed subdued in his father's presence, and though this was a new aspect of Dunster's leading skipper, Finn understood it, and somehow it brought Roddie nearer to him.

The constraint at being in a new house did not irk Finn; it gave him a feeling of being whole and collected; and when Roddie, in due course, suggested that they might have a stroll down to the burn, Finn walked by his side, talking in a normal voice.

Presently they saw Catrine leave the corner of her house and Roddie stopped. "You'd better have your talk together," he remarked. "Your bed is ready for you with us." There was a pause, while they both kept looking across the burn. "All right, then, Finn," and Roddie turned back.

But his cool, responsible tone remained with Finn as he went down by the wood.

Catrine held up her hand against him when he was going to cross the burn to join her. "No, don't come near me just now." Her smiling face made a joke of it. And then she asked, as no one but his mother could ask, "How are you, Finn?"

"Fine," he answered freely.

When she had got answers to many questions, she told him to sit down; so they both sat, talking across the murmur of the water. "She'll be missing me soon," Catrine at length said, with a backward nod of her head. "She's not in great form these days!" Her voice made it the old conspiracy between them.

"Is she short in the temper?"

"Och, she's really not bad. And she's been good to us, Finn. Was anyone asking for her? She would like to hear that."

"Yes, they nearly all asked for her. And there's a man home from the Indies. His name is Captain Mackay. I didn't meet him, but I was told he was asking for her." He smiled with slight embarrassment.

"No?" cried Catrine. "Isn't that grand! What a story I'll make of it!" She laughed. "And is he still a bachelor?"

"I don't know."

"You would probably have heard if he wasn't. So it's a bachelor he is. Good! And were you missing your old mother at all?"

"Och, a little, maybe."

"You're just saying that! I'm sorry, Finn, you can't come home, but——"

"Why not? I can come all right."

"No, Finn." She shook her head, smiling at his concentrated brows. "You see——"

"I don't see why, if you're at home, I couldn't be there too. I could sleep in the barn easily enough."

"Don't make it hard on me. Wait for two days, and then everything will be as before." It was the old intimate voice, warm and light, and more penetrating than anything else on earth he knew. His face grew as sullen as it could look.

"I'll go now, Finn. And if you happen to be down about in the morning, we might have a word. I'm glad you enjoyed your holiday. It's fine to see you again. Good-bye just now."

"Good-bye," said Finn, and he got up and walked away. When he climbed a short distance he turned and found her waiting. She waved and then hurried off home.

He went blindly into the wood, and presently found himself weeping as he walked. He stood beside a tree for a long time, then moved on again. Her hurrying figure going back to that house affected him deeply. He kept to the trees so that no-one would see him, his mind desolate. He had no desire for Roddie's company now, no desire for any company. The only thing that was near him in all the world was his mother's voice; and not only because it was her voice, but because it was the voice of courage in her warm, kind body.

In these moments there was no resentment against her, only a far understanding, beyond which there was nothing.

Crossing the broken ground beyond the wood, he passed the cairn out of which Donnie and himself had taken

212

the rabbit and approached the ruined walls that had protected the House of Peace.

What little wind there was grew still over the small field enclosed by the walls and the long-backed knoll. It was always sheltered here and bright, as if the light itself slept or, rather, lay awake in the dreaming pleasantness that sometimes comes on the body when, bare-legged, it curls in the sun. Perhaps the brightness came, too, from the grey stone; brightness and silence. Finn's mind always quickened as he looked around, and hearing and sight became acute.

By all the superstitions, he should be frightened of this place. And he was—a little, as if a tiny pulse of panic might beat at any time. But he liked this feeling, too. It lay beyond the need to show courage, to have his mind emptied and his body taut, as though there was also a friendliness, and intimacy, withdrawn and evasive.

And, in fact, there was one thing of which he could involuntarily catch a queer glimpse. It was the vision he had had in form and colour (especially in green, a brightness of soft green) when, after hunting the butterfly, he had fallen asleep, and then, in that "lost" moment of awakening, did not recognize this place but saw it as another world.

On his journey to Dale, he had gone out of his way to walk through this field on an impulse as unreasoning as the amused expression that accompanied it.

He climbed the knoll, keeping to the shelter of the birch trees and, on its long back, found the two small circles of stones, all that was left of the ancient cells. The sun had gone down and the faint shadow of evening lay lightly everywhere. He stretched himself out and, staring into the grass, began slowly plucking a blade. Sometimes his head lifted and his eyes turned, but presently his forehead fell on his arms, for he was tired after his long day on the road. It was a great relief to feel himself floating and sinking and the burden of his misery releasing its hooked fingers from his shoulders. All that he wanted on earth was that his

213

mother should escape the plague, that she should live. That was all. He wanted nothing else. He did not tell the knoll this, not specially. He was just letting it be known to and from his mind. And when this had gone from him into the knoll, he followed it, so tired he was.

Now, as he fell asleep, he dreamed, though never in after life could he quite satisfy himself that it was really sleep and a dream, for everything about him was exactly the same, the trees, the situation and the evening light; it was the same moment; and yet like that instant which had preceeded the coming of the known world when he was a little boy, so now he seemed to be awake when he saw standing by the near cell the tall figure of an old man in a white cape with the front part of his head quite bald. The face was extremely distinct, and though it had the dignity of Roddie's father in its expression, the face itself was one he had never seen before. The face did not speak to him or move: it just looked, the body standing still in a natural way.

But the look was extraordinarily full of understanding, and somewhere in it there was a faint humour, the humour that knows and appreciates and yet would not smile to hurt, yet the smile was there. It knew all about Finn, and told him nothing—not out of compassion, but out of needlessness.

As Finn's eyes opened wider, the figure faded, and here he was on his elbows staring at the ring of stones and then all around him. He did not think to himself: I was dreaming; nor—and this surprised him afterwards—was he at the moment beset by any fear. Yet he got up at once to leave the place, and as the ruins fell behind him and he climbed to the top of the wood, a feeling of ease and comfort came about his body and into his mind.

Roddie was at the corner of the house and Finn knew, by the way he turned his head and kept looking, that he was wondering what had gone wrong. But his voice was quite normal when he asked, "Well, how's your mother?"

"She's fine," said Finn cheerfully.

"Good boy!" said Roddie.

"She wouldn't hear of me staying at home."

"Didn't I tell you!"

They both smiled. Roddie neither looked at Finn closely nor asked him where he had gone.

"Can I do anything?" asked Finn.

"Yes," said Roddie. "You can come in for the Books. The old man is waiting. And then you'll go right away to your bed. I want you to be fresh to come down and give me a hand at the shore in the morning."

"That's grand!" said Finn.

After some talk in the gloom of the kitchen, Roddie lit the rush wick and opened the door of the middle room so that his mother could hear the Bible being read and her husband's prayer. He prayed for all those in illness and affliction and asked God in His gracious forbearance to lighten the darkness of the heart's evil and of the plague that had come upon the land. Surely, if God would listen to anyone, he would listen to a grave man like Roddie's father, thought Finn, quietened by the evening's devotions.

In the kitchen there was the same kind of boxed-in bed, with scalloped valance along the edges and short curtains in front, as was in Finn's own house, and when he learned that Roddie and he were to sleep there together, Finn had the feeling that at last he had entered the company of men.

After a time Roddie said, "I think you may as well turn in. You must be pretty tired. I'll wait for a bit because some of the crew are coming over to discuss a little business."

"All right," agreed Finn at once, adding, "the fresh air does make you a bit sleepy."

"That's right. You go to sleep," said Roddie.

But Finn was not in the least sleepy, and he had referred to the fresh air merely to relieve Roddie who, he felt, would naturally rather have him out of the way when discussing private business affairs. He turned his back to the kitchen and tried genuinely to go to sleep, but his mind

was clear and active as an overflowing well. There was, too,
a fine sensation of clarity in all he saw from his mother's
face to the white-caped figure on the top of the knoll. Somewhere between dreaming and waking there was a world
that came or went by the flick of an eyelid. Nothing at all
to be afraid of, any more than of a real dream in the daylight. And one laughed at the most horrid dream in the daylight. But this in-between dream was clear as light. . . .
His mind wandered back to Dale. How frightened they had
been of the plague!—far more frightened than people like
Roddie and himself who were on the spot. If he told Donnie
of the figure he had seen on the top of the knoll, Donnie
wouldn't go near the place alone for ten pounds! Things
were like that. Odd, when one came to think of it. The
great thing was not to be afraid. Whatever took place, folk
must think of him like that—as he had always thought of
Roddie. The only thing he had ever seen in the daylight
that had given him a queer, terrible feeling was the flames
going up from David's house. Angry, blood-red tongues of
flame shooting up above the black rolling smoke. You
almost had the awful feeling that the bodies of David and
Ina were being burned there, though they were both in
their graves. . . .

All at once he felt Roddie standing by the bedside, but
went on breathing as evenly as he could. Softly Roddie
drew the curtains and retired to the fire, leaving Finn so
acutely awake that it was an effort to go on breathing. The
flickering firelight began to die down and Finn heard soft
strokings in the ash. Why on earth was Roddie smooring
the fire if he was expecting company? His curiosity quickened beyond control, turned his head and shoulders and
slowly his whole body without the least sound. Through
the narrow slit where the curtains did not quite meet, he
saw Roddie on his knees before the fire, not smooring it,
but putting it out, extinguishing it, slowly, methodically,
ember by red ember. Finn could only stare in astonishment,
beyond thought, for no fire was ever put out from one

year's end to the other. And with good reason, for the only way to light it again would be by first getting a spark from steel and flint to smoulder in burnt cotton and then . . . but Finn knew this would be so long and laborious a process . . . Roddie, his body getting darker and darker as the fire disappeared, looked like one performing some dreadful, unimaginable rite . . . like one slowly and deliberately murdering fire.

Fear now touched Finn, and when the last red ember was smothered and Roddie was taken up into the darkness itself, he heard the beating of his own heart and was held in panic lest it betray his wakefulness.

After a long time Roddie moved towards the door, paused twice as if listening to the sleeping house, and then very quietly went outside.

The night that stretched outside, stretched to—his mother. Finn's mind now was lost, was imprisoned by the boxed bed, was being smothered like the fire. He put out a hand and separated the curtains—and heard low voices in the night. Then a shuffle of footsteps; and the bodies of men filed into the kitchen.

They spoke in whispers, but he distinguished their voices. Henry and Callum and Rob. All the crew. Clearly they had taken something in with them, for Rob's whisper asked, "Where's yours? Ay, now then. Whatever we do we must keep it going. Now!" There came a soft hissing sound, as of one log of wood being rubbed on another. This went on for a long time without a word being spoken. Then Rob's voice again: "Get your hands on it, Henry. Change!" And for a little time the tempo of the scraping sound increased. Finn was up on one elbow now, and through the widened chink he had left between the curtains could discern the deeper darknesses of the grouped bodies. They were breathing heavily.

That Rob was master of this mysterious midnight ceremony did not astonish Finn. His old Granny had been a queer one, and many of the more knowing had held her to

217

be a witch. Rob, with his solemn dry earnestness had as
many stories about balls of fire, and brownies drinking
milk, and other queer happenings as would fill a book. He
cut his peats or built a turf dyke when the moon was on
the wane so that they would dry into firmness. He lived
with his mother and sister, and followed Roddie.

"Must be damp," Callum muttered.

"Hsh! Be quiet!" whispered Rob. "Keep going."

Except for the soft sawing, there was no sound for a
long time; then suddenly upon the darkness there was a
spark of fire, so clear and white and momentary that Finn
might have doubted his senses, if Rob's voice had not
called in low triumph: "She's coming!"

At that the rhythm of the scraping increased.

More sparks, obscured by moving dark bodies, and
then—flame. A little tongue of flame, dancing flame,
whiter than the new moon. Finn could see the congested
faces in those new-born wisps of fire, fire paler and
brighter than ever he had seen before, dancing in glee like
sprites.

The brightness and whiteness seemed a pure miracle and
struck the men themselves indeed with awe. All of them,
that is, except Rob, who was always matter-of-fact and
soon had the gay tongues leaping up inside a ring of close-
standing black peat. Then he hitched the iron pot to the
crook.

"It beats everything!" said Henry. "From the rubbing
of two sticks!"

"You need two things," said Rob practically, "before
you can get a third."

They smiled in a benign humour.

"I certainly never saw a birth so pure and innocent
before," murmured Callum.

They were in the wonder of mirth beyond laughter.
Finn saw the flames dancing on their faces.

"That's the whole thing," Rob nodded. "Fire must be
put out and created afresh or it, too, grows old and full of

trouble and sin. Did you notice how dark-red, like blood, was the fire over David Sutherland's house?"

Roddie broke the silence by saying, "My mother's father used to do it every year. Then they would make two fires outside and drive the cattle between them."

They all, it seemed, knew something of the same kind, as they sat round the hearth waiting for the kettle to boil. But Rob knew most. He made them listen to the new flames in order to catch the quickness of the flap and the happy eagerness. His dark hair was cut short all over except for the fringe on his brow. When he lifted his eyebrows and looked sideways and downward, as in thought, then something special was coming!

Finn listened with the greatest interest to all they had to say, and felt happy at sight of the new fire. The old and unclean had been destroyed. In the new flame was new life.

Finn liked the expression on Callum's face, too. Callum was twenty-five, with a broad, fair face over broad shoulders. Willing and quick, he had plainly put all his force into the rubbing of the wood; and now wonder sat in his eyes ready for any turn of thought.

Often there was a satiric self-possession in Henry's dark glance, but now it was a gentle, friendly humour. He was three years older than Callum. Roddie was quiet, with the considering smile playing over his face. He was plainly the skipper, who did not subdue the others but, by his very presence, brought out the best that was in them. Their pleasant manhood so touched Finn's body that he became aware of the crick in his supporting arm and noiselessly lay back.

Presently there was a stir in the kitchen and Finn heard Roddie's voice, "Health to you, Callum. Health to you, Henry." A smile on his face, he was whisking a few drops of water on them from the black pot: "Health to you, Rob". "And health to yourself," responded Rob, dipping his fingers in the pot and sprinkling Roddie. Roddie carried the pot in his left hand and when he had put health on the hearth-stone of the house, he approached the bed. Finn closed his eyes tight and when the blessing fell upon him, continued to breathe on. "He's tired after the long tramp," murmured Roddie. Finn had a strong desire to stir and yawn and so appear to awake, for the need to be one of them was powerfully upon him, while at the same time he wanted to deny the silly notion that a day on his feet made him tired. But all this was suppressed in the instinct for harmony.

He heard them leave the house and pass down to the byre. The beasts would be sained, too. Finn wondered that the old folk had not heard the goings-on. What would have happened if Roddie's father had come in?

But here they were, back again. They stood whispering together for a little while, then Rob, Henry, and Callum, in turn took a flaming peat from the fire and quickly left the house. Each would keep his peat alight in the wind of the night until he reached home, where a fireless hearth would be waiting.

Roddie stood still for a long time looking down into the fire, then carefully he smoored the live embers in the ash and the kitchen went dark. Presently he slipped quietly under the clothes so as not to disturb Finn.

In the morning, Roddie had hardly got the fire going when his mother hirpled in on a stick. She was a medium-sized woman, and welcomed Finn in a lively, friendly manner. Off went Finn for water to the well, and when he came back she had the hearth swept and the peats standing round in willing company. He got a quick glimpse of her pleasure in the fire, and for a moment wondered if she knew what had happened in the night. Roddie had said that her father . . . Perhaps Roddie and herself had conspired . . .

It was a bright-blowing morning, and Finn felt happy as they went down by the wood. This time Roddie did not leave him to his mother, and voices as they crossed the water in the burn were companionable. If Kirsty was no better, she couldn't be said to be worse. Finn felt embarrassed in his mother's company with Roddie present, but when she had gone he turned and waved to her.

The water in the burn was almost quite clear again after the recent spate, and as they walked by the pools, Roddie's eyes concentrated in the steely way that turned their blue to grey-green. All at once he stood still without a word, then took out his snuff-box and offered it to Finn. "Do you see him?" he asked. "Yes," said Finn, taking a pinch. As Roddie moved on again he slowly cast his eyes around the braes and along the horizons. Finn did the same. "He's a big fellow," whispered Finn. "About eighteen pounds," replied Roddie. "Clean run on the last of the spate. We'll get him to-night, you and me." The thrill in Finn's heart was a sweet pain. This was the new life, the life of men. His bright eyes rested on the House of Peace. All at once the place was very old inside him, older than peat-smoke, grey and still in the bright morning. "Do you mean in the dark?" he asked Roddie. "Yes," answered Roddie. "He'll lie there now in the fallen water." Then he smiled. "You wonder how it can be done in the dark? Eh?" He was teasing Finn now. "What I really want," he added, "is to send a big slab of the fish to Kirsty. I don't like this loss of her appetite. And I know she has a relish for it." "For salmon?" "Seamen," said Roddie, "never care to mention that fish by name." "Why?" "Why do we do many a thing?" asked Roddie.

A strange world indeed, older than the House of Peace, old as the legendary salmon of knowledge that lay in the pool under the hazel nuts of wisdom, and perhaps older than that, with more mysterious things in it than the mind dreamt of. And how rich the thought of that invisible complexity was on a sunny, wind-bright morning! Everything, even the grey stones, with a hidden life! . . . Not that he completely believed it, but still . . .!

It was the first time that he had ever visited the seashore with a feeling of complete freedom, and despite his quiet movements he was highly exhilarated. No boats had been out the previous night for there had been an ugly swell, and there was still a heavy sea running. The boats had been drawn up, the gutting stations were deserted, and fishermen were attending to nets and gear and doing odd jobs about their craft.

Finn was particularly interested in Roddie's new boat, the *Seafoam*. She was five feet longer than the old *Morning Star*. Rob had stuck to Roddie, and Henry and Callum had come in with a full share of nets. Daun had taken over the *Morning Star*, which was still seaworthy, for Roddie had looked after her well; and Don, the other former member of the crew, had gone into partnership in a new boat with his brother David, now dead, and a first cousin.

Finn looked at the name *Seafoam*, in white against black, under the blue of her gunnel, and could see that this was the largest and finest of all the Dunster fleet. She had, too, some special features, such as sockets for two masts, and a pump. The column of the pump rose into the middle of a thick after-thwart, which had runways for the water to either side. "You have to pour in some water first," Roddie explained, "and then when you start working this handle up and down, she'll suck out every drop until nothing is left but froth."

Finn was deeply interested, and here by the sea Roddie moved in his own element, assured and companionable. The land, with its plague, seemed far removed from the translucent green combers that broke in dazzling foam. The very smell of the sea, through the tangle, was tonic and clean.

Mr. Hendry appeared and began talking to Roddie and other fishermen, who leisurely gathered around. Very soon Finn found that the inn-keeper was disturbed. "The fishing must be kept going, men, whatever happens. Even if some of the south boats have gone home. And the healthiest place you can work on is the sea. You know that. Wick is going ahead, and the trouble is far worse down there than here. . . ."

Finn gazed at the fat, broad, earnest face with the small eyes sharp and full of concern.

"I have my commitments, but it's in your own interests more than mine to keep Dunster's reputation to the fore. You know that."

"I don't think that any boat, unless the trouble touches the crew, will stop fishing," said Roddie. "I think you can rely on that."

How quiet Roddie's voice was compared with the urgency and concern in the voice of the inn-keeper! thought Finn, instinctively aligning himself with the silent fishermen.

When the talk was over and Mr. Hendry seemed reassured, Finn was struck by a remark one of the older men let drop to a friend as they were walking away: "He would be wondering why we didn't go to sea last night." The tone was level, without any emphasis, but its dryness made Finn's eyes gleam with understanding.

That evening Finn felt anxious when his mother did not seem to see Roddie and himself by the edge of the wood. They waited a long time, and then Roddie said, "She must have given us up."

The shadows were heavy in the wood as they silently went along its steep side and came above the pool where the salmon lay. Their idea was to go with a cut of the fish and cry Catrine's name outside the window. When they had made certain, after a quarter of an hour, that no human being could command the pool during the two or three minutes Roddie would be in action, Finn kept watch while Roddie stepped lightly down to the edge of the water. He had a few square yards of old net, and now, with the help of a stick, spread it out over the water and let it slowly sink. He could not see the fish from this side, as it lay against an under-water ledge whose face was turned from him. When the net touched the bottom of the pool, Roddie withdrew his stick and, reaching far out, the water past his knees, gave it a sharp, downward thrust. At once there was turmoil, and Finn saw the flashing silver of the salmon as it bent and heaved to clear itself of the net that ever more maddeningly enmeshed it. It took less than two minutes for Roddie to get his hands on the turmoil. Then he walked out of the pool, with the doubling salmon clasped in his arms, and up into the trees.

Presently Finn led the way back through the wood towards the top corner. The head and gut they buried in a rabbit's burrow, and then Roddie cut the fish in two. "We'll take the tail piece," he whispered; "it's supposed to be more delicate." Hiding both parts for the moment in a small thicket of hazel, they emerged from the wood, full of the pleasantest excitement from the short adventure.

Finn could not see his mother about the house, though now there was a single white cloth on the washing-line near the gable-end, so she must have been out since they went for the salmon. He turned to Roddie to mention this, but did not speak. He had seen that concentrated light in Roddie's eyes once or twice, but never the face turned to stone. Finn felt the chill of the face freezing the life out of his heart.

"Kirsty has the plague," said Roddie. "That's the sign."

His lips scarcely moved. No expression at all appeared on his face as he gazed steadily at the fatal white signal agreed upon between Catrine and himself.

Finn had trouble with his breathing and a sickening sensation beset him internally. Upon the world fell a terrible stillness.

"So it's come," said Roddie, and the breath issued from between his narrowed lips in a cold hiss. He looked down to the burn, to the moor, and back to the house, with its death-white pennant. There was no dismay in the face; only the coldness of stone, a coldness of clear anger that would take the utmost danger in life and break it, if only the hands could get a grip.

"Well, Finn, boy," he said gently, "we have to face this now." He did not look at Finn, because he was not yet thinking about him. "Come," he added. "We'll go over with the fish."

At once he went into the wood, and returned with the tail-piece under his jersey. Finn followed him down to the burn and up the slope to within fifty yards of the house. "You stay here," commanded Roddie, and he went past the gable-end and up to the kitchen window. Finn heard his voice, saw him lay the tail of the fish on the stone sill, and stand back from the house as if he had been so ordered. His mother came to the door and presently leaned outward and saw Finn standing down below the house. She waved to him, with the quick waggle of the hand she used when she was gay. He could see the smile on her pale face. And at that, the strange unreality that had come upon him, behind the sickening, tremulous feeling and the world's stillness, gave way, and he clenched his teeth. His mother, his indomitable mother, waving from the door of death. It was like her.

He kicked the sod idly with his toes, glanced up at them again, and turned away. Though his emotion would have prevented his speaking naturally to his mother, in any case, yet he felt outcast, cut away from them, and somewhere deep in him did not resent this so much as feel futile in himself and therefore empty and forlorn. After all, it was his own mother. Why must he be beyond even what they were saying?

He moved away a step or two, and when he heard Roddie coming did not turn round, though he knew his mother was waiting to wave to him. He wanted to be alone, not to speak to Roddie.

"She's got it all right," said Roddie, lost in himself.

If I don't turn this second, Finn thought, we'll be out of sight. But he could not turn, and the world went desolate.

At the burn, Roddie stopped. "I'm going to get some more of that stuff from Hector Bethune. Will you go up and tell them at home, or would you like to come with me?"

"I'll go up," said Finn.

"That would be better. I'll have to knock him out of bed. And then . . . " He seemed to be thinking at a distance. "I won't be long," he said all at once and set off. There never seemed to be much warm emotion in Roddie. A stone face with narrowed deadly eyes and the voice talking in quiet, friendly tones.

As he went up by the wood he looked across at his home, and its still desolation stopped his feet. The drooping white cloth glowed like a white fungus in the deepening gloom. The house lay to the gentle slope, with curved back like a patient, doomed animal.

Finn did not feel much now. His brain was numb. Indeed, for one moment, he had a sensation of being detached from it all, and of being astonished in a mild way, almost ashamed, that it did not affect him more. His mother came round the corner of the house carrying a bucket. With the graip she dug a hole in the manure heap, and there buried whatever was in the bucket.

As she stood back from the manure heap, she gazed in his direction. He waved an arm. She turned away without any response. He knew she could not have seen him against the dark edge of the wood, yet the disappointment made him more forlorn than ever.

When he told Roddie's father and mother the news they stood in an appalled silence, as if an invisible hand had come down from the air upon them.

"Where's Roddie?" asked the mother in a small voice.

"He's gone to Hector Bethune. I heard at the shore to-day," he added, "that a new doctor has come into the county. He's an expert on the trouble. I'm walking now to Watten to see if I can find him."

"To Watten! Now?" asked the old man. It was well over twenty miles away.

"Yes," said Finn. "It's the new half of the moon." He lifted his round bonnet, shy of meeting their faces, and was turning to the door before they could find words to stop him.

When, at last, they saw not merely that he was bent on going but that he could not rest in the house even until the dawn, the woman started buttering oatcakes and sticking them together. The boy was touched by fate. "What if he's not at Watten?"

"I'll find him," replied Finn simply, "wherever he is."

The eyes glimmered and the bearded head nodded. As Finn took the food, the old woman's hands came on his shoulders in blessing. She could hardly speak.

"May God guide your feet," said Roddie's father from the peat-stack, as Finn took to the moor with the night coming down.

CHAPTER XI

CATRINE AND KIRSTY

❦

Catrine stood by the small window looking out upon the land under the half-moon. It was spectral and very quiet, and when she felt that figures might appear there, she turned to the fire. But the window remained like a face in her mind, and with a dragging reluctance she got up and covered it.

She was very tired, and instead of sitting by the fire, this time she went and lay on her bed. Early, acute terrors of death did not trouble her so much now. When she had got over their attacks, a quietness had descended. For she could never desert Kirsty, not though the love of life sang in each vein and drew her—drew her—to sunlight, to life on the earth, the green earth, to life on quick feet. She loved life. She had always loved it. And only now did she see how lovely a thing it was.

In the quietism there was this strange twilight mood of acceptance, in which she now no longer thought of her own physical death, but of the spirit of death itself, spectral under the moon.

Like all of her generation, she never had any doubts of the existence of God, and the imagination that was strengthened in the stories of the ceilidh-house found little difficulty in seeing the figure of Christ as a child in a manger or as a grown man walking down by a ripe cornfield. The eastern imagery of cornfield and green pasture and still waters was their own imagery, and the desert was the waste of moor turned hot and arid, hot as it often was under

228

a blazing July sun, when the shadow of trees or a rock in a little strath drew cattle with switching tails to its shelter and a human being to pleasant ease on his back.

But religion for the young and healthy was beyond life, beyond the dark instincts, beyond even the superstitions and wild irrational fears that were in such mysterious fashion part of the core and quick of life. Religion was for death, for the unknown hereafter, and paradise a perpetual Sunday school smothering the quick laughter, the gay wonder of human love—should one ever attain paradise by avoiding the brimstone loch of hell. Better not to think about it, to keep it away, and meantime to have life.

And meantime, too, whatever might happen at an infinitely remote Resurrection, ghosts walked. Ghosts, apparitions, spirits of the dead. Men like Sandy Ware said they were evil spirits, phantoms from unholy regions, and if a man stood his ground before them, and called upon his Maker, they would disappear.

Had Sandy Ware ever met—the ghost of love?

Catrine stirred on her bed. Tormad had come near to her again those last few days.

Was this because, in her weariness, the urgency of her flesh had died down and her spirit, purified to lightness for long moments, could wander the woods and green river-flats of Kildonan, and out and in the small cabin in Dale where Tormad and herself had lived on the edge of want that was poverty, but not poverty of life? She loved the thick hair on his black head and the utter generosity of his nature. She felt him with her hands, her fingers going through his hair, sometimes gripping it and hanging on until he yelled and threatened her and they rolled and fought in an ecstasy of living.

Tormad was strong and instinctive, with the moods and graces of the instincts.

Roddie was strong and reasonable.

Tormad was one she had had to deal with, as she often had had to deal with little Finn.

Roddie was like a pillar that she herself could lean against.

More than once she had had an almost overpowering desire to let Roddie take her and so find peace for herself and her body inside the circle of his strength. She could have wished him to break through the barrier between them, even while her face showed how inviolable the barrier must remain. The only thing that kept Roddie back was the thought that her husband might be alive. That was the barrier which Roddie would not break through. And when she saw it breaking down in his eyes, she could restore it with a look.

Yet this did not make the matter clear in itself. She had never, for example, told Roddie the story of Tormad's ghostly appearance to her and her own certainty of his death. Why?

She was weak. She was terribly weak. She feared. She did not know what she wanted. Supposing it had been certified that Tormad was dead, and Roddie then had taken action into his own hands, would she have let him crash through the barrier of strange reluctance? She knew she could no more have stopped him than have stopped fate.

Would she have desired it? Yes, often, madly . . . yes . . . she didn't know.

And now it didn't matter. It was better, indeed, to have the pattern of her past life clear and simple. And that excitement and loveliness of living with Tormad could never have come again. In the ordinary workaday life, with its drudgeries and dependence and hours of hidden misery, here in another woman's home, that early life had often seemed remote and insubstantial. But now it was coming back again, it was stealing in upon her with the quietness of sleep that carries the waking thought into the more vivid dream.

She heard the tapping and wondered where she was; then she hurried into Kirsty's room. The dawn was coming and in its faint light she saw the ghastly pallor of the rigid face. Death, she thought, and when her quick, whispered appeals were unanswered, her heart stood heavily in her breast.

"Were you asleep?" The voice was a thick whisper but the opening eyes glittered in concentration.

"Yes," muttered Catrine, overwhelmed with shame. "I lay down for a minute. Are the pains easier?"

Kirsty's acute attack of what was locally called "the dysentery" and recognized as the onset of "the plague", had been accompanied by an intense nausea and retching. As Kirsty's mouth yawed open in a wild choking effort at vomit which would not come, her abdominal muscles squirmed and griped in cramping pains. A touch of flatulence added to her agony. She complained of a fixed burning pain in her stomach and a desperate thirst. Catrine had bathed her feet in hot sea-water, sea-water that Roddie had brought in a bucket, and given her cold water with a little whisky to drink, all on the advice of Hector Bethune.

But the taste of the whisky, Kirsty bitterly complained, only increased her nausea and turned her tongue cold. She could not go to bed because of the almost incessant diarrhoea. But at last her exhaustion became such that Catrine had had to help her off the floor and into bed.

Now, as her hand came on the bedclothes to smooth them under Kirsty's chin, she found they were wet. Kirsty had been vomiting; and as she glanced at the watching eyes, Catrine seemed to see in them a cold malevolence. She knew how Kirsty loathed this personal uncleanliness, this loss of control. All at once new spasms started. The eyes shut and the body heaved and moaned.

In the use of her capable hands, Catrine regained her assurance. The full kettle was for ever simmering on the fire. She removed the soiled gown and special bed-cloth and washed Kirsty's mouth and body tenderly but firmly, then happed her warmly and hurried out to bury the bed-cloth. The gown she stuffed into a tub of water, astringent from a decoction of roots of the tormentil, which Hector Bethune sometimes used for tanning leather.

While outside, she also sluiced her face and nostrils and hands. Hector had said she should do this always after handling the afflicted body. He had also said that she would do herself no harm by taking a good deep breath of peat smoke, for it might help her to cough up the beginnings of infection.

As the acrid smoke caught her nostrils and throat, she coughed and spat into the fire and felt the better for it. In front of trouble requiring action, she had a native poise and ability.

When she had heated a bowl of milk, she poured a glass of whisky into it, and went into Kirsty's room. "Now, here you are. You'll take this." Her manner was cheerful.

Kirsty ignored her.

"Come away, Kirsty. You must keep your strength up. Come!" She put her arm round Kirsty's shoulders, but they remained rigid against her.

"Leave me," said Kirsty. "I'm dying." The tone was cold and repellent, the face a saturnine mask.

"But you must take something," Catrine wheedled her. "It's your only chance of getting well."

"There is no chance."

"But take it, to please me. Do. Please, Kirsty."

Kirsty now turned her eyes upon Catrine and it looked as if hatred burned in their depths. "I order you," she muttered, "to leave my house this instant." The difficulty she had with her articulation gave the words an almost malignant deliberation.

"But I can't leave you now."

"Leave me," croaked Kirsty, with such harsh anger that her jaw shook and champed. At once Catrine turned and left the room. She placed the bowl beside the fire, and stood still. There was no doubt about the reality of the hatred in Kirsty's eyes. Catrine did not know what to think. It could hardly be because she had fallen asleep for an hour or so.

Suddenly she felt very tired, weary, disheartened. Kirsty
had said she was dying—not as a dying person would say
it—but as if it were her own business. They were perhaps
both dying. But why this misery—this destroying hatred—
now? "Leave my house." Life gave little inward clutches
at Catrine's throat. It might yet be time. Leave the house—
leave it—go over the hills, taking food with you—over the
mountains. . . .

She poured what was left of the milk in the pan into a
clean bowl and added a thimbleful of whisky. As she raised
the bowl her hands shook. She drank it slowly, sitting by
the fire.

She could not feel any more, could not think. For two
nights she had had no real sleep. The sunless dawn was
grey silver over the still land. She listened to the singing of
two larks. Only now and then did one become conscious of
bird-singing, because the place was alive with larks, and
for months the air was rarely free of their mounting wings.
In the grey of a spring morning they became possessed and
all the upper air was a quilted ecstasy. Robins and wrens
had their clear, ringing songs, and chaffinch and greenfinch
their quieter melodies. These smaller birds loved this land
of braes and bushes, of sheltered crannies and ledges amid
grey rocks.

The kitchen was a dim cage shut away from the silver
morning, and because of the strange fatalism and loyalty
bred from her race, Catrine listened to the singing, and its
beauty killed urgency in her.

In her despondency, her body for a little grew light as a
wraith, and she passed on blind feet through singing and
silence, in a vague sad wonder at the ordering of the world.
Then her body came back upon her as she sat before the
fire, her cheeks weighing heavily into her palms and the
flames wavering as if seen through running water. The
milk made her heavy and sleepy and she wanted to slip off
the stool on to the floor and not care if she never awoke.

Finn and the birds. He had always been so curious.

"What bird is that, Mama?" Eager eyes and quick feet, trying to follow the bird to its nest . . . Finn faded; her eyes closed; and she slept where she sat, her head jerking now and then.

At the first sound from Kirsty she was awake and hurrying; assisted her through her dreadful spasms; tidied bed and room, and presently returned with the bowl of milk. "Won't you try a little?"

Kirsty did not answer. She had become dreadfully emaciated. Catrine remained beside her, silent.

"What you waiting for?" demanded Kirsty.

"Try a little," pleaded Catrine, who naïvely felt that Kirsty must get strength from somewhere if she was going to live.

"Go 'way! Get out!" croaked Kirsty.

"Just a little." Catrine put her arm round the stiff shoulders and used some strength. It was a dead heave, but she got the head up and held the bowl to the lips. After a stiff but indecisive moment, Kirsty sucked at the milk. "Again," said Catrine. Kirsty sucked noisily a second time, and then fell back, spilling some milk on her breast. Catrine, laying the bowl down, wiped her breast. "Now you'll be the better of that." Kirsty ignored her, breathing stertorously. In a very short time Kirsty was violently sick and Catrine thought it was the end.

Kirsty recovered, glared at Catrine, and muttered something like, "Didn't I tell you!"

So it went on at intervals all through the day. Catrine could see the flesh wasting away, the bones coming up, hour by hour.

In the early evening, Roddie was waiting below the byre and she told him that it must go one way or the other with Kirsty very soon. They arranged that if Kirsty died, she would put up the white signal.

"Are you doing what I told you and eating your food?"

"Yes," said Catrine. "It gave me something to do. I have been careful."

"That's fine," nodded Roddie. "You have a great spirit, Catrine. Keep it up! And look here—whenever this is over, we have a little place all for yourself for a few days. All ready." He smiled in that diffident detached way that had always attracted her.

"But——" She paused. "Do you mean," she asked, with widening eyes, "that our house will be burned down?"

"Of course," said Roddie. "We'll burn it into the ground." There was an inexorable quality in his quiet voice, a restraint that suggested a terrible strength, a strength balked and turned in on itself.

"I'll have to run," said Catrine. "The spasms come on her suddenly."

His eyes narrowed and she saw that it would not take much for him to walk in, snatch her under an arm, and stride away with her, caring as little for her protests as for anyone else's.

As she ran, giving him a wave and a smile, he stood quite still and, inside, she listened, ready to block the door against him. Once or twice at a market it had taken a few men to hold him. But that was with a drop of drink taken. Now he was sober, and the plague was not a thing he could break on his knee.

She felt heartened and looked at herself in the small glass. She was pale, perhaps, but her eyes were larger and browner than ever, and the lips of her wide mouth had colour still. While she smiled at her eyes, they looked back at her and filled with tears. She hastily wiped the tears away. She was thirty-four, but her skin was smooth as it had been in her twenties. She felt in her twenties, in her 'teens. She moved quickly about the kitchen. She didn't feel she was going to die. She was not going to die. Burn down the house? Her house and Finn's? Somehow that awful thought had not attacked her before.

All day she had kept going, cleaning, washing, looking out sheets and clothes, shifting the tethers, mucking the byre, feeding the horse, and attending to Kirsty, the visits outside being swift sallies from which she returned panting the good air. The early morning tiredness passed away entirely, and she felt she could spend another night without sleep easily.

Only there was nothing much more to do now, except wait for sounds from Kirsty. And outside there was the spectral light again. She feared it. The grey light of dawn and gloaming. The hour when the spirit walked alone— one's own spirit, out through the eyes; and the spirit of a dead loved one, in the strange brightness that can inhabit the grey light, coming down, drawing nigh. . . .

Kirsty's stick tapped, and with a quick catch of breath, Catrine went into her room. Already the face was in shadow, and she lay quietly; then looked up at Catrine standing by her bed, a basin in her hand, asking gently if she felt the spasm coming.

"Why didn't you leave me when I told you?" The voice was clearer than it had been, but also weaker.

"I couldn't leave you, Kirsty. You know that."

"Why?"

"How could I, and you ill? You have been so kind to me, to me and Finn."

"Not been kind. You more than worked your way here. But while I'm alive, I'm mistress here, and you should have obeyed."

"I couldn't. Please don't hold that against me now. Please, Kirsty," pleaded Catrine.

"Very well," said Kirsty. "But I could have died alone. Could you not think of yourself? Isn't one enough?"

Catrine did not answer, seeing in that clear moment Kirsty's inexorable common sense. It was selfless and austere, yet with a final pride in it. Everything had been hard and clear, matter-of-fact and precise, with Kirsty always. Waste not, want not. Her sense of economy was still at work!

"Would you have left me if I had been ill?" asked Catrine.

There was a pause. "Nothing to do with it. The end is not far off now and we have a little business to do. Sit down."

Catrine sat down on the wooden chair beside her bed. Kirsty's hands lay extended on the patchwork coverlet and her eyes stared over them down the bed.

Sometimes her voice was little more than a whisper. She spoke in a monotone, with intervals of silence, and at times indeed it seemed that the spirit alone was talking through the gaunt, exhausted flesh. The eyes were deeply sunk and, in an interval, when the spirit seemed arrested by its own thought, the pupils tended to roll upward.

But the intellect was clear and the burden of what she said was:

"My father wanted you to inherit this croft. That was right. I would not want the home of my people to pass to a stranger. But this was never our home. We, like you, were driven out. But I do not want brother or sister of mine, who left us here, to benefit now. I told my brother that when he arrived too late for his father's funeral. He knows. But when it comes to worldly goods, trust no one. Remember that." Her head nodded slightly but firmly. "So—feeling this was coming on me—I wrote it down on a paper. That paper—in the shottle of my kist. Keys are there, in that small box. Get them."

Catrine found the keys, under some brooches and faded letters, coloured beads and other "bonnie things", surely as old as her childhood.

"Open the kist."

The rectangular wooden trunk was solidly made. When Catrine had lifted its lid, an old scent of wild thyme came up from folded dark clothes. Fixed to the back, like a rectangular sleeve, was the narrow, boxed-in shottle. From this Catrine took the letter.

"Take purse, too."

It was a large, heavy purse, the home-cured leather

darkened and shiny. Kirsty motioned Catrine to put letter and purse beside her and sit down.

She groped for the letter and purse with her left hand and tried to lift them towards Catrine. "Take them—from me." Catrine at once took them. "Yours now. That will save trouble. What I give, I give. You need mention purse to no one. Refuse. It's yours. Understand?"

Catrine understood. Kirsty could do what she liked with her own before her death. Afterwards—it would have been a different matter.

"Count," ordered Kirsty.

Catrine counted forty-one golden sovereigns.

Kirsty nodded. "You will pay funeral expenses. No debts." Then she made a special effort with her articulation: "Always keep a little in the shottle of your kist, so that you may die decently, and be beholden to no one."

"Yes," answered Catrine, troubled with her emotion. "Thank you." She bit her quivering lip.

Kirsty closed her eyes. Her mouth fell open, emitting a sobbing moan and then, after a long interval, another. But presently her eyes opened and her expression seemed to lighten. "If He gave you a soft heart, He gave you willing hands. You have always been a brave, good girl."

Catrine strove her utmost, but it was no use. The sobs came and she got up and turned away, muttering, "I'm sorry."

While she was composing herself, Kirsty had another spasm, but it was not violent, and after it she seemed a little easier.

"Have you thought what you'll do with letter and purse if you get plague yourself?"

There was silence.

"I could," said Catrine, "talk to Finn, when I felt it coming on me. I could—I could put it in a hole in the wall of the little barn. There is one thing of my own I would like him to have." Her voice quickened, almost eagerly. "I could do that. I could easily do that."

CATRINE AND KIRSTY

Kirsty nodded. "Now my mind is at rest."

After a little she said, "You'll never keep that boy from the sea. If you wish him well, don't try."

Catrine was silent.

Kirsty turned her eyes. "You are still against him?"

"I do not want him to go to sea."

"More ugly deaths on this land now than ever on sea. If you put boy against his nature, you'll warp him. Remember that."

Catrine bowed her head.

"Remember that," muttered Kirsty in a little while. "I know."

The last two words came from a distance in thought, and Catrine saw that Kirsty's mind had gone back to the young man who, against his wishes, had been sent to a lucrative position in the West Indies. His mother had high notions of her social position, and Kirsty was not the daughter-in-law she envisaged. The lad's private idea was to save money and return. But the generous hand was native to Hugh. There was high social scandal, and a rumour of Hugh's bitter words on presumably the woman in the case, the last words he uttered: "That scheming bitch", as he went out on the ebb of dysentery, following a drunken orgy.

Catrine had learned all this only a few nights ago; in fact, after she had told Kirsty that a certain Captain Mackay had been asking for her in Helmsdale. The Captain, it turned out, was Hugh's first cousin.

That fairly long, lucid spell was Kirsty's last. Presently her whole body shivered so violently that her lower jaw shook and chittered, and the bed itself trembled. In addition to the warming-pan and the earthenware bottle, Catrine heated two stones, wrapped them in flannel, and put them to the soles of Kirsty's feet. As the shivering subsided, her mouth opened, but her throat, as if plugged, held even her breath back. Her body slowly writhed, the breath came in choking gasps, and she moaned from the pains of cramp.

Catrine massaged the lower part of the shrunken body

as best she could. When she felt the rigor relaxing, she
withdrew the cloths from under the abdomen and went outside, turning her face away, until she got the sweet air.
She felt dizzy for a moment and breathed deeply. It was
now almost quite dark.

Life was so strong in Catrine, she had so healthy and
vigorous a body, that fear for the moment touched her and
she leaned against the door-jamb, breathing the cool air off
the heather. Two peewits started crying up towards the
edge of the moor, a restless, anxious crying, urgent with
life. They drew near and she heard the silken beat of the
wings. They filled her with inexpressible sadness, a sense
of beauty for ever lost; their wings beat in her breast.
They passed over her, and fell away towards the moor.

She leaned the back of her head against the jamb and
closed her eyes. Opening them, she felt cool again, as if the
wings had fanned her face.

She lit a tallow candle (Kirsty had her own mould for
making candles) and went into the sick room. In the indifferent light Kirsty's face was all protuberant bone and
sagging wrinkled skin. Her breathing was slow and very
laboured. Catrine put her hand on the brow and found it icy
cold and clammy with sweat. The lids of the half-closed
eyes lifted slightly, and Catrine, inclining her ear, divined
rather than heard in a gust of breath, "The Books".

The Holy Bible lay on the little rounded table, and as
Catrine set down the candle and lifted the book, she wondered what she would read.

But there was only one thing she could read that would
be real to her heart now, that did not frighten her, that had
peace in it.

"*The Lord is my shepherd, I shall not want. He maketh me
to lie down in green pastures; he leadeth me beside the still
waters.*"

Catrine had not much of a high-singing voice, but, as
Finn knew, she could croon away at one of the old child
lullabies in a way that turned the heart to water and all

rebellions to peace. Her soft voice caught the very core of the lullaby's intention and bore it in a rhythm as natural as the rhythm of a long sea wave. At such times there was an ancient innocence in her voice that was almost too much for the humours of ordinary flesh; in a sense, hardly fair, as of something that could take advantage too easily.

"*Yea, though I walk through the valley of the shadow of death, I will fear no evil, for thou art with me . . .*"

Kirsty heard the words and knew them. Catrine's voice was the stream in Kildonan, a burn in some far comforting paradise. No minister of the gospel could have borne her on the flood of death so softly.

Looking up from her reading, Catrine thought that Kirsty had fallen asleep, for the eyes were closed and the body at rest. She lifted the candle and went into the kitchen. She was beginning to feel an insidious weakness in her flesh, and assured herself it was due to lack of sleep. I am terribly tired, she thought, wanting to throw herself down and let sleep have its way. She had not the energy to wash.

Kirsty's quiet body remained with her, and in a little while she went in again, leaving the candle outside the door so that the light would not fall on Kirsty's eyes and awake her. Kirsty was exactly as she had left her. Catrine did not know whether to take the candle in or not, and retreated again to the kitchen. But now she had no peace, seeing the body stretched out, and soon was stealing into Kirsty's room once more. She listened for breathing but heard none. "Kirsty!" she whispered. Then she brought the candle in.

She's dead! thought Catrine. But how could she be sure? "Kirsty!" She did not know what to do, and her head turned as if she were trapped. "Kirsty!" She put her hand on the bedclothes over Kirsty's chest and pressed the breast-bone. Kirsty emitted a heavy, sobbing breath. It seemed to be her last, for now her breathing completely stopped. Her skin was shrivelled in a livid purple, and the face was so unlike that of the woman she had long known,

that Catrine's fear was touched with horror. A deep, shuddering sob broke from Kirsty again. Catrine gave a small
choked cry. Kirsty's half-closed lids slowly lifted and the
pupils lowered to look at Catrine. There was now such
clear intelligence in the eyes, such sane consciousness, that
Catrine's fist gripped against her heart. "Oh, Kirsty, I
thought . . ." Was that understanding a gleam of the old
grim humour? "Kirsty!" called Catrine. The lids fell and
a shuddering breath came from the livid lips. There was a
long pause, then a final deep convulsive sob.

There was no doubt about death, now that Catrine
looked down upon it.

All at once, outside, several peewits began to cry. Disembodied cries, anxious, frightening cries. Catrine tried to
open the little window. It was stuck. She tugged fiercely,
desperately. It gave—to let the spirit out. She hurried to
the outside door and pulled it open. She hardly knew what
she was doing. What had made the birds cry? In a quiet,
ghost voice from a little distance came the word, "Mother."

CHAPTER XII

FINN'S JOURNEY FOR A DOCTOR

T he resolution to set out to find the new doctor had come upon Finn quite suddenly. He could not have spent the night with Roddie, and wanted to be away before he could return to stop him. So he had gone, and because of his need to be alone, the half-dark of the moor did not at first distress him. The haunted stone quarry—it was a lonely spot—set the hairs apart on his head, but he saw nothing, though a curlew gave him such a fright that his knees doubled in weakness and he felt sickish for a little distance.

As it grew darker, however, he slanted down to the outlying barn of a croft he knew. It was smaller than the one at home, and when he was sure he had it all to himself, he sat down, his back against the wall and his eyes to the door. At first, he lived entirely in his ears, but soon he grew assured, and presently experienced such a strange content in the heart of his misery that his head drooped.

The night was short, and in the new world upon which the dawn came he found a stillness that sometimes enchanted him and sometimes made him a little afraid. He came in time to croft houses strung at a short distance from one another along a road, and they were all so extraordinarily still that they might have contained the dead. Once or twice a dog barked, and he trod the grass on the side of the road very quietly, though his bare feet could have made little enough sound anywhere, and hurried past.

He was now on the road that ran right across the county

of Caithness, from Latheron on the Moray Firth to Thurso on the Pentland, and the great inland moors seemed without end, except far to the west where the Scarabens and Morven marched northward in blue ramparts against the county of Sutherland. As he looked at them, he could see their tops take the light from a sun that he had often watched rise out of the ocean in golden and silver spangles. They had never looked so vast and impressive before, with something foreign about them, as if they were "a mountain range" in Spain or Africa, from one of Mr. Gordon's geography lessons. Such immense vistas as he could now cover quickened all his senses, keeping his head up, alert and questing, and he felt an adventurous traveller.

Now and then he drank out of a burn, and wiped the water from his nose and hair, and looked about him. But at such a time he took only two bites of his bread, and chewed with slow relish. He had never realized before how delicious and fragrant was well-chewed oat-bread with new butter. He had always thought Roddie's mother's oat-bread was thick and tough compared with his own mother's. He had hardly been fair to it; he could see that.

The sound of the little burns in the early morning, over-hanging tongues of peat-bank, sailing bubbles and foam-flakes, all were strange, a little unfriendly, as if brown figures had passed here; yet for moments they were very friendly, too, and the tall rushes with their hairy brown buttons moved suddenly in the air as they did at home. And constantly, never leaving his mind at rest, was the anxiety to be on, to arrive.

He knew the road from hearsay, and began wondering if he would recognize the bridge before Halsary, because it was the most haunted spot in Caithness, with real blood-curdling stories about it. He could go to Mybster and then strike east on the road to Watten, or he could cut in over the moor at Halsary, fetch the Acharole Burn, and follow it to Watten.

But though all this had been clear enough in the talk of

people who had been this way, now in fact everything was on so vast a scale, the road seemed so without end, for ever stretching to far horizons, with lochs bigger than he had ever seen before, and in one place standing-stones, that when at last he came, while it was yet early, within sight of what might be the haunted bridge, and saw furtive human heads bobbing out of sight, his heart began to beat painfully and, almost without stopping, as if he had not seen the heads, he turned to his right and stepped off the road into the pathless moor.

A bridge, to Finn, was a high arch spanning a river, like the one at home. If there was a bridge down there it could be no more than a flat thing of a few feet over the little burn. But he had seen the heads, and not until the spot had fallen from sight behind him did he feel in any way at ease. They might have been poachers, but they looked brown, like heads out of the heather. He was lucky to have seen them in time.

Then he got lost. No matter where he gazed, there was nothing but moor, with lochans here and there. If he kept going straight across country from the Latheron–Georgemas road he was bound in time to strike the Thurso–Wick road somewhere in the Watten district. But such acquired knowledge seemed to have little relation to this vast world of reality. He grew very tired and, sitting down in a sheltered spot, with the sun's warmth on him, he took out his food and ate a third of it. When he lay on his side to rest, his back curved, his knees drew up, and he fell asleep.

Hours later, as he was following a burn blindly, he at last saw a cottage with blue smoke rising from its thatch. Two dogs came barking furiously at him and then a man stood in the door. "Can you tell me," Finn asked him, "the way to Watten?"

"Yes," said the man, astonished; then he stared at Finn closely. He was a big man with a black beard. "Where are you from?" "Dunster." A woman appeared behind his shoulder, and three children peered round their legs.

"Dunster! That's a far road," said the man. "When did you leave?"

"Late last night."

They stared at Finn. "If you tell me the house you are wanting in Watten, perhaps we could put you on your way," said the man.

"I'm wanting to see the new doctor who has come to Caithness about the trouble."

Finn read the fear of the plague in their faces far more easily than he could any story in Mr. Gordon's *English Reader*. The man's eyes hardened like Roddie's, as he said, "If you keep going down the burn it will take you to Watten at last."

"Thank you," said Finn, and started off. He hadn't gone more than a hundred yards when the man shouted and came towards him. "If you wait a minute, we'll get some food for you."

"I have plenty, thank you," cried Finn.

Then he heard the woman's voice. They would be distressed because a stranger—a boy at that—had passed their door without receiving hospitality! He felt sorry for the struggle in their minds, particularly for the red-headed woman, she had such compassionate blue eyes. When he came at a short distance to the bend that would take him out of sight, he turned. They were all standing together looking after him. Finn waved, and at once the man and woman waved back, as if he were their son leaving them on a far journey.

Finn smiled to himself as he went on, heartened by the sadness that would haunt the woman's mind for many a day. And the man would feel the more futile because of his strength. There were kind people everywhere.

The loch at Watten was so big it was like a small sea. Finn had many queer adventures in that district, before he found himself on the road to Wick. He was getting more cunning now in talking to people. This was rich farming land, not like the little crofts dug out of the Dunster moor.

More than once he heard persons crying out to each other in English. They didn't speak a bit like Mr. Gordon. He could not understand them, though he knew a word here and there. What if he could not speak to the doctor? His brow went cold with fear, and he started practising aloud on himself. "Man's chief end is to glorify God and to enjoy him for ever. The word of God, which is contained in the Scriptures of the Old and New Testaments, is the only rule to direct us how we may glorify and enjoy him. The Scriptures principally teach what man is to believe concerning God, and what duty God requires of man. God is a spirit, infinite, eternal, and unchangeable, in his being, wisdom, power, holiness, justice, goodness, and truth."

They were not the words that one ploughman threw to another. So he tried to think of other English Lessons and repeated a little poem to a star. "How are you?" he asked himself. "I am well, thank you. How are you yourself? I come from Dunster . . . "

He got so interested in this, in having English words to tell the doctor exactly what he wanted, that he forgot he was practising aloud, and when the head of a man pushed up behind a dry-stone dyke and stared with round eyes and a silly open mouth, Finn blushed hotly, but kept walking on, gaze front. When well out of sight he could not help laughing, and the laughter grew so catching that he stopped and turned his face to the side of the road to have it out, not loudly, but in soft billows from the chest.

When it's that way with him, a man will go out of his path to find bad luck, as Finn should have remembered, for now, like weasels, young heads popped up behind the grassy bank and stared at him through a fringe of bramble. They were tinker children, of the wandering clan Macafee.

Finn went on, consumed with shame. The children were soon running behind him, laughing mockingly. At first Finn was afraid, but soon his anger began to rise, and when he was sure there were no men with them, he turned and faced the four members of the clan, ranging from his own age downward, one of them a girl. He could see they thought he was silly, and therefore wanted to torment him. But when he had spoken, and picked up two stones from the road, they suddenly broke and ran back, laughing in shrill neighings. Whether it was he who frightened them or the man who came riding on a horse, he never found out.

The number of houses in Wick astonished him, and yet did not much astonish him either. He knew the old joke: you won't be able to see the town for the houses. In his mind Finn could make a famous thing so big that the reality, when he saw it, rarely measured up to his expectations. In any case, the real movement in Finn's mind now was one of fear against so many houses gathered in one place, as if the roofs, huddling together, had a sinister defensive purpose. The fear had in it, however, the tentative smile of shyness, and Finn waited until he saw a small, grey-bearded man in front of a cottage on the outskirts of the town before asking for the doctor's house in his best English.

"Have you no Gaelic?" inquired the old man in that tongue.

"Yes," said Finn, flushing slightly.

"I'll show you where it is, for I'm going that way," and as they went along he questioned Finn.

But Finn was now very unwilling to tell anything about himself or his message, as if by so doing he might let the enemy in on him. The old man did not seem in the least scared of his company. Perhaps in a town, thought Finn, folk were given to asking questions in order to get from one place to another.

"No, it's not for ourselves," replied Finn, "it's for another woman, and I'm just on a message."

"Did you say it was Lybster you came from?" The small dark eyes were quick and curious.

"No, it's farther back a bit. Will the doctor be in, do you think?"

"It'll be Dunster, then. I know the turn of your speech,

248

I was in it once myself, but that was long ago. Well, well. And you have come all that way! Have you many cases of the trouble there?"

"No, not many," said Finn. "Do you think the doctor will be in?"

"If he's not, he will be some time. You look a fine, healthy lad yourself, and long may you be that way."

They came upon houses all stuck together on both sides of the road, with such a press of hurrying people that Finn became confused and self-conscious. The little old man stopped at last. "There's your door. Only two or three cases in Dunster, you say?"

"Yes, thank you very much," said Finn. After all, he was a friendly little man, with his bright, curious eyes, and perhaps so old that he had nothing to do but wonder about death.

As Finn knocked on the door with his knuckles, after a glance at the brass knocker, everything went from his mind but a quivering half-fearful intensity. No-one came to the door. People passed, seeing him standing there. He did not know what to do and felt his body going stiff and queer. The door suddenly opened and a young woman, dressed in dark clothes, with a very white cap on her head, white cuffs, and a small white apron, did not come forward but stood aloofly regarding him. Fortunately, he had his words ready: "Is the doctor in?"

"No."

The rest of his words got scattered.

"Div ye want t' see him?"

"Yes, please."

"He's expeckit back in an 'oor's time."

"When will he be home?" asked Finn, realizing that his English was fabulous.

Her eyes narrowed upon him slightly but with humour. He had such a soft, pleasant voice, and his dark eyes were shy and frightened of her. "I said in aboot an 'oor's time."

Finn now felt desperate. "I want to see him, about my mother."

"Fat's 'e name?"

"Finn," he answered.

She smiled now.

"Far d'ye come fae?"

"Yes, it is a long way," replied Finn.

She gave a little laugh. Finn reddened, body and mind in an agony. An elderly woman's voice called within. "Come back in wan 'oor," said the girl.

Suddenly he understood. "Thank you. I am much obliged to you, M'am."

She was barely seventeen, and he was tall enough to be as old himself. As she closed the door, her eyes threw him a mischievous glance.

When he had separated his head from his heels, he found himself approaching the harbour and soon got so lost in the immense concourse of folk who paid no attention to him that his self-assurance slowly filtered back. He tried not to gape, but his astonishment was very great, particularly at the number of shops and business premises, with their names in big lettering. Once he was caught in a crush of folk in a narrow street and had his bare toes trampled by a seaman's boots. The high tumult of voices speaking and shouting and laughing all at once frightened him, but fascinated him, too. Such a scene his imagination had never pictured. But the harbour itself stopped his breath.

Great stone walls, endless yards and cooperages, immense stacks of barrels, the smell of brine, long wooden jetties, the clanking of hammers, the loud rattling of wheels, warning yells and the cracking of whips, herring-guts, clouds of screaming gulls, women in stiff, rustling skirts, and everywhere men and boats. This was Wick, easy mistress of all the herring fisheries. Her population at the moment was increased by thousands of strangers, not only from Moray Firth ports like Buckie but from far-away townships of the Hebrides.

FINN'S JOURNEY FOR A DOCTOR

By nature Finn would have wished to escape from that tumultuous and even terrifying place—a solitary life could easily get crushed and lost without slackening the onset—were it not for his love of the sea. The harbour basin drew him, and for a time he wandered by the boats, doing his best to note and memorize any peculiarities of construction or colour so that he might have something to discuss with Roddie.

But all this time at the back of his mind was the tremulous fear of going again to the doctor's door. Suddenly he felt he would be too late and hurried away from the harbour. Now, however, he could not find the door. He had lost his way. But the first man he asked told him where to go and—there was the door.

He never told what an heroic effort it cost him to go to that door. From lack of sleep and food and a journey of well over thirty miles on his bare feet, a dragging came to his legs and a prickly heat of weakness to his forehead. But his real terror was lack of English. It was so clear now that Mr. Gordon did not speak in the right way. Sick at heart, but with that frail determination that would not have given in to death, he lifted his hand and knocked.

She smiled, raising her eyebrows in recognition. "He hesna come in yet, but if ye'd care to wait?" She stood aside, and more in answer to her action than her words, he entered.

After an hour in a small waiting-room, with several men and women, all anxious and ill at ease, Finn experienced an increasing light-headedness, and grew afraid he would fall off the chair. Sometimes they spoke to one another, but mostly they sat looking at the door, waiting for the girl to come and call one of them. If only he could have had a long drink of cold water! He grew restless, and an elderly woman asked him if he had come far. "Oh, a little bit," said Finn, smiling but not looking at her. He tried to shut the dumb anxiety of the room, its veiled talk of suffering and sickness, out of mind. He had never conceived life as an imprisoned illness, a closed room. The fear that he might choke and fall off the chair and make a fool of himself started small internal tremors. He sent his thought over the moor, into the wandering wind. The door opened and the girl looked at him.

"Mister Finn," she said, smiling only in her eyes.

He got up too quickly and staggered a step, but gained the door. As she closed it behind her, she looked at him critically. His hands were twisting his round bonnet. She took the bonnet from him. "We'll leave it here," she said, and gave him a smile as if she were one of the girls at home. It was the sensible smile of an ally. As she turned the knob, she kept her face sideways towards him. "Mister Finn," she announced, and then in the friendliest whisper, "in ye go." If she had given him a push behind, it would not have surprised him.

The smell of the surgery cleared Finn's lungs sharply. When he had completed his note, the doctor looked up into Finn's face. "Well?"

"Sir, I have come from Dunster. My mother is in a house with the plague. I thought you might tell me what to do to keep the plague from her."

"Have you walked the whole way?"

"Yes, sir."

The doctor got up. "Sit down there." He went over to a white basin near the window and came back with a glass of cold water. "Drink that. You'll be feeling thirsty after such a long walk. Drink it slowly."

He turned away and did not appear to hear the clink of Finn's teeth on the glass, nor did he see how the glass shook in Finn's hand as he set it down on the edge of the desk. All of which comforted Finn, while the water went down into his stomach like a cool, strengthening rod.

"Now, let me see," said the doctor, looking up from the note he had written, in so natural a way that Finn did not feel frightened of him. "Why did you think of coming to see me?"

"We heard you were the special doctor for the trouble."

"You did?" The doctor touched his top lip with the tip of his tongue thoughtfully. "I see. Well, I will try to help you if I can."

Finn felt a great inrush of confidence, not only because the doctor said he would help him but, more immediately, because the doctor spoke the same kind of English as Mr. Gordon, and spoke it slowly and distinctly.

When Finn was stuck for a word, the doctor found it for him, but casually. Finn, however, could not tell him in what stage of the cholera his Granny was.

"And your mother is still with your Granny, nursing her?"

"Yes, sir."

"I see. Is she doing anything to try to keep the trouble away from herself?"

"She will be washing her hands and her face and she has saltwater for the feet from a man."

"Has she?" The doctor's face brightened. "Who is this man?"

"He's a shoemaker, but he also does the doctoring."

The doctor smiled. "Tell me——" But he was interrupted by a knock on the door. "Come in!" The door opened and a man's head appeared.

"I'm sorry if I——"

"Come in. Here's a young man who has walked thirty miles to see you. Your fame has spread!"

The new-comer looked quickly at Finn, and the doctor, getting to his feet, began explaining. They drifted to the window.

"I wanted to see you before going to Thurso. I'm off in an hour," said the new-comer, speaking quickly. "Whisky, whisky, and if it's not whisky it's smuggled brandy! Is this the universal specific up here? We'll have to wean them off that. I am more than ever satisfied that in the treatment of the preliminary diarrhœa—they *will* call it 'the dysentery'!—the combination of calomel and Dover's powders is *the* thing. I have now tested the calomel and opium separately and combined—definitely not so good. And if you want to keep your fishing going, we must get the people to understand that diarrhœa is not cholera—though it may become cholera if not treated properly and at once. This is very important and we must get it noised abroad. Give the powders and stop the number of stools, then a damn' good sweat and they'll be all right. Let your anxious fish-curers put that around if they want to go on making money! And if only at the same time they could tell them about ventilation—at any and every stage. But the marquee should be an object lesson there. The whole thing arises out of uncleanliness and lack of proper sanitary arrangements. I am convinced——"

"I wonder!" interrupted the doctor. "I admit that in a place like Wick the thousands of incomers have congested living conditions beyond all reason, but in the country, where they're dying in scores, living conditions are as they've always been. And the people are over all a strong, healthy crowd——"

"Yes, yes, but I mean once you introduce the infection. However, we'll argue that again! But I'm particularly optimistic at the moment because the Cormack case is re-acting favourably. He was blue, cold, no pulse, and sense-less, and now he's pulling round under the compound de-coction sarsaparilla. You're taking notes? Grand! I'm going to do the pamphlet along the lines of the four stages: pre-monitory, cold stage, collapse, typhoid stage. . . ."

While this talk was going on, Finn kept his attention to the table beside him so that it might not appear he was rudely listening. There was a white slip of paper on this table, under his eyes, containing the following writing:

> Calomel, grs. 20;
> Pulv. Doveri, grs. 15 to 20;
> ——Gum Kino, drm. $\frac{1}{2}$;
> ——Catechu, scr. 1;
> ——Cretæ Comp. drm. 1;
> Powders, 12.

As Finn could make no sense of this "English", he was again being troubled by the greatness of his ignorance, when the specialist suddenly exclaimed: "But Lord, I must run and you're busy! Give this boy the powders and keep a record of what happens. Results in country cases may be interesting." He paused and looked at Finn on his way to the door. "Have you seen your mother treating the case?"

The doctor was about to intervene, when Finn said hesitatingly, "I saw her burying something in a hole."

"Did you? What was it?"

"I thought it was stuff from—from my Granny."

"Was it? By God, she seems an intelligent woman!"

Finn thought none the less of the specialist because he took God's name in vain. The doctor said, "I'm going to hand him over to my wife. They can tear the tartan between them." And, after taking leave of the specialist who had come into the county to study the disease, this he did.

She was about the age of Finn's mother, graceful in her movements, with a slow, pleasant smile, and at the sound of her voice, he felt shy to respond, his own Gaelic, before he spoke, being harsh in his mind. But she led him to describe his home, and what had happened, and how he had walked through the night at his own impulse. In a short time she had him almost at his ease.

She left the room and returned with two packets of powders and began explaining to him how they were to be taken, how often, and when. "This packet here is for your Granny—because her case is advanced. I'll write 'Granny' on it. And this is for your mother—and, remember, she must take the powders at the very first signs of the dysentery. If it is not very bad, she'll take one about every two hours. But if it's very bad, she'll take one every half-hour. Now let me hear if you have got that right?"

Finn repeated her instructions correctly.

She then told him about bathing the feet in warm salt-water, the importance of raising a good sweat, the need for fresh air inside the house, and other simple precautions.

"When the trouble is gone from the house, your mother must burn all the dirtied clothes. If the clothes are too good to burn, she must boil them in the big iron pot for at least two hours. You understand? Then you'll take all the furniture outside, everything, and leave it for two or three days to air. Then you'll scrub out every corner and whitewash the walls. Only in that way can you be sure of getting rid of the trouble, so that anyone coming into the house will not catch it. Have you got that?"

But Finn could not answer. A brightness was in his eyes. "Do you mean," he asked, with a slight gulp, "do you mean—we won't have to burn down the house?"

"You won't," she said, and the slow, lovely smile came to her face.

"Mother will be glad of that." He flushed and began repeating her instructions.

She complimented him. "And now, won't you need a rest before you start back?"

"Oh, no, M'am. I'll be going now."

"You'll have something to eat, and then we'll see."

"I'll be going now, if you would not mind." He wanted to be off, running. But he did not wish to appear rude. He felt awkward, standing and smiling, the precious packets gripped in his hands. As she remained silent, looking at him, his awkwardness increased, for his eyes were anywhere but on her face. "I'll take the coast road back, and that's much shorter. I won't be long."

"What road did you come?"

He explained how he had taken the roundabout way through the moors to Watten. From there he could have gone either to Thurso or Wick. In this way he was letting her see how sensible he was. He had heard in Watten that the doctor was more likely to be in Wick.

She got up abruptly and left the room, and his heart sank. He must have been rude. Perhaps it was even a greater rudeness here than at home not to accept hospitality, particularly when on a journey. Distress got hold of him. He would do anything for this woman or the doctor, the most desperate thing. Why was she not coming back? What would he do? Perhaps she was telling the doctor! As he began to stow away the two packets, he suddenly paused and regarded them with dismay. It might not have occurred to him that he would have to pay for the doctor's advice, but these real powders . . . !

The door opened and she entered with a smile.

"Here is a packet of sandwiches for the road, seeing you cannot stay for a meal. I quite understand your hurry to be home."

He accepted the sandwiches but remained in an intense awkwardness, making no effort to move. "I forgot," he said in a low voice, "that—that—I forgot—I have no money." Then he raised his face and looked past her. She saw that his teeth were shut against the movement of his features. "We have money," he said, "at home. I—I'll come back to-morrow."

She looked as if she might walk out abruptly again, but the doctor appeared in the doorway and glanced at his wife's eyes. Her mouth gave a humoured twist that he knew, and she remarked, "He forgot all about money. He says he will walk back to-morrow with it."

There was a moment's silence. "Good God," he said. "Haven't I told you the soft disease your folk will die of? Tell him," he added, with a wry humour, "that we usually send a bill." He turned to Finn and stretched out his hand. "Good-bye. If you save your mother, it'll cost you nothing." And away he went.

Then she stretched out her hand. Finn called on his last resources, looked at her eyes, and thanked her. After that he did not see anything very distinctly, until Wick was behind him.

CHAPTER XIII

ORDEAL BY PLAGUE

❧

When Catrine heard the ghost-voice calling "Mother", she turned her head and saw her son's face, ghostly enough, in the dim night-light. He came to within a few yards of her and stopped.

"I have come back from Wick," he said. "I saw the doctor. Two doctors. I havé got the stuff here, Mother, and I want you to understand how to use it." His voice was eager. She leaned against the door-jamb. Something in her attitude struck him. "How is Granny?"

"She has just died."

There was a silence. "How are you yourself?" he asked at last.

"I'm fine."

"Don't give in, Mother." His low voice rose like aı urgent cry. "Don't you give in. Listen to me." He came nearer, but she gestured him off.

The urgency in his voice caught an edge of distress, almost of anger. He began to explain the use of the powders. He emphasized the instruction "at the very first signs" of "the dysentery". He repeated it. As he carried himself beyond the knowledge of his Granny's death, his tone grew commanding. "Do you understand that?"

"Yes."

"Don't give in, Mother." Now he was fighting for her. He knew she could not speak. "The powders will cure any-one, the doctor said. You must think of yourself now, Mother. There's nothing else to do. It's no good giving in. I'll lay them here. Come and take them."

She stepped slowly from the door and lifted the two packets. He explained that one had Granny written on it. That packet was for "the advanced stage". She would not need to use that.

She wept as she turned to the door and gripped the jamb, her back to him. The tears started streaming down his own face, but he stood still and silent.

When her mind was cleared she faced him again. A profound intimacy flowed between them. An eagerness as of happiness went mounting into his head.

"Do you know what they told me besides?"

She waited.

"We won't have to burn down the house!"

It was while he was explaining what had to be done to the house "when it was all over" that she found her voice, and the intimacy between them developed quickly into an air of conspiracy, of hope. They grew eager. Their voices trembled. They smiled.

He told her of the kindness of the doctor's wife and the sandwiches of white bread with meat in them. "The bread was white as snow. Oh, it was good! I went in over a dyke just this side of Bruan and began to eat it, and I couldn't stop until I had eaten it all. Then I'm thinking I fell asleep, though it didn't seem a minute."

He had never spoken to her like this since they herded the cows together on the braes, and when he gave a small chuckle, she responded, urging him on, drinking in his words, like parched land a warm rain.

Presently he said, "Listen, I'll tell you what I'll do, Mother: I'll sleep in the little barn to-night and then if you need me I'll be at hand."

"No, no, you'll go to Roddie's and get a great sleep. You need that, and I'll see you in the morning. I'm not frightened to be with Granny now. After all, Finn, she was kind to us. And wait till I tell you." And she told him of the letter and the money that she had put behind a loose stone just round the barn door on the right. "It's about as high as your shoulder and the second stone. Wasn't that kind of Granny?"

"It was, indeed," said Finn.

"It's not only mine. It's yours. And no-one else's. You understand that?"

"Yes," he said quietly.

"Well, now, you must away. Poor lad, you must be sleeping on your feet. But, oh, you'll never know what good you did to me! I'll do everything you told me. I promise that. Now go, and good night to you, Finn."

Finn got up—and stood silent. Then he said, "I want to sleep in the little barn."

It was the old moody voice of the child. She could have laughed. "I have been out and in there too much. No, no, we mustn't spoil everything now. So off you go. And I'll be looking for you in the morning."

"Are you sure—you won't be frightened?"

"No, no. Off you go."

"All right, then."

"Finn!"

The moodiness went from his voice, as he said again, "All right. Good night, Mother."

"Good night, Finn."

She watched him disappear, and stole down to the byre-end to see if she could get one more glimpse of him.

Now that the tension had relaxed, Finn felt extremely tired and could hardly drag his feet up the steep slope by the wood. Once he had to stop, his heart was beating so strongly, more than after any race he had ever run. When he drew near Roddie's house, he paused and sat down on a heap of stones, withdrawn into the dark of the night. If he went into the house, he would only wake them all up. Instead, he could slip into the barn and curl up in the straw; then he could tell them what had happened in the morning.

His Granny was dead. He should tell them now; should tell Roddie, anyway. There was such a great reluctance on him to do this, that he sat on the stones until he began to

shiver and his head to droop. As he came by the house the
dog growled inside and gave a suppressed bark. He was a
young dog and not well trained.

Impelled by a strange numbness, he lifted the latch
of the door and entered quietly. At once Mrs. Sinclair's
voice, low but clear, came from the kitchen: "Is that
you, Finn?"

She was back in the kitchen bed with her husband, and a
part of Finn's mind wondered if they had left it so that
Roddie could raise the neid-fire. It was very dark, and he
could not see the bed. "How did you get on?" she asked
anxiously.

"Fine. Granny is no more."

"O sorrow on us!" she cried in a broken voice, and
uttered other sad words.

"When did the change come?" asked the old man.

"A little ago," answered Finn.

Then he heard Roddie stirring in the next room. Mrs.
Sinclair was for getting up to make something hot for Finn,
but he said he had eaten plenty and would not hear of it.
Roddie came behind him in the dark and said, "It's all
right, Mother. I'll go over."

Back in the darkness of the inner room, Roddie asked
Finn questions, and got quiet answers, as he drew on his
clothes. "Now, boy," he said in a kind but sensible voice,
"you slip into my warm place and I'll go over and watch
the house through the darkness and see that everything is
all right."

"I'm not tired," said Finn.

"You must be," said Roddie. "That was a terrific journey in the time. You've done all you could, if any boy ever
did it."

When Roddie went out, Finn began taking off his
clothes. There was now so terrible a lethargy upon him
that he could hardly move his arms. His mother should
have let him sleep in the little barn. He shouldn't have
come back here to Roddie's. He should have kept watch

himself. Roddie would be over yonder now, talking to his mother.

All the anxiety, the keenness, the hope that led him on—all went blank in his mind, like a blown-out flame. He felt lonely and outcast. He was terribly tired. His eyes filled and the tears spilled over. His mouth smothered a sob in the bolster and, letting his world go, he sank slowly into the sleep of exhaustion.

In the evening six men brought a black coffin and left it on the bier by the doorstep; then they withdrew a few yards and, led by Sandy Ware, engaged in worship. From where he lay hidden in the bushes, Finn recognized the men, including Roddie. There were some old women, with black shawls round their heads, at a little distance. When the voices rose in the metrical version of Psalm cxxi: "I to the hills will lift mine eyes," Catrine appeared. Eyes glanced at her and the singing died down. As she stooped and, lifting one end of the coffin, began drawing it into the house, the singing swelled. Finn heard the high keening cries of the dark women. The sight of his mother, clear in her purpose, fine in her courage, affected him so strongly that he gripped the withies and bit on the grass.

During the morning he had felt quiet and kept to himself. This seemed natural enough and, anyway, Roddie was making arrangements for a hurried funeral and was absent most of the day. In the afternoon, he had curled up on top of the knoll in the House of Peace. There was a weary, drugged feeling in his body, as if tiredness from the journey was only now overtaking him.

Late in the evening he was careful to see his mother alone. She was so pale and quiet in her manner that her smile was at once very friendly and yet detached.

" You're not worrying about me, are you?" she asked.

"No."

"That's good, because there's no need—not so far," and she glanced at him. There was a humour in her glance, per-

262

sonal to them both, like a game of understanding. Finn felt
deeply heartened.

When they had spoken for a little time, she said, "There
may be one or two keeping the wake during the night, but I
would like you to come by yourself in the early morning. I
would like to have you near me. Could you do that?"

"Yes," said Finn. "Of course."

After that he met Roddie and was happier with him than
he had been for a long time. Some of the old admiration
came back.

"If your mother doesn't object, you must come to sea
with the skimmer. Would you like that?"

"I would," answered Finn at once.

The dry, crinkling smile came to Roddie's eyes. "Special
is getting anxious!"

Finn suddenly remembered that Roddie should have been
at sea and looked at him.

"I made the others go without me," remarked Roddie.

Finn looked down. He was strangely moved. Roddie had
stayed to help his mother.

Between three and four in the morning he relieved
Roddie. "Your mother must be asleep, I think," Roddie said,
"so don't make much noise. I'll turn in for an hour or two."

Finn was glad to be alone in the thin bright light of the
early morning, and listened to a singing lark and looked
now and then at the house. Presently his mother appeared.
She had wakened from a few hours' deep sleep and her hair
was rumpled. There was a faint flush in her face. She was
obviously pleased when she found he was all alone.

After they had talked awhile, she said, "I put Granny
in her coffin last night. Poor Granny, she wasn't heavy.
Then I put the lid on and fitted in the nails. But I can't turn
them far. They're sticking up."

"Wait," said Finn, thinking quickly. "What about taking the coffin out now? It's a fine morning and certainly
won't rain before the funeral."

"Yes," Catrine agreed, "we might do that. I'll try and drag it out. I have it on chairs beside the bed."

"Wait," said Finn. "You mustn't strain yourself." He ran down to the little barn and returned with a large round ball of heather rope. With Finn hauling on the rope and Catrine pushing on her knees, they brought the coffin finally through the door and on to the bier, which Finn had set all ready. "We'll take it over the grass a short way," said Finn, and bent to the rope on his shoulder like a young horse.

"Now I'll tidy up and get everything ready," said Catrine, and with a smile to her son hurried back into the house.

After looking at the nails, Finn wandered down to the barn and returned with Kirsty's reaping hook. It was thin enough near the point to fit the slot in the nail, and Finn was giving a last turn to the last nail when the point bent a second time. As he straightened it between two stones it broke. He gazed at it in dismay. He had been happy because of the eager living look that had come into his mother's face. The blade was worn almost to the backbone. It was done for now. He gazed at the black box and his fear, his hidden hatred, of it parted like a dark mist and he thought: poor Granny! and all but wept.

The burial-ground was over three miles away and men bore the coffin on its long-handled bier upon their shoulders, relieving one another at short intervals. Roddie had provided whisky and oatcake and cheese, and as he poured each man a dram after the interment, Finn came behind him with the bread and cheese. It was the old custom, and the bearers needed the refreshment. The parish minister who had conducted the service outside the house, needed it more than most, for he was hardly off his feet these black days. They spoke soberly, with the restraint that suggested they would go on burying the dead as long as two of them were left. No frightfulness of death would break their strength. Finn felt this, the quiet communion of men. No women ever came to the graveyard.

As Roddie and Finn returned in the late afternoon—for they had helped with another funeral—they half expected to see some of the furniture outside Catrine's door. There was, however, no sign of life. She appeared in the doorway as they approached, looking pinched and ill, but smiling, and warned them off. "I've been scrubbing and I'm tired. I'm going to bed to sleep without waking. Don't disturb me till the morning. But I'll tell you one thing I've taken a fancy for: dulse. I'm longing for something tonic like that. Bring it in salt-water."

They laid a bucket full of dulse and sea-water quietly by the door in the late evening. They said to each other that the request was a hopeful sign, but Finn wondered why she had wanted salt-water.

All morning there was no sight of her. They shifted the stock and at last went to the front of the house. At the kitchen window Finn called, "Are you there, Mother?"

Presently a drowsy voice answered him. She hadn't yet had enough sleep.

In the afternoon they saw fresh blue smoke, and to Finn it had a calm and magical appearance. His heart rose with the swoop of a bird.

But when his mother came to the door in the evening she was haggard.

"I'm all right," she said, and smiled. But a certain wistful look in her eyes cut him like a knife. "Please leave me alone for a while, Finn. I'm so tired."

He had never really thought his mother would get the plague. His mother could not die. Now he saw that she could die, like Kirsty or anyone else. This was a terrible revelation, and when it met the rebellion that opposed it the crash left his body and mind strewn about, with raw bits squirming now and then. Like a stricken animal, he headed blindly for his private sanctuary, and, curled up in the shadows by the round ring of stones, he prayed that his mother would recover, not in words, but in the intensities that words destroy.

In the morning, as Roddie and himself moved towards the wood to get a glimpse of the house, Finn could hardly drag his legs along. Would the white signal be up? His mind's eye saw it.

It was not up.

Neither of them referred to it.

His mother called from inside, "I'm not up yet." She did not come to the door. They heard her trying to make her voice cheerful.

She would not put the signal up—until she was too weak to do it.

That evening, she was still in bed. She asked about the beasts, and had a fit of coughing from the shrill way in which she had to raise her voice.

Neither Finn nor Roddie could go to bed.

In the deep gloaming Finn went to the window. "We're always watching beside you, Mother."

"My darling boy."

Listening, they thought they heard her weeping.

"I'm going in," said Finn to Roddie.

Roddie's face drew firm. He beckoned sideways with his head and Finn followed him.

"You cannot go in," he said. "You know that."

"Why? I'm not afraid."

Roddie looked at him, his cheek-bones smooth as bossed stone, his eyes cold as glass. "It's not you, Finn boy, I was thinking of," he said quietly.

Finn, slim and straight, looked past Roddie, his eyes glancing. All at once he started for the door. Roddie caught his shoulder. Finn whirled it away. They stared at each other eye to eye.

"No," said Roddie. "You can't do that."

"She's my mother," said Finn, glancing past Roddie again, his throat choking with excitement. "I'm going to help her."

Roddie got in his way.

"Let me go," said Finn, his voice rising in anger. "Get out of my way!"

"Not so loud," said Roddie. "Think of your mother."

"She's my mother," said Finn, driving past him.

Roddie held him and Finn struggled wildly, almost losing control of himself. Roddie bore him away in his arms, writhing and fighting.

"Listen, Finn. If you went in, what would your mother say? Damn it, boy, listen to me. Have sense. Do you want to go in and break her heart?"

Finn stood away from him, quivering, his face blood-flushed, his eyes on fire.

"It's nothing for you or me to go in. That's easy. But what would your mother say? If she has the plague, God damn it, man, would it make her end easy to think she had given it to you, her son?" A deadly impatience was in Roddie's voice. His hands were clenched, his shoulders slightly hunched; his eyes had their cold glitter.

Finn hardly heard his words, yet understood them as he might understand unspoken truth. They defeated his purpose, made him tremble, wretched and uncertain, and therefore none the less angry.

"We can't leave her there." His voice cracked. Roddie appeared to think for a moment, then nodded and said in a normal voice, "Perhaps not. Very well. I'll go in and see how she really is." And he turned on his heel and walked towards the door.

For a moment Finn could not move, but by the time Roddie was at the door Finn was at his back. Roddie's hand had lifted the sneck and he was turning to repel Finn, when suddenly it was as if his own hand had spoken to him. He looked at it in astonishment. The door was barred on the inside.

"What do you want?" cried Catrine's voice.

"We were just wondering if we could help you," said Roddie.

"Oh, why don't you go away and leave me for a little? Why——?" Her voice broke in bitter desperation. "Go away and leave me. I'm all right."

"All right, Catrine." Roddie looked at Finn and beckoned him with his head to speak.

"We were wondering, Mother, if we couldn't do something."

"You can do nothing, Finn—except leave me alone until the morning. Then I'll speak to you. Don't make it hard for me."

Finn had the awful feeling that she had overheard the struggle between Roddie and himself. He knew by her voice that she had got out of bed and was standing not far from the door. A deep shame burned his body.

Neither looked at the other nor spoke as they went down towards the burn, where they encountered Wull. Glancing at their faces, Wull said he was sorry to hear the sad news about Catrine.

"What news?" asked Roddie.

Wull glanced at Roddie and became embarrassed. "I didn't know. I heard—— It's—it's sort of everywhere and you can hardly help believing the worst. Did you hear that Margad is dead?"

"No," said Roddie.

Margad was the witch, and that she should die like any ordinary mortal seemed, even at that moment, a dark and astonishing event.

"Yes," said Wull. "A terrible end she had. They had not seen smoke from her chimney for two or three days and sent word to her daughter, Lexy. When Lexy went in she found her lying on the floor, dead, her face half-eaten away. She got into an awful state. Then she saw the black cat, with eyes burning like coals of fire. Suddenly the cat flew at her. They heard her screaming as far away as James-o'-Lachlan's. I saw her hand and neck myself where the claws tore her."

He shook his head. "Terrible times." They all stood silent.

As Roddie and Finn went up by the wood the macabre in the story drew them into talk.

"Perhaps she had no food in the house," said Roddie.

Horror at the cat's ghastly meal emptied Finn's mind.

"I feel I could do with a dram." Roddie stopped. "You wait here and I'll slip into the house."

When he came back he drew a black bottle of "special" from the cross pocket in his trousers and handed it to Finn. "Take a swig," he said, "and swallow it gently."

Finn did this and coughed until the water ran from his eyes. It was the first time he had ever tasted whisky.

Roddie smiled and put the bottle to his mouth. When he had taken a good swig, he said, after a gentle clearing of his throat, "You know fine, Finn boy, that I would do anything for your mother or yourself."

"I know that," said Finn.

Without looking at the boy's proud mouth as it trembled, Roddie said, "Take another wee swig: it'll do you no harm."

Finn was more careful this time. "It fairly burns its way down." He smiled uncertainly.

"I'll have a small one to keep you company, as Special says."

It was after eight o'clock in the morning, when they approached the edge of the wood. Two hours before, the signal had not been up. Now they were going to the house. Half an hour ago, Roddie had privately told Shiela, who was constantly calling for news, that he had no hope.

The first thing Finn saw was the morning smoke curling from the roof. Life, anyway. And then they stopped as if their feet had been gripped. Hanging on to the tether of the red cow, her back against the brute's inheritance of old Bel's wilfulness, was—there could be no doubt about it, no doubt in the wide world—was Catrine herself.

Roddie's throat muttered something that neither of them heard, for they lived for that moment in their gaping eyes. And there was Shiela, climbing up through the bushes from the burn, as if escaping from the water-kelpie itself. And yelling, too, for they could hear her.

Whereupon Bel the Second did a wilful dance: down with her head, up with her hind legs, off flew the tether and high went her tail. There was commotion all over the croft. While dog and cow continued their intricate dance midfield, Shiela, leaning on the stone dyke, called Catrine towards her.

Still Roddie and Finn stood staring. What next? Soon it came. Laughter. Not melodious laughter, but high-pitched squalls of it, shrieks. They saw Catrine double up and lean weakly against the dyke.

"Seems to be a joke of some sort," said Roddie. The truth is they were almost embarrassed, and hardly knew where to look or what to do next, while their eyes glanced brilliantly and their smiles deepened to a warm blood-flush.

The joke was simple enough, but it was heightened in effect by the peculiar circumstances. Catrine had made a dulse soup, knowing her body needed some specific of the sort, but shortly thereafter the two dread symptoms of "the plague", retching and diarrhœa, had assailed her with some violence.

She explained the whole affair to Shiela in detail. She had started taking the powders that Finn had brought. "After the turn of the night, I awoke from a doze, pouring with sweat." Then she went to sleep again and awoke "feeling fine". "If it wasn't the plague," cried Catrine, "it must have been the—the dulse soup!" for they both knew what dulse soup, with a bit of butter, could do. Catrine leaned against the wall. She had lost weight and was as weak as a kitten, but she was well.

CHAPTER XIV

OUT TO SEA

❧

"**G**ive way then, boys," said Roddie quietly, and the four of his crew lay on their oars. There was a crowd on the beach seeing them off, for this was the first time a Dunster boat was to venture beyond the Moray Firth. They were bound for Stornoway, and it was a brilliant morning, with an air of wind off the land. Green had come through the grey of winter, for it was the beginning of May, and a waft of wood-smoke from a cooper's fire brought the smell of summer, as if they were setting sail for it. Finn, whose seventeenth birthday was behind him, kept his eyes sometimes on his mother and sometimes on a dark-eyed girl, while he pulled a slow stroke on his heavy sweep. All at once old Special on the crest of the beach lifted his fist and cried, "Hurrah!" Young men and boys were glad of the chance to show how loud they could shout. The crew smiled in a self-conscious manner. Then Finn saw his mother turn her face away and a man, a stranger, come through the crowd from behind and shake hands with her.

Finn could feel the astonishment in that meeting, emphasized as it was by the way folk turned their heads. It was a particularly dramatic moment for Catrine, who, under the vivid impulse from an old memory (her husband, Tormad, had set out from a beach), had had to avert her gaze to master her emotion—and had stared straight into the face of a man who was looking at her. The man came forward.

"Ronnie!" she breathed.

He had always been quiet and retiring in manner, with

271

grey, intelligent eyes. Catrine had known he had been fond of her. The face was older, with a scar on the side of the right temple, rather distinguished-looking, as if circumstance had etched it firmly and given it an easy poise. But it was the same face, and in particular the same grey eyes.

Catrine was completely, pitifully bewildered, and after shaking hands, stared away to sea again.

When they had gone out some little distance, they got all the wind there was and, shipping their oars, hoisted both fore-lugsail and after-lugsail, and laid their course on Clyth Ness or Clyth Head.

It was pleasant to hear the water lapping and slapping against the bows. One would think the boat herself loved it, for if her head dipped it was only to rise again and be on, as a runner who trips will the more quickly speed. In fact, if you kept your eyes on the peak of the stem you got the impression that, whether it rose or fell, its attention was exclusively fixed on the far horizon. The quiver of eagerness ran along her sides to the rudder, the sensitive rudder that sent the impulse to Roddie's hand, the firm hand under the head whose eyes were on the same horizon.

Pleasant it was to see the land slipping by and the headland of home slowly closing on the stores, the yards, the beach, the river-mouth, like a gate closing in a dream until all their kindred were shut off, leaving them to adventure in the great expanses of the world.

"Well, we're off, boys!" said Callum "We'll have a snuff for——"

"The fun of the thing," said Rob, interrupting him, because he believed it did fishermen no good to be wished luck. They smiled slowly, for there was no hurry and life was long. The sails were drawing nicely and if the wind kept up after the turn of the tide, they would have to put off time to get the first of the ebb through the dreaded entrance to the Pentland Firth. Beyond Clyth Head the seaways would be new to them all, and they had neither watch

272

nor compass. So they had to rely on themselves, and that
was an encouraging thought. If knowledge of their passage
depended on hearsay, well, they had a fair amount of that.
Rob, in fact, was full of it. Where he managed to gather his
vast miscellany of information was a mystery to them all,
after making allowances for imagination.

Sitting on top of the nets, Finn looked at the land, saw
croft houses he knew grow so small that a giant could have
picked them up with his hand and thrown them away. Very
still was the land, and somehow a little sad, held to its own
dream, and never able to move out of the bit.

He half listened to Rob telling a story about the laird,
for along the great rock wall at intervals were castles,
occupied or in ruins. This laird, owner of Dunster, and of
many other lands in Caithness, was an extreme miser and
eccentric. "Sandy Ware, the godly man, had been telling
the people that the earth is the Lord's and the fullness
thereof, but I'll show him and them that Dunster is not the
Lord's but mine," was one of his sayings. He had succeeded
John of Freswick, known widely for his gift of the second
sight, and, having studied medicine and being dark, was
called "the Black Doctor". He moved about in order to
get as much hospitality as possible, but for a long spell at
Dunster he conceived the brilliant idea of cutting down
expenditure to the very minimum by staying in bed and
subsisting entirely on cold sowans (a gruel drawn off the
husks of milled grain). For housekeeper he had Black
Nance, an old woman as eccentric as himself, and when he
had to eat he called her to his bedroom where he kept the
cask of sowans under his eye. When she handed him the
bowl, he supped it greedily, leaving so little for her that
her hunger was merely given edge. Then he closed his
eyes, and when Nance thought he was asleep she would
steal to the barrel. In his bed beside him he kept a long,
black stick, and as Nance stooped over the barrel, down
would come the stick on her head with a hefty crack. It
was his only pastime and he was very cunning at it. Nance

told her troubles to the kindly women of the neighbour-
hood and they would give her food, particularly cheese-
crusts or rinds, of which she was fond. Rob's story concerned the occasion when Nance came to his mother's
house and went away with the whole heel of a cheese. The
Black Doctor was sound asleep and Nance, before his bedroom fire, for there was no other in his mansion, began
toasting the cheese, and was so comforted by the good
food that she fell asleep. "The nostrils of the black fellow
began to twitch in his sleep. He wakened. Ha, what was
this? He slipped quietly out of bed and over to Nance. The
last mouthful of the cheese was going down his gullet when
she awoke. There was the row then! Shaking her fist at
him, she cries, 'No wonder I dreamt the black dog was
upon me!' . . ."

Henry said, "Ay, ay", in his dry, satiric way. "I think
he is nothing but a dirty hound, and if we had any guts in
us we would pitch him over his own rocks, the bastard."

Finn looked at the rocks, the great cliff wall that ran to
Clyth Head, and thought of the Black Doctor's body turning over and over as it plunged downward into the sea, or
smashed on the skerries, where at the moment cormorants
were sitting in the sun with outspread wings like small
black eagles.

He knew why Henry was sore. For the Black Doctor had
driven Henry's people from the pleasant valley lands far up
the green windings of the strath, had cleared them out to
make room for sheep, just as the Earl of Sutherland had
evicted Finn's own kindred from Kildonan and Strathnaver.
Finn could see the new line of cottages by the edge of the
cliff that ran into the headland guarding the bay where
Henry and his inland folk now lived. He remembered how
silent Kirsty and his mother had been on the day when that
bitter clearance took place, as if they were afraid it might
be anyone's turn next. When their rent was put up, they
made no protest.

The strange, dark deeds that could take place on the

land! The year of the plague itself, what a horror, with the
hundreds of dead! And yet he had to admit that in the midst
of it life continued in its own secret ways and he had known
moments of great happiness—particularly when his mother
had got better and he had gone back to live at home. The
harvest, the bringing in of the last sheaf, which his mother
dressed up, the whisky he had produced as the man of the
house, and the grand ceilidh there was afterwards. Often
out of depression a wild gaiety comes upon the spirit. . . .
But the worst time of all, when he had felt the awful power,
the terror, of authority, arose out of the claim by Kirsty's
brother in Elgin, as oldest son of the family, to all the
goods and belongings, the croft itself and, in particular, to
whatever money had been left at the moment of Kirsty's
death. His mother and himself had known one or two nights
of dread then! And that because, in their bones, they felt
the legitimacy of the claim, the blood claim that should
override any other. Catrine had not only astonished him by
her hard, unyielding spirit, but by a cunning that had no
softness in it anywhere. He had expected her to ask the
advice of some of the wise old men—in short, to tell Roddie
the whole circumstances and get him to fight for her. But,
no! One evening she dressed herself carefully and, taking
Finn with her, set out for Mr. Gordon's. "Not a word to anyone till we see where we are. Mind that. You wait here."

She was fighting their own fight! And when she appeared
an hour later, Finn, careful to be at a little distance, turned
his back, because Mr. Gordon was with her. He walked on
slowly, fearing that the schoolmaster might call him, feeling nervous and shy. But in a little while Catrine came on
alone, and when he glanced at her face he thought it beautiful even though it was his own mother's. There was a faint
flush in her cheeks, her eyes were shining, and her lips—
as always when she was gay or excited—were full of fresh
blood.

"I think it will be all right," she said, not looking at
him, head up and eyes front, as if they were returning from

an ordinary visit and any curious onlooker could see there was nothing unusual on hand.

But Finn knew there was something very unusual, and that night it came out. At first Mr. Gordon thought she had no claim at all. She could see he was sorry, but in law the next of kin. . . . And then she had mentioned the letter. "What?" said he sharply. When he had read it, he laughed. "You would think I had given him a present! He tried to explain about Scots law and the value of a letter written in one's own hand. He's a fine man. I never knew he was so nice. He took a copy of the letter. 'I'll write them,' he said. 'You may leave it to me. But cleave to that letter as you would to your life.' Isn't it fine of him? Do you like him, Finn?"

"Yes, I get on all right with him."

"So then I told him everything. What the old man had said, when he was dying. What Kirsty had said, and how she had already told the brother the old man's wishes. And then—I told him of the money.

" 'Very good! Very good! Tell not a living soul.' He rubbed his hands. Then he became thoughtful and he looked at me. I wondered what was coming. 'I do not wish to intrude on your private affairs, Mistress McHamish,' he said, 'and if you do not care to tell me the total sum, you need not. But I have a particular reason for asking!' I knew I could trust him, so I told him it was forty-one sovereigns. He nodded several times. And then said, 'It's enough'."

His mother had hesitated and looked into the fire. "Oh, Finn," she went on, still regarding the fire, "he then said something to me and I did not know what to answer. He said you were his most promising scholar. He said he would take you in hand privately himself with Latin and—and other things. He said the money was enough to—to—send you to the University at Aberdeen. That's what he said." A break had troubled her voice as if she had been about to cry, and she smiled in a strange way. She wiped her nose in the white handkerchief she had specially taken with her. "He asked me to talk it over with you, and let him know."

Finn sat silent. Then his mother turned her head, her soul in her eyes. "Finn, would you?"

He got up, feeling queer and troubled. Her eyes followed him about. "No, I don't want that," he said, miserable and angry.

"You wouldn't think it over? There's no hurry."

"No, I won't," and he walked out of the house.

For two days he hardly spoke to his mother. On the third she said that they could not go on like this. Then very reasonably she told him the position a University education would give him, compared with all this drudgery on poor land. It was for his own good, and the money had come like a sign from heaven.

"And who would do the drudgery when I'm away?"

"It would be nothing to me, Finn. And I could get someone to help me. I was thinking of my brother Augus's oldest son, Alastair . . ." She had it all thought out! She had it all thought out to the very manse where, when she was an old woman (persuasive humour crept into her voice here) she would come and pay him a visit.

Again his feeling grew dull and angry. He would not look at her. She did not give in easily. "All right, then, Finn. Only I thought . . ." And she would come at him in another way, her voice warm, not pressing him, but painting a picture, suggesting what might be, if only . . . until he could stand it no more. As he walked out, she opened her hands to the fire, not to gather its warmth, but to let her short-lived dream go. In face and eyes the new flame was blown out.

It was late before he came home that night, and he was disappointed to find her still up, for he slept now in the middle room. She greeted him naturally and offered to get him something to eat. But he muttered he was not hungry and was going to bed.

"Listen, Finn," she said in a calm voice. "You and I will have to solve our troubles now as best we can, so let us be sensible always. You would like to carry on with the croft?"

"Yes."

"And—perhaps when you are a little older—go to the sea?"

"Yes."

"All right, then. I would never stand in your way. You must know that. I was thinking when you were out that the money would come in very handy, for you would have to buy your own share of nets and perhaps your own share in a new boat. For that, whatever money you need, it is yours."

Then, for the third time, he walked out, but this time into his bedroom. He sat on his bed for a long time, profoundly moved, blinded. Against opposition and difficulty he could struggle dourly, unyieldingly, but against generosity he as yet knew no defence. Not that he thought of giving in. He did not think about it at all, for their quarrel was a small issue in face of this generous greatness that sat in the heart of his mother.

Sailing along the coast of one's native land was a new way of reading its history, a detached way, so that instead of being embroiled in it, one looked on. The page, too, was large.

Here the castle itself, there the ruin, yonder the parish church, and everywhere the croft houses. Morven—the sailor's landfall—was as clear in outline as the nipple of the Pap before it. The long, slow sweeps of the land rose and fell; one saw their beginning and their end, the ultimate horizon line of moor, the near gully that fell into the sea.

The other members of the crew were also caught into this pleasant detachment. The wind was holding, though Roddie looked now and then at the sky whose blue was too dark for his fancy. In his view, the morning sun had been

over-brilliant; like the brilliance after frost, which is inclined to draw mist and fluky weather. But so far they could
not have got a better day, the boat breaking through the
short waves with enlivening speed, living up to her name
by leaving foam in her wake.

This was what Catrine could not understand—this fel-
lowship of men. Who would barter it for intrigue and miser-
liness and cruelty and law-suits and manses, all that is bred
out of the urge for positions of importance? If people strove
to be important like that, let them! But leave Finn with his
own kind, where his heart grew warm. This was a profound, if wordless, impulse in him. Lairds and ministers
were great persons in their own right, and he would shyly
step off the road to avoid encountering them, if it could be
done unnoticeably. But he did not envy them. He just
wanted to have nothing to do with them, to avoid them, so
that he could enter into the comradeship of his own folk.

"Ay, MacProcess they called him," Rob was saying,
referring to the previous minister of their parish, whose
church they could now see, "because he was always having
a legal process against someone. But the heritors were a
bad lot. Poor fellow, he had to screw every penny out of
them. Gordon of Swiney was at their head, and if ever a
profligate got into bed . . . I'll tell you a thing he did once
to a lassie—look! that's her house, with the peat-stack just
showing . . ."

They listened to the forceful details with a smile. For
the minor lairds could, on occasion, exercise a lurid authority over a defenceless tenantry. Though often enough, too,
their more shocking ploys had a wild sanction rooted in the
instincts that left a paralysis of wonder behind rather than
laughter. The art of mean tyranny, exercised with a brutal
lordliness.

Finn could enjoy the stories, but was glad to be outside
their scope. Supposing he had been in the position of
MacProcess, and had to beg money for his salary from a
man like Gordon of Swiney, beg or go to law. . . . Finn

knew he would never beg: he would walk out—or lay
Swiney out! He would hate them, hate their jeering at
religion, their roystering superiority. . . .

"That's why fellows like Sandy Ware and Peter
Stewart are against the—the present state of affairs. No
wonder the anointed themselves are often not much to
speak of. They say there will be a split yet on it. I don't
know, I'm sure," said Rob, "but——"

"It will have to split," interrupted Henry, referring to
the Church. "What has to depend on the cash of fellows
like Swiney or the Black Doctor, that black dog . . ."

They chuckled. They were remote from iniquity, and the
biggest landsmen grow small at a distance and their importance circumscribed and diminished. There was a tatoo
against naming ministers of the gospel at sea, and though
circumlocutary talk could have its own dry humour, Roddie
put an end to it by saying, "Well, boys, you can have a
long look at your native parish, for here's Clyth Head."

It was a large parish, stretching to the high cliff of the
Ord. Once they had chaffed Roddie for walking over the
Ord to his boat in Helmsdale on a Monday morning. This
was reckoned to be unlucky for him, because it was on a
Monday morning that the Sinclairs had crossed the Ord for the
battle of Flodden. Slowly Clyth Head closed on the parish
of Latheron as Roddie fetched a more northerly course.

Off Sarclet the wind began to die away, and before they
had opened out Wick the tide was against them and the sea
calm. Mists smothered the horizon and a haze hung over
the land. They pulled a slow, steady stroke on the four
oars, but it was heavy work and it seemed a long time to
Finn before they got Noss Head on their beam. When they
did, they remained tied to it. Once or twice fitful airs of
wind tempted Roddie to put up the mainsail, but they died
out and the rowing went on.

It was beginning to look now as if they could not
fetch Duncansby Head for slack water at the turn of the
tide—the only safe time for risking the passage through

the Pentland. Roddie was anxious to get through while the weather was good and took his turn at the oar. The whole coast here was exposed, and he could smell a sou'-easterly wind coming. The eyes could foresee it, too, by a raw darkness in the air. If they got the length of Scrabster, they would then be in a fine position to catch the first of the morning tide through the Firth, and with a fair wind they might fetch Stornoway that night. A sou'-easterly wind would suit them grand!

They were all inwardly excited now, though their faces showed little. For long spells no one spoke. They were adventuring into strange and dangerous seas and the haze put a great silence and brooding mysteriousness on sea and land. Finn at the tiller imagined he could feel the kick of Roddie's oar, a discreet explosive kick before he eased up to bend forward again. Without looking directly at Roddie, he could see him, and he knew that what Mr. Gordon had once said of him was true: "He's one of the old Vikings". His hair was reddish-fair and cut close round the ears and back. The reddish tinge suffused his fair skin, too, in a warm blood-strength, faintly stippled with pin-head freckles. His eyes were blue, the hard blue of a winter sea, but seemed to vary a lot, though perhaps not so much in colour as in intensity. He was given to shaving—an unusual proceeding, for nearly all men let the hair on the face grow as it came, merely trimming it now and then with a pair of scissors. He had taught Finn to shave, and they were the only two in the boat with smooth faces. Roddie had, however, left his razor behind.

Finn felt the glow of excitement, a glow that brought him all alive to alertness and wonder and the fascination of danger. Through the haze loomed the shadowy darkness of a distant headland. "Duncansby Head—look!" he called.

"It's a long way yet, boys," answered Roddie. "I feel the tide easing under us. Give her all you can."

"I thought I saw a boat—two boats!" cried Finn.

"It's a long way," said Roddie, his neck swelling under

the pressure he was now putting on his oar. "If we could do it in an hour. After that it's the mill-race. Whistle, Finn —but not too loud!"

Finn pursed his lips once or twice before he could get them to sound. And hardly had the sound died when a puff of wind fanned their faces.

"Wh-whistle again," said Rob.

When Finn got his smiling lips straight, he whistled once more. A dark cat's paw eddied after them. Then all at once there was a breeze.

They had the sails up in no time, and as they drew their shirts from their backs, they referred to Finn with head-shakes and mysterious nods, as to one in dark league with the elements.

But Roddie's eyes were concentrated on the two boats, now quite visible, standing well out from Duncansby. This is what he had been hoping for, and he steered after them. He had known there would be boats making for Stornoway, and the easiest passage is that in the wake of a boat that knows the sea-road. But by the way he once looked steadily back over his shoulder, Finn could see he did not trust the wind.

As the tide turned, the wind fell away. Roddie put them on the oars, without lowering sail, for there were no booms. The wind came again and died. They were making steady headway.

And so at last they opened out the Pentland Firth, the Pentland Skerries to starboard, and saw to the north, their great rock walls looming gigantic out of the haze, the Orkney Islands. They were in it now!

As the *Seafoam* was caught by the suction of the tide, Roddie lowered sail. The last he saw of the two boats they were disappearing round the north end of Stroma Island. "Take it easy, boys, and give it to her when I call on you." He had been told that he could go inshore on the first of the tide, but he liked to have sea-room and, anyway, where other boats had disappeared, he could follow.

The first fright those on the oars got was when the boat

suddenly spun half-round. Roddie gave a small smile. More than once it happened, and raised in the breast a helpless feeling of insecurity. Then when they seemed to be doing well and shooting ahead at a great rate, Roddie sharply called on the two starboard oars. He had the tiller hard over. His voice had such urgency that it exploded in their sinews. Minute—after minute—after minute. And then, "Good, boys! Good! You're doing it!" sang his voice quietly in triumph.

They had left the suction and now saw the whirlpool well away from them. They had only touched its outer rim. They could see the tide behind them and to the left, running with short, piled-up waves like a mighty river in spate. A dull roar came to their ears. Here and there on the surface the water boiled in a whirling eddy, as it does in the tail-end of a water-fall pool. When an eddy came underneath, the *Seafoam* slid sideways on it, raising much the same feeling in their breasts as an earthquake tremor does in the breasts of landsmen. Roddie pushed the tiller from side to side, trying to counter the swinging head but with no effect, until the oars got way on again.

"Half an hour later and we might have been in the Wells of Swinna," Roddie presently said, glancing over his right shoulder, the concentration that had sat in his eyes easing into an alert, smiling, questing look. They could see the island of Swinna (or Swena) on the other side, and Roddie's reference to it was more a jocular reference to dangers overcome than any real belief that they might have been swept so far across the flood.

"If we had been caught in the Wells," said Callum, who had pulled like a hero, "what do you think we would have thrown over?"

"It's no joking matter," said Rob.

"Who said it was?" asked Callum.

"What I told you is gospel truth. Why are they called the Wells? Man, I can see them now! See the foam rushing. Look!" cried Rob. "It's the two whirlpools!"

After a short silence Roddie said, "I have heard of it more than once. If you are caught in the whirlpool you throw a barrel or whatever you have over, and while the whirlpool is devouring that, it keeps quiet, and you slip across it."

"Like giving a dog a bone," said Henry.

"It would be a dog with no bottom to his belly, that one," murmured Finn.

They all chuckled.

"Ah well, Rob, you can thank goodness your kist is safe whatever," Callum added.

"Why would it have been my kist?" asked Rob.

"Because it's the biggest," said Callum.

"It's a great lump of a rock, that," Henry now said, following Roddie's eyes.

"It must be Dunnet Head," replied Roddie, "but we'll know when we get round it, because we should then see Thurso."

Finn was enlivened by his own remark, and so felt more than ever how splendid it was to be adventuring in this wild world of islands and rocks and headlands and dangerous seas. The Orkneys were like a fabulous tale he had heard of in some remote time.

Yes, there was Thurso—Thor's town, as Mr. Gordon called it—with the houses by the beach and up the left bank of the river, and, over on the other side, the tower of the castle.

Roddie kept staring at the land, and after a while said, pointing with his left hand, "Yonder is Scrabster."

A couple of miles or so beyond Thurso they saw it sheltering in its curve of green braes.

"Well, boys," asked Roddie, "what's it to be? We've had a long, heavy day."

No-one spoke.

"It's whatever you say, Skipper, but I'm fresh enough and the evening is long," remarked Callum cheerfully.

"There's just this about it," said Roddie. "We're going

to get some weather, and it would be fine to be a little farther west. Even the Kyle of Tongue, if we couldn't make Loch Eriboll. You can feel the wind, now we're out of the shelter of the Head. What do you say, Finn?"

"Loch Eriboll for me," answered Finn, "and I could whistle if you like."

"The only bit of me that's complaining," said Rob, "is my behind. There's a knot in the wood here . . ."

With both sails up and a wind that was gusty rather than steady, they slipped down the first at a spanking pace.

Henry filled a tin skillet from the small water-cask and they slaked their thirst. They had oaten and bere bannocks, milk and butter and cheese, and part of a haunch of salt beef in a firkin. After their long hours on the heavy sweeps, their bodies enjoyed the luxury of ease, and as they munched they stared at the land with friendly eyes. The sky was darkening, the wind freshening, and now and then a spit of rain hit their faces.

"Boys, we're fairly shifting," said Rob.

"We'll be in the China trade next," said Finn.

They chuckled away as they ate, casting amused glances at the young fellow.

"The China trade!" repeated Rob in his droll, solemn way, shaking his head. A speck of dry bread went down the wrong tube and he started coughing. Callum hit him a great whack between the shoulders.

"What's the d–damn sense in hitting a fellow like that?"

"It cured you, though," said Callum.

As they rounded Strathy Point, Roddie stood into the land a little. By the time they were approaching Roan Island off Tongue Bay they could see it was setting in for a dirty night. But again they held on, for the fine seaway they were making was exhilarating, and now it was going to be a final race with the falling night.

"It will be dark early," said Henry, with a look at the low, ravelled sky.

"It will," said Roddie, without any movement. He sat

upright, his eyes ahead, drawn in on himself, solid and emotionless. As if impelled by something in this carven attitude, Finn looked ahead, too, and again had the impression that the peak of the stem, in a dream of its own, was searching out the far distance with invisible eyes. All at once, he remembered the school-book illustration of the Viking longship, with its high carven head, and in that moment realized with a queer thrill of clear certainty the impulse that in the beginning moved those great wanderers of the sea to carve the lifting stem into a face.

Not a human face, but a boat's face, for Finn felt how heedless the boat was of them in its concentrated onward drive.

As the Kyle of Tongue, with its islands and broken shore-line, its invitation to shelter beneath a glimpse of great mountains, fell behind them and the coast rose up into cliffs, the crew buttoned their heaviest clothes about them silently, for it was getting cold.

Soon the cliff wall reared to a great height and seemed to stretch before them into utmost night. Out to sea the leaden waves, running short, were white-capped and the smother of the horizon drew near. Under the shelter of the cliff-wall the deep water was smooth and black. Roddie kept far enough out for a steady wind, though sometimes it struck him in gusts, from the funneling of hill and cliff.

No one spoke. They could hear the gulls wailing in the cliffs. If the wind had been from an opposite direction what a smashing of seas would have been here! Finn would have liked to ask Roddie how far yet he thought Loch Eriboll was, but he could not. To ask any question would be something worse than futile now. Thus for the first time he got the feeling of the fatalism of the sea. They were committed.

And even when at last that great wall turned and fell inland, they all, by a natural instinct, waited for the skipper to speak. But Roddie was silent. His eyes shifting from feature to feature of the land, until he had fully opened the great sea inlet, when he said, "Yes, it's Loch Eriboll."

They all came alive, yet did not speak very much, for now started the exciting quest, that often grows tense, of finding an anchorage in an unknown place where shoal or submerged rock may at any moment hold the keel to disaster.

When they had sailed for some four miles, they discerned a little bay in front of a river mouth. "It looks a likely enough place," suggested Callum. The night was closing in now and visibility was poor. The rain was not heavy but it was penetrating and cold. An ugly raw night.

But Roddie, after a slow look around, said, "I think we should go farther in. If the wind changed we'd be open here to the full sea from the nor'ard."

"Perhaps you're right," Callum nodded.

So in they sailed between the land until they saw what looked like a small headland or island on their windward or port side. With canvas down, they finally nosed in on the oars, and in three fathoms of water Roddie let the anchor go.

It was the first strange landfall that any of them had ever made, and in the dark and the rain and the flurrying swish of the wind they felt relieved and quietly companionable.

The boat was open from stem to stern, without shelter or berth, but when they had eaten, they did what they could with the help of the sails and the soft bulk of the nets to get into a comfortable position for rest. Finn snuggled down, packed his hip bone, lifted the edge of the sail for breath, and prepared for sleep. But though he felt very tired, he was not sleepy. He was now more than ever pleased at having said things which had made the others laugh. His old shy self had opened, and to his surprise up the words had come. That one about the China trade. You could see it troubling Rob's eyebrows for some time! The rain pattered on the stiff canvas over his ear. How fine it was to be voyaging! A soft warmth from fatigue suffused his whole body; and on a last consciousness of the cradling motion of the boat, he fell asleep. Once he awoke in the thin light of the morning and, poking his head out, saw the humped forms of the other sleepers, the brown heath, the flanks of the barren peat land, the water, and the boat's stem. It was still wet and blowing, and he pulled his head in. After that he felt sure he did not sleep, but only dozed, with long waking thoughts in which figures moved.

Often he was to awake like this in the future, and then, half-asleep, have a dream in which he could to some degree command the actions of the figures but more particularly his own actions.

Now he saw Una before him, and so clearly that the suppressed excitement, which always bothered him in her presence, got such a hold upon him that he could not think of one clever or cutting thing to say, for Jim Dewar, the new fish-curer's clerk (Special's nephew), was always nosing about Una's section of the gutting station when the girls were there. A trash of a young fellow from Wick, with his fine English and fine boots, his laughs and little ready-made jokes! But it was difficult to tell him off, for he would have been quite capable of laughing and saying, "You're jealous!" And at least Finn knew, thank goodness, that he was not jealous. So when he saw Jim making headway in that direction he simply kept out of the way, indifferent. Once Una had flushed when he had come on them together and he had given what he had hoped was an amused, sarcastic smile. "Here, Finn!" Jim had called. But he had answered with a vague salute, hardly turning round: "I'm busy." When he had reached the boat, however, his heart was knocking like a fist on a door. But he had done not badly. If only he could just cut them up with jocular indifference and move on, at some critical moment. . . .

In his morning-dream, the desire to do this became so strong that he heard voices, and when he pulled back the sail and lifted his head, Roddie and Henry were talking together.

More than ever now was it strange to be upon the sea, and at the same time far in between the land. This had struck him last night, but only as part of the background to the long day's end. Here was a new world, with flat shores of peat bog rising on either hand to mountain ridges whose tops were blotted out in trailing mists. There was a chill in the wet wind that was yet soft on the cheeks, and beyond the rising ground on the off side the rain could be seen like a white curtain, half transparent, moving, and yet remaining in the same place. Straight across the loch was a string of croft houses, and dotted here and there were single houses, but no smoke rose from any of them, for it was early yet. A curlew fluted overhead. Finn saw its brown body and long beak, and then along the shore ran the sharp cries of sea-birds whose names he did not know.

Rob poked his head up, blinking and saying, "Uh?" in a comical way, wondering for the moment where he was. The left side of his mouth twisted up, putting a wrinkle under the nostril. Hunching his shoulders, he blew a noisy breath through his lips. But Callum had to be gripped and shaken, when he said quickly, "What? Where? Eh?" and was ready for any attack.

The wind was not so strong as it had been last night. The rain had drawn the sting out of it, and even if, outside, they might have to take a reef in, they could not wish for it in a better airt. The only trouble was the poor visibility. A mile from shore and the land would be gone. But bright weather would now mean a shift of wind.

"We could go out and see what it's like, anyway," suggested Callum, who was fond of action.

"That's what I think," Roddie agreed. "We could always come back."

The decision brightened them up, for to sit here in this weather with no shelter or warmth would become wearisome.

There was no hurry, however, because the tide was flowing, and their minds turned to hot food, which they hadn't had since they left home. They brought the boat in near the shore and Finn leapt, followed by Callum and

Rob. If they couldn't find any life in a croft house, they would be sure to find a dry peat and perhaps a dry stick, and Rob said that, given both and a tinder-box, he would raise a fire at the bottom of the sea—and they had the tinder-box.

About a mile from the boat, Rob fell foul of a collie dog while he was robbing a peat-stack. There was great commotion and much shouting, with Callum and Finn helpless in laughter at a little distance, when a man appeared in nothing but his shirt. High words from him, and Rob started talking in his solemn, natural way. Callum and Finn heard that they had been caught in a terrible storm last night after a long sea voyage and were all but shipwrecked, with two men left on board whose bowels were in a knot for lack of a drop of warm food. "I was half-wondering if I might take a peat from your stack, for we did not want to disturb decent folk at so early an hour, but your dog here. . . ."

After that, it was the inside of the kitchen, with the wife behind the curtain across the bed, and three eager young faces staring at them from a low bed like what Finn himself had once slept in. Only everything here was poorer, more congested. His breeches on, the man was now on his knees blowing the kindling to a flame, when his wife called him. "If you take them out," she said in a whisper they all heard, "I'll get up and have the porridge ready in no time."

Outside, as Rob was telling the man about the Wells of Swinna, Finn, in order to avoid the wink that he knew was waiting in Callum's face, looked away and saw a boat coming clear of a long island in the middle of the loch, and heading for sea. She was plainly a fishing boat of their own class. At the same moment a piercing whistle reached them.

"It's Roddie!" cried Finn. "He'll be wanting to follow her," and he pointed to the boat.

"We'll maybe be back," said Rob to the man.

OUT TO SEA

They hurried over the bogs. Roddie was holding the shore with the boat-hook and they quickly got on board. Up went the sails, and when they had cleared their anchorage they could just see the boat a mile or more ahead. "She's a Wick boat," said Henry.

They lost her for a time, but got a glimpse of her again as the inlet opened. She was clearly holding to the west side and therefore, beyond any doubt, bound for Stornoway. The curtains of small white rain, that made the wind from the hills visible, were troublesome, but in a clear space they saw her standing towards a tall, dark rock (Dubh Sgeir) and, once round it, head for the west.

She was probably a foot or two longer than *Seafoam*, and seemed certainly to have more canvas, for though Roddie gave his own boat all she could carry, he could not reduce the distance between them. For a long time, until they made Faraid Head, they lost her, and Finn called out excitedly when they picked her up again.

But Roddie was saying little. The wind was not anything like so strong as it had been last night. He did not care for the sky. His problem, without a compass in this thick weather, was complicated. He knew that the Butt of Lewis lay pretty nearly west of Cape Wrath, but the westerly stream would take them down the Minch. However, by going straight out past the Cape on the line of the land and then bearing a few points south, it would be impossible to miss the Long Island, the whole Outer Hebrides, which stretched in a line for over a hundred miles! And the distance to Stornoway was not so long as their yesterday's trip.

All the same, his sight strained after the boat in front, and held her, off and on, until she reached the Cape.

Finn had often heard of Cape Wrath and now had plenty of time to gaze on its towering crags against which white sea-birds floated like blown feathers, their high cries sounding afar off and inward, in echo of rock and cavern. It inspired the crew with awe and held them to silence, and none the less because the sea around it was to-day comparatively calm with, however, that ominous long swing and heave of the waters that broke in deep white. Peril was clearly held on uneasy rein, and the rock-brows stared over crested seas to an uttermost Arctic. Roddie alone paid no attention to the precipice and, holding his boat towards the Stag Rock, which was awash in the hollows of the swell, scanned the westerly sea. Then for the last time he caught a glimpse of that fugitive vessel which had led him on so elusively. To Roddie it seemed she was heading straight west. His instinct for a moment troubled him for it wanted to bring the *Seafoam* a few points to the south'ard. He had to make his decision now and he made it without consulting anyone. They saw him look at the sky, searching for the sun, for in between the showers its presence could be vaguely discerned in a dissipated silvery brightness. Then he settled to the tiller, his body upright, his eyes ahead, and followed where the vessel had disappeared. No-one spoke.

As Finn lay against the nets looking back, he watched the Cape slowly being shrouded, until insensibly it passed from his sight, and he shut his eyes and opened them to make sure that it really had vanished. As he gazed around, he could see nothing but tumbled waters over a radius of several miles, it seemed to him, for it was weather that lay on the sea rather than fog. "There's weather on that sky" was the home saying.

Rob broke the spell that had fallen on them:

"Well, I don't know how you feel, but I could do with a bite."

"Trust Rob to remember his belly!" said Callum.

They were suddenly smiling in the happiest mood, munching away at the bread and salt beef, but going canny on the milk, for there was very little of it left. It was a pity, too, that they hadn't at least put some more water in the cask, though no one said as much. Salt beef was bad for raising a thirst. However, by the afternoon or early evening they were bound to hit land somewhere.

"What are you looking for, Rob?" asked Callum. "Expecting anyone?"

"No," drawled Rob, who had been peering over the sea, "not exactly."

Callum chuckled and threw Finn a wink. "Well, you can't say you have been here before."

"No, I haven't been here before," replied Rob, "but I may know about it for all that."

"Know what?"

"You may be a smart fellow, Callum, but your laugh sometimes reminds me on the lad who was living on the island I'm looking for. It's the island of Rona and it lies somewhere in these seas. Have you heard tell of it?" he asked Roddie.

"Yes," said Roddie, "but I hope it's well to the north. Otherwise it's a long trip we're on." Smiling he bit on his bannock, eyes ahead.

"Well, I know, whatever, that Lewis is their nearest port of call," replied Rob, "so it can't be that far away, surely."

"What happened to the lad?" asked Finn.

"It was his first trip to Stornoway, and there for the first time he saw a horse. The horse neighed, and he thought it was laughing at him," said Rob.

"Got me that time!" allowed Callum.

"Ach, it's maybe not so difficult as you think," said Rob, picking a crumb off his breast.

"Is it a big island?" asked Finn.

"No," said Rob, with his slow, sideways nod, "it's only big enough to hold a few families, but they have it well cultivated and they live well enough. They're terrible hospitable, if you land there. They'd kill a sheep for you and give you a bit of all they have. Oh, a fine people, by all accounts."

"I thought they had all died out," said Roddie.

"Yes—and no," replied Rob, screwing his eyebrows. "A terrible calamity fell upon them, but a new lot was set on the island after that; though how they're doing, I haven't heard. But it was sad enough what befell once. It seems that a swarm of rats came from the sea, and ate their grain, and after that some wild sailors landed and killed their bull. The factor of the island reached there about a year afterwards, and found no life, only a woman with a child at her breast, both lying dead beside a rock."

There was silence for a little. "It's the sort of thing a factor would find," said Henry, for he had been touched by the story.

"Ach, well," said Rob, "he couldn't help it, likely. A queer thing how rats come from the ocean in swarms like that. But it's true enough. I have heard of it in other connections. Strange things happen among the beasts of the world, if we only knew."

"Stranger things happen among the humans of the world," said Henry, "particularly when one or two of them have the power and are after the money. The only important difference between the real rat and the human rat is that you can kill the real rat."

"Talking of money," said Rob, "the thing that struck me about Rona—and this is as true as I'm sitting here, for it's all written down—was that they had no money. You see, there was nowhere to spend it, so it would have been no use to them whatever way. Isn't that strange? Yet they lived happy without it, and they had their meal and fish and sheep and cattle—in fact, all the human body needs. But I remember that in particular—how happy they lived. It struck me."

"And how did they pay their rents?" asked Henry.

"Well now," said Rob thoughtfully, "well now, that's— I don't think it was specially mentioned—let me see——"

"Didn't they pay it long ago," said Finn, "in oats and butter and fish——"

"Exactly," Rob interrupted him. "I knew there was something. Man, and do you know what they would put the grain into, for they hadn't bags? It comes back to me now.

They would skin a sheep whole, and then tie up the openings at the legs, and there was your bag! And they would fill that with grain. They would do it while you waited. And, of course, they had the wool for the weaving like ourselves."

"But what would a young fellow do," asked Callum, "if there wasn't a girl for him?"

"I can tell you that, too," said Rob. "It's all written down and it's no lies. They were a good-living people and had their own little place of worship where they said a prayer. And sometimes one would come to see how they were getting on with the religion. Well, once he came. Now there were two young fellows there after the one girl. And one of them said, to him who came, couldn't each of them have the girl year about to wife? But he shook his head at that and said, no, that wouldn't be right, that wouldn't be the thing at all. So one of the young fellows, who was desperate keen on having a wife, even if it was only for a while at a time, was very put out, oh, sore disappointed he was. And then all at once he remembered the shilling he had got from a sailor, and he offered it, saying, Will you buy me a wife in Stornoway for that?"

A gust of wind carried the laughter from the hold, a slash of rain trickled down their smiling faces, the boat rose and plunged, lay over, and Roddie was about to let go the mainsail sheet, when she rose to it and the sting of the gust passed. Passed quite away, leaving a lull. Roddie stowed the after-sail, waiting for the next gust. There were flurries of uncertain wind—and then a calm.

This was what he had feared more than anything else. The wind had blown itself out of the south-east, and so he had lost that steering airt. As they swung at the oars, keeping her, as he hoped, to their original course, he searched the sky. From long practice he could give a pretty accurate guess at time or compass point by glimpsing the sun's position. But there was no sun now. Every minute he expected the wind to come at them from a new airt, but the heaviness seemed to clog even the weather, and their boat wallowed in the troughs of the sea. When this had gone on long past what they felt was the height of the day, Roddie knew that the heavens would not clear and that, as far as making any sure landfall was concerned, they were rowing blind.

It must have been well on in the afternoon when the wind hit them. Roddie judged it to be from the sou'-west, and sailed as close to it as he could, once going over for a reach on the port tack to counter any northerly drift. It started to blow so hard that Roddie had to look out for lumps of sea, and soon it was a fight with the elements. It was good to watch Roddie now, felt Finn. His eyes were like living drops of the ocean itself and you could see the exaltation of the fight concentrated in them. When they judged, and succeeded, the skin sometimes creased in fine ironic lines round the eyes, and once he looked at Finn suddenly, with a friendly smile, and said something with a quiet humour that Finn did not catch.

Though Roddie told them to keep a sharp look-out for land, they neither saw nor heard anything but the sea, and when the light was sensibly diminishing, Roddie's face went expressionless as stone.

CHAPTER XV

STORM AND PRECIPICE

※

All through the night they fought the sea, manning the pump in turns, though they shipped little more than lashings of wave-tops, for Roddie's hand felt for side and crest with a skill that was most part pure divination. It was some time in the first of the night that the seas attained proportions beyond anything they had ever encountered before. Whole hills of water seemed to come at them with great valleys between. For hours Roddie' was cut off from his crew in a darkness as of winter. Once when she staggered as she climbed and they felt for a terrible moment that the wave had got them, was holding them, and was going to throw them clean over, she choked shudderingly within herself, but held, reached the crest, balanced, then quivered as she caught the wind and plunged on, eased by Roddie's hand. Clear and heartening came Roddie's voice: "That was a bad one, boys!"

There were a few elemental jokes of the kind, with words plucked out of the mouth and blown in tatters into the darkness, before the grey of the morning came upon their half-stupified bodies; came to reveal nothing far as the eye could reach but countless herds of tumbling seas. That they had lived through the night seemed now more of a miracle than before.

"Henry," cried Roddie, "some water all round, but go canny with it. I'm dry."

"If you take only a mouthful," called Henry to each, "you can have a mouthful after your piece."

As they munched their bere bannocks, they could not keep their eyes off the waves. But Roddie could now see what was coming at him, and as the light grew it seemed to them that the wind eased.

"Keep your eye lifting for Rona, Rob," called Callum.

"Where do you think we are?" Henry asked Roddie.

"I don't know," answered Roddie, "but I should say we are in the Western Ocean, for I have never seen waves the length of these. Only one thing I know—one while during the night if it had blown any harder we couldn't have done it. And it wouldn't have helped much to try to run under bare poles for the Arctic Ocean! She's a good sea boat, boys. We'll give her that due."

Roddie's simple words of praise for the gallant boat touched Finn closely, and more so as his body was battered into a heavy lassitude, so heavy indeed that when it relaxed completely, it felt light and incorporeal, and there came upon his spirit a fine clarity. He looked at the stem—reaching up the wave, searching the horizon, plunging down—to rise again. On, on, on—that was the song at her heart. So long as the human spirit was equal to the need, she would not fail. With that strange wooden dream of her own besides! Finn felt a softness in him and turned his eyes away to the seas.

For the first time he knew the strange companionship of running seas—strange because lifted beyond the normal into this thin region of the spirit. He had heard of a Gaelic poem that described all the different kinds of waves there are. But no poem could describe them all. Take this one coming at them now—now!—its water on the crest turned into little waters, running, herding together, before—up—up! over its shoulder and down into the long flecked hollow like a living skin. Or that one steaming off there!—a great lump of ocean, a long-backed ridge overtopping all, a piled-up mountain. He drew Roddie's attention to it by pointing. The crew stared. The gleam of a smile lit Roddie's eyes. "We met one or two like that last night," he said. And Finn suddenly understood how a wave, far in the open sea, could catch a boat and throw her clean before it. No small boat could climb that onrushing wall. He watched Roddie's eyes, when they were on the crest of the next wave, peering far ahead. He was looking out for the big ones in the distance so that he might have time to dodge them!

Lying back in partial exhaustion, with the spirit grown thin and clear, Finn felt, coming out of the companionship of these seas, a faint fine exaltation.

He had learned a few things since he had left home! How distant home was—the beach, and the stranger talking to his mother—like something remembered of a foreign shore. His mouth was dry with thirst. There was a well of crystal water not far from the House of Peace. You got down on your hands and knees and then reached farther down with your face. There was the physical effort, before the water lapped your mouth and nose. It was difficult to drink, with the crystal water almost choking your outstretched throat. They had all seen how Henry had had to tilt the little cask, but no one had said anything. There might be a cupful each yet. His teeth began to chitter again, and he moved within his clothes, which were sodden to the shirt.

Presently Roddie started to talk. "We'll have to think of what we're going to do, boys. The seas are running bigger than ever, but the wind has lost its snarl. I think we got blown clean out of the Minch. We probably passed west of the Butt in the late evening. If so, we are now somewhere to the west and perhaps north of the Butt, for we are bound to have made a lot of leeway. I think myself we are well into the Atlantic Ocean."

"It seems to me," said Henry, "that everything depends on from what airt the new wind hit us. It may be sou'-west, but we couldn't swear it is not nor'-west, and when a sou'-east wind dies away—and then the wind comes again—it's more than likely to be from nor'-west than from sou'-west.

Rowing in a calm like yesterday was like walking over a moor in the mist: you cannot keep your direction. We might be well down the Minch, and the long seas may be coming from Iceland. I'm not saying we are in the Minch, but we *might* be."

Roddie nodded.

"Wherever we are," said Rob, "we'll have to think of where we're going, so the sooner our minds are made up the easier they'll be."

"Where do you think we're heading for, Finn?" asked Callum, with an expectant glint.

Finn smiled in response. "My mother's first cousin was taken to Canada in one of the emigrant ships. If we keep going as we're doing we might get some news of him. That would always be something."

"It would, faith!" Callum lifted his broad, fair face in a quick laugh. "You're as good as a drink!"

Nothing happened for a while and then Roddie said, "We'll put her on the other tack. Get ready."

When they were settled down, he remarked, "The sun may help us soon. My own feeling is that we are now heading in a southerly direction. If the sea takes off a little in two or three hours, we'll let her fall off to dead east."

Henry's eyes narrowed in calculation, then he nodded. "That would suit, either way."

But the sky showed no sign of lightening. The weather lay on it, grey-dark and formless.

"It's nothing for a storm in this part of the world to last for a week even in the height of summer," Rob said.

"You for a Job's comforter!" declared Callum.

"It may moderate during the day," continued Rob, ignoring him, "and rise again at night."

"Like a sick man with a temperature," said Finn.

Callum cupped his knees with his palms.

"All the same," added Rob, "it's as well to know a fever when you see it."

After that they fell silent. Callum drew attention to

Rob's head swaying sideways in a doze, but soon his own chin was on his breast. Henry offered to take the tiller, but Roddie answered, "Take a snooze now. You can have your turn later. Pull that bit of stuff over you," he said to Finn.

From a sleep that seemed an endless semi-conscious daze of formless motion, Finn wakened sharply and blinked at Roddie. Henry's lean, black head was up, too. They followed Roddie's gesture and far astern they saw, forming clearly against the misted horizon, a tall ship.

She was life coming after them, she was the spirit of the land, she was comfort and hope, she was the word of direction upon the grey endless tumbling wastes of death, she was a cry they could not yet hear, she was a fine thing to see.

"Wake them up," said Roddie.

Rob screwed his eyes and the left half of his mouth. "It's a big boat," he said, telling them.

Callum had to be shaken strongly. "What? Where? A ship!" He knuckled his eyes. And at that moment a sea hit them and they took in water. Roddie gave a sharp exclamation for he had, through forgetfulness, been at fault. Then Finn noticed the expression that came on his face as he looked at the swinging seas. Not yet! it seemed to say in ironic comment. Not for a while yet! And as Finn glanced away the grey crests seemed to gather speed and fury.

"Lord, I'm cold!" exclaimed Callum. "I was just falling off to sleep when I heard you," he said to Roddie simply.

"It's a good job," said Rob, "that—that you hadn't far to fall." They were all excited.

"Stand by to put her about." Roddie was now satisfied that the approaching vessel would pass well to leeward of them. "We'll keep to wind'ard of her, but as near as we can on her course."

The wind had certainly taken off and the seas were not breaking, though they seemed as big as ever.

Rob ventured the first comment. "She's a Dutch buss."

301

"She's a smack," said Roddie.

"A fishing smack?" asked Finn.

Roddie looked at him. "Yes."

"Why, what sort of smack do you think she would be?" asked Callum, grinning.

"As long as she's a fishing smack," said Finn, colour darkening his face as he glanced away.

They all looked at him, and for a moment felt disquieted. For an old fear had touched Finn, born suddenly out of childhood memory of the first time he had heard how a tall ship had come out of the sea and press-ganged his father. Rob was going to say something when Roddie forestalled him by remarking quietly, "She looks like a Grimsby smack. Some of them come up to the cod fishing at Lerwick."

"Lerwick!" exclaimed Henry. "Are we off the Shetlands then? Or where can she be going?"

"God knows," said Roddie.

"Cold iron!" cried Rob, sharply gripping the point of the boat-hook. They all touched iron, to avert the bad luck that comes from naming God at sea. Finn kept gazing at the vessel over the starboard quarter.

Where, indeed, could this vessel be going? That Roddie had exclaimed so thoughtfully only showed how deeply disturbed he must be.

"I can make out L K," said Finn.

"Lerwick!" Henry's brows narrowed.

"Stand aft here," said Roddie to Henry, "and be ready to shout." Henry's voice was far-carrying. He sang well, if seldom.

The smack was now close and plunging in the seas. Henry was cupping his hands about his mouth when a voice reached them as out of a trumpet.

"Where away?"

"Stornoway," cried Henry. "We're lost. What course?" They could see the crew, a good dozen men, staring at them.

"Dead east!" And the man who shouted threw his arm out. "Lewis—dead east!"

"How far?"

There was a moment or two before the answer came: "Forty miles. Are you all right?"

"Yes."

"Ask him where he's going," prompted Roddie.

"Where you bound?" cried Henry.

"The Rockall."

"Thank you."

"Were you out all night?"

"Yes."

Back came the voice with a ring of tribute: "Plucky lads!"

"Stand by," said Roddie. He was running with the smack and now, watching his chance, brought the *Seafoam* up into the wind smartly and, as she fell away on an easterly course, the crew on the deck of the smack waved their arms and cheered.

It was a genuine tribute, and the men of the *Seafoam*, who could put out a hand and touch the sea at any time, felt it. They waved back and cheered, too, in companionship and gratitude, their faces flushed.

"The Rockall," began Rob.

"He knows where it is!" cried Callum, and doubled over laughing. This made them all laugh, except Rob. And when they saw Callum wiping the tears out of his eyes, they laughed again. The feeling of relief went deep.

"Where is the Rockall?" asked Roddie at last.

But Rob was now apparently in a slight huff. "Och, it's just out there in the Western Ocean."

"Far out?"

"I suppose it is," said Rob. "It's just three hundred miles."

"Three hundred miles!" echoed Henry and, laughing, shook his head. "The farthest out land is St. Kilda—and I doubt if that's farther than we are ourselves."

"Oh, well," said Rob, "you'll know best."

They laughed again.

Finn had been profoundly moved by this chance encounter of the sea. That last shout, followed by the involuntary cheer, wasn't three hundred miles from a lump in his throat and a softness behind his eyes. His body was weak from exhaustion and cold, from lack of food and water. And then to discover that instead of being a ship of war, she was a boat of the fishing folk themselves! What a difference was there! He looked after her, driving into that western ocean, and wished her well.

"Good for the Shetlanders!" cried Roddie. "They're brave seamen."

"They have a great trade in dried cod," said Henry. "They export it all over the world."

"We must go up and see them one of these seasons!" Roddie had not been far out in his calculation of their whereabouts, and was pleased.

"Come on, Rob," he said, "tell us about the Rockall, otherwise Callum will be at Henry for a drink."

Callum shook his head sadly. "My mouth is stuck."

"Stuck!" repeated Rob dryly. "In that case it's maybe been an expensive cure, but I might have stood more for less."

Their ready appreciation of this sally balanced matters, and Rob told them, correctly enough, that the Rockall was a solitary rock in the sea three hundred miles out into the Atlantic, round which there was a famous cod-bank, particularly for large fish. "They get them there up to, yes, over, six feet. A man by the name of Flett, who was a deckhand on a schooner that was forced into Wick, told George Dempster, who is married on a daughter of old Danny Budge, and is a foreman cooper in Lower Pulteneytown . . ."

Finn always got lost in these relationships, though Rob would go into them at a length generally in proportion to the degree of the marvellous in his story.

The *Seafoam* had now a very complicated motion of pitch and roll. Their voices were tired from being raised to carry. Steering was a more delicate art than ever and Roddie's head seemed to get a curious swinging motion from the cross seas that bore down on them. For ever he had to be watchful, with stem or stern ready, and when they rose at a slant over a shoulder, Finn could see the backs of the seas, herds of slate-blue backs, racing over the endless wilderness, a sweep of wind round their mighty flanks, like brutes of ocean, hurrying to some far ultimate congregation. But always, from the lowest swinging trough, rising to out-top them, was the boat's stem, steadfast in its own wooden dream.

Roddie's flanks were beginning to cramp. They could see him slowly straighten one leg and then the other, as he eased himself from hip to hip.

"Will I take a turn?" Henry asked. The others waited in silence.

"Look out!" cried Roddie sharply, and putting the tiller from him, he bore directly away. "I'm going about. Now!" And round she came, so that they were running back on their course. They saw the long-backed monstrous wave coming, and as Roddie brought the *Seafoam* up into the weather, she rode its outer edge, and then fell away on her original course. "Let out a reef," said Roddie. Henry did not ask for the tiller again, nor did Roddie offer it, and so they were all relieved.

Hours later Finn said, "It's land," and Roddie answered, "Yes, I'm sure now."

Callum's lips, pale and with a sticky white munge at the corners, opened: "What about celebrating?" Roddie nodded, sticking his tongue between his own dry lips. For the last hour or two thirst had become a torment.

Henry, helped by Finn and Rob, eased the last of the water out of the cask. There was about a cupful each. It was Roddie first, then Callum, whose hands were in a slight tremble, then Rob, Finn, and Henry last. When Henry had drunk, he said, "I have more than my share. There's a little left." No one spoke. "Give it to Callum," said Roddie. But Callum refused to take it.

"Take it," ordered Roddie.

"I'll divide it with Finn," said Callum. Finn refused.

"Dammit, take it!" cried Roddie sharply. Irritation swept their weakened bodies. Finn moistened his lips and handed the skillet to Callum, who drained it without more ado.

The irritation passed, leaving them quiet and concentrating on what soon were plainly seen to be islands. Roddie kept to windward to have seaway to bear down on them.

As they brought the first two islands abeam, the way the waves broke on them was a silencing sight. Then two more islands—and beyond, to the far dark horizon, nothing but ocean! These were no islands in the mouth of a land inlet. There was no mainland anywhere. No Lewis.

"Have you any idea of what they are?" shouted Roddie to Rob.

Rob stared at the rock-walls with their green tops. The smashing, spouting seas were stupendous. He shook his head slowly. "No."

Roddie stood well away until he was beyond them. There was one larger island and perhaps——

Finn cried, "I see sheep!" White specks against a grey-green. Yes, they were sheep!

"Stand by!" called Roddie sharply. "I'm going to put her about."

Down they came, racing, clearing the water foul with low rock on their port side, heading into a horse-shoe bay, girdled by black cliff.

Calm—in the slow heaving water of shelter. Finn and Callum, each with an oar ready, Rob stowing the sail, Henry forward at the anchor. "Let go!" called Roddie.

"I've got it," answered Henry, holding bottom.

"Thank God," said Callum.

"Cold iron!" cried Rob.

Slowly Roddie got up, after touching cold iron, and straightened himself, his hands gripping the small of his back and working down over his flanks. His face broke. "Boys, I'm stiff." His eyes lifted to myriads of circling, screaming birds. "They seem surprised to see us," he said, and his eyes glimmered.

It was a reconciling smile, and though this looked a wild and haunted enough place in all conscience, still they were here, and that, as Finn had said, was always something. Roddie stretched himself out over the nets and eased his body in rolling motions. For a short while they were full of humour, and lived in its careless moments.

There were some birds which Finn had never seen before and a group of puffins looking over a ledge reminded him of an illustration of parrots in one of Mr. Gordon's books.

"What's that one?"

"That one?" said Rob, screwing up his eyes. "Man, I should know it, too."

"Do you think," suggested Finn, "that we may have landed on an island in the South Seas?"

"No, no," said Rob. "We're just in the Western Ocean."

"Ay, but where? What if that ship was not a real ship at all and we have been enchanted into the South Seas?"

"Hush, be quiet!" said Rob. "What talk is that?"

He looked around anxiously to make sure they had not been overheard by the old dark ones.

And the cliffs were dark enough and mostly sheer. It was a wild, forbidding place, a black jaw, formed as they could now see by two islands, with the gullet at the back, just wide enough to take their boat, twisting out of sight between perpendicular walls, and clearly going right through to the west side because the pulse of the sea came from the channel in undulations upon which they rose and fell.

The reverberations from the pounding waves drummed

307

in their ears and could be felt in their bodies. The black cliffs vibrated. The circling birds had mostly fallen back upon their visible rock ledges where they were better able to keep up the intensity of their myriad-throated screaming.

Roddie lay with his eyes closed as if he had fallen into a deep sleep. They all took their ease and upon them came an insidious lassitude. They gave in to it and lay with their mouths open in such varied attitudes that it looked as if the *Seafoam* had brought to haven a boat-load of the dead.

As each one stirred uneasily he tried to swallow, but could not and that awoke him. Moisture would not come into their mouths. Their tongues and throats felt dry and swollen. They had eaten nothing since a piece of bread in the early morning. The afternoon was obviously far spent. To go out into that sea now would mean, at the best, running upon a lee shore in the dark, a shore that for the most part was bound to be smoking cliff. And in any case the wind seemed to be rising, for they could not only hear the whine of it, but now and then a quicker, intenser whine, as if still swifter hounds of the air were being unleashed to overtake and harry the hurtling grey-backed monsters of the sea.

At the back of their minds had been a vague hope that, where sheep were, human beings might be. When they tried to shout, however, only hoarse croaks issued from them and with such lacerating effect that they coughed in pain. They then bethought them of beating the pot and kettle and tin skillet, of whacking wood on wood, until the fulmars circled in fantastic gyres and the screaming of puffin and guillemot and gull rose to a demoniac pitch, while they themselves, carried away into a momentary frenzy, laughed harshly into the infernal scene.

But Finn had had his eyes on the giddy rock-ledges with their rows of birds. It was the beginning of May. It was nesting time. The cool slither of a sucked egg went down his throat. He would climb the cliff.

He did not speak at once because he wanted to have his

voice under control, so he scanned the wall on the large island to the north for a possible way up.

Roddie began to talk. They were here for the night. He was glad to hear the wind rising, still from the same airt, because there was every chance now that it would blow itself out by the morning. They could not be more than six or seven hours at the most from Lewis, with a half-favourable passage. They would just have to hope for the best and make themselves as comfortable as they could. And the best way was to try to pass the time in dozing. One by one they would take watch through the night.

They were all silent. There was nothing else that could be done. And then Finn spoke.

"I have been looking at that cliff," he said. "I think I can climb it."

Roddie's face slowly drew taut and his eyes hardened. "No-one can climb that cliff," he said.

"Yes, if you landed me there, I could do it."

They looked at the black ledge to which he pointed. The water rose to it, then fell down about twelve feet sheer in sucking, greeny-white swirls, then rose again.

"Are you mad?" asked Roddie, his eyes like glass.

"No, I'm not," said Finn, and felt inside him, small and intense as a needle-prick, an animosity against Roddie. It excited him. His body grew taut in challenge.

"And how would we land you there?" asked Roddie in level mockery.

"Easily enough," replied Finn. "If you shifted the anchor over there, one of you could pay out rope, while the others brought her in stern first on the oars. When you were close to the rock and the stern rose up, I could jump."

It was the clearness of the operation that struck their fancy and kept them silent, but Roddie said, "And what if the stern-post got the rock coming up? What if you slipped? Do you think we could help you then?"

"Someone must take a chance," said Finn, a lash of colour in his cheek-bones.

"Oh? Why?" demanded Roddie.

"Because if I don't do it now, I won't have the strength to do it to-morrow. And you know that." Roddie's tone had whipped him. He shut his mouth to keep more words from boiling out.

"Well, you won't do it now," said Roddie.

"Why not?" cried Finn, in direct challenge. "What are you frightened of?"

"I'm not usually frightened," said Roddie. "I'd advise you to control your mouth. I'm the skipper here."

Finn looked away with a twisted expression. He was trembling.

In their exhausted, thirst-tormented, overwrought condition, a bout of irritation or short temper was understandable enough, but the others felt that what had flared so swiftly between Roddie and Finn was deeper than irritation. They were like two with a blood-secret between them.

"Oh, very well," replied Finn. "I could do it, if you couldn't. That's all."

There was a tense, drawn-out moment and Roddie's fist gripped round the unshipped tiller. Henry broke the silence, speaking calmly. "There's no good talking wild, Finn. Our minds are weary enough. In any case, where would be the point of climbing? We have got to keep reasonable."

"Because there will be water on the top. You saw the sheep. If we don't get away to-morrow—ask Callum what he'll be like."

"You can leave me out of it," said Callum dully.

"We'll wait until to-morrow, and then——"

"And then it'll be too late," Finn interrupted Henry. "I'm weak enough myself and I'm dying of thirst. So are you. Someone should try it."

"Oh, shut up!" said Henry, suddenly overborne.

Rob looked at the cliff and remarked casually, "I never had the head for it myself."

"You're honest, anyway," replied Finn, trying to smile casually.

The silence that fell on the boat now gave them no rest, no ease; worked deep in their minds like a diluted poison. Roddie and Henry closed their eyes to avoid contacts. Callum was slumped against the nets and presently began to moan. His lips were pale as oatmeal. His moaning in a tortured, restless sleep irritated Henry intensely, and he got up and looked at the rock. Presently he had to waken Callum. When Callum first tried to speak, nothing came except a wheeze. But he got a smile through and enough voice to blame the accursed salt beef. He sat up and rubbed his cheeks and ears slowly and pulled at his throat. By the morning Callum would be in a state of acute distress. They could hear the clacking of his mouth as it tried for moisture.

Henry looked at Roddie. "I think I'll have a shot at it," he said, nodding sideways at the cliff.

Roddie removed his eyes and shook his head. Henry had a wife and three of a family.

Henry went silent.

"If the lad thinks he can do it," began Rob, noisily scratching the beard on his jaw, "well—I don't know——"

Finn said nothing, his face to the rock. It was between Roddie and himself, and he was aware that Roddie did not care for cliffs. It was quite possible that he hadn't the head. But, far beyond all that, he knew what was troubling him. Roddie would not like to be the bearer of the tidings of Finn's death to Finn's mother! Something deep inside Finn exulted over Roddie, over his bitter predicament, with a sustained feeling of ruthless triumph. Death itself was neither here nor there, because in fact it never entered Finn's head except as an imaginary counter in this triumph of enmity.

Excepting Roddie, Callum was the strongest man on the boat. But his strength was of the kind that lives powerfully for a short time. His body was broad, and at middle age he would be a stout heavy man. His frank generous nature had a fine simplicity, and now as he stirred and tried to smile, his blue eyes looked as pitiful as a child's. "That salt beef," he croaked. He wanted to lie in the bottom of the boat and not move.

Finn upended the cask and shook it over the skillet. Callum moistened his mouth with the drops and looked grateful and ashamed.

"Well, boys," said Roddie quietly, "I'm willing to hear you."

No-one spoke.

Roddie nodded and looked at the cliff. "Very well," he said. "One of us will try it. Who is it to be?"

"As skipper," said Rob, "you can't desert the boat."

Henry nodded. The thing did not bear discussing, with a young fellow like Finn in the crew. And it was Finn's idea. Rob had spoken because of the look in Roddie's eyes.

There was a minute's long silent conflict in all their minds, then Roddie pointed to the anchor rope. Finn began to strip off his heavy sea clothes.

Henry and Rob on an oar apiece brought her head to where Roddie wanted it. He let the anchor down carefully, holding the rope immediately he felt bottom, and motioned them to row away. Thus he made certain of not fouling his anchor hold, and they approached Finn's ledge, stern first.

Some three yards from the rock, Roddie held them. "Take Henry's oar," he cried to Callum, now on his feet. This was done. "Go right aft, Henry, and let her in as far as you dare."

Finn, stripped to jersey and trousers, took off his boots and stockings, for any climbing he had done had been with his bare feet. With his big toe and the one next to it, he could always pick up a stone and throw it farther than any other boy. This had been often a source of young pride. He knotted his woollen cravat round his neck and stuck the ends down his jersey. Two empty bottles, which had contained milk and bore the label "Special", he placed to one side. Then he stood up and pulled tight over his brows his round bonnet. He was ready.

With left hand up, Henry checked and guided Roddie's control on the anchor rope, while the two men on the oars paddled gently, doing little more than holding the boat straight. Henry was in no hurry. As she rose and plunged on the great impulses of the sea, Henry studied her action and the rock in front. It was a desperate venture, because no two seas behaved quite alike, and the stern was thrown giddily not only up and down but in a swaying circular motion. If she fell fifteen feet on a sharp ledge they would drown like rats. Now the stern began to rush on the cliff-face, then to sag away, while the water streamed from the rock, from the weed, and boiled underneath in seething froth.

For long moments Henry felt he should give up. Or Finn should have a light rope from the boat round his waist. Or—"I can do it now," said Finn.

Henry looked round at him. Finn smiled into his eyes and nodded. Henry slowly motioned Roddie a few inches in. Finn slipped past him and crouched behind the stern-post. Holding on with his left hand, Henry gripped Finn at the waist with his right to steady him. "When she comes up, Finn boy," said Henry in a hoarse voice.

Up she came, rushing on the rock. Henry withdrew his hand. Not until she was a foot from the top of her swinging heave did Finn rise bodily in one swift, easy motion and leap left-footed from the narrow stern-post, and land on toes, knees, and hands, in that order, on the small, rounded, sloping ledge of dark rock.

Down below in the gulf eyes stared up. He held. The boy was ashore. Roddie brought the back of a hand over his forehead.

"The bottles!" cried Finn. Henry threw them, one at each uprising, and Finn caught them against his breast. Then he whipped off his broad woollen cravat, stuck the bottles neck first into the band of his trousers behind, pulled the black jersey down over them, put two twists of the cravat round his waist, and knotted it over the necks of the bottles. Then he looked up the rock, and in a moment was climbing.

Roddie pulled the boat no more than a yard away. The boat-hook was clear. But as Finn climbed on a slant to his right, Roddie knew that the boat-hook would now fail to reach his fallen body.

The shrieking of the sea-birds became an infernal torment to their ragged nerves, and when suddenly Rob seemed to go mad in a high-pitched croak, their hearts leapt as their heads turned—and saw, choking the rock channel, advancing upon them, a gigantic wall of water.

Roddie's whole weight threw itself instinctively on the rope, but it was torn through his hands as the *Seafoam* rose up and up on the towering wave. Along the rock walls it smashed in a roar flinging white arms at crevice and ledge.

Swung seaward on the crest of it, they hung for a dizzying moment on a level with Finn. He had seen it coming and flattened to the sloping rock, gripping with fingers and knees and toes. The solid water swept the soles of his feet, but the white spray covered him like a shroud. Down went the boat, down, down, until tangle, that grew in a sea-green underworld, saw the light of day, and curved over, and flattened like trees ridden by a hurricane.

Then up again, Roddie's hands torn, but the boat well clear of the cliff.

And there was Finn, splayed black against the rock, his head turning cautiously towards the channel. They watched him get to his knees, his feet, pause for an instant to look down on them and wave, before clambering on as if another sea might be coming.

The climbing so far had not been difficult because there was a distinct ridge sloping steeply up the face of the rock for all the world like a narrow, tumbled, broken path. On his left hand the cliff rose sheer, and on his right it fell sheer into the sea. They had seen this formation, of course, from the boat. But now Finn reached a wall in front of him, little more than twice his own height, but to his eyes unclimbable. Here the path ended.

All at once, as he looked up, his vision darkened and his heart began beating at a tremendous rate. He had lived and moved these last seconds beyond his exhausted strength. His skin went cold all over and his flesh started to quiver and tremble in a sickening manner. He lay against the rock, face in, until the silent buzz of the darkness in his head began to subside and his vision to clear. The whistling of his breath made his mouth so much dryer than it was that, when he closed it, it stuck, and came apart again painfully.

As he turned round he saw the upturned faces watching him. He made a gesture of placing his hand over his heart, then he sat down carefully, lay over on one side, and closed his eyes. Deliberately he let his mind sink down in him as if he were going to sleep. For panic was near, the weak nervousness that hates defeat. They would be watching him, too, wondering why he was taking so long, as if he were playing with their nerves, particularly with Roddie's. Well, let them! let them! So long as the panic stings kept off. And actually, for about half a minute, he was invaded by a delicious feeling of languor. He let it soak into his limp tissues. He felt cradled in an eagle's eyrie.

Arising, he looked at the rock. In front of him and on the inward side it was flawless and impossible, but on the outward edge it was notched and in two places riven to miniature ledges. The surface was of a dark, rough texture and dry enough. Without giving himself time for thought, he reached up his right hand and gripped a boss.

They watched him from the boat.

There were moments when the slowness of his movements had, for Roddie, the element of extreme horror that is found only in nightmare. His bare foot would come up, feeling for the crack, pawing the rock, with a suspension of time that must for ever defeat it, while the body hung over the sea, high and sheer over the sea, and in an instant was

going to fall away, fall away with a shriek, to drop, to rebound from the cornice below, to whirl—with final smash
upon the water.

But Finn was still on the rock. And the rock was not his
danger, as he knew. He loved the perilous cleanness of
height. He could go as carefully here as if he were crossing
stepping-stones in a stream. Height invigorated him, made
all his senses sing. What he feared was his staying power,
the trembling fingers, the dark flush.

He rounded the desperate corner, fingers pressing on the
ledge above, toes on the ledge below, and suddenly found
that he had rounded the real danger. His spirit lifted in a
rush, in a silent cry. The rock leaned back. His toe came
up searching for a purchase, found it, felt all round it,
gripped; his right hand moved up and got a hold he could
have swung on; his left hand, his left foot; slowly, with a
certainty of care; up, up over, until he lay on his stomach in
safety, with a laughing ecstasy in his heart.

They saw the broad of his feet over the edge of the cliff.
Roddie, unknown to himself, groaned and sagged, completely exhausted. He had plumbed depths of fear and terror that Finn knew nothing of.

On his feet, Finn looked down at them and waved, laughing, like an immortal youth; then he turned away and went
on up the steep rock with ease, until it gave on grass and he
felt the rush of the wind.

From left to right the ground sloped in a long, upward
sweep. In front the smooth sward was dotted with staring
sheep and rose gently for about half a mile to the highest
and farthest point of the island.

He went up to his right to command the whole island,
and suddenly stood, his heart in his throat, gazing at a
small house. Slowly his eyes searched around everywhere.
There was, however, neither human being nor smoke. He
approached the house. It was dry-stone built, with long
flat stones, as many a house was in Dunster. But it was
small, and not like a house, either. Finn came by the door.

It was a little door, about two feet by three. "Are you in?" he called. There was no answer.

Finn stooped double and entered. Inside it was no more than seven feet long and four or five broad. The vaulted roof was an inch or two above his head. There was a damp smell of the earth or of something very ancient. Finn felt that he was not alone.

He went out quietly and stepped away from that place. There were ruins farther on, up at the high north-west point. The sheep ran wildly before him. The birds screamed. He could feel the trembling of the solid rock. The wind harried his eyes and ears. A feeling of remoteness came over Finn, as if he stood on the last storm-threshed outpost of the world. The warm blood of the heart thinned away. Cavernous screaming of birds like tormented spirits, the whistling wail of the invisible wind, the pounding and booming of the sea, the tremble of the rock, all insecure, on the verge of falling away into gulfs of eternal disaster.

Who could have lived in that little house, sitting there by himself?

The ruins in the high corner were larger. Two rooms, with a low passage between.

Turning away, Finn remembered Rob's story of Rona, the rats, and the dead woman with the child at her breast.

Then he came on the tiny pool, stone beneath it and turf round it. He scooped a little in his hand and tasted it. Sweet, sweet fresh water!

A grand-uncle of Roddie's, a very strong man, had once, long ago, after heavy labour in the height of a summer day, drunk and drunk out of the cold well that is in the brae above the creek at Lybster, and died within an hour.

Finn, flat on his breast, filled his mouth with water, held it a moment, and let it slide down. Ah-h! He filled it again, he worked it round his gums, and let it go. The water was clear and with the velvet softness that peat gives. It tasted like the water in the burn at home; it was full of memories that did not quite come, that stayed on the other side of

knowing, gently as a hand in sleep. "Oh, boys, it's good!"
he said to himself. About to lie over, he pulled up and
brought forth the bottles, as if the little well might vanish
should he close his eyes. After rinsing them twice, he filled
and corked them, then drank again. He could not get the
dry stickiness out of his mouth. Stretching himself on the
turf, he let his nostrils breathe in its earthy fragrance. The
land!

There was no hurry. He needed rest, against the earth.
The sea came, heaving him, a ghostly sea, with all the
boat's motions. And sleep—he had to lift his head, to sit up.
It would hardly do if he fell asleep!

At last he arose with a cool feeling of being renewed.
At the high points to his right, as he faced from the little
house to the ruins, the cliffs were three hundred feet. He
did not care to go too near their edge because the wind was
so strong. But away to the west side the turf sloped in a
gentle breast and there the sea hammered the cliff inward
to a horse-shoe bend, with sheer sides two hundred feet
high. The wind, too, was now in his face, holding him
back.

Finn saw a ledge a little to his right crowded with
guillemots, but knew he could not climb down to it. On his
hips he advanced carefully, however, just to investigate. A
whirl of wind came sideways at him. It was treacherous,
the wind in the rock-faces. But what an incredible number
of birds! On both hands the ledges were crowded with
them. Whole screaming colonies—with each kind keeping
to its own ledge! Finn smiled at that. Each to its own town-
ship, its own parish! Crowded, shoulder to shoulder, and
shouting their rights at the tops of their voices! The
drink was doing Finn good already. His head was clear and
steady, and the flesh on his bones was perhaps fine in the
feel but ready and keen. He had often found that what
looks like the very edge of a cliff a yard away, is not the
final edge when you come to it. So he went on, very carefully, until his feet pushed out over the abyss.

The birds saw him; the guillemots went hoarse, the kittiwakes demented, the razorbills lower down stretched their noisy necks as if fish had stuck in them, the air darkened with wheeling gulls and fulmars, the sea-parrots blinked sideways and bit each other.

Finn saw an egg on a ledge.

The wind buffeted him. It was difficult but it might not be impossible to get at the ledge. He drew back, circled some fifteen yards, and then began again his advance on the cliff.

No, he could not get to that ledge, although it was only just over the crest, because the sloping ground behind was burrowed and treacherous. Still, he could push out, inch by inch. The ground seemed firm enough.

He got within two feet of them, and they still sat blinking at him, broad yellow and red beaks over white breasts, squatting orange legs. They were bird-fools that would not get up. He saw that. He realized that he could catch them with his bare hands.

There were only one or two bannocks of bread left. Under the birds would be their eggs. He knew he was going to take a chance that he should not take. Excitement dizzied him slightly and he lay back to get cool, thrusting out his hands behind, the left one entering a burrow. In the same moment he yelled and whirled over on his face. The back of his left hand was bitten to the bone.

Instinctively he sucked the wound and spat red, his heart hammering. Had this happened to him while he was sitting up peering precariously into the awesome cauldron below, he would probably have gone over. He now drew himself up on his breast until he faced the burrow. Swathing his right hand in his bonnet, he thrust it tentatively into the shallow burrow. Out came the parrot beak. Down came Finn's left, swift as a beast's paw, and caught the head. A twist and a pull, and the bird was dead. In went his right hand, and the fingers touched, closed gently upon, and drew forth an egg, whitish in colour, with vague ashen spots. He gazed upon its miracle of beauty. It was warm. He shook it by his ear. It was firm. He picked up a sharp pebble from the mouth of the burrow and cracked a small hole in each end of the egg. He sniffed, introduced the pointed end to his mouth, and sucked. Slimy, soft as velvet, came the white; a pause, and the yolk broke along his palate in a wave, a choking fullness, a rich gluttony; more wet velvet, and his breath whistled inward through the vacant holes. He regarded the empty shell with a slow smile and tossed it over the edge to play with the wind. His eyes turned, searching for burrows. Most of them were arm-deep, and when a bird shoved out its egg to meet his hand, swathed in his bonnet, he could not help laughing.

In a little while, he was walking towards the boat, with two bottles of water, three dead puffins, and twelve eggs in his round bonnet. As he hove in sight, it was almost ludicrous to see how the four faces were gazing up. He laid his gear at his feet and waved a bottle in one hand and a dead bird in the other.

Their hands rose and fell, but otherwise they showed no animation. For a moment Finn, in the flush of his triumph, felt disappointment. Setting down bird and bottle, he turned away from them back to the well. He was thirsty again, and the two bottles were little enough for four mouths.

The next time they saw him appear he was astride a sheep, holding it by the horns.

It was a joke on Finn's part, for he knew they could do nothing with a sheep. Still, if Roddie showed they wanted the sheep by making to bring the boat in, he could try to force it down, and if it refused to jump, he could give it a push. Suddenly the joke passed from him, and he let the sheep go.

They seemed dull and heavy in that boat! After the run he had had to corner the sheep in the ruins, too!

And how he was going to get this cargo of tender egg-shell and glass down to the sea-edge was a problem!

Roddie was now bringing the boat in below him, lest he fall.

Finn, on his knees, leaned over the short but perpendicular face of rock that had cost him so much dangerous effort in climbing up, and pondered. He had had the vague idea of lowering his bonnet by his long woollen cravat, and trusting the bottles to stick in his fairly tight waist-band. He lay on his breast, holding his scarf at arm's length. It was not long enough to reach the slanting rock track below. And, anyway, the water was more important than the eggs. He must take no risk with the water. But his heart was so set on bringing them the eggs!

There is never a difficulty but there is a way out, was an old saying. He could not take the bonnet in his teeth, with cheek and mouth scraping the rock at the corner. It would, in fact, be more difficult to go down than it had been to come up. Finn knew this so clearly that he did not let his mind dwell upon it. Even the bottles would clog his hips.

And then the idea came to him, beautiful in its simplicity.

Stripping off his jersey, he tied the end of each sleeve in a firm knot and let down a bottle against the knot. The top of the bottle in the right arm he padded with two puffins and set his bonnet of eggs on top. The third puffin he pushed against the bottle in the left arm. Then tying one end of the cravat round the waist of the jersey, he lowered away slowly, lying flat, head and arms over the rock. They touched the slanting track, and by gentle manipulation he got them to incline inward. When they were resting securely, he dropped his end of the scarf.

That's that! he thought. Whatever happened to him now, he had brought them relief, for he had shown them how to land and climb so far.

Sitting with his feet over the edge of the outer rock, he carefully wiped the blood of the left-hand wound from his fingers, until they were dry to the tips. Then he rubbed the toes of each foot against the other leg. Turning over on his stomach, he began the descent, the boiling water green and white far below.

Again Roddie went through his agony; and now, indeed, from exhaustion, the other three members of the crew were caught in the fascination of horror, as Finn moved slowly, with that blind searching and pawing of the toes.

The awful moment came before Finn got his feet upon the under ledge. In lowering from one grip, he had put such stress on his right forearm that he had torn the skin. His body was quivering from drawn-out tautness, as at last he moved sideways, finger-tips on the top ledge and toes on the bottom, his legs straight as bars and hips drawn in. Round the corner, slowly, hanging on, inch by inch, slowly, his breath sticking in his throat now, eighteen inches, a foot—careful, careful—an inch too soon and a bent knee would fling the body headlong—until, gathering all his resources, he lowered himself in a final slow motion of faultless grace. Then he lay back against the dark wall with a sobbing of breath in his throat, an occasional gulping, and a hand that shook as it wiped sweat from a cold forehead.

The faces and bodies in the boat, heaving and falling on the long motions of the sea, remained still and wordless, eyes held by the lad taking his ease against the rock. They were like a group paralysed in a nightmare. Finn smiled, raised a hand in salute, and released them.

But he did not move from where he was until they had the boat in position. He thought to himself, with common-sense, and perhaps a little vanity, that they would understand why he delayed. For it was clear to Finn that the great wall of water which had all but caught him on the way up— a yard lower down, and he would have been swept away like a fly—was one of those monstrous seas, which they had seen outside, happening by chance so to hit the curving rocks on the west side that it was funnelled through the narrow walled channel between the two islands. It would not happen often—but it was bound to happen.

A thought struck his inventive mind and he made a fixed

noose of his cravat, then spreading the weighted jersey against his back, stooping, with right hand free, he made down the slanting broken way as quickly as he could.

"An oar!" he shouted to Henry, who was waiting to receive him, and then made clear his intention by a mimed handling of the noosed cravat. On his knees, Henry stuck out the oar as the boat came up and Finn slipped the noose over the blade, shouting, "Eggs! Canny!" Slowly Henry swung the burden away, over the gunnel, into the hold, where Rob let it come to rest gently at his feet.

"Good, Rob!" shouted Finn and waved an arm in delight.

With his right palm, Henry held Finn back; with his left hand he motioned Roddie still inward. Finn smiled. It was so much easier to leap on to the boat than off it! Then Henry, from the depths, looked up at him with strained face. Finn laughed as the stern came heaving, and leapt. In his anxiety, Henry gripped him and they both rolled head over heels into the hold, where Finn lay choking with laughter.

With an expression arid as the dark rock, Roddie never looked at him; ordered the lifting of the anchor and the rowing to mid-channel.

"What kept you, boy?" asked Rob, in a gentle yet aggrieved voice.

"Kept me?" said Finn. "What do you mean?"

"You were hours. We thought you had gone."

Finn stared into Rob's face and his brain worked. Then he reached for his jersey, as Henry made fast the anchor-rope, and laid out the twelve eggs (two were cracked, none broken), the three birds, and the two bottles of water.

"That's all I could manage," he said, with pardonable irony, and moved up to where he had left his clothes. As his head appeared through the neck of his jersey, it stared out over the sea. Then he sat down and began dressing slowly.

Callum was now in a pretty bad way, because his quick,

self-sensitive mind had endured the agony of having sent
Finn to his doom.

"Finn, my hero," he croaked huskily. "God damn it."
And the tears came down his face.

"Cold iron!" wheezed Rob solemnly.

"Oh, hell," muttered Callum and leaned back, his head
falling sideways.

Roddie came beside Callum and uncorked one of the
bottles. Gently he fed Callum out of its neck as if he were
a child. "Hold it in your mouth for a little," he urged.
"That's the way. Take your time."

"Have you a snuff?" Finn asked Rob casually.

"Surely, boy."

Finn took a pinch and handed the horn back. "Thanks,"
he said, turning away. Leaning over the boat, he washed
the blood from his hand and forearm. Then he made himself ostentatiously comfortable against the nets and lay
gazing out over the stern at the rocks and the screaming
birds.

Perhaps Roddie thought he, Finn, had been deliberately
keeping them in fear, showing off a bit, having his own
back on Roddie in this way. Roddie could think what he
liked; they could all think what they liked—while they
drank the water and sucked the eggs.

He was suddenly maddened at the snuff for making him
sneeze.

He could see that for a long time he had been afraid of
Roddie, of a strange terrible power that was in him. Now
he was no longer afraid. He could hold his own against
Roddie. And would—however the challenge came.

As the flush of anger ebbed, he grew extremely tired,
sick with tiredness, and let his head fall back. Henry called
to him but he did not answer. He could sleep and forget
them all. His re-clothed body was suffused with warmth,
tingling. But anger like a red worm of hate kept threading
up through his mind. He forced his mind from him, set it
against the cliff . . . ranging restlessly, it came on the little

house on the island and almost on the man who rested there. There was the curious kind of feeling he got in the House of Peace. But the House of Peace was pervaded by still grey light. It came out from the stone. The morning they had left home, he had arranged matters so that he could walk down alone. . . . Through the grey light, more gentle than the bitter self-pity that lies beyond anger, he fell asleep.

In the morning, tremendous seas were running and it was still blowing, but the sky had lightened. There was a premonitory freshness in the air, an inwardness of life, of exhilaration. During the long, dark hours, an awakened ear had heard the booming, the ravening roaring winds, as if held to security by a miracle in the centre of a crashing hell. And more than once the mind had rushed on wakefulness in a vast upheaving and plunging recession, a tearing loose, with a blinded moment of dread that could feel no more as it waited the smashing obliterating impact. Then the check of the anchor-rope and the invisible devils shrieking onward round the cliffs.

Roddie had plainly slept very little and was deeply quietened. They were all quietened, with darkened eyelids, but upon their bodies was a half-drugged ease, not unpleasant.

"Feeling a bit better, Callum?" asked Rob.

"I am doing as well as could be expected," answered Callum, taking Rob's simple question in good part. For he seemed renewed, if without the characteristic quickness of physical movement. Henry asked Roddie what he thought about the day. Roddie was hopeful, but it was agreed not to eat meantime.

The sun came out fierily, stinging their eyes. So they closed them, heads back, drinking in the light, lips apart, warmly drugged.

"Keep it from roaring, Rob, will you?" muttered Callum.

"Keep what?"

"Your belly."

"It wasn't mine," said Rob seriously.

They could sleep now. Hours passed before they grew restless again. The sun was high.

Roddie motioned to Henry and a fair division was made of the last of the bread, which was a single bannock of oatcake. Each got a piece bigger than the palm of the hand. There were four eggs left and over half a bottle of water. Henry divided the water into bowls so that each could drink it as he liked.

"I don't want an egg," said Finn.

Henry looked strongly at him. Finn smiled, knowing Henry did not wish him to start trouble again. "I had four yesterday, and last night I nearly spewed."

Henry smiled dryly. "You'll be all right, then."

"If you like," said Finn, "I could easily go up the cliff again." It sounded like a taunt.

Henry turned away, and handed one egg to Callum and one to Rob, but Roddie said quietly, "Keep it meantime."

They could not keep one egg.

"Keep them all," said Callum. "We might want them yet."

"Very well," said Henry.

Finn flushed, and his eyes, flashing, looked through an unnatural smile at the cliff.

But Callum was having no nonsense, and set the talk going as they munched, and they all joined in with a word or two.

No one had asked Finn what it had been like on top of the island, and it was difficult for him to break down his own vanity and tell. Yet he made an effort by starting a private talk with Rob. "Remember your talking about Rona and the dead woman and child? I thought I was going to meet them up there," he began.

"Why that?" asked Rob, interested at once.

Finn told about the little house and the queer feeling it gave when you cried if there was anyone in and there was no one. "So in I went."

326

"Did you, though?"

Then he told about the other ruins and how he found the little well. It was a big island; it was over half a mile long if it was an inch, and one can't find anything just in a minute. Besides, he had thought of Callum, which means, as Rob would understand, that he had thought of his most important part, in short, he had thought of eggs.

"For the belly." Rob nodded. "Man, man, go on."

Callum chuckled. They were all listening eagerly, Roddie with his eyes out to sea.

"So there I was, boy, hanging on by the seat of my pants and by the thought of Callum—when I leaned back for a second, sticking my hands out—like this—and at that moment it struck me, cutting to the bone. Look!"

Finn drew out the mystery and Rob's wonder, until he started laughing himself.

Presently Roddie said, in a gentle voice, "Here, boys, I think we'll give it a trial." And somehow, in a moment, the boat was full of the old well-being and courage.

The masts were stepped, the anchor lifted, and on the oars they nosed out to the running seas. "Look!" cried Finn, pointing to grey seals that plunged off a skerry. A patch of sea had gone demented. Two bulls were fighting. Reefed sails were lifted. The sea, the wind, they heeled over, they were into it now!

The sun was at the top of its arch, due south. When the clouds tore from it, the seas sparkled, a crowning green over deep blue. The wind was on their starboard quarter, strong, but with the snarl gone.

The water swung, raced, glittering, alive. Long waves, not breaking, if with a whiff of drift now and then, particularly when it was a monster, with the little waters running at the top, smoking slightly.

When the boat went clean from them and Rob said, "Ay, ay," in solemn wonder, as if someone had told him a magic tale, Finn laughed from the belly, softly. It was fine being alive again, exhilarated, careless. And Roddie sat upright, drawn into himself, the gleam in his eyes, fighting the seas. He was at home now. He was a great skipper.

Finn did not feel ashamed of the red anger against Roddie in the dark jaw of the rocks. For his challenging manhood was sweet in his flesh. That was past; and before them might be many a strange enough encounter. This weakening lack of food clarified the mind of all vain humours. And where it failed, the sea washed in!

There was no doubt about the mainland of Lewis, when the mountains rose over their starboard bow. That was a lovely sight; and they stared at them as at a vision in a day-dream. "It's the land," said Rob.

As if it might be something else! What a fine sound: "the land". Only men who have been lost at sea know the beauty of that sound as it fades away in silent music through the head. Yet never quite fades, because the eyes continue to hold the wonder of the far blue outlines, un-changing and steadfast. With always that touch of the alien that is at the heart of true wonder.

Roddie held to his course.

Soon the flat land of Lewis was clear stretching far to the north, but not until they could see the waters white against great headlands, did Roddie bear away. "I think, boys," he said, "we'll try for the Butt."

The wind was now almost dead astern and the going easier. It was as well to be done with this ocean! The wind, too, was taking off. Within an hour, Roddie had the reefs out, driving the *Seafoam* all he could. Finn saw the stem lifting and racing, eager now to realize its own wooden dream. If Roddie took a risk he would be ready with a counter. And that stem would help him!

"What about your eggs now, Finn?" asked Callum.

Finn took the four eggs and offered the first one to Roddie.

"There's not one for us all," said Roddie reasonably.

"I wish you would take it," said Finn, his expression darkening.

"Thanks," said Roddie. "Will you break two holes in the end for me?"

This Finn did, and then he handed an egg to each of the others.

"What about yourself?" asked Callum.

"The thought of it still makes me want to spew," said Finn, smiling. "I had four. This is only your third."

"Good health!" said Rob.

"Your very good health!" said Callum.

Henry raised his egg. Roddie nodded and glanced back over his shoulder. Finn felt embarrassed and very happy.

In the late evening they rounded the Butt, but well to seaward to avoid the broken tumult, and as they came into the quiet waters of the Minch, they looked about them with marvelling, humoured eyes.

Small boats out fishing. The entrance to the inlet of Ness. A queer reluctance came upon them to go into any populous place. "They'll talk so much," said Roddie, "the thought of it makes me tired."

A quiet little haven, all to themselves, to sleep the night through, that was what they craved. They were in the mood not to want humanity, to hold by a strange yet comforting perversity to the outcast world they had created about them. Only in that moment did they realize, dimly, the nature of what they had come through.

When the wind died completely away, they took to the oars, shaking their heads over them in arrested laughter as at the final and culminating wonder.

"Queer things happen," said Rob, "if only you live long enough."

Roddie steered into a little creek and ran her foot upon the sand in a slow hiss.

When Callum landed he staggered and fell. They all staggered, for they were weak and light-headed. A trickle of water came down into the creek, forming little pools higher up. "Don't drink too much," said Roddie.

Finn and Henry went up over the rise, and in less than

an hour returned bearing an iron pot between them and a tin pail in Finn's left hand. On the tongue of sward by the strand the others watched and waited.

"It's hot porridge," said Henry.

"And a small drop of milk," said Finn.

"Take off your bonnets, boys," said Callum. "Roddie, say the grace."

Simply and sincerely Roddie said the "Grace before Meat". Their hearts were filled; and then their stomachs were softly and divinely poulticed.

CHAPTER XVI

THE GOLDEN CASK

W hile it was yet early, Roddie woke Henry. "She's
afloat again." Henry sat up, for they had slept
on shore, and looked upon the quiet morning.
The sun was well up and lay in a lively glitter upon a sea
whose surface was darkened by a gentle land wind.

"We've either to put her at anchor or go out," said
Roddie. "It's a fine air of wind."

Henry did not answer. He wanted to sleep.

"We're a few days overdue," said Roddie, "and I would
like to get there myself."

Henry nodded. But the others were almost mutinous,
Callum in particular, when they had nearly shaken the
shoulder out of him.

"This is dam' nonsense," he declared.

Roddie had the water-cask full, and after a little while
they all got on board.

"Didn't the old wife tell you," Callum addressed Henry,
"that there was no fishing in Stornoway in any case?
Surely we could have had one day on our backs."

"You've been over five hours on your back," answered
Roddie. "And when we catch the wind you can go on your
back again."

"Or my backside for all you care," protested Callum.
"What do you say about it, Finn?"

"It's a sort of nice morning, too," said Finn.

"Ach, you! Boys, I can't tell you what like a sleep I
had!" Callum shook his head. "It lasted, at the full, one

moment." He could not close his hands, they were so weak, and, in fact, when the sails were drawing, he fell off as he swallowed the last bite of his share of the two oat bannocks the old wife had given Henry and Finn when they had returned the pot and the bucket and made her a present of the three puffins.

Finn was caught into the peaceful morning and lay half-dreaming as they slowly sailed along this strange shore. It was a different world altogether from the iron-bound coasts of home. There was a softness upon the land, in the air. His blood grew warm and sluggish with dream. It was a world of fable, where the mind was wafted upon its own adventure by the wind of desire. And images formed. One image—very clearly. And there came upon him the intimate wonder of her living face, her dark girl's face, with light in the eyes. Never yet had he given in to it. Not even now would the unfathomable reluctance of his boyhood's independence or pride let him give in to it, let him admit anything. She was not his companion. They could not walk at ease. And her eyes—he could hardly look into them. But —they were there.

Conquering the stormy seas of the Western Ocean, climbing the cliffs of The Seven Hunters (as the old wife had called them), sailing by this far land on a beautiful summer morning—if she could understand that, if someone would tell her, tell her how he had climbed and brought back water (Callum might yet describe in detail how he had been saved, how he owed his life to Finn), then perhaps she would see that a fellow like Jim was not of such great importance after all. That he was of no importance whatsoever. That he would fade out in the glory of this peaceful morning, without Finn's saying a word, because Una's eyes . . .

They troubled him. He saw her hair, like a blackbird's wing, falling away from her neck, the warm, untouchable pallor of her neck. She walked beside him; like two who had met on a journey, not looking at each other, they walked together. They sat on a green machair over a smooth strand, the morning sun in her eyes. They were in a house. They were here, they were everywhere. . . . A salmon in a waterfall pool, a gleam vanishing in dark whirls. . . .

Suddenly it came upon him that perhaps she was for him this gleam; she only. Body and mind went still, banked up in a wave, but his own eyes blinded and the wave burst, drowning all thought. The self-protective wave.

Out of the darkness into which he had fallen from the sudden release of his imagery, he found himself on a cliff wall. For ages he climbed up its perpendicular face. It was a thousand feet high. In over the top was a little house where Una lived all alone, because the men of the place had perished in a cataclysm of storm and sundering rock. There was one enormous vulture-like bird, with a vermilion tip to its black beak, that screamed as it stooped at him. By flattening against the rock, Finn could just avoid its beak, though its pinions threshed his clothes. Una did not know that this was going on. She might never know. That was his agony. As the bird became bolder, drawing time to a climax, myriads of lesser birds circled and screamed overhead. Out swooped the foiled bird from underneath, banking upward in a magnificent wave, holding to the screaming crest, and now—now—coming down—down—straight for him, for his shoulder. . . . He started awake and blinked at Henry.

Henry smiled, withdrawing his hand from Finn's shoulder.

The screaming birds were still in his ears. Finn gazed about him, and saw they had come round a point and were making for a fishing-boat inshore. Wheeling about this boat was a colony of demented gulls.

"They signalled us in," explained Roddie, with the old smile, detached and friendly.

"What for?" And then in a word that was a stroke of wonder: "Herring!"

"By God, cannot a fellow get five minutes' peace it-self?" demanded Callum angrily from the dark fumes of sleep.

"Cold iron!" cried Rob.

"Cold backside!" said Callum.

"Cold iron!" cried Roddie sharply.

"Cold iron," muttered Callum, feebly stretching for the metal. Then he gazed about him and blinked at a boat not so big as their own. She was sunk to the gunnels.

Sails down and oars out, they drew alongside. An oldish man, with sandy whiskers and a pleasant smiling face, called, "Can you be doing with some herring?"

"We can," answered Roddie. "You seem to be in them!"

"We are up to the gunnels, and there are six nets still to come."

"We'll haul them with great care for you," cried Roddie with a smile.

"All right." The skipper nodded, scales to his neck. "Back in and take this lug here."

She had four of a crew, one young fellow about Finn's age. A Stornoway boat, her hold a brimming well of net and glittering herring. As the crew wiped the sweat from necks and faces, the skipper asked where they had been shot last night. Roddie told him they hadn't been shot; they had been coming from the west side.

"The west side?" repeated the skipper.

"Ay," said Roddie; "we went round to see what was doing, but found it pretty stormy. Much doing in Storno-way?"

"No, there's been little so far." He was looking at their faces. "You didn't get caught in the storm, did you? It was blowing terrible strong in Stornoway the night before last."

"We ran for shelter," said Roddie. "We were all right."

"What put you round there?"

"The wind," Roddie answered, with pleasant humour.

"Where did you shelter?" The friendly sea-blue eyes in the ruddy face over the sandy whiskers were charged with curiosity.

"In the Seven Hunters."

"The Seven Hunters!"

Finn saw belief, against their better judgement, hold their staring faces.

As the *Sulaire* drew away from them on four oars, flat as a beetle, Finn said, "Hold your breath."

It looked indeed as if a big breath would sink her.

But they had to keep their laughter and excitement out of the *Sulaire's* hearing. The hold was tidied; their own nets stowed forward; then, grouping aft, they prepared to haul, Roddie and Finn on the back rope, Henry at the sole, with Callum and Rob ready for the heavy weight of fish.

"And you were grumbling at me," complained Callum, "for rooting you out of sleep."

"She's heavy," said Roddie, leaning back with all his weight and strength on a rope that seemed anchored.

"She's solid," said Henry.

In their general bodily weakness, excitement so got the better of them, the excitement of happiness, of wild wonder at this extraordinary conclusion to their extraordinary adventure, that they could hardly pull.

As the first herring came over the gunnel, Rob shook his head in husky beneficence. "B-boys, boys, th-the silver darlings!"

Silver deep in the water, in the air, silver round their feet. All on a glittering silver morning, with the land quiet and the sea quiet; peace everywhere, except in the throats of the flashing gulls. Finn, leaning back on the rope, saw the gulls snow-white against the pale blue summer sky.

They shipped the oars, as a small breeze cooled them off Tiumpan Head, and they half-emptied the water-cask.

Down the Eye Peninsula they slowly sailed until, rounding Chicken Head, they saw the unmistakable smoke of
Stornoway a few miles in.

"We have come at it, maybe, in a roundabout way,"
allowed Rob, with his solemn air.

"I wouldn't say much about that ashore," suggested
Roddie.

Finn knew that Roddie would not like anyone to tease
him on his seamanship. So much had been plain from his
responses to the *Sulaire*.

They were all laughing. Callum's arms fell from him in
helpless weakness. "We're like the one family of kittens."
As they cleared the Point, and stood into the broad bay
that is Stornoway harbour, Roddie spoke to them. "Go
slow, and they won't notice anything," he finished.

"And if they do, we can put it down to drink," added
Finn, filling the skillet once more.

Soon there was no doubt about its being Stornoway.
Beyond a green island in the wide fairway they saw the
piers about a broad rectangular promontory, crowded with
buildings, that stuck far out into the water, the shore curving away to either side from its root. At anchor off this
promontory, Finn counted nine vessels—smacks, schooners,
and no less than two three-masted barks. Straight over
them, on the treeless slopes across the bay, stood a round
tower, and over from it to the right, Stornoway Lodge, the
residence of the island's proprietor.

The harbour wall was crowded as, in a calm, the *Seafoam*
was pulled into a berth by the side of the *Sulaire*, still dis-
charging. There were shouts from the wall, but the skipper
of the *Sulaire* got Roddie's ear. "Are you engaged?" he
asked.

"Well——" Roddie hesitated.

"Because if not, you couldn't do better than engage to
Mr. Maciver. He's a decent man."

"Thank you. I'll go up," said Roddie.

The quay was crowded with men, women, youths, and

girls, in a babble of sound. "You're from Dunster?" called
a man eagerly to Roddie. "You were engaged——" "Oh
let us get out of here," said a second man; "come over to
my office"; adding, as they entered a tiny room, "there's
no need to tell the world our business." He turned to
Roddie, "Are you engaged?"

But the first man at once said: "Aren't you engaged to
Jameson of Wick through your own home curer, Hendry?"

"Well," said Roddie, "Mr. Hendry did say he would
arrange——"

"But you were not actually engaged?" asked the second
man.

"Look here, Maciver, that's not fair. Dammit, you can
see——"

"Keep cool, Bain," said Maciver. "You were not
actually engaged?"

"I am Jameson's representative here, and I hold that
you are engaged——"

"Can't you let the skipper answer for himself?" suggested Maciver, with some sarcasm.

"I was not directly engaged," began Roddie, "but——"

"That's enough," said Maciver. "My point is this——"

"To hell with your point," interrupted Bain. "You're
not the only one with a point. This is a clear case. The man
is engaged to me if ever man was. And, further, let me tell
you this——"

"I know, I know," interrupted Maciver. He faced
Roddie and, speaking through Bain's voice, said, "The
Sulaire is my boat. You have the *Sulaire's* herring. You
were not directly engaged to anyone. The herring therefore
is mine. Do you agree?"

"You cannot agree," said Bain, "if you were engaged
to me. You can go back on your word to Hendry, if you
like, but by God, if you do——"

Maciver saw Roddie's eyes harden, and at once offered:
"I'll give you a pound a cran for your shot, and engage you
at ten shillings and ten pounds bounty."

THE GOLDEN CASK

There was complete silence, for it was a startling offer. The *Seafoam* had thirteen crans.

Roddie slowly faced Bain.

"I make you the same offer," said Bain.

Roddie turned to Maciver and, looking him in the eyes, gave a small smile. "I just did not want to force myself on any curer," he said quietly. "But Mr. Hendry did say he would see me right with Mr. Jameson, and I could not go back on his word. He's been decent to me. Otherwise, you could have had me and my herring."

Maciver, looking narrowly back at Roddie, nodded and smiled. "If you feel bound—that's that." It was a dry smile, but friendly.

As Roddie got back into his boat, the *Sulaire* skipper asked him if he was fixed up with Maciver. "I am sorry," replied Roddie, "but our curer at home had already engaged us to Jameson."

"In that case," said the skipper, looking on Roddie's face, "it couldn't be helped."

"No," said Roddie. "But I would have liked to have obliged you—and Maciver."

"You may yet. Who knows?" said that friendly countenance.

"I hope so."

The crew, sensing disappointment in Roddie's attitude, stood expressionless. He turned to them and said, "Well, we'll get the herring out"; and in the same casual tone added for their private ears, "I have sold this shot at one pound a cran."

They remained quite still. "God bless me!" said Callum.

Rob's reaction took a full two seconds, but the cold iron that had worked so miraculously was not forgotten.

Finn carried with Henry, and once as they tipped the basket into the gutting-box, he slipped and brought a portion of the herring down on top of him. The girls who were gutting laughed, for they were in high spirits at having

338

some work to do. Finn blushed and, stooping too quickly, the blood went to his brain, so that he staggered against one of the girls who was helping to gather the herring off the ground.

"Mind what you're about!" she cried.

"I'm minding," said Finn, smiling and swaying.

There was high-pitched laughter.

"The herring has gone to his head," declared the young woman with some spirit.

"It's not the herring," declared Finn, taking, at last, his eyes off her and turning away with Henry. He had hardly seen her, but in a moment or two his head cleared. Thereafter Henry and himself slowed up the natural tendency to rush with the fish to the station. But the younger women now had him as their mark. "Mind your step!" was the next greeting.

Finn took it all in good part, though once or twice his eyes gleamed, for his exhaustion induced a light-headedness as if he were half-drunk, a carelessness, that gave him an unusual self-confidence or loss of self.

As they emptied the last creel, he leaned for a moment against the edge of the box which came against his thighs, drawing a deep breath. The fair-haired, high-coloured girl of the first encounter now tried with expert inadvertence, as she reached out an arm over the herring, to tip him into the box. To save himself, Finn grabbed her. There was a quick scuffle and, carried completely beyond reason, Finn kissed her somewhere about the ear.

Screams of delight drew the world's attention.

"We're not used to your East-coast manners here!" cried the girl, who had shaken him off roughly.

"You'll get used to many a thing," said Finn, "if you live long enough."

As they walked away, Henry remarked in his dry, satiric way, "You're coming on."

Finn hardly knew whether he was on his head or his heels, for it was the first time in his life he had done anything so bold, but, taking one thing with another, it seemed to him that he might have done worse.

Roddie had returned the six nets to the *Sulaire* and now stood talking on the edge of the quay with Bain, who had apparently forgotten the argument in the office and was, in his quick clear-headed manner, anxious to help.

It appeared that the crew of a visiting boat usually set up a shelter of their own on shore. Mostly it was built of turf and could be erected in a few hours. For that matter, the majority of the croft houses themselves were so built. But, though Roddie was not very communicative, Bain could see that the crew had had a severe passage and said he could get a room for them easily enough. In fact, he brought Roddie along to a grey-haired woman packer and fixed the matter there and then.

"Thank you," said Roddie. "That's fine. We'll go along when we've had something to eat."

Bain smiled with lively humour. "Maciver tried it on!" he said. "He runs everything here—but not us."

"I'm sorry there was trouble."

"Trouble? Yon's the usual!" Bain laughed quickly. He obviously had enjoyed the passage and the defeat of Maciver. "We're striving for the first boat for the Baltic. The fishing has been poor and irregular. But perhaps it's beginning now. Tell the crew to come along and have a dram."

"It's food we need," said Roddie.

"Hits, man! A dram to drink your health first," said Bain briskly. He was a slight man, but with rather broad shoulders and a short, thick neck. He waved the crew to fall in.

They stepped down from the street into a low-ceilinged bar. After the sweat and the heat, it was pleasantly cool and kind to the eyes, even if the nostrils choked slightly at the beery smell. They sat in a row on the form by the wall, staring at the bottles and casks beyond the counter. The glittering brass bands around one small, up-ended cask, with brass cock at its foot, held Finn's eyes. What a beautiful richly-polished little cask it was! As Bain handed him half a tumblerful of whisky, he murmured his thanks.

"Well, men," toasted Bain. "Here's to a good fishing!"

The whisky gripped Finn's throat, but when it was all down, a tingling, followed by the softest languor, spread over his body.

"You'll have one from me," said Roddie, "and then we'll go." When he had ordered the round, he smiled. "We're feeling pretty tired."

"I'm sure," said Bain. "When did you leave? We were expecting you here on Wednesday."

"We took a day or two," said Roddie. "The weather wasn't very good. Well, here's your health! And I hope we do well for everyone's sake."

Finn tried to count. Yes, they had been five days at sea. In a way it felt like a whole other lifetime. Callum was stretching out his legs. Rob was trying to say something. He saw them finish their drink and he finished his own. Bain was telling Roddie about Maciver. The gleams on the cask, reflecting the window-light from their backs, grew big as suns. Callum leaned over against him and then pulled himself slowly away. Rob tried to open his snuff-box at the wrong side. Callum, with the intention of helping him, hit the box down on Rob's knees, where it opened of itself. Sucking his breath in three stertorous spasms Callum let out a mighty sneeze that shook him so far down over his own knees that he couldn't get back. Finn's mind suggested: Slip to the floor quietly; it'll be easier to hold on there. The glittering golden sun of the whole cask drew him to his feet. The sun went out and he fell forward on his face, dead to the world.

CHAPTER XVII

DRINK AND RELIGION

❧

By the following afternoon, Finn awoke finally, ate some boiled herring and potatoes, and felt himself again. A quiet reminiscent humour had descended on them all. Roddie, it appeared, had not only left the *Seafoam* properly berthed and ship-shape, but had brought Finn's Sunday suit from his kist. Finn smiled self-consciously as Callum described how they had taken his drunken body home on a hand-cart with half the children in Stornoway shouting behind. Finn knew that was a lie. Bain had arranged with the landlord of the public-house to let the crew sleep off their tiredness, and he had a remote but indistinct memory of walking like a ghost on padded feet to their lodging.

As they strolled along the south bay towards the pier, the freshness of the air was sweet in the lungs, and the aftermath of tiredness was not unpleasant. Finn looked at the houses and the many shops with their drawn yellow blinds. Seamen like themselves were having a quiet Sunday stroll, gazing at the boats and the water, as if they hadn't seen enough of them. Here and there, persons dressed like ladies and gentlemen, moved quickly along as though they knew exactly where they were going. One beautiful golden-haired girl sat in a gig beside a portly man, with starched ear-collar, who was driving a mettlesome chestnut horse.

"Don't be staring like that, Finn," Callum cautioned him. "She'll think you're from the country."

"She won't be at the gutting, that one, Finn," remarked Henry casually.

"It's maybe as well for her," said Finn.

"Will you look at this!" muttered Rob.

Round the corner of a pile of herring barrels came four young men arm-in-arm, with red stockings, blue breeches, and wooden clogs.

"Dutchmen," said Roddie.

Out of native manners, they did not stare, but Finn was touched by an enlivening curiosity. When they had passed, he glanced at the tall-masted vessels lying at anchor off the pier, and the far shores of the world came in thought to his feet.

"Yes, that's the sloop that carries the mails to Poolewe," a man said in English (more stylish than Mr. Gordon's). "How often?" asked an elderly woman, in a high-pitched voice, as if it didn't matter who heard her. "Twice a week now, but five years ago it was only once a week, and we had a fight with the Government . . ."

As they passed out of earshot, Henry said, "It's a fine thing to own the world."

They all smiled benignly at that. Henry liked to have a back-hander at the gentry.

Pubs, business premises, stores, curers' offices, large printed signs which they all read carefully, half-dried trickles of strong-smelling brine thick with scales which they lightly stepped across, an immense red-rusted ship's anchor that drew them up. They smiled at its size. Finn caught one of the flukes and tried to move it. Callum chuckled. Roddie described the capstan and bars needed to heave that fellow. And so round to the *Seafoam*.

As Finn gazed on her, lying quietly, lashed to the *Sulaire*, his heart swelled. "You can have your sloops and your schooners and your capstan bars," he declared. "I wouldn't give the *Seafoam* for the lot."

"She has a fine heart in her," agreed Callum.

"She stood by us well," Rob nodded.

"She has a way of her own of rising to them," Henry remembered.

"We'll have to take the nets out in the morning and give them a dry first thing," said Roddie with a quiet smile.

Everything seemed set for a good fishing. Already they had had one bit of luck, and they never doubted but that they would get herring. They did not regret now the gruelling time they had had. It was always as well to get the worst over first!

And that was the last day of real peace they knew.

In sunny, windless weather, they laboured at the oars. Herring were on the coast, but only in patches. What were caught were mostly unripe. The curers grew anxious and grumbled. The old controversy got going about the need for closing the whole West Coast fishing for May. Only the gamble of getting the early Baltic market and good prices kept it going, it was said.

But no fisherman ever clearly understood the fish-curer's business. The fisherman could have a good season or a poor one, and he saw that it must be the same with the curer, only on a greater scale. Beyond that lay the private intricacies of business and foreign markets and, naturally, no-one was happier than the fisherman when the curer had a good season. He certainly did not grudge the curer his profits, and indeed was content in the thought that he knew his business, and attended to it, well enough to have the distinction of being a wealthy man. And fish-curers were approachable and friendly, and the best of them would help a deserving fisherman at any time.

On Monday night they drew a complete blank. On Tuesday a fry of herring that could be carried on a string On Wednesday they followed the *Sulaire* a long way to the north. The *Sulaire* had four crans, *Seafoam* half a basket. A few small catches of two to three crans were landed on that day. The herring were on the ground, they were not working. Thursday, however, rumour was strong that Loch Roag on the west side was solid with herring and that

Bernera cod and ling fishermen were hauling them on the beach.

When Roddie went to sea on Friday evening, there was not even one basket of herring to his credit for the whole week's heavy work. An hour or two's sleep had been snatched during the day, when, fully clothed, they had thrown themselves on the two makeshift beds in the single small room. Finn's hands were calloused by the swinging of the heavy oars. What a blessed relief it was when, on the Friday evening, a steady wind darkened the sea under the still bright sky! They all felt a little stupid from lack of sleep and lay back looking at the land and the other boats speeding with them, brown sails bellying and a wafer of foam at the forefoot.

There was never much talk in the boat, and certainly never any argument, as to what they should do or where they should go or in what spot they should shoot their nets. Not that they were content to leave such decisions with the skipper. It was, Finn had discovered the very first night he had been at sea, a much more mysterious affair than that. He had waited for talk, for expressions of opinion, however casual. There had been none. All at once they were preparing to shoot, as if some silent common intelligence had been at work. Surprised at first, he then had been oddly moved by an access of quiet manhood.

There were gulls about, one wheeling vortex of them inshore, where two boats were already putting their nets out. Other boats were running up into the wind and lowering sail. Roddie held on. Finn saw Rob sniffing as if he might smell the herring, which, indeed, sometimes could be done. But herring waited for the passing of the light before they began to "work" or rise from the bottom and so strike into the nets. A school of porpoises appeared near the boat. "Perhaps we'll do," said Roddie, and brought the *Seafoam* round into a wind that was failing. It was going to be a calm night.

Sails and masts down and rudder unshipped, they began

shooting their nets, the flat stone "sinkers", noosed at intervals to the foot-rope, drawing down the meshed wall straight from the back-rope with its many small corks. Finn, who was on an oar, for the wind was now not strong enough to keep the boat drifting, was always attracted by the way Rob dealt with the black, mouth-blown, sheepskin buoys that were round or pear-shaped and bigger than the barrel of his chest. When he had fixed it to the tie-rope between two nets, he threw it upward and away from him with a grandiloquent gesture, never looking at it. It fell on the sea with a splendid splash. Whereupon Rob would blink and sniff, or rub the back of his hand against his mouth and say "Poof!" with a wearied solemnity.

Riding by the stern to the swing-rope attached to the drift, they got out their food. Water, with oatmeal and sugar stirred in it, Finn found a refreshing drink and a good thirst-quencher. Milk was dear in Stornoway and not easy to get. Oaten and bere bannocks, butter and home-made cheese—with these, it did not matter what else was lacking. Loaf bread was fine to have at table, with fried fresh herring or curdled boiled cod, but at sea, loaf bread itself was a vapid food, whereas oatcake was gritty, full of a rich flavour (which the saliva brought out) and great sustenance. As you chewed it thoughtfully, you could let your eyes stray away to the land. Finn had a small smile to himself, for he knew, as clearly as if it had been spoken in explicit words, that the corporate intelligence had a notion that they should have shot farther inshore. It was no more than a notion, uncertain, too weak for the definition of action, but there!

At first, whenever the nets were out, it had been Finn's delight to unwind the ripper and try for white fish. But over-work had soon dissipated that youthful enthusiasm, and now, with the evening lowering its soft shadow on sea and land, they stretched out between the timbers and snatched at sleep.

Finn awoke in the darkness and saw Roddie, his body

bent against the sky, hauling on the swing-rope. Soon he had the lug of the first net lifted up in the usual "trial" for herring. Finn waited, excitement in an instant holding his breath. He knew by a movement Henry made that he was awake, too. There was always this excitement, this momentary expectation, so near sometimes to desperation, in fishing for herring. Supposing Roddie turned round now and said, "Boys, we're in them!" Supposing he, Finn, cried in Callum's ear, "Herring!" Callum would stagger up, ready to overthrow an army!

What was Roddie hanging on to the net for? Could it be? . . .

Finn's mind rose spiring in wild hope. He had felt uncomfortable in Roddie's presence these last days, and had avoided being alone with him. It was something in Roddie, something slowly closing in and terrible.

Henry sat up.

Roddie's arm rose and the net fell with an empty splash on the sea.

Finn's heart sank in him. Henry lay back. Roddie stood upright for a long time. The notion of going inshore was probably still at work! Finn did not feel this with humour but with a desolate bitterness. It was easy enough to haul the nets, tired as they were, and shoot them elsewhere, and perhaps get the herring on the move at the turn of the night. But that same mysterious common intelligence told Finn, as it told Roddie and Henry, that it would be useless. Where they were was as good as the next place. Roddie came quietly back and lay down.

Finn slept but fitfully for the next hour or so, and had many images made strangely intimate and tender because of his desolate mood.

With the first greyness of morning, as the stars faded in the sky, he sat up with a small shiver. The others seemed to be fast asleep. He moved carefully. The land was dark shadow, but boats even at a distance were discernible and very still on the pale sea. This twilight of morning always affected Finn even more than the twilight of evening; it was at once more bodiless and more expectant. Over the water came the plaintive piping of a shore bird. The gulls were awake—they hardly seemed to sleep these summer nights —and their cries moved invisibly, on a haunted note, over against the featureless land. Then one—two—were above him silently, their heads questing from side to side, clear against the sky, and passed on. Passed on—and wheeled and cried, as they saw him move. The morning was coming fast.

Finn caught the swing-rope and began to haul the *Sea-foam* noiselessly towards the nets. How glorious it would be if he had to wake them up with the news of herring! How glorious—but, ah! little hope of that! Hand over slow hand. Little hope. Yet—if only! And one never knew. Never knew with certainty.

Excitement beat up from his beating heart, but his keen eyes caught no silver gleam. And here now—here was the net. Slowly he heaved up the corner and saw naught but the little films of water glisten grey for a moment in the mesh. Deep as his eyes could probe, there was no silver gleam. Nothing. At such a moment a man tended to haul the net up an extra few inches in a forlorn gesture and let it fall with a splash. Finn dropped it quietly and the still water sucked it back.

The land was slowly defining itself, pushing gently away the dark clothes of night from its shoulders. In his disappointment a misery came over him that cleansed hope to an acceptance, a fortitude, that was bitter but somehow intimate and enduring. It was the mood that came from storm and loss and emptiness of all gain. The brow and the eyes of seamen who could not be beaten down, seamen who went quiet and remained steady when death, the omnipresent of the dark ones, felt he could engulf them at last.

Finn sat down on the rudder. He would wait till Roddie and the others awoke of themselves. Some gulls had settled on the water round the tail-end of the drift. One or two of

them, with querulous cries, moved in short, restless flights
of a yard or so. For all the world as if they were seeing
herring! Then Finn did notice a slight bobbing movement
of the last two or three buoys. There was no doubt of it!
All his fine feeling of endurance vanished in a single heart-
beat. He turned round. Roddie was coming towards him.
"We're in them at the tail-end," he said as quietly as he
could. Roddie looked and nodded.

"Well, it's heartening, anyway," cried Callum, as they
began to haul. A few crans to break their bad luck would
be something, even if it only showed that they knew how
to land herring without the help of a Lewis-man!

Empty nets and then the silver glisten here and there.
"Come in, my darlings!" cried Rob to the first-comers.
But one was bitten clean away from the head. Others were
slashed. A hole in the net that Rob could put his head
through. They all stopped as Roddie stopped. Finn looked
over the side and saw the dark swirls, the dark-swirling
bodies of dogfish. The sea by the nets was alive with them,
alive, and evil, and abominable.

A wild rage swept the crew and came out in grunts of
hatred and loathing. When a dogfish, entangled beyond
tearing free, came over the gunnel, Callum seized the tiller
and smashed its head to a pulp.

They hauled the end nets in a frenzy. The last net of all,
which had been very heavy with fish, was torn to ribbons,
torn beyond any hope of mending. It was Roddie's. The
next net to it, also Roddie's, was not much better. Finn's
nets, placed early in the drift, were undamaged. The others
had plenty of mending before them. The last sinker was
dropped into a hold that did not contain a cran of decent
herring.

That afternoon, as Roddie, Henry, and Finn sat in the
Seafoam mending hurriedly-dried nets, while Callum and
Rob were away arranging about getting the drift barked,
Bain, who had been talking down over the wall to Roddie,

was joined by a curer named Duncan, from Fraserburgh, a middle-sized, grizzled, stocky man with small but keen humorous eyes and a complete lack of movement or gesture when speaking.

"It's a one-eyed hole over the week-end is this damned spot," said Bain.

"Nearly as bad as Wick," replied Duncan, "only wi' better scenery."

"Well, there's always some comfort, thank God: it might have been Fraserburgh."

"Ye can leave God oot o't."

"Out of Fraserburgh? He was never in it. And Stornoway, religious enough on the Sabbath, at all events, has gone to the bloody dogs."

Duncan gave a small chuckle.

"Ay, begod, they were pretty bad," he said (dogfish were usually referred to as "the dogs").

After further pleasantries, Duncan admitted, "Ay, I'm beginning to wonder what I cam' here for——"

"Hullo, there's Maciver," interrupted Bain. "You ask him." There was a shout and presently Maciver joined them.

The men in the boat, had they cared to look up, would have seen little more than an occasional head and shoulders as the three curers talked, but they heard their voices clearly enough, particularly when the argument got properly joined.

"No, it's a mistake, an' ye mark my words," said Duncan. "This is playing wi' the foreign market as the dogs played wi' the herring this morning—an' if it gaes on, the market will get torn like the nets."

"Well, your remedy is easy," declared Maciver. "Keep out of Stornoway."

"Ay, ay, that's a' very fine. But we're no' dogs in the net. Ye can come to Fraserburgh ony time ye like. That's no' the point. It's we who made the market. And we made it in twa ways. We made it by getting the Crown brand on oor barrels. Where the German sees that brand he kens exactly what he's getting, kens whether the herring is full or spent, an' he buys an' sells on that brand wi' complete confidence. Now wi' this kin' o' stuff we're catching, we're no' using the brand. We couldn't onyway, because we're afore the time. Weel, it may be a' richt at the moment, but ye mark my words——"

"You're an old Tory, Duncan, who doesn't know——"

"I'm a Liberal, thank God. But that by the way. This is business, an' common-sense, so we can leave yer politics oot o't. As I was saying——"

"Look here," interrupted Maciver, "what's the sense in talking like that? You know that the Germans are anxious to buy these herrings. They'll take as much of this early catch as we can send. Our trouble, as far as I can see, is that we may not be able to get the herring for them. We're not going to be able to meet our on-costs. If the fishing goes on like this, we're each going to be some hundred pounds down. That's what's worrying me. Not your fancy notions."

"Very well," said Bain, "why not close the May fishing down altogether and start some time in June when the herring are herring?"

"Why should I? If you want to do so, nobody is stopping you."

"That's no' the point, Maciver," said Duncan. "We stand for the herring trade. That's oor hale business. It's no' yer hale business. Ye hae yer hand in a dozen pokes, including the ling an' cod trade an' yer ain schooner. Weel, guid luck tae ye! We're no' grudging ye onything. But this is oor business. An' I'll tell ye something, Maciver. I happen to ken that the Glasgow men are seriously thinking o' trying to get this early fishing stopped by Act o' Parliament. An' if they manage to do that, then God help yer poor crofter-fishermen a' doon the West."

Maciver laughed. "You mean the Government would stop them catching herring even as bait for cod and ling?"

"Even for their ain use," declared Duncan (prophetically, as it turned out).

"It's no good trying to talk sense into you, I can see," said Maciver, cheerfully. "I thought you believed in free competition and open markets! You call yourself a Liberal! Well, well!"

"Ay, I'm a Liberal. An' in trade I think it does a man nae hairm should he happen to hae the modicum o' brains that lets him look ahead. My point is that ye're no' looking ahead. What are the facts?"

"Do you think I don't know them?" asked Maciver derisively.

"I'm no' doubting yer knowledge—it's yer application. Here we hae an industry that's going ahead by leaps and bounds. Man, every little village on the Moray Firth coast is like a beehive. I was speaking to my banker afore I cam' ower. He was talking aboot the foreign trade as it affects them in circulation o' notes, a discount at the highest rate on foreign bills, payable in London an' running onything up to from thirty to sixty days. He reckoned that in the three shipping months, through the bank agencies from Peterhead roon to Wick, there must be little short o' £150,000——"

"Well, but isn't that——"

"Wait now. Wait a minute. Ye hae yer productive side going on like that. A' richt. But is yer market increasing at the same rate? What happened four or five years ago? The slaves were emancipated. Ay. An' what happened then? The whole West Indian trade was cut off—slash! Not a barrel."

"The slaves preferred English hams," said Bain, "once they had wages of their own! Do you blame them?"

"By God, this is no joke," said Duncan. "I'm only wanting to see some order. So long as we work through the brand an' the commission merchant, we ken where we are and we can open oot an' expand the Baltic market an' perhaps get a real grip on Russia, which the Norwegians at present hold, mostly wi' spent herring."

"But how can we get a hold on the Russian market, if the Russians let the Norwegian herrings in at a tax of one-and-sixpence on a barrel while they charge us over four shillings?" inquired Maciver sarcastically.

"We can do mony a thing," replied Duncan, "so long as we see what it is we hae to do. That's all I want—to see where we're going, what we're heading for. An' in this business o' the German market, which is oor market, we're heading for a tumble. We'll rush the stuff in, not through the commission merchant, who has his orders from his German dealers, as we hae been doing up to the present, but we'll rush the stuff in on consignment an' that's the beginning o' speculation, an' there never yet was speculation but in the long run, in the long run, it meant smash. Ye run so hard that ye fall ower yoursel'."

"Ah, get away, Duncan! You're the canny Scot—so frightened of running that you stand still. You haven't the spirit in you to take a chance. You're merely frightened. Well, you leave it to men who aren't. That's your way out."

"But," said Bain, "what about the 60,000 barrels we used to send to Jamaica? That's all gone. How are we, with a growing industry——"

"I don't send any barrels to Jamaica," replied Maciver. "I have other markets and they're good enough for me. If you fellows——"

"Canny now," interrupted Duncan.

"Canny!" echoed Maciver and laughed.

"You'll yet laugh oot the other side o' yer mooth, Maciver, when ye stick in the bog o' your ain making. Mark my words. The 60,000 barrels to Jamaica were spent fish. The Germans will hae nane o' that. They're no' slaves. They're an educated business folk wha will only hae the best. An' they are prepared to pay for it. They are the honestest and straightest people that ever I hae dealt wi'. An' everyane in the trade says the same. They are prepared to pay for a good herring because they like it. But they are no' fools. If ye sent 500 barrels on order through a commission merchant, an' then send another 500 on consignment, what happens? Ye sell the 500 on consignment at a cheaper rate. An' the German dealer who has paid the bigger price gets sore. Next time he is no' going to order, he is going to wait, because he sees ye must hae his market at ony cost. When that point is reached, you an' me will carry on blindly until we smash."

"Really! And what do you propose to do about it?"

"Bring a wee thing order an' foresicht into oor affairs. An' the first thing I wad do is cut oot this early fishing. Damn it, man, look at the quality o' the fish. Unripe trash wi' a taste like stale loaf-bread. They winna even carry. Do ye think the Germans——"

"Oh, dry up," interrupted Maciver. "Look at the facts. You know damn fine that we get three or four times more for early fish than for your finest Crown-fulls in the autumn. I was talking to an agent in Glasgow who had been over in Berlin last year. He said that in the expensive eating-places there you pay half a dollar for one early herring. And if you work that out at about three shillings to the dollar it comes, not to twenty-five shillings a barrel, but to over fifty pounds! They eat them with the early vegetables. Very well. What's the good of trying to tell me about the German trade? Do you think I can't see the realities—not your canny policies—but the realities, when they stare me in the face? You may try, Duncan, to frighten me out of a trade you think is your own, but, if so, let me tell you, you have come to the wrong man."

"A' richt, Maciver, hae it yer ain way. If ye think ony o' us in the trade wants to close up a gold mine ye're simpler than I thocht ye. It's nae business o' mine, of course, an' I dinna want ony information, so ye can ask yoursel'—how much ye lost last year, an' by the look o' things, how much ye're likely to lose this year. This fishing shouldna start until the beginning o' June—an' ye ken it. Take Saxony, Silesia, Moravia . . ."

DRINK AND RELIGION

The voices, still disputing, moved away from the harbour wall.

None of the men in the boat spoke. Roddie finished the last mesh of a bad tear, snipped the twine with his knife, held up the netting for a moment and then let it drop, with the gesture of a man letting an empty net splash back into the sea. Finn saw Henry's eyes steal a penetrating glance at him.

"I think we've done enough for one day," remarked Roddie calmly; "fully enough."

Henry did not speak.

"Come on," said Roddie. "We'll have a drink." He got up and stretched himself, not looking at the others.

"All right," Henry agreed, with a glance at Finn.

"I'll just finish what I'm at," said Finn, "and catch you up."

Roddie paid no attention, and Henry followed him out of the boat.

Finn made twice to leave the boat and went back. Somehow the conversation on the pier had been very depressing, and he felt the effect it had had on Roddie. It was as if the dogfish were everywhere, all over the world. Things were brewing in Roddie; working to a head. Instead of being proud, as he might well be, at having brought his boat through the storm on the west side, Finn knew perfectly well that he was touchy about it, as if having missed Lewis and gone out round the Butt was a slur on his seamanship. Those black, unfathomable moments between Roddie and himself at the Seven Hunters. Deep down, like a poison. Henry's glance, before he left, had said plainly: Don't you come. Then the gifted herring—and not even being able to give them to the *Sulaire's* curer. Not catching any herring himself. Blank, blank. And now the dogs, the damaged nets. The curer's talk—with its gloom over this industry, to which Roddie was committed with the strong and single devotion of the pioneer.

Finn felt uncomfortable and restless, vaguely uneasy, and this slowly bred in him a hard bitterness of his own.

Roddie and Henry turned up for supper, with a whiff of whisky on the air. Callum challenged them. Roddie half-laughed, with a gleam of teeth, in apparently fine form, as if the hardness had broken.

But Finn saw it had not broken. It had gone inward in him, a dark rod of iron.

"Eat up, boys," said Roddie. "The curers have been telling us the foreign markets are bitched."

They all felt Roddie was working up to an outburst, not an outburst of words or spleen, but an outburst of the body, a physical crushing of things between his hands. In their bones they knew it was the only way he could find relief. And they dreaded it.

He would have to be left to Henry. Henry had no doubt taken him back to supper. But Henry himself, though satiric and often extremely wise, had his own sort of devilry—after a certain point. Instead of guiding Roddie he might, in a quick shift of circumstance, stand back and look on.

"Well, boys, let us see the sights of the town," said Roddie, rubbing the strong hair on his jaw. Henry, who had finished clipping his beard, put on his jacket and went after him. Callum, Rob and Finn followed at a little distance.

Just as Roddie and Henry turned into the Sloop Inn, on the sea-front, a young fisherman named Seumas Maclean greeted Finn, who stopped to talk to him.

"Where away?" asked Finn.

"I'm going home," answered Seumas.

"What's your hurry?" Finn had a sudden desire to hang on to Seumas, not so much to be away from the members of his own crew as to be apart from them. They discussed some of the week's doings and smiled over the havoc wrought by the dogs. "You have had a drink," declared Finn, "and I haven't."

"No, I must be going," said Seumas; "it's nearly ten miles, and I'll get my head in my hands for being as late as I am."

Seumas lived down on Loch Luirbost, where a religious revival had blown up, and Finn rallied him on it, with Seumas smiling, his grey-brown eyes alive. He was a slim fellow like Finn himself, two years older, with high cheek-bones and dark hair.

"Lord, here's Big Angus," said Seumas suddenly, "taking the street to himself!"

A tall fisherman, fully six feet four, broad shouldered, straight-backed, with a short, curly, brown beard, came along, accompanied by three other fishermen. Seumas stepped off the pavement and Finn was shouldered off.

"They never saw you," explained Seumas, with a laugh. "He's a quiet enough fellow, Angus, until he gets drink. On Saturday night he rules the world, with everyone frightened of him."

"I know someone who won't be frightened of him," murmured Finn, his eyes following the four men until they turned into the Sloop Inn.

They argued until the prospect of some fun was too much for Seumas, and he agreed to go along for a few minutes.

The bar was filled with seamen and voices and drink. The voices broke into laughter and sometimes shouted. More than Big Angus were on top of the world! Finn at last got two whiskies from the landlord, who was a small, forceful man, with a tubby body and a sharp, commanding voice. His clients did not object to his occasional cautionary words, rather liked them in fact, and on the whole obeyed them.

From their stance by the wall, near the door, Finn saw the inception of the trouble. One of the three seamen with Big Angus whispered something to him. "What's that?" asked Big Angus, and had it repeated. Then he turned his face and looked over towards the corner where Roddie and Henry were talking and drinking. Roddie's back was to him. Angus took a sideways step, as if to get a better view, and then laughed. "Missed the Butt!" he said, and coming back to the counter hit it with the bottom of his thick glass. "Another round!" he called. "God, fancy a man missing the Butt!" The humour of it broke from him. He shook his laughing head. "Did you hear that one, Donald George?" he asked the landlord, as he scooped up his change. "He missed the Butt!"

"Now, now, Angus," said Donald George. "That's enough."

"I should think it was!" said Angus, and threw his head back in a hearty roar at his own wit. "It's the best joke I have heard in years."

However Henry tried to hold Roddie's attention he could not shut his ears. The whole room was caught, and eyes gleamed on Big Angus and shot to Roddie, who had now turned round.

His mirth seemed to weaken Big Angus, and he said, "Damn me!" and "Och! och!" Then turning to have another look at the marvel who had missed the Butt, he encountered Roddie's steady stare.

That stare shook some of the mirth out of him, for he was not used to opposition. But he held by his expression as he took a step or two towards Roddie and asked, with laughing curiosity, "Tell me, how did you manage it?"

"Never mind him," said Henry quickly to Roddie. "He's all mouth."

"All what did you say?" asked Big Angus.

"You mind your own business," said Henry, "and we'll mind ours."

"Hoh-ho!" said Angus.

"Now, Angus, that's enough!" called Donald George.

Roddie had never moved. His eyes were glass, his cheekbones smooth. His concentration was so intense that it drew Big Angus fatally. There was a moment's intense silence. Big Angus straightened his shoulders, like a man freeing and gathering himself, and said with automatic derision, "I was only asking him how he missed the Butt."

Roddie's movement was so swift, the smashing blow to the face so instantaneous, that Big Angus was being swayed back on to his feet by the men he had fallen against, before anyone quite realized what had happened.

"Get out of here!" yelled Donald George, fairly dancing.

No-one paid any attention to him. Big Angus, blood on his face, came towards Roddie, his fingers curved, his shoulders bunching. But Roddie did not wait for him; he swept in and lashed out a right and left to the face; then followed up so impetuously that Big Angus, supported by the crush behind, grabbed at him blindly. In this lock, Roddie staggered back to clear himself, steadied, then slowly, his throat swelling, lifted Big Angus clean off his feet and smashed him to the floor, where he lay squirming, like a man in a death-throe.

"Here, by God!" began one of Big Angus's three companions, but Roddie was on him in an instant and the smash of the blow could have been heard down the street.

Roddie had broken loose. Swaying on the outer edges of his feet, fists clenched, he let out a challenging roar. But no-one was interfering with him now. "I'll sail you round your bloody Butt!" yelled Roddie. "Come on!"

No-one, that is, but Donald George, who had a long experience of the moment when, with a few drinks, a client in the pride of his manhood has an urge to sweep the seven seas. He ducked under the flap of the counter.

"Get out of here!" he barked into Roddie's face.

Roddie looked at him for a moment as at something utterly unexpected and strange. Donald George thrust out a compelling hand. Swift as a cat Roddie stepped sideways, caught Donald George by neck-band and trousers-seat, and swung him off his feet, swung him full round, and let go. He passed clean over the counter and crashed into his own bottles and casks. There was a roar of breaking glass and a flood of released whisky.

And at that moment, with the whole company paralysed, it came upon Finn to approach Roddie.

The actuating motive may have been a desire to help Roddie, to get him away in time. Standing before him, he said, "Come on, Roddie. Let's get away now." Roddie's left arm was still outstretched, the back of the open hand towards Finn's face. Through the foot that separated it from that face, Roddie brought it with such explosive force, that the resounding slap almost lifted Finn off his feet. Seumas caught him as he fell backwards; but in a red instant Finn had torn free, carried in that instant beyond all reason, in a stormy madness that cared nothing for defeat or death. For some obscure reason, Roddie did not hit him as he came in, when indeed he might have killed him. Though Finn, for that matter came very swiftly, and did in fact hit Roddie a glancing blow on the cheek. Roddie caught him, crushed him, lifted him up. Finn wriggled and yelled, his voice half-cracked, in a demented rage, clawing madly at Roddie, hitting him where he could. Whether Roddie would have smashed Finn against floor or wall and with what result was never to be known, for Callum leapt clean in on Roddie, and Henry, coming at him behind, slipped an arm round his throat. At that moment, Big Angus gripped Roddie's ankle. Roddie's blind heel shot backwards and hit him in the jaw. He rolled over in a bellow of agony. Roddie thrust Finn down on top of Callum and tore himself free.

"Roddie, boy," said Rob, "you b-b-better stop."

Roddie glared at him, as if he did not know him, and, turning on the men in the pub, let out his challenging berserk roar.

"Don't be a bloody fool," said Callum to Finn, holding him by the throat at arm's length, "or I'll bash you."

Finn's voice was broken, and he was shouting through his insane anger like a tortured child. And though he broke free, Callum, helped by Seumas, bunched him to the door, and finally together they shoved him bodily out.

Seamen were now coming running to the pub.

"Come on!" snapped Callum and, with the help of Seumas, walked Finn along the street. "Now clear out, for God's sake!"

He waited until Finn had gone some little distance before turning back to the inn.

Seumas had him by the left arm, but Finn went quietly enough, head up, his quick breathing broken by panting gulps.

The slow-curving row of houses along the south bay seemed never to end. Seumas was talking quickly and lightly to Finn, and smiling, so that those who looked at Finn's face might be deceived. Once or twice he pointed to a boat drawn up on the black foreshore below the grounds of Stornoway Lodge, as an excuse to avert their faces.

When they were on the country road, heading south, Finn stopped and sat down. He started trembling and, turning over on his face, gripped the heath with his fists. From him came not sobs but dry hacking convulsive sounds. Suddenly he shot up: "I'm going back!" Seumas put an arm round his neck. Finn tried to tear free, but Seumas held him, muttering common-sense gently. "Ssh, be quiet. Here's somebody coming." In time he got Finn quietened.

Finn sat in the ditch staring before him, his eyes bright as in fever. Seumas, with the pleasant lightness of comradeship, more soothing in voice and manner than any woman, told Finn that he was coming home with him to Luirbost for the night. At last Finn said, "Well, I'll be getting back," as if he had not heard a word.

So Seumas put all his reasons forward again, and added, "You can't go back there wherever you go. You'll only start it all over again. And you don't want to do that?"

"I must go."

"You think you're running away. You want to know

what's happened." Seumas looked at him, wondering whether Finn could now stand what he wanted to say, and then he said it: "You're only thinking of yourself."

Finn's face hardened. Seumas laughed lightly. "Be sensible, Finn. You can't pack into that lodging-room now, five of you. Nothing more will happen. It's only a fight. There's hardly a Saturday night in the season but Big Angus is in a row of some sort. Well, he got his gruel to-night. And he deserved it. So leave them alone. Besides," he added shrewdly, "it was clear that Callum didn't want you. It was Callum who told you to clear out. If they don't want you, why force yourself on them?"

There was a long pause. "All right," said Finn.

"We'll have a snuff," said Seumas, "and then we'll take the road. It's a fine night for it."

He was a friendly, lovable fellow, this Seumas, and his voice so full of light common-sense that he broke down Finn's reserve by asking, "After all, Finn, how *did* you miss the Butt?"

So after a vague smile Finn started talking and told of the thick weather and the storm.

Seumas listened with deep interest, drawing him out. And in time they got to the Seven Hunters.

"You didn't climb Eilean Mor?" Seumas stopped on the road and looked at Finn closely, the subtle complimenting friendly manner fallen from him.

"I climbed that rock anyway."

"But isn't there a sheer face? Harris men go out there in the season for a load of birds and mutton. But they take a ladder for that bit, and they're about the greatest rock climbers in the world."

"Yes," said Finn, "a ladder there would save time."

"What did you find on top?" asked Seumas as they walked on again.

When Finn had described the little house, Seumas nodded, convinced at last. "Yes, that's the ruins of the chapel. Long, long ago, a holy man lived there. They called him Saint Flannan. That's why they're known, too, as the Flannan Isles."

"Did he?" said Finn. "I wonder what he was like?"

Seumas looked at him. "No-one knows now. Why?"

Finn half smiled. "I had the sort of feeling that I was expecting him."

"Had you?" remarked Seumas, also smiling, but with a reserved critical look in his eye. As Finn glanced at him, he continued: "An old man from Uig, named Ceit Morison, once told me that he used to go there as a young man. They used to do some queer things on landing. You know how we turn a boat round with the sun: never the other way."

"Yes," said Finn.

"Well, when they got up on top, the leader first of all would say, 'Now, boys, there's to be no relieving of nature here.'"

Wonder came back to Finn's face in a solemn grin. "It wouldn't do, I suppose, after they had got so far safely," he said.

"They didn't want to offend the rock that had been kind enough to take their feet. And it's natural enough."

"That's so," Finn agreed.

"Then they would strip off their upper clothes and put them on a stone before the Chapel. Did you notice a stone?"

"I did."

"They got down on their knees and, saying a prayer, went forward that way to the chapel. Then they went round the chapel sunwise saying a second prayer. And then they said a third prayer by the little door. They did that in the morning, and also in the evening when they had finished killing the birds on the rocks."

"Did they?"

"Yes. Old Ceit said to me that some of them would pray there better in a day than they would pray at home in a year. He said you could feel it was a holy place. Did you feel that?"

"I don't know," replied Finn, thoughtfully. "I felt as if

someone invisible had just left and was maybe coming back. I felt he was an old quiet man. I was a little afraid and yet not afraid. But I have had that feeling at a place at home. What else did they do?"

"You know how we mention certain things at sea by other names? Well, they had queer names like that, too. In fact many of the Lewis seamen have them here. You call water by the name 'burn', and a rock is 'hard', the shore is 'the cave', sour is called 'sharp', you mustn't say a thing is slippery but 'soft'—oh, and a great lot more."

In this way, as they journeyed together, by loch and peat bank, Finn grew calm in himself. But it was a grey calm, thin in texture like the feeling he had awaiting the invisible man, like the politeness that greets a stranger though death sits in the heart.

The night was on them before they turned along the quiet waters of Loch Luirbost, but in it was a dim greyness from the dead day. A sheep coughed, its face ghost-white. Grey, the gable-end of a cottage; and the front of the cottage, like a grey face. Black the peat stack, black the bare peaty soil, grey-green the grass. Stillness everywhere and silence—except for the eternal sea-bird that cried along the shore, drawing the eyes out over the shimmering water.

Seumas had already told Finn about the religious revival in the district and so had prepared him. It was the new evangelicalism rising against privilege and moderatism in the church, and here it had taken an acute revivalist form. Finn believed he had only to imagine Sandy Ware in control.

There was, however, an extraordinary quietism in the scene and the hour that had a new faintly apprehensive effect upon Finn; so much so that for a minute he wondered if he could still retreat. He did not want to lose the core of himself, even if it was a core of misery. Better to be by oneself, lost in the night, in the bog, than to be invaded. Better to gnaw the core of misery to black nothingness and be done with it, than to carry it, shielded over, into an alien night-world where the cottages had faces like masks.

But Seumas was going on confidently, with his light springy stride, and presently led Finn up off the path to a cottage door, which he opened without knocking, crying at the same time, "Are you in?"

Stooping, Finn followed him, and saw a man of about forty get up from a stool by the fire, shadow flickering over his welcoming face.

"What's kept you at all?" he asked pleasantly, after he had shaken hands with Finn. "Was it the inn?" When Seumas said it wasn't, he laughed: "I can smell the black balls on your breath!"

"Would you like one?" asked Seumas, producing a small paper bag of sweets.

"Thank you, thank you. Sit down."

"But aren't you going to the meeting?" asked Seumas.

"Och, well, what do you think? Sit down anyway. I said I would wait for you."

They sat down and Alan asked them all sorts of questions about the week's doings in Stornoway, until at last Seumas said, "I think we'd better be going."

"Ach, you're fine! What's all the hurry?"

"I should have been home before now," said Seumas. "They'll be wondering."

"Ach, all your folk will be at the meeting. My own sisters are there long ago. Take your time."

Finn could see that Alan, for some reason, did not care much about going to the meeting. He had a practical cheerful manner and was full of questions to Finn about Caithness and the way things were going there.

This went on for a long time in a curious mood of gathering tension, in a timeless carelessness slowly being drawn taut, until at last, with a laugh, Alan said all right they might as well go.

As Finn passed over the doorstep, the other two hung behind, and he heard Seumas whispering to Alan.

"Surely, surely," answered Alan loudly, and they came out. He was of average height, with strong bone, and a deliberate walk. From the cut of his shoulders, he would be tough.

They walked about half a mile and came to a thatched house unusually long for this part of the world. Hovering figures melted away into the darkness as they approached it. A little distance from the door, Alan hesitated, and looked at the sky as if wondering about the weather. But Seumas went on and they followed him. "Go in yourself first," Alan whispered intolerantly to Seumas.

Finn had heard the raised voice of the evangelist long before he followed Seumas across the threshold, nor did the voice cease as they unobtrusively joined the group in a deep circle round the peat fire. Room was quietly found for them on the inner circle, but Alan shook his head, implying they were fine where they were, they could stand, and he looked at the preacher as if his interest were entirely taken up. There was a slight shuffling movement and the deal plank by their knees emptied sufficiently to permit them to sit down.

To Finn's astonishment the preacher was not an old man; it was doubtful if he was forty. He had a high brow, with bare temples, and fine dark hair. His skin was pale, almost sallow, but his eyes burned in a black fire from under bony pronounced eyebrows. They had an extraordinary power of concentration, and as Finn stared and listened he found his mind emptying—and reforming far away, as it seemed, in a place where the figures and moods of the preacher came to a compelling life of their own.

He was very tired. The walk for a time had seemed to freshen him, but he had toiled hard and slept very little that week: an hour or two during the day between the spreading and lifting of the nets and again an uneasy hour or two at sea. He had not had his clothes off since last Sunday, and this was Saturday night. On top of all that had come the dreadful struggle in the inn.

DRINK AND RELIGION

For a little while, his exhaustion induced in him a feeling of soft dreamy luxuriousness. This preacher was as expert in his biblical evocations as Sandy Ware, created as intricate a pattern, as rich an involvement, while his intention progressed clearly towards enlightenment, fulfilment, on a tide of emotion that seemed as profound, as inevitable, as a tide in the sea.

Finn began to feel himself sinking. The need for sleep became an agony. The figures that the evangelist evoked grew blurred, wavered, until nothing was seen .but the evangelist's eyes. Far places and figures grew dark and mythical. A wild face raised to heaven, clasped hands, a knife, sacrifice, sacrifice. Angels ascending and descending.

I must keep awake, Finn thought. I must not disgrace myself. He drew a blind over his open eyes and wandered desperately in the hinterland of his own mind, stinging himself awake. This was bitter agony and he wanted to groan and fall over in a dead heap.

Slowly, however, these obscurities of the flesh thinned and he felt easier, and was very glad of this, even if he now experienced the curious sensation of not being quite himself, and at the same time of being more than himself.

He was glad and cunning about it, because he did not want to lose the bodily relief of this state. If he could hang on to it, he would be all right.

But soon the need for such assurance did not even trouble his mind. He was fully awake and followed the evocations of the preacher with clarity and comprehension. He had a deep-sounding voice, as if his chest were resonant. It was the finest, most sounding voice Finn had ever heard, and those rhythms, which flow in Gaelic like the waves of the ocean, or the sigh of the wind, were flawless and inexorable.

This was the case even in his devious attack on the Established Church and its carnal-minded ministers (after reference to the birth-bedroom in Bethlehem's inn over against "this Babel tower"): "When Christ comes to build a house for himself in the soul of man, his first work is, by his word and spirit, to pull down all towers and turrets of man's imaginations and open a door on his heart and a window in his understanding—open his grave that his dead devils may get a resurrection in his heart, mind, memory, and in all the faculties of his soul and body; make his heaven a hell to him, his strength his weakness, his faith his delusion, his light darkness, his sun blood, his moon sackcloth; turn what were once the heavenly meditations in his thoughts into a hell of corruption, and his reformed heart into a cage of all abominations; his spiritual mind, once a library of divinity within himself, now becomes the mail packet to the devil's emissaries; his summer joy is now his winter grief, and he cannot mourn, pray, or sigh, under his sad case, all blasted with the north wind as he is and grown over in his old days with young follies and lusts. Where is this poor man's minister now? Where is the anointed of the church who will lead him at that dread hour through the valley of the shadow? . . ."

Finn saw all the places in the valley of the shadow. He found indeed that he could think of and picture many things, and hear at the same time the words of the speaker and accompany him not only in his thought but in the accent of his speech, the persuasive rhythm of his voice, and still have time to himself, time for meditations between the words, time to look upon his own images. There was one visualization of extraordinary clarity: the terrible magnificence of Roddie in the pub; the flattening of lower lip and flesh over the jaw, the rocking power of the body, the roar. Beyond the littleness of man to-day, looming like the far solitary figure of another place and time. Not evil, not good; imminent and terrible. Even the breath that Finn hardly breathed came in cold upon his lips, while his brain cleared still more. So that he could also look round upon the faces of the assembled folk; and these faces, too, he saw with an unusual clearness.

Not only the faces of the old, with the emotion of the

368

moment wrought deeply upon them, not only that which stirred the lips to a soft moan, the head to shake, the body to rock, but, as if written upon a white page in daylight, the story of their toil and care and pain and forgetting, writ with an iron pencil on the brows, around the eyes, down by the nostrils, at the corner of the lips, upon the lips themselves, in the very shape of the wondering mouth, so that Finn knew them with a profound and loving intimacy—that remained aloof, not intruding. Each face, too, had a physical resemblance to faces he knew at home. He had time to think about this with a faint cool surprise. And the faces of the young, especially of some youths and girls about his own age, were particularly self-revealing. There were two girls of contrasting colour: one reddish-fair, with large blue eyes and a soft formless mouth, and the other dark, with a perfect oval face, a broad face, coming to a pointed chin, with eyes dark and set wide apart. There was a lovely stillness about the dark girl, like still dark water, with a soft tender gleam. He had seen her likeness before in a tinker girl in Caithness, walking the roads with a child, wrapped tightly in a tartan plaid, slung to her back. He had glanced after her and been surprised at the contented look on the pale face of the child that could move neither foot nor hand. This girl had the same kind of dark blue-green plaid wrapped round her, and Finn, listening all the time to the speaker's words and wandering with them in Caithness and Bethlehem . . . the star in the east . . . there was no room in the inn (Roddie flaming magnificent in the inn) . . . suddenly thought of this dark girl before him as Mary, the Mother of Christ. That was so unexpected, so heretical, so blasphemous an image that his own thought stilled—and stilled every other process in the room for a moment that was a very long time. Then the fair girl sobbed. She was a warm-hearted untidy girl. But others had moaned or groaned. The Word was knocking at their hearts. They knew the evilness of their hearts. They glimpsed far, far away, in hopeless hope, "the lovely state of grace".

But the dark girl remained serene, her face a great sweetness, the soft tenderness deepening in her eyes.

Then Finn became aware of another thing: that Alan, though only giving a glance at this dark girl and never a direct one, was bothered and taut in his emotions because of her, and in less than an instant he understood every previous act of Alan—the reluctance to go to the meeting, the haunted uncertainties, the covering laugh, the mask of friendly talk. Alan was probably forty and she was twenty-one or twenty-two. Moreover, the awful fear that held Alan now was that this girl might break down like some of the others.

How extraordinary! For the girl plainly had no thought of Alan's presence or of anything that might disturb him. But how revealing!

An old man prayed, haltingly at first, but then fluently and fervently. The preacher led them in singing a psalm. The music brought into the stream of communion those minds that suffered from an individual hardness. The fervour of the meeting increased.

Time as measurement now ceased. Often, indeed, such meetings, starting at ten or eleven at night, would be carried on until four or five in the morning.

Time was a vanity, with other vanities. Youthful vanity —that sensitive braggart vanity, that hurt in the pride, that rushing in, that screaming and yelling, that clawing of futility on the figure of terrible magnificence.

Time disappeared in a darkness.

But always the dark girl's face looked up serene. She sat on the floor. All the young sat crowded on the floor, their faces hanging down or uplifted.

The tenderness in her eyes deepened and glimmered.

Her shoulders and head uprose like an obstruction, a smooth rock, in the river of time running round and past her. It was shape in the void, it was constancy in the flux, it was beauty's still flower in eternity.

The eyes gathered all the light from the candles.

"There is disputing and anger, there is accusation against false teachers and profane followers, the divisions of Reuben are upon the pinnacles, but oh! how few are our tears for a sight of the beloved Jesus!"

The eyes filled, and down each cheek a tear rolled.

Finn heard a smothered grunt by his side. He turned his face. Alan's head was between his hands, the fingers working in the hair, the left ear showing between curved thumb and finger that closed on it and gripped it. It was like a giant's head in a fable. Finn looked at his own hands in the shadow of a man's back and they were remote from him.

They were in the realm of holiness, of God's holiness, and thought was soft and warm with it. This holiness was in the inner texture of the flesh; like the memory of a scentless incense in the nostrils; it was in all their minds; it was their minds; it flowed upward with the river-movement of light and shadow from peat-fire and candle; it spread under the floor of heaven and outward beyond the confines of the world. They were under the shadow of the wing of God's holiness where all uncertainty ceases. . . .

Finn found himself outside. Seumas was whispering to him, light-toned and friendly as before. "There's no room in our place. But Alan will take you." Personal and detached from it all, sounded Seumas; cool as the stirring wind, with a hidden fun of its own.

All right. He would go with Alan. To go with Alan was what his heart needed. The dawn was in the sky and grey along the grass. But the gable-ends were no longer still and secretive. They went striding away. There was a movement within all stillness. There was invisible movement everywhere. "We'll go," said Alan.

Dark figures pressed through the atmosphere, that was heavy with God's holiness, going into the night. Alan's voice was low but rough and hearty. "Here we are," he said. His two sisters were already inside, and they welcomed Finn with administering kindness. They smiled,

371

their manners practical and friendly, active with quiet grace, the grace of their bodies and the assured grace of God. They gave him to eat and to drink, but his throat would take little, for there was a tremble in his breast, a weariness in his stomach beyond the weariness of death; his eye-sockets were hot as fire and his hand fell heavy on his knee. They were solicitous for him in a kindness that was almost gay. So Alan led him into the little room beyond the kitchen and there they went to bed together.

On his back, at once Finn felt a great peace, a lightening and floating of his body. Outside, larks were singing in the dawn. A curlew flew overhead in the fluting cry of rain. Peewits, disturbed by the dark figures, passed away into the moor. Oyster-catchers—Servants of Bride, Seumas had named them—called piercingly from the shore. Alan was restless and did not want Finn in his bed, did not want anyone or anything but the secrecy of his own dark thought. Finn knew this and knew why. But he could not help Alan —and did not greatly care. If wakefulness came on him now, his eyes would never more close in sleep until he died. The torment was working upon Alan swiftly. His hot breath was holding and quickening. He was in torture, in the torture of desire, of defeat. The desire of the defeated mind, craving in bodiless agony to have, to possess. Young Mary, the Mother of Christ.

"Oh, hell," muttered Alan savagely. "Are you asleep?"

"No," said Finn.

"Could you be doing with one?"

"I could."

"Hush, then, for God's sake! These girls will hear a pin drop." They were as old as Alan himself.

He got out of bed, and when something bumped, he swore under his breath. Softly spoke a cork coming away from something bigger than a bottle. The running spirit glucked quietly. "Here," whispered Alan. "It's brandy."

Finn sat up and took the bowl, Alan on his knees beside

him. The spirit stung the membranes of his mouth, and though he let it down gently, he coughed and Alan had to take the bowl from his hands. "Hsh, for heaven's sake!" muttered Alan and drained the bowl noiselessly. Gluck-gluck. "Will you try another mouthful?"

"I will," said Finn. "I have never tasted brandy before. It's got a nice flavour."

"It's a good drop," said Alan.

"Give me a little time," said Finn.

Alan laughed huskily. "There are three brothers of them. One is a general in the army. One is in command of the Revenue cutter. The third is a ship's master, and he runs a cargo of one thing from here—and he brings back a cargo of another thing with him."

"And the brother on the Revenue cutter has sworn he'll catch him one day, so I've heard."

"He has that," said Alan, on his knees in his shirt waiting for the bowl. "But he hasn't caught him yet!"

"If this is some of it, it would be a great pity if he was caught."

Alan laughed thickly again. "It's not wasted on you!" he muttered.

"I feel the better of that," said Finn.

"You will," said Alan. "And the night is young. I don't hold with drinking alone if it can be avoided. Sometimes it can't." He filled the small bowl again in a profound humour, with a soothed savage happiness. "Your health!"

"Health to yourself." Finn lay back. "Sweet Mary, I'm tired," he breathed.

"What's that you said?" Husky and swift was the voice, and threatening.

"I said I was tired," murmured Finn. "Sweet Mary."

"Who—Mary?"

So Mary was her name! How strange the chance and how true! "Sweet Mary," repeated Finn, caring no more for Alan, "the Mother of Christ."

There was a stark pause. Then Alan's voice rose, harshly

appalled. "By God," he said, "it takes an East-coaster for blasphemy! And you, little more than a boy!"

"Are you not going to sleep in there?" called a voice from outside the door.

Alan remained silent and still for some seconds. Then he said gruffly, "We're going."

"He needs sleep, Alan. He's very tired."

"Go to sleep yourself," growled Alan.

"Alan!"

"Oh, go away!" roared Alan. "Leave us alone!" And he moved about on his bare shanks, muttering. Presently he listened. But the plaintive voice had apparently retreated. "That's them!" he muttered, in a ferocious humour. "That's them, and they hang on to you. Will you have another mouthful?"

"I'll have a small one," murmured Finn. "But it's the last. I'm done."

"Here, then."

After taking a small mouthful, Finn handed back the bowl to Alan. When Alan had emptied it, he sat on the bed, talking in a mutter about women, not directly but with obscure personal meanings and hatreds. Finn's blasphemy had taken a contorted grip of him. Finn knew that Alan hated him for it and yet was fatally attracted. It was an evil mood for Alan to be in and Finn wondered how he would get him into bed. To ask Alan to come to bed now was the only certain way of keeping him out. Finn felt the minds of the sisters in their kitchen bed, sweet in the grace of God, more sensitive than pain, their thoughts crying: Alan! Alan! But uplifted, with veiled lids, towards the region of God's understanding and mercy, uplifted in shame not quite showing, held back into their hearts, hoping that what they shielded might not be seen.

And all at once he saw Alan caught in the tendrils of their mercy, as the sheep of sacrifice was caught in the thicket.

It was a queer, stark, dreadful vision.

Roddie—Roddie—caught in the thorns, too. Years, upon years, upon years.

"Have you no fear of blasphemy?" asked Alan, the harsh laugh held back. "Aren't you afraid you'll be stricken dead? Eh?"

"I'm not afraid," said Finn. "There's nothing a man should be afraid of in the wide world."

"It's the young hero, you are, what! Afraid of nothing?" Derisive laughter tore huskily through his choked throat.

But Finn's mind for some reason had suddenly gone cold and austere. He could not help Alan. He could not help anybody. He was too far away. Here was the calm region of death, cold as a dead face. Of death and of release. No longer any sympathy for Alan, or for himself. An ultimate uncaring. The back of his head fell heavily upon the pillow, his breath came from him in a slow soft stream, and the grey light of the morning passed away.

CHAPTER XVIII

LANDING HERRING

❧

Early on Monday, Seumas and Finn took the road back to Stornoway. Seumas was light and cool as water running in a burn. He refreshed Finn, and chuckled over Alan's brandy.

Finn had not awakened until the afternoon of Sunday. Alan had made a great effort with a wry mouth. "We had a drop," he said to Finn. "We needed it," answered Finn, smiling, "though I could have done without this head." The sisters were as kind as if nothing had happened. A terrible beautiful Sunday kindness. Finn's dazed mind, caught in a thicket of pain and mist, wanted to escape, but Seumas had taken him along and introduced him to his family: the father and mother, three brothers and four sisters. One of the sisters was very attractive, with Seumas's own brightness behind her grey eyes. So Finn hardly looked at her, for she was his own age and it was Sunday, and Seumas and himself went a long walk.

In the evening Alan was moody, and Finn's head was worse. But he was feeling fine this morning, and Seumas's secret news was something to bring back with him. For a man had come up to the Sunday meeting from the east district of Lochs, having crossed Loch Erisort by boat, with word that herring were so thick down Loch Odhairn way, that they had been seen early that morning flicking the water white, like a shower of hail-stones. Seumas, of course, knew the indebtedness of the *Seafoam* to the *Sulaire*, and

when Finn asked if he might pass on the intelligence to the
Sulaire, Seumas said, "Why not?"

Seumas was apparently not deeply impressed by the religious revival, though he did not say much about it, but he
told Finn all about where the preacher came from, who
certain persons were, and many strange stories of that part
of the world. Finn admired his coolness, his light friendly
manner. It made Finn think of having a bathe, and though
Seumas said there was no good place because of the soft
peaty ground, he found a spot when he saw Finn was set on
it, but he would not let Finn swim out lest he should stick
in the bottom.

As they approached Stornoway, a tremor of excitement
caught Finn in the breast and he began to smile in an embarrassed way without knowing it. As Seumas and himself
stood for a moment at parting, a door across the way
opened and the *Seafoam* crew came out. Finn faced Seumas,
saying, "Well, we may be seeing you to-night yet." Then
they caught up the crew and Callum asked, "Where have
you young devils been?" Thus they all came together and
walked on, while Finn told how Seumas had taken him to
his home at Luirbost over the Sunday.

"I thought a lot of preaching would do him good,"
added Seumas.

"And I hope he got it," said Callum.

"Only ten hours of it," replied Seumas.

They laughed at that. Roddie smiled. He was very quiet,
the skin of his face unusually reddened, as if slightly in-
flamed. Finn saw he was gentle as a lamb, and probably in
his own way deeply remorseful, but his head was up, as
always, and his eyes steady.

A feeling of security came about Finn. For he had had his
bad moments about what might have happened to Roddie.
Not but that he would have faced up to anything. Yet it was
good to have the crew together, to be walking to work at
the nets. Callum and himself fell behind as the others went
ahead with Seumas.

"Is it all right?" asked Finn with a glancing smile.

"God knows," said Callum. "We had a terrible time after you left. Oh, terrific. It was the skipper of the *Sulaire* stopped him finally. You wouldn't believe it. Turned him to a lamb. The last man, you would think, seeing—seeing how Roddie was indebted to him. Then they were going to lock him up. Big Angus's jaw was broken. Donald George was a mess of blood and bruises. It was Maciver, the fish-curer, got Roddie free. Bain entered into security for him. But Donald George is swearing now he is going to have the law on Roddie. They say there's going to be a case, and we'll all be called as witnesses. Do you know how many bottles of whisky were smashed? Forty-nine."

"Forty-nine!" echoed Finn.

"It's a good number," said Callum.

"Just one short of the fifty," said Finn.

"You think he should have made it the round fifty?" Callum nearly laughed. Finn smiled nervously. "What the hell," asked Callum, "made you behave like yon?"

"I don't know," said Finn. "I'm sorry. I don't know how it happened."

"Well, watch yourself, my boy. When you didn't turn up last night and we saw Roddie's uneasiness—not that he said anything—I could have skinned you. However, you're here, and, I'm telling you, we have got to hold together now. One of the crew of the *Sulaire* passed us the tip. There are a few men after Roddie. They say they'll get him yet. They say they'll lie in wait for him somewhere and bash his head in. All the fishermen are annoyed. They have a strong belief here that when you spill blood you drive away the herring. I don't know whether there's anything in it or not. But they say it's a fact. And if it is, then begod the herring will be heading for the Arctic for the next twelve-month!"

"Well, they're not," said Finn. "I know where there is herring and plenty of them."

Callum looked at him and, as the others disappeared

round a corner, stopped. "What do you mean?" he asked, his eyes searching.

When Finn had told his story about the herring being in shoal in Loch Odhairn, Callum's expression quickened like a boy's and he jerked his right fist upwards. "If only we get into them!" His broad fair face lit up. "Come on! You'll tell Roddie now."

"You tell him," said Finn.

Callum glanced quickly at him, his brows gathering over sharpened eyes as if he were trying to read in the dark. "All right!"

When the crew were by themselves, Callum said, "Listen here, boys." And he told Finn's story. Roddie looked at Finn. They all did. "It's quite true," said Finn, and gave circumstantial detail. They were strongly moved. "There's one thing I asked Seumas," Finn added simply. "He knew how the *Sulaire* gave us her herring, so I asked if there would be any harm in passing on the news to her skipper, and he said no. So you could tell him if you like," concluded Finn with a glance at Roddie.

Roddie nodded, looked thoughtfully beyond them, then automatically began climbing down into the boat. Callum winked at Finn. "It's a f-fine morning," said Rob, glancing solemnly at the sky.

They lifted the damaged nets on to the quay, with the intention of taking them round to where the drift was drying. Mending could go on there with less publicity and greater comfort.

As Roddie and Henry went ahead, each with a folded net over his shoulders, Finn saw many people turn round and look after Roddie. He noted, however, that they did not stare until he passed.

Callum winked and smiled. "They won't come in his way lightly," he murmured, on a note of triumph 'They'll remember yon fight in Stornoway for a few years! He has no idea of his own strength. He's a terrible fellow." He almost shook his head.

Finn smiled.

"I don't give a damn supposing what happens," declared Callum. "If we get herring to-night—if only! O God."

"Cold iron," said Finn.

Callum laughed as at a hidden joke. Finn laughed, too.

"I'm glad you mentioned about the *Sulaire*. That was a fine stroke," declared Callum. "You have some little sense in you, in spite of everything, I see. Did you notice that knot of folk looking at us and us laughing? They'll be thinking we should be solemn as prisoners going to the jile! Little they know!"

"If they live long enough," said Finn, "they'll l-learn many a thing."

That afternoon, Roddie had a long talk with the skipper of the *Sulaire*. About five o'clock, in a steady sailing wind from the sou'-west, the boats began to put to sea, the *Seafoam* among the first. When Henry gave a final tightening to the halyards, eased the mainsail sheet to a calculated inch, and had everything in the best sailing trim, he glanced at Roddie. Roddie seemed impervious to any enthusiasm, unaware even of the boat in front of him. But Finn saw the stem of the *Seafoam* caught again in her old wooden dream, launching forward, sheering the water in her hissing song, with invisible eyes not for the boat racing there in front but for the horizon beyond. "Let me go. Don't hold me back. Don't hold me back."

"Take her weather," said Henry.

Roddie could not have heard him. The sails might have reefs in. All strife was behind him.

They could see the members of the crew quite distinctly. One of them was the whispering fellow who had started all the strife. Finn recognized him and looked at Henry. Henry gave a small nod, his lips drawn in satire, for it was clearly a matter he could not mention to Roddie.

There was no holding the *Seafoam* back, however. She was overhauling the boat slowly but steadily. "Leave it to me," sang the stem.

"He's cutting you out," cried Henry. "He's trying to blanket you."

But all Roddie did was to fall away a little more, as if giving in. Henry eased the sheet, his face darkening, his lips tight. Not another word would they utter!

Minutes passed. The race was set. Neither crew looked at the other. Nor, perhaps, could the *Dawn*, heading for the fishing ground to the north, be directly accused of cutting her course too fine, or even over much. It was for any other boat to look out for herself. She held the seaway.

It became clear that Roddie must do something, or be knocked off his course before he could over-reach her to leeward. Dammit, he could not let her sit on them like that! They glanced at him surreptitiously, restlessly, tensely excited. Roddie put out his left hand and motioned backward with his fingers. Henry drew in the sheet in imperceptible inches until the fingers stopped him. Roddie's eyes, from the peak of the mainsail, dropped back to stare expressionlessly ahead. He had slightly altered course. Excitement mounted. Neither was giving way. . . . There was going to be a collision. . . . Roddie would ram him!

Roddie did not ram him. He came in on his stern with a yard to spare and took his weather. It was a beautiful piece of seamanship. Two members of the *Dawn* yelled at them in rage, and the whispering fellow shook his fist. The *Seafoam* drew slowly away, nothing now between the singing stem and its beloved horizon. Finn glanced at Roddie's face and found it expressionless and uplifted as the stem. A sudden quick emotion, like a sting of tears, made him glance away—to see Callum giving a quiet shake to the tail-end of the sheet over the gunnel: a request to the *Dawn* if she wanted a tow! He laughed quickly. Henry's eyes gleamed in triumph. Rob scratched his beard noisily.

"She's a dandy!" cried Callum. "I would rather that than a hundred pounds."

"What do you say?" asked Roddie quietly. But they saw

381

the smile in his eyes. Whereupon Callum clean forgot himself. "By God——"

"Cold iron!" yelled Rob.

"Give me the whole end of the boat-hook," said Callum.

"Will you never learn how to behave yourself in a boat?" asked Rob, with loud disapproval.

"A man will learn many a thing," said Callum, "if he lives long enough."

When, well out to sea beyond Arnish Point, Roddie suddenly headed away on a southerly course, a sigh of relief (as Finn learned next day) went over the following fleet. They were well rid of that blood-spiller, if it's herring they were looking for! He was probably ashamed of himself and wanted to be alone! Even the East Coast boats, though secretly elated over Roddie's physical prowess, had no particular reason to believe in his luck as a fisherman. A wild enough devil of a Jonah to frighten any herring! Perhaps the dogs would follow him!

At the tail-end of the fleet, however, were two boats that headed south after him, and one other boat from Buckie that always kept an eye on the lucky *Sulaire*.

Off the islands at the entrance to Loch Erisort, Roddie spilled the wind from his sails. All had gone according to plan, and when the *Sulaire* came up, the smiling skipper gave them a salute. The *Iolaire* was in her wake, and Seumas waved to Finn, as the *Seafoam's* head fell away and followed. Fifty yards behind, the *Mary Ann* was coming quietly, as if she couldn't overtake anyone though she tried. But she had lines to her, as Finn pointed out.

"She could give any of us a clean pair of heels, that one," said Roddie simply.

"Would she?" cried Callum, challengingly.

"She can sail into the eye of the wind as near as makes no difference," added Roddie.

"That's not everything," said Callum.

"She's smart on her feet as the Buckers themselves," Henry said. "And they can handle her."

"They know a boat on the south side." Rob nodded "Do you remember George o' James's, who came from Smeral, and whose son was married on a niece of old Widow Macrae's? Well, the brother of that son, George to name, was related by marriage to a fellow who had a job in the Elgin brewery. . . ."

This involved detail, which he could never remember, suffused Finn's body in a divine warmth. It was Rob's voice speaking. It was the old happiness of comradeship and the sea. If he looked at Callum, Callum would wink, implying, "We'll have him on!" He looked. Callum winked.

They shot their nets not far from the *Sulaire*, which lay inside them in the mouth of Loch Odhairn. The *Iolaire* was over towards the north side. The *Mary Ann* had disappeared round Kebock Head and then come back, and was now shot fairly close into the rocks, where the gulls were very excited and noisy.

"Can you smell them, Rob?" Callum asked.

"Never you mind whether I can smell them or not," answered Rob. "We'll see what we will see."

"Look!" called Finn.

A jet of water rose into the air between them and the *Sulaire*.

"Bl-essings on him, it's himself," said Rob.

The whale! It was the first time Finn had ever seen one blowing.

"How big will he be?" asked Finn, full of the wonder of the sea.

"If he came up under us," answered Callum, "we would fall off his back like a bowl off a table. You better be ready to strip."

Finn smiled and munched away, as the shadows deepened in the great rock before Kebock Head. The sky was overcast and the sea wind-darkened. For weather, it was the best fishing night they had had. They all knew they were among herring. The rest was with the luck they could not compel.

Roddie was quiet in his manner, but smiling now and then. At moments, Finn had seen in him an almost childish poignancy. Because he was strong and had that terrible destructive power, because it was part of him naturally, he was not proud of it. But he would not be abashed.

"We'll stretch ourselves," he now said. "It looks like being a good night."

His voice was quiet and shadowed like the night, pleasant with peace. For a moment Finn felt the loneliness of the human mind. The loneliness of the night. The gulls were crying. The boat moved gently to the swing-rope. Between them and the bottom was an inch of planking, between them and the whale! They were fishing herring, like the whale himself. Over this thought, forming vaguely into a pattern of its own, was a wonder at the meaning of it all. Not a sentimental wonder, but a curious, detached wonder, rather stark, more like a bodiless vision.

It faded before it had quite formed, into the loneliness of himself, the secret companionship of himself with himself, where no-one intrudes—except . . . and there were her dark eyes and the dark hair shadowing the white neck. He never begged of her. Never. But when he forgot himself, she was there. Sometimes his repelling sarcasm was very effective. But with tiredness drugging the body, tenderness has a way of forgetting. . . . He fell sound asleep.

He awoke as if someone had touched him. It was the grey of the morning and Roddie was pulling on the swing-rope. Henry was sitting up. His senses became preternaturally acute. Had Roddie tried the net earlier and found nothing? A slight nausea oalled in his breast. Roddie was slow in his movements, hand over slow hand, his body against the sky. How terrible, if theirs should be the only boat without herring! Upon Finn came the power of the superstition regarding blood. Were they doomed? The premonition gripped him. Their nets hung empty in the sea. They must face up to that, show nothing. Roddie had reached the net. He stooped and hauled, but not far. There was a splash. He stood looking astern, turned to stone. Henry, unable to bear that stillness, got up and in a voice, casual in its supreme control, asked, "Nothing doing?"

Roddie turned. His voice had the smile of a child in it. "We're in them," he said, "solid."

Henry stood dead still. Finn could not move.

"We'll start hauling at once," Roddie murmured. "Waken them up."

Finn rolled againt Callum and, in his ear, cried shrilly, "Herring!"

Callum whirled over, "What? Where?" and grappled Finn earnestly before he came to himself.

There was no doubt about the silver darlings now. In blue and green and silver, they danced into the boat.

"Fair quality," said Roddie, hauling mightily.

"They're good, boy," said Rob. "They're by-ordin-ary."

"They'll pay half a dollar for one in Berlin," said Finn, "and get value."

Roddie laughed. Finn's heart soared among the wheeling gulls.

"The *Sulaire* is in them, too," said Roddie, with light happiness.

"And that's our debt paid to the *Sulaire*, thank——"

"Will you be quiet?" interrupted Rob sharply.

"Thank goodness," completed Callum. "Got him that time, Finn! Do you know what I'm thinking, Rob?"

"It won't be much," said Rob.

"I'm thinking it would be a good thing if Finn went to Luirbost again and prayed for ten more hours."

"That's all you know," said Finn. "I haven't yet told you about the jar of brandy. There was a fellow there named Alan Macdonald and we slept together. He was in a queer mood because certain things were happening to him, and——"

"What things?" asked Callum.

"Never you mind," said Finn. "And he wouldn't go to

sleep. He would keep pouring out the brandy into a bowl and asking me to drink it."

"And you didn't?"

"I had to," said Finn, "or I would hurt his feelings. It's not that I wanted the stuff myself. Not at all. Though it was good enough. I'll say that. It had a nice taste. But you know how it is?" he asked.

"I know," said Callum, shaking his head. "Boy, boy, do you know the road you're taking?"

"You'll be like the fellow from the Dykes of Latheron," said Rob, "big John Angus McGrath—an elder in the church, too. Every time he took a dram, he would shake his head and say, 'Nasty stuff! nasty stuff!' To my father's knowledge he said it for over fifty years."

They laughed at Rob's shortest story.

"Credit where it is due, all the same," said Henry. "I'll stand you a brandy myself when we get ashore, Finn." And his dark face, so often satiric, smiled with such a humoured friendliness that Finn felt his cheeks grow hot.

The sweat was running down their faces; they staggered as they shifted their stance. Then Finn saw the whale heave his great bulk, with wide gaping jaws, quite close to him, and let out a cry.

"Sure, it's himself," said Rob. "I hope you're having a good fishing!" he called to the great beast as it rolled by.

"He'll foul us!" yelled Callum, whose experience of whales was not much greater than Finn's.

"Do you think it's you he's after?" called Rob in sarcasm. "He has better taste."

Roddie was hauling steadily. When it came to the last two nets the whale began to move quickly around them as if in anger at the diminishing store of food. Callum had nothing to say. Finn was dogged by the fear of disaster at the final minute, disaster beyond anything he had dreamed.

As the last net was coming in, the immense brute followed it to the boat's side, feeding on the best herring as they fell from the mesh. He was plainly angry now, setting dark swirls of water about the boat.

"Now, now," called Rob to him. "We have no more for you here. Yon's the *Mary Ann*. Look!" And he pointed. "They're scarcely half-hauled. If you hurry up, you might get something yet." The great jaws closed and the whale turned away in the direction of the *Mary Ann*. "A very biddable beast," concluded Rob.

Yes, the whale was gone! Finn was so relieved that he looked at Rob in open astonishment.

"What do you think?" Henry asked Roddie.

Roddie gazed at the deep well of herring. "Over forty crans," he answered.

Forty crans! They straightened their backs. Roddie alone seemed unimpressed. No quick excitement touched him. Finn saw that his face was quiet with peace.

"The sooner we get them landed, boys, the better they'll cure," he said. And his gentle voice released unbounded energy in their bodies.

They had to row for a time and did not make great headway because the *Seafoam* was deep in the water and the tide against them. But soon a little air of easterly wind sprang up and presently the oars were shipped. The straining on the oars had eased the exuberance in their bodies and as Finn sat where he could get some support for his back, a divine warmth uncurled along each arm and each leg like the snake of life itself. Callum so brimmed over with this lazy warmth that he just winked and gave the small sideways nod that leaves humour lost in wonder.

Finn looked at sea-birds hurrying over the water, gazed at the land, thought of the grey night by Loch Luirbost (which opened off Loch Erisort) and the strange things that happened there. They were not quite real now. They had then seemed more real than life, transcending life. But ah! this was life, this exquisite morning of the world. Alan caught in the thicket, grown by his two kind sisters—a

witchcraft of the night. He turned his head away—and
Callum asked, "When did you learn to tame whales, Rob?"

"I knew about whales before you were born."

"Did you, man? Where?"

"On the sea. Where did you think?"

"Oh, I didn't know. There are some fellows who have
been inside the bellies of whales, and the whales spewed
them up. I didn't know."

"There's many a thing you don't know——"

"But if I live long enough I'll learn?"

"—and there's many a thing I don't know. But there's
one thing I know now that I didn't know before."

"And what's that?"

"That yon whale put the fear of d-death in you."

Callum tried to speak, but no-one would listen to him. It
was Rob's round.

"There's the *Mary Ann* under way," said Henry and they
all looked back. The brown sail of the *Iolaire* was also being
hoisted. But the gulls were still wheeling in myriads about
the *Sulaire*.

"He'll be in them to the gunnels again!" cried Callum.
Roddie smiled.

"He's a fine man," said Rob with his serious air.

"He's all that," said Roddie.

"*Mary Ann* and ourselves for Bain, *Sulaire* and *Iolaire*
for Maciver. It's level going," said Henry.

"It looks as if the boats from the north are blank again,"
called Finn. They had been making but little progress in
the light wind and had seen the bulk of the fleet heading in
past the Chicken Rock but now they were near enough for
Finn's keen eyes to see that the last boat or two sat lightly
in the water.

As they passed Goat Island, Callum said, "Will you
look?"

Convoyed by the gulls, low in the water, they slowly
approached a quay that seemed to be thronged by all
Stornoway.

Finn felt the excitement surging in him, and did his best to look indifferent. Rob scratched his beard. "There seems to be a few folk about," he said casually. After that, none of them spoke, but each sat in his place with calm countenance.

Roddie, the terrible East-coaster, the mad Viking, the spiller of blood, the curse on Stornoway, brought the *Seafoam* to her berth, silver-scaled to his thighs, with a quiet gesture of the lowering of the sails and no word spoken. Glancing up the quay wall, Finn saw hundreds of eyes on them in silence. It was a moment of great triumph.

Bain's voice rose in a shout.

Roddie lifted his face and answered with a quiet smile. Yes, they had a few crans.

"What about the *Sulaire*?" asked Maciver.

"She won't be for an hour or more yet. He'll have to come carefully," said Roddie with a glimmer of humour.

"Good for Macleod!" cried Maciver.

"And the *Iolaire* has a good shot," Roddie added.

Maciver slapped Bain on the back. One up!

"The only other boat that was with us was the *Mary Ann* and she'll be in next," said Roddie. "She was in them, too."

"Hah-ha!" laughed Bain, jerking his head back. Both Maciver and himself had seen the quality of the herring. They were in high feather.

"Kebock Head will be black with boats to-night," prophesied Maciver.

"So long as you have a Caithness man to lead the way," agreed Bain. "I'll stand you a good one to-day, skipper, even if we don't go to Donald George's," he shouted.

The whole quay laughed. Roddie turned away, his face darkening.

"That's him," said a girl's voice. "Throw him a kiss."

Finn, glancing up, saw the gutting crew of three girls with whom he had already had a slight passage at arms. He blushed deeply and looked down. They shrieked with laughter.

As they were unloading their herring, Finn saw people coming up to have a look at Roddie, a discreet wondering look. The story of the Sloop Inn was already growing fabulous. The mass of the Lewis fishermen were glad that Big Angus had got it where he deserved it—in the jaw. But this man's mythical strength, his defiance of superstition, his touchiness over what now was retailed as an incredible feat of seamanship in the Western Ocean, and—confronting them here—his triumph over the fish of the sea itself! . . .

"You mind your step," cried the high-spirited fair girl, as Finn staggered sideways a little in tipping the fish into the gutting-box.

"I didn't mean to touch you," said Finn.

"We've had your touchings before," said she.

"I'm sorry if you didn't like them," said Finn.

She mimicked his East-coast accent. "Mama's pretty boy!"

He stood a moment looking at her, his eyes gleaming over the flush on his face.

"Here!" she called to the foreman. "Watch him!"

"What now?" said the foreman heartily, busy scooping salt. "Going to throw her into the box, my boy?" Swish! went the salt. "She may yet find a harder bed"—swish!— "and not notice it."

Finn retreated. The girls retreated, too, knowing better than to engage the hairy foreman in verbal combat. "He's a nasty old man," said the high-spirited one. "You asked for it," said her companion, a dark merry girl.

"I did nothing of the sort," said the fair one, riding high.

"I think you're getting fond of him," said the dark girl.

"Who? Me?" The blue eyes opened in scorn.

"Hsh, he's coming," said the dark one.

But Fair-face did not even deign to glance at Finn, this time or for several times. Her voice, however, continued to exhibit a considerable gift of mimicry.

"That's the last of them," said Finn, smiling pleasantly to the dark girl. Then in a simple confidential manner, he asked, "Where does she stay?"

"Who?"

"Her," said Finn, with a sideways movement of the head.

"Why?"

"So that I might keep out of her way."

"In that case, don't go near Swordale."

"Thank you very much," said Finn, and off he went.

"You had no right to tell him," said Fair-face, unable, however, to suppress a certain excitement.

The dark girl, bending over the herring, smiled, for though Finn had spoken about her companion, he had spoken with his eyes to herself.

If one lives long enough, thought Finn, as he followed Henry, one learns many a thing.

Bain was talking to Roddie. "Come on!" he said. "No," replied Roddie, "you'll please excuse me. Thank you all the same." Bain looked at him, his eyes sharpened in humour. "Very well," he nodded. "But come on over to the office. I have something to say to you. Come away."

"We'll go over," said Roddie to Henry, and they both followed Bain through the crowd.

"That's done us out of one," remarked Finn to Callum.

"Has it, faith?" asked Callum.

"We'll run the nets out first," said Rob.

"I have a thirst on me," declared Callum, "that would astonish two pints of beer. Are you game?"

"Why not?" said Finn.

"You can't say but I asked you not to go," remarked Rob, pulling down his jersey. "There's a widow woman who has a place round the corner, just short of the Custom House. She's a decent woman; and her husband, who came from Swordale, learned his trade in the Wick Arms, when Danny Sinclair . . ."

Finn began to laugh and waved to Seumas, who cried, "Won't you wait for me?" The four large shots had fairly stirred up Stornoway. There was life everywhere and a buzz of expectation. What one boat got to-day, another might get to-morrow. That the four boats had stolen a day's march on the rest of the fleet was a good joke, for no-one grudged anyone anything so long as herring were about. A man's time was coming! "Boys, will you look at him?" murmured Callum. They went to the edge of the wall and Callum cried, "A few scales on you to-day, Skipper!" The *Sulaire* glittered from stem to stern and her skipper beamed upon them. It lightened the heart to look on that wise, good-natured, radiant countenance, and after a few chaffing words, they followed Rob.

"We'll have three glasses of beer," said Rob to the widow, a buxom heavy-breasted woman, fresh-faced, and forty. She complimented Rob on his shot, and Rob said it wasn't bad, and as they got on the talk, Callum gave Finn a wink. "We'll have the same again, Mistress, if you please." "God bless me, boy," said Rob, astonished, "you're quick with it." "Cold iron to you, Rob—or you're sunk," cried Callum solemnly. Three men came in and the widow moved up to attend to their order. "You're a dark dog," said Callum. "Fancy having all that up your sleeve." "Will you be quiet," muttered Rob, with decent care. "Have you no manners at all?" "Besides," murmured Finn, "he could hardly have it up his sleeve." Callum, caught in the middle of his drink, barked abruptly, spluttered the mouthful mostly up his right arm and went on coughing, Finn taking the glass from him.

"I'm very sorry," he gasped to the lady of the house; "it went down the wrong way."

"You'll have to excuse him," said Rob sarcastically; "he's not used to it."

"Indeed," said the lady, "it's a sore thing." She picked up a mopping cloth. "It's on your sleeve." When he had overcome a second bout of coughing, she wiped his sleeve. He thanked her, pulled his sleeve down, and looked up it.

When at last they left the inn, Finn rolled away laughing, with Rob heavily talking at Callum.

"I didn't mean anything," explained Callum. "If you ask me, I think she is a very nice woman. I don't mean to imply that there is anything between you. There may be for all I know—but I'm not saying it."

"No. But you think I don't follow you. Well, let me tell you——"

Callum stopped. "I don't want you to tell me anything. Don't put any sin on your conscience for my sake."

Finn could see Rob's anger was evaporating, though he still pretended to be hurt. "It's the manners of the thing," he protested.

"Ay, ay," said Callum.

Rob hunched his shoulders and Finn saw a faint new gleam of self-importance come into his eyes. "I was going to tell you," he said, "about Swordale, and how a foreign crew landed there not many years ago, and buried cartloads of silver dollars in the sand, and how the Customs officers got them and found out they had murdered their captain on the high seas, and what happened to the dollars and the crew, but damn me if I now tell you a thing," and he stalked on.

"Man, that's a poor spirit, Rob," replied Callum, winking at Finn, who could have shouted out, for no earthly reason than that he was happy.

But he answered thoughtfully, "I don't agree with you there. After all, anyone could see that the woman of the house had an eye for him, and you can hardly blame him for that. For all we know, he may be innocent. Tell me, Rob, where is Swordale?"

"Do you think you might find some of the dollars?" asked Rob sarcastically.

"I wasn't exactly thinking of the dollars," said Finn.

Callum whistled. "Her husband came from Swordale! Dollars! Not only the woman herself, but her dollars! Finn, this is no company for poor country lads. Let him go on alone." And they stopped, leaning against each other while Rob walked on.

When they reached the *Seafoam*, Roddie and Henry were running out the nets. Rob was explaining to them that he had gone to look after these two, but catch him if he would go again. Callum started a broadside of dark hints. Finn saw that Roddie and Henry, though easy in their manner, were quiet.

And on the way home, after spreading their nets, as Roddie stopped to talk to the skipper of the *Mary Ann*, Henry said: "Listen, boys. There's to be no case. Bain is a decent fellow. He told Donald George that not one member of his crews would darken his doors if he went on with it. But he wants ten pounds. Bain pointed out that the damage done wasn't three pounds, taking the bottle of whisky at a shilling, and it's dear at that. But he wouldn't move. He said it gave his place a bad name and he wanted to make an example. He's just a greedy devil. Bain says he might have got Maciver to talk to him, for he's frightened of Maciver, but, after all, it's our affair, and Maciver saved us already. So there it is."

"I'm glad it's settled," said Rob.

"What are you thinking of?" asked Finn.

"Well," said Henry, "it's a job. You know Roddie. If he insists on paying the ten pounds himself—and he will—then what with expenses and the price of two new nets, he may well go home in debt. For you know as well as I do that the herring is spotty. In any case, we were all in it. The first thing Roddie did when he got his ten pound bounty from Bain was to give two pounds to each of us. And that's more than we should have got. What do you say, Rob?"

"We maybe had a few shillings when we came away," replied Rob thoughtfully. "And we don't settle our accounts until we leave. You can have my two pounds back and welcome."

"Good for you, Rob!" said Callum.

Finn now felt happier than ever.

LANDING HERRING

When they had had their couple of hours' sleep, Henry gave his signal, and waited behind with Roddie.

They were busy lifting the nets when Roddie and Henry came up. In a quick glance, Finn saw the flush in Roddie's skin. As they all came together, Roddie paused, a hesitant smile on his face, and said simply, "Thank you, boys."

The words went straight to Finn's heart. None of them looked at Roddie. Rob scratched his whiskers noisily. Callum's eyes gleamed. They went on, walking up the nets on their bare feet, as if nothing had happened.

And so they settled down to three weeks' fishing. After small shots for a day or two, with the boats going as far south as they could, there was a blank period. By Wednesday, Callum could sleep on his feet, and when he went to bed on Saturday afternoon, he slept round the clock. It was hard work, but Finn liked it, and would have liked it more if there hadn't settled down on the crew a half-drugged lethargy. Finn saw that though mostly due to toil and an absence of the excitements that had hitherto dogged them, this mood was in some degree due to Roddie's quietism. His pleasantness was a mask, the sort of mask one did not try to penetrate. It came and went as required, leaving him with an impenetrably normal expression. Finn felt that he had lost taste for the trip; and though his secret pride might be touched by the way people looked at him, this also undoubtedly irritated him. Instead of soothing, it raised an inward defiance and challenge. Once he had over-heard him say, with his dangerous smile, to a fool of a young fellow who gaped at him, "Yes?" The fool had turned away so blindly that he tripped over his own feet. Two other fools had laughed. But Roddie took no more notice.

Finn's own relation to Roddie changed insensibly, too, changed just enough for him to see again the occasional dogfish swirl deep in his own mind. But any man, Finn was now beginning to realize, will feel like that at an odd irri-tated moment. It was the sort of thing one paid no attention to. More and more he realized that the eagerness and vani-

ties that had beset him belonged to a youth which manhood,
thickening its texture, kept in their place. He became one of
the crew, seeing Roddie as an objective body and presence
with which it was no business of his to interfere. Roddie
wanted no more trouble. Neither did he.

But in proportion to this growing knowledge or understanding, he found in himself a freedom that now and then
realized itself in moments of intense pleasure. The exhaustion following long and heavy toil normally induced stupor
and sleep but it could, in wakeful or half-dream states, arouse
a sensual imagery of sometimes delicious power. There was
one sunrise on a calm morning, of red and gold and ame-
thyst on a wide sea, that had not merely, as usual, drawn a
smiling glance from his eyes, but had held them until the
smile had gone. It was at this hour in the morning, when
expectancy troubled rest, that the images came most clearly. And they did not come in loneliness or austerity, they
came with the girl Una. They were in the core of his body,
secretive, but always human. Yet, whether from lack of
physical experience or other cause, they were never turgid.
The sunrise came about him, into his eyes, drenched his
mind, went about the other boats, where life was stirring,
gulls floating and wheeling, in the calm of a morning
possessed and not possessed. Even when it induced an uneasiness, a dissatisfaction, something at the back of it sang.
For to Finn, life lay in front of him—and he never doubted
but that he would live long enough!

Then towards the end of the second week, a cold nor'-
easter came blowing down the Minch and on Friday night
Finn ran into the dark girl in Stornoway. She was with
another girl and it was Callum who stopped and spoke to
her. But presently she was smiling at Finn. "Not been to
Swordale yet?"

"I went out there on Sunday," said Finn, "but it seems
everyone stays indoors on Sunday in this part of the world."

"Why, don't they in your part of the world?"

"Perhaps they do," said Finn, "but I'm not there now."

"Didn't you go to church?"

"Surely," said Finn. "I went there afterwards, for consolation."

She laughed, sensitive but merry. She looked quite different now, neatly dressed, warm in her attraction, with shy dark eyes.

"Hullo!" And down on Finn's shoulder came Seumas's hand. "Well, well, Catrine! And yourself, Finn! It's a fine night!" He laughed lightly.

"You have your share of it," replied Catrine, flushing.

"Do you think so?" asked Seumas. "Where?"

"That's your concern," said Finn. "We were just discussing the fishing."

"And saying what a pity it is you aren't on the sea to-night! Aren't you afraid of these East-coast fellows, Catrine?"

"I'd be less afraid of them than of many a one I know," replied Catrine, with spirit, for she was annoyed with herself for having blushed.

"Is that a compliment or what, Finn?"

"If you had any sense in you you would see that she is being kind to the stranger," answered Finn.

Seumas went lightly away, laughing. He was back in a moment with others. "We're all going to Laxdale," he said.

"I'm going to my bed," said Callum, and off he went.

There was a knot of eight of them and they kept together going along the road, talking and laughing, and shoving sometimes, for they were all pretty much of an age. The evening was falling and presently they began to sing. Suddenly they all stopped singing and explosions of laughter were badly smothered. The man approached and paused.

"It's a fine night," said Seumas calmly.

"Do you think this is a way to behave in the sight of the Lord on the public road?"

A girl, who had not quite got over her giggles, moaned "Oh-h-h" as if in pain. They all shoved past the man and

397

went on quickly, running against laughter, but it overtook some of them, and though Catrine's eyes were glancing she looked scared, too.

"I know you," the voice called back to them. "I know who you are."

"Ay, ay," said one of the lads drolly, but not very loud.

Soon they stood and chattered like birds, and went on, and stood and every now and then doubled over with laughter.

Finn felt himself the stranger, but not very much, for if they accepted him without any attention, now and then in a glance, a sudden movement, a politeness, they showed they were aware of him in a friendly, inviting way.

The house they entered was a rather poor place, inhabited by an elderly couple, but the spirit in it was rich and soon overflowed. Finn recognized at once that it was a regular ceilidh-house, for the man had little peculiar mannerisms, the eyes of a boy, a tongue for anything that was going, and if it was fun he was happy. Many more came in and when the talk had had an innings, they started singing.

They always came back to singing.

There was one song in particular that Finn did not know and he was greatly moved by it.

They were crushed together, sitting where they could, and mostly on the uneven clay floor. And they sang. Their songs were often charged with sadness and beauty, but, whatever they were, a fond affection was around them somewhere.

From this affection, all the goodness of life flowed like the tide. The songs, indeed, had the sea-tide's rhythm. Even a girl with a sharp mind and personal dislikes and not sitting in the place she wanted to be would be carried away, and presently, what with one thing or another and the way the unseen mind was seen, there would be a movement and a laugh, a skirmish and a change, and likely as not at the end of it she would be sitting in that place, with the man of the house maybe saying something to her and her retorting briskly. For the girls were quick in riposte, having learned the art of it from their mothers and their mothers' mothers at the cloth waulking. And in any case if it was in the nature of a girl to be bold, she would, pushed to it, be bold outright and be done with it. Which was often a merry way for everyone concerned, except perhaps one or two.

And Finn saw that now they were all happy, that life was fulfilled, and if the door was shut it was on yesterday and to-morrow.

Catrine lived three cottages away. Finn and others accompanied her there. Finn thought he had perhaps better not be going farther but be getting back. Which was excuse enough, so it was a quick good night and dark figures swinging on.

"I'll be seeing you," said Catrine, making to move to her door.

"What's your hurry?" asked Finn.

"Hush!" she whispered.

He caught her hand and they stepped back out of earshot of the house. "I must be going in," she said, drawing her hand away. "It's late. I must." She seemed suddenly nervous.

"Why?" asked Finn, and the sound of the word was curious in his own mind.

"Because I must."

"Catrine."

All at once there was something wrong. She glanced at him. His face looked pale. She did not know what was coming, and impulsively said, "Good night," and ran towards the house.

He made no effort to stop her, and stood still until she had gone inside. For some minutes he remained staring at the quiet house.

The sadness of the unknown song came over him in a mood that had something strange and bitter in it. He could have held her in his arms and kissed her; that would have suddenly swamped her nervousness. But at the very sign of

the half-scared spirit moving in her, at the sound of his own
voice calling her by the name Catrine, he found that he
could not force himself upon her, and somehow did not
greatly mind.

After a few random twists of self-mockery as he took the
Stornoway road (Seumas would be no such fool!) he let the
dark girl—brown in her darkness, a mouse-brightness—
fade from his mind, pass away into the outer ring of eternal
beauty and eternal sorrow, the dark outer ring of the song,
where it is lonely to wander, with the wind a cold shiver on
the skin of the face.

My sorrow! My sorrow! said the song.

What sorrow? Sorrow for death, said the words.

But, for the first time, Finn saw it went beyond death.

On the following night, he hunted Stornoway for the girl
with ardent eagerness. His mood was now quite changed.
He longed for her. There was a half-scared, expectant
something in her that he preferred to anything in any
other girl. Not the self-assertive girl from Swordale now,
but this withdrawing almost anonymous girl with her
brown eyes watchful, wondering, quick. He felt towards
her a great tenderness, felt her in his arms; he would kiss
her eyes in grace—as one of the things he had never done
in this life. His body grew warm with the thought of their
growing warm together.

But he did not find her, though he searched everywhere.
On the edge of the dark he walked out to Laxdale, and then
slowly walked back, hoping thus to meet her coming from
the town. He waited outside the town a long while, until
hopelessness made his body listless and tired. This was the
night that, it had been rumoured, some of the friends of Big
Angus were going to lie in wait for Roddie. He did not
care; did not want to be discovered. She had the same name
as his mother. In this hopeless waiting, in his disappointment, there was a bitterness—a bitterness, too, beyond it—
that he could crush away, crush out, if only he had the girl

herself, the two of them, her eyes looking up as his arms closed and his mouth closed her eyes.

He did not want to go back to their lodging, tired of the thought of fighting. Let Roddie fight if he wished, and Henry lash out. He was tired of them, of everyone, and of himself. It was late when he got back and the small room was heavy with the breathing of the four men. He lay down beside Callum and gave in to sleep at once.

By Monday morning his mood was clear and bright, and life was full of expectancy again. The dark girl occupied his thoughts, and when they came in on Tuesday with four crans, he greeted her cheerfully. "Where were you on Saturday night?" he asked through the sound of the pouring herring. "I looked for you all night,"

She murmured quickly, "I was away," her gutting knife never pausing.

"Don't be away next time," he muttered.

"What's that he was saying?" asked the fair one suspiciously when Finn had gone.

"He said that he was over at Swordale on Sunday but never saw anyone," replied Catrine.

"Is that so?" she asked sceptically.

"That's the last of them," said Finn presently, still in a private voice to Catrine, but loud enough for others to hear. "It seems they're a very holy people at Swordale—on the Sunday whatever."

"You would hardly believe it," agreed Catrine, with solemn merriment and relief. She glanced quickly at Finn, her eyes alive. In that glance they had a long talk, and Catrine suddenly knew, amongst other things, that he had never been near Swordale.

Finn now dreamed of her in the boat in the morning in a more intimate way than ever he had of Una. Catrine was like a sweet revenge and he felt very fond of her.

But Wednesday and Thursday were almost blank days. It was the end of the fishing. Henry said he thought they should go home if they got nothing that night, for there wasn't much point in staying over the Sunday. Roddie and himself had a long talk with Bain and so it was agreed.

Finn prayed for herring, but by eight o'clock in the morning they were spreading their nets in the sun, having caught nothing. The morning was all bustle and hurry, and even Callum forgot sleep in the thought of buying presents for his wife and two children. Bain was in good form and very friendly, for he had achieved nearly a full cargo. Their money was paid over, with drams all round and hand-shaking, though Roddie would not give Bain a definite promise for next year. But Bain saw that Roddie was not the sort of man to give a promise lightly.

When all expenses were paid, Finn had over seven pounds to his share. It seemed to him a very great sum of money and as he walked away his feet hit the ground with a solid lightness.

For he had to say good-bye to the girls. But the women had gone home, there had been little to do. However, he ran into the two of them on the street and went up to shake hands, the crew following, and smiling.

"You watch him," cried Callum to the fair one.

"We're not blind," said she.

"Go on, Finn," prompted Callum, "stand them a fairing."

"I will that," said Finn, and looked round for the sweet-shop. "Come along," he called, and they followed him into the shop, laughing. He stood each of them a pound of sweets, and outside again, shook hands.

"Even if you might have been kinder," he said to the fair one.

"You gave a person every chance, didn't you?" she asked, her eyes flashing through the flush on her face. She was a high wind on the sparkling ocean, with all canvas set.

"Are you going to-day?" asked Catrine, her eyes like stars in the night sea.

"Yes, we're off," said Finn. "Good-bye. Will you be here when I come back?"

"I hope so," she said, and suddenly, as if her heart had contracted, her fingers squeezed his hand.

Callum and Rob were waiting for him and, as he turned and waved to the girls, Rob said, "Och! och!" and shook his head.

"Och! och! yourself," cried Finn, in high feather. He stopped. "Have you given the widow woman her mite?"

"Begod!" cried Callum, and for five minutes Rob had a difficult passage, for they could see he was tempted.

"No, I'm not frightened. I might do many a thing, but not in your company."

"We know that," said Callum; "but we never said you did it. And even if you did——"

"Did what?"

"Look here, Rob," said Callum seriously. "You're a man, after all. But we never accused you of it. All the same——"

"Of what?"

"I don't like to use the word, because it's in the Bible, and it's a long word."

Rob looked at him suspiciously. Callum nodded. "You're quite right," he said, "it begins with an *f*. But as I was saying——"

Rob walked away from them in the direction of their lodging. He was a confirmed bachelor, and supported, and was in large measure governed by, his mother and a sister ten years older than himself.

People passing on the street smiled at the happy laughter that shook Callum and Finn. They bought their presents quickly, for Finn knew exactly what he wanted for his mother; and a brightly painted rubber ball, a jack-in-the-box, a small doll, and six cups and saucers, with gilt lines round the rims, settled Callum's problem in a few glorious minutes—until, out of his deep pleasure, he wanted something special for his wife, for she was a good wife to him, none better in the world. But what? Some nice hats. Other articles of feminine apparel. All sorts of feminine garments.

The elderly pale-skinned shopkeeper was quite solemn. They tried to be solemn, too. He had a new line in skirts. Quite new, all ready to wear. Fine and thin. Different from the heavy home tweed. Feel them for yourself. Callum felt them. Yes, perhaps a skirt was as good as anything. "Fashions in skirts don't change," said the man; "a skirt is safe." "I'm glad to hear that," replied Callum. "What's her waist measurement?" "Ah well now, there's a difficulty," said Callum. "Perhaps I'd better get something that never changes at all." Finn pointed to a shawl, feather-light and intricately patterned. "It's like her hair," he said. Callum looked quickly at him, mouth open. "God bless me," he said in wonder. The shopkeeper frowned. They saw he was a religious man and retired politely, shawl and all, thanking him.

Callum was now full of unbounded energy and cried, "Let's go round and draw out the widow about Rob."

As they entered, the bar was empty—except for Rob, leaning against the counter with an owl's solemnity, listening to the confidential talk of the widow woman.

After their midday meal, Roddie said casually, "I think we should lift the nets and go now." They all looked at him, for it had been understood that they were to leave at three o'clock in the morning.

Some sleep first, then the maximum daylight for the passage to the mainland.

"Why not?" said Henry. "It will be the same tide in an hour or two as at three in the morning."

"But we would have the night on us," said Rob, doubtfully.

"Come on!" cried Callum, and all their hearts lifted. They would be off at once, night or no night!

By half-past three, they had kists and nets on board and everything shipshape. Many of the other fishermen were now appearing. Roddie saw Maciver going into his office and went and bade him good-bye. "And thank you very much," he said. "Are you going now?" asked Maciver. "We might as well," said Roddie. Maciver looked at him for a searching moment and smiled. "There's no holding you." He added, "Anything I can ever do for you, I'll do it."

They pushed off and raised sail in a favourable wind, then saluted the watchers on the quay.

"But why didn't they wait until the morning?" asked Maciver.

"Because," said Bain, pointing, "that's what's going to conquer the sea."

It was Monday afternoon before they set past the Old Man of Wick in a sparkling breeze with a fair sea running. They had been becalmed, had had to wait for the tide, had seen the sun rise in splendour behind the Orkneys, had had a thrilling fight to clear the Pentland, with Callum shouting, "Will I throw your kist over now, Rob?" But here at last were the rocks of home.

Finn, lying back, saw the stem lifting now in a racing eagerness. It was going home, back to the old river mouth. It had no thought of them at all, lost in its dream, its eyes beyond the pitch and the roll, rising, ever rising, gallant and undefeatable.

They had been seen coming from the top of the Head, and when at last they opened out the bay, there was a dark crowd beyond the white crescent of surf, for the wind was on-shore.

No-one had known what had happened to them during their long absence, and their women had prayed passionately in the night, when the wind was screaming round the gable-end, that God would spare them.

Week after week—no news. That was good. They did not want news. They should be coming soon. Suddenly they would appear out of the sea—and be there. Like a miracle. Would they? Everyone in the district was concerned in some measure, for this was a venture into the unknown, a new experience brought into their lives.

LANDING HERRING

Here was the miracle coming now! Yes, the whole crew
were there! And Roddie making straight in. He would!
Seamen got ready, for the swell was nasty enough. Down
went the sails. He was taking no foolish chances, was
Roddie! Out came the oars. Pulling back against a comber
. . . pulling on. . . . Then, look out! She's coming! And on
the crest of it she came, while the coils of rope uncurled
through the air from Henry's hand. They took her on the
run. She grounded. They took her again. They got round
her, and she went with them.

CHAPTER XIX

SEA LOVE

At the stepping-stones beyond the Steep Wood they stopped, and Finn refused further help, saying he would take his chest himself, though Donnie was anxious to give him a hand. So he parted from Roddie and Donnie, the chest on his shoulders, and went up the slopes to his home.

His cousin Barbara saw him coming, and, though she was fifteen, she turned and ran to the house, shouting. There was his mother. His heart began to beat heavily.

"Finn!" she said and stopped.

"Hullo, Mother!" He stood, hanging on to the chest.

"Oh, Finn!" she cried, and took her eyes off him in a sudden swirl of action that had the chest on the ground in no time, with Barbara at one end of it and herself at the other. Her eyes were wet; her emotion was very strong; she was laughing.

He looked round the kitchen. "It's the same old place." He did not know what to say, but he had to say something, because of the strong emotion in his mother. It was in himself, too. It was as well Barbara was there, though her presence irked him at the moment. Suddenly Barbara went out.

His mother turned to him. "How are you, Finn?" she asked in a quiet voice, her face glimmering in the kitchen's faint gloom.

"Fine," he replied cheerfully. "You're looking well yourself."

SEA LOVE

"I'm fine." She turned abruptly away. He didn't know
what to do and stood smiling.

Barbara came in with potatoes in the iron pot. She was
thin and dark and moved awkwardly with the pot, which
Finn took from her and hung on the crook, talking loudly
to her, asking how she enjoyed being in Dunster and how
everyone was in Dale. His mother, busy getting food ready,
began to put her word in, and presently asked him how he
had got on in Stornoway. "Not too badly," he answered,
"but the fishing itself had its ups and downs." "You got
on fine?" and she stopped again to look at him. "Yes, all
right," he said, with a careless nod. "I must have a turn
round," and out he went. The cows, and the stirks, and the
few sheep, and the slopes of the brae going down to the
burn. He felt he had been away years from them, surprised
an intimacy that he could not quite catch, like days of long
ago vanishing in the mind. There was something pleasant
about this and also, somehow, sad; something in his mind
that would not form, that he could not speak. The movement of his mother's bustling body and how she felt was
everywhere.

He should go back into the house, but a reluctance to do
this came upon him strongly; so he clapped the cattle, and
examined the tender corn, and went down past the door
noisily towards the byre to examine that. Then he went
into the little barn and got its old, stuffy smell with an
overwhelming familiarity. He handled Kirsty's reaping-
hook, with its broken point, curiously. Standing still, listening, he had the feeling for a moment of immemorial refuge.
Slowly he looked round at the odds and ends and saw them
with an extreme distinctness. He was here and he was not
here, as if there was one world behind the other. But all the
time he knew he must go in. When he came out, his mother
was at the door. "Everything is looking fine!" he called.
She came quickly and took his arm and went walking on
gaily. "Yes, everything is grand," and she began to point
out this and that. "Haven't the lambs grown?"

By the time they came in he felt so relieved and happy
that he began to open his small wooden kist.

"Did you get your things washed at all?" she asked,
waiting to take the clothes from him.

"There's nothing here but a mess," he said, throwing
the cord off and lifting the lid. Then he took out a pair of
shoes and handed them to her. They were black and glistened, with stylish toe-caps neatly patterned. She obviously
had been expecting nothing. Her head bent over the shoes.
Her right hand moved over the smooth leather slowly. Her
upper teeth gripped her lower lip. He laughed. "They're
good and strong," he said. "I saw to that." And from his
box he took a red silk ribbon and two white handkerchiefs
and handed them to Barbara: "How's that?" Barbara's
eyes and mouth opened. She flushed with pleasure. "Oh!"
she cried, "how lovely!" Catrine looked up, smiling, so
pleased at Finn's remembering Barbara that it eased her
own emotion.

Finn was now completely at home and amused them with
a description of Callum's trying to think of something for
his wife. "He was a holy mannie and showed Callum some
queer things. Then he showed him a skirt and Callum
thought that would do fine. 'What's her waist measurement?' asked the mannie. 'You have me there,' said Callum." Catrine and Barbara laughed as if it were the greatest
joke in the world.

"And did he take the skirt?" asked Catrine.

"No, he took a shawl instead. He thought it would be
safer."

They laughed at that, too.

"I thought of a shawl myself," said Finn, "but didn't I
see a woollen jacket, with green in it and blue, that would
be the very thing for you on a cold day. Isn't it bonny?
Look!" And he handed the jacket to his mother.

She did her best, drawing down her top lip stiffly, but
fortunately at that moment the potato-pot boiled over and
she dashed for the fire.

Finn laughed and, lifting the kist, walked with it into his own room.

Late that evening, in the deep twilight down by the little barn, Catrine said, "I have something to tell you, Finn."

He did not look at her, but suddenly remembered the stranger on the shore.

"Just when you were leaving, an old friend of your father's came here to see me. He was with him—in the boat—when they were taken."

The overstress in her mind, the profound affection, he now understood finally.

"When they were taken, your father fought very hard. But—they hit him on the head—and hauled him up on the ship. Five days after that—he died."

Finn kept looking away, his face drawn and hard.

"Was it the blow on the head?" he asked.

"Yes. He—never properly recovered. Ronnie and the others did not see him again. He was buried at sea." Her breath came away quiveringly, but otherwise she made no sound, though the tears were running down her cheeks.

"Why didn't they tell you?"

"They were put on another ship, on different ships. Ronnie said he did write, but——"

"I mean the authorities?"

"Ronnie thought it was perhaps the man he knocked into the sea——"

"Who knocked into the sea?"

"Your father knocked the leader of the press-gang into the sea——"

"Did he?" said Finn. His skin went all cold, and out of a profound pride for his father, tears came into his eyes.

"Yes. Ronnie said he fought like a lion, but they were too many."

"Did he?" He could hardly control his voice.

"Yes." She looked at him, and remained silent. Sud-

410

denly he walked away from her and, when he had gone over
the crest of the brae, sat down by a bush and, lying over,
face into the ground, began to sob bitterly. It was not
death, it was not his father's death, it was the odds against
him. "It was a damned shame!" he cried and clawed the
ground violently.

Presently he became aware of his mother standing near,
and sat up, looking straight across the burn whose little
pools glimmered in the deep twilight.

She sat down beside him. "I always knew," she said
quietly. "He came to me—the night he died."

They sat silent for a long time.

"Come in, Finn. You must be tired."

He got up and as they walked back to the house a deep
feeling came over him of being himself and his own father,
responsible for this woman walking by his side, who was
his mother; deeper even it was than the resentment against
the odds which had murdered his father, and within it, too,
sustaining it, was a strange new element, quiet as this dim
half-light, of peace that was like happiness.

In the succeeding days, Finn found life good. He spent
his time between the croft and the shore and he was busy
the whole time, with preparations for the summer fishing,
cleaning up a new piece of ground on the edge of the moor,
and attending to the new year's supply of peat fuel. Not
even a visit by the ground officer depressed his spirit un-
duly. "You have a good place here," said that reserved
and ominous man. "We're trying to improve it," replied
Finn quietly, leaning on his spade. "It's as well," said the
man, and walked down through the croft, aloof and noting
all things. Finn tore into the ground to ease his apprehension.

"I wonder what he's after?" Catrine came and asked
Finn when the man had gone. She still had the feeling that
they were strangers here and might be driven out. "You
needn't worry," said Finn. "It's money he's after." "I

always feel afraid when I see him," she murmured. "Everyone does," said Finn.

Catrine stayed beside Finn for some time. In the end he had her laughing over his sarcasms. "You'll have old Annie up wringing her hands," he prophesied. "But you should hear Henry on him!" As she was turning away, reluctant to leave him, she cried, "Look! There's Annie coming!" He laughed. Old Annie had a very small holding, but the neighbours helped her to cultivate it, and with a small black cow and some hens she managed along. It was not a very tidy place, and there were many who might be glad of the chance to improve it. We have money! thought Finn to himself, with a grim but easeful humour.

The Stornoway trip became in retrospect not merely an affair full of odd adventure but also a half-secret code of private amusement. "Why did you send her to me?" demanded Rob. "Well," answered Callum solemnly, "she's a widow woman, and if there was a bit of fish going I knew you'd give it to her." In this atmosphere a net seemed to get mended of itself.

Then one day Finn got a slight shock. A boy of twelve had fallen over a rock and broken his leg. That he had not fallen a further fifty feet to his death seemed a miracle. Two boys of fourteen had brought off a daring rescue. And all this, Finn discovered, was a direct result of his own exploits on the Seven Hunters, though he himself had never made any reference to them. He had observed that boys liked to be in his company and were willing to do anything for him.

Catrine had persuaded Barbara to stay on with them over the summer fishing. In this way, Catrine was never alone and Finn was glad of it. Roddie came over once or twice in the evening, but if he had heard of Tormad's death, he made no reference to it and, with Barbara and Finn about, there was a household.

Meantime every day was working up to the climax—that broke over the whole district in the shape of the summer fishing. Life grew hectic. George, the foreman, was full of figures. Everywhere the fishing was growing, was sweeping the villages, the great ports, in a torrent of new boats, nets, curers, men, and banknotes. Ten and even fifteen-pound bounties from the curers were the order of the day. A skipper got his bounty—whether he caught herring or not. Hendry was commonly reputed now to be a wealthy man. Good luck to him! They showed him all the more respect on that acount. His whisky was ever ready, and if he took a note of quantities against their accounts, what else would any natural man expect?

In Wick, the provision of liquor, at a price, was part of a skipper's agreement. It made life seem large and gay and spendthrift. Why not? Wasn't it a grand thing that life should be warm and full of generosity and not for ever dogged by care of the morrow? To walk down the quays in your sea-boots, from a refreshment house, after landing a fair shot, and see the women busy as wrens, the foremen shouting, the salt swishing in showers, the coopers hammering, the fishery officer testing the herring for the Crown brand, was a pleasant experience. You had given them something to work on! Let the world be happy and the hand generous. It's a poor mouth that never sings. Give with lordliness and grudge nothing. Only the mean heart and the mean hand are an abomination in the day of fullness.

Their nets shot, they lay back, eating in the peace of the evening, at sea once more. Not the inlets, the low shores, the islands, the soft wonder of the west, but the grey, unending cliffs of home.

It was the height of summer, and the night never grew quite dark. Finn loved to feel the gentle movement of the boat under him again. It produced, too, the old dreaming effect and passing of images. But the images were altogether from the west now. He had not seen Una since he came home and had no special desire to see her. His cousin Barbara was a friendly, bright girl, and treated him like a brother. He was growing fond of her. But the dark Lewis girl, Catrine, came into his mind now on a few notes of that song which he could not whistle entirely and which haunted him often. In a curious way, however, the influence of the song was stronger than she was. In a few seconds it would grow into a hypnotic tyranny that he could not rouse himself to throw off, and the girl would recede, shadowy, and bodiless.

He saw Roddie trying the net in the grey of the morning and the old excitement crept over him. The net fell back with an empty splash. But he was not very disappointed. The herring were not yet on the ground.

The boats were in early, and while walking with Callum across the flat towards the gutting stations, Finn saw Una. He saw her in the moment that she stepped back from four others, swayed, and bent forward slightly in laughter. Her laugh was not merry and quick; it was slow-noted and rich and rather awkward. Her body swayed, too, in a poised living motion all its own. "Hey, Finn!" called Jim, the clerk, who had obviously made the joke. Donnie was there and the two other girls of Una's crew. "Busy!" called Finn, with a smiling salute, and went on.

A cold flush had gone over his body, and when they reached the store he tried not to let Callum see his hands. The physical sensation was extremely unpleasant and for a little while his brain would not work. He thought of a natural excuse to leave Callum, but could not risk going across the green alone. As the weakening sensation slowly ebbed, anger against himself began to flow. Una had nothing to do with this, or Jim, or anyone else. It was entirely a personal weakness of which he was intolerantly and bitterly ashamed. And even all this he could have overcome, if it weren't that he knew he could not face them and be natural. A horror came upon him that he would be weak and stammer and have the words choke in his throat.

A penetrating hatred of the girl Una assailed him, and the only wary thought in his head wondered how he could dodge her, now and always.

414

When Callum and himself came out the women were gone, and Finn knew a sweet relief. But as they turned the corner of the store, he saw the same five, well in front but over to the left, making for the foot of the green braes. And now a completely irrational desire came over him to hasten, for his path lay up the riverside, and thus he would not overtake them directly but yet might be seen by them. "What's your hurry?" asked Callum. "I thought you'd be wanting your bed," answered Finn. "And anyway, I have a good bit farther than you to go." He made Callum step out and spoke in a loud voice gaily. When he saw out of the corner of his eye that they were observed by the others, he passed a remark about Rob that set Callum chuckling. He himself laughed outright. "You're in good form to-day!" said Callum. At that moment he felt in extremely good form. But his mother thought he was looking tired and packed him off to bed at once. When sleep would not come, he ground his teeth. He turned and rolled. Sleep pierced his eyelids with its sharp needles, but his brain was sharper. It is a great misery for the body to be desperately in need of sleep and for sleep not to come. He loathed the thought of Una and all the appalling nonsense of the green. He heard his mother whisper to Barbara, anxious not to wake him. He had tried not to make any noise. When he could no longer endure the torture, he got up.

Una swayed back and laughed in the half-dream of the grey morning.

Finn knew days of misery, but he won through them to a dull, dogged state. All this time he had no strong desire for Una; he was not even aware of any jealousy or similar emotion against Jim; in fact he would have experienced a desperate relief had Una been definitely attached to Jim. She was like a sickness that he wanted to be rid of; because it was a shameful sickness; a weakness that he had a horror of someone's discovering, and particularly Una and her crowd.

On the fourth morning at sea, Henry said, "They're here, boys." Finn shouted in Callum's ear. "What? Where?" cried Callum, starting up. "So you've come to pay us a visit," said Rob to the silver darlings as they danced in over the gunnel, blue and green and silver.

The old happy harmony came upon the crew. And Finn felt himself renewed, but with the difference that he wanted passively to absorb the fun rather than light-heartedly to increase it. This, however, had a riches of its own. It was like drinking from a cool well on a hot day and lying back. There was a profound satisfaction in it. Callum and Rob were sparring.

"Pull down your sleeve, man, Rob. Your shirt is getting dirty."

Finn was skimming the big herring as they fell from the net, for the catch was not heavy, though of fine, full quality.

"If only the herring had been as big as this in Stornoway!" said Henry.

"I knew something in Stornoway," said Callum, "that was fully bigger, even more developed, as you would say."

"What was that?"

"Ask Rob."

"I knew something bigger myself," said Rob, in his slow, droll fashion.

"No man could have got his arms round anything bigger," said Callum. "Impossible."

"I wouldn't say you could get your arms round it. No, nor your legs."

"But what would you be using your legs for, anyway?"

"Some people use them one way, and some people another, and some people use them to run away on, if they can manage."

"Boys, this is a conundrum!" said Callum.

"Maybe it is a conundrum," said Rob, "and if it is, then it is a w-whale of a one."

SEA LOVE

All of ten crans. It was a good start and many of the
boats were already hauled, like themselves, and making
for home. Finn felt at ease, and knew again in his bones the
peace and companionship of men in the toil of common
adventure.

As he tipped the herring into the box an elderly, quick-
fingered woman said, "Scales to-day on you, Finn."

"A few to keep you going."

"That's what we like." Scores of women were bobbing along the gutting stations, men were carrying
quickly, criss-crossing over the green, in a babel of talk and
cries.

Una was on the other side and to the left and the girl
beside her gave Finn a shout. "You can't see ordinary folk
since you came back from abroad!"

"So long as you haven't forgotten me," he cried, quite
naturally, and as he went back to the boat, with his heart
beating, he felt the stirring of self-confidence. He had not
looked at Una, though he had seen her glance at him. If
only he could carry things off like that!

When they had spread their nets and were returning to
the boat, he said to Rob, "I don't think you should be so
hard on Callum."

"Me! I wouldn't hurt boys, surely."

"If only you would stick to the boys," said Callum, "it
would be all right. Or even the widow women. Look, Rob,
man, at Una there. Wouldn't she make a fine, warm armful
for you now? And she's fond of the boys." He winked at
Finn.

"She might do," said Rob thoughtfully. "She has the
looks."

"She's got more than looks."

"Yes, she's got that loud-voiced gomeril from Wick
with the boots," said Rob.

"But surely you could see the boots off him?"

At that moment, Donnie Grant and another young blade,
Angie Ganson, created a slight diversion and Una stepped

417

SEA LOVE

back with a yelp, wiping a smother of scales that Angie had
deftly smeared on her chin.

"Now, now, young fellows-my-lads, none of that here,"
bellowed George. "Leave honest folk to get on with their
work."

"Who's stopping them?" demanded Angie.

"You keep that, my hero, for the Birch Wood. There's
a place for everything."

In the laughter, Una happened to look straight at Finn's
face. The face was calm and set and she got back to her
work amid chaff from the other women.

As they continued towards the boat, Callum rallied Rob
again, for Una had appeared very attractive, with her flush
of colour and swaying body.

"Ach, she has too many sniffing after her for my fancy,"
said Rob.

"But surely you don't want an easy conquest? What do
you say, Finn?"

With a terrific effort through his choked throat, Finn
answered, "I don't know," and tried to smile.

He felt Callum's eyes narrow on him and knew that the
smile remained stuck in a sickly way on his face. But he
fixed his eyes on a boy and called, "Well, Dan?"

"Hullo!" answered Dan, and he came to walk beside
Finn. Men and boys were everywhere, and Callum was
stopped.

On the way to sea that afternoon, Finn left the path,
climbed over the thick, ruined wall, and came into the little
quiet field that led to the knoll of the House of Peace. The
grey stones were still and silent as they had always been,
but now they seemed immemorially old and heedless,
somehow tired and spent. There was no hidden spirit in
them, no invisible eyes.

All things pass and die; useless stones sink into the dead
earth. There was no sun. The sky was grey. A pace or two
up the knoll, he paused to look back and around. He was

alone, anyway. A stone moved from under the weight of his foot and two red worms, surprised by the light, quickly disappeared, leaving tracks like empty veins. The stone came to rest with the smeared side uppermost.

On top, he sat down at the old spot by the empty stone rings. He thought of the figure he had once imagined here, the figure of the old, quiet man, and his features grew faintly satiric, like Henry's. But there was no bitterness in the satire, hardly feeling of any kind. Even misery was empty of feeling, like a vacant eye. Here, misery itself got drained, as so much folly, leaving nothing at its heart. But in this emptiness there was at least a heedless freedom. He lay back and slowly settled into the earth like one of the heavy grey stones. This was relief and in a few moments he came into the core of himself, where he was alone, and felt strangely companioned, not by anyone or anything, but by himself. The rejected self found refuge here, not a cowed refuge, but somehow a wandering ease; as if it were indestructible, and had its own final pride, its own secret eyes.

Peace might have come were it not for the image which involuntarily created itself inside his head against darkness. This was the appalling trick it had. The inner eye never even focused the swaying body, the sting of colour in the face, the light in the black eyes, the black hair (which, somehow, it saw, although at the gutting her hair was covered). It refused the vision. Yet it was suddenly there, out of direct focus, but there, as if it were thought more than vision. The dark body, with a red flame of life inside it, showing in the face, swaying with the grace of a tongue of fire.

He was past groaning at this affliction. And he would not even allow himself to think that it meant anything. The mere approach of the idea of any such thing as love angered him, maddened him. He was reaping the penalty of having thought so much about her on the sea alone. And he had thought about her because one does think about someone.

Surely love, if there was any such thing, should be ease and tenderness, like the tenderness he had felt for the dark girl in Stornoway. He had confidence there, knew his body's strength, and could have shouldered his way to her past any number of fellows.

But he would get over this disease. And when he did, and had cool command of himself, then—with a laughing, stinging tongue—wouldn't he make them sit up?

He groaned and turned over and lay still. At once he began to sink again and, desiring the sweet luxury of a moment's forgetfulness, fell sound asleep.

His eyes opened wide and stared at the circle of stones. There was something on his face. Rain. He sat up, looking about him. In the second it had taken him to realize where he was, he saw the grass and moss and grey stone and birch tree in a strangely static way, yet with a touch of almost panic intimacy, before their place in the normal world came upon him. He knew he had been asleep for hours, knew it by the very freshness of his body and, picking up his packet of bannocks and milk, went bounding down the knoll. They would be waiting for him. He had never yet been late. Perhaps they had gone to sea without him? Turning a bend, he saw Roddie going on alone a little way ahead. He stopped, panting. He could have been asleep only for a few minutes!

He laughed to himself and, giving Roddie a shout, soon joined him. "I had a grand sleep," he said.

"Good," answered Roddie. "I'm afraid we're in for a night of rain."

And Finn suddenly felt that the long, wet misery of a night of rain would be the finest thing in the world. "As long as it doesn't blow," he suggested.

Roddie gave him a glance and smiled. Finn felt more friendly to him at that moment than he had done for many a day.

There was, in truth, very little time during the rush of that successful fishing season for indulging the luxury of private worries. And with the hard work went a contagious cheerfulness.

In the morning a woman would cry to man or boy, "Are the boats in?" or "What luck to-day?" The questions flew over the land. When the boats were well-fished, hearts were uplifted and the daily tasks accomplished with cheerfulness and spirit. Figures could be seen moving here and there, up the braes, along the paths, dangling a string of herring. There was work for everyone. Along the road from Wick, carriers brought goods at all hours. Crofts would be stocked; a new house built; and, above all, orders placed for new boats, not only in the flourishing yards at Wick but in many a creek along the coast. Young men like Finn dreamed of having their own boats. There was a warmth of communal life in which private worries could be comfortably smothered.

In the evening, when scores of boats headed for the fishing ground, men and women would marvel, looking on that pretty scene, at the change that had come over their coast. No enchanter in the oldest legend had ever waved a more magical wand. In the grey dawn light of a Saturday morning, when the fishermen themselves, heavy from lack of sleep and overwork, saw herring in the net, all their faculties came alive and brought the fish in with avid care, as though after long and ceaseless wandering they had for the first time come upon a silver mine.

For the idea of magic, of possible enchantment, did persist. A crew had good luck or bad luck. There was no certainty. Every night was a new night and every morning a fresh surprise. Lexy had now taken the place of her sister, Margad, the witch, and when she appeared early with slightly stooped body and head wrapped in a black shawl, she had not to ask a skipper for a fry of herring. She was given it freely, and on one morning had sold three crans to a curer at the full price. She was having a very successful season, and who could say but that she deserved all she got? There were herring on the ground, anyway.

One afternoon, as Finn and Roddie were walking together towards the shore, with their food-satchels under their arms, they saw Lexy cross the path in front of them on her way home. They stopped and, pretending they had not seen her, turned back. Roddie muttered under his breath. Finn felt a strangeness go over him and looked at stones and grass and the running water with a queer, arrested smile. The body grew very sensitive, as if the air were suddenly charged with invisible forces.

They walked back over half a mile, saying little, then separated, each going to his own home.

When Catrine saw Finn enter the door, her face went pale.

"It's all right," said Finn, laying the satchel on the table. "Lexy crossed our path."

"Did she!" exclaimed Catrine.

For the witch to cross their path on their way to sea portended bad luck if not disaster.

Finn sat down on a chair and lifted his feet off the ground. Catrine, after standing still a moment, bustled about and brought him some milk and a piece of oatcake. "I wondered what had happened to you," she said solemnly, but with a relieved air, too, as if nothing could be so bad as what one did not know yet half-feared.

When he was ready to depart again, she went out and scouted around to make sure Lexy was not in the vicinity. "Roddie is coming," she said; then looked at him. "Take care of yourself, Finn."

Finn laughed at her concentrated, concerned expression and went on his way.

They were lucky so far, too, in the absence of storms. Rarely a season passed but men and women lined the beach or the cliffs watching the boats fighting their way home. The weather was mixed and not always comfortable, but when the wind did suddenly blow up from the sou'-east it was on a Sunday.

Boats were hauled clean up over the edge of the beach on

which the waves smashed, flinging spume over the curing stations. The fishermen were grouped about their boats, or mending nets and attending to damaged gear, and in the evenings there would be a crowd in and round Hendry's inn. Here George could be heard rolling out his figures of last season's cure from Wick to Fraserburgh, and talking authoritatively of the Baltic trade.

Finn never spent an evening in Roddie's company, going about with lads of his own age, like Donnie or Angie. Jim Dewar had a special liking for Finn and always got into his company if he could. One evening Jim and Donnie and Finn were standing by the river path, not far from the inn, when Jim cried, "What's this I see before me?" Finn turned. Una and Meg and Betz, the gutting crew, were coming towards them at a short distance, obviously on their way home.

"I'm going," said Finn.

"Don't be a fool," replied Jim. "We'll have some fun." He caught Finn by the arm. All in a blinding moment Finn wanted to strike him. But Donnie was in his way, laughing, asking him not to leave. "They'll think you're running away!" And now it was too late.

"Finn was wanting to make off when he saw you coming!" Jim greeted the girls. "Look at him! He's blushing!"

Finn, feeling murderous, tried to smile. A whelming desire came upon him to walk away. His mouth said, "I'm not blushing."

They roared with laughter, the girls excitedly. It made the meeting easy and amusing for them.

Finn's brows gathered over his unnatural smile. His eyes were glancing stormily and he was on the point of saying, "I must see Roddie," and stalking off, when Meg remarked, "Never you mind, Finn. He's always being very clever, by his own way of it."

"Mind who?" asked Finn.

Jim leaned back, laughing, and cleared his throat which was afflicted with phlegm.

"Him," answered Meg, with a sarcastic glance at Jim.

"Oh, him!" said Finn. "Hmf!"

They all laughed again. Finn felt himself trembling. He had not even glanced at Una.

"So you're still feeling sore?" Jim challenged Meg. He was in his element at this sort of badinage.

"Me feeling sore? You fairly fancy yourself!" declared Meg.

Jim stepped away as if she were about to attack him.

All the time they laughed and played in this way, Finn was held in an extreme awkwardness.

"It's time we were home," said Una.

"Right!" cried Jim. "Come on!" and catching Una by the arm he swung her forward. There was a slight struggle until she had got her arm free, and then they walked on, chaffing each other.

"When is Barbara going back to Dale?" Betz asked Finn.

"Not till the end of the fishing."

"We're off," declared Donnie, and he walked away with Meg, who had turned round and cried gaily, "Come on, Finn."

"Your mother will miss her when she goes," said Betz sensibly as they followed the others.

"Yes," said Finn. He did not want to see Betz home. They would pass people on the way. He was wildly angry at having been drawn into this position. Betz was a rather ungainly girl, with big bones and lank dark hair. Her efforts at being amusing were always heavy and out of key; and the thought of Finn's being landed with her now would be a special joy to Jim. At that moment Finn hated her.

And Betz went on talking as if her head were thick and unfeeling as a turnip. Did his mother miss not being able to come to the gutting? Couldn't she have come this year, with Barbara at home? . . . The questions maddened Finn, while he answered them at random. Then an odd little thing happened. He caught in her voice a slight gulp, a

424

catch of the breath, and he knew in an instant that she was sensitive and timid and unsure of herself; realized the effort she was making and the courage that, though hopeless, could still keep going.

He felt mean, ashamed of his own state of mind, yet could not alter it. But he answered her now more fully and even introduced topics of his own. A certain detachment came upon him, covering the mood that went on boiling underneath. Betz made no claims and he suddenly saw her not as a girl, with all the emotions that were supposed to surround a girl, but as a human being apart from him and walking by his side. Presently he was almost friendly, and when she asked, "Did you like Stornoway?" he did not think the question heavy and tiresome. On the contrary, it flashed Stornoway on his memory.

Assurance began to seep back into his mind, and it was not altogether the desire for revenge against present circumstance that drove him on to describe the town and one or two incidents in an amusing way. As this was perhaps beyond what Betz had hoped for, she listened with the greatest interest and the skin of her face took on a faint colour.

The others were not far ahead, for Finn had an urge to keep them in sight, and Jim and Una seemed in a gay mood. When, at last, they stepped off the main road towards the path that led up through the Birch Wood, Jim put his arm round Una's waist as if to help her over the ditch and up the yard of bank. Una drew herself free in a swaying whirl and Jim laughed, glancing back at the others.

"He's showing off," muttered Betz.

"Is he?" said Finn, smiling. "She seems to like it."

Betz crossed the ditch and Finn followed her and they went up the narrow, winding path. The houses lay beyond the wood and presently they saw the four in front standing among the last of the trees. Finn stopped. "I must get back," he said. "These fellows will talk on and on."

"Especially Jim," said Betz.

"You seem to know him pretty well!"

"He is always trying to be clever."

Finn laughed, throwing his head back. "So long as some-one likes his cleverness."

"They think," said Betz, with a sullen humour, "that he's a good catch."

Finn laughed almost naturally. "A cut above the fisher-man?"

"So some of them think. I don't."

Finn saw light in her dumb humour, in her dark eyes. "Rob called him 'that gomeril from Wick with the boots'."

Betz laughed abruptly and deep-throated.

"You might share the joke," shouted Jim.

They paid no attention but went on talking together, un-til Finn said, "Well, I must be off. I enjoyed the walk."

"So did I," said Betz. Her face was now suffused with colour and her eyes deep with a dumb pleasure that sud-denly touched his heart and he shook hands with her.

"We won't look!" cried Jim. But when Finn swung away, he yelled for him to wait. Finn waved and disap-peared, taking the path before him blindly, his mind in an instant emptied of everything but a blazing self-anger. You fool! he muttered. You damn fool!

Nor did he wait to ask himself why he was a fool. He hated what was behind him. He hated intolerantly his own mind, and to avoid it made straight for the inn.

There were knots of men here and there around the inn, arguing, disputing, laughing, engaged in the favourite pas-time of leg-pulling. A penetrating retort was their great delight. For some men took drink as they took heavy seas, with a certain gallantry, swaying, but holding to it and, when they moved, their feet crunched the gravel in a lordly way. A voice called to Finn: "You didn't take long over her!"

"Long enough," cried Finn, and elbowed his way through the door into the packed room.

George's voice was high above the rumble: "That's

the law. The barrel must hold thirty-two English gallons——"

"Gallons of what?"

"Gallons of wine. That's the measure."

"Why not gallons of whisky?"

"We're talking of herrings," said George. "We're talking of a fixed measure—the size of the barrel, as defined
by law."

"But why didn't they fix the size by nips? We know
nips better."

"If you don't look out," cried George, "you'll nip yourself until there's nothing left."

Two Buckie lads welcomed Finn and stood him a drink.
Finn understood the south-side Doric now pretty well, and
they liked to hear his clear Gaelic voice, which emerged,
like his smile, out of a background of personality that was
never immediately obvious, that always seemed to have
reserves. He struck them as having a certain distinction,
both in the cut of his face and in his manner; and none the
less so when he was friendly and fluent and ordered another
round. He was now in the highest spirits. When an alterca-
tion grew too noisy, Mr. Hendry would appear and with
his sharp, small eyes and a "Now! Now!" quieten things
down and draw questions upon himself. The men particularly liked to hear Special being dogmatic.

"Is that you I see, Finn?" asked Mr. Hendry, about to
retire.

"I hope so," said Finn.

"Well, my boy, I would rather not see you here too
much."

"In that case," said Finn in a flash, "I should be obliged
if you would give me a bottle of special and I'll clear out."
From his trousers' pocket he took a shilling and laid it on
the counter.

Mr. Hendry's brows gathered. He was nettled. But Finn
seemed in the friendliest humour.

"I don't think I should give it to you."

"Why not?" asked Finn.

"You lads are too young."

"We're not too young to land herring," declared Finn.

"Now! now!" said Mr. Hendry. "I think you've had enough."

"Enough what?"

"Whisky," said Mr. Hendry pointedly.

"I have only had two nips. Will you give me a bottle of special, please?" demanded Finn, still smiling.

"I don't think I will."

"In that case," said Finn, lifting his shilling amid the silence, "you can keep it," and he turned his back on the landlord and made for the door.

Some tried to stop him, but he shouldered them out of his way roughly. The Buckie lads followed. Along the coast there had sprung up many refreshment houses that sold beer and porter, but at old Mag's there was always an unofficial supply of more potent stuff. Thither they went.

An hour later they were making high carousal when Jim and Donnie walked in, having traced Finn from the inn.

"So here you are!" called Jim, all lit up. "Why on earth did you run away?"

Finn looked at him.

The flash in Finn's face tickled Jim. He pointed to it, laughing. Finn took a swift step forward and smashed his fist into Jim's face. The sound of the blow silenced everything. Jim would have fallen heavily but for the young fellows behind him.

Mag started screeching. "I'll have no fighting here! Get out of my house! Get out of my house!"

"I'm not fighting," said Finn, holding his ground.

"Get out!" she cried. "Get out! This is a respectable house."

"It's all right, Mag," said Finn. "But I don't run away from man or woman." His voice was steady, but his eyes were blazing.

"That was a bloody rotten thing to do," cried Jim, "to hit a fellow when he was not ready."

"Are you ready now?" asked Finn.

"Get out of my house! Get out of my house!" She laid hands on Finn and pushed him towards the door. He caught her wrists. "Stop that!" he called sharply. The others crowded around Mag and began saying it was all right. "We promise there will be no more trouble, Mag." They herded her away. But she swore she would give them no more drink that night, not one of them. There was placatory talk. Everyone spoke. Mag muttered about a decent woman's house. The place grew thick with mumbling and conspiracy. "Give me a bottle of whisky," said Finn clearly.

"I don't sell whisky," she cried, the features of her sixty-year-old face sharp against Finn.

"Very well," said Finn, putting the shilling back in his pocket. "You can keep it."

That fairly roused her ire, but through her screeching Finn said, "Oh, shut up!" and walked out.

The Buckie lads and two or three others followed him. It turned out that one of them had a bottle and it was offered to Finn first with pressing politeness. "Have a swig, Finn lad. I'm glad you sorted that wee bastard." The raw spirit burnt its way down his throat, but he hardly coughed. "Oh, he's all right," he said. "But sometimes he annoys me."

They had seen the flash and movement of the sea in him. They all felt heightened and full of imperious deeds. The bottle didn't last long. The quiet Buckie lad who drained the last of it threw it from him and in the darkness it exploded into many bits.

On the way home Finn chuckled when he side-stepped, for he was pretty drunk. He had never felt drunk like this before, and as a state of mind and body it had its points! For he knew he wasn't drunk really. His mind wasn't drunk at all. It was as sober as the parish minister. Far soberer, begod! It was pleasant to laugh. His mind could go away up into the sky and over the world as though it was light instead of dark. He felt like one who had arisen, had pierced through a sticky covering and was cleaning the stuff from his legs and head. All the tremors and indecisions; all the rank immaturities. Even having said "Shut up!" to Meg didn't worry him, though respect for age was in the essence of living. She had deserved it, screeching like yon!

Behold the House of Peace, lifting its dark head against the faint light in the sky. It was the hour when ghosts walked. A coldness crept over his skin. Very good! He would accept the challenge. He stumbled once or twice and when he got to the top he was sweating.

The place was terribly still. The morning was coming. Devil take it, it was a ghostly enough place. He thought of the headless man. His skin crept and crawled, the sweat icy cold. Something was holding him, stiff as death. No matter. He would not give in. He felt the death-shudder go over his body as the challenge rose in him. Climbing ten thousand cliffs was nothing to this. He drew all his strength into his throat to shout, "Come forth!"

But his throat clove against sound.

Suddenly, however, as though his intention were being answered, there was a grey-white movement and the icy coldness went to Finn's heart. He saw the grey head and the grey beard and went unconscious on his feet. But he did not fall because his staring eyes had seen on their own account that it was Maria's new goat.

He swung from one slim trunk to another and rolled the last few yards. He ran and fell. But he ran, and got over the broad, ruined wall and up by the burnside, before he collapsed. But even then he did not let his mind go from him. Soon he arose and went on to the brae below his own home, where he threw himself on his back and breathed heavily for a long time.

The dawn came and the land was quiet and still under it.

Going on to the house he felt disembodied as a ghost, with
little that was solid in his legs and feet. A couple of peewits
came swooping and crying, bereft spirits that never slept.
The storm was gone. His mother would not be asleep
either. The thought of her lying awake, waiting, angered
him. However, he would slip in quietly. The door was on
the latch. As he turned round to close it noiselessly he
stumbled and it shut with a tremendous rattle. He swore
under his breath. He heard her coming. Groping rapidly
into his own room, he shut the door with a bang.

"Finn, are you all right?"

"Yes," he answered. "Why wouldn't I?" His voice was
impatient with anger—and fear lest she come in.

She did not speak again. She's got the smell of the
drink! he thought in a bitter humour. It was the first time
her son had come home to her in that condition! She
wouldn't sleep now the rest of the night. Alan Macdonald
caught in the thicket by his two sisters. Women! Misery
and wisdom came down upon him, and in their grey air
he saw with a great clarity the meaning and movement of
life. However, begod, he would finish the night as he
began. He would go to sleep and be damned. And he went.

The next day the movement of life was not so clear. His
mother tried to behave exactly as if nothing had happened,
but her voice was distinct, her actions too definite. Barbara
and she were going into the moss to lift the last of the
peats. He spoke readily to Barbara, but didn't look much at
his mother. He had to go to the shore, he said, to get things
ready for the sea, and left the house as soon as he could,
his mother's face going with him, pale as a new moon in the
dusk, filling up the round of his mind and his conscience.

In the afternoon he came back for food and his satchel.
His mother had returned from the moss to give him both.
They were alone. She did not intrude on him, however, but
moved lightly about, speaking naturally. "Well, are you
off, then? So long!" "So long!" he answered, his back to

her, and off he went. Through the remnants of his anger at her delicate manner, he felt deeply moved by it. It was so fine and reticent. A surge of emotion at the fineness of his mother came over him; so swift and keen that it stung his eyes and made them stare ahead.

As he drew near the beach, he saw Jim approaching. Finn began to feel uncomfortable and awkward. Jim seemed uncertain also until he glanced at Finn's face. Then he said, "You're a dam' fine fellow."

"I'm sorry," said Finn, "at the trouble there was."

"I should think you bloody well should be," replied Jim, clearly prepared to be propitiated. "What came over you?"

"I don't know," said Finn. "Special had refused me drink and I was rattled. I don't know. I'm sorry about it."

"Look at the mark you left," said Jim. "Was I angry when I saw it this morning? If you'd even warned me you were thinking of doing anything of the sort."

Finn smiled strangely. "You shouldn't have said what you did just then. That started it off."

"But I didn't mean anything."

"I know," said Finn. "All the same, it annoys a fellow to tell him that he ran away."

Jim laughed as if he had scored. "All right," he said. "But why did you clear off?"

"Ach," replied Finn, "I don't care for girls. They're a waste of time."

This amused Jim very much. "If you had my armful," he said, "you wouldn't think it a waste of time!"

"You're welcome to it," replied Finn. "But I must be going. They're waiting."

That was one point about Jim, thought Finn as he went on: he's a good-natured fellow; there's no real harm in him. The only thing Finn didn't care so much for was his blow about girls, his superior knowledge. He had great stories about two whores in Wick. He liked to impress country lads, to chuckle at their innocence over methods of sexual approach and fulfilment. Then he would step back and laugh and clear his throat of thick spittle. When Rob and Callum had a passage over a widow, how natural everything was, how rich the humour! Two different worlds altogether. Yes, quite different. Finn went on steadily. "If you had my armful." O God! he groaned. But when his brain cleared, he thought that Una herself must have something of the whorish streak about her or she wouldn't let his arms . . . Yes, she must be like that. She was like that. Well, it finished everything so far as he was concerned. He wouldn't look at her now, not though she was crawling on her knees——

"Hullo, Finn!" shouted Callum. "Glad to see you. We heard you had got locked up."

"You'll hear many a thing," said Finn, forcing his spirit high over a deep surge of dismay. Roddie had not yet arrived.

"I'll have a bottle of special, Special!" cried Callum, with a lordly air.

Finn looked at him. "I never said that."

"You never hit Boots in the eye?"

"Well, I pushed him aside——"

They laughed, obviously delighted that he had dealt with Boots; but he could see he was in for some fun now, and if he was, he would not let his side down!

All the same he was flustered, and glad to see the boats setting out over the green water above the sand and the blue-brown over the tangle.

And in the morning all were well fished. There was tremendous activity on the beach and round the gutting stations. "Hullo, Finn!" cried Meg, her eyes merry with knowledge. He gave Betz a special salute. Una did not lift her head to look his way. If he had any misgiving over what he had done to Jim, he let it sink. In fact, there moved in him a devil-may-care swagger. This was freedom and made him feel fine. When the shot was out and he was putting away his empty creel, Meg said quickly in what was meant for an aside, "What's all this I hear about last night?"

"What?" asked Finn.

Betz stood looking at him, having none of the quickness of Meg. Finn gave her a friendly smile.

Meg whispered. But Finn answered aloud: "He has someone to poultice it for him, so he'll be all right," and away he went laughing.

After a quick side-glance at the busy Una, Meg went on with her work, but not before giving Betz a wink.

From that moment, Finn began to feel much better. There was more than one herring in the sea and more than one place to fish them from. Girls were a disease that affected young fellows, and often enough a dirty disease at that. Anyway, it was a grand thing to be rid of—especially with money piling up and his own boat in the offing.

More and more now this idea of getting a boat of his own began to take possession of him. Not a second-hand boat, but a brand new one, longer than the *Seafoam*, in fact —why not?—the biggest boat yet built for a Dunster skipper, with bright paint on her gunnels and a lovely line to her that would take the seas like a bird. Before the fishing was over this had become a secret obsession. It could blot out personal images of the early morning; it was an inspiration far beyond troubles over girls; it made him an expert fisherman with the excitement and niggardly care that hated to see herring fall back into the sea. He was swift in his movements and tireless, and would shout sharply and cheerfully with the best. Herring, the silver darlings, get them in! If the weather was doubtful, Finn was all for chancing it. To be one of a handful of boats that risked going to sea and then to return with a shot—what pride and delight could exist beyond that?

He came to love the sea. It was a great element. He saw now how great and strong it was, with the strength of great men and daring and courage. It was a man's element.

Never before had he seen it quite in this way. It was beyond
even making money out of. It was a stupendous thing in
itself. The mere handling of a boat against it was a thrill
that nothing on land, in man or in woman, could equal. And
the knowledge of all that lifted him above earthly misfor-
tunes.

One early morning he could have laughed, for when he
saw the image of Una it was no longer swaying in front of
his mind, but had receded a long way, so that it was diminished in size and retiring from him into a small local place
of no importance. It might look back if it liked, but he held
the world in front, which was spacious, and into it, over all
its sparkling seas, he would adventure. He had the feeling
of having escaped narrowly. How fellows like to get tied
to girls, their freedom taken from them, shut up in a little
house, was a great mystery. It was true, thought Finn,
marvelling, that if a man lived long enough he learned a
lot!

And Jim, who would one day be a fish curer, a cut above
them all; and George, shouting his figures and spreading
his salt—what were they when it came to the sea itself,
the handling of a boat in a storm, the phosphorescent fires,
the living dance of the silver darlings? They only saw the
herring dead, and lived on them like gulls!

A great accession of strength and assurance came to Finn
in those days. His company was sought after by lads of his
own age and old men liked to draw a laughing retort out of
him. As for sleep, he only needed it when his body was
stupid with fatigue.

On the day of settlement, Dunster became a vast beehive
in swarm. The fishermen were dressed in their best kit and
the gutting girls and women made high holiday. The shops
had laid in special stores from Wick, and the buying of
presents and all sorts of personal and household gear set
money and laughter flowing like the water in the river.
And little of importance could be settled without a drink.
Responsible God-fearing men beamed with the innocence

of their childhood and the instinctive gesture was to put the
hand in the pocket and take out money. It was a day new-
minted, and those who hadn't been seen for twenty-four
hours were strangers to be welcomed. To have money thus
for the spending was a lovely miracle, and as it came under
God's free hand with the tides of the sea, who would
question the order of its going?

With the darkness came gatherings in scores of houses,
leave-takings and songs, and leave-takings over again.
"We must be going." "What's all your hurry? It's not
every day we have a good fishing!" "No, but it's getting
late . . . ." And so out—and to another house.

They sang and they danced all night, and the humour
was robust enough many a time, with the whirl of a girl,
a quick retort, and laughter. Angry voices in a ditch; money
lost and money re-found. And if there was a fight, voices
would placate the combatants through long, intricate argument with slappings on the back and profound expressions
of personal understanding. Any drop of bad blood now
found its letting. There was a ritual for it, with voices ever
ready to serve, for who would leave a bitter man with the
poison of his grievance? And for pledge and healing, behold
the absolving wine in a bottle, the wine of the country.

Finn bade good-bye in the early hours to a bunch of lads
and headed for home, laughing often to himself at one or
other of the queer things that had happened that night. For
one thing sang in his mind. As young men, they had talked
of boats and fishings, and the oldest Buckie lad had said
that he was thinking of getting a boat of his own.

"So am I," said Finn, before he could stop the words.

"Are you?" asked Donnie.

"Yes," answered Finn, "and you and Ian here are coming with me."

For a moment there was silence, then enthusiasm swept
Ian and Donnie. They swore they would put up their share;
they would put it up now. Finn saw that he was their
leader and felt lifted off his feet. "I know the way to

SEA LOVE

Stornoway. I have been in the Western Ocean. Keep your
thumb on it meantime," said Finn, "but by God we'll show
them how to fish before we're done!"

Ian had got so moved that he had thrown up his liquor.

Finn could not help laughing to himself. His mother had
been extremely hospitable to the lads, and Andie, from
Banff, aged seventeen, had been struck by Barbara so
powerfully that, out of politeness, they took no notice. Life
was a queer, entrancing thing.

CHAPTER XX

FINN GOES TO HELMSDALE

T he following week, Finn set off with Barbara for
Dale. It was a fine September day with yellow here
and there on the dark green of the birches and an
air that was fresh and invigorating. The earth looked calm
and lovely, and folk had pleasant greetings, with a smile
on their faces. It was good to go striding down the lands,
to be off on a journey under the morning sun, with a high
heart in a tireless body.

"I'm silly," said Barbara, wiping her eyes.

Finn laughed at her, and from the tears of parting her
face cleared in a bright smile.

"Will you promise me to come back next year?" asked
Finn.

"Yes," said Barbara.

"That's grand," declared Finn. "That relieves my mind.
But remember—it's a promise."

"All right," said Barbara, taking a quick step or two as
his mother did sometimes.

"Did you really like being here?"

"I loved it," said Barbara. "Your mother—she's so
kind."

"And what about me?"

"Ach," she said, "you're—you'll do!"

They both laughed. Barbara was very excited, her dark
eyes bright as sun on peaty water. He teased her and had her
arguing and disputing, but her heart was merry. "You're
glad to be going home," said Finn, "and that's the truth."

"I am," said Barbara. "I'm longing to see them." Her voice was urgent with longing.

"And yet you pretend you're sorry to go!" He gave a sarcastic chuckle

She stopped speaking, her face in front. He gave her a side-glance. Her top lip was drawing down. This amused him. But when she remained silent, he decided to put her at ease again and said sensibly, "I'm only teasing you. It's natural that you should be wanting to go home. It would be a queer thing if you weren't."

But instead of her young face clearing, it tautened still more, and then a gulp of a sob came through. At a complete loss, Finn glanced about him to make sure that no one was about. In a minute she was herself again, and Finn let out a deep breath of relief. He would have to watch what he said.

"You think I'm silly," she said.

"No, I don't," declared Finn. "Honestly."

"You're a great ass," she said, with emphasis.

He laughed, delighted. "That's better!"

But he kept all further teasings in check until they were resting near the far top of the Langwell glen. Then he got talking of the fishings and the gutting, and she said that next season she would be nearly seventeen, and his mother had suggested to her that if she wanted to make a little money for herself, she could do so at Dunster.

"Why, that would be grand!" cried Finn. And she looked as if he had given her a secret present. This amused him. "Ha! Quite!" He nodded enigmatically.

"What?"

"Very likely," said Finn with a serious air, "there will be boats over again from the south side."

"Very likely," she said, with an innocent air.

"Quite so. Special boats with special crews."

"Will there?" She arched her brows.

Would he make her weep? He would. She deserved it. "Extra special crews, with names like Beel and Jock and— and Andie. A nice name, Andie, don't you think?"

She leaned back, laughing. She doubled over, laughing. "Oh, you're funny!" she spluttered.

Finn didn't feel funny. "I think all girls are a bit queer, myself." And when she laughed again, he felt piqued.

"Oh, dear," she sighed; "that was a good laugh!"

"It didn't cost much, anyway," he said breezily.

"Oh, don't make me laugh again," she begged him. "Don't!" Her body, like an opening bud, was immature and tender, a little stiff, but it was full of young life bursting through its restraints, exaggeratedly, but somehow very attractively, too. He helped himself to a snuff.

"Why do you think girls are queer?" she asked.

"I don't know why they're queer, I'm sure," he answered. "It's probably the nature of the animal."

She neither laughed nor protested, but kept her head down, picking at the heather. "Sometimes they may have to do things they don't want to do."

"Have they?" He laughed, out of a great and amusing knowledge. "If so, they hide it very well!" She did not answer. "They hide it so well," said Finn humorously, "that no one would ever suspect it!"

She did not answer. His eyes followed her hand, that seemed nervous, as if her young thought was too deep for utterance. He looked at her head, the parting of her dark hair, the red silk ribbon he had given her keeping it in place. The virgin's snood. A faint warmth went over him, a tenderness for this young cousin of his. As if she felt his eyes, she lifted her head and looked down over the birches and away to the mountains.

"Doesn't the world feel young to-day?" asked Finn in his pleasant voice.

She did not answer for a moment; then she said, "It seems to me very old and wrinkled. It's we who are young."

Finn checked his laugh, in a marvelling astonishment. "You have the wisdom of an old woman!"

She glanced at him quickly, smiling. "Come on, we'll go."

In no time Barbara wàs as interested in the world as a young butterfly. She was attracted by the smallest things, as if the journey were a thrilling adventure. Often they walked in silence. At the Grey Hen's Well, Barbara drank twice. "Once for Auntie Catrine and once for myself," she murmured, wiping the water from her nose.

"Why that?" he asked, astonished.

"This is where your mother rested," she said, "long, long ago, when for the first time she crossed the Ord and entered into a strange land."

He smiled at her legendary tone, but he saw, too, that there was something behind it and, whatever it was, all in a moment it touched his heart. So he got down and drank—hesitated—and drank a second time.

"Tell me," she said, glowing, "—for what?"

But he shook his head mysteriously and went on.

"Oh, Finn, do!" she pleaded, and hung on to his arm. "Do."

"No."

"That's not fair. I told you." She tugged him; she held him back. Her bundle fell from his shoulder as he jerked her forward by the wrist in a rush against him. His arms held her close. "I have you now," he said. "Do you promise to come quietly?" Her struggles ceased. His eyes went over the lonely stretches of moor and hill. "Do you promise?"

"Yes."

He let her go. She did not look at him. She was flushed, but before either of them could think, she cried, "You're mean."

"How?"

"Not telling me."

He laughed and tried to speak in the most ordinary tone, "Well, I'll tell you."

"Promise it's the truth?"

"Yes. Cut my throat and burn my breath."

She laughed excitedly at his gesture.

He hesitated. "I don't know if I will."

"Oh, you promised!"

He acted reluctance for a little longer, then he began to speak in a simple, brotherly way as they walked together, of the sea and boats and the rise of the fishing, how this brought money and comfort to the poor, dispossessed people, and how fine life was going to be on this coast yet. "And so," he concluded, letting his great secret out in an easy tone, "I have been thinking of getting a boat of my own."

"Have you?" she said. "Wouldn't that be fine?"

"Do you think so?" he asked lightly, his ear eager for her wonder.

"I do. I think it would be grand," she declared.

But his ear did not catch the inner tone of wonder, the hush of surprise.

"It's not settled, so you mustn't say anything about it. After all, I mightn't bother."

"But you should," she insisted. "I hope you do. You will, won't you?"

"I'll see," he said.

"I would like you to have a boat of your own. That would be fine!"

"It just occurred to me. But we'll see. Are you feeling tired?"

"Me? No," she declared, with a look at him.

He was going to have suggested a rest, but now he went on walking, talking about several things amusingly. The delicate feeling of harmony between them had gone, and presently, after a silence, when he asked with dry humour, "What are you thinking about?" she answered quietly, without looking at him, "I was thinking about your boat."

This irritated him, so he laughed and asked, "What wonderful thing were you expecting me to say—instead of about the boat?"

She did not answer.

"Come on!" he teased her. "Tell me."

"I wasn't thinking about anything else."

"You were. I know you were."

"I was not," she said.

"Ah, do, Barbara. Tell me. Please." He took her arm. But she snatched it from him. He laughed, and she went walking on alone. He followed, without making any effort to overtake her. Her body was slim and straight, from her bare heels to the crown of her head. He began to make mocking noises in his throat. She sat down, turning her face to the sea. He walked past, remarking politely on the fine weather. In time they grew friendly again. Just before they came to the top of the last rise, he paused, saying, "Now for the first glimpse of the home of your heart!" She hesitated half a second, and ran on.

There it was! He looked sideways, with a smile, at her eager face. "Come on!" she cried and began running; then waited for him.

"Run on," he said. "Don't wait for me."

"You're a great big fool," she said.

"Ho-ho! Why so?"

"Just because you are."

"Enjoyed your walk?"

"Yes, very much. Did you?"

"In bits," he said. "Bits."

"What bits?"

"If you tell me what bit you enjoyed best, I'll tell you my bit."

"I enjoyed many bits," she said.

"So did I," he answered.

"Tell me," she begged.

"No. It's you first."

"Will you guess what bit I thought best and then I'll guess what bit you thought best?"

"You guess first."

She suddenly looked at him, not shyly but in a penetrating glance, with a surprising touch of devilment in it. A certain warmth beset him inwardly, for his mind was running on the moment when he had held her. She looked away. "There's Uncle Angus!" she cried.

"Ho-ho!" he mocked. "You're frightened!"

She turned her head and gave him the same glance. "I'm not guessing," she said. "I know—now. It was when you spoke of your boat," and she ran down the brae-face shouting, "Uncle Angus!"

Finn felt the bottom of the warmth fall out of him.

There was a big change in Dale since the day Catrine had walked out of it. Not that much extra land had been taken into cultivation, for the small plot given to each croft could not grow in size, unless upward into the mountain rock. But the lazy beds, heavy with ripening grain and freshly coloured with the potato flower, lay against the hill-side in an attractive pattern of straight line and serpent twist, like a great quilt. There were more houses, too, small two-roomed thatched cottages, with little or no land attached to them. The real change lay in the comfort of the folk, which they harvested not from the land but from the sea. Many of the young men had left Dale and were living permanently in the rapidly growing village of Helmsdale. They all had a hunger for a bit of land, but seeing it could not be got, they gave more and more their whole attention to the sea. A row of potatoes here and there on a croft each would have, and he gave harvest labour for it, but he now bought his oatmeal. With fresh fish, salt fish, a barrel of cured herring, meal, potatoes, and—for the greater part of the year—milk, butter, and cheese, life was given a solid backing that neither chance nor mischance could affect greatly. A side of a pig, a barrel of porter, meat on more than one day of the week, syrup, eatables bought out of a shop, would be encountered in many a place, and when there was no milk for porridge, children grew excited over the change to treacle, nursing the dark spoonful in the centre of the plate. The rise of the fishing had pushed poverty from the door and beyond the little fields, and though its spectre might haunt the mind now and then, there was a good way of dealing with it, especially when a stranger came, like Finn. It was the hand into the store of hidden shillings then and swift feet for "something special" to the shop. For the women were jealous of hospitality's good name and, to come near the truth, they would indulge in hospitality as men on a market or settling-day would indulge in drink. They loved it, its carefree giving, its talk, its laughter, its swept house, its clean table, its bright face, its delicate pride. "Is it yourself, Finn? How pleased I am to see you! Come away in!"

And Finn knew how to take it all, with a bright voice, a merry retort, a quick movement or sympathetic word, so that they were delighted to see him. He seemed to have relations in swarms, and he wondered if the shillings he had taken with him would cover the youngest of them.

Catrine's mother was now well over seventy, and she looked at her grandson with the clear eyes that saw not only his straight young manhood but the nature of the spirit behind. He knew he was being assessed but did not feel uncomfortable, for the expression of her eyes was kindly, and when she went on talking it was satisfied and fulfilled. He enjoyed the responses that rose in him, an ease of manners, a clearness in the voice. There was an essence of the spirit somewhere that was delicate yet full of life, the gaiety and hope in life, like a song running in the mind. Now and then in little surges it brought a great desire to be generous.

But there was no fear of the spirit taking wings. It was held to the earth by a heavy enlargement of the stomach. Finn had to eat here and he had to eat there until he said to a cousin of his, "As sure as death, if I eat any more I'll burst." So they crossed into Helmsdale where there were greetings and talk and more food than ever. Finn went over the harbour, looking at the boats, agreeing that Helmsdale was far better equipped as a curing station than Dunster, and saying solemnly, "How is it, then, that Dunster so outstripped Helmsdale? It can only be the one thing." "What's that?" "The quality of the men," said Finn. But his Uncle Norman and a few other fishermen did not let him off with that. Then someone mentioned Stornoway, and they turned on Finn in a body, eager to listen to him. But he had no sooner begun than Isebeal appeared, declaring that she could not wait any longer, and carried Finn off, for she was dying to hear about Catrine who was her life's heroine.

Within half an hour, however, the men began to file into Isebeal's kitchen until it was packed, and then Norman said, "You'll begin at the beginning, Finn." The ceilidh was set and Finn began.

It took him two hours to describe the trip, for he was listened to by experts both in boat-sailing and story-telling, who let him off with nothing. "We left on the Tuesday morning. It was a good morning, clear and bright, with a fine breeze off the land; so we put both sails up and set our course on Clyth Head." "How was the tide?" asked Norman. So Finn described the state of the tide, explaining how necessary it is to get the first of the ebb through the Pentland Firth if you hope to get through at all. "In fact, when we got there——" But Norman pulled him up. "We'll come to that," he said. In this way, any self-consciousness that Finn might have, talking before so many people, was taken from him and he entered into the telling of the whole story as if it were happening before his eyes, which indeed it was. When the wind died away and they got on to the oars, feeling now they would never make the Pentland in time, Finn communicated the anxiety that came over them in a vivid manner by introducing bits of talk between Rob and Callum. He interrupted his story to describe Rob and Callum, and this light relief in the tension of the race for the tide was greatly appreciated. They laughed. They repeated the sarcastic or witty saying. In fact, Finn himself found that something which had not appeared very comical at the time seemed now the very essence of the comical. Then back to the oars, straining at the oars. Would they make it? "It did not seem like it," said Finn. Their eyes were on him. An old man, who had been a drover in the days before the clearances, sat with his chin on the crook of his stick, his eyes burning under hooded brows. Boys were grouped spellbound on the floor. He had not yet started his story and they were frightened he would hurry.

It took him a long time to get through the Pentland, and indeed to satisfy men like Norman he drew a chart of the passage with his finger on the floor. The swiftness of the tide like a mighty river, the ripps and boils. "The boat goes from you," said Finn, "as your heels go from you on a bit of ice." They shook their heads. The wonder of the world was without end. The Wells of Swinna and the need to throw a chest overboard enthralled not only the young. "Get your chest ready, Rob," said Callum. "Take your own chest," said Rob; "there will be more food for his belly in it, if I know you."

The night in Loch Eriboll, the fun of the milk-hunt, the departure, the Cape, the Minch, the short strong waves, the mist. "We were lost," said Finn.

The night of storm and the great long seas.

He laid Henry's and Roddie's theories of where they might be before the seamen around him. "You see how difficult it was?" he asked with an eager smile. "No land, nothing but these tremendous seas coming at you like the hills of Kildonan, with great straths between. In the darkness of that night there were many times when I thought she was away with it." "She had a great seaman at her helm," said Norman. "That's true," agreed Finn. "Roddie was great. He sat there like one of the Vikings of old, never moving, only his eyes watching, hour after hour, through the dark of the night and the long hours of next day." They saw him and were deeply moved by the ring in Finn's voice.

This was one of the old stories, going from wonder to

wonder, for now a ship appeared on these lonely wastes, and Finn said the sight of her frightened him a little. His voice grew modest, with a smile in it, but most of them had known Tormad well and they liked this reticence in his son. They were greatly relieved to find she was a friendly cod-smack and lingered over the vision of her ploughing into the Western Ocean. "The Shetlanders are daring seamen." "They are known for it." They nodded their heads.

"So we thanked them, and Roddie, watching his chance, put her about in the running seas, and we bore off, and at that the whole crew lined the deck and gave us a loud cheer."

His listeners shifted restlessly. "You deserved it," said Norman; "I'll say that." "You did indeed." "Yes, yes." They took a moment or two to settle, for they were moved strongly. But Finn had them laughing at the way they now decided to celebrate in drinks the emergence from their troubles, quoting Callum and Rob to suit his purpose. "It's a terrible thing, thirst," said Finn. And he smiled, describing the way it attacks a man. And then—then they saw land. "Callum fairly revived at that!"

He would! He would indeed! And it was not before time!

And so Finn brought them, not to land, but to a place of dark fantastic rock, and anchored them there.

Never before had Finn known the power of the story-teller. The smashing seas, the screaming birds, the black rock-faces, and the terrible thirst that had come upon them. Someone would have to try to climb the rock. "For we saw that by the morning it might be too late."

The rock-face, the mystery of the little house, and—the water. The rock-ledges, the birds, and his astonishment at the bite that nearly put him over the cliff. They laughed in relief at that. And then his problem over getting the eggs and bottles down the rock. "I was completely stuck," said Finn, "and I was anxious, too. I didn't know what to do. I hated to be beaten. And they were not the sort of things you could throw down!"

This was a story and more than a story, and when at long last Finn brought them to the *Sulaire* and the silver darlings, that last surprise of all had their eyes shining in wonder and satisfaction.

The night was now far advanced, but the listeners were only settling down, for Norman and the fishermen wanted to hear what happened in Stornoway and to ask a hundred questions. But Isebeal said no, Finn would have to go, for Granny would be sitting up for him.

"Be quiet, woman," said her husband. "The night is young." Who bothered with time, anyway? "Sit down, Finn boy."

"No, I'll have to be going," said Finn. "I'd better be going."

"Nonsense. Never mind that woman. She would have to be putting her word in."

"Finn will come back to-morrow night," said Isebeal, "and he can stay till all hours then."

"No, I must go home to-morrow," replied Finn.

"Nonsense," said Isebeal. "You know you haven't to go."

"I said I would."

"You didn't. You said you might. And your mother said to you that if you didn't come she wouldn't be expecting you."

"How did you know?" asked Finn. And they all laughed.

Out in the dark, beyond the door, the drover put a finger on Finn's breast. "You gave me a vision—of the youth of Finn MacCoul himself." And finger and man withdrew into the night.

The next morning Ronnie called for Finn. "I was sorry I missed you last night," he said. Finn liked his quiet manner, and thin, distinguished face. Close-cut grey hair over the ears, a red scar below the bone of the right cheek, and grey eyes that seemed washed. He had a very slight stoop of the shoulders and his body was thin. All in a moment Finn felt that this man had something not to tell him but to give him. It was a curious feeling, and made him at once eager and shy.

When Ronnie suggested that they might take a long walk up the strath of Kildonan, unless Finn had something special to do, Finn answered readily that he had nothing to do and would be glad to go. So they set off, and when Ronnie said, "Your father was my greatest friend," Finn was strangely moved, as if the unknown and the half-known in time and the world were coming upon him.

"This was our world," said Ronnie, and as they walked along he described scenes from the early life of Tormad and Catrine and himself, the world before the clearances, in its pastoral ways. His voice was even and pleasant; and when he described the harrowing and brutal scene of their eviction, it was not vindictive; as though brutality were the common-place in' life, out of which the poor man gathered a few joys like odd jewels—if he was lucky. And Ronnie had had the luck of his youth. There was something spent in Ronnie, like a spent wave, but he had come up clean.

Finn sailed the seas with Ronnie, and names like "The Indies" had an enchantment for him. The exploits of the *Seafoam* were little enough now! Finn would have been ashamed to talk about them before this man. There was a strange dividing in his mind, and he moved in its two worlds—the world Kirsty had talked about, with its lairds and captains and foreign adventures, the very same that this man Ronnie, his father's friend, had sailed through, and the world of home with the simple common people who were known to him and stirred in human warmth.

The far world seemed bright and full of great adventure; the land of home awkward and dull-minded, without knowledge.

"There are a great many things in the world we don't know about here at home," said Finn.

"That's true," agreed Ronnie. "But I wouldn't say you'd gain much by knowing about them."

"I wonder?" murmured Finn, sceptically.

"Looking back on it now," said Ronnie, "I can say that there was more wonder in one year of my young life here than in all the years I spent on the high seas and in foreign places."

"But you have been to those places," said Finn.

Ronnie smiled. "It's a delusion, Finn," he answered quietly. "It may be pleasant to see new things, but they pass before the eyes. Your own nature remains. Human nature does not change—except often for the worse. There were days of such tedium that they were a horror in the mind. Men craved for anything, for fights, for drink, for death, anything to break the horror that discipline kept rigid. There were only the two ways out: brutality and foul language, and they went together. They were a great relief. They were like a vomit that cleared you. They were helpful many a time."

"Were they?"

"For a while I had the name of being the greatest swearer on board. I have seen an angry Englishman look at me in wonder and say ' *Holy Jesus!* ' and laugh.

Ronnie's mind, opening in this unexpected way, kept Finn silent but anxious to hear more.

"For it's an odd thing," said Ronnie, "that in our own language we have no swearing of that kind. So in English a swear to us hardly seems to be a swear at all, you sort of know what it means, but it's funny, too. It's new. A new sound. That's about all. I have seen English sailors laugh at swears in Spanish in the same way. The worst fight ever I saw was between a Devon man and a Frenchman. There was a devil of a fellow in our crew, whose whole aim in life was to cause trouble. A 'practical joker' they called him. Well, he got hold of a simple Devon man, a nice fellow, and dared him to repeat two French words on shore to a French sailor. The knife was out before you could wink. What a night that was! There were fifteen casualties. It kept us going for two months."

"It must have been exciting often."

"It had to be," said Ronnie. "Even when one or two of our own fellows got clapped in irons and we muttered to ourselves and swore and threatened mutiny—that was relief, too. A month of it; a year of it; year after year after year. It's a long time—when your heart's not in it."

"I suppose so. Were there fine fellows among them, too?"

"Oh, yes. One or two of the world's best. But you see, the fellows who would be your friends would be the fellows whose hearts were not in the business either. So you would talk of your homes and the old life. There were nights often enough when the strath of Kildonan ran through my mind like the glen of Paradise."

"Did it?"

"It did."

Out of the silence Finn asked, "What was the worst thing?"

"There were many things," said Ronnie, "but the worst was the thing that was always with us or in the offing. I have taken part in it myself. I could be as good at it as at the swearing. And often it did me good. But too often it left a sickness in the heart, a bitterness of gall in the stomach. It was that awful, bloody thing, brutality. Jesus, I hated it. I never got used to it."

Finn was silent.

"They can talk about religion, Finn, and the sins of the flesh, and the Ten Commandments, and good and evil, but there is only one sin and one evil, and its name is brutality. I wear its badge. Look!" And, taking off his bonnet, he showed Finn a little silver clasp in his skull. "Some day I may tell you the story about it, but not now. It does me good to touch it sometimes, and to remember how I got it. The children like to see it." He smiled drily.

They went miles up the strath, talking of many things, for Ronnie would point to this or that and tell Finn something about it. Finn, too, remembered some of his mother's stories.

"Your mother was a beautiful young girl. She was so full of life," said Ronnie. He talked simply and frankly about her, not concealing his admiration, until Finn felt slightly embarrassed. "But I had no chance with her, when your father was about!"

"Hadn't you?" Finn tried to smile.

"No," said Ronnie. "I used to think about her often when I was away." His tone was clear and frank and transcended Finn's embarrassment. "The autumn is on us," he said in the same tone, lifting his face. "The rowan berries are red."

Finn looked at the mountain-ash with its load of berries, blood-red berries over green leaves in the September sun. Their stillness and silence touched him, as if they were waiting or listening.

"We'll sit in their shadow for a little," said Ronnie, "for I'm feeling a bit tired."

The moment had now come, Finn knew, when Ronnie would tell about the death of his father.

As Finn listened to the description of how the line stuck in the bottom and they thought they were in a whale, he could not help laughing, for Ronnie himself was smiling; then the first white fish; and finally, in the dawn, the herring. He could understand the excitement, and wanted to prolong the moment, for he knew what was coming. But like fate it came, and when Finn heard how his father had behaved, his heart was bitter and proud, and the emotion that rose in him would not let him speak. He saw it all with a terrible clarity, and fought beside his father as he would beside a great hero.

"We had not much English, and not the kind they spoke anyway, and we did not answer them but remained dumb. That has troubled my mind often since. Perhaps they used it as an excuse not to know or report anything about your father. There was a dumb anger in us—and we paid for it before they broke us. Your father was buried at sea. O God, that was a terrible moment when we realized who it was.

Terrible beyond telling. I was always a peaceable enough man, but murder dwelt in me for many a long day. However, it's no good going over all that. No good at all, Finn boy. Young Torquil—he broke out. They put him in irons. I thought he was going off his head. We were separated in the end. Time will do anything to a man. For we come of a tough enough breed, a breed that has endured a lot. Never mind. It all comes back to the one thing, Finn —brutality. Compel people into a position where they have to use the brute that's in them in order to live and the brute will waken all right. When the brute is naturally strong in a man—that's the man who becomes the leader of the press-gang. And there you have it. Where all is compulsion and enforcement, it's the bully that rules."

Finn sat silent, a dark flush on his face.

"Life is a strange thing, too," said Ronnie. "At first there is anger and murder in your heart. You feel that you'll yet get your own back. You're young. You can endure. You'll have your revenge. But it does not work out like that. Not in life itself, Finn. Why? Because of this terrible thing—that the years pass. You had thought that you would work through it and get what you wanted yet. You even work out years of service and a pension and a cottage of your own. But all the time the terrible thing that's happening is—that the years are passing. I have the little pension and the cottage but—the years have passed."

"But you are secure now," said Finn, under the shadow of his father's death.

"Yes," said Ronnie.

Finn felt uncomfortable.

"All I wanted to say, Finn, was that you are doing fine here. You stick to it, boy. This is a full enough life for any man. You have everything here—and freedom besides. Don't go hankering after the wastes of the world. They were telling me of your story of adventure into the Western Ocean."

"That was nothing."

"It took you to the edge of death—and further than that no adventure can travel in this life."

"Oh, I don't know," said Finn, feeling restless.

"I know," said Ronnie. And he added, with a quiet finality in his voice, a summing up of wisdom, "We were driven: you went."

Silence fell on them now and Ronnie lay back against the slope. "It's fine here," he said.

But because of the mood that was on Finn, he felt in Ronnie's simple words a deep, incommunicable sadness.

Ronnie closed his eyes, Finn and all the brutalities of the world washed from him. Finn glanced at the face and saw it strange and remote, the skin taut over the bones beneath, the scar a shiny red, the whole fixed and set as in death—like a face washed up by the tides of an invisible sea.

Finn began breaking a little stick in his fingers. It was dead and broke readily. He became aware of Ronnie's eyes but did not like to turn his head and look.

"It's fine lying here. Man, I enjoy this," said Ronnie, in a cheerful half-sleepy voice. When at last he got up and gazed at the tree, his whole manner was friendly and bright. "Look, now. What about taking a sprig of these berries home to your mother? I'm sure she would like you to take something to her from her beloved strath."

"Do you think so?"

"It would show her you remembered her."

With a slow smile, Finn pulled down a cluster of the red fruit.

On the way home the following afternoon, Finn was in grand heart. He had thoroughly enjoyed his stay at Dale and felt now as if he had grown larger. Everyone had been extremely kind to him. Ronnie had come some distance with him and before saying good-bye had spoken of the change on the coast. The picture of a people happy again, with the coming of prosperity from the sea. The sea did not belong to any landlord and the use of the press-gang was

dying out. By the new Act of Parliament, a man press-
ganged could not now be held more than five years. But
everything depended on the young men. "It's for fellows
like you to lead, Finn; to build up the ways of our folk once
more. Your father and myself started—but we were beaten.
You are the new generation. Justify your father, boy, before the world. And look after your mother, who suffered
more than you'll ever know."

It was good fun to think of these words now. Like
marching to a tune. And Barbara—they had made Barbara
blush. She had snatched her hand away at leave-taking. He
laughed, thinking of it. He had a lot of news for his mother.
He would lay himself out to tell her about everything!
Ronnie—Ronnie . . . and his mother? His brows gathered
over a smile. The idea that anyone like Ronnie should think
of marrying his mother! *Holy Jesus!* as the Englishman had
said. Finn felt hot and laughed. Old people had no sense.
But, of course, Ronnie never meant—really. He couldn't.
He was too—too wise and fine a fellow, with fun in him
besides. Good Lord, no! And, out of a sudden driving
exuberance, Finn took to his heels and ran, and freedom
ran with him.

He would be home on the edge of the dark.

CHAPTER XXI

CATRINE AND RODDIE

❦

When Finn and Barbara had disappeared, Catrine turned and found she had the whole croft to herself. It was suddenly both intimate and vacant, and over her came an urgent impulse to work. Chairs and stools she whisked outside; the beds were stripped and armfuls of blankets spread to the. sun; everything was shifted or taken down, until the whole household was in an uproar. Then she settled to the attack.

A fine girl, Barbara. Youth was away on the road.

Bran (successor to Oscar who had died from injury) lay at a few yards on the grass considering her now and then with some misgiving, but keeping well clear of this odd frenzy that attacked humans occasionally. The cock was astonished as usual. One or two of the hens croaked in the quiet, reflective way they had at times, speaking to themselves like old women, while two or three young ones indulged in a luxurious bath near the peat-stack, fluffing now and then the fine black dust through their feathers.

Not that she wanted to be with Finn and Barbara. She was well content where she was. Though it would be lovely, too, to see her mother. There was a queer pleasure in having the place to herself. It was like having herself to herself. The byre was empty. The little barn. There was a silence in Finn's room; and in the guest-room. Kirsty's wooden trunk looked at her. She got the key, sat down on the floor, pushed back the lid, and forgot all about her labours in the very middle of them.

The past came back with a sweet sorrow. A brooch of Kirsty's was a love-token from a life beyond her own. All hers; the trunk itself; not Kirsty's now, but hers. Yet it would never be hers as it had been Kirsty's. All that was really hers were the little precious things of her very own that she had hidden away here. Green . . . cairngorm-yellow. . . . At the sight of them, she began to weep; and she wept heavily, like a child, the tears flowing copiously.

She wiped the tears away and smiled, but with little embarrassment, for she was not ashamed of herself. She knew perfectly well that all this was weakness and senti-ment. But there was no-one in the world to see her. So what business was it of anyone? She could weep if she liked. And enjoy it, too. There were little things that could break the heart; that could make the heart young and break it.

She felt young. Perhaps it was the sight of Barbara and Finn setting off. . . .

Catrine was now thirty-eight, a fully-developed woman, her shoulders rounded and firm, her chest deep, her face more full than it had been in the old days but with the eyes still large and the mouth red. The texture of her fair skin retained much of the smoothness of youth, of girlhood. Life, too, had taken care that the texture of her mind would not grow insensitive or complacent. At times, indeed—now, in a measure, by Kirsty's old chest—her eyes would quicken as in clairvoyance and her whole body grow alive to a con-dition or emotion remote from her in time or place. The fire could sweep her, not so recklessly as in youth, perhaps, and not so often, but sometimes with a deeper force; for—as Ronnie had said—the years pass. . . .

She had been sorry for Ronnie. Oh, desperately! He would never know how profoundly she had understood him. She had come nearer to an understanding of life, of that ultimate something final and tragic in it, than ever she had before. Sorrow had not burdened the mind and blinded the eyes, but had been seen clear in its pattern, beyond chance or mood, distant and fixed as an outline of the Kildonan hills.

Ronnie could not expect her to understand this. Yet in his way, he had understood, too, and that somehow had been the hardest part to bear. She had seen it coming from the first moment she had met his eyes. "Catrine!" "Ronnie!" And there it was. How confused she had been! The past calling to her, rising in a wave. She had turned away to look at her son in Roddie's boat, leaving her for the West. That was excuse enough for any emotion. And when the boat had disappeared beyond the Head, she found herself all in a moment delighted to speak to Ronnie, anxious to speak to him, with the terror of what he would have to tell her about Tormad—and then about himself—making her eyes brilliant and her body bloom. There had been early moments when she had been almost overcome with excitement, with intolerable suspense.

But Ronnie had been so wise and practical that her gladness at seeing him increased. Barbara was there, too, and that was good for restraint; so he could stay for a day or two, as he had intended, quite well. Of course he could. She would hear of nothing else.

The first night Ronnie had told her of the manner of Tormad's death. He had told it so simply and straightforwardly, that death was given a dignity, a heroic air. "We are no longer children, Catrine. These are the chances that come to life. They are bitter, but we learn to face them. It took me a long time, for I slept with murder many a night."

When she wept, he offered no sympathy. His voice remained quiet-toned, distant from her a little, but gentle with understanding. That delicacy—afterwards, in the sleepless hours of the night—had a curious steadying effect, for it was as if she remembered it without having noticed it at the time.

The following day he was interested in the croft, and she showed him everything. He was a fine companion now, full of life and little jokes, delighting in the land, staring at the tender corn with a smile, hearkening to the birds, talking of nests with a half-amused, half-adventurous expression, clapping the cows when she milked them—as though he could not get quite used to the old wonder of it all. His sailor's eye saw things crying out to be fixed up, or battened down. She saw life taking root in him and growing before her eyes, life and hope. This excited her deeply. She laughed too readily and too much. Her anxiety now was to keép him off, and yet by the very way she set about it, by the gaiety that was meant to avoid the serious, she drew him powerfully, and knew she did but could not help it.

On the third night, with Barbara up at Shiela's, he spoke to her, again with one of his simple questions, without intruding, in the quietness of the kitchen, their minds alive as the tongues of fire: "You would not think of getting married again, Catrine?" Not looking at him, she had answered, "No."

"Why not? If you care for me at all?" His voice had shaken. "I hàve always cared for you. Never anyone else. Couldn't—couldn't you think of it?"

She had shaken her head.

The dumb gesture had encouraged him. He had drawn nearer, close to her. "Catrine, why not, my white heart?" An arm went round her shoulders. "Our lives are before us. I could make you happy. Listen to me, Catrine. Many a long night did I think of you. Catrine, together we could make up——"

"Oh, no, no, Ronnie!" and she turned to him blindly and buried her face against his breast in a storm of emotion.

He had clasped her now in both his arms, and kissed her hair, and murmured words into it. But she had drawn away from him, and in a moment felt tragically calm.

"I'm sorry, Ronnie—to behave like this—but it cannot be. It couldn't."

He did not give in easily. This had come too quickly upon her. But in time—perhaps in time—give time a chance.

She did not answer him.

"Do you not care for me?"

"It's not that." Her voice and manner were fatally calm.

"What is it, then?"

"I don't know." But she knew, oh, she knew now. She would never get away from the past with Ronnie. He was its ghost. The strath, the outline of the hills, Tormad, the red berries—with the life that ran through them, the flame of youth, quickening, terrible, enchanting. Ronnie would lead her back there, remind her. It could not be borne. And because of this revulsion, knowing now how he had suffered, seeing his mind and hope with a dreadful clarity, seeing both of them caught like this in the ways of fate, of a past inexorable fate, wanderers akin in spirit and in circumstance, she almost loved him. But they could not wander in that place. It could not be borne.

It was out of a silence that he had said the words which desolated her and haunted her for many days, the simple words, but awful and final for him, "I see it is too late."

For at that moment she knew he was thinking not of her but of himself, of his past life, the bitterness of the defeated years.

And fate had singled her out to tell him of his defeat, to show him the bitterness.

Catrine closed the lid of the chest.

But she could not get up, all power of volition being drained from her body. The stillness that had come upon the kitchen, with Ronnie sitting motionless, came now upon her mind, and she saw their two figures as in a quiet but terrible dream. Ronnie had got up and said he would go out for a little walk, had stood for a moment staring at the grey light in the window, and then had gone.

Catrine leaned over the chest and her head dropped heavily between her arms, thought draining away from her, as it had done when, Ronnie gone, she had crouched in the empty kitchen.

Presently she sat upright again, listening to the sounds

about the croft. She knew them all and at first they were
strange, but in a moment like little living things they came
running into her heart, and she got up, went outside,
looked around the croft, at her beasts, at the fields, found
she had the whole place to herself, and set about her cleaning with a renewed strength in body and arms. She was
scouring a tin milk-pail outside, when suddenly there came
upon her from nowhere a feeling of extraordinary happiness. Such an access might have at the core of it a sadness,
but not so now. It ran through her flesh, her blood, in
promptings of laughter. Must be the sun! she thought, and
began to hum away to herself as she worked with force.
Her body was full of strength, delighted in its strength,
could have scoured the bottom right out of the pail! "What
are you looking at, you old fool?" she called to Bran. He
got up and came towards her doubtfully, with an uncertain
wag of his tail. "Off you go!" she cried. And back he went
with resignation. "Poor Bran," she said. "Come here and
I'll give you something."

In the late afternoon, as she was making up the beds,
Shiela looked in, and when Catrine told her how she had
spent the day, they both began to laugh. "Look, I scoured
a small hole in the bottom of the pail!" But Shiela could
not hold up the pail against the light for laughing. And
when Catrine began to chew a little oatmeal with which to
plug the hole, Shiela got a stitch in her side and Catrine
spluttered.

Shiela loved laughing and often had tremendous bouts of
it. Her mind was quick and intelligent, and her eyes a
lively bright brown. From laughing she could pass to
solemnity or a tender look in a moment. Her house was
never very tidy but it was always warm. She could make
life itself glow almost at any time. "We'll hurry up and do
your milking. And then you'll come up with me and spend
the night."

They were like children again, Catrine quick on her feet
and Shiela with a story about Lexy the witch that she let

out in explosive bits. All the affairs of men and women, in sex and at market, were given by Shiela a consuming humour, particularly if they were outrageous.

About nine o'clock Roddie dropped in. Shiela had seven children and the youngest of them welcomed their uncle with delight. "Yes, you're coming on," said Roddie to little Art, feeling the right bicep. "Another year or two and you should about do. In fact, I think you could almost hoist a sail yourself now."

"Oh, dear, that bairn!" exclaimed Shiela. "It's nothing but boats with him from morning to night. Sure as death, I never get out of the bit with this swarm."

They all seemed to do as they liked. There was continual turmoil and often, to be heard, a grown-up had to shout. When there was a fight on, Shiela would give one of them a clout. But Mairi, aged four, was a solemn child and would stand by Catrine or sit on her knee, saying nothing indefinitely. "Now, Mairi, what would you like?" "I would like a little song." "What about you singing me a little song? Come!" And Catrine started humming and prompting. When Mairi was at last persuaded into a few notes, a mocking laughter stopped her, and her lips began to tremble. Then Shiela set about the Philistines.

"How thankful you ought to be that you're not burdened like this!" cried Shiela, her voice breaking in laughter.

About ten o'clock, Roddie saw Catrine home. It was dark, with a slight ground mist after the heat of the day. Roddie was friendly, and they talked amusingly about the children. Once or twice Roddie took her arm to steady her on the uneven path, for they could not see the ground, and her heart was glad and relieved when he naturally withdrew it. But the stones over the burn were a more difficult matter and he had to take her hand and then almost lift her up the yard of bank.

"Thank you," she said. "It's not lighter I'm getting!"

"You're just a sound, reasonable weight," he replied critically, and she laughed.

"Finn will be with all his relations now," she said, and went on talking brightly about them. Soon they were at her door. "Is it too late to ask you in?"

"It's not too late for me—but thanks all the same!"

"That wasn't a nice way of me to put it, was it?"

"We'll take it that same way."

"Well, come in."

"That's better! But it's getting a bit late, Catrine. Don't you think so?" His voice was friendly and sensible.

"Perhaps it is late."

"Yes. I think so. Some other time. Well, I'll be off. You're not afraid to spend the night alone?"

"Oh, no."

"You're plucky!"

"I just don't think about it."

"I don't know of any other woman who would do it—apart from Lexy!"

"That's a nice name to couple me with!"

He stood quite still. She could hardly see him, but in his stillness there could always be something strong and ominous. Had it been Ronnie she would have known exactly what he felt. She was never sure of Roddie.

"Good night," he said in the same clear voice, and walked away.

"Good night," she called and, going inside, quickly found her hands fumbling with the bar, and her heart beating as if something tremendous had happened from which she had narrowly escaped.

Quiet-footed she entered the kitchen and stood against the wall beside the window, listening. The fire was low. When it seemed his footsteps were gone from the night she drew the window-blind and, getting down on her knees before the fire, began to build it up. But why was she building it up? It was time for bed. She thought: I'm all through-other! and tried to smile.

There was nothing tangible in her mind to explain this heart-beating and feeling of escape. Something had happened—and was over. She began to realize that Roddie had made up his mind to leave her alone. And that somehow was astonishing. She hardly knew what to do with the fire; whether to walk or sit. He had never mentioned Ronnie's visit—nor referred to Tormad's death.

So then at last she was free of the dark image of Roddie. It was all over. Astonishment was not only in herself but in the air about her, in the squat stillness of the low three-legged stools, in the table, by the quiet bed.

She did not ask herself questions, because this, as yet, was something she could not think about. Behind thought was feeling, charged with deeper meaning than thought. And this meaning was alive and immanent.

Suddenly her thought accepted the full meaning: this was the end of another chapter in her life. It was the end. For long years Roddie's life had run parallel with her own, ready to touch it, for ever threatening to touch it, and in some way this had been part of the rich troubling excitement of life. She had not desired it, often feared it, always was concerned to keep it at bay. Naturally enough, for there had been no absolute certainly of Tormad's death—as Roddie knew; naturally enough, for that reason alone.

But she was not thinking. Her mind in the kitchen was like a bird astonished at finding itself in a cage. The past was known, and had not to be thought. She was all alone in the kitchen and no-one would come.

Sleep was so far away from her that it was no good going to bed. She did not know what to do and felt helpless. It was a pity she had not taken Shiela's oldest girl, Janet, who was twelve, down to stay with her, as Shiela had suggested. But she had laughed and said no she did not mind being alone. For some unaccountable reason she had actually looked forward to being alone, to being all by herself, as if the essence of some long-forgotten pleasure might arise and surround her, like the scent of honeysuckle in the air.

She began to be afraid, not merely of the emptiness in the house, but of something nameless and dark and looming, coming out of the night and out of her own mind. Images tended to form quickly and pass. She was not afraid of Ronnie; he could enter with assurance and stay. They had understood each other so utterly. But all at once she saw Ronnie's face and heard his words: "I see it is too late," and she was appalled.

For now the words had a new power, a different meaning. Before, they had made the tragic pattern of life clear; they had set things at a distance: Tormad, herself, Ronnie, and the paths they had travelled, the paths traced by fate, awful and inexorable. But they had been seen with clarity, with the ultimate understanding that accepts. So figures are seen moving below in a glen of the memory or on ridges against the sky.

But now the words were not spoken by Ronnie but in the dark recesses of her own mind, and they came upon her with a sense of immediate horror. The clear picture was blotted out like a piece of sentiment. *Too late—too late—for you, Catrine.*

Roddie had nothing to do with this. It was far beyond Roddie. It touched the ultimate loneliness of herself.

It was her first real intimation of Death.

Her eyes brightened and glanced in fear. Her mind flew hither and thither. Would she—would she go out and run —run—all the way to Shiela's? She could say she would rather have someone; take Janet back with her. She didn't know what to do, and stood helpless, staring towards the door through which she should pass. Her eyes went beyond the door into the little room, Finn's room, and saw Kirsty lying on her death-bed. The vision was so stark that she had to stare at it, unable to drag her eyes away, as though by doing so she might commit some appalling wrong against Kirsty. At last she withdrew her eyes from it, decently, if under a terrible strain. As she set one live peat against another, she found she could not lift her head to look at the door. Kirsty was standing there. She raised her head. There was no-one there. The tongs fell with a clatter from her trembling hand. She bit her lip against the scream that rose. She got up and backed away from the door. Bran moved from her blind feet with a little yelp. "Oh, Bran! Bran!" She had forgotten the dog and now, stooping, fondled him with an erratic hand, her eyes on the door.

The dog twisted about her legs, licked her hand, and she told him to lie down. She spoke in a loud, reckless voice, filling the house with her voice, so that everything could hear it. When the dog had yelped, her eyes had blinded. In this way she got back a small measure of assurance. Now, she thought, with Bran it would be easy for her to go through the night to Shiela's. She would hold on to the dog.

She was trembling all over. The dog was no real company. If she went into the middle room and assured herself that Kirsty was not there, that the bed was empty and everything normal, she might be all right. It was her mind that was going to bits. She found, however, that she could not go into the room; and, with the shawl tied round her head, she found she could not go out into the night. She thought: This is madness! She had not been afraid even when Kirsty was lying dead in her room, not afraid in this way. She was losing her courage. She was becoming hysterical. She would move about exactly as if everything were normal; smoor the fire and go to bed.

She took off the shawl, hung it up, and went about the kitchen, tidying and putting things straight. Her body remained tremulous, felt very light, and presently she had to sit down. But she could not lift the tongs; had not the power to lift the tongs and smother the light.

What had gone wrong with her? "The years pass . . ." Ronnie's voice. Not death—but the death of the years. While you still have the years, everything is possible, everything can be encountered, even death. But with the years gone, with the years dead, all that was possible is past, and ahead, ahead in the lonely darkness, is Death.

She raised her head and all over the skin of her face ran

living pain. She pressed the back of her right hand fiercely against her mouth, and when she drew it away there was blood on it. She stared at the blood, as at a terrifying portent, for she did not know how strongly she had bitten her lip when the dog had yelped. This bright red occasionally affected her because of its colour link with the rowan berries. She now started to her feet, crying out, small strangled cries. Bran whined. She encountered her face in the little looking-glass, saw the blood on her lip, and realized she must have bitten it. But the face was dim in the glass and flickered, and she turned away from the eyes, quickly, as if someone had stood behind her. Mid-floor, tensely listening for she knew not what, she heard two faint footfalls outside. Even before Bran growled, she knew it was Roddie. He was coming back; he could not leave her as he had done! She stood unmoving, unbreathing. His fingers would tap at the window or tap at the door. Now . . . now. . . . He would be waiting, wondering, his hand ready; standing there, ready to tap. She felt the blind darkness of his body come against her face.

But no fingers tapped. A long time she stood, held by the presence outside. At last the thought was born: could he have gone? She went to the door and, holding her breath, listened. A small sigh from the night went past the door. She swung the bar and pulled the door open. "Who's there?" she asked. But no-one answered. "Go in, Bran," she said to the dog in a formal voice, closed the door on him, and stood outside. It was pitch dark. "Who's there?" she asked more loudly. She stepped along the house as far as the window, with a courage stronger than fear, a desperate courage. "Who's there?" she cried, but her voice was thin and high and would not carry far. For she had to control it.

There was a heavy stillness in the night; an absolute silence. A cold breath came on her face, damp and clammy; a faint sigh ran along the edge of the thatch. The night pressed her against the wall. She turned for the door and

tried to walk slowly, normally. But once inside, she banged
the door shut and hurt her finger-nails clawing for the bar
and swinging it into position; then leaned against the door
with her shoulder, with all her weight, breathing heavily.

As she came into the kitchen, Bran was waiting for her,
his head slightly lowered, his eyes gleaming with an un-
human intelligence, blue-green fires, lit from inside the
skull. As she stared at him, his tail moved slightly, but his
lowered head remained still, the eyes watching her.

From a recess in the wall, she took a tallow candle, lit it
at the fire, and, holding it before her breast, went towards
the middle room. As she pushed its door open, a cold
obliterating sensation crinkled her temples and ran down
her back and left side. The draught flickered the candle
flame and for a moment she saw nothing but swinging stab-
bing movements in the dark. Then the room settled and the
counterpane on the bed was as she had left it, drawn smooth
as sleep, passive as death, a waiting place for sleep and
death. By the foot of it was Kirsty's chest, a dark wooden
box, holding "the bonnie things" from her life on earth.
And holding—already—a few of Catrine's own.

Behind her Catrine drew the door shut quietly and
glanced up the dark passage towards the guest-room. But
there was no need to go there. In the kitchen, however, she
stood with the candle in her hand, staring over it, her lips
apart. She tried to think of the inside of the guest-room
clearly, but could only see the movement of dim figures,
several figures, bending over and whispering. She turned
and went up the passage, hesitated before the door and
cleared her throat, her flesh running icy cold. Then she
pushed the door open so that the candle flame hardly
flickered and entered. But as she entered, while the leaning
flame straightened, she thought she saw, over against the
farthest wall, the figure of Kirsty's father, standing quite
straight, with a look of remote yet infinite understanding in
his grey face. As the figure faded from the shape of things
hanging on the wall, a swooning sensation beset her. The

candle swayed, and when the hot drops of grease stung her hand, she screamed. The scream set her in a wild flurry and stopped her from falling. She got along the passage in a way that she never afterwards clearly remembered, and came back to herself lying on her own bed in the kitchen.

As her mind cleared, the omnipresence of terror lifted somewhat also, as if her visit to the two rooms had in some measure cleared the house of it. But she remained in so highly sensitive a state that if anything else happened, even a small thing, the sensitiveness would snap. She knew this, and told herself about it, trying to rally her dissolving spirit. For a long time she was conscious of this struggle going on inside her, and the temptation not to struggle, to let go, to give in, was at moments extremely strong. But she held on against this seductive desire to let dissolution have its way, and presently the wild wave receded, the tumult subsided, and she began to breathe with some ease in exhaustion.

Slowly upon her there came a mood of quietism, and she wondered if it was the old man she had actually seen or just the pattern of things on the wall. She had not been thinking about him at all. He would not do her any harm. He would only help her if he could. But she was afraid of him now, she did not want to see him, because he was dead.

So the living forgot and feared the dead. The thought touched her heart's sympathy and strengthened her a little. But it did not take away the fear.

It was extraordinary how Kirsty and her father had come to life in her mind and in the house as they had never done since their death. The years pass. . . .

The years pass. She saw them pass. Year after year after year. They took her with them. She was walking with them on the road, the road vanished, and there was Kirsty on the bed, dying as she had seen her die, with her dreams, the bonnie things, locked in the wooden chest by the bedside.

She was on Kirsty's road. . . . But she rebelled at the thought, and with that came a greater access of strength.

She was young. She felt so young. In her mind and her body she felt like a young girl. She was no older than Shiela, who was in the midst of life, a warm swarming life.

But self-pity would not come; neither self-pity nor tears. Her mind had travelled too far and seen too much. She was terribly exhausted. Her head fell over and she breathed in gusts. After a little time she sank into a fitful sleep, but towards the morning she slept heavily.

When she arose and dressed and looked out of the window at the sunlight on the grass, Catrine was conscious of an extreme relief and happiness. She smiled, remembering last night, believing it hardly possible that she could have worked herself up into such a state! She went into the middle room, where everything was quietly awaiting Finn's return. He would probably be home to-night. She suddenly longed for him. It would be fine to see him coming walking up, tall and slim, but getting broad-shouldered—and very good-looking! She would run out and link her arm in his. So long as she did not show any particular emotion, any real affection, it would be all right! She gave a small chuckle of a laugh. Up now she went to the guest-room. It was perfectly normal, too. Though it was always somehow a trifle solemn, with a sort of Sabbath air about it. Hardly troubling to glance at a certain spot on the farthest wall, she closed the door and shut the room away. The beasts were waiting for her, outside where the sun was shining. The ground mists were clearing. It was going to be another glorious day. She milked the cows and tethered them and fed the hens. When Bran and herself had something to eat, she would clean the byre, churn a bit of fresh butter, get everything clean and tidy, and, later on, do some herding down at the lower end. The corn was beginning to turn. She loved the harvest season. She did not even mind lifting potatoes to Finn's graip. And she would have all Finn's friends around; this was his home; they would have a spree, a real Harvest Home.

She was sitting by the burn at the lower end of the croft, knitting a strong pair of socks for Finn's seaboots, when she observed Roddie coming down by the Steep Wood. Without lifting her face, she saw him look towards her home and then, missing something, pause—until his eyes picked up the cattle—and herself. She gave him a gay wave. Slowly he approached the wall against which Finn had blown his trumpet in a dream. "Some of the boys have gone out in the small boat. If there's a bit of fish to spare, I'll remember you."

She thanked him, drawing near the wall, her eyes bright, her mouth red. He leaned on top of the wall, the slow characteristic smile clearing his face. "You don't look as if a night alone had disagreed with you."

"Don't I? What makes you think so?"

"You look so fresh."

"Thank you! I hope you had a good night yourself?"

"Not bad, considering."

"Considering what?"

"You would like to know, wouldn't you?"

"Not if you don't want to tell."

"Ah well, there are worse things than a good sleep. I see you are giving them an extra bite. They look pretty well, too."

"Yes, don't they? But then everything thrives on our croft!"

"Apparently. You'll miss young Barbara."

"I do indeed." And so they got talking in a natural friendly way about everyday affairs, until he said that he would have to hurry if he was going to be in time to catch the boat coming in.

Two hours later, the twilight falling, he appeared at the end of the house with a string of fish as she came out of the byre. "There's just one for you," he called, and, laying the catch on the grass, slipped a large codling off the string.

"Thank you very much. That's lovely. Won't you come in?"

"No thanks, Catrine; they're waiting for me at home."

"It's very good of you."

"It's nothing at all."

"I'm sure you would like a dram?"

He looked at her. "Well, now!" And he smiled back.

"Come on," she said gaily, and turned and went quickly into the house. He followed slowly, wiping his hands on a bunch of grass.

When she had poured him a stiff glass of special, he wished her the best of health and luck and drank half of it.

"Won't you sit down?"

"No, thanks. I'll have to be going."

"All right." She was very glad to have him in the house like this, with no difference or difficulty between them. She would hate Roddie to feel any restraint just because their relationship had taken a certain final turn. She had deliberately overcome his reluctance to enter in order to restore the old friendliness, and now she felt happy and completely unselfconscious.

Roddie sat down. "Faith, I'm tired being on my feet all day."

"That's right!" said Catrine brightly, and offered him a piece of crisp oatcake, as was the custom at such a moment. He took it and his lips curved away half-humorously from his even teeth. It was his most attractive expression.

She kept the talk going without any difficulty, and felt even a little excited at doing her hostess's duty so satisfactorily.

"So you weren't frightened?"

"Not I!" said she. "Though I confess my heart did miss a beat once."

"Did it? When?"

"Just before going to bed. I thought I heard footsteps round the house."

"Did you?" he said, and moved his head sideways with a curious half-mocking wonder; and all in a moment her ease left her.

She talked quickly and laughed. "Bran heard them, too, so I couldn't have imagined it."

"And what did you do?"

"Oh, I just waited and—and nothing happened."

"What did you think it was?" he asked, looking at his whisky.

"Must have been someone taking a short cut home, of course. Who else?"

He nodded. "I can understand that it would frighten you all the same." His voice was easy, but amused in its inscrutable way, and he looked at her.

She could not now meet his expression and busily bent down to place some peats against the bank of fire, talking as she did so and laughing. She was beginning to feel nervous.

"Had I thought you were frightened I might have come over and given you a call," he suggested.

"Not at all! Not at all! I wasn't frightened. It was just eerie a bit. You know?"

He was silent. A premonition of something about to happen, of a word and movement by Roddie that she could not cope with, overcame her, and she said blindly, brightly, "I'm expecting Finn any minute," and busily swept the ash back off the hearthstone. Then she had to look at him.

"Oh, are you?" He drank off the whisky. "In that case, I'd better be going."

"But there's no hurry."

"Thank you for the dram." He was on his feet, smiling. "It was good."

"But—but there's no hurry." She could not think of anything else to say and her brightness was now forced.

"You'll be wanting to get things ready for him," and he went unhurriedly out at the door, smiled, saluted her, and walked off.

She went back into the kitchen full of intense dismay. She could not read Roddie; she had no certainty about him. He had behaved normally, but—— She sat down, and in a little while her mind began to clear.

CATRINE AND RODDIE

It was Roddie who had walked past the house last night. There was suddenly no doubt about it. It was Roddie. She let her mind hearken to the footsteps again, let it hang on to them, because of the new terrible thought that was waiting to be faced.

"No!" she cried, before she faced it. It was nonsense! But certain little acts and attitudes of Finn towards Roddie, small intangible affairs mostly which she had put down to manhood's normal growth in her son, now became clear. Finn was jealous of Roddie; and Roddie was intolerant of Finn. Because of her!

Her heart began to beat in an extremely agitated way, accompanied by an emotion of outrage, such as had never before touched her; outrage and a strange burning shame, as if her body were being exposed. She could not get over it, could not think, got up and moved about with wide-open eyes, picked up the milk-pail and went to the byre.

She milked so erratically and nervously that Bel refused to let down her milk. For Catrine always hummed her a milking-croon, pulling the teats to its rhythm, when the beast stood in a half-swoon, loving the caressing luxury of it. Catrine tried to hum, but Bel was now out of humour. Catrine grew angry and slapped her on the haunch. Bel moved restlessly, whisked her tail into Catrine's face, and grew stubborn.

Her mind would not rest. It was the absurdity of the whole thing! she thought, getting the fish ready for Finn's supper. He should be coming soon, if he was coming at all. It was getting dark. What was keeping him! Perhaps he was staying another night. She had told him to stay, but he had said that wasn't at all likely, in that slightly sarcastic manner he now had at times.

When she had eaten some of the fish, drawn the slip of blind, tidied the hearth with its glowing bank of peat, and looked around the cosy home she had for Finn and herself, she felt much calmer. Indeed she was presently aware of a feeling of profound ease, of deep luxurious comfort. For she realized that she loved her son, loved him beyond anyone or anything else in the whole world, and he so cared for her that he was jealous of the intrusion even of Roddie, who had done so much for him and had meant so much to him. It was stupid; it was absurd; in some way it made her feel foolish; she was ashamed of it; but now, in this calm rich moment, waiting for Finn, she realized that, after all, it was the way life went, and it was no good crying against it; what she had to do was to put it right—and that should not be difficult! She would be able to reassure Finn without trouble. And already Roddie was standing off! In her wisdom she smiled, somewhat self-consciously, like a woman who had trafficked in thought with sin. She looked very attractive.

More than once, of course, she had contemplated the future with common sense and even a little misgiving. But in fact there was no sign of Finn's becoming attached to any girl. If Finn got married she would not want to be in the way, in the same house. But the only thing that Finn was thinking of marrying was a new boat! How secretly and strongly his mind ran on that—as it had once run on the trumpet! He thought she did not understand. She smiled to her knitting. But she had not gone far enough when she had recently told him that half the forty-one pounds was his. When he came home, she would hand him twenty sovereigns, make him take the money. If there was this folly between Roddie and himself, the sooner he had a boat of his own the better.

This thought pleased her so much that she got up, hunted out the old leather purse, and divided the contents, making his share twenty-one. She would present them to him in the purse. It was nearly enough to buy a boat in itself, and he had a few pounds of his own stowed away. Once he had given the order to have the boat built, he would become a grown man and the real head of the house. How sweet it would be to mother Finn through years. Years, anyway.

CATRINE AND RODDIE

She felt the rich flow of life in her flesh. Lately her body
had had this deep warm feeling of well-being very strongly.
Her skin had the fairness that holds light. Her hair was fair.
In the peat fire, her brown eyes looked black and gleamed
with lights. She sat with an easy poise, not quite upright,
her back curving over into the firm pale nape of the neck,
her face lifting and sometimes glancing about the kitchen
as she withdrew a needle to start a new row. She looked
like a woman whose mind is made up, who is content, because she is waiting for her lover. There was that faint,
expectant, almost wanton air about her.

But Finn did not come that night.

Next day she knew he would come, and set about her
ordinary tasks in special preparation for his arrival. If
Roddie moved in her mind, it was as a rather ominous force
far in its hinterland, and she did not mind him. Why should
she?

In the late afternoon, she went several times down to the
edge of the brae to see if Finn was coming. He had probably been held up on the way by Callum or others, anxious
for the Helmsdale news. Finn was a favourite with the
regular fishermen, and none of them had any great idea of
time. She forgave him, feeling happy that he should be so
well liked.

With the evening at hand, she thought: I'll get the cows
in and have the milking over. And immediately she became
very busy, her feet light as they had been in her twenties.

Bel, whom she always milked last, stood with her eyes
shining, in a dumb ecstasy, listening to Catrine's voice
keeping time with the old Gaelic air as her gentle hands
firmly and rhythmically drew the milk dancing into the
pail.

She was at the long last squeezing strokes, the melody
slowing up, dying, when a footfall at the door fell like a
blow on her heart. She glanced sideways and saw Roddie,
his face shadowed from the dim evening light behind him.

"Hullo!" he said, in a smiling but husky voice.

She could not speak, pressed her forehead against Bel's hide, drew on the empty teats, then said, "Now!" and got up, the milk-pail in one hand, the little three-legged stool in the other, and turned to Roddie, deathly pale but smiling. "Hullo!"

"Finished your milking?"

"Yes."

He did not give way and she stood before him, knowing that the awful moment of decision had come at last. He bent down to take the pail and stool from her; but she hung on to them, saying, "No! no! It's all right."

Gently but firmly he took them from her and set them down to one side.

"Roddie, no!" she said, feeling the dark force of his body coming at her, pleading wildly out of the weakness that was melting her flesh.

"Yes," said Roddie, enfolding her. "Yes, Catrine." His voice was laughing-gentle, thick with breath, terrible. In the crush of his arms, she felt herself fainting, and lifted her hands and gripped him behind the neck.

The strength of her body, that for these last few days had played such strange pranks with her thought, now completely deserted her, and she hung limp in his arms, her mind blinded. He carried her over to the stall with the straw, where Finn had been born.

CHAPTER XXII

FINN DENIES HIS MOTHER

{*}

Finn would have arrived at the byre a little before Roddie had he not been deflected from the river path by a sudden desire to cross over the knoll of the House of Peace. He had always been slightly ashamed of the impious visit under the influence of drink, and to-night, because he was feeling so happy after his highly successful Dale trip (the drover had been there the second night, and asked, "Are the days of Finn MacCoul coming back upon us?") he wanted to be at peace with the world, even the other world. To have shouted "Come forth!" would have been such bad manners. The thought of it more than once had made his sensitiveness wriggle. But he had not shouted it, and he was convinced now that it was not fear altogether that had kept him silent, but consideration for the figure he had once imagined there.

In the usual spot, by the little flat stone circle, he sat down and looked about him. The natural tiredness of the body after the long walk disposed him to pleasant ease. And, besides, there was this odd feeling of fulfilment in the simple fact of being back home. Here was a difference not merely in the stones and the trees and the shape of the ground but in some influence that came out of them, old and friendly and known. At no hour was this experienced so much as at the approach of the twilight, when a tenuous darkness came into the light and made grey rock or autumn-tinted leaves glow faintly as from an inner radiance. The robin's song was full of impersonal reflection. Above the rising broken rocks across the little gully, a rowan-tree hung with its load of brilliant berries. From his pocket he took and examined the sprig he had brought with him from Kildonan. The tiny stems had gone soft, but the berries themselves had not wilted. It was a curious present to bring back to his mother. He smiled but put the berries carefully back in his pocket, seeing Ronnie's point now. They were quite valueless, and it seemed to him amusing that they yet could convey something. But they did, and he would produce them with a smile. Precisely how? Would he mention Ronnie? No. In an offhand way, as if he were discovering them in his pocket. . . .

He got up, went down through the birches, and walked across the little field. He had not let the "Come forth!" incident even enter his mind, but he now knew that it was washed out—as if one existed here not in words or even in silent thoughts but in states of mind. Not that he worked it out clearly, or worked it out at all. The mind was in a new condition and the eyes glimmered.

The two long pools, the Steep Wood, the wall that his trumpet had shattered, and now the rising slopes, the roof, his home. His heart began to beat. His mother would come rushing out. It's a wonder she wasn't on the watch! How unsuspecting the house was of his near presence! He would approach quietly. There was Bran—ah, now he had seen him. Bark! bark! They met at the byre door, and he spoke in a loud voice which his mother could hear in the kitchen. She couldn't be in. And she wasn't. The kitchen was empty. At once he turned out again—and there were Roddie and herself at the byre door.

In a very short moment of time Finn's mind was invaded by a shattering tale of action that had had a beginning, a middle, and now an end. Their faces, looking towards him, their arrested bodies, cried the story aloud in that small moment. And when, above it, his mother cried "Finn!" and came towards him carrying the milk-pail, with an exaggerated eagerness, a hurrying trepidation, he stood still, his mind scattered, smiling awkwardly.

Roddie slowly followed her.

"Oh, Finn, how are you?" she cried, her eyes glancing. She looked confused, but eager for him. He had taken her at a disadvantage but—but—that was all, was what her manner was crying out. "You must be famishing. Come away in and get some food," and she made to bustle in at the door. But Roddie was still there.

"Perhaps," said Roddie, "I'd better be getting home. You had a good trip?"

"Yes," answered Finn, not looking at him.

"Come away in," Catrine cried eagerly to Finn, cutting Roddie away from them.

"Don't you think——" began Roddie; but she interrupted him, as though she had not heard him, crying over her shoulder, "We'll be seeing you soon."

Finn followed her and, after standing a moment, Roddie walked away.

In the kitchen, she bustled about, getting food ready. "I've been watching for you ever since last night." She talked without looking at Finn as she hurried, talked quickly. "And how are they all?"

"They're all right."

"And had you a good time?"

"Yes."

"I missed you this time a lot. The house felt quite empty. For the two nights I could hardly sleep. I was frightened!" Her hurried voice was laughing. "No-one came near me until Roddie looked in at the milking to-night."

"What did Roddie want to say?"

"When?"

"Just now, when you stopped him."

"Want to say?" She stood and glanced at him, as if hitherto unaware of his cold peculiar manner. "I didn't notice he wanted to say anything."

"You know he did."

"Finn, what do you mean?"

"Oh, nothing," he said.

"You must mean something. I don't think that's right."
She was bustling about again. "I don't know what's come
between you and Roddie. But—but—you make me feel
awkward. And I was so looking forward to you coming
home." Her voice had risen in distress.

He did not speak, but stood staring at the patch of window, with a gloomy mocking expression on his face.
Through her distress, she glanced at him acutely.

But Finn could not help himself. His brain felt dull as if it
had been struck a heavy blow. What he wanted to do was
to walk out and leave her. She was acting, lying, trying to
get round him, to smooth things over. Something had happened. She was hiding it. She was all strung up. Why had
they taken so long to come to the byre door?

"Here's your supper." Her voice was calmer. He felt the
quiet desperation in it. The blame was falling on him. He
did not want his supper. If he would not speak to her, she
would not speak to him now. This could not be borne. He
stirred, putting his hands negligently in his pockets. The
right hand pulled forth the sprig of rowan-berries from
Kildonan. He regarded them on his palm with a slow sarcasm, then pitched them towards the fire, but with a physical indifference that let them fall short, an indifference that
yet had in it an odd perversity, as though he would not
quite destroy them, but must let them be seen.

He was aware, too, that his mother was watching him,
for there had come an extraordinary stillness upon the
kitchen. But he could not turn and look at her now. All at
once an element of fear touched him and he swung round.
Her eyes were on the berries, her face death-pale, her lips
apart, her fingers against her breast like claws. She collapsed so suddenly that she fell her length before he could
stir a foot to save her. She hit the floor with a solid thump,
and lay with the crown of her head a couple of inches from
the sharp edge of the hearthstone.

Finn had never seen anyone faint before, and now got into a state of extreme anxiety. "Mother! Mother!" he cried sharply, on his knees beside her, shaking her. He touched her face. It was death-cold. She had stopped breathing. When he lifted her head and shoulders against him, the head rolled away and the arms slumped. Was she dead?

"Here, Mother!" he cried into her face. He did not know what to do. He could not leave her and run for a neighbour. His voice broke. He gathered her up against his breast. Would he try to lift her into bed? "Mother! Speak to me!" O God, what would he do? As, beside himself, he began to lift her, getting to his feet, her soft body slid heavily down through his arms. He felt he was choking her and laid her out on her back. Rob had once told a story of how cold water . . . Before the memory was right born, he dashed for the bucket. His intention was to sprinkle it, but from his cupped hands the cold well water fell in a splash on her face and trickled down her neck. He had done it badly! But as he hung in desperation, he saw her eyelids flicker. Quite suddenly her eyes opened, and stared, and glanced from side to side. She did not know where she was, and in a moment was in a flurry of terror, as if she were being attacked. He tried to soothe her crying, "It's all right! It's all right, Mother!"

She grew calmer. "I must have fainted," she said.

"Yes. Come, and I'll help you into bed."

"Wait a minute. I feel strange." Her smile came strangely. "Did I give you a fright?"

"You did indeed! But look, it will be softer for you in bed."

Slowly her face turned to the fire. Yes, the berries were there. She began to tremble. Finn put his hands under her armpits and would no longer be denied. His right arm round her waist, he guided her to the bed and heaved her legs in. "Now! You just rest and you'll be all right," he said comfortingly.

She lay on her back and closed her eyes.

"I'll tell you what," he said brightly. "I'll go for Shiela. You'll be all right until——"

Her scared expression stopped him, and he at once assured her he would not go away, but would get her a hot drink.

"Don't tell anyone," she implored him in an exhausted voice.

"No, no!"

"Where—where did you get the rowan-berries?"

"I got them in Kildonan. I—I thought you might like to have them from there."

"Finn."

"Yes." He lowered his head towards her weak voice.

"Please leave me for a little."

"Yes, Mother," he said at once. "Try and get a little sleep."

But before leaving the kitchen, he picked up the berries. It was now getting quite dark outside. A surging passion of affection for his mother moved in him. Her death-pallor, her helplessness, had wrung his heart. A profound feeling of responsibility, transcending every other consideration, walked with him. He did not want to be seen; he wanted to hide what had happened from all prying human eyes; and crossing the pasture lands above and to the back of the house, he came among the bushes where his mother used to play hide-and-seek with him when he was a little boy. Down below, the small pools of the burn were grey from the last of the light in the sky.

For a little time he lay without thought, moved only by emotion for his mother. Gradually, however, his mind darkened with the foreshadow of thought. He felt it coming, and began to breathe more quickly. It came in the shape of Roddie, at whom he would not look. But though he avoided looking, because the conflict would be too destructive even inside his own mind, he still apprehended the coming. And now an odd limitation of vision beset him. There was no need for the body to have a head. Headless, it drew near him, dark-clothed, physically rank, imminent, awful, abominable, and in a paroxysm of revulsion and hatred, he slashed and destroyed it.

When the paroxysm had passed, he found his hands smeared with the crushed berries. He wiped away the sticky red stuff on the grass and then, moved by fear lest his mother came upon the crushed mess, he hid it under a bush and covered it up.

After that his expression grew cunning and full of a bitter mockery. But he could not think. Everything stopped on the edge of thought, of apprehension. For he could not penetrate beyond the vision of Roddie and his mother at the byre door. Some ultimate loyalty to the thought of his mother would not let him penetrate.

By the time he went back to the house, he was tired, and weary of his own mind. His mother was up and greeted him quietly. "You must be very hungry."

"No, not very," he replied in an indifferent voice.

"Sit in." She placed his chair.

Presently, she referred to the folk in Dale.

"They are all well," he answered. "They were asking for you."

"Were they?"

"Yes." He knew she wanted details, wanted him to talk. The food was sticking in his throat.

"How is Granny?"

"Fine."

"And Isebeal?"

"Quite well. I spent the evening there last night."

"Did you? Were there many in?"

"Yes. The house was full."

"Did you enjoy it?"

"Yes; it was all right."

She did not encroach on him; did not press him. She seemed pleased with the few crumbs of talk.

"I'm feeling tired." He pushed his chair back. "I think I'll go to bed. We were late last night."

"All right, then."

Once behind his own door, he stood stock still, wishing he could have said something natural and kindly to his mother. But it had been beyond him. He sat down on Kirsty's chest and began to breathe heavily, as if he could not get enough clean air. His hands were shaking, his chest was restricted, he was beset by an impending darkness of guilt and horror.

Next day, Finn and his mother had a quietened attitude to each other, and went about their tasks in a fatalistic manner. Folk behaved so after or before a death—but not with this underlying consciousness of estrangement, of secretiveness. There was a feeling of waiting, of watching, that soon would become intolerable.

Catrine, however, hung on to the mood, playing for time. She must keep Roddie and Finn apart, and allowed this to become an obsession, obscuring her own personal problem, keeping it under, where she need not see it. All day she was in terror lest Roddie appear, and made work in places where she could command his approach.

At their midday meal, they spoke little to each other, but reasonably. Catrine said she would do some herding in the afternoon down by the burn, and Finn thought he would go along to see Henry. They were glad to get away from each other, from the strain of being calm and reasonable.

When Finn disappeared, Catrine lay beside a whin bush and closed her eyes. She would have these few minutes to herself. Blessed minutes, they lapped her about from the grass and the heather, from the spaces beyond men. They came pressing upon her in a soft darkening, pressing on her eyeballs through the lids. When Roddie awoke her, she grew agitated and confused and glanced about half-terri-fied, pulling her clothes straight.

"Who are you frightened of?" he asked, with that faint humour that could come into his steady eyes.

"I fell asleep," she answered, flushed in astonishment.

"Didn't you sleep well last night?"

"Not very." She hadn't slept a wink.

"Anything wrong?"

"No oh no." She was restless, ill at ease in his company, as if she wanted him gone.

"Was Finn a bit difficult?"

She kept looking away. Lack of sleep and involved torturing indecisions made her eyes brilliant, her fair skin very delicate. She bit her lip.

"Catrine," he said gently, sitting down, "you must tell me." He was deeply moved by the vivid troubling spirit of life in her.

"I am afraid of Finn," she said, swallowing.

"How afraid?"

She looked down at her restless hand plucking the grass. "I don't want you—I want you to keep clear of him. If there was any trouble between you—it would kill me."

"But why should there be any trouble?"

"He's young. I'm his mother. Oh, Roddie, promise me!" And she looked swiftly at him.

"All right, Catrine. I won't cause any trouble."

"Yes, but—do you understand?" She searched his eyes with a feverish penetration.

"Yes, I understand. Don't worry about that." Into his voice had come a cool amusement.

"I don't want you near the house for—for a little time."

"You're wrong. It would be better to get it over. I'll speak to him myself."

"No, no; you mustn't! Promise me!"

"Oh, all right. I don't mind." His smile was hardening. "So I'm not to come near the house?"

She could not speak.

"Don't you want me to come?"

"I don't think I do!" she cried, and suddenly buried her face in the grass.

"That's bad," said Roddie thoughtfully. "You're upset, I'm afraid. However, there's one thing you needn't be frightened of. I have too great a respect for you ever to do anything to Finn. You can keep your mind easy on that score."

"Oh, I'm glad!" she muttered, and, after she had wiped her eyes, sat up again, deeply confused but brighter and happier than she had yet appeared.

"He's a lot in your mind, I can see," said Roddie.

"It's—it's difficult to tell you."

"You needn't," said Roddie. "I was on my way to the shore when I saw you lying here, so I thought I'd waken you up for fun. But I must be off." There was now a penetrating coolness in his light pleasant tone. "I may see you sometime, then. So long!" And he walked off.

Catrine sat quite still for a little while, then suddenly shivered.

She had wanted to cry to Roddie, to get up and call him back so that he would understand, but had been unable to stir a hand. Roddie could not discuss and recriminate. In the pleasantness of his tone had been a bitter anger.

A feeling of intense shame came upon her, of awful, of obliterating shame. Visions would come back. She crushed them into the grass. Everything was wrong. Life was ugly and miserable. She had been so happy with Finn alone.

But behind this emotion her mind was gathering its cunning, which knew neither shame nor bitterness, only the real knowledge of life as it was, of the day as it came. And for the first time she felt in touch with Roddie's inner mind, with the pride that would stand provocation and not break. She admired it—and was glad to take advantage of it, to save Finn.

When the folk had cured their supply of herring for home use through winter and spring, the next excitement was the appearance of schooners to carry the thousands of barrels to the foreign market, mostly the Baltic. They were vessels of about a hundred tons burden, and the sight of one of them anchored in the bay made a truant of every adventurous boy.

Transporting the barrels in the local boats from the beach to the schooner's side was a merry job, and Finn had lads of his own age with whom to raise a laugh or crack a joke. Occasionally, too, a schooner was well-found in brandy, and brandy was a novelty. When Rob rubbed his beard and admitted judiciously, "Yes, it was a good drop," and then, on walking away, side-stepped, Callum and Finn rocked with laugher.

"By God, you're drunk, Rob. What'll your sister say to you when you get home?"

"Me drunk?" inquired Rob, turning upon Callum with slow care. "It would take more than that to-to-to make me turn a hair."

"It's not your hair, Rob; it's your feet."

Rob looked down at his feet.

Callum and Finn swayed.

"I know you," said Rob, offended. "You think you're a wh-whale of a fellow. Both of you think you're wh-wh-whales. But I could tell a different story." He nodded and walked on with a serious air.

Finn could hardly tear himself away from the beach. Because he hated going home, he hung about avid for any amusement or hilarity. Sometimes he grew quite reckless, and was the leader in any ploy where brandy was concerned. He reckoned he knew something about brandy! Three other lads and himself did a bit of secret trading at night, and succeeded in concealing on shore a gallon of fiery cognac.

The sea was his element. "The sea is our salvation," said George.

"Our worldly salvation," corrected Finn solemnly.

"It'll be the only salvation most of you young devils will ever know unless you mend your ways," retorted George.

"I doubt if it can last," said one man in a dubious tone.

"Last!" exclaimed George. "I've just had the figures

489

from the Fishery officer, for this parish alone, although it's not all in his *jurisdiction*."

That was a cracker of an English word! Their eyes gleamed.

"What figures?"

"The figures for the season just ended. We had 73 boats fishing out of here. We had 94 boats out of Lybster, 30 boats out of Forse, we had 49 boats out of Clyth and 15 out of East Clyth. Altogether we had 305 boats for this parish coast alone. What do you think of that? We had 1,257 fishermen actively engaged; we had about 900 women, and 160 labourers of one kind or another."

"You wouldn't count the coopers?"

"And," continued George, "we had 99 coopers—the only skilled men in the whole business for without them there would be no business at all. A total of 2,400 persons —not counting the 45 fishcurers."

"Why don't you count them?"

"Altogether there was cured about 40,000 barrels of herring—and that doesn't include the 3,000 barrels that must have been cured by all of us for our own use nor the hundreds of barrels that were sold fresh. The average price of the cran here was nine shillings, and the price of the cured barrel was one pound."

"But what price did the curer get when he sold abroad?"

"That's his business. Do you grudge it to him?"

"No, och no. We only want to know."

"And what do you want to know for?" demanded George.

"Just to make sure that the poor man was not out of pocket."

"Some of you are not worth talking to, upon my word," cried George against their laughter. "You cannot understand the bigness of what's happening before your eyes. Even if the curer got two or three pounds a barrel—what would that mean? It would mean that from the coast of this poverty-ridden parish, with its calfie or its stirkie—its calfie or its stirkie," he repeated derisively, "it would mean that there has been exported—*exported*, do you understand?" he boomed, "about £100,000 worth of fish. About £100,000!"

It was an astonishing figure. Its size warmed them. They felt friendly to George. Thier eyes travelled out to sea, while they moved restlessly, prepared for more wonder of the kind. But George now seemed to be on his high horse.

"Ay, but will it last?" asked the man, who had asked it before. He was a small round-shouldered man, inclining to pessimism, with a large wife and a large family of daughters.

"By the look of things, it will last as long as you whatever," retorted George. There was a smile all round at this thrust, for they wanted a large optimism, not the crofter's niggardly fear.

"You cannot tell that."

"Can't I?" said George. "Believe me, I can tell you a few more things besides. What goes on in your own house through the winter and spring? Do your family spin hemp and make nets or do they not? And if they do, is it found money?"

"I'm not denying that. I never said——"

"No, you wouldn't. And yours is not the only family nor score of families. What do I do myself, and the whole squad of coopers on the station from now on? We make barrels— and get paid for it. All the thousands of barrels we need are made on this same strip of coast. Last! Will it last? Huh!" barked George. "You can take it from me—it will last as long as we have the spirit to make it last. The spirit!"

A droll voice made the inevitable reference to spirit in a bottle and the pleasant fun increased.

Finn always felt invigorated by George. The sight of the sea brought him out of himself. He did not want to think of his mother and Roddie. He hated to think of them. Going back home was like retreating into a dark silent hole.

So he recounted George's talk to Henry. "They're want-ing a deck hand on the schooner," he added lightly.

Henry looked at him. "Thinking of going?" he asked in a quizzing tone.

"You would never think of going, Finn? Surely not!" exclaimed Henry's wife, with a touch of dismay.

Finn had become very friendly with Henry lately, finding relief in his dry satiric manner and the real ability and generosity underneath it. Henry had three children, with another not far off, and the second boy, Andrew, was Finn's favourite. His wife was fond of company and Finn could be so gay that he seemed not to have a care in the world. She was always glad to see him about the house.

"Why not?" Finn smiled at her. "It would be fine to see a bit of the world. I would like to go up the Baltic."

"You're not serious?"

"I am—unless Henry here falls in with my plans for the cod-fishing."

"Oh, you and your schemes!" she cried, relieved. "Henry is worse than yourself, I do declare." She laughed.

And so, in good humour, Finn started out for home. But as he approached the Steep Wood in the gathering dusk, the usual nervous tremoring began to affect him.

It was now nearly a fortnight since the incident that had estranged his mother and himself. For a few days she had left him alone, and he could see she was hoping that time would heal the difference between them. But something was hidden in her mind, something more than the resigna-tion the difficulty demanded, an inner troubling, and now and then she did not seem to care whether he spoke or not.

Sometimes his heart cried out to her, but in a moment there would follow a relentless feeling, a deliberate vindic-tive pleasure in the thought that she was being hurt. It usually eased the stress on the knot in his mind, but left his mouth bitter.

What he really feared as he came by the Steep Wood was that he might meet Roddie, or might meet both Roddie and his mother in some moment of secret communion, and he did not know how he himself would behave. There was that occasion in the public house in Stornoway when he had lost his head. He did not care to remember its hysteric weakness.

These last few days, too, a change had come over his mother. Her preoccupation with herself had increased. Instead of the gradual re-establishment of the old relationship, there was suddenly a deepening of the existing trouble. He had seen this in Roddie too; a gathering of him inwardly into a relentless strength.

As he came up to the dry-stone wall, he heard his mother's voice cry out, beyond, amid the salleys by the stream. It was a strange, sharp, heart-wrung cry. Roddie's head and back appeared. He had Catrine in his arms, bearing her lightly, and he was laughing.

Over Roddie's shoulder, Catrine saw Finn. She was borne several steps in Roddie's triumph, before she could cry to him to let her down. She struggled violently. "It's Finn." He set her on her feet and turned round.

Finn was standing motionless behind the wall, his face white. There must have been something uncanny about his head and shoulders, of the nature of an apparition, to Catrine, for her voice, breaking in distress, emitted half-whining sounds.

"All right," said Roddie coolly. "We'll tell him now."

Finn's face turned away, and in a few steps his head sank below the top of the wall, and he was walking down the burnside. Roddie's voice cried to him sharply, but he did not rightly hear it and continued on his way.

In a wood of small birches, he lay until it was quite dark. Occasional spasms of violence forced his fingers into the earth and contorted his body, but they were formless and without any conscious cause. For the most part he lay in a quiescent state, and more than once a queer ultimate sensation of solitariness touched him.

In the star-lit darkness, he could walk anywhere without

fear of being met, for most people were afraid of what might be encountered in the dark.

There were two ceilidh-houses where folk gathered at night. Outside one of them, Finn listened to the singing of a traditional song, until he could no longer bear it. Then he drifted away. At various places he appeared, and had anyone seen him drifting away voiceless they would have said it was his wraith. Out of the moor, miles distant, he came down on Una's house and from a hundred paces stood looking at the glimmer of light in its little window.

He went up to the window on quiet feet. The slip of blind had not been drawn, for busy folk used all the daylight they could get, and in the slow change to the peat light would sometimes forget the blind altogether. There was a young woman with her back to him, sitting on a small stool just beyond the fire, making a net. Her right hand was extremely dexterous and the white bone needle flew out and in. The mother was spinning and humming. Duncan, Una's brother, was helping his father to make a heather rope. There were others, but Finn could not take his eyes off this stranger, this dark young woman with her hair up. All at once, she turned her head over her shoulder and looked at the window. It was Una. He saw her eyes open, her expression grow rigid in terror, and at once he tip-toed away. A dog barked.

Surely she could not have seen him! But he knew by her expression that she had seen something.

When a young woman hears her name called from outside at night and no-one else hears it—and there is no-one outside—it is a sign of her near death.

But he had not called her name. She would think it was his wraith!

From the land, he turned at last to the sea and appeared among the looming bows of the boats drawn up over the ridge of the beach. He leaned against one of them for a while, then, going down into the mouth of the river, unfastened a small boat, slid her as noiselessly as he could into the water, and began to row out towards the schooner.

When he drew quite near, the man on watch cried, "Hullo, there!"

"Hullo," answered Finn.

"Who is it?"

"It's me. I heard——"

"Who are ye?"

"I'm a fisherman. I heard you were wanting a sailor."

"Oh, is that it? Well, ye're too late, my lad. A young fellow signed on this evening."

Finn sat quite still. The man spoke again, but he did not answer.

"Hullo down there?"

"Hullo," answered Finn. "You don't want anybody then?"

"No. Ye're a bit slow, my lad."

"Thank you," said Finn, and he rowed away.

The small boat was old and heavy and altogether beyond Finn's power to haul up the steep slope. He hunted about for wooden rollers and when he had got her three-quarters out of the water he fastened her short painter to a boulder. The tide was making but had still some three hours to flow. After he had stood for a while in the windless night by the sea, he began to shiver with the cold, and, going up among the boats, climbed into one and huddled up on the planking between two timbers.

That the schooner had been unable to take him deepened his misery, but somehow now he did not greatly care and closed his eyes in a weariness beyond thought. Every now and then, however, he found himself regarding figures with an extreme clarity. His mother's heavy elderly body—so it struck him—in Roddie's arms, with Roddie's laugh, the laugh that could harden into a cackle, like a gull's, the whole action had for him elements of the obscene. The revulsion blotted out the picture. Una did not trouble him much. She was Jim's "armful". Obscene enough, too.

Suddenly there were footsteps and low voices—of two men, who came and stood on the other side of the planking. They talked for half an hour and revealed to Finn a harrowing story of secret family trouble. Finn knew the family, and wouldn't have believed the story possible. "For God's sake, never by word or look . . ." The footsteps died away.

After a time, Finn went to the small boat and found her afloat and wet his arms to the shoulders getting the painter off the boulder. When at last the tide was full in and he had made her fast, he turned for home. As he approached the house, the old trepidation beset him, but now his mother would be in bed for it must be three o'clock. All at once he stood still, unable to move, for he imagined Roddie and his mother sitting by the fire, waiting for him. It was an extremely strong visualization, and may have been prompted by an instinctive knowledge of how Roddie would act. And indeed Catrine had had great difficulty some hours before in getting Roddie to see the wisdom of his going home. Finn approached the blinded window quietly and listened. The fire was not smoored and there were no voices. The silence affected him in an appalling way, and he had the desperate sensation of pushing noisily against it, slowly, in at the door, and into the kitchen.

His mother rose from her stool and saw him glance about the kitchen.

"You're late," she said quietly.

"Am I?"

"Would you like something?"

He did not look at her and turned for his own room.

"Finn!"

He stopped.

"This can't go on," she said. "I can't——" She had meant to be calm, but now her voice had suddenly risen and threatened to break.

"Good night."

"Finn! You must listen to me. You must. I—I have something to tell you. We can't go on like this."

"What is it?" He half-turned his head but did not look at her.

"Why are you—why do you make it so difficult? Cannot you understand——"

"What is it?"

There was a moment's silence. Then she said, "Roddie and I are going to get married."

There was a further and complete silence.

"Finn," she said appealingly, desperately, "why are you against me? If you are to be against me, life will be unbearable." Her voice went on, suddenly released, and then abruptly stopped, as if she were on the verge of a breakdown and a storm of tears.

"It's got nothing to do with me what you do," he said, and walked away into his room and shut the door.

She could weep herself to death for all he cared. He did not even listen. "I don't give a damn," he muttered, and pulled the blankets around him. If she came to the door, he would drive her out—as Alan had driven his sister. She did not come to his door, however, and when at last he had to listen he heard a silence intense and desolate.

CHAPTER XXIII

THE WRECK

❧

Roddie and Catrine were married within a month. The wedding was popular and exceptionally gay, for Roddie was looked upon as the leader of the herring fishers and his old saying that he had "wedded the sea" was used against him with sly fun. In fact the best of it was that Roddie, who normally had a reserve one did not intrude upon wantonly, now seemed open to any attack, so delighted with himself did he appear to be. And his pride in Catrine was no less obvious than his happiness. It was he himself who said, "There's no fool like an old fool," with the smile curling from his teeth. And no-one thought him old, not even the young, because of his great strength and fabulous fighting powers.

The wedding took place after the grain had been harvested and, with everyone free and in the mood for merriment, it lasted several days. Roddie's house was open to all Dunster and a large party came from Dale. They danced in the barn, they danced in the kitchen, and the Dale folk slept in the barn, together with others who were not in the mood to go home, men on one side and women on the other, upon new straw. The presents of dressed fowls, butter, cheese, eggs, bannocks and other foods were sufficient to support a small army. Hendry sent twenty bottles of "special", and old Wull, the smuggler, brought a two-gallon cask of his finest "run". Roddie was now reckoned to have "a good bit of money behind him". And if he had, they added, he knew how to spend it.

THE WRECK

"This is a real wedding," declared Wull, his eyes lit up at the merry sounds and the whirl of the young bodies.

"How do you make that out?" asked an elderly solemn and argumentative man.

"Because", said Wull, "I hold that a wedding is a public affair. They should be married not only in the sight of Him above, but also in the sight of us below. And when I say married, I mean married."

The solemn man nodded. "I think I see what you mean."

"How do you see it?" asked Wull.

"And then we know and it's settled for good," nodded the solemn man, following his own thought. "Quite so. At the same time——"

Wull laughed. "You're drunk," he said.

"What's that?"

Wull gave his neighbour a dig with his elbow and cried to the solemn man, "You're drunk. You're as full as the Baltic."

They all laughed.

"Me drunk? I'm not in the least drunk."

"Can you stand on one leg?"

"Yes, and on two legs."

"Ay, but can you stand on one?"

"Why couldn't I?"

"Ay, but can you? Let's see you try."

The solemn man paused to think this out, as there might be a catch in it somewhere. He was only sixty and regarded Wull as a wily old fellow who was worth the watching. He did not mind standing on one leg, which he knew he could do easily, but if so, then Wull would have to stand also. Only thus could he be sure of getting the better of Wull. But in the contest his one leg proved less biddable than usual and he was getting ready for a second effort when Wull overbalanced against him. They continued the argument on the floor. "You pushed me," alleged the solemn man.

This little incident was used as a text by Sandy Ware. But no-one bothered about Sandy at the wedding. A dry harvest was gathered in. The fishing had been good. The long winter nights were before them. And here was a wedding, wherein the happiness of their lives was gathered in warmth, with creation beyond it.

"Why don't you give Una a dance?" Meg asked Finn.

"Why should I? Isn't she getting plenty?"

"Yes. But you might give her one."

"Do you think she would like it?"

"I'm sure she would."

"She'll be feeling lonely now that Boots has gone back to Wick? Very hard on her."

"Hard on my granny!" said Meg.

Finn laughed. "It's difficult to get near her—there's such a run on her." He added, "There's the same run on yourself—but that's different," and he gripped her firmly. "How's Donnie doing?"

"I can't make you out," said Meg.

"That's pretty cool—seeing all the chance you give me."

In the whirl and intermingling of the fast set dances there was little opportunity for talk. Twice Finn went to take Una up, but was forestalled by quicker feet. He did not try again.

Once he heard Una sing, for all the company contributed to the evening's entertainment in song or chorus. A remark by Wull stuck in his mind, worrying him: "She has the richness of the blackbird." He was sorry he had heard her.

It was a great relief to him when the wedding was over and he had no longer to argue himself each evening out of secret rebellions, and appear among the company, laughing and prepared to take part for appearance's sake. He was now completely detached from his mother and Roddie; felt he had no interest in them, never wanted to have anything more to do with them, had for them a cold distaste.

In this last month he was conscious of having aged a lot. He was barely twenty, but it was as if the very flesh on his bones had lost its softness and drawn taut and sinewy. There was a similar change in his mind, and where formerly he would have been deeply moved to sympathy or emotion he now could harden his eyes and know only an impulse of intolerance.

Barbara and her mother remained with him for a fortnight and then an aunt, a widowed woman of over fifty, came to stay and help him run the croft. Her husband had been drowned on the Guillaim off Cromarty and her son and daughter were both married. Elspet was a medium-sized woman, with grey hair and a slight stoop of the shoulders from being perpetually busy. She had by nature a pleasant disposition and was an excellent housekeeper.

At first Finn had refused to take the croft from Catrine. Roddie's mother had died some years before, but his father was still alive. Finn derisively understood Roddie's pride. He had not married Catrine for her croft! He was taking her to his own croft, his own home, and Catrine would look after his father as was the custom in such a situation.

Finn had told his mother they could have this croft, too, for all he cared. His mother had produced the purse of twenty-one sovereigns. Finn had refused it. She had dropped it on the table. "It's yours, not mine."

"I don't want it."

"I can't help that," said his mother calmly.

The money lay there for nearly a day.

"I don't want this money," he said angrily, shoving it aside.

"You can put it in the fire, for all I care," she answered.

He returned late that night, and in the light of the morning saw the purse with the money on the shelf by his bed.

Night after night he kept away from the house, but from the moment his mother had said she was to marry Roddie a steadying sense of finality had come upon his mind. At first the general greeting: "I hear you're getting a new father, Finn!" had been bitter as gall, and if his laugh had been awkward, well, folk realized it was an odd joke for Finn right enough! What grown son or daughter liked a mother to get married? Naturally they couldn't see the

force of it! But Finn had played up well enough and now it
was all over.

There had come a decisive turning point at a critical
moment when Finn had all but made up his mind to clear
out of Dunster and might readily enough, in a chance encounter with Roddie, have fatally lost his head. It came in
the form of a question. There was Kirsty's money; there
was the croft. It was one of the best crofts in a district
where the smallest plots of land were coveted. For the
population had greatly increased since Finn had been born.
Many who had been evicted in recent years—for these evictions were still going on—from the Heights of Kildonan
had come to Dunster. Finn saw all this in a sudden clear
light; his mind hardened in acquisitiveness; and he asked
himself, "Why not?"

Why not? There was a coldness of revenge in the question. He would take these possessions. They would be his.
His own croft, his own house, his own boat. He felt them
surround him and give him power. At that moment, a cool
shiver cleansing his skin and his mind, Finn entered with
clear consciousness upon the estate of manhood.

The winter and spring fishing was entirely for white
fish. There were "small lines" for catching haddock and
"great lines" for cod and ling. A winter season for netting
herring was still far in the future. Finn's long discussion
with Henry had been devoted to a thorough prosecution of
the cod and ling fishing, for, as Finn had said, there was
money in it if they went about it in the right way. While in
the Lews, Henry himself had observed how large was the
trade in dried cod and ling. The folk of the Western Isles
had taken no great interest in herring except as bait for
their great lines. And look at the Shetlanders! Herring on
the West were uncertain, but cod and ling were constant,
were sure money. That was what the Lewis people knew.

Now they had been catching cod and ling, splitting and
drying them, in Dunster, but in Finn's view the business

had been too easy-going, not taken seriously enough. They should use only their biggest boats, so that they could stand up to dirty weather, come to an arrangement with an export merchant in Wick at an agreed price, and then get going in real earnest. At an average price, say, of sixpence a head for each dried cod or ling, they might make something that would astonish a few people at the end of the season!

During the white fishing, the herring crews got broken up, because an ever increasing number, with no stake in a boat, engaged themselves only for the summer herring season. From the west of Sutherland and other distant coasts men appeared in early July prepared to hire themselves to skippers at £4 to £5 for six to eight weeks. When these "hired men", including those from the local country districts, had dispersed at the close of the herring season, the real fishermen were left, and, to form crews for the white fishing, had to band together, so that two or more skippers might find themselves on the same boat.

In this way, Finn was able to break with Roddie without rousing any particular comment, for about the shore Finn and Henry had voiced their ideas whenever discussion got going, which was about as often as a group gathered to look at the sea.

It was cold, dangerous, and incessant work, but it suited Finn, though he was troubled with one or two bad cuts on his hands that never got time properly to heal. But they were making successful headway and other boats of the larger type began to follow their lead.

Roddie took no part in this leadership, and fished as one of a crew of five in the regular small type of winter boat. The four others were older than he, and prepared for reasonable work in reasonable weather. This suited Roddie who had never greatly cared for the white fishing, and whose home life now absorbed him. His marriage had had a deep effect upon him, far deeper than ever he had conceived possible; and whoever wanted to kill themselves splitting cod were welcome to the job! Indeed, he might have left the sea largely alone that season were it not for the pleasure he found in coming home.

Once, well into the spring, on returning home in the forenoon, he discovered Catrine waiting for him by the Steep Wood. Her face was white and large-eyed and his wits scattered as if he had been struck a blow on the head.

"Are all the boats safe?"

He hardly heard her. "What's wrong?"

She read his face and tried to smile. "Nothing. Are all the boats safe?"

"Are you sure there's nothing wrong?"

"No. The wind woke me early, and I was frightened. Oh, Roddie, I cannot tell how glad I was to see you!"

"Are you sure that's all?"

"Isn't it plenty?"

Roddie blew a slow breath. "You fairly gave me a fright!"

"Are all the boats in?"

"I think so," he said. "Why?"

"It felt up here like a wild storm for a while."

"It blew a bit. But nothing to be upset——" He stopped and looked at her closely. "There was something?"

The wind blew fair strands of hair over her brow. She looked in front with an awkward smile. "I awoke out of a dream where I saw a boat being smashed. I got frightened —it was so real. I'm glad you're home."

"Now, my girl, you mustn't be getting these fancies. They're not good for you. You know that. You'll end up by making me frightened myself!"

"Are you ever frightened of the sea?"

"I wasn't thinking of the sea. You can leave the sea to me."

She smiled as they walked on, but her eyes were troubled. "I'm sorry," she said, "but—I can't help it. The old fear of the sea is coming back on me."

"You're just having fancies!" he said with meaning.

She flushed.

THE WRECK

He dropped the string of fish outside the door and followed her into the kitchen. The old man was still in bed,
for he had been weakened recently by a heavy cold and did
not get up until the afternoon. The porridge pot was plop-
ping over the fire. "So you're having fancies!" muttered
Roddie, as he hung up his heavy jacket. He was going to
tease her still further when, as if unable to bear it, she suddenly gripped him and dug her fingers into the flesh of his
back and buried her face in his breast.

"Gosh! you're hurting me," said Roddie.

She did not speak.

He laughed gently, derisively, into her hair, then picked
her up in his arms to relieve the sheer stress of pleasure
that came over him.

When she was pouring the porridge into his plate, he
said, "I'll bring you home a rope from the boat."

"What for?"

"You could then tie me by one leg to the end of the
house as you do a hen with chickens."

She turned away, confused.

But Roddie smiled. He felt he understood her far more
deeply than she imagined and enjoyed keeping the knowledge to himself.

But if Roddie for the time being was thus losing grip on
the sea, Finn was being drawn to it ever more elementally.
The weather was often wet and stormy, and occasionally it
was intensely, bitterly cold. For spells, feeling would desert
his hands and even the flesh on his back, and the cold would
crawl along his bones. Working in the sea water, his fingers would experience the smoothness of washed stone—
at a little distance from him, flexible like tangle-weed. They
could only feel a hook-point dimly. The men were heavily
clothed, however, and in frost, with a creeping haar, Finn
sometimes achieved a sensation of bodily misery that was
ultimate and strangely bearable. Not only his hands but his
mind seemed washed by the cold sea water.

Then in April something happened which drew Finn into
an even closer kinship with the sea.

Already Roddie had let it be known that he was not
going to any West Coast fishing in May. He said he didn't
think it was worth it, and doubted if there would be much
doing in any case, because curers seemed dissatisfied, unwilling to take bounty and other risks, and doubtful of the
wisdom of a too early fishing. He was going to give it a
miss for this year anyway, he said. But Finn guessed correctly
what had happened. He was about the last to discover that
his mother was going to have a child. For two or three
months, he had seen very little of her. The estrangement
between them was such that when they did chance to meet
in Elspet's presence they could talk to each other with that
appearance of distant ease or restraint not unusual in members of the same family whose interests have diverged. When
he suddenly found out about the child, he had a revulsion of
feeling strong enough to snap the last cord between them, to
make the estrangement complete. When the revulsion had
slowly ebbed, he felt glad that the whole affair was over, that
he was finally cut off from any consideration for his mother.

And he could afford to smile with contempt at the
thought of Roddie, the great seaman, being overcome by
his wife; Roddie making excuses—because he must stay at
home! He even heard Roddie suggest in a very roundabout way to Henry that he might take his place with the
curer. For Henry was expecting his own new boat within a
week. Things had come to a pretty pass with the great
Viking! But it suited Finn excellently. He would never
have dreamt of going with Roddie in any case. Now Henry
and he would carry on the winter partnership into the
West, for which there was growing within him a deep
nostalgia. He was longing to get away, longing for the
sea-inlets of the West, the glimmer of twilight in the quiet
nights, remote from Dunster. It was like a land that existed
in a dream, though he never had the felicity to dream of it
except with his eyes open.

And then the incident happened.

Dunster had been luckier than many places on the rocky coasts of that northern sea in so far as loss of life was concerned. Hardly a season passed without its storms and alarms, but actual tragedy had been rare. Perhaps Henry and Finn had set a high standard of daring against the weather, and though there was little overt rivalry among boats, yet no skipper liked hanging about the shore when another was at sea, not unless his weather judgement had been proved in the past and was respected. However that may be, several boats were at sea in the dawn of a darkling April morning, when an easterly gale sprang up. Henry and Finn had been a little uneasy, because the sea had a nasty "lift" in it; there had been a "carry" on the sky they did not like, and they could smell bad weather about. But in the winter-spring fishing particularly, such an uneasiness was not unusual, and did little more than keep the eye lifting and the ear alert.

They were about to start hauling a great line with its hundred hooks on snoods a fathom apart when they saw and heard the wind coming. Such an onset occurred frequently enough to have found a common form of description in the mouths of the fishermen: "A lump of wind struck us". The lump now struck them with a sweeping flattening violence, and Finn and another threw themselves on the loosely stowed canvas. Henry's face was into the weather. "It's coming, boys!" he cried, when he had assured himself of what was behind the lump.

They were about five miles from Dunster, and Henry's decision to leave the line and make for home was immediate. Over the blackened water, scuds of drift were racing. With a peak of sail to give steering way Henry ran his *White Heather* dead before it. The uneasy sea began to rise with great rapidity. But they were not frightened of the sea; what sat in Henry's mind was fear of the shore, where in no time the rollers would be breaking. There was no harbour, no breakwater, nothing but the open beach and the stony river mouth. And apart from that crescent of beach, with some deathly skerries beyond its southern horn, there was nothing but gaunt cliff, whose base far as the eye could reach was already white spume. That the tide was low was an added anxiety.

They could see the other boats making for home. None of them had been so far out as the *White Heather*, and already several were approaching the bay, and three more, a little to the south'ard, were fighting hard against the drift for the wind was a little north of east. Two of them should make it, but the third, some distance behind, would have all she could do to keep off the skerries. Yes, it would be touch and go with her!

The crew felt exhilarated. Already in their bodies was the fight with the beach, the leaping overboard, the gripping of the gunnel, the heave upward of the bow to keep the bottom planking from getting stove in. To save the boat each in risking his life would know a high thrill. For the boat was more than all, it was their challenge to the sea, arousing in them not thought of risk but an exalted courage. And Henry was there, jealous of his seamanship, anxious in the moment of test that he should acquit himself creditably before his fellows.

Finn glanced back at him. Henry's thin face was set, calm, but its lines held as in a faint fixed smile, the irony that was characteristic of him. Somehow this touched Finn with the old emotion of comradeship and he glanced away —and saw well to the west and fairly low in to the rocks the heaving darkness of a small boat. He cried out and pointed. They all looked and their faces quickened, for they knew on the instant that that boat was doomed.

"It's Daniel Bannerman," cried Henry.

Their hands gripped what they rested on. They looked from the distant boat to the beach and back to the boat again. They could see her losing way as if they were hanging on her iron-held oars. She was done for!

Now they wanted to give their own boat more speed.

There arose in them the urge to land swiftly. They had no
fear of the sea. Its spray stung their cheeks and eyes. The
wind roared and whistled past them. Henry stood close into
the Head to get what eddying shelter there might be by the
river mouth. Bursts of spume were flying up the rock-face.
Yes, he could save himself from landing on the beach. He
could take the river-mouth. They could do it! Yes, they
could do it with ease!

"The oars clear!" cried Henry, his eyes narrow and calculating.

But they hardly needed the oars, except, at the last, to
hold her from broaching to, and, as her forefoot grounded,
they jumped. There were some men on the water-edge. She
was gripped, and went with them in their midst until only
her stern was washed by the breaking waves.

The cry now rose about Daniel Bannerman. Already folk
were appearing from the crofts, men and women and boys.
Small boats were being drawn up the beach by seamen wet
to the waists. Women with heads tightly shawled leaned
against the storm, their wide skirts flapping. The seadrift
whistled past in a stinging rain. Blobs of spume big as gulls'
eggs caught the ground, shivered and burst.

As Finn joined the surge of men along the crest of the
beach the last of the three boats that had been seen fighting
for the bay was being driven on the skerries. Seamen were
leaping the boulders towards the black rocks, sloping like
wedges into the sea, upon which it was now clear she would
be piled up. Standing on an outer skerry, each wave as it
came seething white round his feet, was a tall commanding
figure with a coil of rope in his hand. Though at a considerable distance, Finn, running, knew that figure. It was
Roddie. Then, through the roar of the breakers, he began
to hear his voice. His left arm was out, directing them,
indicating by a sweeping peremptory motion the narrow
channel they must take between two skerries. Now could
be seen the power of the storm and the desperate effort of
the four men on the oars, pulling out to sea with the utmost

strength of their bodies, pulling into the eye of the wind
and being driven before it, keeping the ever-lifting stem
into the weather while trying to guide the stern between
the two skerries, which every surge of the sea submerged
in bursts of tumultuous water. When at last she caught the
ground-swing properly she came in a rush and crashed
against the western skerry. The man on the bow oar was
unseated by a severe blow on the chest from the end of his
oar as the rock smashed its blade against the gunnel. The
boat shot off the skerry, still plunging inward, and would
have smashed her stern in on the living rock, had not the
sucking recession of the water begun. As it was she
shivered from the crack. There were cries as the men
gathered themselves from the bottom boards, and Roddie's
voice rang out with the uncoiling rope. A side channel to
the left gave on a sandy pool, but all human effort at direction was futile in the heave of the sea, and as she struck
again she began to fill with water. But Roddie had now
belayed the rope round a corner of the rock and managed
to heave her nose inward to the channel; heaved her farther,
until, taking their chance as it came, the five men, assisted
by Roddie, scrambled on to the rock.

"Come on!" cried Roddie, leading the way. There was
shouting behind him. He turned round. It appeared the old
skipper was not going to come. Roddie strode back and
yelled, "Come on!"

"It's all right," said the old man calmly. "Be you going.
I'll stand by her for a little while." He had to lift his voice,
but his manner was quiet as if he were talking from his
croft door.

"By God, you'll come now!" cried Roddie in an anger
suddenly flaming because of what moved in the heart of
this old man.

But the old man began pulling on the rope. "Be you
going," he said. "She's been a good boat to me." There
was an extraordinary, an incredible calm on his face, a
gentle expression that smiled.

THE WRECK

Out of the flowing tide the sea answered, but Roddie gripped the old man and together they clung to the streaming rock. They climbed upward on to the skerry whose top ledge was several feet above high-water mark (here, perhaps, the skipper had thought he might weather the tide), and down again, and inward, until they met the sea coming from the other direction in that welter of rock. In crossing the narrow channel to the beach the youngest of the crew was swept off his feet but he could swim and, gripping the strong tangle-weed, soon heaved himself out. A few minutes later, the passage could not have been made, except perhaps in a headlong dive by a strong swimmer.

There were high cries for the crew from members of their families. One man's face was streaming blood where the skin had been scraped away by a barnacled ledge, and another had his head bent, coughing painfully, his hands against his chest. But apart from these minor bruises, they were all safe and sound, which was miracle enough.

"You'll come now, Hamish," cried his old wife to the old skipper.

"Be you going, Nanz," answered the old man. "I'll wait a little while."

"You will not," rose her shrill voice, "and you wet from head to foot! You'll come now, this minute!"

"Ah, be going, woman," said Hamish austerely. "And leave me alone. What's a little wet?"

Finn followed the others, but as he was making for the steep green brae above the beach, he had a sudden thought and began to run towards the store by the gutting stations. He emerged with his head stuck through a heavy coil of back-rope. On the slanting path up the brae, he was overtaken by an elderly fisherman who had been delayed securing his boat in the river mouth, and, after some talk, this man went back for more rope.

Soon two men from the hills, making for the shore, ran into Finn, and when he had given them the news, they carried the rope between them, thus giving Finn a rest and increasing speed.

As they left the braes behind and came out on top of the cliffs, they saw the crowd at a little distance and Finn, because of his knowledge of that coast, was aware in a momentary deep inward sinking that boat and men were doomed.

He knew the crew well. Daniel Bannerman, who had been evicted from the Heights of Kildonan, was a tall man of sixty-three, sparely built, patriarchal in manner, quietly religious, and, as it was solemnly said, "highly respected", for he had a considerable formative influence on the life of the people beyond the Birch Wood; Oscar Sinclair, in his forties, robustious in action, with a red beard and the nature that got pleasure out of giving a neighbour a hand; Tom Dallas, a steady dark lad in his twenties; and Una's brother, Duncan, a year older than Finn.

They moved, living, in Finn's mind, and it was incredible to him that they should now die, smashed against the cliffs and drawn down into the green water.

As they approached at a trot they knew from the high desperate cries of the women and the wringing of their hands that the boat was foundering. Men were shouting and driving the adventurous back, for the grassy turf sloped gently downward a few yards to the edge of the sheer cliff and was thus a place of great danger, for the wind as it struck the rock face was thrown upward and created a suction behind it that might draw anyone over the edge.

A woman clasped her hands and lifted them and her face to the sky and in a high voice cried, "O God, save them! Save them!" The desperate appeal affected many, and several women got to their knees and added their entreaties to the grey storm-driven sky.

It was in that terrible moment, when grown men felt the drawn-out appalling nature of their own impotence, that Roddie, turning round like a trapped animal, saw Finn and the two men with the rope. He stood stock still, and Finn went straight to him.

"Is she in?" asked Finn, glancing at the same time down at the cliff-edge and even taking a careful step forward. But no boat was now to be seen.

"She has just gone in," said Roddie evenly, as Finn turned to him again.

Finn met his piercing eyes.

"I'll go down on the rope," said Finn, "if you hold on." Roddie's face paled in a drawn concentration.

Finn sat down and began to take off his boots. He liked to feel the rock with his bare toes. In trousers and jersey, he stood up lightly.

Roddie turned on those pressing about them. "Get back!" His voice cracked like a whip-lash, and even old men took a backward step as if the primal force in the man had struck them.

"Are you ready?" asked Finn, and he met Roddie's eyes.

"Will you try it, boy?" asked Roddie, and his voice was gentle.

It was a moment of communion so profound that Finn felt a light-heartedness and exaltation come upon him. This was where Roddie and himself met, in the region of comradeship that lies beyond all the trials of the world.

Finn saw the final struggle in Roddie's nature and saw him overcome it. "Very well," said Roddie.

When they were satisfied that the rope was long enough, Roddie picked his team of men. Everyone now knew that Finn was going over the edge, and the clamour rose and stilled.

"When I give two tugs on the rope, you'll haul away," said Finn to Roddie.

"If you want more rope, give one pull," said Roddie.

Finn nodded.

Roddie looped the rope under his armpits.

"Take care of yourself, Finn," Roddie said.

Finn knew he could not say more and smiled to him. "I'll go to the edge first and perhaps come back," he said. "I'll see." Then on his bare feet, Roddie paying out rope, he walked down the grassy turf.

THE WRECK

At the sight of him walking down with the rope round
him, the women began to weep aloud. Roddie took the
strain as Finn, standing on the edge, leaned over the abyss.
It was clear he saw something below by the quickened way
he began examining the edge, foot by foot. Roddie knew he
was looking for a smooth hard place for the rope. He
stopped, turned round, and signalled Roddie that he was
going down. As he met the eyes upon him, he could not
help seeing Una's astonished face, and, before dropping to
his knees he gave the pleasant characteristic salute of farewell with the left hand. In a moment he had disappeared.

"Don't hang on the rope," shouted Roddie sharply to the
men behind him. "I want to feel him." They obeyed him
instantly, holding the rope lightly, while Roddie paid it
out hand over hand, his heels dug in.

At last the rope slackened. There was a single pull.
Roddie lowered away a yard or two and held. Another pull.
Through sensitive fingers he let the rope go again, and
then held it, his head turned sideways as if listening to its
message. But no message came up. All at once there was a
single wild pull and Roddie, instead of paying out rope,
hauled slowly. "Don't pull!" whipped his voice. The rope
eased and in a moment he paid out a yard, while the expression on his face cleared. All eyes were on his face, as
though, through his hands, it could divine what was going
on down below.

There was no doubt about the two tugs when they came,
and Roddie began hauling, checking the eagerness of the
men behind him. Tension now rose to a high pitch. Twice
Roddie stopped the rope and eased it before hauling away
again. Was it Finn coming back—or the crew? He must be
near now—near now . . . and then suddenly before their
eyes, coming up over the crest, a red head. It was Oscar
Sinclair.

"It's Oscar! It's Oscar!"

"Give him time!" yelled Roddie.

Oscar tried to get to his feet, but he fell, and they hauled

514

him up the gentle slope on his stomach. Again he tried to get
to his feet, floundering like a wounded animal. But Roddie
got down on his knees and caught him, trying to gather the
meaning of the desperate urgency in the thickened voice.
"Hurry up! Other rope! Send down two ropes! They'll be
gone!" He clawed the ground, his eyes wild and roving.
Just then, the man whom Finn had sent back for more rope
arrived, accompanied by two young lads and a new coil.

Already Roddie had shouted, "A stone!" and men had
scattered. Before he had the two coils in position and
knotted their ends, a dozen stones were at his feet. Swiftly
and securely he attached one to the double rope, and shouting, "Pay me out to the edge," walked forward with the
double rope round his back and under his armpits. A yard
from the brink he got down on his stomach and pushed the
stone before him. His right leg took a holding twist on the
rope behind, as his head craned over. The base of the cliff
did not, as it chanced, go sheer and deep into the sea, but
broke into a welter of riven sloping ledges upon which the
waves mounted and smashed, throwing great plumes of
foam that hung on the air, falling slowly, to be renewed
again, like smoke from an inferno. Bits of planking and
gear from the smashed boat heaved on the rock, rushed
back, and swung on the water. Of human life there was no
sign.

Roddie pushed the stone over the spot Finn had chosen
and, drawing himself backward, returned without help of
the rope. His face was hard and expressionless. All saw its
deathly message, but no-one dared question him.

His relations had removed Oscar to a little distance, and
now there arose a crying and keening. Daniel Bannerman
and Tom Dallas were gone!

In a moment everyone seemed to know what had happened. The boat had piled up on a ledge and heeled right
over as the wave fell from her, throwing them all backward
into the boiling sea. The next wave had heaved Oscar
again on the ledge and the receding side-swirl had washed

him into a cranny, from which he had all but been torn away by the impact of Duncan's body. There was still life in Duncan at that point. From this cranny Oscar had half-dragged Duncan to a small crevice two yards higher up and near the base of the rock, where they had lain face down, holding on, as inrushing swirls swept over them. Then the life had gone out of Duncan. Finn had taken his, Oscar's, place, but he could not hold it long, not on a rising tide. One big sea would sweep them both away.

The men behind Roddie said, "Daniel and Tom are gone," in the quiet voices of fatality, but all Roddie said was, "Leave the rope to me," and he let the stone take it through his hands. Down it went, down, down.

Una was now standing five paces away from Roddie. She was fond of her brother Duncan. Her face was death-pale, and once she turned and looked at her mother, and for a moment it seemed that the unnatural tension of her mind would snap. But her mother's still anguish steadied her. Una was breathing quickly and her hands opened and shut in spasmodic motions, sometimes tugging her clothes outward from her breast. Her eyes were black. Her whole body was a suppressed cry.

The rope slackened. Roddie waited. There was no response.

Second followed second, while Roddie waited. He eased the rope under its own weight. All who were watching saw that there was no response. Finn's friend Donnie came forward and said he would go. . . . An explosive "No!" choked the words in his mouth, and he fell back a pace as if Roddie had struck him.

Roddie began to pull on the rope slowly, patiently, took in about half a dozen yards of it, glanced over his shoulder to make sure no-one was holding it, then let it run out over his open hands under its full weight. This time it went nearly a fathom farther before it slackened. Roddie's eyes glittered.

They all saw the jerk on the rope. Finn was still there!

Roddie seemed to grow taller and rock a little on his feet, his head to the gale, his face, though hard and smooth as bossed stone, imperious and exultant.

The double pull came, and now Roddie led his strong crew with his great strength gathered into his sensitive hands; eased them, checked them, and hauled away again, until the heads of Finn and Duncan came above the brink. Duncan's head was lolling. He was clearly unconscious or dead. Finn had him gripped from behind, and now, removing his arms, signalled Roddie, who at once lay on Finn's rope and helped him over the edge. Finn leaned down, got a grip of Duncan, and, aided by the pull on Duncan's rope, eased him carefully on to the grass, and supported his head and shoulders as Roddie drew them up the slope.

Finn, breathing heavily, looked up into Roddie's face. "There was no sign of Daniel and Tom. They're gone," he said in a strange defeated quietness.

"You could do no more, Finn," said Roddie.

Before the ropes were right off the lads, Duncan's mother and Una were pressing in, but Roddie pushed them back firmly, and, on his knees, set to work on Duncan's body, which he stretched out on its face and then began to compress and relax as if he were working a slow bellows.

There was a great crowd above the cliffs now. Indeed half Dunster seemed to be gathered in the mouth of the gale. The heavy sky was low and darkened the air, and this darkening was a sadness for ever streaming by.

A little boy, whose parents had deserted him, stood behind a turf wall, and wondered if the folk yonder were making a new market-fair. A man came hurrying down and the little boy called, "Is it a market-fair?" but the man did not wait to answer. So the little boy started out on his own. Presently he came on small groups standing at a distance here and there as they did at a market, looking and looking towards the main scene. All at once a young woman, walking reluctantly some paces in front of him, stopped and began to cry and wring her hands. Her companions tried to pacify her, and said, "Come on!" But she would not be pacified and she could not go on. The boy saw that she was terrified to go to the market. "I can't go!" she cried in distress. "Oh, I can't!" and all at once she got to her knees, and when it seemed she was going to weep heavily in that attitude, she threw herself on the ground and rolled over on her face, clutching at the grass. The two other girls got down on their knees and tried to pacify her, but they, too, now seemed strangely affected. Their skirts billowed and flapped in the wind.

The boy had not greatly liked the look of the market from the beginning. The bodies had seemed to him dark and small under the awful wind like black birds. It was like a market round the corner of the eye, where queer things often are, because you see them backward, in a light that is clear but not bright.

When now he adventured out from the shelter of the turf dyke—for he had come so far secretly and carefully—he was suddenly caught by the wind more fiercely than at the gaps in the dyke and began to be blown away. At that, the ominous black-bird terror came full upon him from the market, from the awful market, the terrifying market, lifting him in the horror of its wings under the dark streaming sky. One of the two girls ran after him, clutched him, and cried in his ear, "What are you doing here, Ian Angus?"

At that moment Roddie had been working unceasingly on Duncan's body for thirty minutes. After five minutes, no-one could believe that any life was left in the body. Roddie lifted his own head, working patiently at the same time. "Donnie, change that hand," he said; and Donnie at once forgot the hurt of the lashing "No!" Una took the other hand, because Finn was wet through and now, after the exhausting effort of the rock, could hardly keep his teeth from chittering as he lay on the ground. Others made a wind-break, and in a deep half-circle the crowd stood looking and waiting. Then they saw Duncan's mother do a

thing that silently and strangely moved them all. Antici-
pating Roddie's order to chafe the feet, she stripped the
boots off and the two pairs of thick socks, and then with a
curious whimper, she unfastened her bodice and placed the
cold lifeless feet between her deep breasts, and covered
them over with the bodice, and pressed them inward, while
the tears flowed down her face and she murmured, "My
boy! my own boy!"

At the end of twenty minutes, which seemed to everyone
a much longer time, they were satisfied there was no hope.
Heads were shaken. Folk felt that Roddie's patience was
being overdone. This was a refusal to recognize death, a
taking away from its dread dignity. The slow incessant
handling of the poor lifeless body . . . it was time Roddie
gave up.

But Roddie did not give up, and no one dared to suggest
to him to do so, for though patience could dwell in this man
as in a stone, there could at the same moment be in him
the explosive lash.

Then Finn gave up hope, and he saw that Una had no
hope left either. The hands were limp and cold, the hands
of the dead. He had never seen her as he saw her now, all
the movement of her mind, its emotions, its courage, its
fear; the sudden access in which she pressed the hand
against her face, against her neck, and then continued to
chafe it upward as Roddie had told her.

"You'd better go home, Finn," said Roddie, looking at
him.

"No," answered Finn lightly, and clenched his hands and
gritted his teeth to keep the idiotic trembling within
bounds. At that moment he encountered Una's eyes and
they looked at him directly, knowing him, and he was
aware of a movement within him, profound as tragedy, as
death, before her eyes fell to their task.

Then hope went from Roddie—not, after the first few
minutes, that it had been very strong. But the curious
automatism that his mind could achieve in certain situa-

tions, when time became obliterated in endurance, decided to keep him going for still a little while. But conscious hope now left him, and if the father of Duncan had told him to desist, he would have done so.

Only the mother had any hope left, and it was hardly hope so much as a blind surging effort to give warmth back to the cold body. She nursed the feet against her breast as if she were giving them suck of her heart's blood. She lay on her side, curved inward towards them, and the father who had to endure this strange sight, got held as in a trance, for he knew the warmth of life there was in this woman, and how as a woman she was the great fighter of death.

And then it was, when hope was going to sink away from her also, that she roused herself against death, and called from the deeps of her spirit to her son, pouring her life into him, and for answer she felt a pressure of the cold feet against her breasts, and she gave a great cry to her far-wandering son, guiding him back to her.

Roddie saw the slow tremor pass over the body, the lips part, and the head reach forward a little in a motion of vomit.

"Dear God, he's living!" he said, in a harsh voice of wonder.

They bore him to the house of the little boy, who had thought the crowd on the cliff-head was a market, because it was the nearest house. The mother now walked beside the father with her eyes to her son's ease, but the father and Roddie and two other men carried him with such tender hands over the broken places that he floated as on a bed.

Many went with them, but the great crowd stayed behind.

Meantime the woman of the house and her daughter had hurried home to prepare the kitchen bed for Duncan, who had relapsed into unconsciousness. The daughter was a young woman of twenty, buxom and light on her feet and

full of swift energy. As her mother drew the peats together into leaping flames, she swept the blankets off the
bed and with outstretched arms held them to the fire, her
brown head thrown back. As they brought Duncan in, she
flung the warmed blankets back on the bed and straightened
them out. When the father and Roddie began to strip the
wet clothes off Duncan she left the kitchen with all the
others except the man and woman of the house and Duncan's mother.

In a minute or two the three men came out. The man of
the house said in a quiet voice to his daughter, who had
prepared the bed, "They're wanting you inside."

"Go in, Una," said Una's father calmly at the same
time.

The two young women glanced in a startled way, then
dropped their eyes and went quietly in at the door, closing
it behind them.

All the others now looked away towards the crowd on
the cliff-head. Some of the younger men could be seen
stretching out on either hand, to get a view of the rocks
from another angle, and Roddie, who had the little boy in
his arms, said, "I hope these young fools will watch themselves."

"They can do nothing now," said Una's father.

"Whenever it shows signs of taking off, we'll get a boat
out."

They glanced at the sky, standing back out of the wind,
which came whistling round the corner of the house.

"It won't let down until the rain breaks it," said a man.

"In that case, it shouldn't be long," said another.

The weight of fatality was heavy upon them and made
their voices sound light and pleasant.

"I'll go in," said Una's father, and the man of the house
went with him. The little boy now struggled to get out of
Roddie's arms, overborne by a desire for his mother, and
as Roddie set him down, he ran after the two men and went
in with them, holding fearfully to his father's hand.

"How is he doing?" asked Duncan's father as he came by the end of the bed.

"There is no sign yet," said his wife.

The father leaned over the bed and looked at the bluey-cold pallor of his son's face. Behind it was the dark head and flushed face of his daughter, Una, and in front the warm face and glancing eyes of the brown girl, whose name was Janet Calder.

"Do you feel any heat in him yet?" he asked gently.

"No, Father," said Una.

Outside, Roddie said to Finn, "It's high time you were home."

"Yes, indeed," said another man, looking closely at Finn.

"Sea-water never did anyone any harm yet," remarked Finn, for it was held, out of experience, that no ill-effects followed immersion in sea-water. But now there might be another meaning to Finn's innocent words, for the sea-water had proved fatal enough that day, and Roddie asked, before the thought could be born, "Did the stone stick before it reached you?"

"Yes," replied Finn, twisting his body to keep the chitters from it, "yes—it stuck on a little ledge above. I saw it stick."

"That would be an anxious moment for you?"

"It was, " said Finn, smiling, "—especially when I saw it going up again."

"It would be."

"Yes. I thought it was all up with us then."

"Boy, boy!" said a man, in thoughtful wonder.

They glanced at Finn.

"Did you see any sign of the others?" asked Roddie.

"Yes, I got a glimpse of Tom's dark head a few yards out, but when I looked again, as the wave went from us, it was gone."

They stared towards the dark figures on the cliff.

Duncan's father came out and said to Roddie, "He's coming to himself now. He'll be all right."

"That's fine," said Roddie. "Well, we'll away home, Malcolm, because you know how anxious folk can get when they don't know what's happening."

"I can only thank you, Roddie."

"It's little I did," said Roddie, as they shook hands.

As Malcolm shook hands with Finn, he suddenly, in a warm movement towards his youth and courage, brought his left hand over to his right, and cupped the lad's hand in a pressure of deep emotion. "We won't forget, Finn," he said, smiling.

"Och, it's nothing," said Finn, and if the words could hardly have been more inept, they were understood profoundly.

Roddie and Finn and Donnie and three others now set off for the Dunster bridge, Roddie setting up a swinging pace, for the thought of Catrine and the rumours that might reach her ears had troubled him for some time.

They had hardly got properly under way, however, when a soul-stirring sound came upon the wind and drew them up. For a moment it was like a surge of unearthly voices under the sky, but in a few seconds they recognized the swell and rise of the old Psalm tune to the words, *O God, our help in ages past. . . .*

They listened for a little to this singing from the cliff-head, then in silence moved on again.

CHAPTER XXIV

AS THE ROSE GROWS MERRY IN TIME

T he bodies of Daniel Bannerman and Tom Dallas were recovered two days later, and a few days after their burial, the *White Heather* lifted her brown sails in the bay and, rounding the Head, set her stem on Clyth Ness.

"Boys, this is good!" said Finn.

"Rob's kist is still the biggest," Callum observed, "and he had a narrow squeak with it last time."

"If it's big it's valuable," replied Rob, "and if there's to be any squeaking, we'll throw the rubbish over first."

Henry smiled. There were only the four of them, which was the normal size of a home crew, unless for a young lad at the skimmer. And though they were now going to a distant shore, they reckoned they knew the way well enough to manage by themselves! A lad of sixteen who had been going to come with them had at the last been overborne by his mother, who was sister to the mother of the drowned Tom Dallas. They had refused other lads, for Henry said that this was only another voyage of exploration, as Stornoway had not yet awakened, and if Roddie's news from Wick was anything to go by, might again be dead to the herring world as was all the rest of the Hebridean West.

But, meantime, it was fine to watch the new *White Heather* going through her paces in a choppy sparkling sea. It was worth while setting an adventurous course for that alone! It was the real May weather, too, with a brisk wind out of the nor'-east and a bright sky.

Henry drew her so close into the wind that Rob, lips apart and eyes on the sails, at last shook his head in admiration. "She's good. I'll say that."

Henry smiled and eased the tiller a little.

"It's long legs to-day, boys," said Callum; then he winked at Finn. "Can you remember, Finn," he asked solemnly, "the name of a public-house in Stornoway where —tuts! what's its name?—it's an awful thing, the memory —but it was run by a very pleasant, rather stout armful of a widow woman . . ."

When life is good it is warm. Its warmth came about Finn's heart, and it had known the cold for many a long day. These days had culminated in the drowning of Daniel Bannerman and Tom Dallas, and in that hour, as he had clung to the crevice in the rocks and held his breath against the swirl of the water and its lung-stinging suffocating spume, he had know the final coldness, the coldness that is washed and cleansed of all warmth and feeling, the death-coldness of the sea.

Afterwards, he could feel himself rise out of that tragedy, with the cleansed, cold feeling that bound him to the sea, that took fear away, for beyond what he had seen, which was death, there could be no further earthly experience. The sea had drawn close to him, close as the bone-skeleton that held the mesh of his warm flesh. When all doors were closed—there was that door to the sea. Whatever should betide him, there would be the sea always.

The sparkling laughing sea, throwing its little bursts of drift about the stem, a new stem but with the same eagerness as the stem of the *Seafoam*, with eyes for nothing short of the horizon. It was the way to travel and to sail.

The parish fell away behind them as Henry put her on the last long leg that would bring Clyth Head abeam; and, as on the previous trip, they had the odd sensation of seeing all that belonged to it both diminished and made clear in its proportions. Feeling in particular was eliminated, and Elspet's hauling the recalcitrant Bel by the tether that sometimes got round her skirts was a picture pleasant and laughable to the inward eye. Barbara would not arrive until the end of the month, and would then stay on for the summer gutting.

He was glad, too, that he had got through the business of saying good-bye to his mother quite naturally. Roddie had been there, and that had made man's talk easy. He felt that he had nothing against his mother now. He had somehow just lost taste of her. That was all. His desperate, terrifying feelings had been an odd sort of madness, so odd that a sudden thought of it could still close his fists and grip his body in a slight rigor. But all that was passing. Growing pains! A man had to live long enough to learn many a thing! All that was really left over from it was a feeling, haunting him now and then, of incommunicable loss. Not the loss of his mother, but the loss of something from his own life. And even that was fading.

Not that he even thought of it to-day, for his mind refused to contemplate his mother and Roddie about their own home; or, rather, banished the thought as not worth bothering about. For it was extraordinary to Finn himself how, despite that moment of communion with Roddie on the cliff, when their spirits had been held, known each to each, finally, as if the gale had calmed in a little still circle of eternity, they had thereafter withdrawn into each other, man apart from man, and the old relationship had been established, but with the difference that they could now talk when they met normally if not readily or lightly.

White round the foot of Clyth Head, and now no more legs but the wind on the starboard beam and the *White Heather* flying. "They'll be talking about their steamships," Rob remarked with his droll air.

"A great day!" murmured Finn, smiling abroad upon the sea and looking back at the land.

"I bet you, Rob, he's thinking of that girl in Stornoway?"

"Which one?" asked Finn.

Rob shook his head sadly.

"Between them both and their women," cried Callum to Henry, "O God, we'll have——"

"Cold iron!" yelled Rob.

When they had gripped iron, Rob turned on Callum with some anger. "What's the good in behaving like that? Surely you're old enough to know better and this a new boat. There's many a man would refuse to sail with you for less."

"I'll hold the iron till it's warm," said the abashed Callum. "It was the thought of you and Finn with your women did it."

"If Finn and me need women, we won't shout for anyone's help," replied Rob with crushing sobriety.

Rob was a great stickler for the old beliefs, and Finn thought of last night's doings when Rob raised the neid-fire. Henry had had to lead the way to the shore in the dark to sprinkle some of the water on the bow of the *White Heather*. Many said they no longer believed in these old superstitions, and the Church was against them. All the same, when the affair had been carried through in complete secrecy, there had followed an inflow of comradeship and confidence, a gaiety that made them feel ready for anything. And even if no more than a feeling, still it was a pleasant one! There was little point in being on the wrong side of the dark ones.

To be on the right side of the dark ones, and to have the bright ones, from the fields of the sky, driving over the blue ocean with a white mane showing here and there—and the *White Heather* bounding onward trying to keep up—made a day of days.

As they brought Wick abeam, Finn thought of his boat now building there. She was to be ready for the first week in July and he would be the youngest skipper in Dunster.

"What are you going to call her, Finn?" asked Callum.

"Keep the name to yourself until you christen her with it," advised Rob darkly.

"I'll do that," agreed Finn.

"It's a difficult thing to get a name that suits you completely," said Henry.

"Perhaps so," said Finn, but with a smile, because his mind was made up to call her *Gannet,* the white bird that lives in far and stormy seas and is a great fisher. Not a warm name, perhaps: cold and white and distant, but of the sea's core.

The Orkneys rose from this deep-blue sea and the Pentland Firth like a vast river in flood. Finn liked the way the islands lay in the water, with their great rock sides sheering to headlands as the sides of a boat to her stem. Mighty monsters they were, guarding the Beyond.

Henry said they would dodge about until the tide turned, and offered Finn the helm, "just to feel what she's like".

"In a boat like this," said Finn, "I would sail round the world."

Callum and Rob mocked him.

"All right," said Finn. "Watch me."

After a while Rob's brows gathered. "Where away now?"

"Course set for the Fair Isle! Shetlands beyond!" sang out Finn. Presently it got beyond a joke when cross seas set up an uncomfortable jabble. They shouted at him. "Are you frightened?" challenged Finn. When they threatened to rush him, he put her about smartly. "One year, boys, we'll go the Shetlands. What do you say? Isn't it a great thing to have the whole ocean for the wandering over?"

When fishermen arrived at the Pentland Firth and found the tide had been running for two or three hours at full spate westward, they gave their boats to the stream and, with wits and hands ready, hoped for the best. But now, as the tide turned along shore, Henry could afford to take the passage inside the island of Stroma without any risk of having the tide turn against him before he was clear of the great stream.

"Boys, this is like a holiday," said Callum, as they sailed by the white strand of John o' Groats, with its fabled shells. They looked inquisitively at all they could see, discussed the condition of the crops, made comparisons with Dunster, and remembered what someone had said sometime. As Holborn Head shut Scrabster away, Rob got slowly launched, through intricacies of relationships, upon an ancient story about a bishop who had been roasted on his own fire in these parts, and Finn, settling down, listened, until the voice seemed as far back in time as the characters it evoked.

The wind died away in the evening as they entered Loch Eriboll, and over the quiet, dark waters they pulled their oars to anchorage. The birds cried along the shore. The air was soft. After the hot day, the mountains were hazed as by a faint blue smoke. The sound their oars made travelled a long distance, and when at last they stood up and listened, they heard the silence going farther and farther away. A slow glimmering came into Finn's eyes. They had reached the land of peace, the long sea-inlets of evening and morning, the world of the West.

"We'll go off to yon crofter that Rob hauled out of bed in his shirt to see if the porridge is boiling yet," said Callum. Finn was the first to jump.

The darkness was fallen and Henry asleep before they came back along the shore, making much noise, for the hospitality had been good, as the folk in this region held the curious belief that barley had been created by God and not by the London Parliament, and if so it wasn't God that had made the regulations and charged the whisky duty.

Finn suddenly gripped Rob by the arm. "Listen!"

Rob half-cowered from the leap of the dark, breathing, "What is it?"

"It's the silence," said Finn.

"The what?" breathed Rob, looking over his shoulder.

When, from their gay voices as they moved on, Rob began to understand what Finn had said, he grew angry and hinted at unnameable things that would yet astonish them. "You'll remember my words, maybe, when it's too late."

So that Henry had some difficulty in wakening them in the grey of the morning. Callum he gave up, but Finn brought his mouth to Callum's ear and shouted, "Herring!" Whereupon Callum threshed about him, muttering, "What? Where? . . ."

The wind came cool from the morning's mouth behind the hills. Round the Cape and out into the Minch they sailed in a gentle breeze, and lifted the coastline of the Lews, and marvelled at the ease of this trip compared with the last.

"It just shows you," said Rob, with his sideways nod of wonder.

"What does it show you?" asked Callum.

Rob ignored him.

"Never mind, Rob," said Finn. "You sang well last night. You kept up the honour of the boat."

"Sang?" repeated Henry, raising his brows in real surprise.

"Don't you listen to them," said Rob. "They're trash. They haven't the manners of my foot. There we were, being entertained by decent, honest people, who gave us food and a song, and when they asked for a song back, which was but right, you would think it was two of Dannie Sutherland's stots I had with me."

"So you gave them a song yourself?"

"I gave them a stave or two," admitted Rob. "What other could I do?" His shoulders hunched in ill-humour. "Oh, I'm seeing you winking all right," he added to Callum.

"And they never sang at all?" asked Henry.

"Sing, is it?" and Rob snorted a ruthless sarcasm. "Once they plucked up courage from me, it wasn't the singing then; no, it wasn't the singing."

"What was it?" asked Henry.

"It was the getting them to stop," replied Rob. "I thought that fellow there," nodding sideways at Finn, "was going to throw the lassie through the roof."

"Through the roof?"

"With the dancing that was on him," said Rob.

"She was a fine lass," murmured Finn, "with a soft eye."

"Soft eye, my—huh!" said Rob. "And it wasn't the eye that was bothering you, moreover."

In past Goat Island to Stornoway itself.

After over two weeks in Stornoway, the crew of the *White Heather* were wondering if they would clear their expenses. They missed the hope and enthusiasm that sustained their own home coast even when herring were not on the ground. There was a half-hearted air about the whole undertaking and disputation amongst those on the curing side. Maciver had suffered financially through the loss of an uninsured trading schooner, and the small type of fishing-boat out of the creeks round the coast, not lured by bounties from "the Stornoway financiers", preferred the tolerable certainty of the cod and ling fishing, backed up, as June came in, by the kelp-burning.

"Besides," said Henry, "they're too poor to buy nets and their boats are too small. They'll never do anything of themselves, never a dam' thing."

"It doesn't seem to me they could do much whatever," said Rob. "You cannot catch what's not in it."

"I must say I think it is a bit early myself," said Callum. "The fishing will come on all right, but by that time we're getting ready for our own home fishing. And there it is."

"But when the fishing comes on here, why don't they fish it?" asked Henry.

"You need curers for that—and the curers are on the East Coast then," answered Rob.

"They had bad luck in the days of the Government

bounty," said Finn, "and they've never got over it. There were fellows then, calling themselves curers, who were just pure chancers. They had no money, and all they were after was the bounty. Seumas was telling me about it."

"They're too poor and landlord-ridden, if you ask me," said Henry. "They strike me as a people who have lost hope. And I don't blame them. Take the kelp-burning itself. Was there a single landlord from here to Barra Head who didn't make a fortune out of it—before the tax came off the barilla? The crofter and his family worked like hell, gathering the seaweed off the beaches and out of the sea and burning it—and at the end they would get three to four pounds for a whole ton—which the landlord, who hadn't done a hand's turn about it, then sold for twenty pounds. And even the herring itself down the coast—there are places they can't even sell them except through the landlord or his factor. It's a bloody shame," declared Henry.

"Well, they don't get four pounds now," said Rob.

"No, they don't get two, and the landlord makes out he's a fine, helpful fellow because he only gets four. He's just allowing them to carry on for their own benefit. Saves him having to give them meal when they're starving."

"Ay, ay," said Rob.

Finn laughed.

"What are you laughing at?" asked Rob.

"There's nothing else to do," said Finn. "Are we going to sea to-night or not?"

"Why?" asked Callum. "Anything on?"

"You never know," said Finn.

Henry looked at him. "We'll leave it to you."

"In that case we'll go," Finn said promptly.

They eyed him, then Rob scratched his beard. "There's a dirty bit of sea running, and it's worse it'll be before it's better."

"We'll go," said Henry, whom talk of landlords always put in a bitter humour, "if you're all agreeable."

"I don't mind," said Callum.

"We come from a rock-bound coast," said Finn, "and here there's always a hundred places to run for. At least let us show them an example."

"Ay, ay," said Rob.

Finn laughed and winked to Callum, who asked him, as they walked along behind Henry and Rob, if he really had had anything on.

"I had, as a matter of fact," replied Finn. "But only if we weren't going to sea."

"And you're sorry now!"

"Not a bit! Dammit, let us give things a chance. It's the sea first."

"You'd better watch yourself with that lassie."

"Which one?" asked Finn largely.

Callum laughed, for Finn in this humour always enlivened him.

A few fishermen were hanging about, some making fast their boats against a blow. When they saw the *White Heather* pushing off, they were astonished. "You're not going out this night, surely?" called the old skipper of the *Sulaire*.

"We thought we might go out and see what it is like," answered Henry.

"Well, boys, I don't think you should," replied that wise old man.

Bain now came over to the wall and shouted.

"We'll give it a trial," Henry cried back.

Bain stood still for a moment and then saluted them. They knew he would now boast to Maciver about the East-Coast spirit.

Once outside the Point, they found a nasty sea running, as if it were catching on the bottom and falling over itself into breaking water and long swinging troughs. But they had experienced this peculiarity of this part of the coast before, and kept her heading into it, until they began to open out Loch Erisort.

"I'm afraid it's not to-night we'll shoot nets," said Rob.

The wind was a little south of east, blowing fairly strong, and if they did not want to go back to Stornoway now, they could run into Loch Erisort. No one spoke, however, and Henry drove on.

"I'll tell you what I was thinking," said Finn. He could see they were now out of humour with him, holding him responsible for this foolish adventure. "What harm in running south—even a long way south—if only to find out if there's herring on the coast?"

"And what good will that do us?" asked Henry.

"Well, at least we'd know," said Finn.

Rob's breath left his nostrils in a noisy snort.

"You mean down Harris and Uist way?" asked Callum ironically.

"Why not?" challenged Finn. "What's the good of sitting in Stornoway?"

"And supposing we found herring, what then?" asked Henry. "Where would we take them?"

"It would be fine to see them, at least," replied Finn, with a sudden smile, for there was no answer to Henry's question.

But Henry, looking at Finn, suddenly liked the humour in his smile, its air of daring, of taking a chance first and finding out what would happen afterwards. There was the old memory of Kebock Head, which they could now see; there was last week's rumour of herring off the Shiants. The weather was getting no worse, though the sky was ugly. "We'll hold on a bit, anyway," said Henry.

They held on past Kebock Head; they opened Loch Sealg, with the Shiant Islands some five miles to the south. The wind was moderating. They might yet shoot their nets inside the Shiants and perhaps fetch Stornoway on the morrow with a good shot!

The darkness began to dim the sea. There were porpoises about. The wind died away suddenly. "I don't like it," said Henry.

"If it doesn't veer round and come in a sudden lump," said Rob.

And veer round it did, and came with terrific force, smothering the half-light and blotting out the land.

The following day they fought their way into a small creek, and when Henry asked the man who helped them to make fast what the name of the land was, the man answered that it was called North Uist.

"You've got your wish," he said to Finn.

"Thanks to you," answered Finn quietly.

The nights they spent in that remote place were never to be forgotten by Finn. They had the influence on his life of a rare memory that would come and go by the opening of a small window far back in his mind. Through such an opening a man may see a sunny, green place with the glisten on it of a bright jewel, or a brown interior place and the movement of faces, or a strand in the darkening and the crying of a voice, but whatever the sight or the sound or the moment, it is at once far back in time and far back in the mind, so that it is difficult to tell one from the other. Indeed, an odd commingling seems to take place, and a curious revealing light is not even thought of, yet had always been there.

They were a friendly, hospitable people, full of an extreme inquisitiveness. But their curiosity did not offend the four men from Dunster. On the contrary, they understood it, and Rob's intricate and circumstantial way of telling all that could be told pleased them highly. Henry's reticent irony was understood also, and sometimes one of his dry sayings would be appreciated like a proverb; while Callum's friendliness, particularly with children, was welcomed by the women, who greeted him in the most cheerful way. Never before had Finn so clearly seen how different each one of the crew was from the other.

If they questioned Rob, Rob did not fail to question them. Their circumstances were poor and their houses more primitive than anything now in Dunster. They lived under a system of rack-renting that made Henry's eyes glisten, and when he questioned them, after telling how his own people had been treated in a clearance, they gave him an old saying to the effect that it was bad enough to be a tenant, but to be a sub-tenant was the evil of the Evil One. A great landlord would lease swatches of his land to relations or other tacksmen, and these would screw out of the sub-tenants everything but bare life. Yet they had no active grudge against landlord or tacksman, who in times of great scarcity might give them meal, and who, for the rest, seemed in some strange way to be related to them like fate. No, they had never tried the herring fishing; they hadn't the boats or the nets for it, and, anyway, there had always been the kelp-burning at this season, and the coming of the crops.

The crops looked healthy enough, but the patches of land were tiny for the number of houses squatting about them. From a slight eminence, it was a world of sea-inlet and fresh-water loch and peat. There were moments, then and afterwards, when to Finn it seemed a forgotten place that had lived on.

But however all that may be, there was no lack of hospitality for the strangers, though it was the poorest time of the year for grain, lying between the last year's crops that the spring had lived on and the new crops that were not ready. But oatmeal and beremeal bannocks there were, and some milk and butter and cheese, dried cod and ling, and a fresh egg, for the hens were laying fairly well even if here and there a squawker had to be shoved under a basket to put the brooding off her.

What is misfortune to one may be fortune to another, they said pleasantly, for the storm had thrown much tangle-weed on the shore, and when the crew of the *White Heather* had had a good sleep, they gave a hand in the gathering of the tangle, distributing their efforts amongst their hosts in the fairest way they could. When it seemed the storm was going to take off, it would start to blow again, not strongly but with the persistence of an anger that could not get rid of its grudge.

Finn enjoyed this work. There was much merriment amongst the young folk down on the sea-edge, racing in, gripping the tangle, and getting out before the wave overtook them. When a boy was worsted by the wave and the others laughed, he would snatch the long, sinewy arm of a tangle by the root and switch sea-water from the frond into their faces. Some of the young girls would scream, but always one here or there would cry "Stop it!" in an imperious voice. From a wary distance, a boy would ask, with false concern: "It's not wet you are, Alastair?" until poor Alastair would be near dancing with rage.

All the same it was good drying weather for the seaweed. They spread it on the machair, and particularly wherever there was an edging of bank to let the fronds hang down. Finn became interested in the process of kelp-making, and visited the places reserved for the fires, and handled the ten-foot poles with their iron hooks, for when the sun had dried the weed, just enough to make it burn, it was gathered and heaped upon the long, narrow fireplace—anything up to six paces long and nearly one broad—and set alight. Great is the labour and intense the heat, said the old man with the stoop to his shoulders, when the kelpers set about stirring up ash and ember with the iron hooks, keep on working up the whole mass, thickening it, until it becomes like the ball of dough a woman makes for the baking. A long time the grey mass takes to cool, and then it is heavy as stone. Ay, when the season is wet and the drying not too good, it will take twenty tons of the weed to make one of kelp.

And so the pleasant, informative talk went on through the hours, and the old man, in whose house Finn slept, liked talking for its own sake.

"You have a great lot of ponies among you," said Finn to him.

The old man paused and regarded Finn.

"Yes, we like our horses, and we like to ride them, and at Michael's Feast on Mary's Strand over in the west of the island, there are exciting races, with the girls riding as well as the lads. It's the great pity you were not here then, for by the look of you, I think you would do well at the games."

Finn smiled and asked him more about this Feast. And as he listened he saw, as if he had seen it before, the concourse of the folk on their little horses in processional pilgrimage round the graves of their fathers; the games, with the lads in shirt and short trousers and a whippy tangle-stalk in the hand, racing their horses amid the shouting of old and young; the dancing all through the night, when "You give a gift to her you are fond of and receive from her a gift that her own hands have made". But this old, stooping man of the bright eyes talked about the angels in heaven as naturally as of the lads on horseback, and brought the Victorious Michael flying over the machair on his white steed, until Finn felt the olden strangeness getting a grip of him.

Much knowledge Finn received from this old man, who was one of the three story-tellers of the district. He could have listened to him for hours on end, because as he listened something in himself that had hitherto been dry, like dry soil, was moistened as by summer rain, and became charged with an understirring of life and with an upper movement of wonder like fragrant air. There was perhaps some special concentration of the self in it, too, for the old man's first name was the same as Finn's, which was likewise Finn MacCoul's, the great hero of the noble Fians, whose marvellous exploits were this story-teller's province in learning and art. The story-teller, Hector, specialized in romance and would draw his own followers; and the third old man, and the oldest, whose name was Black John, cared most for the sonorous flow of certain ancient epic poems.

The coming of the four seamen, from the continent beyond, had a quickening on the lives of these folk as they gathered in the evening, anxious above all things in the world for news, their faces bright and expectant. They were greatly astonished at the amount of money that was being made at the East Coast fishings, and questioned Henry closely, and shook their heads in wonder. There was a man up from South Uist on a visit to his mother's sister. "Myself," said this man, "I come from Lock Skiport, and the day before I left, and it's no lie, the water was white, as if you were beating it with thongs, and that from the playing of the herring." Henry's eyes gleamed as he asked, "What did you do?" The man explained how they had shoaled many on the shore with bits of nets and blankets and other gear as the tide ebbed. Henry nodded twice as he looked at his crew with his slow, ironic smile. "What did you call the place?" he asked. "Loch Skiport," answered the man. Far in the years to come, with his son setting out to fish for a curer in Loch Skiport, Henry was to remember how and where he had first heard that name. But now he thought of Bain and how he would move the fish-curers. The West was waiting.

That they were good seamen, Henry knew, for he had already found out that boats ran dried cod and ling to Greenock and Glasgow, and Callum had discovered from the women that young bustling men would come from Lochmaddy and buy up their eggs at twopence a dozen and send them to the same markets. "In what size of boat?" "There will be one or two fully seventeen feet." "In that case," said Henry, "we have little to tell you of seamanship."

But they would not listen to this, and when these matters had been discussed back and fore, it came about that, to entertain the company, Finn had to start on the story of their first trip to the West.

By this time, Finn had gathered a few special sea names

and terms, mostly Viking, used by the people, and he introduced them skilfully. He had, too, the experience of having told his story to seamen in Helmsdale, and in the simplicity of his recital he smiled when the danger was at its worst and became grave when about to include Rob or Callum in a jest that made the company cry out with pleasure. His reward came when he saw Rob's mouth fallen slightly adrift and his eyes set in solemn wonder.

Before Finn went to sleep that night on his heather bed, old Finn-son-of-Angus said to him: "You told the story well. You brought us into the far deeps of the sea and we were lost with you in the Beyond where no land is, only wind and wave and the howling of the darkness. You kept us in suspense on the cliffs, and you had some art in the way you referred to our familiars of the other world before you told of the figure of the man you felt by the little stone house. There you saw no-one and you were anxious to make this clear, smiling at your fancy. It was well enough done. It was all well done. It was done, too, with the humour that is the play of drift on the wave. And you were modest. Yet—all that is only a little—you had something more, my hero, something you will not know—until you look at it through your eyes, when they are old as mine."

"What do you mean by that?" asked Finn.

But the old man shook his head and turned away. "Go to your sleep, my boy. Many a one may come," he muttered to himself, "in the guise of the stranger."

The third night started as a merry night, for it looked like their last. Finn was now deeply interested in the customs and ways of the people, for the more he knew of them the more he seemed to discover what had long lain hidden in himself; and that not seriously, but with a humour prompting his eyes to glisten or his mouth to laugh. This was the night that revelation came upon him, and as with most men who are strongly male in themselves, it came through a woman.

It started with dancing. Hector, who had the great fund of romance stories, was ever curious to compare one place with another and to gather new material where he could. "Are you telling me that?" he would ask, with a deceptive air of wonder. "Now what . . ." And so in a moment he was at the heart of what he was after, his eyes watching.

When the talk had gone a little way on dancing, he asked, "Is that all you have? Do you mean to tell me you know nothing of the real ancient dances like, say, The Fight of the Cocks?"

"No," answered Finn. "What's that?"

"Do you know the dance called The Waddling of the Ducks?"

"No."

"Nor The Reeling of the Blackcocks?"

"No," answered Finn, laughing.

"Ah, well, you'll know The Old Wife of the Mill-dust?"

"No."

"Well, well. It's little of the meaning of dancing you do know." He shook his head. "Our world is passing away. It is going from before us. And soon, maybe, here itself all you will have will be an old man telling of the dances he once saw in his youth that are now no more. And already—already, my grief!—there are places in these islands where dancing of any kind is stopped by the new ministers. A terrible blight is coming upon the happiness of the human heart and upon the happiness of the world. Ai, ai, and you tell me you have never even seen The Old Wife of the Mill-dust?"

"No, but I would give anything to see it," said Finn.

Hector cocked his eye at a young woman, and in a few moments she took the floor, followed by a tall fellow who was handed a short stick. She was fair and he was dark, and Hector tuned his fiddle and smothered the tail-piece in his bushy, grey beard.

Finn never before or after saw any dance like it. The

dancers faced each other, struck attitudes and gestured, with vigour and decision, speaking at each other through their bodies and arms, interjecting with the stamp of a foot, parting, quick-stepping, exchanging places, the man swinging his stick over his own head, over her head, until in the climax of that first part he brought the stick down with skilful lightness and stretched her dead at his feet.

His sorrow now when he sees what he has done! Round her he dances, gesticulating wildly, sadly. He looks upon her; gets down on a knee. He lifts her limp left hand and stares into its palm. He breathes on the palm and touches it with the stick. At once the hand comes alive. The hand goes up and down, to left and right, up and down, to left and right, keeping time to a music as old as the dance. With this sign of life the man is delighted, and dances round the figure in joy. Now for the right hand . . . the right foot . . . and now all four limbs are active. But the body—the body remains dead. Down over it the man kneels, and breathes the breath of life into its mouth and touches the heart with the druid's wand. Whereupon the woman leaps to her feet, and together they dance as in the first part, with vigorous happiness.

After that, the woman who next moved Finn was a girl of no more than nineteen, though she looked older because of the strong bone in her face. From the very beginning Finn had thought the face unusual and even remarkable, though he had not been particularly attracted by it. She had a pointed chin, high cheek-bones, a broad, rather low, forehead, and eyes large and set wide apart. Her hair had the blackness of peat in the moss, but her eyes were blue, with black lashes. There was at once something a little ungainly about her and at the same time very old, archaic, a dark one out of the old race. Though usually those of this race are noticeably small in stature, and dark-eyed, Matili Maccuithean was, in height, above the average of the rest of the girls and rather slower in her movements. She was a grand-daughter of Black John.

From actual dancing the talk had turned to fairy-dancing, and Rob had upheld the honour of the strangers with an extremely circumstantial story about the origin of the little people themselves, told to him, he said, by his mother's mother, who had heard it from her mother's mother in a little hollow of ground on a summer's day, and the hollow is there yet, and that wasn't yesterday. But if Rob knew a thing or two about fairies, it was nothing to what they knew in North Uist, where there was one family itself called Black-fairy. And for all they knew about fairies, it was little enough compared with what the fairies themselves would be up to, especially when it came to stealing human children.

There was a little old woman, Hector's sister, who put a quickening down Finn's spine by introducing into her story the golden butterfly that is man's soul. "And if you catch that butterfly and kill it you kill the soul in its flight. Like God's fool, it flits . . ."

Finn listened, fascinated, and when they turned to Matili and asked her to give them a song, he gazed at the girl with such concentration that he saw for the first time the antique beauty of her features. When she had sung two notes, all his skin ran cold.

The song was a lullaby that illustrated in its own way the subject matter under discussion. But for Finn it was charged with a power that held his quivering body in its invisible hand. It was a lullaby his mother had sung to him on the green brae with its bushes and birds above the little stream in the time of the herding.

Matili sang it as if the song were evolving itself, effortlessly, out of a memory so old that it was quiet with contemplation. The girl's voice had in it the innocent note of the child, and surrounding it the primordial innocence of the mother.

For Finn the evocation of his mother was so strong that

he had the extraordinary sensation of smelling her breast and breath as a child, and in the same moment of recognizing her withdrawn destiny, without losing his own identity as the grown man.

At first it was the mother and child in communion, but, as the rhythm went on, the mother's face lifted from her child and stared away over the green braes and over the burn. And the child felt this withdrawnness in the mother and felt it too in himself, yet could neither protest nor move, held by the song's intangible loveliness with the half-terrifying, sweet sadness at its core. And the child was apart from the mother, and the mother from the child, though he was sitting on her lap, close, close to her.

The effect upon Finn was deep and self-revealing. Love for his mother cried out in him, the love that now understood the withdrawn fatality of the mother. He had been blind, blind. The awful inexorable simplicity of the singing became too much to bear. He tried to put it from him, not to listen; he moved his head and pressed his right heel into the clay floor, so that his body be kept within control. He wanted to cry out, for the relief of the cry. They were all so still, listening to the girl singing the old lullaby of the mother whose child was stolen by the fairies:

> *I left my darling lying here,*
> *A-lying here, a-lying here,*
> *I left my darling lying here,*
> *To go and gather blaeberries.*

> *Hó-van, bó-van, Gorry óg O,*
> *Gorry óg O, Gorry óg O;*
> *Hó-van, bó-van, Gorry óg O,*
> *I've lost my darling baby, O!*

> *I've found the wee brown otter's track.*
> *The otter's track, the otter's track;*
> *I've found the wee brown otter's track,*
> *But ne'er a trace of baby, O!*

I found the track of the swan on the lake,
The swan on the lake, the swan on the lake;
I found the track of the swan on the lake,
But not the track of baby, O!

I found the track of the yellow fawn,
The yellow fawn, the yellow fawn;
I found the track of the yellow fawn,
But could not trace my baby, O!

I found the trail of the mountain mist,.
The mountain mist, the mountain mist;
I found the trail of the mountain mist,
But ne'er a trace of baby, O!

Finn shook his head with a strained smile when they asked him to sing. "The only one who sings here," he said. 'is Rob."

"That's what they said the last time we were in a house," Rob explained sarcastically. "But when I did sing a stave or two—the trouble then was getting them to stop. No, no. It's not me that will be taken in again."

This drew the whole house upon him and it was a packed house. Rob was at last clearing his throat, when he saw Callum wink to Finn. "Look at him winking. If he can wink he can sing." He shut his mouth.

For some reason this set up a wave and a roar of mirth, and the girls in particular would not leave Rob alone.

Finally he gave in. "Well, if I give you a verse it is on the one understanding: that we haven't to listen to them for the rest of the night, because if so I'm going home now."

Rob had a harsh, tuneless voice, concerned with the story in the words rather than the music. As he started to sing, he stared straight before him, and did not break the look until he had finished. When the girls joined in the chorus he was so inspired that at the next verse he went off the key and his voice cracked, but back he came and found it again. Before the compliments that fell on him, he scratched his beard. "Och, it's not often I do much at it," he said negligently.

"But when you do you make up for it," observed Finn, who seemed extravagantly happy.

So nothing would do but that Finn himself must sing.

"Well, with Rob's permission——"

Rob groaned. "Didn't I tell you? I'm off home."

The girls pressed down his shoulders as he made to get up.

"This", said Finn, "is a song I heard from a woman in my native county of Caithness, and the name of it is: As the Rose Grows Merry in Time."

"Say that again," requested Black John, looking at Finn.

"As the rose grows merry in time," repeated Finn, smiling.

Black John savoured the words in sound and meaning. Finn saw that the house was caught by the surprise that the words had first roused in himself. The bright eyes of old Finn-son-of-Angus were on him.

The melody was not much in itself, but it did contrive a persistent, hypnotic effect. And Finn was able to give it full value, because of a quickening deep in his personality, and a nervous radiance above. The last two lines of each verse were repeated:

As I came in over yonder bill,
As the rose grows merry in time,
I met a fair maiden her name it was Nell
Saying, an you will be a true lover of mine,

You must make unto me a cambric shirt,
As the rose grows merry in time,
Without one stitch of your own needlework,
Before you can be a true lover of mine.

AS THE ROSE GROWS MERRY IN TIME

You must wash it in yonder well,
As the rose grows merry in time,
Where water ne'er flowed nor dew ever fell,
Before you can be a true lover of mine.

" It's questions three you have put to me,
As the rose grows merry in time,
But twice as many more you must answer to me
Before you can be a true lover of mine.

" An acre of land you must plough to me,
As the rose grows merry in time,
Between the salt waters and sands of the sea,
Before you can be a true lover of mine.

" You must plough it with a wild ram's horn,
As the rose grows merry in time,
And sow it all over with one peck of corn,
Before you can be a true lover of mine.

" You must reap it with a wild-goose feather,
As the rose grows merry in time,
And bind it together with the sting of a nether, (adder)
Before you can be a true lover of mine.

" You must build it on yonder sea,
As the rose grows merry in time,
And bring in the last sheaf dry unto me,
Before you can be a true lover of mine.

" You must thresh it on yon castle wall,
As the rose grows merry in time,
And mind on your life don't let one pickle fall,
Before you can be a true lover of mine.

" And—when you have finished your work,
As the rose grows merry in time,
You may call upon me for your cambric shirt,
And then you can be a true lover of mine."

The following evening the wind died away, and though the sky remained overcast, Henry smelt a warmth from the brimming tide. "The turn has come," he said. The words were hardly out of his mouth when lads who had been fishing at the far point came running with the magic cry: "Herring!"

Willing backs got under the *White Heather*. She took the water and, followed by a few ancient small craft, headed for the sea under her slow, heavy sweeps. At first the crew had been doubtful of the news because one of the lads had said it was as if big drops of rain were falling in a shower, and that looked like mackerel, but soon all doubt was put aside. "They're here, boys," said Callum, and excitement ran along their veins in fire, the excitement that never staled in all the years of a man's life.

There was a motion in the sea, a darkened sky, and the daylight was going. Perfect fishing weather. "We'll shoot only half the drift," said Henry, "'till we see."

As they lay to the nets, Finn asked, "Did you feel that?" It was a fitful soft air out of the south. They all nodded.

"If only we could do it!" exclaimed Callum.

"Be quiet, will you?" said Rob, who was against all expressions of luck and hope—as a temptation to the perverse ones who might overhear. For though nothing had been said, they all knew why Henry had shot only half the drift and what a southerly breeze would mean. With twenty crans, the boat would not be so deep, but that a following wind might see her in Stornoway before to-morrow was dead.

If there wasn't much light when they began to haul, it was enough for Rob to speak like a father to his children: "Come, my little dancers; come, my silver darlings—steady, now—up!—that's you!" His voice was very matter-of-fact. "Are they any size, Rob?" shouted Callum, winking at Finn wildly from habit. "They'll pass," replied Rob. "Yes, they'll pass. In fact, I have never seen anything like them. Not on this coast." "They're what we have heard about but seldom seen, eh?" "You mind what you're doing," answered Rob. They were drenched with excitement and sweat.

About twenty-five crans, reckoned Henry. The two sails were hoisted and the four oars began to pull away.

"I'll tell you what you're thinking, Rob?" cried Callum.

"Is that so?" replied Rob.

"You're thinking it's the great pity to be leaving all that fish in the sea."

"The sea will keep them."

"Till we come again," said Finn.

As the world lightened the wind strengthened. "Take a snooze when you can," said Henry. "We have a long day before us."

"And maybe a few blisters," smiled Callum, settling himself.

But sleep was far from Finn. The good weather was cleaning the sky and the land had colour and the stillness that never failed to move him. It was the stillness of sleep, not sleep as one knew it on land, but sleep as a magic arrestment, observed from a boat sailing by islands and inlets in the thin clear light of early morning. The gulls were white with this sleep.

Finn closed his eyes, so that Henry might think he was sleeping.

The antique features of the singing girl came before him, and presently he experienced again the feeling that had been roused in him about his mother, but with the bodily detachment of the light before sunrise. He was fond of her, would ever have for her a natural affection, but he saw her now as a woman under the spell of her own destiny. And that somehow was eternally right, like the movement of a figure through the mesh of fate in one of Hector's old stories, or like a swan on the Irish sea in the legend by Finn-son-of-Angus. And this brought to him, beyond understanding, a cool aloof relief.

This was the way in which he had seen Roddie, once when he was at the tiller, upright as if carven, during the storm in the Western Ocean, and again in the moment on the cliff-head, when eternity had put its circle about them, and he had known the ultimate companionship of men, had seen the gentleness, profounder than any crying of the heart, at the core of male strength.

Finn experienced this far more surely than could ever be thought out or expressed in words. Perhaps here was the education that came from no schooling, came from the old stories by men like Hector and Black John and Finn-son-of-Angus, none of whom could either read or write. And the girl, not teaching, but singing the experience of the race of women in tradition's own voice.

It was enough, anyway, for Finn, even in its symbols, like the swan, as though nothing profound is ever finally and materially clear, but only glimpsed in its symbols; and as certainty stirs delight, delight obscures the symbols, leaving behind the sweetness of delight, as a flower leaves its fragrance.

Opening his eyes, he saw the islands in the Sound of Harris. Presently, getting up, he said to Henry: "I can't sleep. You go and have a couple of hours. Come on!" He refused to be put off, and at last Henry took Finn's place and in no time was as fast asleep as Rob and Callum.

Finn now felt completely happy. The sleeping men left him in loneliness to his secret waking thoughts. He kept the stem, the lifting racing stem, on the farthest headland he could see.

As the sun rose, the wind freshened. He was young, and the dark face of Una that had so long and so often haunted his thought came to him with the exhilarating rush of the boat and the glittering lights of the sea. She was fated, like a woman in a story. And if so, he thought . . . and let the thought rush from him. He could not conquer or hold that thought.

He generally kept it from him, banished it away, and if

it came in on him unawares, or was suddenly gnawing out of sight, he could always give it the heel of his temper.

He had said to himself the night before he left that it might look a bit odd if he did not call and see how her brother Duncan was. The real reason for calling was, of course, that it would provide an excellent excuse for meeting her in her own home and showing her that she meant nothing to him, less than nothing.

The visit had been a trifle embarrassing all the same, because he quite forgot the part he had played on the cliff and they hadn't. There was a meal prepared for a hero, and Una had been rather quiet and pale. Finn himself had talked as if his nerves were full of fun and ignored Una completely. But at the first chance he had got up, pleading the preparations he had to make that night. The mother shook hands with him warmly. Then Una held out her hand and looked at him and, damn him, if his hand, by an unspeakable treachery all its own, hadn't sort of half-squeezed it. Duncan and his father both accompanied him to the edge of the wood, but he had no memory afterwards of what they had said. He had been extremely angry with his hand. It was the sort of idiotic treachery, the silly trifling little thing, the infernal weakness, of which he was entirely made up. He was a born weakling: that was the whole trouble. Only in the whirling of the wood for the neid-fire did he work the fury out of himself, and remember Una's pale, strange look.

What the true cause of that look was he did not know, but like the memory of a person under sorrow, it quietened him.

It quietened him still—and made him wonder. Anyway, he thought, if it meant that she was remembering he had helped to save her brother's life, well, she had had plenty of time to let her memory cool!

The stem of the boat went leaping and plunging over the sparkling sea, and Finn put from him the thought that would not go away and the resolution that had been made without being made. But he had become adept at doing this as far as Una was concerned. High time it was stopped, and, O God, he was going to stop it! Leaning forward, with a smiling, reckless gleam in his eyes, he touched the iron end of the boat-hook. But his body had the last laugh at him, for it was quivering and by no means so bold and certain as Finn might care to make out.

Life (according to Mr. Gordon, the schoolmaster) was full of many entrances and exits, but if so, the entrance into Stornoway between four and five o'clock that afternoon took them by surprise—and they had been prepared to make a fair show. Rumour had it that the *White Heather* had gone down off the Shiants with all hands. A crofter had seen her one moment and not seen her the next. Certainly she had made no known anchorage as far south as Tarbert Harris. And if she had, the weather had not been so bad but that she could have struggled home the day before.

The fishermen were getting ready for sea when word went round that the *White Heather* was in sight. The word sped up into the town, into shops and private houses, where folk were glad of a bit of excitement at any time, and down they came, crowding the pier.

"It's the whole of Stornoway," murmured Callum, and at that their faces took on the cast of indifference. But there were some boys on the outmost edge of the long crowd and, not being trained in reticence, what should they do but let out a cheer when the *White Heather* came abreast of them. The cheer ran along the wall like quick flame. Not a face but was smiling or laughing. And then, on top of all, the incredible news that the *White Heather* had arrived with a shot of herring!

Here was Bain, elbowing folk out of his way, lord of the town. He wanted to hold converse with seamen, real seamen.

And there were the four men, quietly and normally

bringing their boat to the landing berth, with the remote cold air of the sea about them.

"Welcome back!" shouted Bain.

Henry lifted up his thin, dark face and smiled. "I hope," he asked, "that we are not too late for you?"

"Late? You'll never be too late for me!" shouted Bain. Then he let out a roar to his foreman to gather the gutting crews. Anyone would think he was putting the sea off his bows.

Henry now looked satisfied, as if this was all that had been worrying him—as indeed it was.

"You have thirty cran?" cried Bain.

"Barely," said Henry in the slow sea voice. "But they are good herring—the best I have seen here."

"Where were you shot?"

"We shot last night off North Uist."

North Uist! A deep murmur ran along the mouths of the fishermen.

The skipper of the *Sulaire* asked, "Where were you in the gale?"

A smile of humour softened Henry's features. "Running before it," he said, "under bare poles."

"By God!" said Bain.

Then he shouted the crew to come up and have a dram. But Henry said he would like to get the herring out first, and have an hour or two's drying on the nets.

"You have the whole evening for that," shouted Bain.

"Not if we're going to sea to-night," said Henry.

Bain's mouth opened, but no word came through.

Finn was in great feather now, and the dark girl, Catrine, was as busy as a wren.

"Do you think she was missing me?" he asked.

"I think she was," said Catrine, nervously merry.

"You fairly fancy yourself," said the fair one with a toss of her head.

Finn laughed and retreated with the creel.

For in these questions, and others like them, Finn and the dark girl Catrine spoke indirectly to each other, and this was a delightful game.

"Do you think she really cares?"

"She might. You never know," answered Catrine.

"I wonder how I could find out?"

"I'm sure I don't know." And the herring flew from her quick hands.

"I'll have to think it over," said Finn seriously.

A dark swift glance like an electric spark shot into his eyes and vanished.

He hove away a trifle excited, and remembered Callum's suggestion that he had better watch himself. But that was always the sort of suggestion people did make. There was a profound humour in this. And, anyway, how could a prick of conscience produce such a pleasant sensation?

With the herring out and Henry in Bain's office, Callum had very clear ideas on a pint of beer. His flesh was wrung dry and his mouth like leather.

But Rob was wary. "Where to?" he asked.

"You know fine where to," replied Callum. "So don't be wasting time."

"Well, there's a place here——"

"There's nothing of the sort," said Callum. "You're a dam' fine fellow anyway. Have you no thought for the woman who has endured all these nights wondering if you were drowned?"

"If that's what you mean," said Rob, stiffening, "I'm not going. And that's short."

Callum winked to Finn, who took Rob's arm. "Come on, Rob, never mind him."

Rob drew his arm away abruptly. "Will you be quiet," he said harshly, "and the people seeing us."

"What do we care for the people?" asked Callum. "We have nothing to be ashamed of. At least—I hope not."

"Go away!" growled Rob, growing angry. Then he

scratched his beard and looked at the sky, so that decent folk might see they were only discussing the weather.

Callum laughed. "If you don't come, then we're going, and by the lord we'll tell her."

"It's a good drying wind that," said Rob, walking on, because one or two youngsters had stopped to listen to the daring seamen whom folk had thought drowned. "I'm ashamed of you," muttered Rob, "that you don't know how to behave in a strange place. Black affronted. I'm going home."

"I hope," said Callum, "that we know how to behave ourselves as well as you. This way."

"No. I'm not going," said Rob. And they stood still again.

"Very well," said Callum. "If you're frightened to face the woman, that's your concern. But——"

"What was I going to be frightened of?"

"Well—why not come?" asked Callum.

"I must say, Rob, to be candid," admitted Finn, as if more than a little hurt, "that I don't like you sort of implying that we don't know how to behave ourselves in a decent woman's house. I don't think we deserve that."

Rob looked at him with a suspicious snort. "I know you," he said. "And moreover I know both of you."

"I hope so," said Callum. "Are you coming?"

"If you say anything out of the way," threatened Rob, "it'll be the last that ever I'll have to do with either of you. Take it or leave it." And he strode on towards the widow's public-house.

Callum gave Finn a sharp dig with his elbow and his left eye disappeared completely.

CHAPTER XXV

THE BIRCH WOOD

Their reception on the beach at home was far beyond anything of the kind ever experienced before. One or two of the women started waving and crying in a hysterical way. The tears streaming down the face of Henry's wife brought a shamed darkness to her husband's features. The assumed pleasant indifference of the crew was pierced through at first by awkwardness and then by dismay.

They had not long to wait, however, to learn the reason for this extreme behaviour, for it so chanced that Mr. Hendry was among the crowd and he greeted them with direct words. Indeed his words were in the nature of a short speech of instruction and reprimand. His importance carried off the occasion in some measure, for he was a fish-curer in a large way now and spent much of his time in Wick where, it was rumoured, he would one of these days take up his abode permanently.

But there was some general impatience with him, too, for what cared Henry's wife whether her husband had written or not, now that he was safe? Or Callum's wife and children? Or anyone else, for that matter? News had filtered through from Poolewe that they had been caught in a storm off the Shiants and had all perished—and lo! here they were, each one of them, safe, and walking in life.

It was a tremendous moment for those who had gone through days of fear and despair, and why should they restrain a few tears and much enthusiasm and laughter now? It was not every day the beloved dead come home alive.

The crew filtered through the crowd, and here was Meg, running. "Hullo, Finn!" As she shook hands, she looked him over. Yes, he seemed to be in it! "Have you brought me a present from Stornoway?"

"Nothing but myself—if that's any good to you?"

"That's all you know!" She lifted her voice in a yell: "Una!"

Una approached, smiling, a little gravely, and shyly. "Welcome home."

"How polite we are!" exclaimed Meg as the two shook hands.

Finn's colour deepened and he turned to accept other greetings.

But on the way home, he said abruptly to Donnie, "One minute," lowered his end of the chest and called "Una!"

The five in Una's group stopped as Finn walked towards them. "He wants to speak to you," said Meg quickly, and with the other three moved on.

"I forgot to ask you how Duncan is?"

"He's fine, thank you," said Una.

"I'm glad of that," said Finn. "I just wanted to hear."

"Yes, he's fine."

"That's good. I just wanted to know."

"Yes, he's all right."

"That's fine."

"Yes."

"You're all well?"

"Yes, thank you. We're all fine."

"That's good. Well, I'd better be getting up." And, with the grimace broadening, he glanced at her face.

Beneath her expression there was the movement of the spirit that he had once glimpsed on the cliff-top, a movement that had seemed to him then as profound as tragedy or death, but that now was caught in a strange pallor behind her smile.

557

"I'll be seeing you," he said, with an almost uncouth manifestation of his usual easy manner and turned away with a hearty salute.

"I forgot," he explained to Donnie largely, "to ask how Duncan was."

"He must be at the peats, or he would have been here," said Donnie.

"Yes, the peats," nodded Finn. "Lord, there are a few things to do! . . ."

Donnie insisted on coming right to the door of the house, and here was Barbara flying—and Elspet on the threshold.

When the greetings were over and the peat smoke of the kitchen in a swirl, Finn asked, "And how's everyone?"

"You haven't heard?" cried Elspet, looking at him shrewdly while Barbara glanced sideways.

"What?"

"That you have got a new brother."

"A what?"

"Your mother has had a son, a real fine boy, a little treasure."

"Oh! And is she quite well?"

"They're both as healthy as trouts. Now, isn't that fine news for you?"

"It's news certainly," said Finn.

"You must go up and see them whenever you've had something to eat," suggested Elspet. "You'll do that, won't you?"

"Surely," replied Finn. "We must inspect the marvel."

"He's a little darling," said Barbara, with a swift rush of feeling that sounded like relief.

"Did you ever hear of a baby that wasn't?" asked Finn. "However, first things first." And he began to unrope his chest. "How is Roddie taking it?"

There was a distinct cackle from Elspet. And at that weird sound, Finn laughed.

.   .   .   .   .   .

THE BIRCH WOOD

Supper over, Elspet reminded him about going to Roddie's. "Right," said Finn. "Coming, Barbara?"

Barbara hesitated, but Elspet told her to go.

"I'll take my present with me," said Barbara swiftly.

Finn's mind was kept on its toes by Barbara's presence. He was fond of her, and she obviously thought no less of him than before. In front of the house Finn saw Roddie lifting a bundle in his hands and gurgling up at it. Barbara's eyes troubled at the harsh sarcastic sound from Finn's throat.

Roddie saw them and shouted.

Inside, Catrine heard the shout, and, glancing out of the window, beheld Finn and Barbara coming. She went pale and short of breath and pressed a strong palm against her heart. Drawing back a pace from the window in the instinctive movement of one who would not be seen, she remained still, feeling slightly faint.

"Hullo, Finn!" cried Roddie. "Welcome back!"

"Hullo!" answered Finn.

"What do you think of this?" asked Roddie. "Eh? Look at him!"

"So this is him?" said Finn. "Hullo, boy!" And he inspected the child with a critical half-amused look.

"Isn't he a great fellow?" asked Roddie. "Eh?" Then he spoke to the child. "This is Finn. Yes, this is Finn, back from the sea, far far away."

The small head waggled in little jerks, the unwinking eyes stared, lifted to the sky, fell to distant vistas of the moor, to Barbara (who thereupon chortled at him) and once more to Finn.

"Ah, he's beginning to know you!" cried Roddie with triumph.

Finn's scepticism issued in a soft gust. Roddie, the great seaman, the Viking, carrying on like a silly woman! This sort of behaviour embarrassed Finn at any time, for he had never seen a child of this age that didn't look like a skinned rabbit. He was always relieved when the thing was taken away.

"Who do you think he's like?" asked Roddie.

Even that question!

"It's difficult to say yet," replied Finn. "But I believe the poor thing is in for it."

"What do you mean by that?" demanded Roddie.

"There is a certain vague but general resemblance," said Finn, "to yourself."

Roddie laughed. Suddenly the tiny features were congested and the mouth opened and yelled.

"Do you hear that?" cried Roddie, lifting the child beyond Barbara's reach. "Hasn't he got great lungs? And the strength that's in him! I can hardly hold him! As sure as death!"

Barbara took the child. "Now watch you don't let him fall," Roddie cautioned her. "Well, Finn, and how are you? Come away in. We've been hearing already that you have had a fair fishing."

As Finn entered, his mother was standing by the window. She said quietly, "You have got back?"

"Yes," replied Finn, shaking hands and smiling as he glanced around "And where is himself?"

"He's keeping to his bed," answered Catrine. "He hasn't been too well."

"I'm sorry to hear that," said Finn.

"That lassie will never stop the bairn crying," remarked Roddie, hearkening to the row outside.

"Yes, she will. Just leave them," said Catrine. "And had you a good season?" she asked her son, as if he were a stranger.

"Just fair, I think," and he addressed Roddie, "that the West is going to be worse before it's better."

The two men discussed the fishing and Stornoway in easy tones. Catrine sat still, listening, saying no word.

"Was Bain as large as life?" asked Roddie.

"Larger," said Finn. "When we came in with the shot that time after the storm——"

"Ay, we just heard you were caught in a bit of a storm,"

interrupted Roddie, with a secret wink to Finn, who thus became aware that the news had been kept from his mother until that moment.

"Oh, it wasn't much," said Finn. "But as I was saying about Bain . . ."

Roddie kept putting questions to him, and Finn responded with more and more humour. "Yes, Rob was in good form, but we pressed him hard sometimes. It wasn't fair. Remember the widow woman who has the public-house?"

"Yes." Roddie laughed, and then explained the position to Catrine, as if he were an interpreter.

Finn smiled. "There's something in it."

"No?" cried Roddie.

Barbara came in with the pacified child and stood near the door.

Amid the amusement he drew from Rob's indirect courtship of the widow woman, Finn began to open his brown paper parcel. "I'm the great one for the presents," he said to Roddie humorously.

"You might have a worse fault," answered Roddie.

"This is for you," said Finn to his mother, handing her a large brown Shetland shawl, cunningly knitted and light in weight.

"Thank you," she said. "It's lovely." She bent her face over it and smoothed it with her hand.

"And look! What do you think of this for winter foot-wear?" he asked Roddie. "Remember the old fellow in the shop? . . ." He handed the boots to his mother negligently, saying, "Now, what do you think of this?" and exposed for Roddie's critical admiration a small curved horn snuff-box.

"Well, isn't it a neat one!" declared Roddie.

"I thought you would like it," said Finn.

"Do you mean it's for me? God bless me, boy, you've been fairly going it!"

"Haven't I! But I owe you a few snuffs in my time. And

561

talking of snuff, I have an ounce here for the old man himself. Oh, special stuff. There's some of it in that horn of yours. Try it."

Meantime Barbara had drawn near to Catrine, anxious to show her own silken present, holding it out in its brown paper for Catrine to unfold. As Catrine lifted her face, the eyes were wet and very bright, and the lower lip held. There was a softness and beauty about the eyes that went straight to Barbara's heart, a nearness of emotion that made her want to weep.

"Good, isn't it?" asked Finn.

"Extra special. Fragrant," agreed Roddie, sniffing with deep appreciation.

"Well, that's about all," declared Finn, "except for one small thing." And now he did not look at any of them, as he lifted an article wrapped in tissue-paper. "You have all," he said largely, "heard of the horn spoon of our forefathers and of being born with a silver spoon in the mouth. Now, didn't I happen to see a little horn spoon with silver at the end of the handle—look!—and I thought, well you never know but it might come in handy sometime. And here it is. It's for the little fellow himself," and he handed the spoon to his mother. "Do you like it?" he asked practically, picking up the brown paper.

Catrine did her best. She strove hard. But the held breath broke through her nostrils in two terrible sobs and, getting quickly to her feet, she went blindly from the kitchen.

Barbara followed, weeping. And presently the wails of the little fellow rose upon the air.

"God save us, boy, it's the howling match now! You'll have a dram," said Roddie.

"A small one. I'll be getting down. I can do with a good sleep. Stop!"

"Ach, it'll do you no harm. We're glad to see you again." He hesitated a moment, and about his face came the old remote smile. "I would rather you had done that than a thousand pounds. Well, good health!"

When Finn had paid his respects to the old man, Roddie accompanied him to the top of the wood, discussing the fishing, and what had to be done to-morrow at the shore.

As Finn went on alone, he felt tired and life seemed fairly empty. But the remoteness, the feeling of loneliness, was not altogether unpleasant. He was glad he had done what he had done. A great desire for sleep came over him.

A week later, Finn sat alone on the Knoll of Peace. He was feeling tired and wretched, his finger-tips burning from the handling of sun-dried peat. This mood was the more inexplicable because in less than two days now he was going to Wick to bring home his new boat, the *Gannet*. The thought of this culminating act in the growth towards responsible manhood had so often excited him that perhaps he was now suffering no more than a temporary reaction. Often a person before running a race or starting on some perilous adventure experiences an almost sickly apprehension. In fact, when Finn lifted his mind, he saw the clean green seas running, and knew that freedom was there, and adventure, and the song of man's strength. He would be all right when he looked at the lifting stem of his own boat. Then would come upon him a freedom that would have in it the gaiety of revenge over all the cluttering doubts and anxieties of the earth.

The earth was very still in those long summer nights that never grew quite dark, still, and full of a peace, a waiting, a green light, queerly alive, like something hearkening. The sea rushed and was tumultuous, or lay glittering in the sun, its waters clear, its depth known. Here was the stillness of mystery, like God's thought, or the reverie that comes upon a woman with a child in her lap.

Finn wanted his mind to be at peace.

And all the Knoll said to him was that it would not be at peace until he had cleansed it of a certain haunting misery.

Cleanse it of that, and all the seven seas are yours. But Finn knew as much himself and did not thank the Knoll. The longer he stayed here, the stronger this knowledge grew, the more pointed its thought, until Finn could not bear it any longer and got up and walked away. It was the first time the House of Peace had failed him.

So completely had it failed him that he could not go home and in a desire to get away altogether from his human kind, he struck up the neighbouring strath and ultimately came out on the moors among the sheep. He took the lonely ways, looking every now and then over his shoulder like a sheep-stealer. As he came down at last upon some scattered croft houses, he began to skulk, and spy, and slip on like a hunted criminal, until, breathing heavily, he gained the shelter of the Birch Wood and threw himself down, out of sight of the path.

His wretchedness now was gall in his mouth, bitter as poison. He shut his eyes and ground his teeth and tried to blot himself out, blot out the burning shame he had of himself for behaving with such utter and appalling weakness. For it was no good hiding the truth from himself any longer. Jim had come up from Wick for the new fishing season. That was all.

This sort of behaviour destroyed a man's manhood. It destroyed him inside, in the places of his spirit. It made a wretched mess of him, and instead of turning away from it he could not leave it alone; had to turn back, nosing it out, like a dog.

But there was one positive point, with the prospect of relief in it. Once he was sure, dead sure of a real relationship between Una and Jim, then he could cleanse his mind finally. He could and he would! he swore, the skulking feeling of insecurity heavy upon him. He would finally be rid of the whole damned mess. Deep in the dark centres, he felt unclean and ashamed.

Voices in the distance coming up the path through the wood. He could hear Jim's laugh.

Jim and Donnie and Meg. Not a fourth voice. Then there was a fourth voice. The voice of Betz, sounding sarcastic and sullen.

"What about going and rooting her out?" asked Jim.

"I'm going home," said Betz.

"I must say you're a pleasant one," declared Jim.

"The same to you," said Betz. "Stop it! Good night."

When the girls had gone, Jim asked, "I wonder why the hell Una didn't come to-night?"

"I don't know I'm sure," said Donnie. "Perhaps she couldn't get away."

"Did Meg say anything?"

"No."

"She did," said Jim. "I know by your voice. You must . . ."

As the voices receded, Finn raised his face and the marks of small twigs were bitten deep into his forehead.

He sat up and stared like one whose mind was wandering. Then he went to the edge of the wood and gazed after the two girls, who seemed to be going direct to Una's house which was the nearest and not very far away.

Round the gable-end came Una and her mother, and Finn heard greetings and laughter. The mother was sent inside and the two girls helped Una to carry some wool dyed a vivid blue over to a low turf wall. But they did not start spreading the wool to dry. Meg had too much to say, and her body swayed every now and then with high laughter. To be working so late—for it was nearly eleven o'clock— to complete a task was nothing unusual at this time of the year. Presumably Una, who had been busy and was now getting the news, had been unable to go with the girls to spend the evening visiting friends.

When the fun was over, Una would not allow the others to soil their best clothes over a job that would take her no time, and after two or three false starts, Meg and Betz actually departed.

Una was down now at the little wall all alone spreading

the blue wool. He watched the movements of her hands and arms and saw her dark head. The birds had stopped singing, except for a corncrake in a little field over on the left. The night was very quiet and the light a dim green. Una kept working all the time, with never a sound from her, down there by the little wall. Finn wet his lips and let out a low clear whistle. As Una looked up, he walked out just clear of the trees, stood still, and beckoned.

He saw her face whiten as she started back. He heard the smothered cry. "Una!" he called, loud enough for her to hear. She stopped. He beckoned again. She stood staring at him, looked over her shoulder at her home, around her, and slowly returned to the wall. He beckoned her to come to the wood, come to the wood, where they would not be seen, his body standing still against the darkness of the trees.

She crossed the wall and went up towards him, but slowly, watching him, like a woman in a trance. As she came near and he saw her eyes, he stepped back into the shelter of the trees. She followed him and they met.

"Hullo, Una!" He looked into eyes that were still upon him—not shyly, but in a strange searching manner. Then her expression broke and she glanced away, her body twisting. She smiled. "I wondered who it was," she said. She began to breathe heavily. "Phew! I'm tired," and quite deliberately she sat down. She did not seem self-conscious or greatly concerned about his presence. "Oh, I'm tired," she repeated, and threw herself down and turned over on her face.

Her neck was white beneath her black hair. His eye ran along her body to the blue stains on her bare legs and feet. He was profoundly moved by whatever had happened to her. For in her flesh, in her eyes, even in her awkward movements, there was the warm soft darkness of appeal, of grace, the emanation that haunted him, that would never leave him alone.

He sat down feeling remote from her, not knowing what

to do, but so near her that he touched her shoulder lightly, and murmured her name. Then he spoke more firmly. Was she crying? He lay beside her and listened. "Una," he said into her hair.

"Leave me," she muttered.

He sat up and waited; and presently, somewhat shame-facedly but not weeping, she sat up beside him. Her face was now hot with blood, her eyes deep. "You gave me a fright. I was not sure who you were."

"Why, did you think I was someone else?"

At that she turned her head and looked at him, looked into his eyes, with an assessing woman's look in the midst of her warm emotion, and looked away.

"Why don't you answer?" asked Finn, losing his bearings.

"I'll have to go," she said, as if he had fallen out of her thought. "They'll be wondering where I am."

"Answer me: who did you think I was?"

"Why do you question me?"

"Never mind. I'm questioning you."

"I'm going home."

"No, you're not."

"Who'll stop me?"

"I will."

She laughed a queer note or two and got to her feet. But he stood in her way.

"Answer me," he said.

"I will not answer you."

"Answer me," he said coldly, angrily, his expression drawn and inclined to quiver.

Not looking at him, she strode on. But though she was a well-built girl, Finn pinned her arms and broke her strength. In doing this he grew very excited; he forgot himself altogether, and kissed her hair and her ear. But when her strength was broken, he felt ashamed of what he had done, not only to her but to himself. His loss of self-command increased his deep misery and wretchedness. He let his arms fall. "All right," he said indifferently, yet with deep underlying enmity and anger. "You can go."

But she continued to lie against him, breathing heavily.

"Why don't you go?" he demanded, and put his palms against her shoulders. But she would not be shoved off. She gripped him, hiding her face. He felt its pressure against his neck.

As he gazed over her head, his eyes narrowed in an intense woodland look. Then he gazed at her hair. "Una," he said in a low voice. She gripped him more strongly as if she felt what was coming. He pushed her head back relentlessly. She struggled against showing what he would find in her face. But he found it and the world went blind against her mouth.

Some time thereafter, as they lay side by side on the floor of the wood, they heard her mother cry her name.

"I'll have to go," she said. "They must wonder where I am." The wonder lay warm in her voice and in the soft beauty of her face. She did not stir.

"Never mind them."

"I must." She smiled.

"Do you want to go?"

She glanced at him. "You're a terrible one for questions."

"You know it's not that."

"What then?"

"I cannot believe it. I want to be sure."

"It was awful of you to think I would come for anyone else."

"But—you said—you wondered who it was."

"I wondered—if it was you."

"Did you think, then, it was someone else?"

"No."

"I don't understand."

"Una!" called her mother anxiously.

Una watched her two fingers pick amid the little dead
568

stalks. "Once," she said, "one night, I saw your face at our window. I saw it quite clearly—and then it vanished."

"Did you?"

"Yes."

"You must have got a terrible fright. What did you think?"

She did not answer. "To-night, *when I heard my name called*—and looked up—and saw you standing still against the wood, with only your hand beckoning me——"

A small shiver went over Finn. "And still you came?"

She nodded.

CHAPTER XXVI

FINN IN THE HEART OF THE CIRCLE

❧

"I t's not the best of weather," said the owner of the shipyard who had handed Finn back a pound as luck-penny.

"But good for her baptism," answered Finn lightly.

"You'll tell me how she does?"

"You can rest assured I'll do that—one way or the other!"

The boat-builder laughed. "You're a hardy lot out of Dunster. I'll say that."

"Nothing but the best for us," answered Finn. And then with a swift smile, "That's why I went to you."

"Well, you didn't go far wrong, my boy. The best that could be put in her is in her. And sea-knowledge besides."

"I am well satisfied, thank you." Finn turned and in the quiet voice of the skipper said, "Give way, boys."

There was a stiff breeze blowing into Wick harbour, with dark clouds massing. But Finn's crew were like horses before a race. Up went the sail, and the *Gannet*, standing aback for a small shuddering moment, then lay over and dipped in salute to the sea, rose, gathered way, increased her way, and was off.

Finn knew that many were watching, for Wick was already stirring into the tumultuous life of the summer fishing. He beat out, and in due course prepared to put her about. Up into the eye of the wind, acknowledging the helm, pressing her weight against it to feel the assurance of Finn's hand, up in a slowing but steady sweep, up and round and falling over, and again gathering way, increasing her way, reaching out . . .

Finn's heart sang in him, sang back to his boat in pride, The crew made their compliments. Finn replied gravely, "She answers very well."

But his heart was singing, and when they got outside he put up the mizzen, although there was a fair sea running and smashing on the skerries.

"We'll see what she can do," he decided. They saw his eyes gleam through the faint smile on his face that was lifted to the horizon. And he put her into it; he baptized her; he brought the strong spray over her bows; he lay her over until the sea seethed along her lee rail, but whatever he did, she answered him with increase, giving herself to the elements for which she had been created, assured of his hand.

Finn felt the sea-exhilaration come upon him. The wind was strengthening under the dark clouds. The crew sat very quiet, beyond comment. He should have been running before it for Clyth Head. But Finn and the *Gannet* had their own fight with the sea, before he said calmly, "I think she'll do."

She was very clean and sweet in her gleaming tar and new paint and grained wood of mast and oar, as she turned and flew before the wind.

"She is well named," said the stranger of the crew, a middle-aged hired man from Stoer on the West Coast.

"You think so?" replied Finn, gratified.

"There's nothing in Dunster will touch her for speed," said Ian, on a lifted note of enthusiasm. "Nothing at all!"

"She has good lines," nodded Finn.

"She's as big as anything in Wick," declared Donnie.

"I believe she is," agreed Finn lightly. He was yet to own a boat of over forty feet, all decked, but such a boat for the herring fleet was still far in the future. "South-built", with 30 feet keel, 34 feet 6 inches over all, and open from stem to stern, she seemed a large and splendid vessel to her crew. Finn would not have thought twice of reaching for the Baltic!

But now he was reaching for home. The headlands, cliff walls, slopes, inland valleys, Morven—the fisherman's mountain, the whole flow and shape of that stern land looked well to Finn. An attractive country, very agreeable, thought the new skipper with appropriate calm; but, inside, his heart was singing, because his heart had fallen in love with his boat and his croft and—and everything. For they were a grand folk, taking them all in all. They moved in procession, many and differing characters, on varied occasions, from the old smuggler Wull to the youngest lad hunting a rabbit in fear.

"See the Bodach now!" cried Ian, interrupting Finn's thought. And there was the needle rock standing out from the headland.

But Finn lifted his face to Morven, ran his eyes along the saddle-backs of the Scarabens to steady them on the Birch Wood.

"I suppose that will be your landfall," said the Stoer man to Finn, gazing at Morven.

"Yes," said Finn, gazing at the Birch Wood

"You'll be able to see it a long way at sea?"

"You see it," said Finn, "when you see nothing else." And he smiled.

"Look at them waiting for us on the shore!" exclaimed Donnie.

Finn's body quickened and his eyes gleamed.

That opening season turned out a good one for the *Gannet*. It was altogether memorable for Finn. The old crew had got broken up, except for Rob who was still with Roddie. Callum had gone half-shares in a boat with his wife's brother, and they engaged two men from the West Coast to complete the crew. Roddie had two men from Harris. There were not sufficient local men now to man all the boats during the summer season. The number of "hired men" from the West Coast was steadily increasing, and Finn, because of his early wanderings ever had for them a special affection.

It was a pretty sight to see the boats reaching for the herring grounds, and folk would involuntarily stand and gaze: "The boats are going out." At the ceilidh-house, a voice would say, "The boats are shot close in to-night," or "The boats are shot off ――――" naming this cliff or that area. "Any word of the boats to-day?" "The boats were in early." "The boats are coming in." The boats. The boats.

George the foreman's voice shouting, men quick-footed with the brimming creel, cascades of silver fish, bright eager faces of women and their swift hands, voices from Lewis drawn-out and soft and rhythmic; voices from Wick uplifted, direct, ironic; voices from Banffshire easy-going and full of diminutives. Bodies threading the maze of the busy hours of landing and gutting, the gleam of human life.

Una was there, and Meg, and Barbara, and Betz, and a shoal of young women besides, with older women, too, and greying-haired women tight-shawled and quick-tongued. And amid this plenty, the witch drew her share, for when it came to the hidden forces and the dark ones, as they affected the sea, the men of Banff had knowledge over all others, and the Lewis men had special knowledge, and ach, dash it! the sea loves the spendthrift hand anyway!

"Well, Finn, what luck to-day?" shouts Meg.

"Not bad," cries Finn.

"What'll you do with all your fortune?"

"You'd wonder."

"Not for long," answers Meg.

Una flashes him her dark smile. The excuses he makes to pass her way wouldn't deceive a kitten, though he must think they do, for sometimes he passes without either look or speech. He just passes.

But, over all, it was not a markedly successful season and the *Gannet* was only one of the many fairly well-fished boats. Roddie was leading Finn by thirty crans. To every fisherman, however, there comes, some time or other, his stroke of luck, and to Finn it came in the very last week of the fishing, and in so striking a fashion that he was never to forget it.

When, the nets shot, his crew had eaten their bite, pulled a fold of sail over them, and gone to sleep, Finn was invaded by a sleepless calm that left him inclined to sit and stare. Perhaps it was an aftermath of the sunset that had turned the clouds into vast banks of fiery red. The sky had indeed come alive in a wild and menacing beauty, and all the sea had run red in molten currents, and the red had come off the sea and shone in the faces of the silent crew and glittered in their eyes.

Now the last blood-flush was dying from a cloud in the east, slowly draining out of it, as Finn looked, until nothing but the leaden death-hue remained, and the cloud hung cold and still.

There had been a touch of menace in that red—though of what none of them could have said. Nor did they refer to it. For it raised up no definite thought or image; just as a chance glance at the eternal Book would raise up no definite image of desert sands, or sacrifice, or crucifixion.

The flat sky deepened its cold leaden hue and the water darkened under fitful movements of the dying wind. Gulls still cried in the cliffs not a great distance away, yet in cries distant and cavernous and forlorn. Once, by some trick of reflected light, Finn saw three of them float ghost-white against the black rock.

As he turned his eyes eastward, he saw over a hundred craft, masts lowered, riding to their nets. Those in the distance seemed very close together, but Finn knew there was little likelihood of their drifts getting entangled because along this coast—unlike the bays and inlets of the West— the tide moved in a slow steady stream. He was still haunted by the feeling that he had come too far west, for he was indeed the westernmost boat in the fleet. Yet there had been that curious secretive impulse to get into a clear space

of his own, the impulse that had often haunted the boy.
Over and above, however, there had been another impulse
springing out of a superstition that he would not have put
words on for worlds. As they sailed out westward, he had
kept her going, while boat after boat took up a fishing
berth, until, with Tomas from Stoer restless and Donnie
on the verge of comment, Finn opened out the western side
of the Birch Wood and so, in his mind's eye, Una's cottage.

Night settled down on the sea and the near boats loomed
indistinctly. A haze smothered the wood, and wiped away
the image of the cottage, and slowly but surely carried
away the hills. Finn did not feel that he was being unfair to
Una. It would not occur to him to blame her as an unlucky
talisman, should he draw blank nets and the other boats be
well-fished. This was only his fancy; this was a secret tribute from far down in the deeps of his mind. As he thought
of her, he saw her eyes darker than the night, but, unlike
the night, they were dark wells of light. They glanced and
lived, flashed away and came back, smiled and grew warm.
He could see them now without seeing any other part of
her.

He stirred restlessly. High time he was asleep. But now
at sea, when her eyes came before him like this, they exercised an extreme entrancement.

Held in this thrall, time, too, for Finn was wiped away.
He was brought back to his normal self, however, by a
curious phenomenon, which his eyes had been staring at
without consciously seeing. It was a large patch of glassy
light on the dark sea. To his staring eyes it was like a window let into the blackness of the water. Not that in form it
was square. On the contrary, it was irregular, but rounded,
too, into a clearly defined shape. It was when this shape
took the likeness of a woman's head and shoulders that Finn
was wakened by the finger of wonder. The woman's head
was bowed; beneath the face was an inlet of darkness; then
the light came again on her breast. The likeness was in fact,
quite clear, and Finn's preoccupation merely gave it a vivid

and personal quality. But, astonishing as this phenomenon was to him, what next affected him was even more astonishing. They had, of course, shot their nets across the tide and nets and boat were slowly ebbing eastward. But this great figure—it must have been thirty yards across—was coming *against* the tide and towards his drift of nets. It was visibly moving over the windless sea. The head of the woman bowed right down as her breast touched his nets, and in a sinuous movement the whole rounded form flattened and ran along the drift. As Finn watched, first one buoy, then another, gave a spasmodic upward jerk, like a living head struck under the chin, then fell back and slowly sank.

As if struck himself, Finn fell upon the dead men and shook them to life, his voice harsh with triumph. "Boys, we're in them!"

There was excitement then, but in restrained low voices, lest mystery or wonder overhear and be frightened away. Finn began to haul on the swing-rope, and at once in the water it turned into a rope of fire, a rope that threw off phosphorescent flame, streaming downward, as Finn put forth his strength; when the pressure came on the first net, the flame ran into sheets, swift evanescent fires, with the pale green light that is sometimes seen in the moon; but more intense, and always vanishing, elusive, instantly evoked and blown out by the uncanny magic of the undersea.

But the meshes of the net came up into the hands black and dripping and empty.

Then, fathoms away, there was a gleam from a solid silver bar, and amid the swirls of light that glowed and died it remained constant. It came with the net, came up out of the sea, in a little silver dance, and passed down into the hold.

It was not, however, until they began to haul the third net that they struck the first of the shoal. And now the silver bars formed in banks, banks of show that swayed in living mass, throwing off spindrift of elfin-green light. The crew's excitement increased as the weight called forth their strength. Slowly and carefully, now, steadily. Here they come! And they came in their companies, fluttering up out of the sea, the silver darlings, dancing in over the gunnel with small thin cries.

The great happiness that came upon the crew was kept in control by their eager labour, drawn taut as the back-rope upon which Finn and Tomas hauled, hauled until their necks swelled and the blood congested in their faces.

Now Finn felt like a great hunter, like the leader of hunting men. Assurance of his strength and power was in him like a song. But when he spoke, he spoke quietly, as if deep in his throat was a gentle laugh.

And still in the nets the banks of fish glittered, and from the banks shot away pale green arrows of light—the herring that had not been meshed and now vanished into the black deep.

Altogether out of that small shoal they drew, Finn estimated, about thirty crans. When the nets were hauled, they rested from their labour for a while, but in silence, listening.

"I can't hear any of them moving at all," said Tomas.

They would not wish poor luck to any boat; still, as they hearkened to the dead silence, a glee of conspiracy and close comradeship came about their hearts.

"I'm thinking," Finn said, "that they are maybe too far east and a little too far out."

"They may be indeed," Tomas admitted, "though one never knows."

"We know one thing now whatever," said Donnie, and each face smiled in the darkness.

"We have drifted a good bit, hauling," Finn said presently. "It's yet only the dead of the night. What do you say if we go west, a little beyond where we were, and shoot again?"

There were now, however, no landmarks to be seen, and none of the boats carried riding lights. Finn had accordingly been careful to note many small signs such as the direction of the last net, a scarcely discernible lightening in the sky that could be the rising of the waning moon, an occasional wash of water like a soft choking sigh from a skerry this side of the Great Cove. The sweeps dipped and stirred the water into vortices of silver that swirled towards Finn as he leaned forward, his right arm along the tiller.

Black the water, invisible the black rock, gone every last outline in the black of the world's night. Finn felt this deeper darkness come from impending cliffs. It shrouded away his crew so that he lost sight of them, lost sight of that lightening of the sky which he had imagined in the east, lost sight of everything but the radiant pearls that fell from the oar blades, and the two whirling silver cones, and the vanishing flames, spectral green.

"Stop!" he cried softly, and for a hushed moment they floated at the core of darkness.

"Ah!" said Tomas, hearing the faint wash of the sea over the cliffs' feet. There was relief in his voice at the known sound. They had it on their starboard side where it should be. Its faint murmur felt solid to them as a tow-rope.

The sun rose out of the sea to find the fleet hauling their nets. The sky was high and arched and of a blue lighter than cornflowers. The clouds had been herded away to the west where a last few galleon sails were going down the horizon. The dawn spangles glittered upon the water, and the level light was reflected in the chilled faces of the fishermen, who acknowledged its thin warmth in a delicate shudder.

"It's a fine morning," said a mouth in one boat or another, and the words were quiet as a line of poetry.

Presently an air of morning wind darkened the surface of the sea and here and there a brown sail went up.

On the edge of the beach in front of the gutting stations, girls and women and a few men slowly gathered in prospect of the day's work. But the boats first to arrive were blank. Then one came with three crans and her skipper said the herring were very spotty. Callum had two creels and Roddie four crans. When all the boats had returned, except one, the fishing was seen to be very light. The biggest shot was eight crans.

The boat that had not arrived was Finn's. But after an hour or more they saw her coming. At once there were many voices, crying: Look how low she is in the water! But George's voice rose above them all, triumphantly applauding a young runner in a great race. The girls of his curing station laughed with excitement. One gutting crew had their arms interlocked, and the middle one of the three, with dark eyes and flushed face, had to suffer elbows in secretive merry stabs. She swayed like a young full-foliaged tree, lissome and lovely in the warm morning sun. "Be quiet!" she said to Meg.

But as the *Gannet* drew near, drew slowly near, helped by two sweeps, for the wind was light and she was indeed deeply laden; as she drew still nearer, slowly and inexorably, with Finn's head and shoulders steady and his arm along the tiller, and a voice crying, "She has over fifty crans if she has a creel!" there came upon Una through the expectant silence of the crowd a momentary strangeness and everything stood still in that moment as in a fated land. The dark eyes glimmered deeply, and an irrational happiness quivered, all in an instant, on the verge of tears.

As Finn dropped a net from his shoulder on to the drying green, he saw Rob and Callum approach. He expected that they would express their congratulations by way of pulling his leg. And this they did. But then Rob began to scratch his beard and Finn grew wary.

"Of course there is a saying," said Rob, "that the man who goes forth always with his net will catch birds now and then."

"Why birds?" asked Callum.

FINN IN THE HEART OF THE CIRCLE

"Haven't you been hearing anything?" Rob asked him in solemn astonishment.

"No. What?"

"Oh, in that case, nothing," answered Rob, "nothing. Only a fellow will be hearing a thing sometimes."

"Who were you hearing it from?"

"Och, maybe it was just only a small bird," replied Rob, with the wrinkled face of his special brand of antique humour.

"A small bird? Oh?"

"Ay."

"And where was the small bird from?"

"They say she's got a nest up somewhere about the Birch Wood——"

Rob yelled as Finn tackled him, and his voice grew angry, reminding Finn that this was not Stornoway and that he should be ashamed of behaving in such a way before his own people. The gleam, however, remained in his eye, and Callum's delight was absolute and complete.

On a harvest evening, Finn moved stealthy as a wolf through the Steep Wood, over the grey dikes, round the edge of the little field, and up on to the knoll of the House of Peace. There, lying flat, he gazed around with a hunted look, and down towards the river path, commanding the approach to his home.

When he was assured that no-one was after him, he performed the mental act of describing the circle of sanctuary around the ground on which he lay. Then his eyes fell on the circle of low flat stones and he crept into its heart.

At once the hunted look caught a gleam of cunning relief. They would never find him here. They would never think of looking for him in this haunted spot. He would escape them yet.

The way in which men who had been his friends had specially leagued against him produced a new vision of humanity. He saw their dark relentless bodies, conspiring against him, not to be deflected from their purpose, mercilessly closing in, like that image in the Bible of the fowler with his net.

From his own home he was an outcast. He had seen the alien gleam in the eyes of women; even in the eyes of his mother, conspiring beyond him.

He had caught a glimpse of her standing still, looking away to the moor, with the calm reverie which the singing girl of North Uist had evoked by her song. Her happiness had been so calm and profound that it had touched the fringe of sadness, of fatality, as in the song, as appeared to be the way with women. His mother would never alter. She would deepen and grow in her own wisdom. Beyond the accidents and tempers and fatalities of life, she was encompassed within herself, the mother-woman he knew, different from all other women, and between them the blood relationship of mother and son. But she was distant from him now, completely apart, and this estrangement was cool and whole, leaving the relationship of the blood imperceptible as a sleeping instinct.

"She's a fine girl. I am very happy about it."

"I'm glad you like her," he murmured in reply.

They hadn't spoken much more about it, for he had felt a certain restraint in his mother's presence; but as he had been going away, she had said: "Take the sweetness of life, Finn, while still you have it."

The sweetness of life!

Excitement stirred him in the circle of stones. He felt very nervous. Curse these fellows! He had seen Rob and Callum as thick as thieves, conspiring. They would go to Henry, to Roddie. Donnie and Ian and Davie and Duncan . . . right up to old Wull the smuggler. Hundreds of them, without decency, without mercy.

"We'll see you married and properly married," Rob had said.

"What do you mean by that, Rob?" asked Callum.

FINN IN THE HEART OF THE CIRCLE

"Marriage," said Rob, "is a *public institution*. That's why I never went in for it."

"We know the way you went in for it," retorted Finn. "And I tell you now that if any of you try on any tricks, I'll break your necks. Now I'm warning you. I mean it."

"But what trick would we try on?" asked Callum innocently. "Dammit, it's not us who's going to do the trick whatever."

"Let us hope not," said Rob, "But however that may be, the point is that marriage is a *p-p-public——*"

"Not a public-house, Rob. No, no," intervened Callum sensibly.

"A *public institution*," proceeded Rob, "and as such it has to be—to be——"

"Ay, ay," agreed Callum.

"I forget the *legal* word," said Rob, "but it means that it has to be it before—before all, so that no question can arise b-but that—that—it was it."

"That's enough, Rob. You're making the poor boy nervous," said Callum. Finn strode away.

This was the night before his marriage, and Finn knew that if they got him in his home they would put him through certain heathenish practices. He had more than once assisted at them, and assisted with great glee, and the harder the prospective bridegroom raged and fought, the deeper the glee. They made him one of the company of men, beyond all false pride, before they were done with him. But now Finn saw the whole proceedings in an entirely different light.

The wedding would last for days. And they were not beyond certain stealthy forms of semi-intrusion on the marriage bed itself. This was what Rob had been hinting at.

Finn curled up like an adder that had accidentally stung itself.

But he was safe here meantime and he needn't go home to-night.

Underneath all this, a turmoil of happiness seemed for

582

ever to wash up in his breast and recede like a pulse of the sea. There had been one moment of revelation that would outlast all others. It occurred in the Birch Wood. Una and himself had been sitting talking, and from them all self-consciousness, all stress, had fallen away. She was talking quietly of something they would do together, when suddenly he did not hear so much what she was saying as the tone of her voice, and its intimacy put about them a ring of silence. They were within this ring alone, in league for ever, the two of them, cut off from all others in the world. An intimacy, a trust, clear as her unselfconscious voice, clear as a singing in the hills, near as the deepening tenderness in his breast. She turned her head, for his silence had touched her.

Finn turned his head and looked at the grey-lichened stones. They were very old, and their age gave him a feeling of immense time on whose threshold he lay. What he had lived of life was only its beginning. Its deeper mysteries were ahead.

As if all hitherto had been but accident and skirmish, there came flooding through him a deep blood-warm realization of the potency of life. It uncurled in his limbs stretching them in slow strength, in a divine feeling of well-being. Odds and ends of vision touched his thought from his own boat, the sea, the busy communal life; flashes moving him to restlessness. George's voice, declaiming his congratulation: "There's nothing like marrying young, and I'm telling you your children and your children's children will see many a great change. . . ."

His children and his children's children! These old fools could think of nothing but children! A touch of Rob's antique humour came through the confusion of Finn's thought and expression. He saw himself as an old enough man by that time! a white-haired old man, head of a tribe, sitting on this knoll in quiet thought, his sea days over! How distant and fantastic—how pleasant and amusing, with kindliness about it and peace! Like the figure of the

white-haired man he had once imagined here. . . . Finn's
thought suddenly quickened, and for an intense moment
the knoll took on its immemorial calm. Time became
a stilled heart-beat. Stealthy, climbing sounds. Finn's body
drew taut, heaved up on to supporting palms. Whisper-
ings, the movement of the top of a small birch-tree here
and there whose trunk invisible hands gripped. The
hunters in their primordial humour were closing in. Life
had come for him.

ff

Faber and Faber – a home for writers

Faber and Faber is one of the great independent publishing houses in London. We were established in 1929 by Geoffrey Faber and our first editor was T. S. Eliot. We are proud to publish prize-winning fiction and non-fiction, as well as an unrivalled list of modern poets and playwrights. Among our list of writers we have five Booker Prize winners and eleven Nobel Laureates, and we continue to seek out the most exciting and innovative writers at work today.

www.faber.co.uk – a home for readers

The Faber website is a place where you will find all the latest news on our writers and events. You can listen to podcasts, preview new books, read specially commissioned articles and access reading guides, as well as entering competitions and enjoying a whole range of offers and exclusives. You can also browse the list of Faber Finds, an exciting new project where reader recommendations are helping to bring a wealth of lost classics back into print using the latest on-demand technology.